The Alpha Enforcer and His Dancing Warrior
Volume 1

By Amanda K

Book 7 in the Ribbon Series

Cover art by: Allison Richardson

Dedication

To my husband and boys who are my world, I love you three.

To my loyal editor and the fact that you just went with the direction I took this first volume after decided we needed to go further back into this story and give some details.

To my BAGG thank you doesn't really cover it! I hope you enjoy the angst of this story. You will go through a lot of frustration but you learn so much ☺

Author's Note

Hello Reader,

I just wanted to say this book will have some time jumps in chapters. We do NOT cover everything that the main characters go through in the age listed.

Also, this book deals with physical and emotional abuse (starting when Melanie is fourteen years old). She has some suicidal thoughts (When she's sixteen). So, if those moments trigger you, please skip them and think of your mental health first and foremost!

Table of Contents

Prologue

Alpha Ezra was gleeful. I clarified, "And you're sure it all worked?" The Ring representative rolled her eyes at me. My wolf broke free of the hold I had on him. He asked, "What is this you're thinking about? You can't do this! NOT TO A PUP! I AM AN ALPHA WOLF AND I WILL NOT ALLOW THIS."

I simply dosed him with some wolfsbane, and he was back to being quiet. He'd forget all about it too and his memory was all foggy. He didn't know over half the things I did. Nor could he tell another wolf if he remembered.

The Ring woman raised an eyebrow at the pressure syringe I used. I snorted, "You people provide us with these and then looked confused when we use them." She shrugged, "I would never hurt my counterpart. You just have to reason with them." I didn't know what she was, and I didn't care. I explained, "An Alpha wolf would never agree to hurt a pup as we plan to do."

She shrugged, "So, you have a holier than thou wolf. You just need to find the right thing to convince him this is what's right." He could not be convinced, like some other Alpha's wolves I knew. Our brother, we didn't know about dying didn't do it. Us not getting money out of those filthy rich bastard allies didn't do it. I didn't even get answers until the Ring approached me. I was never getting what was due to me until they showed up.

I waved, "This isn't about my wolf. This is about my revenge. Are we sure that no one met the pup?" She said, "I'm told the pups name is Melanie." I knew that. I just didn't care. I got her damn birth announcement three years ago because I was pretending to be Red Run's ally for information.

I asked, "How is that pup's name relevant? It's not. I've known it for three years; I just don't care about her." She waved, "Yes, well as you know the second you told us about Sam's heat and possibly trying for another child we got some spelled cookies into her at the grocery store. They were samples she tried. Once she did that, she had to have them. We even signed her up for delivery direct to her house."

I grinned, "So no one will question you because you have her signature. Are you keeping up the deliveries?" She winked, "I have for three years. The pack loved it when we showed up with the cookies when she was pregnant because she couldn't keep anything but our cookies down. It was all part of the plan." It was honestly thrilling to me how much I was getting past Drake McAlister. He had no idea, but one day I would shove it all in his face.

I grinned, "So, you spelled Sam. We need more than that to convince them of all our plans. I've been trying to tell you that. She wolves are fiercely protective." One of my own pup's mother's was annoyingly against my ideas.

She had Alpha blood, and I knew our pup would be my strongest pup. She just fought for him every step of the way. Tao could be great, and she wanted him to be good, just like Alpha Eric Conners. It made me sick. Her mate stood up for them both. I couldn't believe him. I'd raped his mate in front of him while he was sedated and he still wanted Tao. He was infuriating.

The woman in front of me nodded, "Yes, we found a couple that had a child with Werewolf blood." I cut her off, "I told you it was important my brother's line was involved in this." She grinned, "And this child IS related to him." I asked, "How?"

She huffed, "So the she wolf he had a child with impregnated a human." I wanted to grimace. She said, "Your brother was twelve at the time." I shrugged. She continued, "That human gave birth to a girl who had a teen pregnancy with another human." Disgusting. She added, "If you care, they ended up being mates." I did not care in the slightest.

She replied, "The pack wouldn't accept her, so he rejected her." I frowned, "And?" She replied, "She gave up that child who went into foster care. This child is that child's daughter. The family is quite young and very happy to have a steady income for something simple." It seemed to be a problem with that group to keep having kids young. At least it helped serve my purpose.

She asked, "Do you want their contact information?" I scoffed, "Why would I want that?" She answered, "They are relatives of yours." I explained slowly, "If I am seen with them, the allies will catch wind of it all. What's the plan? Walk me through it." Because we were hammering out the details and we disagreed on a main sticking point of mine. I wanted Melanie here and hidden. They did not.

She sighed, "Ok, so now that we know Melanie's talent, we…." I snorted, "No pup of Drake McAlister's will have any talents of note." She sighed, "Yes, well you do realize he's somewhat a genius himself?" I dismissed her with a wave.

She told me, "Ok, well by all accounts Melanie is smart like Drake is, but even more so." That wouldn't be hard since he was an idiot. She continued, "She's also a dancer." I snorted, "She's three." She grinned, "We have a teacher in the dance school on our payroll and she slipped us the tape of Melanie's class. She's amazing." I rolled my eyes knowing they were wrong.

She continued, "We plan to have the pup you are related to wear this necklace." She held it up saying, "She'll look like the McAlister girl. I took a hair off the baby when I delivered Sam her cookies three years ago. I told her that I'd heard she'd given birth and made an extra batch for her. We'd packed those with some sedatives to knock her out. It was improv on my part."

I growled, "The pack OB could've discovered the whole plan!" She rolled her eyes, "They didn't. Plus, they had already did all their bloodwork. I am NOT a novice." I said, "You have a counterpart but you have Witch powers." She winked at me, "It makes me effective, doesn't it?" She was annoying and I wanted to rip her apart.

She waved, "Come on, admit it. I'm helpful. I kept Sam secluded her entire pregnancy." I snorted, "It was only three months, and you want a damn crown. It was also three years ago." She rolled her eyes, "Yes, I do. That's not easy to do for someone who is a social butterfly like Sam McAlister. I even kept her best friend away." I outright laughed, "Chelsea Hanes has absolutely been around Sam." She frowned, "Valerie Bi…" I cut her off, "I know who Valerie is. I know who everyone tied to that family is."

She said, "Well, to this day Valerie has not seen Melanie. Nor has anyone outside of the pack, because Drake has been influenced to be even more overprotective than his instincts call for." I asked, "Cookies again?" She grinned, "No, it's in his coffee." I wanted to say she'd probably gone overboard because she clearly didn't know how much coffee Beta's drank, but I didn't really care. I kind of hoped Drake sounded so paranoid that Alpha Peter removed him as his Beta.

She said, "Now, we'll have the pup cross the border. We have hit a possible, and very large, snag." I snarled, "WHAT?!" She explained, "The pup in the pack that's your blood…" I cut her off, "If he's befriended them, I'll kill him."

She gasped, "Wow. Overreaction much? No, it's the opposite problem. Your son and the McAlister's don't get along, especially our target." I sat back humming, "Good boy." She rolled her eyes, "Yes, well it's how we discovered Melanie believes Alexander Conners is her mate."

I asked, "And?" She snorted, "Now, we need to keep them away from each other. Along with his family. We don't have powerful enough spells for the Princess though." I questioned, "But you do for Alpha Eric?" She replied, "Well, it's a stronger batch and being tested right now in their pack. So far, it's only kept him from directly interfering with things surrounding Melanie.

" I scoffed, "How did you get it in?" She answered vaguely, "We have a mole in their pack." I asked, "Who?" She shrugged, "I can't tell you." I snorted, "As if I'd tell them." She laughed, "Well, until Cassandra Conners died it was her." That actually pulled me up short before I busted up laughing so hard I hit my knee. I cackled, "You turned CASSANDRA CONNERS?" She grinned, "They had her over a barrel, but honestly she was more than happy to help. She gave us so much information on Melanie it's crazy."

I conceded, "She would. She hates Fairies." She waved, "Yes, well now there is another." I asked, "Who? I might need to assist them." She sighed, "Her name is Patricia. She's quite money hungry and has an expensive shopping habit. She thinks she's passing information to the Supernatural Council." I asked, "Is she?" She chuckled, "Yes, but it's also us." I didn't care enough to ask how.

I urged, "Back to our plans." She nodded, "Yes, and I know you won't like this. So, just hear me out." I sat back in my chair and gestured for her to go ahead. She cleared her throat, "I've taken care of the

McAlister's phone by getting them to a great dark Witch. No one outside the pack can see pictures of Melanie, they are blurs. With this Conners possible mating, we need a bigger spell. So, that's being worked on."

I nodded, indicating with my index finger she needed to keep going. She explained, "We can't have the Conners seeing what she truly looks like for all this to work. Given her abilities in dancing that's how we are going to get them to believe she's left the pack. Sam will be spelled when Melanie gets older to push for an Arts school in New York. Your relative is going to take her spot."

I asked, "Can this other pup involved dance?" She shrugged, "It will likely be for acting, but we'll cover the bases." I asked, "And the McAlister's are going to be fine not speaking to their daughter? You guys suck at planning. No wolf would be ok with that."

She rubbed her temples complaining, "You are a terrible listener. We have the plan all laid out. We have a way to get in their phones just briefly. They will think communication is coming from other Alpha's." I glared at her.

She huffed, "For example, we will send a text pretending to be Alpha Eric to Drake when Melanie is older about no popping to their kids. Alpha Eric is going to decline to talk about it. Drake's phone is not as protected as Alpha Eric's, so we are going to do a fake call from Alpha Eric to him. We will be quite busy intercepting calls, but in the end, no one will be able to come to Melanie when she needs them." I liked that a lot.

I said, "That's great and all but I need her here to turn her evil. I want to bring her into the Ring. She needs to be conditioned then we will have her bringing other wolves into this life." She sighed, "Yeah, I'm not done explaining the plan." I shrugged, "Fine."

She grinned, "Thank you. Anyway, Sam is going to be heavily spelled…" I cut her off, "Then you need to keep Ryan Bishop away from her or he will be able tell." She huffed, "I'm telling the story! The Bishop's can't tell if she's ingesting it. The necklace she has that has her paranoid about Melanie is always hidden under her clothes, Ryan Bishop will never see it." That sounded like a possible risk, but I gestured for her to continue.

She huffed, "Sam will be compelled to convince Drake to let Melanie go to the school when she's thirteen." I asked, "Compelled? Sam is a Werewolf." She groaned, "And we know a Vampire that can compel Werewolves."

I grinned, "So, compel Drake to let her go." She carefully replied, "If that's necessary we will." I laughed, "This is sounding better and better." She continued, "Anyway, you told us about crossing the border, so we are going to have to keep that up. We'll have to trial some test runs attacking Red Run when they leave Melanie behind. We haven't decided those events yet, but the point is they will be test runs."

I pressed, "For when?" She grinned, "Elise and EJ will have some big events at Black Mountain. We will choose one of theirs. We plan to make sure Melanie doesn't eat the cookies. She already calls them mom monster cookies. She positively hates me."

I laughed, "You've been spotted by a pup." She rolled her eyes, "A genius pup, but the cookies make Sam angry any time they are mentioned. She does NOT care for being called a mom monster." That was actually funny.

She continued. "So, we pick an event. We will engineer a massive fight over the border ordeal. A Beta pup will be upset that they don't believe her, yes?" I nodded, "Oh yeah, super pissed. Especially if she has proof."

She grinned, "Good. So, they have a big fight then we will put the pack into a trance and convince them Melanie left for New York for school. Just ran off." I grinned, "That will kill Drake." She frowned, "I doubt he will die." I sighed, "Metaphorically."

She nodded, "Oh well yes, he does seem to love her quite a bit." He was weak and didn't see pups for what they were. Mindless drones whose opinions you could form and shape. He was stupid and these people thought he was smart.

She clapped, "Then we will put her in an illusion. She will believe her parents and one brother return to talk to her. Hunters are coming so they will be attacked. We have to knock her out…" I cut in, "I want her hurt very badly." She offered, "I guess she could take a non-fatal shot." She wrote that down. She asked, "Which brother do you want her to believe turns his back on her?"

I thought about it then answered, "To believe they shipped her off being unable to care for her having any shot of her believing that would have to be Jason McAlister. Tristan is training to be the Lead Beta of their pack so she'd know he could do it with her there." She nodded and took that as another note.

She said, "Ok that's all good stuff. We'll have her see them die in the illusion." I grinned, "Then she comes here." She snorted, "No, she is already aware never to trust you. She'll never believe her family sent her to Alpha Ezra Knight. Drake tells all his children not to trust you." The bastard.

She said, "We are going to send her to Black Path. It's all worked out and their leadership agreed to our plan." I snarled, "THE HELL YOU ARE! SHE IS MINE TO TOY WITH!" She sat back calmly saying, "Which is why we have agreed to let Black Path have their justice. Yellow Hills killed your brother and your nephew is down there."

I growled, "I know." He'd been set on being a good person, so I lied to him when he was young. His mother and mate loathed me, but I didn't care. She nodded, "Yes, well you kept their pack in the fold because we weren't making headway with that Alpha and Beta until you turned Booker. So, we are going to give Melanie to Trevor to mark."

I snorted, "What?" She grinned, "Well, we are going to suppress Melanie's wolf on her sixteenth birthday." I was now leery of her. I asked, "You can do that?" She snorted, "Me? No. A very powerful dark Witch can." I grinned, "Valdoma."

She nodded, "Yes. Anyway, Melanie will be subjected to the teachings of the Forgotten packs and placed with Hunters." I grinned knowing Drake would lose his shit. She said, "She'll help them and every mission she helps with we will have documented to give him eventually. She'll kill innocents and let Omegas die."

That was a direct slap in the face to the allied beliefs. I said, "A Beta isn't just going to believe her family turned on her." She waved, "We have plans for that with fake letters and phone calls. We will steal Alpha Peter's official Alpha seal once she's in Black Path."

I instructed, "Do so during a pack party. They will brush it off as the pups pulling pranks." She took that note down too. She said, "We will have her convinced they blame her for the death since we plan to have her think they came back because they fight with her." That was all brilliant.

She added, "A suppressed wolf will die if they are marked by someone other than their fated mate." I grinned, "You'll kill her wolf?" She nodded. I sighed, "I still want her here." She said, "I know that, but think of the revenge you get on them all."

I growled, "It's better revenge if I broke her and turned her against them." She argued, "Yes, but think of the possibilities here. Melanie could be Alpha Alexander's mate which means once she's discovered as a Huntress they still can't touch her. They'd have trouble going after her considering she's Drake's daughter, but if she's truly Alpha Alexander's mate alliances would crumble when people rightfully wanted her dead because of those she kills." That would be hilarious.

She added, "Plus, the Princess will talk about her mental health and what was done to her as a pup. We will have the perfect tool to hold over their heads. It will KILL them to see her out there." I asked, "And you think she's going to reject Alexander? Or since she's mating Trevor, he just gets a second chance." She grinned, "Valdoma speculates that through a series of technical things you won't understand, he will still know she's his."

I laughed, "And you think Trevor won't die when he finds out?" She shrugged, "I don't care if he does or not." I admitted, "Neither do I." She grinned, "I didn't think you did." I said, "Drake will never let it fly that Melanie doesn't come home. Other than that, it's not a horrible plan."

She rolled her eyes, "It's a great plan. The pack is going to be compelled by the Vampire that compels. Drake will be horribly sick every time he thinks something doesn't make sense." I snorted, "A Beta wolf? Are you insane? They will know something is wrong." Wolves didn't get sick.

She shrugged, "A doctor will find nothing wrong with him and they will be compelled not to mention it to the Princess." I said, "You should probably make them have everyone making Alpha Eric's mate feeling crazy for asking questions about Melanie, because she will ask them. If everyone gaslights her, she'll be suspicious but she might think they are pranking her if they all do it." She took that note too.

I asked, "How are you going to get to an Alpha, Beta, Gamma? Hell, the entirety of their pack?" She grinned, "You are going to meet your son. Do what you do best and piss him off. Get him on our side. He can help with the cookies. We even want him to date someone in Black Mountain to easily get the cookies there. He can pick the girl so long as she's good at cooking. We can compile a list for him."

I snorted, "I won't have a pup of mine mated to some Omega cook." She rolled her eyes, "I said date, not mark." I nodded, "Fine. I guess I could go see him. He'll be easy to manipulate if he's anything like Skyler." She nodded, "His mother." I snorted, "She actually thinks I don't know she had my pup." She shrugged like she didn't give a single shit.

I agreed, "Fine, I'll get my pup onboard. He will NOT mark the Omega though, so do something so she doesn't press him to mark her. You should probably suppress her scent too or her mate will take her away." She sighed, "You always give me more to do." I winked, "Sorry about that." She rolled her eyes, "I know you aren't."

I chuckled, "So Sam McAlister is already a paranoid nutjob and her own daughter dislikes her." She answered, "No, Melanie loves her mother." I pointed out, "You said she calls her a mom monster." She nodded, "When she eats the cookies, yes. She still loves her mother." The pack would probably think Sam had lost it though. She'd become less likable to them, which would make Drake's life harder.

I asked, "What about Alpha Eric?" She winced, "Yes, he'll have to be compelled to." I pointed out, "If that goes wrong, we are all dead." She huffed, "We are getting everything in place. We will mute his bond. There are those in the Ring that know how the Princesses bond was muted from her Hackura Family. We are in the process of getting a bracelet like that for the process. We will figure it all out."

I reiterated, "I still want Melanie here at some point. If she turns thirty-five and is unmarked, I get her." She snorted, "Thirty-five?! Trevor is going to mark her when she turns eighteen." I laughed, "You think a daughter of a Beta will let that hapless pup mark her? She won't. She's already a trained fighter and better than him." She explained, "When she doesn't shift, we are going to tell her she's not Drake's daughter."

I shrugged, "Ok. That will hurt her, and I do like that, but you are discounting the stubbornness of Beta blood. I'm simply saying if she's unmarked at thirty-five I get her." Because it would KILL Drake if I marked his daughter, and she was mine.

She snorted, "It won't happen but fine. If she's unmarked at Thirty-five you can take your turn." I grinned and she looked at me oddly. She asked, "Why do you look so happy?" I winked at her, "It's nothing for you to worry about."

It was because that meant Melanie would be mine to mark. Trevor would not convince her to be his, ever. Especially if he was mean to her and abused her, which I planned to have him do starting the second he lays eyes on her. A Beta pup would NEVER stand for that. She knew what fated mates looked like and she knew he would never be able to raise a hand to her if it was true.

The representative stood and shook my hand, "I'll be back to discuss the plan as it develops. Goodbye Alpha Ezra." I dismissed her with a curt, "Bye." She snorted, "You could use my name." I called over my shoulder "I didn't bother to learn it."

I left with a smile on my face knowing one day Melanie McAlister would be mine and it would send Drake into an early grave. Melanie would be my evil mistress, and it would send Alexander Conners into a spiral, along with all the allies. It was certainly a good day to be me.

Mom Monster Cookies

Melanie is Seven Years Old

Melanie was pacing in her room. My Xander was going out on his first ever mission with his brother EJ. They had been ready for two years, but they were finally going. I was so nervous I could barely stand it. I'd tried to distract myself, but I couldn't concentrate on my book.

It was from my favorite series, the *Thoroughbred* Novels, and normally I could lose myself in the story, but not today. I told my Xander wolf, "I should be with Elise and Cassie having a sleepover, waiting in Black Mountain for them to come home."

I grumbled, "He's my Xander and I'm JUST as nervous as they are. It's really unfair when you think about it… except he doesn't know I'm his…. like I know he's mine. UGH!" I jumped on my bed and clutched my stuff wolf to me.

I whispered, "Keep him safe, ok." I groaned berating myself, "The wolf is with you, not Xander." I should've insisted Elise take him this time. I'd tried several times, but she always said my Xander would want me to have him.

Well, that was silly because I was NOT going on a mission. Why were they off school for a random holiday that had no assigned meaning? Why couldn't their mission be on the WEEKEND like NORMAL missions? I would have a dance competition and that would distract me then but NOOOOO.

My phone rang and I noted Tiffany, another dancer, was calling me. She lived in New York, but we went to competitions together. She was my toughest competitor. She loved competing against me and vice versa.

I answered, "Hey, Tiff." She said, "Your text was all over the place, per usual. Your Xander is what now?" I squeaked, "He's on his first mission and I have NOTHING to do!" She snorted, "Was world denomination off the table?"

I grumbled, "I can't take over the whole world." She argued, "I mean, I think you could. You're seven and you already have a secret network of dancers to keep you clued into rumors about those you love." I blushed loving that it was true.

I muttered, "It's hardly my fault that people want to talk to me… or that other pups love to have something to come tell me. I just pointed them all at things that would be helpful… and pups are unassuming… people talk in front of them… and stuff. Something people should consider but don't… because they are pups. Which works for me…as I am also a pup."

She snorted, "Yes, well you've gotten some good tips to pass off." Most never checked out, but a few had. It made me feel like I really was helping when it came down to it. Everyone said I was just a pup and never let me offer suggestions. Even though I'd been tested and was on a genius level, surpassing my dad's I.Q.

That wasn't easy either. My dad was very smart, he was just better at not rambling than I was… and lying… and talking to people in general. Everyone said that would come, but I wasn't sure. I just didn't see the point in not telling people the truth. They'd learn it eventually, but I could acknowledge I could easily have finesse. Beta's all had that in spades, but not me.

Think about my network had me thinking of an encounter in Minnesota when Tiffany covered for me.

Flashback

Tiffany whispered, "Ok, your mom is talking to mine. Go." I nodded, "Thanks." She added, "For the record, this is crazy." I replied, "I'll be back before my dance slot…and if anyone thinks…I mean I've got it worked out." Tiffany chuckled, "Go. I'll say you have a new dancing ritual and no one can see it. Your mom will buy that." I knew that since we'd worked it all out.

I went into my dressing room, which I'd gotten through my reputation and someone working here being a fan. I'd set it all into motion last week when I'd had a pup ask me if I was interested in something they overheard about my Xander. Of course, I was.

This dressing room had a door to a different area, but that wasn't well known. Only the working maintenance crew knew about it. Since I had sources, I did too from a pup whose dad worked here. I changed into bulky clothes and pulled a hoodie over my head.

I had my bus pass ready to go. I was heading for Arden Hills. It was a lesser known suburb of Minneapolis which worked for me. Bloomington was the most popular one. I pretended to be asleep and heard the Demons behind me.

One grumbled, "I'm going to figure out how to kill that Angel." I slit my eyes open and the Angel a row in front of me turned and winked at him. The Demon growled, "Stop stealing my girlfriends." The Angel laughed, "But it's so easy." I knew how to kill and Angel.

A plan formed in my mind. I already had a few secret history books from other Supernatural groups and a security box for them. It was the first time I'd implemented Prince Gunner Cambridge's word as gospel and it worked. The security box was under an alias I'd set up using his tips.

I only had two lesser known history books from other supernaturals so far, but some of the books I'd read in Faerie led me to believe the Angel's might have a secret history book. I really wanted it. I wondered why they kept it so secret. The book had to have that answer....right?

This wasn't a Fallen Angel, so he might know about the history book. I did know how to kill an Angel, and he never needed to know that I wouldn't actually tell that Demon how to kill him. Both of them got off in Arden Hills, which was perfect.

I jogged after the Angel. I called, "Excuse me, sir." He turned, "Pup." I hummed, "So, I have a question." He snorted, "Ok." I asked, "Do you know about the secret Angel history book?" He gasped and grabbed me by the arm. I hit his elbow instantly making him let go.

I surmised, "So you do...or you wouldn't have done that. I want it...or a copy is fine..." He cut me off, "Why the hell would I give you a copy? And how do you know about it?" I hummed, "Yeah...I'm not answering the second part...except technically you told me...so...I guess I will answer. I suspected... your actions confirmed. Anyway, I want it and since I know how to kill and Angel...I think you'll tell me.. since you don't seem to want to die...and that Demon wants you to."

He gasped, "Are you threatening me?" I corrected, "I'm blackmailing you...there is a difference since... I'm not going to use the knowledge of how to kill and Angel on you...I'm giving it to someone who wants to kill you."

He demanded, "Tell me how to kill an Angel then." I conceded, "That's fair to ask." He asked, "Why the fuck would you care about being fair?" I answered, "Xander does." He blinked several times. I waved, "Anyway, you can kill an Angel not a part of Michael's line with a phoenix thread, phoenix feather, a drop of demon blood, venom from a werebasilisk, a drop of a Leviathan's blood, fur from a bunyip, shavings from a wolpertingers shed antlers, and a flaming sword."

He ordered, "Keep your voice down." I said, "No one is nearby." He clenched his fists asking, "How did you come by that knowledge?" I answered, "Uhh other secret history books...and umm...hacking." The Hackura knew how to kill Angels and...I'd seen that record.

He rubbed his temples, "Look, I have a reason to mess with that Demon." I shrugged, "Ok. That's not really pertinent information...to this conversation." He snorted, "Yeah, I'm pretty sure you wouldn't tell him how to kill me. You're not an Angel though so it's not a big deal if you have the book. Keep it a secret."

I agreed, "Sure...I have a lot of those...plus...I'm a pup so no one really listens to me." He snorted and waved his hands around and handed me the book that appeared in his hands. I asked, "Umm how did you do that? Angels don't have a conjuring ability." He replied, "The answer is in the book. Stay out of trouble. You're definitely the most interesting person I've met in a century or two." I grabbed the book and thumbed through it.

I ordered myself, "Focus…do what you came her to do…even though this side mission was TOTALLY awesome…and…focus." He chuckled and I ran off with the book. I would give my tip and get back in time to dance. I was just going to cut it closer than planned.

Flashback Ends

Tiffany's chuckled pulled me back to the present. I groaned, "I need something to do." Tiffany suggested, "Go dance in your field." I jolted up, "Yes! That's brilliant, that's what I need to do… I only hadn't because T's not available but…"

She jumped in, "Maybe wait for him." I snorted, "Then what would I do?" She sighed, "So, you're going. Just record it for me since I bet it will be good." I agreed, "Yeah, you shoot me your inspiration week dance too." She laughed, "You know, you keep dancing fun because we do this. I think I'd be burned out if not for you."

I asked, "Burned out? We are seven." She snorted, "And more mature than the other seven year olds, even for Supernaturals, and in more hours of practice because we can handle it. Humans can't understand my intellect and abilities let alone your freak of supernatural natural ones."

I snorted, "Well… ok that's probably true… and they do call us both prodigies." She admitted, "We are even for supernatural's. Ok, I'll go choreograph. You do the same." I would. I grabbed an old phone of my dad's that he loaded every type of music on for me.

I went out into the main area of the house. No one was here so I just left a note on the fridge that I went dancing in the field I loved. They knew which one it was. I skipped out with my Xander wolf and my Xander wolf shirt. I'd scoured the internet for it then showed Grandma Esther. She understood me almost as much as my dad did.

I was positive, even though no one said it, she was genius too. She got me better than most people. She bought it for me with a smirk on her face saying it would be my protector wolf shirt. I saw several people on my way out there and waved to everyone.

Several called, "Hey, Ladybug!" Some pups stopped to ask about dancing positions, and I helped them all. I couldn't keep the smile off my face because I truly loved this pack. Most of the pack members were nice, but not all of them were.

I didn't focus on the negative ones though because they were few and far between. I did see a dad push his teenage son into the gym when he growled. His eyes were zoned in on my Xander wolf. My face fell because I knew people didn't like it.

Zane, our Male Lead Warrior, paused and knelt down. He put a hand on my shoulder, "Ladybug, you're allowed to have your stuffed wolf." I whispered, "I know but I thought everyone would be used to him by now."

A delighted smile filtered across his face. He asked, "Him?" I nodded and watched him try to suppress his smirk. He commented, "I see. Does your dad know the wolf is a he?" I pointed out, "I mean… it's black… and white… well… I guess all Alpha's including she wolves are black… but my wolf….I mean I know I don't have her yet…but she probably wouldn't like a she wolf Alpha… since… well… I like guys… so I feel it's obvious… that…"

Adeline jumped into view commenting, "It's totally obvious." I squealed, "ADELINE!" She laughed, "Hey, what are we doing?" She linked, "Distraction time?" I nodded. She knew Xander was out on a mission, and I was nervous.

Zane asked, "Why do you have an old phone AND a tablet?" I answered, "Well, the old phone is for music to choreograph… the new dance I'm thinking of… and the tablet is in case…" Adeline said, "Someone needs her to come home."

He replied, "Uh huh. Sure it is. Linking would work." I stammered, "Umm… I get lost in dancing…" He interrupted, "I noticed." I rambled on, "And sometimes… dad says I lock out links… which like… I shouldn't be able to do as a pup… but when you think about it… I can do a lot… so who knows… maybe it's not really that crazy… and… well…"

He held up his hands interrupting "I have to coach a practice that has some individuals who need to run some extra laps now. Have fun with whatever you're doing while you dance. Try not to take over the world." I grumbled, "Why do people keep saying that to me? I have never, even once, tried to take over the world." He snorted and jogged away.

Adeline looped her arm in mine. She surmised, "So, you're nervous?" I admitted, "I am… it's just that… well… it will be fine… but I should be at the sleepover too!" She pointed out, "There was no reason for Elise to get you there other than to say you wanted to go. You didn't think your mom would say yes." I muttered, "She might have if not for the mom monster cookies."

Adeline replied, "Even without one, it was a stretch of an ask." I pointed out, "But it SHOULDN'T be. Black Mountain is even more protected than our borders and really, it's just… insane to think I wouldn't be safer there than here." She agreed, "It kind of is. Are we going with the angsty playlist?" I nodded and set up tablet to record for Tiffany.

I also set up a few alerts. I'd followed Prince Gunner Cambridge's steps to monitor some things. I knew that my dad and Jason would be notified when EJ and Alexander were back. Jason was going to see Alexander and mayyyybbbeeee

I was hacking them to make sure my Xander was ok. Which was fair when you thought about it… I would get grounded for forever if they found out… but it was TOTALLY for the greater good.

I got lost in the music until Adeline called, "I've got to go home for dinner. You dance so beautifully. I'll see you tomorrow!" I replied, "See you later, Adeline!" She was easily my best friend in the pack. I kept dancing until

I heard a ping on my tablet. I squeaked and ran over. My Xander was texting my brother. I read the messages as if I was Jason since that's who I'd hacked.

<u>Best Bro:</u> I'm back man. Wanna come celebrate?
<u>Me:</u> Be there soon.

I sighed desperately wishing the me was actually me and not Jason. I snorted, "You have Xander saved in your phone as 'Best bro' really Jase?!" Oh well, now I had his number. Well, for now. According to the files… I totally got the right way and not hacking that time… he was going to change his number several times. He'd get his permanent one when he was eighteen.

They did have charms so any number they wanted to be able to text them would be forwarded from the old one. It was an impressive security measure that I really liked. I should do that… if I ever got my own phone… but my mom would eat her mom monster cookies…so I never got one.

Her argument mostly made sense because we didn't go to an actual school until we were eleven years old for middle school. So, I was usually with family, and I really didn't need a phone since I had my dad's old one with all the music.

They definitely didn't know all the things I had access to on my tablet. Which at this point, was definitely for the best… when you thought about it. I powered it down and took off. I was running along when I realized I was being herded. I was hit from behind then on front.

I screamed, "What are you doing?" They ripped off my brand new Xander shirt. Robert growled, "Next is that stupid stuffed wolf!" I screamed and punched him and kicked his other goon in the balls. I snarked, "You'd think you would learn, I'm better than you are." This wasn't the first time they'd pinned me down, but they'd never ripped off my shirt before.

He snarled, "I'll rip that stupid wolves head off." I screamed, "NO! HE IS MY WOLF!" I scooped up Xander wolf from where he fell and ran. Robert yelled, "Yeah, you'd better run! That wolf is going to be shredded next time. Don't you dare tell a single soul about this."

I snarled, "You've been trying for four years to tear him up and he's still fine!" He growled, "But not your shirt." Grandma Esther had bought me that shirt. Tears sprung into my eyes.

I found my dad's shirt lying around when I got farther away. I knew, as they did, that I could outrun them. I put it on and let myself cry into my Xander wolf. I whispered, "What will I tell Grandma Esther?"

I powered up the tablet and ordered a replacement shirt. I'd just keep it in my closet. I shivered remembering the look in Robert's eyes when he ripped it off. He was officially unhinged.

I began to pace. Logically, the right thing to do was go to Alpha Peter… but they never believed me when I said I didn't cross the border. Plus, this wasn't really an emergency… when you broke it down. I needed them to believe me if something REALLY bad happened.

If my bullies were upgrading to ripping my clothes off and that was not a good escalation in pups' behavior according to the papers Princess Luna Haley's psychology group published. It wasn't even just her that had written about concerning behaviors to look for and seek help on.

Literally all across the globe people were backing her up and conducting their own studies. Robert and his friends just made a very bad move in their progression to Supernatural's who turn angry, bitter, and abusive.

The thing was those people were often… well more often than not… the ones that ended up getting killed because our way of life didn't lead to everything being fine, if you were a jerk.

For example, if my Xander knew he was mine, Robert would've died for what he just did. I rubbed my face berating, "He doesn't know though… and you need the adults to believe you if they do something worse… I have no bruises, and they definitely do. If they say that I did it… would everyone believe them?"

I had a dance competition I didn't want to risk not going to. I'd invited Xander… and I wanted to win. I took several deep breaths, clutched my Xander wolf tightly, then began to run home. I didn't hear anyone chasing me so maybe they gave up.

Once I got closer to my house a Warrior stopped me. He asked, "Ladybug, are you ok?" I squeaked, "Ok… huh… obviously … it's totally…" He checked me up and down. He questioned, "Is this the Beta's shirt?" I answered, "Umm well yes… it is… and…."

He grabbed my shoulders gently. He asked, "Are you ok, Melanie?" I had to decide right now if I was going to tell anyone. I nodded, "Totally… I'm so beyond fine… I mean… the Beta is my dad… so this is not weird…."

He frowned, "First, I know you're lying because you're bad at it." I winced. He continued, "Second, you have no reason to change into your dad's shirt that he lying around. I can smell that shirt has been outside and you haven't shifted yet. So, there is literally no need for you to find his shirt and put it on." He made some very valid point.

He sighed, "I'll escort you home. Ok?" I nodded and he jogged home with me. It was moments like this that made me love it here. Even though Robert was awful, and so were his friends; they were the outliers.

I nodded, "Thanks, Harrison." He asked, "You know me?" I answered, "Yes because you train with top ranked Warriors… and I might… well… I kind of… spy… is a harsh word, but…" He laughed, "Come on and join us next time, Ladybug." I squeaked, "Really?" He grinned and nodded.

I ran into the house past my mom who just laughed. It wasn't uncommon for me to come home in a blur of movement. I burst into my room and checked my email.

I did a little dance because Xander had signed for the dance competition ticket I sent him. His signature wasn't legible, which was odd for a supernatural, but he was probably in a hurry. I pulled up my app to talk to Tiffany. She answered my video call.

She greeted, "Hey Mel, I've got a few minutes before I have to go." I whispered, "He signed for it." Her face fell, "Ok, but he's signed for several now." I grinned saying, "I know but he could come this time." She winced, "Just don't get your hopes up." I waved, "I know. He's really busy and…" She cut me off, "He's twelve."

I nodded, "Yup… yup… I know. He's got future Alpha stuff… training… He's a double Duke… So, like I do get it and…" She cut me off, "You shouldn't get it. He's TWELVE therefore he has time." I frowned, "I mean not really…" She jumped in, "Then stop saving your money and sending him tickets." I shrugged because she didn't know I invested my money. It wasn't really…. in the realm of being legal.

I didn't use the investment money to send him tickets though. I saved my allowance, which is what Tiffany was talking about. I shrugged, "It's my money." Her face softened saying, "And you work hard for it with all the chores you do. You should do things you really like." I whispered, "I'm meeting him this week." She rubbed her face, "I really hope you do. I hope those jerks don't lie again." They always did, then mom ate her mom monster cookies and stopped believing me.

I admitted, "I'm planning to throw the mom monster cookies away." She laughed, "Then you'll get grounded." I muttered, "Not if she doesn't eat them." I heard a gasp and looked over towards the door. I told Tiffany, "I'll talk to you later." She waved, "See ya at our next competition!" I waved back and ended the call.

I went downstairs and found Mrs. Dutton there. I asked, "Where's my mom?" She waved, "Oh, a situation came up and she and your dad went to handle it. Do you know why Warrior Harrison was trying to talk to the Beta before it all happened? My husband said Harrison said it was important before they got pulled away."

I squeaked, "Huh? What? That's… well…" She snorted, "Did you beat up one of the Warriors he works out with?" I answered, "No… but he did say I could come to practice…" She laughed, then Grandma Esther came into the house.

Grandma Esther announced, "I've got my grandpup, you can go on about your day." Mrs. Dutton nodded and waved to me before she left. She warned, "If you go to that practice make sure you tell your brothers or your parents." I was going to go and I would tell them. They were never weird about me practicing. They were proud of my skills.

I asked, "What's going on?" Grandpa Esther answered, "Boring adult stuff. Which means we are having a grandparent's night. Let's pack your things." I squealed and went upstairs to grab all my stuff. I packed an overnight bag and ran back downstairs. She smiled at me, "Let's go, Ladybug."

I took her hand. I asked, "So, you're not going to tell me what happened either? Because… something did. I heard mom gasp and…" She paused and took me over to the porch swing and sat down and patted the seat next to her. I jumped up beside her.

She started to rock the swing back and forth. She said, "You know, you remind me so much of your dad. He was just so curious about life and able to understand things better than other people." I giggled, "Because you do."

She grinned saying, "I am not as smart as you or your daddy are. My brother was and I saw how it frustrated him when people gave excuses not to answer his questions. Or didn't have the answers to his questions." I knew that.

I asked, "Where is your brother?" She'd never mentioned him. She sighed sadly, "He was killed by rogues because he had questions no one would answer. He went out in search of those answers without understanding what he was doing. It's why your parents react the way they do when the Warriors say you've crossed the border."

I made a face grumbling, "But I don't." She grinned, "I'm not looking to start a debate about that." I asked, "Did my daddy know your brother?" She nodded, "He did. He adored him and they understood each other in a way none of us did. Your daddy was ten when my brother died, and it devastated him. Did you know your mom's aunt and cousin died because of a rogue attack?" I shook my head.

She sighed, "Her cousin crossed the border, and her mom took off after her. The rogues killed them before the border patrol got there. Sam was in their pack visiting and ran as fast as she could to try and help them. Her Uncle tried to hold her back from seeing, but she saw their dead bodies."

I gasped, "That's awful." She agreed, "It is. Families have their fair share of tragic stories because of rogues. It's what scares us so badly about you." She tapped my head, "You have such a gifted mind, and while that's a beautiful thing it can lead you into dangerous situations."

I argued, "Anyone can go into a dangerous situation." She agreed, "Yes, they can. Rogues and border crossing are just hot topics for our family." I concluded, "So, someone crossed the border." She nodded, "Yes, a group of pups dared their friends to cross. Sharon popped the pup to Haley to try and save him. He was still alive, but the rogues ripped his arms and legs off the second he stepped over our border."

I asked, "Why were they lying in wait? I mean… one of them couldn't have done that before our patrol go there based on the times they run. Dad has a whole system so that…" She interrupted, "There were five of them and because of how your dad has the patrols run, they got there before one could rip his throat out." I emphatically stated, "He will be fine."

She sighed, "I hope so." I shook my head, "No, the Princess will heal him and he will be fine." She kissed the top of my head, "I hope he will be. I've seen that woman perform some damn miracles in this life, but this would be one of the most amazing."

I argued, "Hmmm no it would not." She asked, "Oh?" I explained, "I read the report about when Alpha Eric got shot. That's how I know she can do it. Plus… Xander is there. So, if she needed help, he would assist. No Werewolf should've been able to survive that shot Alpha Eric did."

She winced admitting, "That's true. Your parents are comforting the pup's family and praying with several others to the Moon Goddess the pup lives." I asked, "Shouldn't it be Azoney? The Princess is using her Fairy powers and Selene has no control over that."

She chuckled, "See? That brain just works on another level. That's an excellent point. Come on, let's go make some cookies." I nodded even though I wasn't a fan of mom monster cookies, I did like cookies. Especially sugar cookies. The mom monster ones were peanut butter flavored.

I asked, "How old is the pup who crossed?" She answered, "He's four." I nodded and we walked over to my grandparents' house. When we walked in my Grandpa Ben scooped me up and hugged me tight.

My Aunt Melinda squealed, "They brought Melanie over MaryBeth!" My Grandpa sighed and put me down. I ran and hugged them both. They were my aunts but we were really close in age so we were really good friends.

I asked, "How are you guys?" MaryBeth grabbed my bag and yanked me upstairs. Grandma Esther yelled, "We are making cookies in fifteen minutes, girls. Then we are having a movie night." Grandpa Ben laughed, "And I need help turning the living room into a fort."

I turned, "I actually thought of a…" Melinda snorted, "Yes, we know. You'll have some revolutionary way to do that, but right now it's girl time." Grandpa laughed with Grandma. I watched them kiss for a second before I turned and followed my aunt's into their room.

They'd chosen a joint room even though they were always told they could have separate ones. The room was literally two different personalities. I asked MaryBeth, "How's Dane?" She sighed dreamily, "He's perfect."

Melinda snorted, "He needs your help though because he's getting a C in math." MaryBeth snorted, "Not everyone gets math. Ok? It's no big deal." I grinned, "I'll help." She hugged me, "I know because you're the best." Plus, he was older than me and I loved doing higher level work.

I added, "Not that anything is wrong with a C…. Does he want to work harder? Or is he in trouble…? Because a C is passing and…" Melinda cut me off, "He wants to do better personally. He's not in trouble." I agreed, "Then I will definitely help." They both grinned at each other.

Melinda whispered, "Did your Xander sign for the ticket?" I clapped and giggled, "He did." We all jumped around squealing. MaryBeth said, "Maybe he will come this time." I nodded, "I sent him a note, like always. If I meet him this weekend, then we could talk about what he was doing at the past events."

Melinda frowned, "It doesn't really make sense that he doesn't reply to the note. He's so nice." I shrugged, "He's busy." MaryBeth snorted, "He could still show proper etiquette and reply with a no or yes. I hate that you get your hopes up and then he doesn't come." I shrugged, "It's totally fine and…" Melinda groaned, "I thought we discussed what a bad liar you are."

I gasped, "I've been working on it!" MaryBeth said, "It's not working. Your whole countenance dropped, and your face fell. In fact, you look near tears." I pointed out, "But I didn't sniffle… or start to cry… so that's obviously progress."

Melinda snorted, "You take the smallest steps as progress." I reasoned, "Well, of course I do… because that's the definition of progress. It's not measured by big leaps…. any sort of little step is…" MaryBeth groaned, "You always lose me with these explanations."

I grinned, "No I don't." She giggled, "No, you don't. You're so smart and interesting to listen to. Some smart people are SO boring. You're always fun and your explanations are hilarious." I frowned admitting, "My teachers tell me I'm not succinct enough."

Melinda snorted, "Screw them. They are jealous you are smarter than them. Your brain just doesn't work like theirs." I admitted, "I could probably… pause before speaking. It's what they all say.. a lot… daily even."

MaryBeth gasped, "NO! That's the charm of Ladybug. I will tell daddy to GET them. They can't do that! I love how you talk and explain things. How dare they try to change how you talk!" I pointed out, "Well… my rambling is all they can help me with."

Melinda cut me off, "You don't need help with your rambling. Your thoughts work differently than most people. That's not wrong, it's just different. Don't change who you are for anyone. Especially a teacher who is probably just jealous you correct them."

I pointed out, "Not everyone finds my rambling endearing." MaryBeth stated, "Then they are stupid." I gasped, "You can't say that!" She boasted, "I just did. We love you for who you are. If you want to change, then that's fine. I'd be sad, but other people shouldn't be trying to change you. You're awesome." I hugged them declaring, "I love you guys."

Grandma called, "Let's bake everyone!" I asked, "What's MaryBeth going to do?" She gasped, "I'm helping." I raised an eyebrow, "Uhh… that's like a… I mean not the worst idea… but it's kind of up there." She stomped her foot and ran downstairs.

Melinda snickered, "It really is." I whispered, "She nearly burned the house down the last time she was in the kitchen." Melinda laughed and took me downstairs. I was right though, she literally burned part of their house down. Sharon had to fix it.

MaryBeth glared at me as she put the storebought cookies onto the sheet. My heart sank into my feet when I saw the dough the box came in. The mom monster cookies were now being sold in dough form. I asked, "Can't we just make them from scratch? Even if MaryBeth puts a whole thing of sugar in…" MaryBeth gasped, "I wouldn't do that." Everyone made a face and Grandpa laughed.

Grandma said, "Well, I thought these would cheer your mom up. She loves them and she and your dad are doing a hard part of the job." Melinda linked, "Wait, the mom monster cookies come in dough form now?!" I replied, "Evidently."

Grandpa jumped in, "I need to borrow Ladybug since she looks like she's about to be more bug than lady." That's how I got my nickname. Tristan had come up with it saying sometimes I was a dream pup but when I was mad, I buzzed around like a bug. Hence, Ladybug.

Grandpa Ben took me outside. He asked, "What's with the face? You look betrayed." I whispered, "Those are the mom monster cookies." He winced, "They are just cookies." I pointed out, "There are so many brands out there, and I hate that one. I hate them! You guys act so weird when you eat them." It was true, they just affected my mom the most.

He sighed, "Ladybug, they really are just cookies." I snorted, "I really don't think that. I wish you'd ask Ryan Bishop about them." He raised an eyebrow, "You know your brothers call him Uncle. I find it odd you don't." I retorted, "I've never met him. How he could he be my uncle?"

I heard something drop. I turned and spotted Uncle Duncan standing there. He'd dropped his bag. He was staring between me and Grandpa Ben with confusion written all over his face. I squealed, "UNCLE DUNCAN!" I ran off the porch and threw myself into his arms.

He caught me, "Opf. You're getting so big. Look at you!" I heard Melinda and MaryBeth scream, "DUNCAN!" He put me down and caught them both. He said, "I swear to the Moon Goddess my little sisters have GOT to stop growing."

I muttered, "Or you could stop leaving so much… that's a thing… that feels like it could happen." He ruffled my hair, and we went inside. MaryBeth didn't seem to notice she was given tasks away from the oven. I didn't help with the cookies at all.

That made me feel bad, but they didn't need me to help. Plus, I refused on principle. Everyone always changed their mind about things after they had those cookies. Something was wrong with them, and I knew it. Plus, the lady who delivered them was evil. No one agreed, but I knew it.

I helped Grandpa Ben turn the entire living room into one big tent. They acted like it was revolutionary, but anyone could do this. They just needed a different support system. Uncle Duncan brought me popcorn because everyone else was eating cookies except the two of us.

Melinda and MaryBeth fell asleep, so they turned off the movie. I pulled out my ideas notebook and I started to write everything down I was thinking. Uncle Duncan whispered, "I think you're supposed to be sleeping." I admitted, "I've never figured out how to sleep when my mind is running with ideas."

He commented, "Finding a way to use jewelry to alert Supernatural's to elements that could hurt them is ingenious. It sounds quite complicated. You and your dad's brains just work on a different level." I boasted, "He's the smartest." He winked, "You've got him by far, pup."

I didn't think so. He was better with people than I was. He snorted, "You know, even when you say nothing, you're a bad liar. Your face literally details your thoughts. Your I.Q. is higher than your dad's and he's possibly the proudest of you for it."

I pointed out, "I'm bad at telling people things… I just say it… and I never gather my thoughts…" He jumped in, "That's not a bad thing." I whispered, "It is for a Beta blood." He scoffed, "Says who?" A lot of people but mostly Robert.

He frowned asking, "Melanie Jane, did someone say that to you?" I answered, "Yes." He growled, "They are wrong." I shook my head, "We are supposed to calm people down, but my way doesn't do that."

He argued, "That's not true. Sometimes you shock people into inaction. Every Beta has their own way of doing things. Any of the Kyle's would be lucky if you were their Beta, but between you and me I think you'll be doing something else."

I whispered, "I kind of want to work in the new lab at Black Mountain… or… be a Lead Warrior." He chuckled, "I think you'd be a good Luna." I squeaked, "Luna… that's… I mean…" He grinned, "Ladybug, I know my older brother and even sister in law are blind to who that little wolf looks like, but I'm not." I blushed, "I… umm… that's… well…"

He added, "Plus, I heard Jase say that Alexander left a sweatshirt at your house, and it was just put in the laundry. It had no scent before it went missing. I just so happened to see the hoodie in your room under your bed."

My face flushed, "Why were you under my bed? That's… weird…" He laughed, "I was putting a load of laundry away and the sleeve was out from under your bed skirt. I put it back, so your secret is safe." I muttered, "I just wanted to know what he smells like, and no one will say. It didn't even work…since it didn't have a scent."

He winked, "You'll find out one day, pup." I grinned, "Orrrrrrr you could tell me… because it's just fair…" He cut me off, "You'll find out at the picnic and Fairies are the ones who care about being fair. Not Wolves." I snorted, "You think I'm going to the picnic?" He answered, "Of course you are." I scoffed, "After they ate the mom monster cookies? I doubt it…" Tears filled my eyes.

I whispered, "Why can't I meet my Xander?" He asked, "Mom monster cookies?" Had he really not heard me say that? He frowned, "Wait, why did you say you haven't met Ryan Bishop earlier?" I answered, "I haven't."

He argued, "Valerie and Ryan used to come over to see you all the time." I snorted, "Uhhh no they didn't. Valerie calls mom to complain that they haven't met me a lot. Mom laughs and says she's sure she did. I got grounded from the last ally outing because I agreed with Valerie when they hung up."

He blinked, "Sam wouldn't ground you for that." I muttered, "Once she eats the mom monster cookies she does." He nudged me, "I'll look into it. Ok?" My face fell. I whispered, "That means you're leaving again."

He grinned, "I'm going looking for my mate this time. I'm not scouting anything dangerous." Uncle Duncan did a lot for the pack that was dangerous. Grandma Esther called him her daredevil. I stared him in the eyes, "Promise."

He grinned and held up his pinky finger, "Promise, Ladybug. It's not dangerous. I just want my other half." I gave him a hug. I whispered, "I'll miss you." He teased, "I'll be back." I shrugged, "Yes and no." He laughed, "This is going to be good."

I explained, "You'll visit but you'll leave the pack when you find your mate. I just feel she's in a position you won't make her leave. It's why you don't take a Beta or Warrior position here. You want to give your mate the option of where to live… so… you'll leave when you find her."

His eyes softened, "I'd never really leave you, Melanie Jane. You'll always be my favorite niece." I blushed, "You're not supposed to have favorites." He winked, "Yeah, but Allison's girls aren't you. I love them, but you'll always be my favorite."

I asked, "Promise?" He grinned, "I'm doing that a lot tonight, but I promise. Nothing could make me not love you. I came back to see you, didn't I?" I pointed out, "You came back to see everyone." He laughed, "Keep it between us, but I really came home to see if you took over the world. I'll keep an ear out about the cookies. Ok?" I shrugged knowing he wouldn't hear anything about it.

He asked, "What world domination ideas do you have these days?" I rolled my eyes, "I don't want to rule the world. I mean… I'd probably be bad at it… since my goal has been to meet my Xander forever and I never get to."

He disagreed, "You'd rule the world better than anyone else would. What papers have you read?" I grinned and launched into the papers coming out of Faerie and the Hackura realm I'd read. With more details than he probably cared to know.

He nudged me, "See? You combine papers, themes, and ideas no one else does. We have hybrids but everyone still sticks to what they know. You're the smartest pup there is." That seemed like an exaggeration. Grandpa Ben called, "Duncan, where's my grandpup?" He chuckled, "Busted."

We walked back inside, and he snorted at us. Grandma Esther announced, "The pup was healed by Haley." I frowned, "I told you he would be. I'm not sure why anyone… well no… his family and the people who saw it… but he was still alive when they got him to the Princess Luna… so… I mean he was going to be fine."

Grandma Esther added with a wink, "Alexander had to help but Haley and he were able to regrow all his limbs." I pursed my lips because I knew that would affect Xander. The bond he shared with his mom was a balance to each other, but it made him feel his siblings and his parents better than anyone else. He must have felt he needed to pop to her.

Grandpa Ben ordered, "Now, you go get to bed before your parents say no more sleepovers because we beyond missed your bedtime." I blushed, "I mean… I never go to sleep when they think I do…" They stared at me while Uncle Duncan smirked.

I continued, "Like when I was little… I would just close my eyes so mom would leave the room, and I could work on my ideas and…" Grandpa groaned. Uncle Duncan busted up laughing. I gasped, "Please don't tell them that until after the picnic." Grandma Esther said, "Yeah, I'm not telling them they didn't sneak anything in during that time."

I shrugged, "It's not like I haven't heard people having sex… and…" Grandpa Ben yelled, "No! No! No! Ladybug you are NOT talking about sex." I pointed out, "It's perfectly natural… and supernatural's have higher…"

Grandma Esther cut me off, "Loveable little Ladybug, go to sleep. Actually sleep this time. That big brain of yours needs rest." I grumbled, "Fine." I had more ideas to work out, but I did try to lay down. I tossed and turned until I wrote three more ideas down then my brain quietened. Then I was able to fall asleep.

When I woke up, Melinda and MaryBeth were still asleep. My Uncle Duncan raised his coffee to me and inclined his head. I jumped up and ran over to him. He held up his finger to his mouth and we crept out of the house. He handed me the coffee and I slammed it.

He grinned saying, "There's that Beta blood. Step back." I did and he shifted then knelt down. I greeted, "Hi Jinx." I climbed on his back, and he took off for a run. Pepper joined us and I squealed, "Daddy!" He purred and we kept running.

When we got back, I got off Jinx's back. They shifted back, grabbed shorts, and my dad slammed into Uncle Duncan. He laughed, "You snuck back into the pack, little brother." Uncle Duncan teased, "Which you knew." My dad gently shoved him, "Of course I did. I always know what you're doing. It's my job as the older brother." He put Uncle Duncan in a headlock and gave him a noogie.

My mom yelled, "Melanie Jane!" I turned and waved, "Hi, mom." She sighed, "You can't just go somewhere without telling your grandparents." Uncle Duncan said, "That was my bad, but I left a note." My mom sighed, "She knows better." She ate a cookie while talking and I nearly cried.

I waved to Uncle Duncan, and he yanked me in for a hug. I whispered, "Good luck on your trip." He ruffled my hair, "Thanks, pup." I ran back inside and got my things quickly. I hugged Grandma and Grandpa. Melinda and MaryBeth squealed and hugged me.

Melinda linked, "I can't wait to go the picnic." Yeah, neither could I. My parents took me home where my brothers were waiting. My mom cooked us all breakfast and everyone was laughing and talking. My heart fell when my mom ate five mom monster cookies. I was barely talking, which had my brothers looking surprised and concerned.

I had to bite my tongue several times, but I wasn't going to wake the mom monster. Peter came in and called, "Drake I need you." My dad kissed us all on the head. Chelsea called, "Sam!" My mom laughed, "I'm called into action too. You guys stay out of trouble." She pointed at me, "I'm looking at you Ladybug." I nodded, biting my cheek so hard I drew blood.

I literally NEVER caused trouble. I waited until the door shut and pushed my chair back so hard it fell. Jason yelled, "Mel!" I ran up to my room and slammed the door then screamed into my pillow in anger. My door flew open. Nosey big brothers.

Tristan asked, "What the fuck was that?" Jason snorted, "You aren't supposed to curse." Tristan shot him an annoyed look. Tristan growled, "I smell your blood." I replied, "I bit my cheek so she wouldn't ground me for saying I NEVER cause ANY trouble. I do everything I'm supposed to and it's not going to matter." I began to cry.

Jason sounded mortified, "Hey, don't cry Ladybug. Please. T, help me out here man." Tristan sighed, "Mel, mom wouldn't have grounded you for that." I snorted, "She's snarfing down mom monster cookies with Grandma, Grandma, Melinda and MaryBeth. They come in prepackaged cookie dough form now." Jason groaned.

Before he could say anything, Tank called up, "Jase, we've got practice to get to." I hugged him, "I love you, Jase." He agreed, "You too." He asked, "You've got this right, T?" He nodded, "Yeah, I got it." Jason left and we heard the door slam.

Tristan said, "Mom loves you." I replied, "I know that…it's just that…" He cut me off, "It's just nothing. I know Grandma told you about the deaths rogues have cost this family. I was hoping that would help you understand their reactions better, especially mom. She saw the mangled bodies of her own family." I argued, "But I'm NOT crossing the border, I swear!"

He hugged me acknowledging, "I know you're not." I yawned. He laughed, "Why don't you take a nap so you're ready for the picnic?" I whispered, "We both know I won't get to go." He gasped, "Where is the positive version of my sister? You're always adamant you'll meet your Xander."

I gasped, "SHHHH! You're not supposed to say that so loud." He replied, "We are the only ones here. Take a nap, Ladybug." I nodded, "Ok." I set my alarm so I could get up and get ready in time. I went to sleep and dreamed of the moment that Xander and I met.

My alarm blared and I sat up. I whispered, "It's time." I jumped in the shower and flew over to my outfit. It was a black skirt with red flowers and red top. I smoothed it out and glanced at the clock, a little surprised no one had come to get me.

I ran outside hoping that they didn't leave me. I found my family gathered and everyone looked sad. I asked, "What's wrong?" Everyone turned and Tristan winced. My mom crossed her arms with tears in her eyes. I took a step to go towards her, but she held he hands out in a stop motion.

My dad whispered, "Sam." She asked me, "How could you?" I noticed there was a bit of a crowd, and several people were looking away. A few had hats in their hands wringing them. I asked, "What did I do? I just took a nap and…"

Mom screamed, "STOP LYING!" I stared at her asking, "About what? I literally haven't said anything that…" She warned, "You were seen, just admit it." I frowned, "I don't know what you're talking about… I just woke up and took a shower."

She shook her head, "I know your grandma told you what happened yesterday. I know you know about our family members, and you selfishly crossed the border anyway!" I gasped, "No, I didn't! T, tell them."

I turned to my brother who looked near tears. My mom said, "Melanie Jane McAlister, you know full well he had to leave. Don't you even put him in this position." Tristan jumped in, "She was asleep when I left." My mom waved, "You left her a note."

I blinked at her but her anger remained. I didn't do anything wrong. I scoffed, "You still don't believe me. I didn't do it! I never do it." She warned, "Do NOT start. Do you know your dad and I saw that little boy yesterday? Can you imagine our terror? Of course you can't, because you don't have pups."

Saying I was too young would probably be a bad idea. Jason linked, "Don't say it. I see the thought on your face." I replied, "I didn't do anything wrong." He sighed. She wiped away tears. I whispered, "Mom, I…" She sighed, "Just admit what you did."

I repeated, "I took a nap and a shower…. In that order." She sighed, "Sometimes, I really do try to understand that you're a pup and you don't understand selfishness like adults, but this is beyond what is acceptable." Dad jumped in, "Sam, that's not fair."

I bit my tongue again because not talking was getting hard. I knew what she was going to say. She said, "You've yet again made Mrs. Dutton stay with you. She was coming today to the picnic today, ya know? Now, she'll be with you because you're grounded. I cannot understand how you could be so hurtful and selfish."

I exploded, "YES YOU DO BECAUSE YOU ARE THE ONE WHO IS SELFISH AND HURTFUL!" My dad warned, "Melanie Jane, don't talk to your mom that way." I pointed at her, "You know I didn't do anything wrong. You always do, then you eat your mom monster cookies."

"You don't even care that I hate them! You don't care that I'm TELLING YOU something is wrong with that lady who brings them. You love me until you eat them, then suddenly I'm selfish and terrible. You punish me for things I didn't even do." I wiped my tears away as she gaped at me along with everyone else. I usually just ran away in tears, but not today.

I shouted, "It's not fair! I'm sorry about what happened to that little boy, and I'm sorry about our own family members that rogues killed BUT I AM NOT THEM! I'm tired of being punished for YOUR fear. Everyone gets to meet the allies and your friends BUT I DON'T!"

"I get to live a half-life, hearing about everything from everyone else. YOU are the one who isn't FAIR AND YOU ARE THE ONE WHO IS SELFISH AND HURTFUL! You look into EVERYTHING Jase and T say is off EVEN WHEN THEY ARE WRONG BUT YOU WON'T DO IT FOR ME!"

My dad growled, "MELANIE JANE!" I asked her, "Are you happy now? When is it exactly you'll be happy? I told T you wouldn't let me go. Ask him. I told him before I took a nap it wasn't going to happen because you wouldn't let it."

"He said I needed to be positive, but I knew the second you all ate those mom monster cookies I'd be staying behind. AGAIN. Blame yourself for Mrs. Dutton not getting to go to the picnic. She doesn't need to stay since plenty of people could guard the prison cell you CLEARLY think I belong in." I didn't wait for a reply.

I ran into our house, but I didn't stop there. I was done with this. I ran out the back and went down into the cells. They could all panic wondering where I went. That was mean, but they were mean too. I got down here and NO ONE noticed. I could cross the border without them noticing too. They thought I was stupid.

I wiped at my tears. I didn't do anything and now I wouldn't meet my Xander again. I went into one of the cells and burst into tears after I closed the door. My dad linked me, "Melanie Jane, where the hell are you?" I replied, "Exactly where she wants my hurtful, selfish self. It should give you ALL pause no one knows the answer of where I am except me. Because I AM A GENIUS! I can get around people."

I laid down on the dirt floor and hit the ground. It wasn't fair. Tristan linked, "Ladybug, this isn't funny! Where are you?" I retorted, "Who said it was funny? I'm not selfish! I would never throw their pain in their faces. I'm not stupid!" They all just thought I was when it came to emotions, but they were wrong.

It hurt that my mom would never do any of these things unless she ate those cookies. She'd never hurt me this way. I heard a sigh I knew well. Peter said, "Melanie Jane, you don't belong in there." I whispered, “Please leave me alone, Daddy Peter.” He practically threw the door off the cells. He picked me up and I cried into his neck. I sobbed, “I didn’t do it.” He hugged me tightly and rubbed my back.

I was near hyperventilating, “They think… I’m a bad person… that I would hurt them… and I wouldn’t… I would never hurt them… I… No one would cross a border after what just happened… why does everyone tell me how smart I am then act like I’m an idiot?”

My dad growled, “Why the FUCK was she in a cell?” Peter said, “You know why.” My mom sighed, “Melanie Jane, this was not an appropriate response.” I muttered, “Sure it is. If you think I’m that bad of a person, then I should be in a cell.” She jolted back as if I slapped her when she was the one who kept hurting me.

She whispered, “That is not remotely what I said.” It was but maybe the cookies made her not understand that. Something WAS wrong with them. I scoffed, “So, intentionally causing your family pain because you are not a person with feelings no longer makes on a sociopath then. Because that’s what you think I am.”

Mom gasped, “MELANIE JANE, I DO NOT!” I disagreed, “You do if you believe that I or anyone else crossed the border today or for the next month. I’d be longer than a month but on a statistical average a pup would forget the pain and terror of yesterday in a month.”

She growled, “I never said you were a sociopath nor do I think it.” I told her, “Maybe ask the Princess Luna, since she’s your friend, the definition of the world. Because is the person you are describing. A lack of empathy and disregard for social norms is a sociopath.”

She asked, “Can you really think I believe that?” I replied, “Your statements say that you do.” She started crying but I was right. She basically called me an emotionless robot. Peter said, “No one called you an emotionless robot.” I grimaced, “Did I say that out loud?” He nodded. Great.

Jason announced, “I’ve got this. You guys go. Jared will pop me in.” My mom said, “We aren’t leaving like this.” Sure, they were. I actually laughed. Mom asked, “What now?” I said, “You always leave me like this….maybe not in the dungeons…but you meant emotionally….So, why would today be any different?” Her jaw dropped.

Jason whispered, “Mom, it’s only going to make it worse. She literally threw herself into a cell without anyone noticing. Just let me work some of my big brother magic. You can talk to her when she’s calmer. Go to the picnic.”

I muttered, “Like you know you have to because you’re the Beta Female of this pack and dad’s the Beta.” Peter winced. My dad said, “I don’t give a shit about that.” I shrugged because it was one of his duties to the pack so he should care. It didn’t make sense that he wouldn’t.

My mom touched my shoulder saying, “You, T, Jase, and your dad are the priority to me. Your dad feels the same way.” I didn’t even look at her. She sighed, “Ok, we’ll go. I love you, Melanie Jane.” I knew she’d go. I also knew she’d love me again in an hour or two, but I didn’t believe the mom monster loved me.

My dad hugged me whispering, “We love you so much, Ladybug.” I hugged him tightly and heard my mom sniffle. Peter kissed the top of my head, “We will be back.” Jason clearly linked Jared who popped down to us and popped us to my room.

I whispered, “Just because it’s nicer doesn’t make it not a prison cell.” Jared winced then popped out. Joy. Another day of everyone feeling sorry for Melanie and claiming I don’t understand human emotions when it was them that didn’t understand.

Jason walked past me and turned on my bathtub. He came back out, “Why don’t you take a relaxing bath?” I took a shower before I went downstairs. Did he not hear me say that? I snarked, “Why don’t I go prove I could cross the border, so people FINALLY believe me when I say I don’t?”

He growled, “Mel, no.” I cried, “Why not? Give me one reason why not. I’m already accused and convicted. My words protesting my innocence do not matter. I am convicted with no trial or evidence. Only eye witness accounts are about fifty percent inaccurate…I could cross the border and not get caught.”

Tristan answered from behind us, “The reason is because you would never be that cruel and you’re not a sociopath. Plus, you were right. No one would cross after what happened yesterday.” I cried, “Then why don't they understand that?" He said, "I'll talk to mom. You know that shook her yesterday and she's not thinking clearly."

I knew that because she was eating mom monster cookies. I nodded to them. Both came and hugged me. Tristan said, "You are beyond loved." It didn't feel like it today. I muttered, "I will be in a few hours when someone asks mom at the party and they call her on this insanity. Then she'll bad, bring me a piece of cake, and act like nothing happened."

Tristan said, "You can't know that." I replied, "Statistically speaking, I can. It's what happens every single time. Just watch. I'll be right." They both glanced at each other but left. I went and got into the tub since I might as well.

I took a deep breath and went under. I came back up and grumbled, "I should've just convinced Elise to come home… which wouldn't have been fair… she got to see EJ… but I just want to see Xander." I got out, towel dried my hair and put on comfy clothes.

I grabbed my Xander wolf and cried into its fur. It was probably filled with my tears at this point. A soft knock came, and Mrs. Dutton came in. I sobbed harder apologizing, "I'm sorry you always have to miss out and watch me and miss out on everything." She came over and sat down on my bed.

She took my hand saying, "I'll let you in a secret, I volunteer if someone needs to stay with you or anyone else. I have serious social anxiety, and I keep that very well hidden. I've been working with the Princess Luna on opening up about it. Your parents don't even know, only Luna Chelsea does. I don't mind staying back with you, and it's not a punishment for me like it is you."

She hugged me, "I don't know what's going on sweet girl, but I know your mom was just scared out there. She heard you crossed the border, and she went to her knees in a panic. The Beta calmed her down, but she was scared."

She rubbed my back saying, "That doesn't excuse some of the things she or you said. Just keep it in that brilliant mind, words can't be taken back. My mom always said words are like toothpaste, once out of the tube you can't get them back in."

She paused then added, "But I have to say that's the first time I've seen you get upset like that. It tells me a lot since normally you just run back inside, and I find you here with your stuffed wolf." She kissed my head and went back downstairs.

I waited five minutes until I heard her show on, then crept out of my room. I went through the kitchen and found all the mom monster cookies and the pre-made cookie dough. I gathered them all up into a garbage bag and threw it over my shoulder.

I called, "I'm taking out the trash." Mrs. Dutton gasped, "Goodness gracious pup! Stop reading about how to be like a ninja! Make some noise." I snickered because I did read a bunch of papers put out by the Hackura on how they stayed in the background even when they weren't faded back.

I went outside and jogged to the dumpster. I tossed the garage in whirling when I heard a growl. Rober mocked, "Poor little horrible Beta blood. One has to question if you are at this point." I hit him square in the face. He screamed, "MY NOSE!"

I scoffed, "Yell, louder so someone comes… that seems like a bad plan." He growled, "You're NOTHING!" I rolled my eyes, "Literally no one is nothing… even you… that's just… an asinine statement … even for you."

He warned, "Everyone is beginning to question if you even have Beta blood." I disagreed, "Everyone knows I do! My mom would NEVER cheat on my dad. HOW DARE YOU SAY THAT AND QUESTION HER CHARACTER!" I snarled and jumped on him.

I hit him several times before his friends dragged me off and I hit several of them while I was at it. One yelled, "Damn! Come on, Robert. That was over the line. No one doubts she's Beta Drake's daughter. Even if we did question Beta Female Sam's integrity, which we don't, Melanie looks just like Beta Drake but more feminine."

Robert yelled, "Shut up!" Someone argued, "You shut up, man. That's not cool to say to anyone, but especially about the pack leadership." I said, "I could cross and not get caught and… honestly everyone should know that." He taunted me, "Then do it."

I scoffed, "Uh huh… sure… like I'd believe you wouldn't rat me out. Gosh, people think I am so dumb… when I was literally tested." He got in my face and whispered, "Yet you haven't figured out what's really going on here. I'm running circles around you, and you can't even figure it out."

I shoved him back, "If you're caught lying about me… I mean… you have to know that's bad for you." He winked, "I'll never get caught." His friends finally looked nervously at each other. Whatever he was talking about, they didn't know about it.

Tank, Jason's friend, yelled, "Hey! What's going on over there?" They took off running while Tank jogged over. He asked, "Why do you have blood on your hands?" I said, "Uhh… well… you see… what had happened was…" He groaned, "Goddess above, pup. Come on." I started to speak, then said, "One second."

I pulled open the bag I just tossed and took out some of the cookies while Tank raised an eyebrow. He could do that all he wanted but I was going to send them to Ryan Bishop. He could figure this out. I was going to prove there was something wrong with the cookies. He could help me do that.

Tank teased, "You just like to cause chaos." I snorted, "I don't cause chaos… it seeks me out… even when I do nothing but try and exist." He ruffled my hair. I sighed, "Have you met Zippy yet?" He laughed, "That's quite the name. I can't say I've even heard it."

He'd transferred to our pack with his family a couple years ago. I said, "She is my best friend Adeline's sister. She is doing a foreign pack exchange program, but she'll be back in six months. You'd like her." He admitted, "I'm confused as to how I haven't met her when I know Adeline."

I explained, "She travels during the summer and keeps doing exchange programs. Her family goes to see her. She wants to get her… well she says travel bug… out of her system before she meets her mate. You guys would be cute though."

He winked, "I'll see if I can get a picture and let you know if I agree." I squealed, "One second." I ran inside to my room and brought out a picture from a pack picnic he and his family weren't at, because they'd visited their old pack that weekend.

He grabbed the picture and pointed to Ziggy. He asked, "This is her?" I nodded, "Yup." He asked, "And is Ziggy a nickname?" I grinned, "Nope." He admitted, "If anyone else said that I'd say they were fucking with me."

I explained, "It's the name of one of their ancestors. Their mom got super into researching their bloodline. Her name is to honor a name that had been out of their family for centuries. She found German ties, plus… it means Victorious Protector…. and Ziggy is fiercely protective of anyone she loves… so.."

He asked, "And what does one have to do to convince you to give me her number?" I said, "Uhh well I don't have her number… but I have her email address, and you could… well…. I will give it to you if you tell me what Xander smell like?"

He winced, "I promised Jase I wouldn't say. You got anything else that would convince you?" Dang it, Jason! I bit my lip. I couldn't tell him about the Robert deal. I clapped, "You go to Harrison's Warrior classes!" He nodded, "Yeah."

I grinned, "He said I could go… but no one will partner with me when I fight… will you?" He looked like he felt sorry for me. He agreed, "Of course, Ladybug. I thought everyone wanted to be your partner." My face fell, "Uhh well… no. No one likes being my partner… which… well I win… so…."

He laughed, "Then I look forward to the challenge of getting better when we fight." I nodded and went back to the house and wrote down her email. I walked back out and handed it to him. He said, "I don't know why but I feel like you just handed me my forever, pup."

I pointed out, "Well, you aren't eighteen and neither is she… so…" He grinned, "Yeah, I know. It just feels like it. Can I keep the picture?" I nodded, "Sure… oh… and maybe should it come up…for reasons… I might have mentioned you to her in an email and attached a picture of you and Jase….and she thinks you're hot. Ok bye." I shut the door in his face, and he laughed really hard.

He knocked and I winced opening it. He said, "If you ever want to talk about whatever that pup and his disaster friends are doing, I'm here." I hung my head saying, "No one will believe me." He frowned, "What does that mean? I thought they left you alone." I shrugged, "Well…"

Mrs. Dutton came in greeting, "Oh hey, Tank." He nodded, "Mrs. Dutton." She said, "You should get moving. The McAlister's can't find out I let her run around while they are gone when she's supposed to be grounded."

He nodded then linked, "I'm always available if you need to talk. Also, your parents didn't leave when you told them to. They waited until your brothers came outside from talking to you. Neither were willing to leave, but your brothers convinced them to. I know this is not fair, but they do love you."

I wanted to keep him on my side…especially since no one believed me…and he seemed to consider my innocence at least. Plus, I really did think he'd be cute with Ziggy though. I replied, "They always leave. They will come back with cake and apologize saying they didn't know what they were thinking. Or that they weren't thinking. It's what happens. I appreciate you telling me they didn't just leave though." He nodded.

When he left, I grabbed a note and found an old box to send to Ryan Bishop. I found his address in my mom's address book. I went over to Peter and Chelsea's house. There was a place to put mail to go out. I put my priority sticker on it. I had an account, so I just printed it out. He'd have to sign for it and I put my email in there so we could talk.

Robert yelled, "I see you, Melanie Jane!" I groaned and jumped off the porch and ran back to my house. He yelled, "Yeah, you better run." A Warrior shouted, "Excuse me?" He replied, "Uhh, cause she's grounded." The Warrior hummed at him. Yeah, have fun with that one Robert.

Mrs. Dutton chuckled, "Pup, you are too busy for your own good. Go dance in your room and consider world domination." I muttered, "I might have to actually take over the world, so people believe me about things." The phone rang a few minutes later and I heard Mrs. Dutton answer.

She greeted, "Duncan, hello. Well yes, I am. She's upstairs. Yeah, again. I know. I feel so bad for her. You should know it was bad this time. Consider linking your older brother. Well, she put herself in the dungeons and no one noticed. Alpha Peter found her down there." She paused, "Yeah, Beta Drake was held back when they found where her scent led. Beta Female Sam was beside herself."

She paused, "Honestly, I've never seen Ladybug lash out like she did tonight. She even threw all the cookies away in the house. There's nothing you could've done if you were here. It was hard to watch, everyone felt bad."

She scoffed, "Robert reported it, but I just don't believe a word out of that pup's mouth. His friends all backed it up with one adult saying they did see her headed in that direction. The thing is you know she's a bad liar. It just doesn't make sense. I'd bet my bank account she didn't do it. Yeah, I'll tell her you called. Good luck finding your mate this time, Duncan." I closed my door and let my tears fall.

I whispered, "Some people do believe you, Melanie. Ryan Bishop is family to us, even though he doesn't know you yet, he'll help." Great now, I was referring to myself in the third person. My hope really did lie with Ryan.

So of course he never signed for the package and the tracking number I got said it was lost in transit. It was just me against the mom monster cookies.

Everything Changed

Alexander is Twelve Years Old

Alexander was excited. I glanced at EJ and sent my uncle's the fact we knew they were here in the bond. They sent their amusement in response. EJ linked, "So much for coming alone." I replied, "We knew they'd be here."

Honestly, Cassie should be here too. She was ready just like we were, but as the only girl besides mom in the Cambridge line, it wasn't happening. My mom had argued with them repeatedly, but it just wasn't sinking in for them.

Oden snorted, "That doesn't upset us." I replied, "If Cass was more upset about it, I would be too. She's really fine with it and understands." I just hated it for her. At the same I'm relieved. It made for some interesting feelings.

My dad sent me his feelings to focus and to knock it off. Oden linked, "Thor said mom is pranking everyone." I linked EJ, "Ask Brutus about mom's pranks." He replied, "All he will say is that there are pranks." I winked, "I think this mission should get dragged out. One must be thorough after all." He grinned and we both chuckled.

My dad sent a warning that whatever mischievousness we were feeling needed to stop. My Hackura Uncles were basically shaking their heads at us. I feel like they understood the feeling better having grown up with my mom.

Our mission was fairly straightforward because EJ and I were simply observing today. We all knew this mission wasn't a priority. From the files I'd read our family's first missions tended to have something go awry that Uncle Bjourn or Grandpa Titus blamed themselves for.

It seemed to me like Aesir's hand was in all but Uncle Harper and Uncle Gunner's first mission. That was clearly foul play. The rest seemed like well timed warnings to stop things from spiraling out of control for our family. Because of that I was on high alert, and I'd told EJ to be the same.

I'm sure that added a level of pranks to my mom's hijinks she was pulling. She'd had our bond close to her for weeks in anticipation of our first time out. She'd know we were prepared for everything to go haywire and have to step in more than just listening. I could tell my dad wanted to link us and check to see how we were doing, but he wasn't going to.

Oden linked, "I'll let Thor know we are fine." I grinned because I truly loved my wolf. We'd been together all my life, which was unprecedented for Werewolves until me and my siblings were born. My cousins had them too, but we were the first.

I knew people were jealous that we'd had our wolves our whole lives. We had a link and bond with them most didn't have for quite some time. EJ and I faded back the second someone came near the tree we were in.

The guy looked up and snorted, "Damn being the low guy on the totem pole." He yelled, "I don't know what the fuck kind of joke this is, but no one is here!" I sent EJ my confusion in the bond. Someone yelled back, "Well, the note we have says there are two men here listening to us."

He scoffed, "Well, they aren't." I linked EJ, "Mom gets notes that appear out of nowhere and now those notes are trying to ruin our mission?" He snorted, "You know as well as I do who those notes are from." I did because they were always from Alania Holloran.

The guy huffed, "I repeat, no one is here." He muttered, "Damn notes appearing and making me work my ass off even more than these people do. I'm only here because they've got my girl. Now, I'm their fucking errand boy."

I linked EJ, "We have to help him." He reasoned, "We aren't supposed to." I asked, "Can you let this go?" He admitted, "Nope. I feel my Alpha and Hackura blood firing, but so does everyone else." He was right about that.

I wished I could wall myself off to get this done like my mom could. I hated that ability she possessed more than any of my siblings. My mom and I had an empathic connection, so I could tell when it got cut off easier than they could. I could literally feel the walls snap into place.

Moments like this, I was jealous I didn't have the ability like she did. I used to think it was a Fairy power, but I'd researched that at length in Faerie. I couldn't find a single thing about it, so I'd asked a Fairy. They'd snorted and told me it's not an inherited ability then all but ran away from me. I could've chased them, but that told me it had something to do with being a Fairy but not a power.

We were still faded back but I got down to follow the man running around. The guy in charge stared right past me. He asked, "Well?" The guy replied, "Like I said, no one is there." He put a finger in his face warning, "Your girl loses a finger if you mess up."

The guy stiffened, "I don't even know what the fuck you do here! I still don't know why you took her or why I'm here." The man replied, "And you never will. Do what we want, and she'll be free." I linked EJ, "So, they are setting him up as the fall guy? Because I caught that evasion."

He snorted, "Warlocks never understand Fairies always catch their evasions." The guy sighed, "I just want my girl back." The Warlock replied, "Then do what we are asking." The frustrated man yelled, "I AM! I do everything you ask and all I get are hair and pictures! She hates getting her hair cut. She cries every goddamn trim and now…"

I nearly gasped out loud because that likely meant his girl was a partial Fairy. Oden growled, "We have to get her to mom." I linked EJ, "I have to get her. Come with me." He put a hand on my shoulder, and we walked away.

My Uncles were getting worried, but my mom shot her belief in us. It felt like a warm blanket telling me to follow my instincts and she knew we'd do the right thing. I faded in with EJ and we nodded to each other before we popped to the girl.

I faltered realizing I had made a false assumption. I thought when the man said my girl, he meant his girlfriend, wife, or partner. He meant his daughter. Oden snarled, "SHE IS A PUP!" She was maybe five years old.

She stared at me and EJ with curiosity. I put a finger up to my mouth to indicate she needed to be quiet. She grinned, nodding at me. EJ and I hid as our uncles were practically cursing at us through the bond.

I knew several were trying to link us, they'd joined the pack for the ability to do so. Oden said, "I have it blocked out." I knew that too. A guy came in, "Ok, little freak here's your cold ass food. You can warm it up yourself. Don't even think of pulling your freaky tricks on me. I won't be scared this time, I'm prepared."

She must have used her Fire powers on him. I grabbed him by the neck whispering, "Boo mother fucker." He tried to scream for help, but EJ shifted into Brutus and killed his backup. The little girl clapped, "Go wolf man!" We probably did look like men to her.

I asked, "Do you know what you are?" She shrugged, "Daddy says I'm special. I miss him, but they won't let him visit." EJ picked her up and we popped back to where her dad was. I grabbed him and popped back to where my uncles were.

The dad groaned and fell down. His daughter screamed, "DADDY!" He managed to sit up and hold her tightly. I greeted, "Hey Uncles of ours, fancy seeing you here." My Uncle Bjourn yanked me into a hug. He asked, "What the fuck, Alexander?" I said, "They had a girl they were holding hostage."

Uncle Evin said, "Yes, a partial Fire Fairy." Her dad snorted, "I'd say you were full of shit, but she does love fire. If she gets mad enough, she can melt things." She pouted, "I didn't do it right in that house though and I tried. I got PLENTY mad they wouldn't let you visit."

I consoled her, "I'm sure they were putting iron into your food. I'd like to heal you." Her dad agreed, "Please do it." I let my healing light take over. When I pulled back, she was perfectly fine. Her dad asked, "What do we do? They will come after us. I don't know why they wanted us."

Uncle Bjourn said, "They will be taken care of." The dad asked, "Were you two the ones the note said were listening in?" Uncle Harper grunted, "Note?" I snorted, "I think we all know who the note is from." I felt their lancing anger in the bond.

I told her dad, "I'd like to take you to meet my mom." The girl squealed, "Sure. Is she like us?" I knelt down, "She's the Princess of the Fae." She gasped, "Does she know my mom?" Her dad made a face. I asked, "Where is her mom?" He answered, "I don't know."

The little girl said, "She loves me a lot, but she had to go." The look on the dad's face told me he'd lied to her. So, we'd have to get that story. Fire Fairies loved partials though. EJ linked, "I sense a little earth blood in her." Still, she was mostly a Fire Fairy.

We popped our group to my mom. She grinned, "You're back!" She jumped and hugged me then EJ. My dad came running into the room. He linked, "Oh hey dad, we are back. No worries, we are just trying to give you heart palpitations on top of the pranks mom is pulling." He yanked me into a hug first because mom still had EJ.

I whispered, "Hey, dad. We are back." He snorted and clapped me on the back then yanked EJ into a hug. My mom said, "And you brought guests. Hello, cutie." She knelt down and tapped the little girl on the nose.

The little girl asked, "Are you the Princess?" She answered, "I am." My dad said, "Maybe do not say who you are in front of him." He pointed at the dad, who was human. I said, "He knows." My dad groaned, "Great."

The guy said, "It's not like I'm going to call you all crazy. I knew my daughter was special, so I understand all this. Honestly, it's nice to get her around people who understand her and I." The little girl grinned, "It's me and daddy against the world."

My mom said, "Well, now you're with us. So, you two are with us against the world." To my shock, Lindsey Sherwood burst into the house. My mom asked, "Lindsey, are you ok?" She growled, "MINE!" Holy shit. The human guy was her second chance mate. He shrugged, "Sucks to be you fellas because I'm pretty sure that beautiful woman is talking about me."

I snorted, "She is." The girl jumped up and asked, "Are you my mommy? Did you finally come back? I've seen you before." Lindsey asked, "You have?" She nodded, "In my dreams. I'm positive you're my mommy." Lindsey picked her up and went over to the man.

She introduced herself, "I'm Lindsey Sherwood." He kissed the top of her head then shook himself. He apologized, "Sorry, it just felt like…" She interrupted, "Don't apologize, I liked it." He said, "Well, I'm Tenn. My mom thinks she's funny."

My mom asked, "What does his name have to do with his mom being fucking funny?" I answered, "He's from Tennessee and his name is Tenn." She didn't make a face, but I felt in the bond she thought that was kind of silly. EJ chuckled out loud.

Lindsey asked, "Where is your mom?" He admitted, "I told her to get out of the state when Lark got kidnapped." My mom physically jolted. I felt her walls slam into place quite firmly. I asked, "Mom?" She whispered, "Lark?" The little girl said, "Momma named me. She gave me this too." She showed my mom a necklace.

My mom conjured a different one. She said, "What if we traded? This one is very shiny and from Faerie." She squealed, "OK!" She took the necklace and handed my mom the other one. Tessa, our Female Lead Warrior, came in.

She announced, "I hear there's a special little girl that needs to see the pack." Lark asked, "Me?" She nodded, "Yup. I've got a group of pups clamoring to meet you and go on a tour." She whispered, "They are my hellions." Lark giggled.

Tessa winked, "We call them pups, but I'm certain mine are hellions. They have never seen a clean area they did not make messy." My mom snorted, "That's just children in fucking general." Tenn agreed, "Preach, sister." My mom said, "I am not a pastor." I bit my lip. Tenn chuckled, "You're quite literal." Lindsey assured him, "She really is."

When they left my dad asked, "Angel?" She said, "I know the family the name comes from." My Uncle Aiden popped in. He asked, "What's going on?" She showed him the necklace and he reached for it, snatching it away.

He whispered, "Where did you get this?" She answered, "From the little girl my sons brought back from their mission." He asked, "Where is she?!" I asked, "What's going on?" My mom assured him,

"She's fine, Aiden. She's being shown the pack." Tenn asked, "Do you know her mother?" Aiden answered, "I know the family she came from." Tenn muttered, "Her name was weird."

My mom snorted, "Of fucking course it was." He admitted, "I was shocked Lark had a normal name. She just left her on my doorstep. I knew she was pregnant and went to her appointments. It wasn't some love affair or soul mates. She was just a one night stand I was trying to do right by. She ran off on me, then left Lark. I had the DNA test confirm she was mine. I can take care of my little girl, I swear."

I said, "You obviously can. Sadly, you were just up against Supernatural's without any other than your partial daughter on your side. That's who took her." My mom said, "They are likely adjacent to the Ring." That had all our attention.

I asked, "Huh? What's the Ring?" She answered, "Bad people that we fight against." I asked, "How do you know that? The mission we were on wasn't that high level." She answered, "Her name is Lark." Ok? Oden told me, "If it helps Thor is very confused."

I asked, "Are we related to Lark?" I didn't get a very comforting sense in her presence, but I'd been distracted. Uncle Aiden answered, "No, she is related to me." Tenn snorted, "And are you the King?" My mom answered, "He is."

Lindsey caught him when his knees buckled. He insisted, "I was JOKING!" Uncle Aiden said, "Well, I was not." I asked, "What the fuck is going on?" My mom explained, "There was a group of your Grandpa Fenilton's family that did not side with the Holloran's when we rose up against the previous family."

Mom had met Uncle Aiden's dad in the Beyond and he requested to be called our Grandpa. She agreed so that's what we call him. I wished we could've met him when he was alive because he sounded awesome.

She sighed, "There was a Hayes mated to one of their earth family members. Her name was Lark, and that necklace was given to signify the Hayes and the earth family's lines. The woman who went against the Hayes' and your Grandpa Fenilton was named Lark."

I asked, "What the fuck were they doing with the Lark we found then?" Uncle Aiden answered, "They were going to have her father killed and have her moved back to their facilities more than likely. Based on some research I read, they were toying with what a child with love versus not could do." My mom's walls clamped down further.

She said, "Don't worry Tenn, we will make sure nothing happens to Lark." Uncle Aiden said, "I will destroy this necklace to send them a message she's ours now." He asked, "Who the fuck are these people?" Lindsey assured him, "We will protect Lark. I know that Fairy family is truly awful on all levels, but we will protect her." She'd see her as her own pup now.

He asked, "And what are you? Do you melt things too like little Lark?" She snorted, "No, I'm a Werewolf." He nodded, "Sure, why not. Fairies and Werewolves." I said, "You were being forced to work with Warlocks." Several people groaned.

My mom yelled, "ARE YOU SERIOUS?! WARLOCK WARTS?! MOTHER FUCKER!" Uncle Bjourn said, "Don't you dare leave, little one. We will DISCUSS this, and those Warlocks are already in our custody." Or they would be shortly. They were definitely being watched.

I asked, "Why haven't you popped to the people who betrayed Grandpa Fen if you knew they did?" My mom answered, "We haven't been able to, but you and your siblings have always been an exception to that." I knew she was proud of us for that, but it worried her.

We'd been met with resistance a few times. Others we'd been able to get close by, but not all the way through. Uncle Aiden snorted, "And I mistakenly assumed they would not be out there having kids with humans." Lindsey was rubbing her hand up and down Tenn's back.

He said, "It was an Oops. Nothing quite nefarious like you seem to think." Uncle Aiden snorted, "And how long was your one night stand?" He winced, "It was more than a night, she was crazy." I laughed, "Wait until Faerie hears a human lasted through her concupiscence." He snorted, "She used toys when I needed to sleep." Still, it was impressive.

Lindsey growled, "I want her dead for trying to kill my mate and take ou…" She trailed off then said, "his daughter." I linked her, "I actually don't think he'd mind if you called her yours." She said, "Well, we tend to take things much slower with human mates than this." I reasoned, "He's got a partial Fairy daughter so the rules probably don't apply to him anymore." His daughter was even from a very powerful and Royal family line. Two technically.

He said, "Gosh, I'm just falling all over this beautiful woman." He straightened. She said, "You're my mate. I know that probably doesn't make sense to you, but it's everything to me." He snorted, "Things have not made sense to me for five years and change. My daughter was a preemie."

He paused then admitted, "Well in my mind she is, but the doctors said she was fully developed. I argued with them something fierce about it too. I could tell they thought I was a sap until the DNA test came back that she was mine. They were stunned."

He snorted, "Then things started to melt around my little girl if she got too mad. Plus, she made her bottles appear to her if I took too long. She smirked at me as she did it too. She did that for about two weeks and I'm certain it was a game." It definitely was.

He added, "I think she thought it was funny how I jolted awake when she cried. I also never changed a poopy diaper. She did NOT like poop touching her skin. At first, I was worried she wasn't pooping. The doctors again thought I was a wackadoodle."

My mom asked, "They hit you?" He snorted, "No, they thought I was insane." My mom shot my dad a look and he just grinned. Tenn waved, "Anyway, I'll have to tell my mom I've got Lark back. I thought for sure I was going to die."

Lindsey growled. He chuckled, "Damn. You really a wolf. Alright. Anyway, I didn't want to do what those people asked me to. I have no idea what they were doing, I just wanted my little girl back. They got her signed out of her school when I was at work. I would've died before I let anyone take her from me."

Lindsey assured him, "No one here doubts you. Haley is our Luna and Eric is our Alpha. The two boys that brought you here are our future Alpha's." He snorted, "You're saying they are teleporting Werewolves?"

I let my eyes blaze, "And we are Hackura." He said, "I have not heard of that one." Uncle Bjourn replied, "And you wouldn't have if you weren't brought into the supernatural world." He chuckled, "And let me guess, you're the King of the hack…." He trailed off then waved at me, "Whatever he said."

Uncle Bjourn answered, "I am." He snorted, "You're shitting me." I bit my lip knowing my mom was about to say something. I felt amusement all around the bond. Mom asked, "What the fuck? You want him to shit on you?"

Tenn groaned, "No, absolutely not. I was just shocked." She grumbled, "This fucking realm and its damn sayings." Uncle Aiden said, "I would like to meet Lark." Tenn asked suspiciously, "Why?"

Uncle Aiden assured him, "I would not hurt her. She's a child and she's my family. Fairies do well around their family, and I would like her to meet hers. She's from the Royal Fire line in my realm."

He asked, "My Daughter is Royal?" He answered, "Yes, she is a cousin of mine." He pressed, "A Princess went rogue in your realm?" Oden snickered. My mom said, "Rogues are Werewolves not Fairies." Tenn rubbed his temples clearly trying to adjust to my mom being extremely literal.

Uncle Aiden explained, "Your daughter is Royal among Fire Fairies but her family line is not considered the rules. Her mother was not a Princess. We do not view cousins as they do in this realm. Any child of a cousin is just a cousin to us. It was my dad's cousin that went with the former ruler family instead of the Holloran's."

Tenn asked, "Is that family like Voldemort and you all don't say their name?" Oh no. My mom yelled, "DID YOU JUST COMPARE US TO THE WITCH BITCHES AND WARLOCK WARTS?!" My dad grabbed her around the waist.

He said, "Tenn has no idea how you feel about Witches and Warlocks." Tenn said, "I'm on her side with that since I was clearly working for the Death Eater type versions." Lyndsey purred, "You like *Harry Potter*." He laughed, "I am a very big fan." So was she.

My mom was slightly mollified by his comments, but I could tell she did not care for the comparison. Uncle Aiden said, "I understand the comparison, but we don't say their name for different reasons. We do not fear them by any means. My sister and I are the promised siblings, they could not take power from our line. We do not say their name because of the devastation they brought to our realm for centuries. They hurt many people and that hurt still echoes among the remaining generations."

Tenn nodded. He agreed, "You can meet Lark. I'm sure she'd like you. Is my daughter going to get wings or some shit?" My mom let hers come out and flew into the air with my dad since he was still holding onto her.

Tenn said, "So, yes." Uncle Aiden laughed, "Not necessarily. Hers would look something more like mine if she did get them." His came out and EJ and I grinned at each other. Tenn gasped, "Holy shit. His wings are fire. Do you see that?" He asked Lindsey.

She admitted, "I've seen them quite a bit actually. It continues to be impressive every single time you see it." He whistled, "I'll be." Uncle Aiden commented, "You are a very understanding human." He shrugged, "Like I said, I always liked the fantasy type books and worlds. I like them better than ours because it makes life more fun." Uncle Aiden chuckled.

Tenn added, "Plus, there's only so long you can blame sleep deprivation for thinking your baby never pooped and could make her bottles appear out of nowhere." My mom came down and said, "It's called conjuring."

He shrugged, "Sure. I'd like to learn all I can for her. I just don't want her to know that her mom abandoned her. She's just a little kid. A smart, very advanced kid." Uncle Aiden interjected calmly, "Supernatural's progress through stages faster than humans." He snorted, "No joke. Anyway, I just…." He trailed off and Lindsey rubbed his back.

He said, "My dad left me, and I was old enough to understand that and it fucked me up. I don't want that for her." Lindsey said, "We can ease into it. She will need to know that she can't trust someone who says she's her mom. She needs to know when she's older, but there's nothing wrong with letting her think her mom did want her. That is clearly true. She came to you on her concupiscence." She growled that part and tried to reign it in.

My mom agreed, "Lindsey's right. Her mother did want Lark, that's not a lie." Uncle Aiden hummed, "And her name was?" He admitted, "I think it's made up. I just didn't care about that at the time to be honest." Uncle Aiden sighed, "It's probably not."

He shrugged, "That's what you say now, but she said her name was Guardiolagea." He nodded, "Yes, that's a family name." His eyes widened. He muttered, "I would've changed Lark's name if she'd picked something like that."

I chuckled, "Fairy names are usually very out there." He jolted, "You heard that?" I grinned, "Werewolves have excellent hearing." My mom grumbled, "That I don't have, which is still utter fucking bullshit."

She waved, "Boys, you should go celebrate your first mission. You can debrief with your uncle tomorrow, but you'll need to celebrate this moment." She hugged us both again, "I am so very proud of you both. This was beyond the expectation for your first mission, that your sister should've been on to share in this moment with you." Everyone groaned but I sent my mom all my love.

She winked, "But you should go see Cassie and Elise. I know for a fact that both of them are very anxious for your return. They will be so proud of you, like your dad and I are." My dad agreed, "We are so proud of you and not at all thinking of ways of getting you back for your brief consideration to draw the mission out before you heard Tenn talking."

Oden snorted, "As if he could out prank us." No joke. I grinned, "Bring it on, dad. We could run laps around your pranks." My mom commented, "That would not be a good prank, Eric. They already run a lot because of Bjourn's program and yours. You can't prank them with running." I winked, "Yeah, dad." He rolled his eyes at me but sent me his love.

EJ and I popped upstairs to Cassie. Elise was in his arms in seconds. Cassie raised an eyebrow at me because she felt the tinge of disappointment I'd felt. I'd felt that since Melanie McAlister was born. Almost every time I saw Elise, I hoped Melanie would be with her. Sadly, she literally never was.

Flashback

Alexander was running laps in the gym. Oden asked, "Can we run outside next?" I agreed, "Of course." I finished my laps and waved to my dad who grinned at me. Dylan Frost screamed, "DID EVERYONE SEE THAT? HE IS SPLITTING HIS FACE AGAIN!"

Several people chuckled and my dad rolled his eyes. He shot back, "I smile all the time, Dylan." Dylan gleefully said, "Now, you do. The thirty two years and change you lived without smiling means that the rest of us have to shout it when you smile now. It's your own fault. Maybe when you are sixty-four we can stop."

I chuckled as I ran outside to shift. I heard my dad shout, "SIXTY FUCKING TWO?! ARE YOU SERIOUS? LACY, CORAL HIM!" Lacy just laughed and I didn't blame her. I could tell you that Dylan Frost would continue doing it past when my dad was sixty-two. It was probably going to go on for centuries.

Oden chuckled, "It definitely is. Fang found dad's reaction hilarious." Jesus Christ. I had just reached the top of the mountain when I felt it. Everything in my entire world changed. I went on alert as the wind blew, caressing me.

I called, "Mom?" She wasn't there though. The bond told me that. I conjured my phone to look at the time, noting it was just after noon. I linked EJ and Cassie, "Did you guys feel that?" Cassie answered, "Feel what?" I would've accused her of being evasive, but the bond told me she was sincerely confused.

EJ asked, "Alexander, are you ok?" I pressed, "You guys really did sense a change of any sort?" They both replied, "No." Oden said, "They are wrong, everything in the world just changed." I asked, "But what was it?"

EJ and Cassie popped to me. EJ asked, "What's going on?" I answered, "I just feel like everything just changed." They both exchanged glances. I shrugged, "I dunno what changed. I thought everyone felt it." They both shook their head.

Cassie made a plan, "Ok, Alexander go ask dad. I'll go ask Uncle Aiden if you could've developed a Fairy type power, and EJ will ask mom." I grinned, "You're such a planner." She snorted, "You make battle plans, and I get us answers. It's what we do." I'd bet money her mate was a Hackura.

I was actually hoping her mate was Cayden Crawford. Time would tell though. It was weird she'd never met him, but we had. Oden huffed, "Let's solve our mystery instead of their weird scheduling conflicts." He was right because I wanted to know what had changed.

I nodded to my siblings and popped back to my dad. He looked confused asking, "Alexander, are you alright?" Dylan cooed, "Do you bring a mystery with you? Fascinating." My dad groaned, "Will you go find Wesley and Buttercup before I hit you."

Dylan snickered, "He jests so, but he's never punched me. He's punched people FOR me though. It's so sweet of him because WE ARE FAMILLLLYYYY YEAH YEAH!" My dad shouted, "CALEB!" His Beta had resigned and now it was Cousin Jim, but Caleb still did a lot.

Caleb smirked, "Yes?" My dad said, "Make him go away since Jim and Nick are busy and Lacy just left after laughing at me." Caleb laughed and grabbed Dylan. Dylan cooed, "What do you do in retirement? Because you still do a lot of things. You know you're going to get scooped up for the Werewolf Council with your pups. You should relax and go to a beach until that happens."

My dad grabbed my hand and led me into his office. He said, "I know you want to ask me something." I nodded admitting, "I do. Did you feel a change in…?" I trailed off. He pressed, "In?" I shrugged, "I don't know the universe, world, the realm, territory, or all the realms? I don't really know but I felt everything change a little bit ago. EJ and Cassie said they didn't feel anything."

He tilted his head, "I felt like something happened and so did your grandpa, but not the world changing." I asked, "Grandpa Nathan felt it too?" He said, "We both felt like something significant happened, but not like the world changed"

I asked, "Did the wind caress you too?" He answered, "Uh no. It was just like a moment where it stilled." Stilled? Everything came alive in that moment. I sighed, "We didn't feel the same thing then." He said, "Or we did and it's just different to you."

I asked, "Did anyone else feel it?" He answered, "Not that I know of." I asked, "Why would it be us three?" He shrugged, "Again, I don't know." Theirs didn't feel like mine did either. He said, "Sometimes, we just feel things. I know I got a jolt that now I recognize as my Supernatural side calling out to your mom from the moment her name was announced to me. I always sought out information about her because she was my destiny."

I nodded, "I know." He talked about that a lot. He asked, "Are you ok?" I shrugged, "I thought something really happened. Everything feels different." He urged, "Let's get in the ring and fight your anxiety off, pup." Oden purred, "Yeah, let's."

I figured he'd want to go for another run later. We got in the ring and I fought my dad. I got a shot in, and he grunted. "Damn pup, you pack a punch." Several people had stopped to watch us. We sparred and I heard someone cheering and clapping for us both.

Oden purred, "Mom is cheering us on." That was very much like her. My dad pinned me eventually. I winked and popped out from under him. He laughed, "Cheater." I asked, "Is it cheating to use what I can do?" My mom popped in and kissed my cheek then hugged my dad.

She answered, "No, it's not. In a fight that's not a friendly spar, you should open a portal. Their ass would drop into the Hackura realm, and they would be ripped apart." I laughed but stored that knowledge away for later use.|

The rest of the day passed and Oden and I were still thinking about earlier in the day. When my phone rang, I answered, "Hello." My friend Jason McAlister sang, "Guessss whhhhhattttt?" I laughed, "Ok. My guess is that your mom is going to show up to an event."

He said, "I'm sure she will since she's not sick anymore." I replied, "She's been sick her whole…." I trailed off because I was about to say pregnancy. I asked, "Did your mom give birth?" He proudly answered, "Yup! Melanie Jane McAlister was born at noon." I nearly dropped the phone.

NOON?! When everything in my entire world shifted? Oden purred, "I love her name." I did too. Was this like my dad seeking out things involving my mom? Was Melanie mine? Oden said, "We will find out soon enough." That was true. If Sam hadn't been sick, we'd already know because I'd have been around her.

I said, "Congratulations man. Can I come see her?" He sighed, "I wish but mom's being all protective she wolf right now. She barely let Chelsea, Peter, Elise, Dakota, and Dalton in to see her. My grandparents, even my mom's parents, haven't met her yet and neither has Uncle Duncan. Aunt Allison is traveling with the pups since my uncle can't leave the pack yet. He'll be here next week though." Damn it!

Oden purred, "We still will meet her soon enough." I asked, "How? We barely go to Red Run." He reasoned, "EJ does." That was true, he did. I said, "Well, I can't wait to meet the newest McAlister and I'm happy for you."

He boasted, "She's so cute too, man. She's got a head full of really pretty raven black hair. Mom and dad think it will lighten out, but I just have a feeling it won't. I swear her hair is thicker than mine." I was soaking up every detail about this pup I'd never laid eyes on knowing Oden was quietly doing the same.

He added, "Oh and her eyes are like the coolest ever! The pack doctor said they will probably change. He mentioned something about eyes changing in the first three months, but I hope they don't. Her eyes are the palest green I've ever seen. Not to brag, but she's the most beautiful pup that ever lived."

I chuckled, "I'm sure." Oden purred, "I am also sure." We talked for a bit longer before I hung up with him. Oden purred, "Our mate may have been born." I said, "Let's temper that until we meet her. Ok? We like her name." He added, "And we felt everything in the world change the literal minute she was born." So, there was that. Dad and Grandpa Nathan felt it too though.

My Grandma Cassandra linked, "Are you coming tomorrow to Grandma Cassandra day?" I answered, "Uh huh." She snarked, "Be sure to lose that attitude when you do." I shot back, "I will when you do." She growled, "Well, I just never…" Her voice faded and I chuckled. That was a short argument for her.

Oden said, "I shut her out." He didn't like her any more than I did. I shoved her out of my mind and pulled out a sketch book. I had a slight talent for drawing. I sketched a pup like Jason described. I whispered, "Hi Melanie Jane. I hope to meet you one day soon."

Flashback Ends

Alexander blinked when Cassie touched his arm. She asked me, "Are you ok?" I nodded, "Yeah." She said, "I texted Jase you were back." I hugged her, "Thanks, sis." She asked, "So, how did it go?" Jason and Tristan came in with Jared. Jared must have popped them here.

We got into all, and Cassie whistled. She groaned, "Damn it! Aiylee said she could tell my path wasn't on that mission. I'll get another one, but that was juicy!" So, that's why she'd let it go she wasn't allowed to come with us.

Oden snorted, "Plus her and Rain are the biggest daddy's girl." That was true. Jason said, "Congrats man, that's a hell of first mission." My guard, Egres, faded in. He hummed, "It certainly was. Next time, send a smoke signal and we will go to the unknown place with you."

I winked replying, "That hardly sounds fun." He disagreed, "It sounds like so much fun." He handed EJ and I whiskey. It wasn't our first time trying it since my dad had let us have it on occasion. He said, "This is from your Uncle Bjourn." He winked and faded back.

We drank it and talked with our friends. EJ snuck off with Elise and I was certain they were going to have their first kiss or something. Maybe not. We weren't like other Hackura. A full blood would need to work off the vigor they felt from completing their first mission. I felt that in my Hackura blood, but I just called up my other sides.

My Wolf and Fairy sides were firmly in control. I didn't have anyone I even wanted to make out with because any time someone would offer, the sketch I drew of Melanie Jane McAlister flashed in my mind. Oden didn't want anyone else and neither did I.

Oden grumbled, "I still can't believe we haven't met her." Yeah, I couldn't either but that was all changing soon. I felt intense horror from my mom and then I could sense she was using her healing light. I asked, "Who got hurt?" Everyone shrugged then Tristan's phone rang.

He answered, "Hey, dad." He stalled, "Uhh no, we came to Black Mountain. Jared popped us in and…" He gasped, "What? No, I'll go check. I promise I'll stay in the borders. Do you have eyes on Ladybug?" Oden went still and Cassie shot me a look.

Tristan sighed, "Yeah, that's good. We will plan to spend the night here." He hung up. I asked, "Did someone get hurt in your pack?" Oden said, "If Melanie is hurt, we need to help heal her." My mom's light would tug if she needed me, but I really wouldn't care if it was Melanie that had been hurt. I would help her and heal her faster.

He shook his head, "A pup crossed the border in our pack and rogues came at him hard. It's like they were just waiting outside our border for someone to cross. Dad said they ripped his arms and legs off, they are preparing for the worst. Sharon brought him to your mom." I was gone in the next second to my mom.

My dad said, "Alexander." Her light hadn't called to me, but it would've. She could regrow limbs, but it would be easier with me. We were in an operating room which I found odd. There were doctors waiting all around us.

I announced, "He's going to make it." I put my hands on him and my healing side felt his intense pain. I could practically taste his terror of thinking he was going to die, but my mom and I weren't going to let that happen.

My mom had regrown one arm and a leg and healed some internal bleeding and damage. I finished his other leg and fixed some arteries and bleeding on that side. Then I faltered backwards. My dad caught me and shoved food at me. He ordered, "Eat."

I whispered, "I need to help mom." Uncle Aiden emphatically stated, "What you need to do is eat." I pressed, "But mom will pass out." Uncle Aiden said, "Maybe not since you helped her." I felt my mom tapped into my Grandpa Titus and Uncle Bjourn's strength to keep going.

Uncle Aiden rubbed his temples. I asked, "What's wrong?" He grumbled, "Just the fact she could do multiple sessions instead of pushing herself. They could keep the pup sedated. She could simply take some breaks to eat, but it's not in her nature. Goddess, I miss Arion." I felt the feelings from my dad that it annoyed him that he agreed with Uncle Aiden.

I knew something went down with Uncle Arion and my mom. I just didn't know what. I knew my dad had begrudgingly, over the years, slowly admitted Uncle Arion would've been helpful to have around. I whispered, "How old is this pup?" Oden growled angrily because we could sense he was pretty young, maybe even three.

My dad answered, "He just turned four yesterday." I snarled, "HOW DARE THEY! Are they dead?" He replied, "Yes, they are. Peter, Drake, and their border patrol handled it." The need to rage and fight was now firing on all sides.

When my mom finished she nearly hit the floor, but my dad caught her. I conjured her a bunch of pizza and she smiled at me weakly. I cupped her face and kissed her cheek. She whispered, "You did so good." Uncle Aiden snorted, "If not for him, you'd be unconscious."

Our pack doctor, Ethan, snorted, "Yes, well thank god she's not." My dad growled, "Hey!" Ethan was unfazed. He shot back, "You are a holy terror when she's unconscious even though you know me and my staff can't do much more than give her fluids."

My dad retorted, "You've helped her several times." Ethan shot him a look before replying, "Not when she passes out from a healing, which is what I was referring to." Ethan walked over to my mom and grinned.

He teased, "How's my worst patient?" She grumbled, "I cannot be the worst." He laughed, "The Alpha's do give you run for your money, but I get to treat you more than them. I would like to run an IV on you." She waved, "I can feel that will make Eric feel better so go ahead." She turned to me, "Go do what you need to do." My dad looked torn.

My mom touched his shoulder and inclined her head back to the corner. I turned and saw my Uncle Bjourn. I smiled at him. He nodded, "Your mom pulled me letting me know you needed me." He assured my dad, "I've got him, I promise." I felt my dad's absolute faith in my uncle and actually wished Uncle Bjourn could feel it. I knew it would mean a lot to him. Both nodded at each other.

My dad said, "I'll come see you later, son. I'm very proud of you." My Uncle hustled me out of the room, but I still heard the pup scream in terror when he came to. I saw his parents with Peter and Chelsea. I said, "His parents should go back, he's freaking out. Which is more than fair, but he's perfectly fine."

The parents ran and hugged me before going back to their pup. Peter and Chelsea hugged me next. He said, "It's always amazing what you and your mom can do." I shrugged, "She did most of the work." He said, "But you helped, and you weren't even asked to. You are amazing pup, and you get more impressive every year."

He squeezed my shoulder saying, "Go on and do what you need to do. It's not just your Hackura blood here. I'm sure your dad will be there for you and Oden." He would. Oden snarled, "I want to RIP those rogues to pieces." I did too.

When we reached the gym, everyone gave us a wide berth and Liam nodded to me. He was my cousin's mate, which to me made him a cousin as well. Uncle Bjourn and I got in the ring. Eventually Liam threw us bamboo sticks and Uncle Ubbe showed up to fight too.

After several hours I felt my eyes stop blazing. I whispered, "He's only four." Uncle Bjourn said, "And he's ok because of you and your mom." It still gutted me that it happened and that it was in Red Run.

Uncle Bjourn ordered, "Pop us to the mountain." I did. He asked, "What's the rest of this feeling you have?" I whispered, "I feel bad." He sighed, "I know that, but I don't get why." I winced, "Because I'm glad it wasn't Melanie. What kind of person does that make me?"

He answered, "A normal one. You saved that boy and you're glad Melanie didn't get hurt. I'd bet several people feel the way you do." He nudged me, "You're meeting her soon." I snorted, "Provided she comes."

He said, "Well, no one in that pack is crossing the border for at least a month or six after that." It was true. Pups never crossed the border after a rogue attack, especially a brutal one like that. He nudged me, "I'm proud of you, but I know you're still restless."

My mom popped in with my dad. Her coloring was back, and she looked much better. She kissed the top of my head urging, "Go with your dad. Your Uncle Aiden and I are going to center ourselves with the earth." Uncle Aiden popped in and winked at me. I hugged my Uncle Bjourn. I whispered, "Thank you." He said, "I will always be here for you, nephew. I love you." I replied, "I love you too."

He backed up and my dad shifted into Thor. I let Oden come out and he dug his claws into the dirt and growled. Thor inclined his head, and we took off running. He linked me, "We have some reports of rogues near some borders. We are going to find and kill them so what happened today does not happen again." I was all about that plan.

We ended up near Alpha Theo's territory. It had been his brother's until he went crazy, and Lucas had to kill him. I scented them before my dad and took off. He was right behind me, and we had killed four when more surrounded us.

One took a swipe at my dad that he avoided. I snarled and pushed at them. They went down whining in pain. Alpha Theo joined us with his Warriors. I exploded two of their heads seeing the horrible things they'd done.

The other two were just broken and crazy, but they hadn't hurt anyone though. I shifted back and conjured a sword beheading both. Alpha Theo said, "Well, that makes my life easier. How is the pup you saved doing?" I didn't answer because all I knew was he was alive.

My dad told them, "He's good and my wife set him up with a pup psychologist that's the best in trauma. He's obviously traumatized, but thanks to Haley and Alexander he is alive." Alpha Theo clapped me on the back, "Good job, pup. What's the difference in the kills here."

I pointed, "Those three raped several humans in no man's land. One might have even killed the woman. Those two were just crazy, but they hadn't hurt anyone yet. It was getting close though." Oden snarled in anger.

My dad asked, "Did you get a sense of when? We'll need to watch out for pups." We usually had couples offer to adopt if the humans got pregnant and elected to keep the pregnancy. We never judged them if they terminated, chose adoption, or raised the pup. We understood their feelings no matter how it turned out.

I said, "It was within the last few weeks." He nodded, "I'll have Jim look into hospital records." I knew he'd handle that. I just hoped they'd all made it. Rogues tended to attack humans instead of Supernatural's because they were easier targets. Plus, they wanted to avoid packs. Alpha's would put them down. It made me feel bad for the humans.

I said, "We need better protection for the humans in no man's land. It's not their fault rogues are running around, and they live in unclaimed territory." My dad winced, "That's complicated but I will work on a solution. I'll set up some businesses and Lucas has some shelters. We will rotate wolves interested. I'll put up a hotel and we can staff it. That way we'd catch a scent."

Rogues weren't smart enough to get around that system. Other Supernatural's could easily. We couldn't monitor no man's land for that. I felt the Alpha blood in me settle because I knew my dad would work to better protect them from Rogues. That's what we could do.

I just felt horrible for these people that had no idea what they were up against. Those poor men and women who suffered because rogues were avoiding packs. My dad put a hand on me and discussed everything with Theo before we shifted and ran back.

Oden felt much better and so did I. I shifted back and my dad did the same and snapped us clothes. He nudged me, "Snap us some whiskey." I did and he clinked my glass before he drank it. He said, "God, I would give anything for you not to have to deal with things like that today. Hell, I'd give the world, so your mom didn't. You are just a pup who shouldn't have to deal with seeing things like that."

I replied, "But I will always come to mom. Plus, I didn't see him ripped apart like the pups with him had to of." I didn't even see the limbs. He nodded, "Yes, but you can feel the damage done to him. Your mom says she can sense how terrified someone is when they are hurt." I nodded, "That's true."

He sighed, "I hate that for you guys, and I wish with everything I have in me that I could change it. At the same time, I've seen pups hurt the way that one was. I've seen a dead pup and consoled other Alpha's when it happens to them. We do our best, but we can't always be perfect. Ever since I met your mom, that has changed. She does amazing things, and you do too. I felt your conflict in feelings earlier."

He paused probably wondering if I'd explain it, but I remained quiet. He continued, "I feel that same type of conflict because I wish this burden wasn't put on you or your mom, but I remember those days before you guys were here. When we lost innocent lives to rogues, and I am happy that pup will get to go on and live his life."

I nodded, "I get that." He chuckled, "I know you do. It felt like you came earlier than when your mom's light tugs you." I admitted, "I came when T got the call about what happened. I knew she'd need me, and I preferred not to wait before she was fatigued, and her light called." He hugged me and we walked back into the house.

I tried to fall asleep but tossed and turned until I felt someone beside me. I whispered, "Mom." She said, "Sometimes the healing can haunt you with the ghosts of feelings. The horror his body felt echoes in ours and I didn't want that to happen to you today."

I snorted, "You were going to try and do it on your own." She acknowledged, "I was but that's not the point. Right now, the point is I'm holding my baby boy until he falls asleep." I snorted, "I'm taller than you and I'm not a baby."

She kissed my head, "No matter how big you get you'll always be my baby. All of you will. Even though I have to fly up to kiss your heads or cheeks when you don't bend down. I have wings so I'll use them to my fucking advantage." I laughed, "That's so you, mom." She hugged me and held me tight.

Somehow, despite the fact that she reeked of my dad and I could smell what they'd been doing, I finally fell asleep with her holding me tight. When I woke up, I could smell my parent's scent strongly in my room.

I opened my eyes a slit and my mom smiled saying, "I conjured you breakfast." We ate it together before they went on about their days. Everyone always thought they couldn't pay attention to all the pups they had so far, but everyone was wrong.

No one managed their time better than my parents. I loved my family and knew they'd have more pups because my second sister wasn't born yet. I was more than happy to have more siblings. All of them were great.

I got up and ran some laps. Theo, my little brother, joined me. I winked, "Hey, little brother." Oden grumbled, "We should run with Barker." That was my brother's wolf. He was actually named after Alpha Theo because he was friends with my dad.

It did confuse people because we had a lot of people with the same names running around. Which all of us with Fairy blood found deeply amusing. We messed with people about it too.

Theo greeted "Hi, big brother. Why are you so keyed up?" I winked, "I'm excited for the big picnic later." He gave me a measured look, "Umm ok." I asked, "Do you want to go for a run? Oden wants to run with Barker." He grinned, "Let's go."

We barely made it outside before our wolves ripped out of us ready to run. Brutus joined us and so did Leif, my brother Julian's wolf, and Morris, Maverick's wolf. Maverick and Theo were twins. Oden howled happily that Lief was out here. Julian leaned more Fairy than the rest of us, so he didn't run as much here. He usually shifted in Faerie. Leif howled back and we ran together.

When we arrived, several people were pretty somber. I linked EJ, "Who peed in the punch?" He replied, "I don't know." He went and found Elise, she'd been here all day but he'd left her to join us, who he got to smile before he shifted back. He popped her away and I felt his incredulousness along with intense disbelief. They popped back.

I teased, "Hey Elise, where is the imaginary Melanie?" I was trying to goad her and the other Red Run wolves into producing Melanie. I didn't actually believe that she was imaginary like my mom did. Oden purred, "Because she's probably ours." I really hoped so.

Elise sighed, "Well, she's not coming." Oden muttered, "Of course not." EJ shot me a look over my disappointment in the bond. I didn't bother addressing that. I tapped my chin, "Let me guess, she's getting the Nobel peace prize. What about some science or math award?" EJ snorted, "Alexander."

I said, "No, she's getting a Pulitzer winning literature prize." The science and math award had been mentioned for her absences. Oden chuckled in my head. Wesley said, "Come on, Alexander. You know it will be a competition she entered in last minute." I snapped my fingers, "There it is. A good old classic, Wes." Several people snickered.

Elise winced, "She's grounded." I asked, "For? Because this will be good. I'm expected a top tier excuse." She winced, "She crossed the border." Even Wesley snorted with me this time. I teased, "Oh come on, you can do better than that." She frowned, "Huh?"

I said, "No pup would cross your border after what literally happened last night. Let alone the Beta's daughter, who was probably told what happened." Elise admitted, "She was told." I snorted, "So, that's a bullshit excuse. What else you got?"

She insisted, "Some older pups said she crossed and a parent confirmed they saw her headed in that direction." I asked, "Why would anyone believe that? No pup crosses right after a rogue attack, let alone a genius."

She rubbed her temples, "Well, Mel doesn't really get social cues sometimes." I raised an eyebrow. Wesley asked, "Does she have survival instincts?" Elise went to answer but he held up his hand, "It's a rhetorical question because all Supernatural's do. I'm merely pointing out this excuse is insane and inaccurate."

My mom popped over. She asked, "What's going on?" I said, "We are trying to help Elise come up with a better reason Melanie isn't here." She waved, "It's because she's damn prank and they won't let it fucking go."

She kissed my head, "Don't feel bad they got you. They are just being sore losers because I'm better at pranking them. They might want to watch it because I'm going to go Fairy Hijinks on their ass because they won't let this one go." She popped away.

Elise insisted, "She IS real." Oden said, "Push her on the subject! She's so annoyed right now." I teased, "Sure, she is." She shouted, "SHE IS!" Wesley jumped in clearly picking up on my feelings. He said, "I dunno. You want us to believe a genius has zero supernatural survival skills or that she can't cross a border without getting caught. Humans can do that. She's supposedly a genius."

Elise retorted, "She's LITERALLY a genius." Wesley grinned, "Then tell us the real reason she's not coming. Because it's not that she crossed the border. Literally no one believes that." She stomped her foot, "That's what my dad said the reason was."

EJ growled, "Guys." He knew we were pushing but Elise was getting agitated, and I didn't actually want that. I said, "Sorry, Elise. I'll leave you to your prank ponderings. You should warn your pack, my mom really will get you guys."

She sighed, "It's just a weird coincidence you haven't met her." Wesley said, "I mean she's supposedly seven, so it's past weird coincidences and now is in the quite intentional realm." I tended to agree with that.

Oden huffed, "Who cares? Let's just leave. It's a picnic like any other and we've been to those." I wandered away from the group and ended up in the gym. Liam joined me. He questioned, "Alexander, why aren't you enjoying the picnic?"

I hit the bag grunting, "What's to enjoy?" He answered, "The sunny day and your Earth side." I grunted and hit the bag again. He got behind it and let me continue to hit it. My dad came in and took his place.

I commented, "You're supposed to be out there." He chuckled, "I don't actually do what I'm supposed to most of the time. I do what's right and I don't care what that looks like." Dylan yelled, "HE SO DOES! HE HAS BEEN BUCKING TRADITION SINCE HE WAS A WEE PUP!"

My dad groaned, "Will you just go back to the party?" Dylan huffed, "Fine. I'll leave you to your moody pup who is a member of the OG triplets." Oden snarled at him. He pointed, "See? Moody." I rolled my eyes. He called, "Catch ya later, Moody Triplet." I glared at his retreating form.

My dad asked, "What's going on?" I shrugged, "I don't like being lied to." He tilted his head, "Neither do I." I said, "Then you get it." He disagreed, "I don't think I do." I snorted, "Did you hear why Melanie isn't here?"

He sighed, "Uh huh. Your mom asked when they got here and she linked me for thirty minutes full of cursing about how pranks are supposed to be over at some point. She also claims if certain people can't get a handle on that she will launch a longstanding prank war the likes of which we have not seen."

I stalled my hit, and he nodded. He commented, "Yeah, words do NOT express how much I don't want that to happen." Oden said, "I kind of do. Then they'd have to produce Melanie." That was actually true.

My dad pointed at me warning, "Don't you dare push her into doing that. I feel you thinking it's a good idea to nudge her into doing it." I laughed, "They'd bring Melanie then to prove she's not a prank then though. Wouldn't they?"

He agreed, "Yes, but eventually she has to show up to things. Elise considers her a sister." I asked, "What do you really think is going on?" He replied, "I think Drake is very nervous about Melanie's safety and the Warriors and other pack members pick up on that. They all worry for her because they do love her, and they are doing what they think is best."

I gasped, "You think they are lying." He shrugged, "Pups are curious. I'm sure she has crossed a few times, but she got caught. Do I think she crossed today? No. Literally no one thinks that. Sam and Drake have trauma associated with crossing the border. So, I think they believe it."

I asked, "What trauma?" He answered, "Deaths in their family prior to you or your mom coming into our lives. It happened more than we cared for it to. They get so triggered about it because it's happened to them before. Both of them having those stories make them react harsher. Sam saw her family members' bodies, and she's been on scene at several pups in Blue Moon dying. One of her best friends did run away at one point and keep everyone at arm's length before she left. Sam has a lot going on."

I snorted, "That's not Melanie's fault." He agreed, "It's not but something I have come to understand is it's very important to talk about your trauma because it shapes our reactions to things. I don't even know if Sam could control that response at this point. She's afraid for her pup and she's seen the aftermath. Considering it was right on top of what happened yesterday, I wish those that reported it had used a different made up offense." Me too.

It was insulting they believed it. Oden grumbled, "That means Melanie is probably insulted too." I didn't like that. My dad said, "Let's head back out there." I nodded and walked back out into our pack. I'd try to have fun, but it didn't hold a candle the excitement I'd had thinking I was going to meet Melanie today.

Helping My Way

Melanie is Eleven Years Old

Melanie was nervous. My network of people listening out for rumors that I needed to warn people about had grown exponentially. Pups were unassuming and people talked around us. Plus, I was certain some of them were in bad packs.

My network was of dancers and general word of mouth. This tip was important because I'd verified it… Ok, I verified them all. I should feel bad because, well in a way I was taking advantage of those pups… but I was helping. No one ever wanted to let me help.

So, I might have had a network listening for subjects I wanted to know about. Did they do that because I'm kind of an amazing dancer? Well… yes. I did talk to them though… so it wasn't all bad. I watched the clock, ready to finish this experiment.

My dad was coming to pick me up from school then I was heading to my dance competition in California. That's where I'd enact my plan to protect Xander. I had to. I was finalizing my competition experiment for the science fair next week when I got back.

I wanted to check my financial portfolio before I left though too. I'd been investing since I was little. I felt a little bad I'd used a fake I.D. but I mean… I had to, when you thought about it. My parents gave me an allowance… and they did have a lot of money. No one took me seriously though and I wanted to prove I could invest and make my own money.

So, I used my allowance as my spending money. All the money from my grandparents at Christmas and my birthday I'd put into investing. My grandparents on my mom's side always gave me money… because I guess it was hard to buy me presents.

Me, Jason, and Tristan were their only grandpups since my mom was their only pup. They were rich too…and I did know that made me very privileged… but I'd turned quite the profit. I smiled to myself because I was a millionaire, and no one knew it.

I had a diversified portfolio, and I even set up a profile using Prince Gunner Cambridge's tips, to advise people on their finances. I hired a guy who was the front guy, but the ideas came from me. Those genius genes from my dad really came in handy.

My mom is smart too though so I should thank both of them really. My dad says I'm smarter than he is which feels like a tradeoff… because he's better at not saying everything he thinks out loud. I'm bad at it… like very bad. I love it when people say I remind them of him though. I'm a proud daddy's girl.

My teacher came over and hovered in close. He inhaled, "Hmm, that's brilliant." I muttered, "It's not done yet." I was working on a tool that identified elemental components. I wanted to turn around and use that and combine with jewelry for Supernatural's. Uncle Duncan had been there when I thought of it, but I hadn't worked on it until recently.

If I could it worked out Supernaturals could know if they were around something that hurt them. My teacher trailed his finger down my arm saying, "It's brilliant. I love the way your mind works." Because I was smarter than he was.

Ok, that sounded mean, but it was true. I was much smarter than this human teacher. He groaned, "Wow, you smell good." I made a face because humans weren't supposed to have an enhanced sense of smell, but I'd found a lot of them liked my scent.

I smelled like strawberries so I could understand people liked it. It was the scent of candles, bodywash, shampoo, condition, perfume, lotion, and all kinds of other things humans sold. I was about to say I used strawberry shampoo….which was true when I heard an all out snarl. My dad was early. Good.

I jolted up and my teacher jumped five feet back. I grabbed my backpack, "Hi, daddy! Let me clean this up and…" He ordered, "Go outside." I frowned, "Oh…umm well… it's just class procedure to clean up your…" He growled, "Outside." I blinked in surprise at Pepper. My dad's wolf was firmly in charge now. I quickly left the classroom, but I heard him hit my teacher.

I linked Peter, "Umm…" He laughed, "What's wrong?" I admitted, "I'm not sure, but… well so… Pepper is beating up my human science teacher… he definitely growled… and…" He popped in front of me with Warriors, Garrett, Sharon, and Zane, our Male Lead Warrior.

Peter ordered, "Sharon stay out here with Ladybug." He pointed at two Warriors, "You too." I offered, "I could help." I could. I trained with Zane, my mom, Chelsea, and former Alpha Nick Kyle. He was like my grandpa though.

We trained with Elise too. She was the best! She was practically my sister. Peter didn't answer me and took off. Sharon asked, "What happened?" I explained what I'd been doing and she winced. I asked, "What? I don't understand what's wrong?" She chuckled, "Oh, Ladybug." I hated when people said that.

It was the tone that said I was so cute and didn't understand. I didn't like not understanding things. It irked me. She ruffled my hair, "One day, you'll understand. You'll be getting a new teacher though." I shrugged because he wasn't really a good teacher. I basically did his job and taught the class.

I must have said it out loud because she asked, "You what? What do you mean you do his job?" I admitted, "Umm… well, I plan the lessons because… through a series of events… we already learned what he taught prior… so I plan his lesson and give it to him for the week… and…"

She cut me off, "Why didn't you say anything?" I answered, "Because I liked the challenge of planning the class." She asked, "Was this just for your class?" I admitted, "No… it's… well… it's for all his classes." She rubbed her temples, "Goddess that won't help the situation." I wasn't even sure what the situation was.

I whispered, "Will they make me stay home from the competition? Because I…" She cut me off, "No, you're still going. Why wouldn't you? You didn't do anything wrong." I pointed out, "I never do, and I still get punished all the time… like literally… all the time." She winced and made a face I knew all too well because she knew I was right.

It was maddening that I followed the rules all the time, but I was punished for breaking rules I never had. I was tempted to break them to prove I could. Because I TOTALLY could break them and get away with it.

Someone definitely didn't want me to meet my Xander. That was the only explanation. I'd bet it was Robert. He was the worst. You'd think people wouldn't listen to him though. We had a history of disliking each other. He was the one with the problem though, not me. I just defended myself from him and annoying Charline. She was SO obnoxious that even ROBERT thought so.

Sharon tugged my hair asking, "Where did you go?" I shrugged saying, "No where… just thinking about how people don't like me." She knelt down, "Everyone likes you, Ladybug." It was crazy she believed that. She couldn't lie since she had Fairy blood. It was obvious people didn't like me… especially Robert.

Though I stopped telling them when he bothered me. So, maybe she did believe that. Well, she had to believe it. Obviously….the whole can't lie thing. We waited and chatted outside for over an hour before my dad came back out. He knelt down and picked me up and squeezed me so tight it was hard to breathe.

I whispered, "Daddy." He pulled back, "You'll never have to see him again." That definitely meant the teacher got fired, but it could mean he killed him. I still didn't get what happened. He put me in his SUV, and we drove away.

I asked, "Did I do something wrong?" He answered, "No, you did absolutely nothing wrong. That man will never be near you or another pup." I questioned, "Is he dead?" He gripped the wheel hard before he answered, "No, he's alive." Huh. I definitely thought given how he squeezed the wheel the teacher was dead.

Humans would consider us over aggressive, but we lived by a different way of life. Plus, ya know… they were human, and we weren't. We were supernatural's and it was still very much a different version of justice we lived by.

Humans had to wait a very long time for justice with the court system. I felt sad for them with that. Even if we waited for the Werewolf or Supernatural Council to render a verdict, it was swift. Sometimes Human cases went on for years.

When we got home my brothers were outside waiting with my mom. She urged, “Hurry up and pack, Ladybug.” I quickly ran inside, not mentioning I was in fact packed. I went and checked my portfolio. I’d had a massive cash influx from a stock when I’d first started everything. I traded some and bought another startup company’s stock that I saw going places.

Prince Gunner recommended real estate purchases, but I hadn’t done that yet. I checked my boards to see if he’d put out another paper. He was my hacking and computer skills mentor… he just had no idea that he was.

Which was totally a thing in my head… but probably not really. He hadn’t put out a paper, but my Xander’s dad did. I quickly downloaded his latest paper and noted King Aiden Holloran, my Xander’s Uncle, had put out another paper one second before Jared popped into my room.

Jared winked at me, “Do you have my paper I gave you to proof?” I handed him his research paper. He took and snorted, “You changed the entire paper I gave you. You were just supposed to edit it.” I frowned, “I did… I mean… it’s just that the parameters could be expanded and far more interes…”

He cut me off, “I believe you.” He conjured a duffle bag of books from Faerie. He winked, “I went to a new section for you this time.” I grinned and gave him a hug, “Thanks, Jared.” We’d had this deal since I was two. The first book he’d given me was a Fealish dictionary and we went up from there. I’d learned for my Xander.

My mom called, “Ten minutes, Ladybug.” Jared winked at me then popped out. I pulled out my packed suitcase from under my bed and my backpack. I put a few of the books from Jared’s duffle back into them and unplugged my tablet that had the two new downloaded papers ready to view. I pulled out my Xander wolf and put him under my arm and smiled at him remembering the day I got him.

Flashback

Melanie was so excited. I’d convinced my mom that I wanted to go to the toy store. I’d earned my allowance from my chores, and I knew what I wanted. I felt a little bad… I had kind of tricked Elise… but she didn’t know.

So, that was ok. I hoped… it seemed ok. Ever since I could remember, I knew Xander was mine. Now, I knew what his wolf, Oden, looked like because she told me. I hadn’t met my Xander yet, so I wanted something to remind him of me.

I loved stuffed animals, so we were heading to the big store around here that carried all a bunch of toys and stuffed animals. My mom asked, “Are you sure you want to spend your allowance?” People would’ve considered me young for one if they knew how old I was.

I was three and I was certain people didn’t think I could hear them whispering that I was genius pup like my dad. That made me want to impress them even more. I wanted to be just like my dad. I knew that if I lived in a different realm, I’d probably already be working my way through high school level classes.

I could already speak three languages… but… well… no one knew that. Except Jared. Well, he knew I could speak two. English and Fealish. I just also knew Latin because of my Xander. He spoke all three so I wanted to as well.

My mom parked the car, and I scrambled out from the back. She laughed, “The store isn’t going anywhere, Ladybug.” Yeah, well she hadn’t eaten the mom monster cookies yet today, so I needed to get this done.

I hated those cookies because she ate them, then never believed what I said. I didn’t trust the lady who delivered them, but she was friends with my mom…. I guess. Mom always said that when I told her she was shifty.

I’d get in trouble if I said it after she’d had a cookie that evil lady brought. I’d tracked them back to the grocery store. The whole pack raved about them, and sadly I couldn’t prove they were evil. I was hoping I could when I got older. Plus, she clearly wasn't my mommy's friend. They were acquaintances at best. Mom never hung out with her or went to the allies day with her.

I couldn't wait until I got to go those. Xander's mom hosted them rotating through several realms, and they all whispered about how much fun they were. Elise got to go since she was EJ's. I was Xander's but I was the only one who knew that.

When I was older, I would get to go. It was probably how I'd meet Xander at this point. I blamed Robert and the evil cookie delivery lady. It was definitely their fault. Robert was a pup in my pack, but he eyed me weirdly and said mean things to me.

He liked Elise and was mad I'd told him she was EJ's. I warned him he'd better leave her alone. He made fun of me because I didn't get all the words right. It annoyed me that I could read all the words but somehow, they didn't come out right. I sounded better than other pups my age, but I could think all the words they just came out wrong.

My mom took my hand, and we walked into the store. I went over to the stuffed animal section; they had a massive wolf one. The humans thought they were just popular in this area, and had no idea they were so popular because pups wanted wolves that they thought would like them one day or their parents' wolves.

My mom cooed, "Awww, this looks just like Pepper. How about him?" She held him up and I shook my head continuing to go through the bin. She chuckled, "You seem to be on a mission." I nodded and kept going.

She gasped, "This one could be what your wolf will look like." It was a brown wolf with little white spots on it but I shook my head. Although, she was right. It probably was what my wolf would look like. She snorted, "Fine, he's a light brown one. I just think my Warrior blood will get in your wolf, and you'll have a white paws or a white spot."

Warriors often had white in their coats. The only ones who didn't were Alpha bloods, even if there was Warrior blood in their DNA. Except my Xander. He had a white underbelly and paws. He was special because he was an Alpha Enforcer, and he was poised to be the strongest one ever. I'd tell people he would be, but they wouldn't believe me.

I'd read about it in one of the books Jared brought me. Ok, so it was also a hypothesis based on the book… so it wasn't really anyone else's fault they didn't know about it. My mom laughed, "Mel, are you going to pick one?" I huffed once I got to the bottom because there were a lot of all black wolves, but none that looked like Oden.

Tears filled my eyes because I just wanted to get something that would remind me of my mate. I whispered, "They don't have it. Let's go." She knelt down, "Mel, they have lots of wolves." I shook my head, "They don't have him." She chuckled, "Him?" I nodded. She winked, "Let's keep that between us girls." Ok?

A worker came over asking, "How are you ladies finding everything?" My mom glanced at me then said, "I don't think we found it today. We'll come back another time." The worker frowned, "What are you looking for?" My mom turned asking, "Mel?"

I answered, "A bwack wolf with white paws and white chest." The worker tapped his chin then clapped. He said, "You know what? I think we actually got one like that, but it was a manufacturing defect, so we were going to send it back." Why would they do that?!

I gasped, "Pwease! Can I see it?" Ugh! I needed to stop talking because that wasn't coming out like I knew it was supposed to sound. Why couldn't I get all that right?! I curse not living in a different realm. I would talk at a high school level if I did.

The worker nodded, "Wait right here, I'll go look. It might have gotten sent back already." I bit my lip and shuffled my feet. My mom said, "Don't worry, Ladybug. If they don't have him, we can just order it online." I'd looked on the tablet I had. They had parental controls on the old one I got to use, but I could get around them. I hadn't found the wolf I wanted anywhere.

The worker came back twenty minutes later with his arms behind his back and a big smile on his face. Happiness filled me knowing he'd found it. He pulled it out and winked, "It was all packed up and ready to go, but I called the store owner. She gave me permission to sell it to you for the same price as the other wolves." I squealed, "Twank you!" I hugged my Xander wolf tightly and we skipped to the counter.

My mom already had my allowance, so she paid for it. She chuckled, "Well, you were dogmatic, but you got exactly what you wanted." She took a cookie out of her purse and ate it. I deflated and knew my normal mom would be replaced with the mom monster. I hated when that happened, and I hated the evil cookie delivery lady. It was HER fault my mom turned into the mom monster.

I silently told my Xander wolf, "Once I have my wolf, I'll eat the cookie delivery lady. You'd be on my side about it. You'll protect me, won't you?" I hugged it tightly and we got back in the car. I was quiet on the ride home, so I didn't provoke the mom monster.

As long as no one said I did anything remotely bad, the mom monster didn't activate. Well, unless someone asked to take me outside the pack. Then the mom monster raged. I decided today I didn't care because I got my Xander wolf, and he was everything I wanted. I hugged him tightly as we drove back to the pack.

Flashback Ends

I shook off the past and quickly ran downstairs so I could say goodbye to everyone. All before the evil cookie lady showed up. She was here less often, but those cookies were still EVERYWHERE. ALL THE TIME. Did anyone but me find that weird? Nope.

I had this all timed out today because we could NOT have the cookies on this trip. I had things to do and that didn't involve being foiled by mom monster cookies. I had to get word to the Faries and Hackura stealthily. I had a whole plan mapped out that came straight from multiple papers of Prince Gunner Cambridge.

I could admit I was nervous to see if I could pull this off. I'd pulled papers that were decades apart, so I was hoping they didn't check it all. I knew I had to be above reproach and there was no room for mistakes because I was going up against the best of the best.

My own mentor… who still didn't know that's what he was to me…. Put all the papers out. I'd done test runs and checked everything more than I needed to, but this was important. It was for Xander. I slid down the banister like I always did.

My mom gasped and grabbed my dad's arm tightly. She didn't like when I did this, but if she didn't have a mom monster cookie, I didn't get in trouble for it. I jumped off at the end and into my older brother's arms.

Tristan chuckled, "You go kick ass, Ladybug." I whispered, "I wish you were coming, T." Jason snorted, "What I am? Chopped liver?" I jumped into his arms next, and he squeezed me tightly. I linked him, "I know something is going on with T while I'm gone. I know you're staying to have his back. Link me if you need anything."

Tristan and Elise had their wolves now, so they were included in more stuff than me and Jason were. Jason linked, "You know it." I knew he wouldn't actually do it. He'd just say he would. They were very protective of me.

I squealed, "MELINDA! MB!" They were my aunts technically speaking. I called MaryBeth, MB since she liked it right now. They both laughed and gave me a big group hug. MaryBeth said, "Go win that competition and come back with a big trophy and medal." Melinda agreed, "For sure!"

I asked, "Where's Uncle Duncan?" They all looked at each other. My dad cleared his throat, "He'll be here when you get back." I frowned because that was evasive. Uncle Duncan always said goodbye before my competitions. Maybe he was out looking for his mate again.

My Grandpa Ben chuckled, "Get over here, Ladybug." I squealed and went to hug him. He swung me around. He whispered, "Go take on the world, Ladybug." It was the world championship competition. I was the only dancer in our academy that was going. Four of my teachers were coming. Mostly that was fine, but one I didn't like at all.

Mom said I had no reason not to like her, but I disliked her a lot. I told the Warriors to be weary of her, but I feel like they just thought I was cute. Grandma Esther hugged me next. She whispered, "We will be watching on some link T set up." I chuckled. One, because Tristan didn't set it up. Two, because she was just as savvy as us pups were with the internet, but she played like she wasn't. I think I was the only one who knew she was just messing with them besides Grandpa Ben.

Tristan snorted, "I've already cleared out time for you to be confused and me to have to go over to your house and set up it." She muttered, "It would be easier if we just put it on the big screen in the main house."

Peter and Chelsea came in. He agreed, "It would be. That's probably why I reserved it." I giggled, "Daddy Peter!" He held his arms open wide and I ran into them. He linked, "Go do us all proud, you always do."

We were like family, which was very common between the Alpha and Beta families, even the Gamma's. They entered next. I smiled because everyone was coming to wish me good luck. I hugged Chelsea, Garrett, and then Sharon.

My mom laughed, "Alright, we've got to get going." My watch beeped and I knew she was right. I agreed, "Yup… gotta go… for sure… last one to the car is a rotten egg!" I took off for the SUV. The Warriors going with us raised an eyebrow. I threw all my stuff in the back.

My parents came out and my dad got into the driver's seat. He was taking us the airport. I waved, "BYE!" People from the pack were outside with posters and banners to wave us all out. I held my breath as we left, knowing we had thirty seconds left. I breathed a sigh of relief when we made it past the main entrance of the pack.

My dad asked, "Are you ok, Ladybug?" I squeaked, "Who me?" He chuckled, "Yes, you." I nodded, "Uh huh… sure… totally fine." We locked eyes in the review mirror. He told me, "It's ok to be nervous. You're going to win though." He winked, "You always do."

I was relieved that he'd assumed I was nervous about the competition instead of the cookie lady because that would've led to a blow up about her. I saw a few Warriors glance at each other. I was certain they knew. Maybe my dad did too, but he wouldn't have been mad about it mom would've.

We made it to the airport, and got checked in. My dad sighed, "I wish I was going." My mom put her forehead on his and they rocked together. I was pretty sure that was unconscious on their part. My parents were fated mates, just like Xander and I were. I loved their relationship and hoped Xander and I would have what they did.

They kissed before my dad kissed the top of my head. He said, "You've got this, Ladybug. I'll probably growl about your costumes. Don't think I didn't notice you nor your mom showed me what they looked like for this one." I chuckled, "I didn't pick them out."

My mom gasped, "Don't even imply I did! I had NOTHING to do with it." I snorted, "That's true. The teachers picked them." The Warriors with us snickered. My dad hugged me one last time then mom and got us to the TSA line.

He walked away muttering, "Why do those dance teachers want me to lose my goddamn mind? She's just a pup and she looks damn near twenty years old when she's done up in the makeup and the hair, combined with those outfits. I swear they want to give me heart palpitations."

My mom and I both busted up laughing. I asked, "Daddy knows you do my makeup, right?" She winked, "Of course he does. I've been doing makeup since I was in high school." She was really good at it and often did it for she wolves for fancy events. She just also had an accounting degree and was really good with numbers.

I knew at one of the BAGG (Bad Ass Girl Gang) day's she'd done everyone's make up. She loved doing it. She was certified and everything. We made it through the security line and to our plane. We were flying back on Peter's private jet.

I was shocked mom didn't have Sharon pop us into the competition this time. It told me that something was definitely up in the pack though. I pulled up my tablet and started reading through Alpha Eric's paper first. He was giving out battle strategies.

I pulled up my notes on the side and began to type them out with my questions. My brain also formulated additions to the offensive and defensive strategies Alpha Eric put out. I got lost in the paper and my thoughts.

Our flight was called, and we all boarded. It seemed silly since it was a private flight for it to be called, but that was just me. We got settled in and I finished my notes and reading on Alpha Eric's paper. I filed those away and got to King Aiden Holloran.

He had interesting papers on hybrids I read, but also full bloodied Fairies. No one paid attention to those but me. I monitored his tracking for analytics on them. The Hackura were the only ones who read them. It seemed silly because he was telling people they were dangerous, and no one should cross them.

Somehow people didn't seem to understand or comprehend they should NOT mess with Fairies. There were a lot of times the freak weather reports were them because people weren't listening. Xander's brother, Max, could cause earthquakes. Cassie could create tornados and there were others. Julian had a lot of earth powers, but people respected that.

For some reason, it didn't occur to them to respect the Fairies that had more capabilities than the Conners. Or stronger earth powers. It was maddening to me, but I would imagine it was more so to the Fairies themselves.

Well, that wasn't true. I think they kind of enjoyed it. People STILL didn't suspect them of the things they did. The overall characterization of them was that they were flighty, uncaring, and fun loving. So, no one suspected them of being serious.

When in truth, they could be quite serious. Also, their versions of pranks were insane. You did NOT want an angry Fairy pranking you, but no one seemed to get that. I found that odd since Xander's mom, Princess Haley Holloran Cambridge Conners, had beyond proved that.

She was even nice with most her pranks because of Alpha Eric and his alliances. She still got people good, and they seemed to just think she was extreme. She was quite tame by Fairy standards to anyone who was allied with Alpha Eric. They just didn't seem to get that.

They clearly didn't know how she pranked Fairies. Which was totally NOT something I knew because I'd put a device I was working on a book Jared returned. It did NOT help me piggyback onto their system and hack some files. That's not a thing that I did. Nope. Not even kind of.

We were landing before I knew it and I huffed because I had to put my Fealish book away. I'd been taking notes on it. I stowed all my stuff, and we got off together. We were waiting for my teachers who came on other flights. The last one that showed up was the one I didn't like.

She plastered on a fake smile, "Hey little tiny dancer." I frowned, "Litle and tiny imply the same thing… so it's not necessary to say both and…" My mom cut me off, "That was rude, Melanie Janie. Say sorry." I sighed, "Sorry."

She was right. It was rude but I REALLY didn't like Miss. Janie Loperstom. That sounded like such a fake name, but I hadn't been able to prove it was. I mentally grumbled that if I knew Prince Gunner, he could prove it. Or his son, Micah. He could totally prove it too.

We loaded up in the SUV's my dad rented for us and took off for the hotel. My plan was going to come into play tomorrow night. My teachers and my mom were attending a parent's night out deal the competition was doing. I was going to be "asleep" when they left with Warriors on the door. I had everything to get that done.

My mom clapped, "Ok, we get to the hotel, check in, and we will get you ready for the afternoon competitions." I nodded because I knew that. I was more relaxed when all the teachers got their rooms. Miss Janie Loperstom was arguing with the front desk because her room wasn't near ours.

My mom chuckled, "I wonder why she's not by us." The Warrior who checked us in answered, "Beta Drake got you the penthouse. Alpha Eric owns this hotel, and he worked it out with him." I gasped, "He did?" My Xander's dad gave us the penthouse? He winked at me and nodded.

Janie Loperstom squealed, "That's great! We can all share!" I linked my mom, "Who tells her when she's rude? Because… that was totally rude. You always say I can't invite myself places." My mom's lips twitched trying to hide her smile.

My main teacher, Miss Becky Saveron, gasped, "Janie! You cannot invite yourself into their room!" Mis Janie argued, "They have a whole penthouse, and we were supposed to be on the same floor to work on the routines."

I snorted, "Huh? I know all the routines… because I choreographed them… I've practiced them for almost half a year… so… working on them doesn't make sense." The most senior Warrior with us, Tom, said, "Sadly, we cannot accommodate more in the penthouse. We will all be up there and there are additional guards coming."

Miss Janie squeaked, "WHAT?!" My eyes narrowed in suspicion because she sounded nervous. I wasn't the only one that noticed this time either. Tom said, "Alpha Eric has wolves that work security for the hotel, and they will be joining our detail for the competition at his insistence." I hid my grin behind my stuffed Xander wolf.

My mom said, "Well, that's very nice of Eric." Yeah, she was allowed to call him that. Miss Janie wasn't, and I bet that made her mad. Miss Becky dragged her to the opposite elevator. When I noticed no one was watching me I stuck my tongue out at her and made a 'I'm watching you gesture.'

She narrowed her eyes, but her glare stopped. She quickly looked away. I glanced over my shoulder and nearly groaned. Tank was watching the two of us. He had just graduated high school, but he'd always hung out with Jason and his friends. Jason was mature for his age.

Well, we all were… and Tank watched me a lot growing up once he moved to our pack. He was officially on my sometimes detail when he passed his next level Warrior class, that solidified he could go out as a guard once he graduated.

We were led to a different, private, elevator. Ok, this might make this all harder to get out. It was SUPER cool though. I just needed to tweak a plan or two… because I had studied the blueprints of this hotel. I knew who owned it and everything.

I squeaked when our key worked, and we were taken to the top floor. The elevator doors opened, and I gasped, "Oh my gosh! Do you guys see this?! LOOK AT THE CITY! Are those flowers? And chocolate? Ohhhh energy drinks!" My mom laughed, "Oh no! Tom, do NOT let her have one." I pouted and she led me into the bathroom.

She said, "This one can be yours. Get in the shower and I'll do the same." I nodded and she left. I waited to get undressed because I knew who was coming. Tank slid into my room and crossed his arms. I bit my lip, but he just kept standing there, waiting.

I blurted out, "I don't know why you do this… I mean I do… you want me to talk... and it works… because you know that I hate silence… which makes it kind of mean that you keep doing this… and I have TOLD everyone Miss Janie is bad."

"She's clearly bad… like she was obviously nervous when there were more guards mentioned… it's like she had some other plan. But when I say that… I'm crazy… or the bad guy… which is crazy because you saw that look she gave me… and her voice squeaked! Everyone says when my voice squeaks it says I'm nervous… or lying and…"

He cut me, "I'm watching her, don't worry." I grumbled, "If only you were with me all the time." He said, "Well, if I submit a report she needs to be watched, she will be." I grumbled, "Because people listen to you when I've said for years…"

He cut me off, "One day soon pup, everyone will be listening to you. I can feel it." I huffed, "I'm sorry you got pulled away from your mate…you guys just found each other and…" He laughed, "She's coming out here tomorrow so it's not a big deal."

I squealed, "Ziggy is coming?!" I ended up being right about them being cute together. I had a few more people I'd mentioned they'd be cute too and they acted like I was right since I was about Tank and Ziggy.

Tank admitted, "She has strict instructions from Adeline not to forget a single thing about you taking home that trophy." I grinned, "I hope to." He snorted, "You're going to. Now, get in the shower and avoid that teacher." I muttered, "I always do."

He caught my arm. I frowned, "Umm…you said to shower, and I was just…" He asked, "What do you mean you always do? The reports I read said she's your favorite instructor." I snorted, "Does my mom not read these reports? Or my dad? Because they know she's not. I literally hate her… mom says that's a strong word, but I do."

He frowned, "I need to call Lead Warrior Zane." I muttered, "Well, you should know that if Kenso overhears you… he'll be mad and…" Tank cut me off, "Why would he care?" I answered, "Because they are sex buddies." He groaned "Tell me Kenso did NOT teach you the words fuck buddies."

I blushed, "What?! I said sex buddies… you said the other one… not me… I didn't…" He shook his head, "That's what most people call it." Yeah, well if I cursed the mom monster cookies got me. Non mom monster cookie mom didn't really care.

I just didn't want to do anything to bring out mom monster when she had those cookies. Plus… I could say a lot of other things. So, it didn't really bother me. Tank waved me into the shower as if I had not been heading there in the first place.

I quickly jumped into the shower after throwing my hair up into a bun. It was easier to style when it was a little dirty. Mom would probably do my hair herself. She'd gotten really good at it with all the competitions, and I preferred that process done with just her and I.

She was waiting when I got out of my shower. She shook her head, "The Warriors are whispering and on the phone." I didn't want her to find out why, so I just shrugged. She laughed, "That tells me you did something. Come here." She pointed to a seat, and I hopped into it.

She winked, "Make up first, I think. We get to do bright red lipstick with this one." It wasn't my normal shade, but it was red. I winked, "Miss Becky came up with this costume." My mom grinned, "Do you want to know who she called to ask for it?" I asked, "Who?"

She grinned answering, "A shop owned by Haley." I screamed, "CONNERS?! DID SHE DEISGN IT?" My mom laughed, "She did because the shop didn't have anything like what they asked for." My Xander's mom designed my costume. I jumped up and grabbed my Xander wolf.

My mom quickly got into braiding my hair and pulled it all back. Then she did my dramatic dancing makeup. Once I had that done. She pulled out the garment bag with my first day costume in it. It was a bodysuit missing a large chunk in the side. It had clear beads that bled into red ones with fringe ride going to the other side. It did have two straps.

My mom chuckled, "Your daddy will hate the back." I replied, "He'll hate the whole thing. So will the Warriors." She winked, "I thought of that." She pulled out a sweatsuit that I definitely didn't need as a Werewolf, or in California. It had the dance academy's name on it though. I hugged her, "I love you, mom." She hugged me tightly, "I love you too, Melanie Jane."

I loved when it was us like this. No mom monster cookies and fun times. I felt like it showed me my real mom. I had her most of the time to be honest, but if any event was coming up those cookies seemed to multiply.

She helped me into my costume and made sure the jewels holding the back of my outfit on were secure. She handed me my sweatsuit and we walked out. My mom asked, "Are you boys trading secrets?" Tom answered, "Nope."

Kenso looked around at all the confused. That was smart of Tank to keep him out of it. Huh. A Warrior who actually listened to me. That was weird. I'd have to tell Adeline her brother in law was the best.

We went downstairs and were joined by more security. Fifteen additional Warriors seemed like overkill, even for Alpha Eric. I shot a look at Tank who avoided my eyes. I glanced at my mom, but she seemed confused too. She'd link my dad later if she wasn't already.

Our teachers were shuffled into a different car being driven by someone from the hotel. Kenso huffed, "I thought we'd get to drive with them. I drove them over here." Tom said, "Stop thinking with your dick. You aren't here to guard them." My mom cringed and my eyes widened.

Kenso jolted, "Of course, you're right. I'm sorry." He actually looked contrite, and I winced feeling bad for him. He was always nice to me, he just defended Miss Janie. I didn't mean to make anyone be mean to him. I bit my lip and chewed on it.

My mom linked me, "Whatever is going on with them is NOT your fault. Don't take that on, Ladybug." I asked, "What if it is?" She replied, "It's not. Tom was harsh, but it's true they are not here to guard your teachers. Ok?" I nodded and we drove straight to the underground garage at the convention center.

Alpha Eric's guards walked around the area before we got out and then I was ushered quickly inside. I linked my mom, "What's going on?" She admitted, "I don't know but everything is going to fine. Ok?" I nodded. I took off my sweatsuit.

Tom groaned, "Beta Female Sam, you have GOT to be kidding. My voicemail isn't cleared, and Beta Drake will fill it about that outfit." My mom replied, "When he calls, you answer and say that you're guarding OUR daughter, like WE asked you to. Add that her outfits are NOT up to you. Besides, she looks beautiful." She winked at me while I grinned. He grumbled, "Yes, she does."

She put on my music, and I began to practice my routine. Miss Janie snarked, "Clean up those lines." Mis Becky said, "It's not a classical routine. She's in the freestyle round first. She can't be robotic." I blocked them out and performed the routine I'd choreographed for Xander.

I'd invited him to this competition. It was a long shot he'd come, since he didn't come to the local ones I'd invited him to, but he did sign for it. He must always be in a hurry when he signed because it was the sloppiest squiggly line.

Adeline told me I should stop inviting him once she'd found out Tiffany agreed with her. They were worried about me wasting money, but to me it wasn't. He could show up one day, and his dad did do all this for me. Maybe he was coming.

When I finished my mom gasped, "Ladybug, that was beautiful!" She fanned her face, and two workers came over with paperwork for the teachers to fill out. Another grabbed my mom and whispered, "She's on in ten minutes." My mom waved to me and then walked with me and Miss Becky to the stage.

Miss Becky said, "You have this routine down pat. I'll be in the audience watching. You've got this." She hugged me then dashed off to film. My mom hugged me and kissed my hands like she always did. She said, "Gosh, you're growing up so fast." I teased, "I'm growing up at the same rate everyone else is."

She laughed, "Not with that big brain in there, you aren't. You are so wise and strong for your age. I'm so proud of you. Go out there and do what you love. You shine every single time that spotlight comes up on you. Your daddy and I love you so much, Melanie Jane."

I threw myself into her arms, "I love you too, mom." Tom cleared his throat, "I'll get you to your seat, Beta Female Sam." She asked, "Who is staying back here for Melanie?" Tank answered, "Me and the least talkative of Alpha Eric's group." My mom cackled, "You're doing an initiation on them?" He winked at her.

The men in question looked at each other in confusion. I explained, "It's because I talk… a lot… probably more than all of you combined could talk… so she means getting an initiation because you'll be back here after my first dance and in the room with me once I change… because I have another dance… ok… I have three more but…"

Tank cut in, "They get it, and your mom left laughing." Oh. The stagehand announced, "You're up, kid." He pushed me and Tank didn't appreciate that. One of Alpha Eric's guys grabbed me and glared. The man held up his hands, "Sorry, the teacher's notes say she has stage fright and needs a shove." Tank grabbed his clipboard nearly yelling, "What?!"

The other guy said, "Go out and there and dance. I've been hearing it's like magic and I'd like to see some." I frowned, "Uhh… then you totally knew you were on this detail for a while… and you've been at the venue… which makes this all a plan…. by Alpha Eric and…"

He winked, "That's a cute stuffed wolf the man named Tank is holding." I blushed but it was a tradition that my Xander wolf was waiting off stage, so the Warriors held him for me. He whispered, "Maybe other people think so too." My jaw dropped and I quickly took off for the middle of the stage.

I got into position and glanced down the row my mom was sitting at. She waved at me and blew a kiss. The seat next to her was empty though. I deflated a little because I'd hoped that Xander was the one who liked that Oden looked like him.

I shook that off because he was probably just busy. He was the Duke of two Kingdoms, and he was already the most feared and talented Alpha Enforcer the Werewolf community had ever known. The music started and the lights came on and I lost myself in the dance to honor Xander. They were all to Xander, if I was being honest, he inspired me. I'd picked *Crazy Stupid Love* for this dance.

When the song came to an end I slid across the stage on my knees. The auditorium exploded in applause. I saw my teacher going to get my score sheet with the comments. I grabbed some flowers thrown and did a quick bow.

I ran off stage and Tank handed me my Xander wolf. I hugged it tightly and they led me back to my dressing room. I quickly changed int my white two piece outfit. The top was bedazzled with white and varying shades of light pink flowers and jewels. The bottom where shorts with pearls on them and a partial tutu covering the back.

I changed the music to the classical solo I had. I opened the door to Tank and my security could come in. I began to review my dance. When I finished Tank whistled, "That may be the best classical routine I've seen you do." I blushed. He told the other guys, "That's not a low bar."

The one who had commented on my Xander wolf replied, "I believe you." Tank asked, "What inspired that dance, Ladybug?" I squeaked, "Huh? What? Why would you ask that? I mean it could... be like anything... or just like it came to me... it totally just came to me... In a dream... while I was sleeping... that's definitely a thing that happened."

They all started laughing. I asked, "What's so funny?" A stagehand knocked, "Hey, you're up in a few kid." I nodded, "Ok, thanks." My guards were still laughing. I yelled, "Hey! What's so funny?" Tank said, "Your ability to lie has gotten worse." I gasped, "That's not true!" Another guy said, "Your heartbeat was going a million miles a minute..."

I cut him off, "That's not even remotely possible." He winked, "Yet it happened, and your voice cracked and somehow also squeaked. Just say you're keeping what inspired you a secret. That way your voice doesn't crack." Ok, that was actually good advice.

Tank snorted, "She can't do it. Trust me." My jaw dropped. I could TOTALLY do that! He ushered me back to the stage, where the stand hand did NOT push me onto the stage. *Footprints in the Sand* began to play and I let myself get lost in the music. My classical dance felt like it went even better than my first.

I ran off and hugged my Xander wolf again. Tank announced, "We've got Jazz and hip-hop left, right?" I nodded and ran back to change into my Jazz outfit. This one was an actual bodysuit. It had gold and green sequins on the top half. My favorite part was the collar that wrapped around my neck and the bottom two layers of fringe.

I opened the door and Tank sighed in relief. I asked, "What?" He said, "I'm not going to get yelled at down the link by Jase for letting you outside in this outfit. Your brother did NOT care for your first two outfits." I giggled because it was so like my brother. My brothers and my dad were silly.

That routine passed without incident, and I ran back to get ready for my last routine. This one was a two piece. I had black leggings with cutouts all up the legs and a black crop top that was tied into red bows on my ribcage. I let my guards in so I could practice.

Tank bobbed his head back and forth. He said, "This one is fifty-fifty but I feel the first two outfits tip in the favor of them liking it." My mom entered the room and rolled her eyes, "I swear the overprotective males act like she's not been doing this since she was three." She took off my lipstick and put on my favorite shade.

She told me, "You're doing amazing, Ladybug." I admitted, "It's fun." She winked, "I know they picked black shoes, but I knew my pup would want these." She admitted, "I had Haley conjure these too." I threw open the lid to the box and gasped. They were sparkly red high tops with black laces and accents.

I squealed, "Mom, I love them." She winked, "Haley also used some charm, so they are worn in." I hugged her, "Thanks!" She hugged me tightly, "Knock 'em dead, Ladybug." She was escorted back to her seat, and I knew that dance was easily my best when I finished. I squeezed my Xander wolf extra tight and was ushered out of the building.

Once they got my mom in the car, we were off. She chuckled, "I feel like we are the most important people on the planet with this escort." I did too. We got back to the penthouse, and she helped me get all my make up off.

She asked, "Are you ready for bed?" I could tell she hoped I wasn't. I winked, "Not even a little." She jumped, "I'll get the chocolate out and order the burritos!" On my long competitions we always had mom and daughter nights. Burritos and chocolate may sound like a weird combination, but they were our tradition.

I skipped out into the main room once I'd showered quickly and put on comfy clothes. Tank was waiting with a box of sugar cookies. I squealed, "SUGAR COOKIES! THESE ARE MY FAVORITE!" He laughed, "Beta Drake researched the best places for sugar cookies out here weeks ago." Of course he did. I could hear my mom talking to my family and I ran into the living room with my cookies.

Everyone saw me and yelled, "THERE SHE IS!" My dad asked, "How's the best dancer in the world?" I blushed, "Dad! I mean… the world… gosh… that's a lot of people and…" He cut me off, "And you're the best." I held up the cookies, "Thanks." He winked, "I'll always make sure my little pup is taken care of."

Tristan yelled, "You were great!" Jason agreed, "Yeah, maybe mention to your teachers' costumes don't have holes." Grandma Esther slapped him on the back of the head. He yelped, "Ouch!" She snorted, "You looked beautiful, Melanie Jane." My dad and Grandpa said, "Yeah, and much older." I asked, "Is Uncle Duncan back yet?" My dad answered, "Not yet, Ladybug." I nodded and we talked for a bit before they logged off.

My mom handed me sparkling rose. I winked, "Ya know, I could shar with you and…" She snorted, "You drink your sparkling rose little lady." I made a face before admitted, "It is really good." She fixed my chipped nail polish.

She casually asked, "So, who's a hottie in your class?" I groaned, "MOM!" She chuckled, "All my friend's pups had crushes by now." I shrugged, "I don't like any of the guys in my class…. I mean as people, they are fine… I mean everyone thinks I'm super weird and…"

She cut me off, "Melanie Jane, you are not weird." I admitted, "I mean… I kind of am and…" She cupped my face, "No, you are NOT kind of weird. You are amazingly smart, talented, and gifted. Sometimes other people can't see that. Your dad worked really hard as a pup to figure out a balance." The thing was he had, and I couldn't seem to.

She kissed the top of my head saying, "If the stupid boys in your class can't see how amazing you are, then someone else will." I gasped, "You're not supposed to say stupid." She agreed, "Nope, but anyone who calls my pup weird IS stupid." We both giggled.

We ate our chocolate and watched a movie together snuggled up together under a blanket. I asked, "Mom, do you think I can help with the pack stuff…like everyone keeps me out of it and… well it's just that I'm really good at fighting."

She tucked my hair behind my ear and tapped my nose, "I think you can do anything you want. I've never seen you set your mind to something that you don't accomplish." I grinned at her. She added, "It's your time to be a pup, but I feel it in my bones, and Sugar agrees, that you're going to change the world."

The world might be dramatic. She continued, "All those inventions and ideas you have rolling around in that big brain will be the next biggest things to hit the market outside of the things your dad invented." I puffed up. My dad had invented a lot of things that humans and supernatural's used.

She hugged me, "We just want you to have your childhood and not grow up too fast. The bad people in this world will always come at us, and sadly that won't change when you're older. I wish it would because I don't want you, Jase, or T to have to deal with them. It's just not realistic. You guys will all make your mark on this world. It just doesn't need to be today." Well, I kind of already was.

We hung out for a few moments longer before I went to my room. I packed my bag and the one I was going to hand off. The Warriors wouldn't find this weird because I always gave younger pups little dancing kits. I started that before then it turned out to be an easy way to pass off information.

This folder was going to the portal Faerie had here. I had all the details, and it was going through several people before a dancer's brother was dropping it off. He was actually a supernatural courier, and his sister was going to add it to his route.

That meant Faerie would get the details. I went over my plan and carefully got into the cameras. I went over the blueprints and figured out the new facet to my plan. I only went to sleep once I had it all done.

The second round of competition was all day with more down time for me, which I did not care for. I did not like being bored. I read more of my Fairy books and kept making notes. I'd do my dances in between them. I passed out several of my dancer's kits to pups, and made sure two went to one who passes Tiffany the one with information.

When we got back to the hotel, I didn't have to feign being tired. My mom said, "I can stay back with you tonight." I shook my head, "No, you deserve to go have fun!" She hugged me, "You did so good today. One more day."

I whispered, "I miss home." She hugged me, "Oh, Ladybug." I always got homesick on longer competitions. I missed my home and how everything was there. My routine. I missed my family and my pack lands.

I watched her get ready and clapped when she was done. I told her, "You look amazing!" She laughed, "It's a Haley creation. I figure I should wear them since I get them." I agreed, "You should. Her creations are amazing." She spun around before she gave me a hug. She whispered, "If you need me to come back, just call or link me. Ok?" I nodded, "Ok."

I quickly went to my room after she left. I took a deep breath and got dressed in all black and put on a brown colored wig, making sure my mane of raven black hair was tucked in. I took off all my makeup and used it to make myself look different, complete with black lipstick. I put in a fake lip ring and pulled my plans back up.

I went through Prince Gunner's checklist that I'd made from all his papers. I had the loop of my heartbeat to play through the Bluetooth speakers that would play for several hours so if anyone came by, they'd hear that.

I had the pillows situated so it would like me, complete with black hair, in case they peeking in through the door. It obviously wouldn't hold up if they came inside but it was good for a peek. I had spare cash to use so nothing could be traced.

The big one was the loop on several security cameras. Prince Gunner had it down, so it was seamless, and I'd added a step. They could see a brown hair girl with a lip ring out but that wouldn't set off any alarms.

I'd looped the security feed for the hallway of the penthouse. I'd even sent a message to housekeeping to come up now. I had my spare hoodies under the one I had on, so I'd appear bulkier then thinner through my stops.

I began to debate my plan to call the Hackura directly. If I left the Werewolf Council a message that wouldn't be as direct in Prince Gunner's face. Yes, that's what I'd do. I started a timer on my watch and went out the adjoining door room and hit play on the heartbeat.

I used my no scent spray and prayed it worked. The testing phase wasn't exactly ready for field testing, but having a faint scent was better than nothing. I quietly went out the other room's door into the side room where the housekeeping laundry bin was in.

I got inside and put the dirty ones on top of me and waited. I heard housekeeping knock and come in. I took a deep breath once I was rolled into the working elevator then waited until I didn't hear anyone coming. I looped this feed and left before letting the real one come back. I kept my head down and swiped an employee card.

I went out the back and found the bike one of the local dancers left for me. I quickly took off and hid it behind a dumpster before getting a cab. I paid the cabbie in cash and jogged five miles back to where I was going to make the call. I kept the hood down but made sure my lip ring could be seen.

I dialed the anonymous line for the Werewolf Council. I used my voice modulator, "A bounty has been taken out on future Alpha Duke Alexander Conners. They plan to get him when he's alone at his brother's sports practice. Protect him." I slammed the phone down while my heart pounded.

I ran all the way back to where I'd stashed the bike taking a few different routes and shedding hoodies in various dark spots as I went. That's what Prince Gunner called spots where there was no surveillance. I grabbed the bike and made it the rest of the way to the hotel.

I swiped back in with the employee pass and went back to where housekeeping was. They were taking new towels, per the system request said came from my mom for this timeframe. I got into the cart of the assigned housekeeper and closed my eyes. She took me right back up and I slipped out soundlessly, then back into my room. I put everything away then jumped into bed. I took several deep breaths. I whispered, "I did it!"

Someone knocked. I called, "Come in." Tank came in and said, "Your heartbeat sounds very fast. Are you ok?" I nodded, "Uhh yeah… I'm totally fine… and it's just…" He snorted, "Ok, well someone wants to see you. He pushed the door open, and my jaw dropped.

I squealed, "ADELINE!" I jumped up and hugged her. She laughed, "I came with my sister to surprise you." I admitted, "I'm surprised." She squeezed me tightly, "I'll let you get back to sleep, but I'm here to root you on for tomorrow."

I hugged her again before getting back in bed. I muttered, "That was close." An unforeseen factor was something Prince Gunner's papers talked about preparing for, but I wasn't sure how I was supposed to prepare for that.

I woke up the next day and got ready with my mom. We made it to the facility in record time. My mom went to talk to some other moms, and I went into my dressing room. I heard a growl and whipped around.

Tank was holding some guy back. He yelled, "What the hell, man?" He snarled, "She shouldn't have that wolf!" I grabbed my Xander wolf and held it tightly. Alpha Eric's guy grabbed him, "You're an Alpha, get it together." His gaze was locked on me though.

I wasn't about to show him any fear. I could take him. Whoa… hello insane confidence. I was good… and sometimes I could beat Alpha Nick… but thinking I could take this guy was overconfident… but right. UGH!

I heard a growl I knew. I squealed, "DADDY!" The Alpha jolted and found himself staring down my dad, brothers, grandparents, Peter, Chelsea, Sharon, and Garrett. I happily jumped up and down, "You guys came." I went to run to them, but Tank held me back a second before I could pass by the Alpha mad about my Xander wolf.

My dad warned, "Get out of here and expect a HELL of a complaint from our pack. OR you can get your ass kicked here and now by me." Peter added, "And me." Garrett chimed in, "Me three." The Alpha held his hands up and walked away. I noted several people surrounded him and escorted him out.

I repeated, "Daddy! You came." I ran and jumped into his arms. He hugged me tightly, "Of course we came, Ladybug. Did you really think we wouldn't make it out?" He winked at me. He said, "I'll go find your mom, but these are for you." He handed me a big bouquet of flowers. I blushed, "Thanks."

I put them in my dressing room and tried to ignore that my security had doubled. This time, they were Warriors who had clearly been popped in from our pack. I flew through my dances, worked on my experiments' notebook, and read books on my down time.

My teachers never allowed anyone but my guards to come back and talk to me during the final competition. I won all of my routines, and my family cheered so loud I couldn't help but grin. We were heading back home once I changed, and honestly I was ready to be there. I'd helped Xander and won my competition. It was a solid weekend.

Promises Can Hurt

Alexander is Sixteen Years Old

Alexander was annoyed. I threw the *Thoroughbre*d series book down I was reading. I started it because I heard Elise say Melanie read it. I rubbed my face and pulled out the *Long Falls Dance Competition* hoodie.

It barely held her delicious, tantalizing strawberry scent now, and I was certain I imagined that it still had it. It mostly smelled like me but for a while our scents mixed on the material. Which made it the best smelling object to ever grace any realm. The day I'd found it was permanently in my mind.

Flashback

Alexander questioned why he was even here. Oden snorted, "No you don't. We hope to meet Melanie." He was right, I did. Plus, EJ met her. I knew he did. I stole his shirt when he came back from going to Red Run. I'd surmised he learned how a dance for Elise, but her scent captivated me from the brief hint of it on his clothes.

I'd been consuming strawberries because I hoped the scent would stay on the shirt, which was literally insane. Since they didn't have the exact same scent, it was just what I had. I got out of the car and barely held my shit together.

Oden howled, "MATE!" I reasoned, "You don't know that just because she smells good." He snorted, "Good? The air is permeated with strawberries. I could find her room so fast." I reasoned, "That would make us weird." He snorted, "No, it wouldn't since she's ours."

I groaned, "You are a new wolf, so you don't know that." He retorted, "I know how every older wolf, including Thor, described the smell of their mate over others. It's intense." He was right, but at the same time we weren't the only ones who liked Melanie. There had been problems her whole life with possessive men.

Oden growled, "Then get inside and you'll stop doubting me." I barely managed to walk inside instead of running. I could tell EJ was suspicious. Oden snorted, "Yeah, Brutus noticed us sniffing the air." Damn it! Be stealthy Alexander. Oden huffed, "We don't need to be stealthy about our mate."

We walked inside but Melanie's scent was faint here. Oden reasoned, "She might be at her house." Yeah, but the sinking feeling in my guts was saying something else. The McAlister's knew I was coming. What if they got her out of here?

Oden asked, "Why would they do that?" Because they know we could take them if we wanted her. He growled, "We would never do that." I sighed, "That was an internal thought, not a conversation. Also, just because WE know that doesn't mean THEY do." That upset us both because we loved Red Run and them thinking badly of us chaffed at me.

Drake said, "You boys look nice. Cassie, wow, you look beautiful." She really did. My sister, bless her, asked, "Where's Melanie? Elise said she'd be here today." Drake sighed and I knew it was coming. Oden whined in my head. He announced, "She's at a competition with her mom."

I couldn't stop myself, "What? I thought you said she didn't have one tonight, Jase?" He didn't miss the accusation in my look or tone. My dad's curiosity was spiking over my feelings. My mom had her walls down, but I could feel the guilt and the debate she was having right now.

She wanted to come to me because of what I was feeling. I sent her the feeling to stay put. She practically pursed her lips, but she was respecting what I wanted. I needed to collect myself.

Jason held his hands up saying, "She didn't, then one came up." One came up? Came up? Oden growled, "How dare they keep her from us!" I whispered, "What if she's not ours and we are just a possessive asshole like the rest?" He insisted, "We aren't! I know it." But people we loved and respected didn't.

EJ was studying me, but I didn't have the mental energy to spare him a second in my mind. Keeping the façade and secret about liking Melanie from him was exhausting and I was tired and hurt. I just wanted to end the constant adrenaline state that was thinking I'd meet Melanie that always ended in disappointment.

Meeting her was LITERALLY the reason I was here. I'd lost all interest in this dance. When Jason said, "You look beautiful, Cass. I'm a lucky guy." I smarmily agreed, "Yes, you are." Oden had a bit of bite, so I practically growled at him which drew several concerned looks.

Peter Kyle stared at me in surprise then looked like he was trying to solve a puzzle. Oden scoffed, "Thunder will have no luck with that if Pepper doesn't help and Pepper is confused." Drake did look perplexed, and Pepper was his wolf. That would mean he didn't know why I was mad though. Was Sam the one keeping Melanie away from me then? Why would she do that?

Jason looked taken aback, but he always did when I was snarly with him. So, was he clueless too? Or a good actor? He was supposed to be my friend. Why would he keep Melanie away from me? I know seeing your sister mated would be hard, I did. I was worried about Cassie's mate, but I was confident Aesir would make sure he was worthy of her.

I'd also seen him with his tongue down my sister's throat so what the hell was his problem?! Oden said, "Ajax is asking if we are mad at them. He's also going over everything they could've done. Nothing with mate is in the list." Ajax was Jason's wolf so maybe he really didn't know.

Oden was now dead set Melanie was our mate. He growled, "Because she is." I worried my crush had influenced him as a new wolf and I'd set him up for heartbreak. He insisted, "You didn't." Maybe I did. I was so utterly dejected right now I wanted to pop home. That wasn't fair to Charline though.

My dad linked, "Son, are you alright? Your mom is ready to wage war and come to you." I replied, "I'm physically fine." He snorted, "I know that's an evasion. If you need to leave, I'll call and lie about needing you home." It warmed my soul that he'd do it too. He'd take the heat for me backing out of the dance. I said, "I'll be fine. It's just a dance and I agreed to go with Charline." Like an idiot.

I told Charline, "You look lovely." She blushed but didn't reply. Ok? Maybe she was just nervous. Oden huffed, "Her wolf is already apologizing for what this evening will be. Her human thinks we will fall in love with them and make her ours." I wanted to cringe. Not that I wasn't used to that.

My last name came with people coming for us. No one was deterred by the fact that we knew if they were our mate, or not, the second we met them. It's why I tended to be a recluse in the dating world to a degree. The other part of it was because of Melanie.

Ever since I heard her name, I was intrigued. Being with someone else didn't appeal to me but right now it felt disingenuous. I felt like a total ass because Charline was into this date already and I was merely physically present. She didn't deserve that.

Oden snorted, "Her wolf said she kind of does." Well, I didn't agree. I should've known better and not come. She had false hopes. I steeled myself to be a good date. She deserved that and my parents raised me to be a good person.

Drake said, "Alright, let's load up. I'm your driver for the evening. Drop off and pick up." Maybe if I showed him what a good date I was, he'd let me meet Melanie. Oden scoffed, "He knows we are a good man." I wasn't so sure he did, but at this point I had no idea what was going on.

The excuse about a dance came up out of the blue was new. Melanie had competitions months, almost a year out, in advance. Yet they wanted me to believe this competition came up right around when I asked Charline to the dance.

Oden conceded, "That is suspicious." I knew that. Chelsea yelled, "Wait! Drake, you can't go yet. We have to take pictures." I groaned because I didn't need to commemorate the moment at all. Charline nudged me, "It will be ok. Plus, it will look cute in the future." The future of what? Oden said, "Obviously, we will look cute in the picture in the future. We are handsome."

I linked Phil, "Question." He snorted, "Are you going to explain your emotions? Or are we still pretending I don't know." I huffed, "Say what you want to say." He took a beat then said, "I'm sorry

Melanie isn't there. Why isn't she there?" I answered, "A dance competition came up." He shouted, "ARE YOU KIDDING ME?!"

I snorted, "Nope. It's bullshit. She has events on her calendar almost a year in advance. The ones that come up come up months in advance. I ask Charline to the dance and a random competition opens up." He replied, "That can't be it."

I asked, "Do you have a better reason?" He insisted, "It has to be a coincidence." I reasoned, "Well, Elise was telling EJ how excited Melanie was to be here and meet us. She wanted to see her in her dress." He groaned, "I don't know what their problem is. What was your question? Because I know it wasn't about that."

I questioned, "Why would someone say pictures will be cute in the future? She's attractive and I'm obviously handsome. They will be cute now." He snorted, "Charline is hoping to show your future pups." I reasoned, "She's not my mate."

He groaned, "I swear you all need a manual for life. Let me tell you from the depths of her soul, she doesn't care. She wants you to fall madly in love with her. I know you're not going to, but I'll say this directly. Don't have sex with her. She'd take it the wrong way."

Oden growled, "Not happening." I agreed, "I can't be with her. She's in Melanie's pack and it would hurt Melanie's feelings. I won't do that, and I don't want to." I literally had no desire to sleep with her. Oden snorted, "Yeah, you can't have sex with a flaccid dick." I yelled, "ODEN!" He cackled like he'd told the funniest joke. The fact remained I was not turned on.

Phil linked, "Hello?! I'd be worried but your feelings tell me you weren't considering it. Color me shocked." I huffed, "Your sarcasm is noted. Also, no there's no chance of that happening." He laughed, "Not aroused then, cousin?" I retorted, "Shut up!" He said, "I bet you'd be all kinds of excited thinking about a certain dancer." Damn it if my dick didn't jump.

I linked, "Please stop talking before my date gets the wrong idea." He chuckled, "I'm sure she'll say something that will deflate you. Grubby title chasers always do." I wasn't sure she was one. It was something about my last name that sometimes had people acting unlike their usual self.

We got done taking entirely too many pictures and were ushered outside. The second the door opened Oden took over yelling, "MATE!" I practically made sonic waves to the back of the car. I quickly conjured the most amazing smelling hoodie to my room at the house.

Phil asked, "Uhh you stole a hoodie. That's so normal. So, she's yours?" I replied, "Oden thinks so. She smells so good." He said, "I mean, she smells like strawberries." I asked, "Doesn't it smell intoxicating to you?"

He laughed, "I'm so glad the answer to that is no because you'd kick my ass. I put the hoodie in a baggie for you and then placed it under the bed." I replied, "Thanks."

Oden asked, "Will you listen to me now?" I said, "As soon as we meet her, it will be official. Phil's never been interested in Melanie. I'm not tracking down someone else who is and making them answer if it smells good to them. Do you want that?" He snarled, "NO! Our hoodie and OUR mate." I knew he'd feel that way, and honestly, I did too. I just needed to be certain. I needed all shadow of doubt removed.

The dance went by in a blur. Charline made several comments that grated, and Oden was totally done with this ordeal. He told me, "I dislike her a lot. Something's off about her, and I don't like how she's looking at us." I couldn't say that I blamed him really.

When EJ danced with Elise my suspicions raised. Oden whimpered, "He met mate, and we didn't." It was obvious he did, but that meant he'd say Melanie was real. Maybe my mom would demand to meet her and solve everything.

Oden snorted, "She would if we'd just tell her Melanie is ours." I asked, "Do you want to risk that and disappoint mom?" He whined and I knew he didn't. We just need to lay eyes on her then this would all make sense.

Charline had barely left my side. I'd danced a few times, but she made it awkward. She would grab my dick and yank it. Oden snarled and it had slipped out which is why we were not dancing now. He was angry enough that he might take over and yell at her.

He grumbled, "She deserves it!" Probably, but I didn't need Red Run to have a reason to keep Melanie from me." He admitted, "You have a point." We both usually did. We had a great balance together that came from being together my entire life.

Cassie was dancing but suddenly EJ took off. Elise had left a little bit ago. Oden linked, "Brutus is on alert." Which put me on alert and now I was conflicted. After a second, I decided to follow EJ out of the dance. Cassie linked me, "What's going on?" I answered, "I don't know, but I'll find out. Stick with Jase and don't leave his side."

I stayed back far enough, then realized EJ was too upset to smell me. I popped around the corner from the trophy case. My heart stopped when EJ told Robert to leave Melanie alone. He wasn't? Oden growled, "We kept an ear out for rumors about that! Everyone said it was done and over with." Clearly it wasn't if that's what EJ was saying.

Oden snarled, "How did this escape everyone in Red Run's attention? They claim everything they do is to protect her! She can't leave the borders because they want to protect her but she's getting bullied BY THAT MOTHERFUCKER?!" I wasn't about to talk him down because I was just upset as he was. I peeked around the corner and saw red. Elise's dress was ripped.

My parents were pinging with concern over my feelings. He'd ripped MY SISTER IN LAW'S DRESS?! THAT FUCKER! Oden growled, "You seem to have GLOSSED over the part where he said all black wolves weren't Alpha's! He told mate we weren't an Alpha!"

A rage I'd never known filled me at the thought of Robert bullying Melanie and laying one hand on her beautiful raven black hair I'd never seen. He was trying to take her stuffed wolf from her. I knew it looked like Oden.

My dad said Robert and his asshole friends didn't like that it didn't look like their wolf. Oden snarled, "BECAUSE IT IS WHITE AND BLACK! I AM WHITE AND BLACK AND I LIKE THAT HER STUFFED WOLF LOOKS LIKE ME!" His possessiveness was coloring mine.

Now, I had the attention of most of my Hackura family. Hastein, my oldest cousin, sent me the feeling to do what I needed to do. He'd fix it if need be. I sent him back my love and decided that Robert would be set straight before we left this building.

He would never touch Melanie again or go near her. Thankfully, EJ turned to leave expecting Robert to follow him. He was taking care of Elise, just like he should. Oden linked, "And we are going to take care of our mate like we should." I didn't know if she was ours since we hadn't actually seen her yet. I did know that I was going to make sure Robert steered clear of her.

She deserved to walk around her pack without being bullied. Especially since she was clearly hiding it was happening. I couldn't stand the thought of that. Of her suffering in silence. I could even imagine why she did. Oden snorted, "Yeah, no Beta needed for that. I don't even need to ask Phil myself."

My dad linked, "Son?" Oden snarled to me, "She doesn't tell them because they never believe her when she says she didn't cross. Our mate is SUFFERING because they are lying about her. She doesn't think they will believe her." Which pissed me off for her.

The thing was, I knew Peter would believe her. He'd use an Alpha Command on those she said bullied her. It was standard practice. Did she not know that? Oden scoffed, "Obviously not. She doesn't want them to call her a liar." I needed to find a way to get that information to her.

I couldn't stop my growl when Robert took a step to follow my brother. My dad linked, "Ok, seriously are you about to commit murder at a dance? I'm not saying don't, I'm just wondering why. I can be on cleanup; I just need a heads up here. Also, your mom is going to rage in a second based on your feelings." EJ and Elise had gotten far enough away they couldn't stop me.

I was pissed and grateful Robert took that damn long to follow my brother's order. I'd be more upset if it meant I didn't get to achieve my own goals. I popped in front of Robert enjoying how terrified he looked.

Oden took over and threw him into the trophy case. I told him, "I assure you Robert, I'm a fucking Alpha." Then punched him in the face. Cassie sent me her feelings that I was an Alpha and to kick his ass. Oden told me, "I assured Rain that we will." I spoke our space unheard chant. No one needed to hear what we were going to say.

My dad linked, “Alexander, I need a response of some kind.” I sent him my feelings that I was taking care of shit. He said, “Ok, I’ll take feelings in the bond. Oden could talk to Thor too, that’s also acceptable. Who are you debating whether or not to kill? And why?” I sent him the feeling that I was debating killing an idiot. He groaned.

Phil linked, “Uhhh are you going to kill a grubby title chaser? What did she do?” I snorted, “She grabbed my dick and squeezed it. I worried at one time she’d snap it off. She’s lucky neither EJ nor Cassie spotted it. I’m also not with her.” He hummed, “I’m confused. Explain more.”

I snarled, “Robert IS STILL BULLYING MELANIE! Find out why we don’t know that because the only reason I can ascertain is because she doesn’t think they will believe her.” He sighed, “I hate that you figured that out without me finding the right way to frame it.” Oden shouted, “I KNEW IT!”

I told Robert, “You’ll leave Melanie McAlister alone.” Robert snorted, “What are you going to do about it? It’s not the pack you’ll be an Alpha of.” I slammed him down on the ground hearing ribs crack. I pointed out, “It’s not yours either you little shit. You’ll go back and an Alpha Command will get used on you. Or my sister will make you tell the truth then they will know. You’ll have your every move around Melanie watched.” He paled more than I thought was normal.

Oden reasoned, “We are terrifying, and your eyes are half black and gold right now.” Because he was just as much in control right now as I was. He just wasn’t fully in charge. EJ linked, “Don’t kill him.” Seriously? The world would be better off if I killed him.

I could easily AND Hastein would have my back. Hastein clearly had a hold of our bond because he again sent me the emotion to do what I needed. Everyone else was sending caution. I noted there was a Fairy here recording me.

One day it would stop surprising my Uncle Aiden had people everywhere all the time. I shot the Fairy and annoyed looked, but he simply smiled back at me then flashed his Royal Guard seal. Fuck. He wasn’t going to leave.

Oden asked, “Who cares? GET THIS WHELP!” I asked, “What’s his wolf saying?” He answered, “He’s groggy. Like they are drunk.” I didn’t smell any alcohol on him. Maybe they’d taken drugs. I used my pushing power on him.

He must have been thinking about Melanie because I heard them talking. I also didn’t need anyone to tell me it was her voice; I knew it was. “GET RID OF THAT WOLF! YOU’RE NINE YEARS OLD YOU PATHETIC WIMP!”

Her voice sounded beautiful as she replied, “I’m a wimp who can kick your butt! It’s my stuffed wolf! Peter said I could keep it so you can’t take him!” Robert snorted, “You’re mine to toy with, mine to bully, mine to lie about.”

Melanie snorted, “I’m so beyond not yours… it’s just… no. I am someone else’s. You like Elise anyway… which like everyone knows. literally everyone. Why don’t you just say that out loud so EJ can just kill you, and you’ll leave me alone!”

Robert snarled, “Elise is different from you. I love her. You’re just my possession.” I let him go because my own possessiveness fired. Oden snarled, “MATE IS NOT HIS! ELISE IS OUR SISTER IN LAW! HE CAN’T TAKE ELISE! BRUTUS WOULD KILL HIM! HE’D RIP HIM TO PIECES! HE CANNOT HURT MY BROTHER!” I assured him, “He won’t take either of them.”

I snarled, “MELANIE IS NOT YOURS! DO YOU HEAR ME?!” Robert’s eyes widened. I continued, “Leave her alone!” Robert smirked, “You’ll never know if I do or not. You’ve never even met her. Which means she wouldn’t tell you. I don’t know how EJ knew, but I’ll make sure she’s quiet about it again.”

My dad linked, “Alexander Marcus Nathan Conners, you answer me right now about why you are so upset.” I replied, “Robert thinks Elise is his and she’s not!” It wasn’t a lie; it just wasn’t all of the truth which my dad called me on. He sighed, “I’m begging you to tell me all of it. I know there’s more.” I couldn’t.

My mom linked, “I don’t know what the FUCK is going on at this school dance, but I know you. I don’t give a mother fucking shit if you kill someone. You make your point no matter what that means. I will back you up and have your six. Do you hear me?” I replied, “I hear you.” She replied, “Good. Tell your dad what’s going on. If you need me, I’ll be there.” I grunted, “I knew you would be.”

I pushed at Robert again. This time I heard Melanie scream and hit the ground then I heard ripping. She screamed bloody murder, and I heard punches. She shouted, "NO! HE IS MY WOLF!" Then I heard feet pounding on the ground. She must have run away.

Robert yelled, "You'd better run! That wolf is going to be shredded next time. Don't you dare tell a soul about this!" I could hear her crying but heard her snarl fairly impressively. I was too angry to hold onto the memory, so I let him go.

I snarled, "DID YOU TOUCH HER?! What was that?!" Robert explained, "I didn't really touch her the way you mean! I'm not a pervert. I just ripped her shirt off while my friends held her down. It pissed me off and matched that stupid colored stuffed wolf. It was prominently featured on the shirt and I'd already ripped the first one off her. She didn't learn her lesson! What was I supposed to do?"

I ordered, "LEAVE HER THE FUCK ALONE! YOU REALIZE THAT WOLF LOOKS LIKE MY WOLF!" He blinked several times as if that had not occurred to him. Or that Oden would have the opposite reaction to his wolf being featured and ripped to shreds. Oden snarled, "OFF OUR MATE'S BODY TWICE! HE HURT HER!"

Oden took over and punched him. He snarled, "LEAVE HER ALONE!" Robert was still holding on to consciousness and looked like he was hiding something. So, I pushed at him again. I heard him and his friends planning, "She'll be dancing in an hour, and T has a big project he's working on. He won't be with her. We can split up, destroy the wolf, and watch her cry."

Oden slammed me forward and we lost the rest of the hold we had pushing at Robert. He was shaking now and a little blood trickled out of his nose that he quickly wiped away. I snarled, "Robert, let me make something clear. if you EVER make Melanie McAlister cry or destroy that wolf, I'll take you to the Hackura realm where no one will ever bring you back."

I practically vowed, "I'll torture you for a decade before I kill you, and I WILL kill you if you touch her again. Are we clear?" He stared at me like I was the crazy one here. Oden scoffed, "He's a perverted deviant and we should RIP HIS THROAT OUT!" My mom did say I could.

Uncle Bjourn's feelings told me was leaning towards I should do what I wanted and Hastein's feelings told me he practically on my six. I replied, "EJ said not to kill him." Oden grumbled, "I could explain this to Brutus, and he'd change the order."

He might but he was saying it because Peter was his father in law, and this was Peter's pack member. I didn't need them to be upset with us. More specifically, me. I needed the McAlister's to let Melanie near me to end this 'what if' game.

Oden grumbled, "It's not a what if game. Melanie IS ours. Her scent tells us that." I reasoned, "It won't be certain until we see her." He huffed, "You're going to be a stickler about this. I do know why, but I know you. I've been a part of you since you were born. You do not have a bad bone in you. We are not a possessive asshole."

I grabbed Robert by his shirt and snarled in his face. I warned "If you see her walking towards you then you walk away. If someone mentions her name you shut up and leave the general area saying NOTHING about her. Or you will be the target I use to practice the torture techniques my Uncle Bjourn has. I haven't even seen them all, but I bet in a decade I'd learn." Robert paled but said nothing.

I stared at him for several minutes. Eventually I asked, "What will it be? I'll open a portal right now. EJ only said I can't kill you. I doubt he'd feel the same way in a decade, and if he did I could just have my cousin H torture you until you died. I really don't care which option you choose. In fact, I prefer the one where you DARE to say you won't follow this order."

Robert frowned saying, "So you're possessive of her too." It cut at me that I was lumped in with them. My mom shouted, "WHO HURT YOUR FEELINGS?! THEY ARE FUCKING DEAD!" I loved that she felt that way.

My dad growled, "Who hurt you?" I said, "Sticks and stones, dad." He scoffed, "I note you did not reply that to your mom." No, but maybe I should. The rant about earthly sayings would be hilarious.

I told Robert, "Don't compare me to yourself. I'm nothing like you. I don't want someone who is already mated TO MY BROTHER!" I'd just ignored how we were alike in being possessive of Melanie, but I was protecting her. He was going out of his way to hurt her. There was a clear difference.

Oden snarled in our link, "She's ours and he can't have her. We are possessive, but she's OURS. So, you are right, there IS a difference. It's just more than what you are thinking. We ARE protecting her, but she's also ours." We'd find out the second we met her.

I told Robert, "Don't look at Elise either. She's my brother's. He may have the strength to hear sides and shit, but I do not. I'm going to be his Enforcer, and you know it. I do things he cannot do. I jump to action before the rest because I know a threat when I see one." He paled again.

I vowed, "If you touch Elise or Melanie ever again, you will understand the wrath of the Hackura. Are we clear?" Robert nodded saying, "Yes, I think we are." Damn. I was kind of hoping he'd say no. Oden said, "I wish he had a wolf. I didn't like his tone when he said, 'I think we do.' He seems too pensive about something." He did but Phil wasn't here to walk me through it.

I wanted to kill Robert more than I'd ever wanted to kill anyone. My dad linked me, "Are you just going to mostly ignore me all night?" I replied, "I'm just dealing with trash." My dad told me, "Your mom is worried." I answered, "I can feel her, and I've been linking her. Tell her not to be worried. EJ told me not to kill Robert, so I didn't."

My dad snorted, "I don't care about that nor does your mom. Kill him or don't, it doesn't matter. I know you won't because EJ said not to, but that doesn't mean I don't feel you think you should. You are so angry right now. I know you said this is partially about Elise, but will you please tell me all of it?"

He's right, I was very angry, and it was about how they treated Melanie. Melanie. Plus, Robert wanted Melanie, and he couldn't have her. She was mine. Oden sighed, "FINALLY! Go get our mate!" She wasn't in their pack, and I couldn't pop to her.

Oden reasoned, "She might be back from her competition." I argued, "The universe hates me at this point, so she definitely won't be back." Oden grumbled, "Point take BUT her hoodie is in our room." That was true.

EJ popped next to me. I guess it was time for people to hear us again. I knew one thing. I'd have an ear out, and if Robert went near Melanie again, he'd simply disappear from this realm. Forever. Hastein would help me and back up along with my mom. I'd take the three of us versus anyone else any day of the week.

Flashback Ends

Alexander shook his head. I had to mentally push that memory away because now I was furious. I popped to the gym and began to hit the bag. Liam asked, "Do you need a fight, Alexander?" I agreed, "Yeah, let's go." He nodded to some of our elite Warriors. He said, "I have an appointment I'm stepping out for, but if you're still going when I get back, I'll jump in."

I walked over and nodded to my cousin, Cory. He took his spot to work out with them. It was just understood I had the ability to lead this class because I had been able to since I was ten. Oden said, "Because we are elite." We really were. Even Uncle Bjourn said so.

I asked, "Have you warmed up?" They smelled like they had. Everyone nodded at me. I ordered, "Come at me." They looked at each other. I growled, "NOW!" Several of them rushed me and I took out two of their legs before slamming another to ground. I ducked, spinning around before taking down another. I took them all down then ordered, "Again."

We went at that for over an hour before Liam came back and stepped into the ring with me. After we fought my mom popped in and smiled at me. She conjured me a bamboo stick and we fought. I felt calmer when she called the fight.

She said, "Let's take a walk together." I agreed, "Alright." Oden pushed, "Tell her so we can meet mate." I replied, "My answer is the same and so is yours. We don't want to disappoint mom if we are wrong. I don't want her to be disappointed in me." It might kill me if she saw me as a possessive jerk because she was the most understanding and loving person on the planet.

We hiked to the top the mountain in silence. She asked, "What's wrong?" I admitted, "I was thinking about Robert, and it made me mad." She frowned, "I know that you know I know what you're doing."

Evading. She put her hand on mine saying, "I will burn down fucking realms for you. I hate feeling this hurt from you, and I want you to know I'm here."

I nodded, "I know you are." I didn't continue and I felt her put her blocks up. I turned, "Mom, what's wrong?" She asked, "Why would anything be wrong? Feelings are tough and I know when you're ready you'll talk to me." Oden whimpered because it probably hurt her feelings I wasn't confiding her. Maybe I should've told her when I was younger. It would be understandable then.

I asked, "Do you think anyone looks back on their life without regrets?" She answered, "No, I don't. It's unfuckingrealistic to think otherwise. You can be confident in a decision and believe it was right, but then things are revealed and you're not as confident anymore. No one is perfect, though I think some people are damn near it. It's not an attainable goal to be perfect."

She added, "We are Supernatural's, but we are also human. Everyone makes mistakes, that's life. No one makes perfect decisions twenty-four seven. We don't always have all the information available to even make the best plan. We do what we can at the end of the day. We try our best, but will there be something that haunts you? Yeah, there will."

She sighed, "I wish I could take that from you and your siblings but it's not possible. Even if you're making great decisions in your life, maybe those decisions affect someone else. Especially as an Alpha. There's a lot on your shoulders because of the names you carry."

"I fucking hate that, but I know you kids will do everything in your power to be good people. You'll stumble and maybe fall, but you bet your ass I'll be right there behind you to pick you the fuck back up." I grinned and bumped her, "I love you, mom."

She put her head on my shoulder, "I love you too, son." We sat there in silence watching the sun go down. I was practically itching to watch Melanie dance in her competition. I knew she'd already danced, but tomorrow was the finals.

I just wished I could be there for her. I'd almost bought a ticket and popped in, but not wanting people to think I was a creepy weirdo stopped me. Oden snorted, "And it was sold out." Yeah, that too. I'd decided not to buy a ticket but still waited in the queue when they went live.

They were all sold out when I got in there, which annoyed me even though I'd decided I wasn't going. My head was a confusing place to be. My dad found us and sat down without a word. I cleared my throat, "I'll be back. I'm going to the Hackura realm." They both nodded to me and sent their love in the bond.

I sent it back and popped out. I groaned, "What are you doing Alexander?" Oden snorted, "Despite you talking in third person, I approve of this plan. Do it!" I was in the technology building and let Oden come forward. Micah Percival, my cousin for all intents and purposes though it wasn't biological, was working here.

He was quite talented at hacking, and I knew he could do what I wanted. Plus, he'd keep it private. I found him hunkered over, rubbing his head in a room where the techs went to get a break. I knocked calling, "Hey, Micah." He looked up and his eyes widened. He nervously greeted, "Hey, Alexander. Are you here with your brothers?"

I grinned, wondering if he had a crush on one of my brothers. Max and he would make a striking pair. Oden chuckled, "Do not play matchmaker. It's not our forte." He was right. I'd leave that to Angela and Cassie. Even at two Angela was better than me at it. Then all of us except Cassie really.

I told him, "I was wondering if you could help me." He agreed, "Of course." I winced, "Hold that thought because I need you to keep what I'm asking secret and not ask me questions." He snorted, "Do you know what most of my job is?" I answered, "Yes, hacking." He laughed, "Yeah, but I keep a lot of secrets and rarely ask questions. It comes with who we are. What do you need?"

I conjured my computer and handed it to him. I explained, "I need you to put a backdoor on my computer to Jason McAlister's that he can't trace." He made a face and stared at me. He held my gaze and nodded, "Alright. Are we worried about Jason being a traitor?" I scoffed, "No."

He laughed, "Is this for a prank?" I answered, "Also no and I'm not going to do anything bad." I'm just going to use his link to watch Melanie dance. He shrugged, "Ok." He got to work, and I sat down feeling everything settle in my gut. I'd finally lay eyes on her.

Oden huffed, "Will you admit she's our then?" I snorted, "We have to see her IN PERSON, and you know it." He argued, "A lot of Hackura say when they see a LIVE video feed, they know." I shot back, "Two people is not a lot."

He groaned, "Come on!" I said, "Once we see her in person, it will all be settled." I closed my eyes and couldn't help but think of the biggest shot to our family regarding the McAlister's before the dance in Red Run, that felt like it set a new tone to our relationship. They hurt all my siblings' feelings, but it shot through to my heart in a way I couldn't explain.

Flashback

Alexander was curious. My dad had gathered all of us with mom. She was locked down in the bond and I hated that. I raised an eyebrow when my youngest siblings so far popped in. We need our three year old brothers here for this?

I picked up Grant and nuzzled his nose. He giggled, "Alexander!" Bryce and Bradley popped into my lap. I teased, "You guys are getting too big for this." Bradley gasped, "But not really, right? You jokin'." I grinned, "I'm pretty sure I'll always be bigger than you guys."

Bryce scoffed, "Never." My mom was pregnant with my little sister and brother. She rubbed her tummy, and I saw a calm come over her. I was certain my little brother was an empath and helped mom. I just wondered why she wasn't calm right now. In fact, I was certain she was hurt.

My dad cleared his throat, "Since we are all here, I do have something I need you guys to give me a promise about." My mom turned her head, but I saw the face she made and I could feel her better than my siblings. She did not agree with what we were about to do.

EJ asked, "What's going on?" He sighed, "I have had a discussion, that I don't agree with the outcome of. I just want to say that. I don't really understand where this is coming from, but I don't think it's about us." Everyone frowned and I felt my sibling's confusion.

He explained, "Obviously before your mom came into this pack, as Wolves, we didn't really rely heavily on magic." I snorted, "That's a way of saying how things worked in packs. Turning into a wolf is magic." My dad nodded saying, "No, you're right but we didn't use teleporting or charms to get things done." Ok?

He ran a hand through his hair and the bond told me he didn't want to have this conversation. He felt this was unjust and could hurt us. That put me on alert because I didn't want any of my siblings to have their feelings hurt. I sussed through my bond with my dad. I was shocked to find he was mostly worried about me and EJ.

It revolved around how we'd take this news more than my siblings. There was a tinge of it around Cassie too. My mom said, "Just tell them outright, Eric." She whispered, "They will take it better that way." It was already clear this dealt with our Fairy side. I wasn't aware packs were still being weird about that.

My dad nodded at her saying, "Your mom already made the promise to our allies." Her jaw locked and I felt how much she hated it before she locked down. I asked, "What the fuck is going on?" My dad answered, "I need you to promise not to pop to the McAlister's or into their home unless Drake declares it's an emergency."

My heart literally faltered in my chest. I could feel my heartbeat in my ears. My mom popped beside me. She urgently grabbed my hand, "Alexander." I couldn't pop to Melanie? Oden growled in anger. He'd been silent until now. We'd been trying to meet her for years to no avail.

Oden snarled, "We will just have to go the dance. Elise said that Warrior's daughter wants to go with us. Accept." I was actually thinking it was the only choice. Preston asked, "Why?" My dad explained, "He doesn't want his pups to rely on magic. They don't have any and he wants them prepared to act without it." That made sense and didn't.

Cassie said, "They have a Fairy family in their pack. Their Gamma's even." My dad nodded, "This went out to all the packs, and they don't want to discuss us." Too fucking bad. I asked, "Are you saying I can't ask Jase what the fuck their problem is?" My dad nodded and I could tell he felt it was bullshit.

I pointed out, "He is my friend." EJ said, "Elise is my mate, and I won't hide a damn thing from her." My dad replied, "I very much doubt she'll say anything about it to you, but if she does I am not going to police the conversations you have with your mate."

I scoffed, "Just us our friends." He winced. My mom said, "It's not his fault and I know you understand that, but you will not talk to your dad with that fucking tone. Do you hear me?" Guilt flared up in me. It wasn't his call, but I took it out on him. I nodded, "Yes, mom."

I set my brothers down and popped to him. I whispered, "I'm sorry, dad." He hugged me tightly. When I pulled back, he looked into my eyes worriedly. He said, "I don't give a shit who relies on magic or not. I would never ask this of you guys. I just can't tell someone how to raise their pups because I sure as shit won't listen to anyone else about how to raise mine. The McAlister's aren't in our pack."

Maverick said, "But they are in our sister in law's pack." It was an astute observation. My dad nodded, "And this promise doesn't involve Elise." But it did include Melanie. Julian glanced at me then asked, "And if someone in this family ends up mated to Melanie, should she exist, then what?" My mom scoffed, "She's a damn prank they won't let go of."

Julian pressed, "But if she IS real." My mom snorted, "If Melanie is mated into this family, I will personally hold Drake's feet over an actual fucking fire until he releases all of us from that promise. It won't happen because she's a damn prank. I'm very sorry they are putting this on you guys. They seem to think they can take the prank master title from me."

She scoffed again, "They are going on about this one and it's not even fucking funny. Eleven fucking years and they use insulting reasons as to why we haven't met her." I agreed because several of their reasons insulted our intelligence, but she was real. I knew she was.

Oden agreed, "She is real." I agreed, "I know buddy." He whispered, "But we can't pop to her and she's probably ours." I reasoned, "Mom will fix it." He said, "I know this hurts you a lot." It did. Theo said, "Well, I've never popped to them or their damn house. So, I promise not to pop to a McAlister or their house unless it's declared an emergency."

One by one my siblings all agreed and left the room. All were offended and hurt. Cassie begrudgingly agreed as did EJ. Both shot me glances before they left. My mom ground out, "Eric…" He cut her off, "They are our allies." She said, "Alexander, please give us a second." I stood and went outside the door.

When she was angry enough my mom forgot I could still hear her even if I left. She hissed, "Don't make him do this." Dad sighed, "I don't want to make any of them do this. It feels like bullshit. I don't understand where it came from. It feels like there's a threat I don't know about. The McAlister's asked for me to say they all promised."

She yelled, "SO FUCKING LIE! You have the ability to do so. Alexander doesn't want to do it. He can just give us his mother fucking word that we both believe in. He can't lie so if he says he won't go, he won't. As I said multiple fucking times not having us be able to pop to them unless ONE goddamn fucking person says so is a bad…." She trailed off then groaned.

She continued, "That's not a good enough word, catastrophic is." My dad agreed "Yes, but none of our Fairy relatives are making this promise. I have to go ask the Henderson's, but no one asked Aiden. He could go to them if they needed help."

My mom snorted, "Sure, because they can link YOU and you can link our sons. All that can be done without a FUCKING PHONE! They have to hope they can get ahold of us, because my brother is NOT answering their calls. Then get Drake TO AGREE before they can pop there. Do you know what that means? SOMEONE COULD FUCKING DIE!"

He whispered, "Come here." She must have popped closer to him. She cried, "He doesn't want to say it, and I may not understand the feelings behind the why of it; but it's important to him. So, I can't ask him to do it. We shouldn't be asking any of them to do this. It's wrong. Popping into their home, fine. Them personally? I just don't understand what the fuck is going on."

It had to be me. Maybe they suspected I'd be possessive of Melanie like the other guys. Oden growled, "That's not true." It had to be what they suspected though. I hated hearing my mom cry. My dad whispered, "I don't want to ask him to do it either." I could feel he truly hated asking all of us to do it.

Oden was quiet in my head letting me think through it all. Dad said, “I can’t let relations with us and Red Run go sour because of EJ and Elise.” My mom argued, “That’s exactly why it won’t go bad. Elise and EJ are mates.” He replied, “But if we balk then other allies could and that could affect their relationship with Red Run. I can’t have Elise in jeopardy.” Shit, that was a good point.

My mom repeated, “So fucking lie. You can.” I came in saying, “I won’t make him do that.” My dad stood, “Son, I’ll lie for you pups on any day ending in Y.” My mom snorted, “That’s all of them.” She blinked then said, “Oh, well I agree with that sentiment. Fucking A.” She smiled at me, “You young people say that, right?” I bit my lip.

I nodded, “I have heard that around my school.” My dad asked, “Where did you hear that, Angel?” She replied, “He just said the teenagers say it at that human school they go to now for high school.” That was evasive but mom had some sources in the pack. It stood to reason one was a teenage pack member.

I whispered, “I promise not to pop to the McAlister house or…” I trailed off. My mom jumped in, “That’s good enough and I will fucking fight anyone that says otherwise.” I grimaced, “Or the McAlister’s themselves.” I popped out right after.

I felt my dad yank at me to come back. My mom was more understanding, leaving me to my feelings. I stalked into the Hackura gym. Cayden glanced over but didn’t really take me in. He greeted, “Hey, Alexander. Is Cassie with you?” He looked over when I didn’t answer. He blinked, “Holy blazing eyes.”

Aaron whistled then said, “Ok, Cayden get out on your mission. I’ve got Alexander until the Royal family portals in.” Uncle Bjourn said, “I’m already here.” He hugged Cayden and turned to me. He ordered, “Walk with me.”

I argued, “I came here for a fight.” He agreed, “You did but I have a partial Fairy sister. From what I understand that’s the side of you hurt right now. Which means we have other priorities before we get in that ring.” I glared at the ring but nodded.

He portaled us to a bar. I asked, “What’s this?” He answered, “Cali and your mom’s new business venture.” I conjured us whiskey and slammed mine. He followed my lead, and we kept drinking. He easily matched me. I asked, “Why are we doing this?” He simply shot back, “You tell me.”

I whispered, “I promised not to pop to her.” He blinked several times then sat back. He said, “Since you are not talking about a mated woman, this is about Melanie McAlister.” He tapped his chin, “Your wolf has a different reaction to her wolf looking like yours I take it.”

I conjured another glass of whiskey then confessed, “Yes, but it’s more than that.” He inclined his head and waited. I slammed another drink before saying, “You can’t tell anyone.” He raised an eyebrow telling me, “All of you know you can tell me anything and I won’t share that if you don’t want it shared. I am not only your Uncle, but your King. As long as you aren’t in danger, it’s between us.”

I admitted, “Since the day she was born, the world changed for me.” He asked, “In what way?” I shrugged, “I don’t know. No one else felt it besides dad and Grandpa Nathan. It felt different to them than me. They felt something change, but to me it was the whole world. Then Jase called and told me his sister was born the very second I felt everything change.”

He whispered, “Alexander, why have you not said anything?” I snorted, “Because I assumed, like an idiot, I’d meet her.” He put a hand on my shoulder, “Hey, you’re not an idiot.” I snorted, “Aren’t I? What if they are scared of me meeting her?” He questioned, “Why would that scare them?” I snorted, “Think about how many people are possessive of her.”

He practically growled, “And? I’m not getting it here.” Maximus, my cousin, faded in, “He’s saying he thinks they are scared he’d run off with Melanie and be possessive of her. How can you say that about yourself, cousin? Anyone would be lucky to have you as their mate and in their family. They should parade her in front of you to see if the weirdness around her stops. She’s clearly yours.”

My Uncle studied me then asked, “Is he right?” Maximus snorted, “You know I am.” I muttered, “What he knows is you’re the stealthiest of my cousins to exist because you have Uncle Logan’s talent for it with your Demon side.” Maximus rolled his eyes saying, “I won’t say anything, cousin.”

I sat up and pushed all my feelings at him. I emphatically stated, “I knew you wouldn’t. You heard me say I didn’t want it discussed.” Uncle Bjourn said, “Maximus is right. Anyone would be lucky to have you in their family." Maximus added, "Plus, I can set people on fire if they try to keep you to that promise once you declare her yours."

Uncle Bjourn snorted, "Maximus." Maximus innocently asked, "What? I can. It's a skill that I possess and I'm quite good at it." He did the impossible and made me laugh. Uncle Bjourn said, "You'll meet Melanie and Maximus will not be alone in making them back off that promise for you, your mom, and your siblings."

I snorted, "Mom was talking about literally holding his feet to the fire." Maximus clapped, "Ah ha! You see where my fire throwing abilities will come into play. I can scare them by throwing it NEAR them, then make Aunt Haley her fire to hold his feet over. The plan is cemented in my mind for possible use if necessary. Levi seems to believe the McAlister's are reasonable people though, so it may be for nothing."

He tapped his temple, "The plan does have merit for certain situations though." Uncle Bjourn pointed at him saying, "Do NOT have your Aunt hold people's feet over a fire." I snorted, "That was way too vague." Maximus grinned replying, "It really was. Bye!" He shimmered out.

Uncle Bjourn snorted, "You all live to give me a headache. Do we need to get in the ring?" I answered, "No, I need to go home and see my dad. He's upset." He put a hand on my shoulder advising, "Tell them what's going on." I snorted, "I can't." He argued, "You can."

I shook my head, "It's bad enough you'll know. If she's not mine, I'm just another possessive jerk." He stared at me in disbelief. He blinked before saying, "I can understand why you think that, but not one person in this family, especially your parents have given you the idea that was true."

I changed the subject, "Have you ever had the cookies from Red Run? Sam gets them delivered. Jase gives them to me too." He snorted, "I don't give a fuck about cookies. I care about you." I told him, "I'm sure Levi has had them. Mom doesn't care for them since they have peanut butter in them. They were the only things that made me feel better when Red Run showed up without Melanie and Sam when she was first born."

My Uncle looked at me worried, "What does that have to do with this conversation?" I admitted, "I could use a cookie right now. They are always a pick me up when I'm down." He rubbed his temples. He said, "I'll get you a cookie then." I teased, "It wouldn't be the right cookie."

He blew out a breath then said, "Go home and talk to your dad. Also, yes. I've had the damn cookie you're talking about and they do make me feel better too." I asked, "Did my dad link you?" He answered, "More than once." I hugged him, "Thanks for letting me get this out." He replied, "I'll always be here for you, and you know that." He kissed my cheek then I popped home.

My dad was waiting in my room. He handed me whiskey saying, "I'm guessing you've had a few based on the scent." Oden chuckled, "He knew before he scented us." I told him, "I'm sorry I snapped at you." He shrugged, "It's ok."

I argued, "It's not. You didn't want to ask us, and I could feel that. I understand why you did. I didn't think about Red Run's relationships with other packs and how that could affect Elise. I don't want that to happen."

He said, "Bjourn said you mentioned cookies. It just so happens Elise had them at their house and EJ swiped them. I got us two." I took it and said, "There's just a lot of feelings with everything going on. Uncle Bjourn said…" I trailed off and took a bite.

I questioned internally, "What the hell am I doing? I was about to shame myself in front of my dad. I was about to tell him I'm a possessive ass." Oden snarled back, "We are NOT a possessive ass, but maybe now isn't the moment to tell him."

My dad urged, "Uncle Bjourn said what?" I answered, "That he's always here for me." He'd said that many times over the years. My dad agreed, "He and all your uncles are. You know that." I agreed, "I do." He hugged me, "I love you and you can tell me anything."

I nearly told him again, but the doubt creeped in. Could I handle seeing disappointment in his eyes? The answer was emphatically no. I never wanted my dad to think I was a bad person. I replied, "I know I can, dad. I love you." He hugged me again then left before my mom popped in and crossed her arms.

We had a stare off and she wrinkled her nose, "Those cookies again? I swear they popped up nine years ago and they refuckingfuse to leave." I replied, "They are pretty good." She disagreed, "They look dry and crumbly. Also, they stink."

I laughed, "You just don't like peanut butter." She grumbled, "I don't like dry ass cookies either. They taste like ash in your mouth." I shrugged, "I didn't like my first bite, but it grew on me." She snorted, "You do not have cookies growing on you."

I hugged her saying, "Never change, mom." I felt her confusion, but she agreed, "I won't." She paused then added, "I'm here if you want to talk." I whispered, "I know." She kissed me and left me alone to my spiraling thoughts.

Flashback Ends

Micah cleared his throat and handed my computer over. He came around to my side and explained how it all worked. He said, "That back door goes into his computer. He won't detect you there." I asked, "And if I wanted to take a screenshot or put a file onto my own computer?" He snorted, "Just pull it onto your desktop, like this." He showed me.

I stood, "Thanks, man." I walked out then turned, "Have you met all my siblings? We are basically family." He blushed, "Uhh no not all of them." I said, "I can get them here if you tell me which ones." He waved, "No, no, no, you're busy. Everyone's busy and my break is up. Thanks, I needed the distraction."

I yelled, "You realize I know that you don't have designated breaks times." He called, "Later, Alexander." I rolled my eyes. Oden said, "He's definitely into Magnus." Magnus was Max's wolf. I said, "Well, Max's middle name is Harper and that's an amusing tie in to Micah." He chuckled in agreement.

Uncle Gunner was Max's dad, so he wasn't actually related to us since Uncle Gunner was related to us by his marriage with Uncle Harper and Aunt Calista.

Oden urged, "Let's get back so we can set everything up." I agreed and opened a portal. I used a charm so no one could just come into my room. I conjured a forty-nine inch computer monitor and the cables to plug my computer into it.

I pulled up the link through Jason's computer and displayed it. I growled the second she appeared on stage. Her outfit was stunning, and possessiveness flared through me. Oden snarled, "OURS!" The need to go to her was so high, but that promise I'd made kept me in my seat. Oden grumbled, "Stupid fucking promise." It really was. I was so mesmerized by her dancing everything else faded away.

When she finished, I found myself clapping in my room on my feet. She was an amazing dancer, and I knew one day she'd be all mine. Oden grumbled, "Please hold onto that feeling." It was true I waffled and grappled with self-doubt, but I touched the screen when she ran off. I whispered, "I'll meet you one day, Melanie McAlister." I meant it with my whole being.

Data Sets and Percentages

Melanie is Thirteen Years Old

Melanie jumped out of the car. My mom laughed, "You could wait for us to stop." I would've teased her back, but she'd eaten the mom monster cookies out of a baggie in the car. She'd probably get mad and ground me, so I gave no reaction but a meek smile.

Tristan linked me, "What the heck was that?" I answered, "What? I didn't say anything… no words… which is…" He cut me off, "Weird." I huffed, "She ate the cookies on the way home." He winced. My dad shot looks between us.

Chelsea cleared her throat, "Someone wants to talk to you, Ladybug." I asked, "Who?" Elise answered, "Me." Chelsea held up her phone and Elise was on FaceTime. I squealed, "ELISE!" She told me, "I'm engaged!" I was confused. I said, "Umm well of course you are because… like…. you're marked and…" She laughed, "I'm so glad it's logical to you that I'm now engaged. I want you to be a bridesmaid."

I screamed, "YES!" Several people laughed. My mom chimed in, "She doesn't have time." My jaw dropped and tears filled my eyes. My dad winced, "Sam." Mom groaned, "I hate having to be the bad guy, but she has several dance practices, a paper due, and a math competition to prep for."

I quickly said, "I did the paper… like… weeks ago… and I'm ready for the competition… I always am and…" She cut me off, "You haven't done all the prep." But I had. I knew that Elise would be having her mating ceremony, and I wanted to make sure everything was done so I could go. I had no idea she'd ask me to be in the wedding.

Sam added, "Plus, I really don't want her traveling that much during the school week for all the events Elise will have for the mating ceremony." Elise said, "She doesn't have to come to them all." Mom argued, "That's not fair to you to have someone that can't do all that with you." Elise replied, "I'm fine with it though. She's basically my little sister."

Mom sighed, "I'm sorry, but the answer is no." I dropped my head and subtly wiped my tears. Tristan squeezed my shoulder. Jason said, "Hey, you won your competition." I nodded, "Yup." Elise angrily said, "Well, she's coming to my mating ceremony. Correct?" My parents answered, "Of course."

Elise didn't let it go. She demanded, "Swear it to me." Peter rubbed his face. My dad said, "I promise she'll be there." Elise prodded, "Sam?" Mom winced saying, "I promise she'll be there. One day if you have a little girl, you'll understand being the parent with the hard line sucks, but these men are all saps for their little girls." That was true, but right now this was about the cookies. I knew it was.

I whispered, "Thanks for asking me, Elise." She said, "You are my little sister. I'll send everything we are doing. You're invited to all of it." My mom groaned. Elise ignored her, "Anything you can come to would be great. I love you, Ladybug." I replied, "I love you too." Chelsea walked away with the phone shooting my mom a confused look. It was going to set her off.

The cookies ALWAYS did this. She'd get defensive, more so than she would without them. I kept waiting for Ryan Bishop to come in with answers, but he hadn't yet. He hadn't even answered me so far. I felt bad for mom because it wasn't really her fault. It was the cookies… which sounded insane, but I knew it was true.

I tagged Jason and yelled, "You're it!" I took off running and everyone laughed. Jason shouted, "That's not fair! You are FREAKY fast!" Dalton and Dakota ran off their deck and shifted. Dalton linked, "Hop on Caulder's back." I jumped on and he took off running. I giggled as he ran around and looked back.

Our parents were laughing now instead of staring awkwardly at each other. Tristan linked, "You know, it's ok to let everyone call mom on that bullshit excuse." I replied, "She'd just get mad." He asked,

"And?" He didn't get it even though I'd explained it all a million times to them. Everyone thought I was wrong, but I wasn't.

Apollo ran up next to Caulder. He whined and I knew he wanted me to ride on his back. I giggled and jumped over. Cooper ran and jumped on Caulder. Jet, Dakota's wolf, whined because no one was riding him. Ajax, Jason's wolf, huffed in annoyance. I teased, "But you're it, Ajax." He howled and began to try and tag everyone.

Eventually our parents joined. I jumped on Pepper, my dad's wolf's, back and squealed. I even switched to my mom before Jason linked, "No more riding wolves!" I asked, "Really? Because… ummm you can't catch me… so this way makes it better and…" Several of the wolves laughed because I'd linked everyone playing our game.

Jason retorted, "I can catch you." I frowned saying, "Uhh no you can't… like… that's literally never happened… I'm faster and…" He growled playfully. I shrugged, "Ok… but I feel like this will make you mad… so…" I jumped off Sugar's back and started to run.

I had juked Ajax several times making most of the pack chuckle. Eventually my dad linked, "Alright, you two that's enough. Melanie, you're it. Give everyone a twenty seconds head start." I grinned at Ajax who ran up and nuzzled me before he took off.

I counted slowly in my head before I took off running for them. Tristan linked, "Maybe get me first since Ajax will pout if you get him first." I corrected, "Jase will pout. Ajax wouldn't care." Apollo barked out a laugh that let me know I was right.

I went after him and got him first, then Dalton, Cooper, and Dakota. I got Peter, Chelsea, mom, and dad before I got Ajax. Jason shifted back and grabbed shorts. He yelled, "She got all of us in under three minutes. Where did her flash genes come from AND WHERE ARE MINE?!" Everyone started laughing.

Tristan gave me a noogie and we went home. My dad hugged me, "I'm so proud of you, Melanie Jane. Congratulations on winning the competition. Not that there was doubt in my mind." I agreed, "There shouldn't be. Statistically speaking, I've never lost. The odds were high I was winning, plus Tiffany didn't compete and…"

He cut me off, "Statistics don't come into play. You're my pup and I'll never bet against you." I pursued my lip, "But statistics…" My mom picked me up and swung me around and turned on the speakers with a remote. We all began dancing in the living room. Jason and Tristan moved everything out of the way.

I teased, "You'll have to find the exact spots those came from because of the…" I trailed off realizing I'd been about to bring up the cookies. My dad swooped in saying, "Sometimes, Ladybug, you have to make the world your dance floor."

He tapped my nose, "Especially you. You'll change the world, and we all know it." I blushed and he spun me before we all started dancing again. I quickly made up a dance they could copy as we made the living room our dance floor.

When we went upstairs Jason nudged me. I asked, "What?" He said, "You really can make the whole world your dance floor." I said, "I mean… not really, because…" He cut me off, "Yes, really. You're going to do big things in this world."

I pointed out, "It's not like anyone lets me help with anything now. I have all these ideas and…" He interrupted, "We want you to be a pup, but the day is coming when you'll shake up the Supernatural world. I want you to know on that day I'll be cheering you on." I smiled at him replying, "I know." They thought I was brilliant, and it was true. On paper, and the ideas I had said I was brilliant.

I went into my room and worked on the formula for the contacts I wanted to give the Hackura to protect Xander. I had it so it would stop them from turning gold done, but I wanted to give them colored eye color options.

I was frustrated because I couldn't get the blue right, which was important. Xander had blue eyes, and the contacts turned green when the gold entered into the equation, which was no good. Even humans would notice someone's eye color changing like that.

I fell asleep with my face on my notebook. I heard a throat clear and jumped up. Dakota grinned at me. Tristan asked, "What's that?" I held my notebook to me, "Uhh what? This? Nothing?" Dalton snorted,

“Ladybug, your voice jumped six octaves, and you asked a question.” I explained, “Just some stuff I’m working on for… reasons…” Jason snorted, “Well, we thought we’d go for a hike.”

I thought about it then nodded, “You’re trying to distract me because Elise is having a mating ceremony function today and I don’t get to go.” Cooper laughed from the hallway. He shouted, “I told you guys she’d know!”

Tristan snorted, “You guys get everything packed up for our picnic and we’ll join.” The Kyle’s all left. Tristan sat down on my bed and so did Jason. Tristan apologized, “I’m sorry you can’t go.” I shrugged, “I never thought I’d be going. I really do have everything done because I didn’t want it to be a reason I can’t go to Elise’s mating ceremony. I’m literally going to glue myself to dad and mom’s side the day of so no one can lie… which might sound dramatic but I’m doing it.”

Jason said, “It’s certainly one way to stay out of trouble.” I told them, “I love that you’re doing this to distract me though. It’s really nice.” Tristan kissed the top of my head, “We love spending time with you, Mel. So do the Kyle’s.” Jason jumped in, “Because we love you.”

I asked, “Are MaryBeth and Melinda coming?” Jason answered, “Dane’s going so MaryBeth is, but Melinda has homework to finish.” I waited but he didn’t continue. I added, “Plus, she doesn’t really like going on hikes.” Jason frowned, “Of course she does.” I snorted, “No, she doesn’t… it’s super obvious… because… well… it is.” They both looked at each other.

I reminded them, “She got a tick the last time and it really freaked her out… she hasn’t gone hiking in five years… since… the whole tick thing… so it’s obviously about that… when you think about it.” They stared at me and Jason ruffled my hair.

He commented, “You just notice things.” I said, “I’m working on a Supernatural bug repellant… because she used the human one… and we get ticks and bug bites…. I’ve worked with another scientist on a study about how our blood is sweeter… which makes sense…”

Tristan interrupted asking, “What scientist?” I continued, “Under an alias… because…. Obviously, I didn’t use my name… but Earth Fairies don’t get bitten…. we’ve been trying to ask other Fairies… I have lines out to the ones who still live in Ireland…. even though they go back and forth… they really won’t answer though and…”

Jason cut me off, “Whoa, you’re like running a whole study with people we don’t know. That’s crazy, Ladybug. You can’t do that.” I asked, “Why? I’ve done it… a lot… like… for years…” Tristan yelled, “YEARS?!” He was mad?

Dalton came back in and looked around. He asked, “What’s going on?” Jason answered, “Ladybug is talking to randoms online.” I said, “I mean… scientists… that like… I researched and have boards with… some college students… that might also think I am one… but we have research projects going… so…”

Tristan gaped at me. Dalton asked, “Are you serious?” I frowned. He waved his hands groaning, “Never mind, I already know you are.” Jason asked, “How the hell did you get an alias?” I answered, “Uhhh I made a bunch of social media pages for someone to look at with student profiles…” Jason asked, “Don’t you have to get into college to have one?”

I replied, “Technically…. maybe…” Tristan groaned, “Stop asking questions about how she did it. Just stop talking, Ladybug.” I asked, “Why?” Dalton said, “Because you don’t know who is out there on the internet.” I replied, “I didn’t work with anyone I didn’t research… and I’m better at it than they are… I looked up credentials… ok my alias has put out a lot of papers at this point…”

Jason groaned, “Please stop talking.” I pointed out, “That’s not really a forte of mine… which you know.” Dalton agreed, “Let’s just go hike and talk about other things.” I asked, “Like what?” He replied, “Anything.” I pointed out, “That’s kind of a broad topic.”

Dalton said, “We can talk about that fancy school they are saying you are going to in New York.” I replied, “It’s not fancy. It’s a performing arts school. Fancy would be a boarding school in Europe which I’m certain if mom had a cookie, she’d send me off to as well.”

Tristan argued, “No, she wouldn’t.” Cooper shot me a look that said I wasn’t exactly wrong, which I knew. The mom monster cookies had special abilities that everyone discounted, but I didn’t. I still knew there was something wrong with them and they’d refused to acknowledge that throughout the years.

I got lost in my thoughts while we walked. None of the Covens I'd sent them to ever got back to me. That was weird enough, because protocol said they should reply. Ryan Bishop should've replied because of protocol and his wife being my mom's friend. Not that I'd ever gotten to meet her, but it was true.

Something was going on with those cookies and the coven's not answering me about them proved it. Maybe one or two got lost in the mail, but fifteen letter requests to look into them didn't. That was just math and logic.

Dakota asked, "What are you thinking about so hard?" I answered, "Huh? What? Me? Do you mean MaryBeth?" Marybeth snorted, "He does not mean me. I was kissing Dane." Jason said, "Which I was ignoring so thanks for pointing it out." She winked, "You're welcome, nephew."

I asked, "Is Uncle Duncan coming for Elise's mating ceremony?" Tristan answered, "We don't know. He's invited, but he's on a mission with his mate." I reasoned, "We could link him." Jason replied, "You know some packs ask families not to link their family members on missions once they join a new pack. Uncle Duncan's is one of those packs."

I muttered, "Which is a dumb rule." Dakota chuckled, "Ladybug, you're being more bug than lady today." Dalton teased, "You have NO idea brother." I followed them to the path and grumbled, "No, I'm not. I'm being right. Which I am….a lot."

"It's silly to ask us not to link him. It makes me wonder why we can't. Because he's not obligated to reply to a link so he'd just have us in his head which would soothe his wolf in any situation. It feels shady… and it's not a protocol either. It's just that pack's rule. I checked."

Jason stopped and turned around. He said, "Whoa, hold up. You checked what?" I answered, "The Werewolf Supernatural clauses for packs… and the Supernatural Council's. There is no rule that dictates that. Some packs have adopted it, but most are considered shady by the Werewolf Council." Tristan groaned, "You can't call Uncle Duncan's pack shady."

I said, "I mean… technically the Werewolf Council did….and I just repeated it. Which doesn't really feel the same. Plus, it's not like they consider the Nashville packs. Or even some in Louisiana. They are just in the murky area, not fully bad… but..."

Jason groaned, "No but's." I pursed my lips. MaryBeth nudged me, "Tell me about the shady, murky areas. I'm all ears." Tristan huffed, "No, you're not." MaryBeth retorted, "I will protect my brother how I like. Tell me all the statistics Ladybug."

I shrugged, "I don't have enough data sets for statistics yet, but I can say that over one hundred transfers got cut off from their families. All because they started out doing missions when they joined and abided the rules about no linking while on them."

Tristan stopped walking and so did Dalton and Dakota. I added, "Uncle Duncan's missions on average are two point five weeks longer than everyone else's. For the transfers his are three point six days longer. I could give you the hours if you'd like." MaryBeth shouted, "WHAT?!" Dane wrapped his arms around her.

I replied, "He said he's better trained than others." Jason groaned, "You told him?" MaryBeth snorted, "Of course she did." Tristan said, "He's right. He is better trained than they are. He's a Beta wolf." I argued, "No, that's not right either. They've had Alpha blood's and other Beta blood's transfer too. Their Gamma blood's aren't sent out as much as Uncle Duncan either. Uncle Duncan is the one closest to his family though… which is an interesting data set point."

Tristan gently said, "You don't have an unobjective point of view in this." I replied, "Which is why I have another group observing my data sets." They all yelled, "WHAT?!" I frowned, "I mean… it's true that my objectivity in the study is clouded. So, I gave the data points I had collected to a third party using code names and situations. It's a psychological group study project. They haven't rendered their findings… but their analysis is leaning towards me being mostly right."

Dalton asked, "Mostly?" I said, "Well, they didn't get my analysis… where I might… have called the Alpha a few names… along with their pack leadership… so yes… mostly, their analysis is trending towards agreeing with mine. They just don't feel as strongly as I do about it."

Jason said, "You can't just share pack data." I pointed out, "They aren't in packs." Tristan groaned, "You gave the data to humans?" I replied, "Well, there is a human in the group, but he's mated to a

Supernatural. It's a Supernatural college group. It's not a big deal… since they don't know who I am… or that it's a pack. They think it's a human study."

Dalton asked, "Did you tell them that?" I said, "I mean… I implied it in the email… we don't talk on the phone or anything… because…" Tristan snorted, "Because we'd hear that." I argued, "Umm no… because it's a chat group… for ideas and stuff… so… like… the chat is online. They don't have each other's numbers…" I did have theirs. I hacked all their information using Prince Gunner Cambridge's papers.

Jason sighed, "Don't use Uncle Duncan's life for research." I pointed out, "Someone uses everyone's life for research. There are roughly over one million scenarios used in the psychological world, human and Supernatural, about Princess Luna Haley Conners. If someone is going to run them on our family… I really feel like it should be me."

Dalton gasped. Tristan blinked several times and everyone stopped walking. I pointed out, "It will take us a very long time to get to the destination of this hike if we keep stopping." Jason asked, "Are you serious? Someone is using Haley's life like that? Does she know?"

I replied, "If she looked at the studies she would? Prince Gunner definitely knows because he has keywords searched and some of the papers didn't publish… because the author died… suddenly… which was totally them. She's a public figure, even to humans. Her background fascinates people. Alpha Eric has killed a lot of tabloid stories and gossip about her…"

I added, "Plus… some were killed via King Aiden for sure… based on the patterns of elemental problems that followed the story or data cancellation." MaryBeth asked, "So, you think Alpha Eric knows about them?" I answered, "All of them? No. He'd have killed a couple… I might have sent some to people… for reasons… and things… maybe…"

Jason groaned, "You emailed Eric?!" I snorted, "Uhh no." MaryBeth snickered. Cooper asked, "Who did you email then?" Dane answered, "She'd have emailed Prince Gunner, Caleb, or Aiden." Tristan sighed, "She'd have Aiden's email because she reads his books from Faerie." I said, "His email is not in those books, or everyone would email him… and he doesn't know I emailed him."

Dalton busted up laughing. I asked, "What? He doesn't. He could suspect… but he didn't come ask me. No one did. You didn't even know about it. I'm not grounded for life for helping… so they definitely don't' know about it." Dane said, "She's not wrong." Obviously.

MaryBeth said, "Well, this is a cone of silence thing then. Get me everything about my brother's pack and the data sets. I'll talk to him." I shrugged, "He didn't seem to care and thought I was 'cute' for doing it all." Jason rubbed his face.

MaryBeth gasped, "You put cute in quotes! HE SAID YOU WERE CUTE!?" Dane rubbed her back, "MB." She shouted, "CUTE?! That information isn't cute. He's a Beta blood, he knows better." I agreed.

I said, "Yes, well factoring in the mate bond… and the fact that I am biased… with my age because people love to point that out… I'm hoping the new analysis from the online group gets him to see it better." Tristan instructed, "You guys keep moving. Ladybug, hang in the back with me."

The group started to leave but he stayed back with me. I pointed out, "They can hear us back here." He said, "I'm just going to try an explain something." I gestured for him to continue saying, "Ok." He said, "You can't just analyze people's lives and tell them they are wrong. It's rude."

I replied, "It's rude to use people and alienate them from their families. It's actually textbook gaslighting, narcissism and abuse." He sighed, "Ladybug, people make choices in life. You can tell them how much you love them and point things out, but if you constantly tell them they are wrong they will cut you out of their lives." I frowned.

He added, "It hurts to hear you're wrong all the time. I know you understand when to back off because unless you're pissed you don't mention the cookies to mom. You've realized where that gets you. That applies to more than cookies." That was magic… or it had to be… I was pretty certain. The probability was ninety nine point nine nine nine percent.

I said, "I'm not saying his mate is bad… just the pack." He reasoned, "A pack he wanted to join for her." I asked, "And?" He said, "These are his choices to make because it's his life. We have to respect the choices people make." I opened my mouth to argue but he held up his hand, "Even when you think it's the wrong choice."

I snorted, "People tell me not going to New York would be a strategically stupid decision and waste of my talents because I don't want to go. So, why doesn't that rule apply to everyone else? They use feelings as their argument. I have literal data and facts that prove I'm right. It's a psychological study so there is a margin of error based on perception, but it's still a data set instead of feelings. I added factors."

He growled, "Who the hell said that you?" Robert. All the time with his friends. I answered, "A lot of people." He said, "You don't have to do anything you don't want to do, and we will all respect the choice to make about school." I asked, "Even if I say I don't want to go, and mom makes me?"

He said, "I promise you that if you end up at that school and you don't want to be there then I will bring you home." Jason called, "Same!" Dalton and Dakota shouted, "What they said." MaryBeth scoffed, "I have a whole plan if that happens, and it involves Dane, so he agrees." Dane chuckled and pulled her in for a hug.

Cooper added, "I'd help too." I shrugged, "Well, then know now I don't want to go." Jason argued, "You could change your mind." I replied, "I won't. I've already decided." Tristan linked, "Don't make that decision based on Alexander." I wasn't going to argue with him because it did have to do with Xander, but I also didn't want to miss everyone here.

Out loud he said, "Jared would pop you back and forth with Rena and all their siblings. You could still live here and go." I shrugged, "I still don't want to." He rubbed my shoulders, "Why don't you focus your data sets on whether you should go or not?"

I frowned, "I obviously already did that… I mean… I'd think that was obvious… plus, dad doesn't want me to go…" I trailed off when he looked away. I asked, "Right?" Everyone had stopped again. Jason said, "Dad wants you to be safe." That was evasive which meant my dad did want me to go. He was the one adult in my data set that was on my side. My data was wrong. Tristan whispered, "Ladybug."

I turned and ran from the group as fast as I could. They all shouted after me, but I was a lot faster than all of them. MaryBeth linked, "I don't want you to go." I couldn't answer her because my chest hurt. Mom ate all those cookies, and sure dad did sometimes I wouldn't deny it, but if dad wanted me to go then I was getting shipped off to New York. No one could stop it because Elise was in her own pack now.

I went to my dancing area then climbed the tree I had hidden an emergency speaker in and connected my phone and began to dance. Everything swirled around in my head as I danced. My dad wanted me to leave. If he agreed with my mom, then I'd be gone. I'd miss everything here and my home. This was my home. Why did I have to leave when I didn't want to?

I dropped to my knees feeling it hard to breathe. I got home sick on long trips, and they want me to go New York?! Suddenly out of nowhere Peter grabbed my face demanding, "Breathe right now, Melanie Jane." I gasped, "I… can't…." He Alpha ordered, "Breathe." The confusion of that command not taking hold had me letting out a breath. Why didn't that work? He was my Alpha.

He asked, "What are you doing here? I thought you pups were going on a hike." I cried, "Daddy wants me to leave." He jolted, "What?" I said, "They were all evasive which means it's true. Daddy wants me to leave and go to that school and I can't breathe… which makes… no sense… because there is air here and… I… don't make me go. Please, Daddy Peter."

He hugged me and rubbed my hair. He ordered, "Get out of here." He must have been running a patrol. He said, "I will never have a pack member doing something they don't want to or hate. Ok?" I nodded. He said, "If you decide to go, and you hate it I'll bring you home." I hugged him tighter.

Tristan said, "I knew you'd come here." Peter turned around and I could see he was pissed. Tristan sighed, "Mel, it's not like how you think it is." I snorted, "So my data sets and telling people they are wrong isn't getting me sent away?" Tristan flinched.

Peter asked, "What?" Tristan pointed out, "We didn't know about that until the hike." That wasn't true at all. They did know that. I told people based on the math and science they were wrong… dang… ok it was a lot… but… I was just trying to help.

Peter announced, "Drake is on the way so you might want to speed this talk along, T." I pointed out, "It's not his fault… because… dad should've told me he didn't want me here." Tristan growled, "Melanie

Jane, it's not like that and you know it. He wants you to have the best opportunities. It's not like everyone can just get into that school."

I argued, "I don't WANT the opportunity." Tristan argued, "You could probably go to Julliard." I replied, "Just because I enjoy dancing and competing…doesn't really mean I want to go to Julliard. It's unfair… on every level. Because a human would lose out… I'm naturally more inclined to be better at dancing than someone who works hard and…"

Tristan jumped in, "You work harder than anyone." I disagreed, "I practice more. I do not work harder. Dancing comes easily to me." My dad said, "And you shouldn't have to settle and not take opportunities because that's true. You compete against humans in competitions." That didn't make it fair.

He continued, "You also do supernatural competitions, and you win. You are immensely talented." I wiped my tears saying, "You want to send me away." He wrapped me up in his arms. He cupped my chin and said, "No, I'd wrap you up here in bubble wrap if I could. That's not fair to you though."

I muttered, "Neither is acting like you aren't letting me go to compete for a spot then… just… telling everyone else you want me to go for my safety." He snorted, "I think someone has been eavesdropping then, Ladybug." Tristan said, "Yeah, Jase and I have."

My dad jolted then growled, "You told her?" I answered, "No, they evaded because I was so confident you didn't want me to leave." He repeated, "I don't want you to leave, but I don't want you to miss the chance to make the world your dance floor."

I cried, "I could do that here." He said, "But you could do it there too. We have Fairies who could bring you back. There are planes, trains, and automobiles that could keep us together. My insecurities about you leaving this pack have kept you here a lot. This is a big opportunity for you, and I can't hold you back as much as I'd like to."

I asked, "So, if I don't want to compete, I don't have to then." He replied, "I think you should compete." I continued, "Then I can decline the spot if I win." He winced, "I think you should give it a chance. There are times when you're young you make decisions, then live with what if's. I don't want that for you."

I asked, "What's your what if then?" He locked his jaw. I nodded, "You don't have one." He reasoned, "Just because I don't doesn't mean other people don't live with them." I whispered, "I'm an annoying know it all who rambles and talks to much… I get why you want me gone." It just hurt.

He snarled, "T, WHAT THE FUCK DID YOU SAY TO HER?" Tristan growled, "I didn't say anything like that!" I agreed, "He didn't." Peter asked, "Is this about those bullies you didn't tell us about? They filled your head with that bullshit? Because that's exactly what it is."

I frowned, "I do ramble and talk a lot. Plus, not to brag… but like, I am right a lot." They all busted up laughing and I actually smiled. My dad said, "I would not change a single hair on your head or anything about your big brain. All pups talk a lot and blurt things out. It's part of life."

He tapped my nose, "You are different. You're a literal genius and your brain doesn't work like ours. Even mine. You're smarter than me and I'm damn proud of you for it. Everyone in the pack is." I mean that was definitely not true. Robert hated that I won stuff, but for the most part my dad's statement was accurate.

My dad said, "I don't want you to hate me later for holding you back." I gasped, "I could never hate you." He laughed, "You could." I said, "Holding grudges and hating people takes effort. It's silly to waste time on it." Tristan pointed out, "She does say that a lot."

Because I was right. I would have to REALLY hate someone to decide keeping the grudge and hating them was worth the effort. Like the Ring. I hated them for how much they were trying to hurt Xander. That was worth the effort, but that wasn't something I needed to say. Since technically speaking… I wasn't supposed to know they existed since I was 'just a pup' or whatever.

My dad said, "I don't want you to think anyone WANTS to send you anywhere. I want you to take on the world and conquer it. I want you to have zero what if questions about opportunities. I want you to have the world if that's what you wanted." I wanted to meet Xander. That's what I wanted.

Tristan said, "That's what we all want, Mel. We just want you to be happy." I repeated, "I'm happy here." Peter said, "That doesn't mean you won't be happy there." My dad admitted, "Knowing people don't treat you well here did influence my decision." I gasped, "That's not that many people. Statistically…" He laughed, "I know the numbers, I just hate it for you."

I hugged him, hoping I could change his mind. He asked, "Will you at least compete?" Mom was dead set on me going. I pursed my lips. I said, "If I get to decide if I accept the scholarship or not, then yes." He sighed. I pointed out, "We can afford the school without a scholarship. They would invite me to come dance even if I didn't compete." I could afford it myself, but they didn't know that.

He said, "I'll talk to your mom about that." I groaned "So, no." He cupped my face, "I love you so much and if it were up to me, you'd stay here forever." I shrugged, "Ok, let's do that then… when I meet..." Tristan jumped in, "Your mate might not live here." He didn't.

My dad chuckled, "That's true. Your mom told me about the dress you want for your mating ceremony. I may have had to sit down thinking about it, but it sounded beautiful." I couldn't stop myself returning to that day in my mind.

Flashback

Melanie was in the hotel with her mom. We'd had so much fun this trip. She hadn't had a single cookie, and I loved it. She twirled my hair, "So, why haven't we had any conversations about your crushes?" I frowned, "Because I don't have any." I held my Xander wolf tightly against me.

She prodded, "No boys have caught your eye?" I answered, "Nope." Xander was a man by Hackura standards and had been for a while. She asked, "What about girls?" I sighed, "I like men, mom." She cooed, "OHHHH men, huh? Here I was talking about boys."

I blurted out, "I've thought about my mating ceremony a lot." She grinned asking, "Have you? Tell me about it." I sighed, "I have this dream about my dress, but I don't think it exists." Xander's mom could make it though, if I told her about it. Mom said she conjured things all the time. Everyone did.

Mom urged, "Tell me all about it." I grinned, "Ok, so it's a two piece dress." She chuckled, "You want to set your dad off already. I love it." I said, "It covers way more than my dancing outfits so… he should be fine with it." She hummed and smiled at me.

I continued, "The top would be a nude sleeveless top with a red lace overlay of flowers. The bottom would be on my waist with a red band at the top and the skirt would be white." She admitted, "I thought the whole dress would be red."

I blushed saying, "Nope. The flowers would start at about my thighs and scattered throughout the bottom until the bottom where it just looks died red, but really it's flowers." I paused, "It sounds silly." She argued, "No, it sounds beautiful and utterly you. Does this top show off your boobs?"

I flushed, "No. It wouldn't be straight across like the bottom of the top. It would look like this." I quickly drew it for her. She teased, "Is there nothing you can't do? I didn't know you like drawing." I mean, I could somewhat draw.

I said, "They teach art in school." She asked, "Do you want me to put you into art camps then?" I answered, "No." I wanted to draw with the Conners. They'd be the best teachers anyway. She nudged me, "So, no boys for you then. Only men." I nodded, "That about sums it up… really."

She grinned, "I feel like that means someone has your eye. They aren't mated, right?" I gasped, "Of course not! That… I… would never…He's… ummm…." She clapped and exclaimed, "AH HA! So, there is someone specific." I gasped, "You tricked me."

She winked, "It worked, didn't it?" I blushed. She told me, "Your mate is a lucky man. Anyone you like and give your attention to is lucky. Do you hear me?" I replied, "You're my mom… so you have to think that." She laughed, "No, I don't. It's just true. You have a beautiful mind and heart. I pray to Selene for Robert's mate. The poor girl. Although, if he's actually gay, it wouldn't shock me."

I snorted, "MOM!" She shrugged, "He's so angry and I have to wonder if that's not about himself. There's no shame in who you love or who you are attracted to. I just hope if that's his problem, he can accept himself. Now, having said all that I hate him and hope he chokes on his boogers." I cackled, "His boogers?!" She winked, "No one hurts my pups and has me in their corner."

I pointed out, "You're his Beta Female... so you have to be." She said, "I do not. Sharon deals with anything that has to do with him." I asked, "Really?" She nodded, "And she hates it, but she thinks it fair that I don't since he's a bully. Who happens to have come after my pup." She hugged me, "I never want anyone to hurt a single hair on your head, Ladybug. You're my little girl." I hugged her tightly wishing this moment would never end.

Flashback Ends

I admitted, "It's not a real dress. It's just an idea I had... or vision... or a daydream... definitely a day dream." He chuckled, "I don't care what it is. Your mom and I will make sure you get every single dream you want." Why didn't they understand they were making that school to be something bigger than it was?

Tristan grabbed me and we walked off. He said, "I'd rather take a punch then hurt your feelings. All of us would. We want you here. Period. End of story." I asked, "Then why is everyone so determined I go to that school? It's weird... right? It's definitely weird." He sighed, "It's a little weird. I'll look into it."

I teased, "You look into so much though." He winked, "I guess I do, but you're my little sister. I'll always have your back." I replied, "Levi would say six." He agreed, "Yes, he would because any Hackura would say they'd have your six."

I sighed, "I haven't seen him before or since I didn't get to go to Xander's birthday party." He snorted, "Uh huh. You mean you saw him that day." I frowned, "No, I met him that day." He rolled his eyes, "Ladybug, you've met my best friend."

I agreed, "Yes, because he came that day." He waved me off saying, "Surely you met him before then." I muttered, "No, I didn't. I haven't met a lot of people." He snorted, "Alexander doesn't count." I argued, "He definitely does, but I meant other people." He prodded, "Like who?"

I answered, "The Bishop's." He laughed, "Dustin and Aubree live around here so you'll meet them." I said, "Not them. Valerie and Ryan." If I met him, I could get his number and call him about the cookies. He said, "You've met Valerie, you just don't remember." I argued, "I have not met her."

He shrugged, "She came to help mom out when you were born." I disagreed, "I doubt that since I've never seen the picture of her holding me. There's one of you and Jase, but not me... which leads me to believe I didn't even meet her as a pup." He frowned saying, "I'll hunt down the picture, we have to have it." We didn't because it didn't exist.

The rest of the week actually went by quickly. We had some Warriors get in a scuffle and they took on silver. Xander was on his mission and Haley wasn't around either. They Warriors weren't in danger of dying so Alpha Peter didn't link Alpha Eric about it. They planned to link him once Haley was back.

This was the perfect time to test my chocolate to help silver poisoning. I went into the hospital with a book. A nurse spotted me. She greeted, "Hi, Ladybug." I waved saying, "I'm just going to..." She chuckled, "Read to the unconscious Warriors. That's good."

I went to Mr. Dutton's room first. Mrs. Dutton was asleep in a chair by him. I fixed her blanket and looked around. I quickly popped the chocolate in his mouth. It would dissolve quickly. I read him a chapter and went to the next person.

I hid in the hospital lab where they were running there labs. One tech said, "I'll be damned. I ran it four times. It doesn't make any sense but it's true." Someone asked, "What is?" He said, "The Silver levels on our Warriors blood panels jumped lower than they should. Those doctors are going to be on our asses, but it's true." Yes! It worked.

When they huddled in a group to talk about it I snuck over and read the results. I just needed to up the dose and they'd wake up without needing to be healed. I left and went to find Tank. He was with Ziggy and Adeline. Adeline linked, "Did it work?" I nodded.

Tank groaned, "Oh god. What have you two done?" Adeline looped her arm with mine, "We have a project we need you to take us to the school to finish." He sighed, "Fine." Ziggy laughed and he drove us to the school.

Adeline and I went into the science classroom. I gave her goggles and instructed her on how to help. She whispered, "So, it really helped?" I nodded, "Yup. I heard them say it and I checked the results personally." She gave me a high five. We left that lab and went to the other side of the school for the oven. Once the chocolate was done we found Tank. He raised an eyebrow at us but Ziggy kissed him and we left.

The next day I repeated my process. While I was reading to the last Warrior waiting for the chocolate to dissolve people started yelling. Mrs. Dutton shouted, "He's awake! He's awake! Thank Selene!" I did a little dance in my chair.

I stood and peeked out of the room I was in. Mrs. Dutton was fanning her face. She did a double take when she spotted me and I squeaked then took off out of the hospital. I was almost to my house when Tank found me.

I waved, "Umm hi…Tank." He hummed, "Yeah, how did you that?" I asked, "Do what?" He said, "I know it was you." I squeaked, "Huh?" He started to say something when my mom yelled, "Melanie Jane, come clean your tornado of a room."

I waved, "Bye, Tank!" He said, "This conversation isn't over." I pointed out, "It never really started…when you think about it." He laughed, "You're amazing, pup. You did a good thing." I knew that.

I made it back to my house thinking normally, leading up to when I was supposed to meet Xander it was slow. This time wasn't because of my side chocolate mission that I now had very real data on. Plus, our family was spending a lot of time together.

I was still angry but not surprised Uncle Duncan's pack wouldn't contact him about Elise's mating ceremony. He was going to be upset when he came back. He probably wouldn't do much though because he was dead set on living there.

I guess, based on what Tristan said, we had to let him make those decisions. Everything had gone really well and maybe I hid all the cookies… Ok, I did hide them but not all of them. Technically, I sent more out to other covens farther away. I sent one to Megan in Black Mountain. She could figure it all out, provided it actually got to her.

I should've sent them for signatures, but I didn't have time. I had to get them out quickly when everyone fell asleep. Today, I'd been doing homework for next month while sitting with my dad. He chuckled, "Ladybug, you don't have to stick with me today." Peter had already gone in Black Mountain with Chelsea.

I shrugged, "I don't mind… plus… I just want to be here…. so… you see me… and…" He raised an eyebrow, but I cut myself off. I was pretty proud of me for that too. He said, "Well, I see you." I got back to doing my homework. Then helped him file paperwork. He was finalizing the patrol schedule when I finished.

My mom came in and laughed, "You need to go get ready Melanie." I squeaked, "What?" She laughed, "Drake, you and the boys should go without us. We are easily going to be late." I gasped, "No, I'll get ready so fast!" My dad laughed, "We can wait." She urged, "Go on, we'll be right behind you if she plans to get ready at the speed of light."

I pointed out, "Sharon could snap me ready." My mom laughed, "Their whole family left already." Well, linking was an option. My brothers came in. I linked, "Don't go without us, T. Please!" He said, "You'll be right behind us. It's fine." Except it never was. Literally not once. I wasn't even going to get in the dang car, and I'd been so hopeful since I'd been hiding all the cookies.

My mom took me back over the house. She chuckled, "Impress me with your speed." I was definitely going to. I ran upstairs and turned on the shower. I linked Rena, "Can you snap me ready in like ten minutes?" She asked, "Why not now?" I answered, "Because I'm going to shower." She agreed, "I have a timer on." I grinned and jumped in the shower. I'd washed my hair last night so I wouldn't be too long.

I'd just dried off when I was snapped completely ready. I ran back downstairs, and my mom gaped. She shook her head, "Ok, I think you need to tell me about all your inventions because you got ready faster than I would've thought possible. Let's go." I gasped, "Really?"

She laughed, "Of course. We will be a little late, but we should make it before Elise walks down the aisle." I squealed and ran to the car. The pack was practically deserted because everyone was going to the wedding. I buckled myself into the car and grinned. Oh my gosh… we were really going!

I watched her start the car with bated breath. I linked Tristan, "We are actually driving! We are on the way." He replied, "Of course you are. It's Elise's mating ceremony." I squealed, "I'm going to meet Xander!" He cautiously said, "I know. Just don't be too disappointed if that doesn't work out." I shot back, "It will, because he's my mate." He just groaned. No one got it, he was mine and I knew it. It wasn't a crush because he was my mate.

I shoved all that aside when we left pack lands. I grinned at my mom because I was so excited. I was actually in the car on the way to Black Mountain. I was really going to EJ and Elise's mating ceremony. I looked down and smoothed my gold dress out. I was meeting Xander. This was really happening.

My mom asked, "Why are you so nervous, Ladybug?" I looked over, "Well… I finally get to meet everyone and it's an important day for Elise. I haven't gotten to see her much… which I understand, she's busy… but it's just so different without her there and…" My mom reached over and squeezed my hand.

She said, "You and Elise will figure out the balance. Elise has a very large pack she's in control of as a Luna. It may not yet be official with the hybrid style they are doing, but she's running things already basically. Even if it's not her name on it yet."

I whispered, "I know." I understood that all, logically speaking. I really did. I just missed her. Normally, she was just across the yard in her house and now she was gone. That was all about to change though. I'd get to see her more once Xander realized we were mates. Then we could all hang out.

I took a deep breath while my mind spun with questions. Would he like me? Would he be happy about the fact that we were mates? Would he hug me? Maybe he'd kiss my cheek. I blushed at the thought. Before thinking of getting my first actual kiss on the lips. I was a woman by Hackura standards. Actually, by all of them besides humans.

My mom laughed, "What's that blush?" I looked over stammering, "Umm nothing… I… it's nothing." My mom reminded me, "You're a horrible liar." No one needed to remind me, but they felt the need to do it constantly. No matter how many papers or books I read about how to lie, I still couldn't master it which was annoying.

Mom questioned teasingly, "Do you have a crush I don't know about?" My blush deepened. Mom gasped, "Oh my god, you do! Tell me everything. I have to know so I can keep your dad and brothers calm." I was about to say something when headlights blinded us in the rearview mirror.

My mom yelled, "What the hell? Why would someone use their brights when we are right in front of them? Learn how to drive, you asshole!" She muttered, "I would totally flip him off if I knew who it was."

She turned to me, "It's easy to get angry and react in emotional moments, but you have to remember that people are fucking crazy. You never know who is driving around you, or what they will do. I never want to lose you or your brothers to road rage. Do you hear me?" I nodded.

She sighed, "They are so fucking lucky I can see." Given we were Werewolves our eyesight was better, but a human would be blinded right now. I turned around in the seat. A sinister smiling face I knew greeted me. Why was he following us with his brights on? Dad wouldn't have him guarding us, and he wasn't even a Warrior; let alone a Guard.

Then I realized he was speeding up. I yelled, "MOM, LOOK OUT!" before he hit the back panel of our SUV. I screamed as the back window exploded. My mom shouted, "HANG ON, MELANIE JANE!" She was trying to keep the car straight, but we were hit again.

She glanced at me, and I saw the panic on her face. She said, "You're going to be fine, baby." Then she lost control, and the SUV rolled. Glass exploded and I squeezed my eyes shut and I felt the car spinning and rolling around.

When we stopped, I screamed, "MOM!" She didn't answer me. I cried, "No, mom please answer me. Are you ok? Because… you have to be ok… mom…" She didn't say anything. I cried, "Please, mom." My mom had to be ok.

I turned to try and see her but there was a tree in between us. Did the car split in two? I tried to yell louder, "MOM!" All I heard was the wind in reply. I went through the statistics on car crashes. The tree was in the middle of us so only a branch could've impaled her and at this angle it was more likely the car spit in two.

Everything was trying to fade away from me. I ordered, "No Melanie… stay conscious… use your Werewolf vision… and move forward around the tree." I put my hands down on the roof and moved as far forward as I could.

I looked over and screamed, "MOM!" The SUV was completely in two pieces but her side was just in front of the other side of the tree. She wasn't moving and there was blood dripping down her face, but she was breathing. I yelled, "SOMEONE HELP US!" My head was pounding but I heard footsteps coming.

I instantly quieted. What if the other driver didn't keep driving? I closed my eyes, pretending to be unconscious. I smelled him outside our window before I felt a sharp pain in my head. He'd hit me hard enough I couldn't hang onto consciousness anymore.

I heard beeping. It wouldn't stop and it was annoying. Was I dead? I sat up. Someone said, "Whoa, take it easy. Do you know where you are?" I forced my eyes open. I looked around the hospital. A quick inhale told me this was a human one. Seriously? Why were we taken here? Wasn't I with my mom? What was I doing before this? Surely, I was with mom.

I asked, "Where's my mom? What happened?" I couldn't remember anything. I saw my gold dress in a bag with blood on it. That was the dress I'd picked out for Elise's mating ceremony! I remembered we'd been driving.

I announced, "There… we were in the car…" I looked at the nurse in panic. I asked, "Where is my mom?" She said, "You need to calm down." I could hear the beeping on the monitor increase, so it was a heart or blood pressure monitor.

I repeated, "My mom…" The nurse interrupted, "Please take a deep breath." She wasn't listening to me! I yelled, "I WILL TAKE A DEEP BREATH WHEN YOU TELL ME WHERE MY MOTHER IS! Where is she?! She was hurt!" I started to cry.

I screamed, "MOM! MOM! WHERE ARE YOU?!" She'd hear me with our hearing. She had to and she'd answer me. Who were all these people? I cried, "Where is my dad? I don't know you." Several people ran into the room, but none were my mom.

She didn't answer my screams either, which logically meant she wasn't on this floor. Or she couldn't hear me, which I was rejecting even though the probability she was unconscious was rising. Someone put something in the IV that I had in my hand.

I looked at them and yelled again, "Where is she?! Why won't you answer me?" They looked at each other and frowned. Someone said, "That should've knocked her out." I pleaded, "Just answer me! Where is my mom? She's ok, right?" They still didn't answer me. Bile filled my throat and I felt extremely dizzy.

I started trying to yank everything off me, but they held me down. I could get them off me, but it would hurt them. They were humans. I screamed, "LET ME GO! Why won't you just tell me where she is?! I want my mom! Is she ok? Why won't she answer me?"

I heard a growl I knew and cried, "Daddy!" He was running down the hall clearly based on the sound. He still ordered, "Get your hands off my daughter RIGHT NOW!" Tristin yelled, "Mel!" Jason growled, "Let her go!" They all filled the doorway.

I looked up and cried, "Dad, they won't tell me where mom is… or if she's ok… she didn't answer me… and the likelihood she's unconscious is… around seventy percent…" The nurse said, "How? She wouldn't have heard you. You didn't yell that loud." Not to her, she was human, but my mom wasn't.

My dad ran into my room and glared at several people. He came right to my side. He whispered soothingly, "I'm here. It's ok, Ladybug. Your mom is in a different room on another floor. I'll go see her in just a minute."

I asked, "Is she ok? She wasn't moving and she wouldn't answer me." They were all in tuxedos. It felt like a weird thing to notice because surely, I saw them before they left. Didn't I? What had I done with my whole day? Why was everything a blank with sporadic pockets of information? Like I knew mom didn't answer me in the car. I knew that tree split the SUV. I knew we were hit. Everything else was gone.

My dad explained, "The call I got was that both of you were stable. I'll go check on her as soon as I know you're ok." Tristan urged, "I've got her, dad. Go check on mom." My dad kissed the top of my head. I whispered, "I'm fine. T is right, go see mom. Please. They won't tell me how she is."

Tristan asked, “How are you feeling?” I admitted, “My head really hurts and I feel dizzy.” Tristan frowned. The doctor came into the room. He raised an eyebrow looking around. Eventually he said, “I wasn’t aware the on call doctor was called for my patient. I’ll need to know what happened in here.” My dad was going to sue them is what happened.

The doctor turned to me saying, “Your disorientation makes sense. You have a severe concussion, and your equilibrium will be off. The accident damaged your inner ear.” I frowned, “But I have a dance competition…”

The doctor interrupted, “I’m sorry but there will be no dancing for at least a few months” I gasped and looked at Tristan in panic. I whispered, “But it’s a big competition next weekend and…” Jason jumped in, “Mel, we can have our doctors at home look at you. We will get a second opinion.” The doctor here wasn’t a wolf.

How did I get taken to a human hospital without ANY supernatural’s running around? Or at least one on my medical team. The likelihood of that happened was literally next to none. I’d helped out with a college study on it. It was literally unheard of to have a team of doctors in human hospitals without a Supernatural on it. Especially for me when I’d clearly been admitted here. Something was off about all of this.

Tristan said, “It’s going to be ok, Ladybug.” Except it wasn’t. I’d invited Xander to my competition because it was a big one. I’d mailed him the invitation personally and everything with a note like the other times. I’d specifically said this was a big one though.

I felt hot tears slipping out of my eyes. Tristan hugged me whispering, “I’ve got you, little sister.” I held onto him tightly. A nurse asked, “Does she have an aversion to sedation or pain medicine?” Tristan admitted, “She has a high tolerance for medicine.” I knew that because after I’d separated my shoulder, they’d barely able been able to take the pain away at our pack hospital.

The nurse nodded as my dad came back in. He quickly announced, “Your mom is fine, and your grandpa Ben is with her. Your other grandparents will be here shortly.” He meant my mom’s parents. He growled, “Sam’s asking about my daughter since she wasn’t told immediately when she woke up.” He glared at the doctors.

The one that was my actual doctor frowned. He apologized, “I’m sorry that happened. I’m sure she was very worried.” Tristan and Jason scoffed, and I knew why. They were lucky my dad and grandpa got to her when they did, or she’d have gone momma wolf on them.

Sugar would’ve taken over and the question was if it would’ve been in wolf or human form. If she’d shifted, Fairies would be here erasing memories. My dad turned to the doctor that had apologized and inclined his head outside.

He told me, “We will get you and your mom home.” I asked, “What happened? There were lights and… I can’t remember anything.” Which was annoying. I remembered everything, even when I didn’t want to.

My dad explained, “It was a hit and run accident, but I promise you we will find out what happened. Peter knows you guys are ok and will receive the full report later. Garrett is on the scene and working on everything with Dylan Frost.” I’d missed meeting Dylan Frost again? Man!

Jason walked out with him. I whispered to Tristan, “Do you think Xander will come heal me?” Tristan sighed, “It’s not an emergency, Ladybug.” It felt like one. Actually, it felt like I was going to throw up. Why couldn’t the Moon Goddess give me a break? I just wanted to meet Xander. I reached for something, and nurse handed me a bag that I threw up into.

Tristan asked, “What’s going on?” The nurse answered, “The concussion, or her inner ear issue could cause this. It’s quite severe.” Tristan said, “I don’t know what an inner ear issue means.” I answered, “Balance problems, vertigo, dizziness, hearing issues, nausea and vomiting, ringing in your ears, headaches, earaches and so on.”

The nurse chuckled, “You’re smart.” I muttered, “I’d have to lose over twenty I.Q. points to be classified as smart.” Tristan’s tone was full of amusement when he admonished me, “Melanie.” I said, “Well, I would… and…”

The nurse said, "Some of the hearing loss could be permanent." Tristan asked, "Did you hit the tree, Mel?" I closed my eyes and tried to remember. I remembered looking around the tree to see mom. I whispered, "I don't think so."

Tristan linked me, "The hearing loss, if you have any, won't be permanent." I replied, "I hear just fine… she's annoying… and I don't like her. She wouldn't answer my questions." He teased, "And you don't like people not answering your questions."

I retorted, "That's literally in my blood." He ruffled my hair. The nurse said, "She threw up again." Again? When did I throw up before? The doctor nodded, "They are transferring her to a private hospital nearby where they live." She shrugged and left the room.

The doctor went through a bunch of stuff with my dad when I smelled my mom coming. I burst into tears when Grandpa Ben wheeled her in. I sobbed, "Mom!" Grandpa wheeled her next to me and she took my hand. She whispered, "I'm so sorry, Melanie Jane."

My dad growled, "It wasn't your fault, Sam. Some jackass t-boned you guys, lost control and hit you again, then left you guys down in a ravine." I hummed, "It's very rare for Harbison's Hawthorn trees to be in Tennessee and we hit one."

My mom snorted, "Great. It's rare and we just happened to find one." That seemed very strange and unlikely. I added, "They are actually rare and endangered in this state… it's a large tree for a ravine… they are large and…"

The doctor chuckled, "She certainly knows facts." I did and they weren't adding up here. Something was going on and I needed to figure it out. I'd just add it to my growing list of things to figure out. My mom squeezed my hand, and I squeezed hers. We were ok and that was what mattered.

Killing Spree

Alexander is Eighteen Years Old

Alexander was furious. I hit the heavy bag harder than I had been. EJ was off with Elise after their mating ceremony, and I was glad he wasn't paying attention to my feelings. Melanie didn't show you for their damn ceremony or reception.

Hell, neither Sam nor Melanie showed, and it was BULLSHIT! Oden growled, "She was supposed to be here." She was always supposed to be at something then she never was. My dad came into the gym, and I noted everyone else left.

He got behind the bag and let me keep swinging. Then he ended up holding the bag up himself when I knocked it off. He said, "Your Uncle Aiden and Uncle Bjourn have things for you to do." I snorted, "I'm here because EJ is about to go on his honeymoon." He replied, "Neither will take you long and I'm here. You'll need the missions."

I faltered then asked, "Why?" He set the bag down then slowly answered, "Sam and Melanie were in a car accident. That's why they didn't make it to the ceremony." Oden snarled in my head. I asked, "Is she ok?" My dad raised an eyebrow, "Both are healing." I nodded, "So, mom went to heal them."

His jaw locked, "No, it wasn't an emergency." I asked, "WHO GIVES A FUCK?!" He replied, "They do." I questioned, "What are the injuries?" He answered, "Sam had some cuts from the glass that are already healed. She had a concussion and some other injuries that will take some time for her wolf to heal."

I waited for the injury listed we both knew I actually wanted. He sighed, "Melanie suffered a very bad inner ear problem." I didn't know what that was. Oden chimed in, "I don't either." I asked, "What does that mean?" He admitted, "I'm not entirely sure."

I called my Uncle Bjourn and he faded in. My dad snorted. I asked, "What does it mean?" He would've heard us talking. He said, "There are differing severities." I said, "But Uncle Gunner got into the chart, so you know how severe it is."

He agreed, "I do, but their tools are primitive compared to ours. The scans were awful." I snorted, "Pack hospitals…" I trailed off when they shot each other looks. Oden began to growl. I demanded, "Why did you two just look at each other like that?"

My dad answered, "Because they were taken to the human hospital in Blue Moon's territory. Drake is filing a lawsuit against them." I snarled, "WHY?! Did they hurt her?" Oden came forward and my hands began to shift.

Thor ordered, "Pup, calm down. She is fine." Oden let me take back over. My dad asked, "Would you care to comment on what just happened?" I answered, "No. What did they do?" He answered, "They wouldn't give him details on his wife or pup's condition. They were holding Melanie down instead of simply answering if Sam was stable, and threatening Melanie with restraints."

I growled, "Did they bruise her?" Uncle Bjourn answered, "Yes, they did." They were dead. I was going to get their names and kill their human asses. I asked, "What's inner ear damage mean?" He answered, "It can cause hearing loss, dizziness, balance problems…" I interrupted, "She's a dancer!" He winced, "She won't be dancing for a bit."

I demanded, "Call them back and say I'll come heal her! She loves to dance. They can't just take that from her because they don't want our help. That's not fair." My dad agreed, "I'll call them again." I nodded, "Thank you. Is that all Uncle Bjourn?"

He groaned, "No. It can cause nausea, vomiting, ringing in the ear, you can feel like the ear is full of something, and it likely will give her a headache." I growled, "For how long?" He sighed, "If I could scan her with our tools, I could give you a better answer. Levi is going to try, but they've locked her down for now. Drake is full wolf dad mode and none of us can blame him for that."

Oden snarked, "I can blame him for not wanting us or mom to heal her." Yeah, we could. Uncle Bjourn admitted, "From the hospital records, they estimated a year of issues, but they think she's human. They also think there is permanent damage, but she's a Supernatural. It could be four to six months before she's fully recovered." I sent my fury to both of them.

I ground out, "She LOVES to dance!" My dad said, "We know that." I snorted, "Someone should mention to Drake she can hardly fight and escape the people who bully her if she's FALLING OVER BECAUSE SHE HAS NO BALANCE!"

Dad argued, "That's not happening anymore." That was because I'd threatened Robert within an inch of his life. I said, "The point stands. If they are attacked, she is vulnerable." Which was something I could not allow. Dad inclined his head, "I'll call him again. Ok?" I nodded, "Thank you." He left with my uncle.

I went to find my mom because based on her feelings, she knew our healing had been turned down. I found her on the mountain. She greeted, "Hi, Alexander." I grabbed her hand and popped her into the house.

I snapped us drinks and urged, "Out with it. You have sorrow to share, and I know you're blocking most of it off from other people. You can't with me because this is about our healing sides." Something I enjoyed her being unable to do, when it was our shared power. I hated that she could usually do it about everything else, though.

She replied, "You have feelings about this I don't understand." I winked, "But I asked you first." She sighed, "I thought Sam and I were friends." I replied, "You are." She scoffed, "Then why is it always me?" I asked, "What do you mean?" She answered, "They don't care when Emmaline uses her powers. Nor do they care when Sharon and her kids use theirs."

She added, "Which I think is great for my cousins. I love that they accept them. It just fucking sucks no one can ever fucking do that with me. You want anyone else to use their power? Yes, everyone wants that. Me? Nope. Why the fuck would we do that? Let's only do it in life or death situations. That's not harder for me to fucking heal or anything. Let's have people suffer unnecessarily. That's obviously the better options."

I sipped my whiskey, "Sarcasm noted." She winced, "Why don't they like my powers? I just don't fucking get it. I'm fine to use in battle but not every day. I've healed countless fucking wolves, and other Supernatural's, who had trouble conceiving. I have bent over backwards, fucking literally, to block people from getting Sam in battle. Then they practically smack me in the face with their rejection of my powers."

She slammed her martini and conjured another one. She snorted, "No one else has to sensor their powers around them. We all can't fucking pop to them and that's bullshit but whatever. No one else ASKS to use their powers."

"They all clamor to hear Emmaline whisper mated pairs. Don't get me wrong, I do too. I fucking love her power. They have Sharon's pup using water powers, and hers, all the damn time. Why the FUCK doesn't anyone ever accept me for who I am?"

I hugged her, "Because they are fools. We love you." A few of her tears fell. She whispered, "I have tried so hard to…" She faltered then straightened, "I'll talk the rest over with Lexi. You are their ally and this hurt you too." I replied, "I can take it, mom." She smiled sadly, "I know you can."

I said, "It's like a sucker punch they'd rather Melanie not dance for months, and Sam heal slowly from whatever is wrong with her." She snorted, "Just another reason on top of ALL the reasons that confirm that child does not exist. Who wants their child to suffer unnecessarily? No fucking one. Especially NOT Drake and Sam. They are good people."

Oden whined, "Mate is real." I replied to him, "I know she's real." Phil came in with Lexi Scott. I stood and hugged her. I greeted, "Hey Aunt Lexi." She wasn't actually related to me, but she was family in all our minds. She winked, "I've got your mom." Phil saluted me, "And by the fact I'm your Beta and cousin, I've got you."

My mom argued, "If you could give us a minute, Alexander was sharing his sorrow." I shrugged, "I'll tell Phil." Her face was blank when she nodded, "Of course." She hugged me and linked, "I'm always here for you. You can tell me anything." I replied, "I know." I felt her eyes on me as I walked out of the house.

I grabbed Phil then faded back. I heard my dad arguing, "Drake it's just that…" Drake's voice cut him off, "It's not an emergency." My dad sighed, "I understand that but…" Drake's voice crackled, "It's the rules." My dad asked, "Are you ok? Your voice sounds off." It really did. He said, "I need to go. Sam needs me." He hung up and I heard my dad slam his phone down.

I left and went outside. I called Jason. He answered, "Hey, Alexander." I asked, "Is your dad ok?" He answered, "He's stressed but he's fine. It's my mom and sister that aren't." I offered, "I can heal them." He sighed, "I wish." I pointed out, "I am offering." I heard someone call him. He said, "I gotta go."

Karina, an Omega, walked by with a plate of cookies and handed a few to Phil. I said, "Drake's voice sounded weird, right?" Phil agreed, "It did. It was like static over the line." I scoffed, "Which wouldn't happen. Uncle Gunner is all over the networks and cell towers in this area."

He ate a cookie then offered me one. He said, "It's not that weird." I scoffed, "What the hell are you talking about? It was really fucking weird then dad called him on it, and he had to go. That's convenient." Oden growled, "Something is going on." Phil urged, "Eat a cookie." \

I grabbed one and snarfed it down grunting, "There. Happy?" He winked, "And now your hangry ass isn't ready to detonate." I deflated, "You're right. It's just a coincidence." He agreed, "Exactly. I have your missions from Uncle Bjourn."

I asked, "Do you have the one from Uncle Aiden too?" He said, "No, the secret Fairy that lives around here, but isn't actually a secret yet hangs onto that notion he is, does." I snorted, "You know his name." He agreed, "I do." I added, "And there is more than one." He retorted, "But there is a main one." There was.

He handed me a file. I opened it and grinned, "I get to kill someone." He snorted, "Shocking. I also have the schedule for your squadron practice in the Hackura realm." I'd taken on a bigger role there than I'd planned to do. That bitch started messing with my sister and I needed to be there more often to watch over Cassie.

I took it and reviewed everything. Phil said, "And the secret Fairy approaches." The man in question chuckled, "Hello Beta wolf who knows my name." Phil rolled his eyes saying, "Your name is absurd." I shook my head and linked, "Now, he's going to want a nickname." Which he had, but I don't think Phil had said it around him.

Ailbhe laughed, "Do I get a nickname?" Oden took over, "You have had one and have for years." Phil groaned, "Oden!" Oden retorted, "I am not in a good mood, and I want to go kill people. He has the file, and I want it." Ailbhe asked, "What's the nickname?"

Phil sighed, "He can't even ask the right questions. He didn't ask why you want to kill things." Ailbhe replied, "He always wants to kill things, but as I hear things being around as I am. I suspect I know why he wants to kill things." He winked at me, "Which I agree you should do. The nerve of people to decline your and your mother's healing. Fools." He was somewhat right.

He pressed, "And my nickname is?" Phil sighed, "We call you Abe." He laughed, "That is amusing. Here you go, Duke Alexander." He handed me a file. I flipped it open and grinned, "Another person to kill." He hummed, "Yes, your Enforcer blood Fae and wolf should be very happy. Take care." He popped out.

Phil asked, "So what is it?" I replied, "Ariena has taken a new lover." He snorted, "Can you not just kill the evil Fairy instead of her lovers?" I replied, "We can't pop to her because she has something magical that prevents it." Ariena was working against my family and had been trying to garner support to overthrow the Holloran's. Which I would never let happen.

She'd kidnapped one of my cousins when they were little, but they'd outsmarted her and got away. I was pretty sure she'd been pouting about that for years now. If only she'd slip up and do more. He asked, "Have you gotten any further on her last name?"

I snorted, "If they weren't all dead, I'd guess the ruling family before us. Maybe some escaped." He shrugged, "Maybe. I find it weird no one mentions her last name." I admitted, "I asked mom, and she didn't know either."

He hummed, "That's weird." It was. I just didn't currently care. Oden growled, "I want to rip someone's head off." I asked, "In wolf form? Or half shifting?" He growled, "Both." I linked my dad, "Is anyone having a rogue problem?" He snorted, "I'll look into that. You be safe on your missions. Ok?" I agreed, "I will."

He said, "You know, spying on my phone calls was annoying when you were a pup. Now, it's just insulting you don't think I know you're here." Damn the bond for giving me away. I sighed, "Mom is going to need you. This hurt her." He replied, "And it hurt you."

I snorted, "Yes, but not in the way it does mom." I knew why they didn't want me to heal Melanie. They were scared of me. That was abundantly clear at this point. He asked, "What do you mean?" I explained, "She thinks they don't like her powers."

He shouted, "What the literal fuck?" I reasoned, "She has a point. They let everyone other Fairy use their powers, and they ask Cousin Emmaline a lot about mates. Mom has her hang ups because she wants to be accepted." He growled, "I've got her." I knew that.

He added, "But seriously, your ass will kill those people and not get a scratch on you. That's not just an order from your dad either. I'm saying it as your one day Council leader." He was going to join the Werewolf council when we took over after taking some time off. It was all but guaranteed.

I teased, "You could've just said as the Alpha." He snorted, "I'm currently a figure head. You and EJ are in charge." We were but we weren't. EJ suggested a hybrid style that was brilliant, but that was EJ for you. I decided to use every advantage I had and popped to Angela.

TJ winked at me while my sister smiled. I teased, "Were you waiting for me?" TJ shrugged, "Yup. Ang said you were coming." Angela said, "The Fairy has a weapon under the pillow. It wasn't going to hurt you, but his face when he reaches for it on the path where I tell you about it and not finding it is pretty comical. You even smirk." I threw my head back and laughed.

I asked, "And the other one?" She made a face, "He's a very bad guy." I knew that. I told her, "You don't have to look into his path's little one." She sighed, "I was curious, but he is very bad. There is someone you need to save with him. She's locked Underground. Call Iblis when you find her, he will help." So, it was a Demon. Which wasn't surprising since I was going to kill one.

I asked, "Is Maximus going to show up?" She laughed, "You're killing a Demon. Don't ask such silly questions." I grinned teasing, "Right? What was I thinking? Of course he shows up." She hummed, "I just don't know sometimes what you all are thinking."

I asked, "Do you know who our cousin's mate is?" She replied, "Maximus asked me not to look." I raised an eyebrow and TJ snickered. She huffed, "Maybe I peeked. She's hidden somewhere and the paths about how she comes into our lives are confusing."

I questioned, "Confusing how?" She said, "Some are blurry for some reason. Others we are A LOT older. The blurry ones keep firming up." Which would drive her crazy. I asked, "When did they sure up?" She admitted, "Earlier." Earlier when Melanie and Sam got into a car accident? Oden growled. I shook myself. That was a crazy thought. The two were not related.

I assured her, "You'll figure it out. No one can keep you locked out. You're our little one and you're stubborn." She beamed at me, "Thanks, big brother." I kissed the top of her head, "Anytime." I decided to do the Fairy mission first. Maybe Ariena would be there. Probably not if Uncle Aiden was sending me in, but I did have a lot of questions for that Fairy. Mostly what the hell her problem was.

I popped nearby the place where my target was. I noted that it was pretty well hidden, but I could tell there were more people here. I linked my Uncle Aiden, "Was my target supposed to be alone?" He answered, "Yes. Why, are there more people with him?" I answered, "I sense five people here, but Angela didn't mention it." Which meant she didn't know. He said, "I'll call this off."

Oden scoffed, "Nope." I agreed. I faded back and went inside and conjured the Fairy man's weapon away. I flipped on the light and he called, "Ariena, you're back very early. Are you ready to be my bad girl?" I said, "I have literally no interest in that." He jolted and grabbed for his weapon, and I had to admit Angela was right, his face was comical.

I was on him in a second. I said, “For your crimes against the Holloran family, you are sentenced to death.” He faltered, “I…” Oden scoffed, “He didn’t even pop to give us a challenge.” Yeah, that was sad since I didn’t hit him with iron.

He declared, “I won’t turn on her.” I laughed, “She didn’t tell you anything worth knowing because she didn’t care about you. You think you’re special, but she knew we’d get you like we have the others, and she left you which meant we could find you. She didn’t care.” I ripped his heart out his chest and he turned to dust.

My Uncle Aiden popped into the room looking angry. He linked, “You weren’t supposed to come in.” I winked before answering, “That didn’t sound like any fun.” My cousin Figert popped in and wiggled his eyebrows. We moved silently through the house. I made clear signs to the closet in a room that look abandoned.

I called to the wind to blow the door off and gaped. Uncle Aiden whispered, “Goddesses above.” I asked, “What’s on their wrist?” Uncle Aiden made a sound I didn’t understand. I looked at Figert, but he shrugged.

My Uncle answered, “It’s why Angela didn’t see them.” Ok? Figert offered, “I feel like that requires more of an explanation.” My Uncle agreed, “It does but these are one of the ways to interfere with sight. They are incredibly hard to put together and it blocks sight entirely.”

I pressed, “So, not blurry?” He snorted, “It’s just a blank to them with this.” Figert knelt down saying, “You are all safe now.” Oden snarled, “THEY ARE PUPS!” Yeah, they were. They were terrified partial Fairy children.

I linked my mom, “We need you.” She popped in a second later with my dad. She gasped, “That evil BITCH!” They children actually snickered. My dad hugged me, “I’m proud of you.” My mom ranted, “I will HUNT that Ariena bitch down.”

Uncle Aiden said, “We haven’t been able to.” She hissed, “She is trafficking children!” He replied, “We are trying to locate her.” My mom scoffed, “Well, fuck that bitch and whoever is FUCKING hiding her!”

I linked her, “You’re right but the kids need you right now.” She blew out her breath and nodded to me. She kissed my temple then said, “You are an amazing man and I’m so incredibly proud of you. Go do what you need to, son. I can tell this isn’t over for you.”

I shrugged, “This was easy. Maybe the next guy will at least shimmer away and give me a challenge.” Her lips twitched into a smile. Dad growled, “What? NO! You don’t let him shimmer! Just kill him.” My mom replied, “He’ll win the fight.” My dad gaped at us both and we started laughing.

He shook his head and linked me, “You kill him quickly because if you get hurt…” I cut him off, “I won’t get hurt.” He sighed, “Fine. I’ll kick your ass if you do. I’m one of the few who still can, you know?” I admitted, “I know.” I gave him a hug then my mom, Uncle, and cousin. I watched for a second while my mom literally crawled into a closet to comfort those kids.

I popped out and took a few deep breaths. Oden growled, “Someone is messing with our sister’s sight, and I don’t like it.” I snorted, “You can say who it is. We both know.” He snarled, “Alania.” Yeah, she told someone how to do it. I replied, “Angela will get the last laugh. She’ll best them all.” Oden purred, “She will. Our sister is the best.” She was.

I made my way to the Demon portal. I picked the one on a mountain because I wanted the hike. Something Melanie couldn’t do right now because they wouldn’t let me heal her. That pissed me off all over again. I faded back when I reached the top and waited.

It was only five minutes before someone came. I grabbed the back of their shirt without them noticing and walked through into the Demon realm. I let go and trekked to where the man who needed to die lived. I easily felt Maximus nearby and sent him annoyance. He sent impatience and concern back. He’d expected me earlier. I assured him I was fine.

I went in through an open window in the target’s home. A silly mistake really when you lived how he did. I found him eating dinner. I commented, “That’s really not a good last meal.” He whirled, “You’re not the first to come and you won’t be the last.” He threw a knife. Oden scoffed, “Pathetic.” I called the wind and blew it away.

He frowned, "King Aiden sent you." I let my eyes blaze, "Guess again." He gasped, "A Conners child?" Oden grumbled, "Let me rip his throat out for that disrespect. We are a man." I simply stared at the Demon before popping behind him.

I partially shifted and let Oden rip his throat out. Oden muttered, "Again with the not shimmering away. No one wants us to have any fun." I had to agree with him. Maximus shimmered in complimenting, "Well done, cousin."

I said, "Angela says we have to find someone Underground. We should start in the basement." Maximus nodded. He commented, "I hate that she sees so much evil like this. Do you sense someone else here?" I admitted, "Nope. I don't hear a heartbeat or anything. Maybe it's a Vampire."

He stopped walking then said, "You should get out of here then." I replied, "No." Oden took over saying, "Our sister said we'd call Iblis, not a Vampire. I doubt it is one. Maybe there is extensive soundproofing in the underground room." That made more sense. Angela would've warned me if it was a Vampire. My wolf was definitely right about that. He snorted, "Of course I'm right."

We moved silently down the stairs. Maximus snorted, "He wasn't even hiding it." There was a massive door with a lock on it. I conjured it off and opened it. I announced, "I hear the heartbeat now." I followed it past the underground rooms.

I asked Maximus "Is it me or is this like some sort of time warp?" He said, "It does have everything looking very human realm nineteen fifties, just underground." That was weird. I kicked the door off the hinges, and I heard a scream.

She sobbed, "I did everything the book said. Please, just check. Don't be mad at me again." I gently said, "He's gone, and he can't hurt you again." She shook, "He is my master, and I love him." She was lying.

I glanced at Maximus and sent him the emotion this man must have tricked her about getting saved before. He went over and used his abilities to undo the chains. They were Demon made and required a strong fireball. My healing light told me she had high levels of copper in her system.

I told Maximus, "I'll need to heal her while you call Iblis." She whispered, "My master would not allow such things. Please put the cuffs back on. I will not be tricked by a fake rescue again." Oden growled angrily in my mind.

I asked, "Do you know any Fairies?" She admitted, "No." I said, "Well, I have Fairy blood so I can't lie. I promise you, this is not a trick. I killed the man upstairs." I grabbed her and popped her up to him. She swayed on her feet as Maximus shimmered in.

She saw the Demon with his throat ripped out and a giggle bubbled out of her. She pointed and laughed so hard she clutched her knees. She waved, "You ripped his throat out. It's too good." I looked at Maximus, confused. He shrugged and pointed to his phone.

I told her, "I'll heal you now. The copper will be out of your system soon." She snorted, "It's been there so long I barely even notice anymore. At this point, I wouldn't know how to use my powers if I tried."

I assured her, "You will." I healed her and stepped back. Maximus handed me a sandwich which I gratefully accepted. He said, "So, that wasn't good." I said, "He abused her and was making her Demon weak. I thought I'd have to call in mom." He ordered, "Conjure yourself more food. How long has she been here? Could your healing light tell?"

I admitted, "I hope I'm wrong." He asked, "Why?" I said, "Because I think some of those injuries were twenty plus years old." He jerked, "Good god. Iblis's son was looking for him. Hopefully he will…" He trailed off and we both drew weapons as a shimmer started.

Iblis raised an eyebrow, "You did call me, young Maximus." Maximus snorted, "I am not young." He glanced past me and grinned. He said, "I see Bjourn had you kill him. Good." He hadn't noticed the woman who hadn't regained consciousness after my healing.

Iblis asked, "Why on earth are you eating so much, Alexander?" His eyes looked like a flame when he asked, "Did this whelp hurt you?" I answered, "No, we found her." He turned and gasped, "Asmodeus, above." I asked, "You know her?" He nodded and tears filled his eyes.

He picked her up and she blinked. She snorted, "You look like King Iblis. Not that I met him. I was going to, then I was put into this hell." He said, "I am Iblis, and my son has not been the same since your death." She snorted, "Uhh I did not die."

He admitted, "He did not believe you had, but we found all the evidence. Your family buried what was determined to be your burned body. My son has not stopped searching the realms for you and we thought he'd gone mad."

Which son? Oden snorted, "There really is no way of knowing since he has so many." Maximus offered, "If you'd tell me who to call, I'll get him." Iblis said, "You've never met him. We've barely seen him because he refuses to quit searching. My children wanted me to order him to do so, but I could not. I have given the full funds to continue his search to do what he feels is needed."

She sobbed, "He got close several times. I miss him so much." Iblis said, "He loves you and you both already had my permission to be spears then, and now that can happen if it's what you wish." Oh shit. Someone faked the death of Iblis' child's chosen mate?!

Oden snorted, "He's lucky we ripped his throat out then." My dad linked, "You felt weak earlier. Why? Are you ok? You feel shocked now. What's going on?" I answered, "Maximus and I liberated a woman whose been in captivity for quite some time and she happens to be someone a child of Iblis' wanted as his chosen mate."

My parents popped in. My mom glared at Iblis. She pointed, "You know if people would FUCKING TELL ME SHIT, I would solve their damn problems." He explained, "She was supposed to be dead. We had evidence. My son couldn't let her go, or so I thought. He had no proof she wasn't dead. Or none that he gave to me. I would've asked you to pop to her if I thought she was alive."

My mom sighed, "Fine. I accept that answer because you mean it. Which son?" He admitted, "You never met him." She muttered, "Because you have so many damn kids." He laughed, "You are one to talk." She snorted, "Are you fucking serious right now? You have A SHIT TON more kids than Eric and I." He winked at her and fired off a text on his phone.

He admitted, "I don't know if he'll read it. He's out of touch a lot." My mom rolled her eyes and popped out and back with a man. He said, "I don't know you and..." The woman whispered, "Astaroth." He whirled and put a hand to his heart before grabbing her out of his dad's arms.

He held her tightly as though she may disappear. He sobbed, "Lamia. I knew it. As Asmodeus is my witness, I knew you were alive. I have been searching for you far and wide across all realms. Time has stopped moving since you were taken from me. I'm so sorry I didn't protect you."

She told him, "You kept me going." He asked, "What happened to you? What are you wearing?" She snorted, "That evil spawn preferred human women from the fifties. I guess he fancied himself in love with my grandmother, who smiled at him in school once for the week he was there. He decided to take me and turn me into the perfect nineteen fifties human wife. Though I don't think he understood humans back then. It didn't go well."

I asked, "How long have you been down there? The injuries I healed suggest at least twenty years." She answered, "Twenty-three years, nine months, and twenty three days. I would tell you the hours, but I only got calendars, not a clock. Maybe because I had one and cracked the glass and cut him. One could not say."

Astaroth laughed, "Did I not tell you about her fire and humor, father?" Iblis kissed his son's forehead, "You did. I am sorry I did not believe you, son." He looked pretty upset with himself. Astaroth said, "You thought I had lost it yet you gave me everything I needed."

He squeezed his dad's hand saying, "Many called me crazy, but you simply called me your son. You were worried about me and gave me everything I needed to do what I had to do. You argued I had to do this and let me do so. Thank you for coming to her."

He turned to me and Maximus, "You both have a marker from me for anything you need." Lamia cried, "A marker? For me? After all this time?" He said, "I will love you through space, times, realities, and one life to the next. You are it for me and you will always be. I pledged that to you then and I meant it. I truly never stopped looking for you."

She said, "I knew you had because we moved multiple times." I said, "It's probably why he had such intense soundproofing. I couldn't hear her heartbeat upstairs. My sister saw her when she heard about my mission and told me to save her."

My mom handed her a card. She said, "I will speak to you anytime you wish, free of charge." Iblis replied, "I will pay you, Haley. She has the weight of my family behind her. I was going to mark her as one of mine and give my son permission to take her as his spear. Astaroth told me how much he loved her, then proved it every single day for over twenty years."

My mom shrugged, "It's not necessary." He disagreed, "It is." He turned, "Lamia, you are now a daughter to me." He marked her as one of his and nodded to his son. Iblis asked, "What do you want to do Lamia?"

She snorted, "Are you serious? I want to have sex with my man. Do you know nineteen fifties women aren't allowed to masturbate and that fucker wanted me to beg him to have sex? When I tell you your son is magic between the sheets, I mean it. I haven't had sex since I was taken."

Oden blew out a sigh of relief and I had to admit, I did too. I would've hated for her to be raped. My mom busted up laughing. She waved, "I'm sorry. I can just imagine how fucking pissed off your captor was when you refused to beg." Lamia winked, "It was the highlight of my day."

My mom squeezed her hands, "You're a warrior and a survivor." Lamia's eyes filled with tears while my mom continued, "When you have times where you fear this is not real and you're not free, call me. Or speak to Astaroth. Find your person to center you and remind you this life is real. I struggled with that myself when I went to my Hackura family."

Uncle Bjourn portaled in and asked, "Little one, are you ok? You pulled me and Gunner had your location with Alexander and…" He trailed off and asked, "What's going on here? Astaroth you're…" He stopped talking when he eyes landed on the woman in his arms. He asked, "Is that Lamia?" I answered, "Yup." He rubbed his temples.

Iblis said, "I find myself wondering if anyone is really dead. I need to go to speak to Asmodeus." He turned, "Are you ok, son?" Astaroth grinned, "For the first time in a long time I can tell you I am fine." Iblis nodded, kissed the top of his son's head, then shimmered away.

My dad put a hand on my shoulder. He said, "You did really well tonight." I asked, "And where are we on the rogues?" My mom shot a sharp glance at me. My dad replied, "I have places for you to go if you need to do that." Oden growled, "I do."

I whispered, "She was a prisoner so long, but he never gave up. Even when all the odds were stacked against her." My dad hummed. I added, "He never stopped loving her." He nodded. I vowed then and there, I would be the same way about Melanie that Astaroth was about Lamia.

I would meet Melanie one day because I was stubborn, and I wasn't giving up on her and us. Oden grumbled, "I'm so glad you admit that she's ours now." I said, "We will know in person someday, but there is nothing to say if she's not we can't be chosen mates." He hummed, "Except she's ours."

Either way, I didn't think it could go any other way at this point. We were both set on her, much like my dad was set on my mom. Oden growled, "Yes, because like Mom and Thor SHE IS OURS!" I had to stifle my smile at that.

My dad linked, "There's a pack in Nevada that needs help, Shine Low Pack." I nodded and popped out. The Alpha jolted. He snorted, "Damn if you're not your dad's mini me." I admitted, "We all are. Why haven't we met?"

He answered, "We don't make it to Summit's because it's always on the same dates that are important to our pack that we celebrate." I hummed, "Well, I'll just see if we can't change that." He laughed, "Wow. You are like your dad."

I asked, "How do you know him?" He answered, "He took over this pack and had me put in charge. He was my Alpha once upon a time. He gave me the opportunity to come out here and now everything I have is because of him." He put out his arm and his Luna came over to him.

She was pregnant. I congratulated them, "Congratulations on your little one." She laughed, "This one is a surprise. Our oldest pup is seventeen and wants to run around with you tonight." A male voice chimed in, "I want to go too!" The Alpha chuckled, "That's my son, he's sixteen." Their daughter walked over and nodded to me.

She said, "I'm going to be the Alpha around here and I'd like to see how you handle the rogues since your dad said that's why you were coming." I replied, "I can stick to wolf moves if you'd prefer." Oden snorted, "We were doing that anyway." I had planned to kill a few in human form.

She shrugged, "Do what you want. I can learn and adapt. We have partial Fairies in our pack too. In fact, my pups will be partials themselves." I laughed, "Your mate is a Fairy?"

A man popped in beside her and to my surprise I didn't know him. Given my mom trained partials, I'd met most of them and he was one. He answered, "Yes, our kids will attend the trainings your mom holds."

I asked, "Did you? I don't recall seeing you." He winked, "But I remember you. You were a very cute baby, but your sister was adorable. I hope my kids have that cherub look she did." Ok. I said, "Then I hope they do too." The Alpha sighed, "Yeah, them meeting is your dad's fault too." I threw my head back and laughed.

The Fairy asked, "Are you off on your adventures, love?" She kissed his cheek, "You bet your Fairy ass." He said, "Be very careful and learn from the best." He turned to me, "You may be my Duke, but I warn you now not to let any harm come to her." I replied, "I won't." She sighed, "He's protective." I shrugged, "He's a mate."

We shifted and took off. Oden snorted, "Does the younger one think we don't know he's following us?" I popped behind him and his sister doubled back. They were probably linking but he ended up staying. I let Oden follow the scent to an actual pack of rogues.

I linked my dad, "Did you know the rogues are making packs? Because this is one." He growled and he and my mom popped beside me. I linked, "We could handle this." The pack showed up with the Fairy mate. Oden linked, "They should've heard all that. They are too far gone as rogues." There might be some that weren't though.

We surrounded them with the pack, some Fairies, Hackura, and our Warriors. I linked the Warriors from our pack, "NOW!" We jumped into the fray. I heard my mom yelling at some, "Stand the FUCK down! They are fucking children!" I went to the Alpha of the group with my dad.

He snorted, "The Conners have dared to show up. You're too late. I'm too powerful!" Angela linked me and my dad, "YOU NEED TO MOVE! PATHS JUST CHANGED!" A group of them threw a pot of wolfsbane at my dad. I shouted, "NO!"

I jumped in front of him and screamed in pain as I shifted back. My dad roared in anger and jumped on the Alpha. I whispered, "Oden." He whimpered in pain. My mom screamed so loud I not only heard it but felt it in my soul. The sky crackled with her anger.

She popped to me, but a rogue was coming at her. I pulled up my Hackura side, conjured a weapon and popped behind her and killed the rogue. I screamed out a war cry and let my rage loose. How dare they try to hurt MY parents.

I was cutting through the rogues knowing my mom was on my six. I noted my brothers had shown up along with several of my cousins and all of my uncles. I pushed at several rouges and saw them taking orphaned pups.

"Come with us and have a family. You have those genes you don't understand. We can help you." I yelled out another war cry and pushed harder letting their heads explode. I took a deep breath when my dad came into my line of vision.

He ordered, "Alexander, let your mom heal you." I grabbed him, "You're ok." He gave me a look replying, "I am fine." He linked me, "If you EVER jump in front of wolfsbane for me again I'll kick your ass. I can take it." But I couldn't. My senses would go haywire if my dad got hurt.

My mom's healing light enveloped me. When I came to, she was cradling my head in her lap. She kissed my forehead. She linked, "You were very brave and selfless to save your dad that pain. Just know that we are the type of fucking parents who would save you kids that pain every damn time."

She added, "I'm so proud of everything you did tonight. I know there are other emotions driving you, and I'm here if you want to talk about them. I'm also adding a part of your training for your Fairy abilities. You could've called the wind, or me, instead of jumping in front of the wolfsbane."

I argued, "I had a second…" She interrupted, "And you acted exactly how I fucking would've. I've done that exact move, and your Uncle Bjourn had my ass in training. So, you'll do the same. Ok?" I nodded, "Alright." I was proud to be like her.

My dad helped me stand and yanked me into a hug. He clapped me on the back, and I did the same. EJ was standing there to my shock. I asked, "Brother?" He glared at me snarking, "Yes, brother. WHAT THE FUCK?!"

Cassie snorted and I hugged her and nodded to Cayden who was standing behind her. I told her, "You go home, and I'll be there tomorrow." EJ sighed, "I see we are ignoring our big brother. Something clearly happened tonight that SO MANY people have to explain to me."

I urged, "Go back to honeymoon. I didn't mean to interrupt you." He yanked me into a hug. He linked, "If you think this is the end of this conversation then you have not been paying attention. What happened?"

I replied, "You were missing two guests at your ceremony and reception." He growled, "You're fucking kidding me!" I snorted, "They actually have a reason this time, but Elise might want to give her parents a call." He pulled back and hugged everyone before he popped back out.

Max asked, "Why did dad have to go all Alpha rage on the asshole who threw wolfsbane at him and my brother? I wanted to hurt him." He kicked an arm, and I noted that my dad had literally ripped the man to pieces.

I asked, "How did he know our wolves?" My mom snorted, "You're fucking bigger than every other damn wolf. Plus, Oden is distinctive." Oden was black and white so that was true. Uncle Bjourn answered his phone, "Gunner." He hummed, "I see."

I asked, "What's going on?" He said, "There were funds this Rogue Alpha had to support them, but they were donated to charities that you support within minutes of the news going out about what happened here." I clarified, "My charities?" He nodded.

My mom questioned, "Who the fuck did that?" Uncle Bjourn answered, "We don't know." My mom scoffed, "What?" He nodded. She waved saying, "Harper's boytoy lover will get the answer." My Uncle admitted, "The answer comes back to him, but he didn't do it." I rubbed my temples asking, "Huh?"

He explained, "The signature on the bank codes is your Uncle Gunner's. I'm sure someone in the technology division took it upon themselves to do it for him. He's pushing to get the station now, but it's handled."

My mom snorted, "You think an overfuckingacheiver did it, then didn't announce it was them? No. Absolutely not." His phone beeped again, "Yes, that's what happened. The man went to the bathroom and everyone was congratulating him when he came back." My mom raised an eyebrow, and I could tell she didn't believe he did it, but said man would tell Uncle Gunner if he hadn't.

I felt my mom's gaze and turned to meet it. I saw confusion on her face, but didn't know what it was about. Theo hugged me tightly. Angela popped in with tears in her eyes. I linked, "Little one, it wasn't your fault." She hugged me tightly and the whole family ended up in our group hug minus EJ. TJ even popped in.

Angela linked, "I'm so tired of assholes changing their mind and plans at the last freaking minute!" I agreed, "People suck." She huffed. I said, "People changing their minds is not your fault." She whispered, "It was so awful. Dad got hit in some paths and you did in most. I don't like seeing you hurt."

Eventually, we were ready to leave. The Future Female Alpha I'd been running with called, "Hey, Alpha Alexander." I turned and she stuck out her hand. I gripped it and she whispered, "Thank you. We had no idea it was a whole pack. When I think of what could've happened here…" She shivered and assured me, "We are making plans not to brush off attacks like we had and beef up our patrols."

I assured her, "There was no way you could've discovered them like that. I found them because I have a better sense of smell." She nodded, "Well, my mate is going to implement some intense protections around here." I agreed, "That's a good idea."

She added, “My parents are quite taken with a few of the siblings that were from the orphanage they took these pups from. They were from Maryland, but I just bet they stay here.” My mom said, “We will find placements for them, and I have several families that already want to meet their adorable fucking asses.”

She’d started a Supernatural site that linked same sex couples, couples that wanted to adopt, or people that didn’t want to be a parent, but were willing to be surrogate, donors, or looking for other types of situations.

The families and pups had profiles, and they could chat and find the right fit for everyone. My dad was wrapped around my mom nodding at her every word. A pang hit my heart because I wanted that, badly. I wanted to be like that with Melanie.

Oden grumbled, “We would if you’d just go demand to meet her.” I argued, “That would not help with the current situation where they are scared of me.” He snorted, “They can be scared all they want. She’s OURS.” Hopefully. He sighed, “And we are back to that word.”

Phil punched my arm. I asked, “What?” He growled, “WHAT? He says what!” His brother, Jeffery, chuckled, “Little brother, he’s an Alpha blood.” Phil said, “When one encounters a Rogue PACK, they call THEIR BETA WHO IS ALSO RELATED TO THEM!” I said, “I don’t exactly have my phone.” I didn’t when I was out, so I had a bracelet with a tracker.

He hit me again while Jeffery laughed. I asked Jeffery, “You even came back from your mission, cousin?” Phil yelled, “YOU ARE KIDDING ME! LINKING ALEXANDER, IT’S A THING!” Jeffery snorted, “He’s not. As far as my mission, I felt your pain. We ALL came the second we felt that. I’m sure Elise was either sleeping or she’s kicking and screaming pissed off at your brother that he left without her. She’s such a fighter, our lead Luna.”

I snorted, “She’d be asleep. She’s an Alpha who can handle herself so EJ wouldn’t have left her behind if she wasn’t.” I checked my bond with EJ feeling every sense that I was right. Angela called, “She was sleeping, but she gets mad he didn’t wake her up.” She’d be more focused on Melanie and Sam soon enough.

Hastein faded in and I hugged him. I nudged him, “So, the realm has go getters anticipating Uncle Gunner’s orders.” He shrugged, “So it seems.” I snorted, “You and mom seem to have a whole other theory.” He said, “I’m certain I have different suspicions than she does because I know more things. She suspects something like I do, but she doesn’t have the who.”

Phil rubbed his temples. I asked, “Who do you think did it and lied to Uncle Gunner?” He said, “I’ll have to ask said person when I go home.” He wasn’t going home for some time, and this wasn’t a high priority. He walked over to talk to my Uncle Bjourn.

I linked Phil, “Who do you think he thinks did it?” He scoffed, “Oh, so NOOOWWWWW you want my help? NOWWWWW you can link me? Sure. Let me just answer ALL your questions. He thinks Melanie did it. Why? I don’t know but he clearly does.” I snorted, “She isn’t a hacker.”

Oden purred, “She could be.” Yeah, but not good enough to hack into the Hackura and make it look like one of them did it using Uncle Gunner’s code. No one was good enough to fool him. Phil said, “See, here’s the thing. She’s a genius. So, could she be a hacker? Sure. Obviously. She is not like us mere mortals.”

“Do I think she’s good enough to hack into the Hackura? No. Give her time then maybe she will be. Especially after you two meet and she becomes my official Luna. She’ll hang around and the minions in her brain will have her hanging out with Gunner.” I snorted at him.

He asked, “What? Geniuses totally have minions in their head that make them do all these things. Maybe someone looked up things about highly intelligent people. Maybe in doing so I have found I am not the only member of the family doing so.” My jaw dropped.

He continued, “I know you’re thinking obviously your dad does, and he so did. He’s just not the only one doing such things. CAYDEN, and yes I do mean your brother in law, is looking up these things. You are so not as subtle as you think.”

I replied, “Cayden thinks he knows, but that doesn’t mean that he does.” He sighed, “Literally the only person without a clue, and mind you that will come back to haunt us all, is Cousin Haley. I’m certain that's because for some reason when she says Melanie isn't real, we don't insist she is. Seriously though, the fact your mom doesn't know will end up being the worst thing ever. I see horrible, horrible pranks in all our futures. They will probably be legendary."

Oden growled, "I could just tell her." I asked, "And you want our mom to be disappointed she raised a possessive jerk?" He replied, "We are NOT a jerk. Obviously, she knows we are possessive. You are aware I'm an Alpha wolf and she's mated to one." I sarcastically replied, "You know, that escaped my attention." He scoffed, "I'm beginning to think that it did."

I sighed, "I don't like fighting with you." He admitted, "I don't like it either. So, just admit I'm right and everyone gets to be happy." I smirked. Phil said, "Rocket is saying interesting things." My mom popped over asking, "About what?" He lied, "Geniuses and minions in their brain."

She tilted her head, "Do you mean that movie about the little yellow people working for Gru?" Phil laughed, "Yes. Can we get those to come to life?" She answered, "Of course." He grinned, "That should be a party idea. We can even have them plan to steal something. Think of how much pups would love that!"

My mom's eyes gleamed with the party idea. She admitted, "That could be a great joint party for Elise and me to have to transition the pups looking to her instead of me." She hugged Phil then me. She said, "Thanks for the really brilliant idea. Fucking genius." She popped away.

I smacked him across the chest, "Minions! The pups are going to be working on stealing something with minions." He laughed, "This is going to be hilarious, and Dylan will be jealous." I admitted, "I can't believe this hasn't been done before." He shrugged and I knew he was too, but then again, my mom didn't really watch many movies unless Cousin Miley had her watch them.

I linked him, "Why do you think Melanie would move the money around? I'm certain she can't look at a screen with her injuries right now?" He replied, "I swear you are so dense about her crush on you." I retorted, "Because she doesn't have one?"

He snorted, "Riiiggghhhhttttt. Whose wolf does her stuffed wolf look like again?" Oden purred because it was us. I said, "That's a coincidence." He snorted, "Cousin, you are overlooking way too many details. It's not a coincidence."

Jeffery commented, "Silent conversations make Beta bloods curious. What's up with you two?" We both answered simultaneously, "Nothing." Jeffery rolled his eyes, "Even without a bond, I knew that was a lie. With it, I know. Don't worry, I'll figure it out. There is clearly something going on that several people know about that I don't. How exciting."

Oden growled in my head. I shrugged, "It's not really that exciting." Jeffery grinned, "Sometimes I think I have more Fairy blood than you do, Alexander." I rolled my eyes, "You don't have any." He laughed, "Yet I have more fun."

Dylan shouted, "ENTER ME! I did that! I cultivated the fun gene in the Beta's with my classes with you adorable pups running around." He waved at me, "I cannot be faulted that he's his father's spitting image."

He whispered, "Even if I do blame myself for making sure little Wesley was fun. The Moody Triplet was always a lost cause though. He's been like his dad since birth." My dad was walking over with my Uncle Harper.

I winked, "Thanks. I'll let my dad know you think so highly of us." He snorted, "As if he needs the ego boost of knowing I think he's a good man, Alpha, mate, and father." My dad replied dryly, "And now I can die happy."

Dylan squeaked, "TRICKERY!" He winked at me, "Check out your Fairy DNA coming out. Yet it was to my detriment, which shows SGAP DNA." He turned, "Hey SGAP, did you know the masses are worried about your lack of leveling up in your name?" My dad sighed.

Dylan continued, "You're basically a slacker at this point and people question your power." My dad rolled his eyes, "Yes, well I'll continue not losing sleep about a nickname you gave me not growing." Dylan sighed, "I know. It's so concerning. What's the matter with you? I'll schedule an appointment for a physical. Poor Ethan is just backlogged in your area with all the people he has to help."

I replied, “Our pack doctor is doing just fine.” Dylan snorted, “Yet this lack of leveling up has gone on unchecked. This is the man who had to take over as the youngest Alpha in years, and not even out of necessity. SGAP has been stagnant for SO LONG! I worry his level up days are over as he heads into retirement. Or he’s holding onto a doozy.”

He pointed at my dad, “Don’t you even think about it!” He snorted, “I just came over here to ask my son and cousin why, dear god why, they are having my wife throw a minion party.” Dylan jumped up and down.

He answered, “Because they convinced her you truly are evil! She wants to steal the moon! No, you want to steal the moon.” Dylan gasped, “Is that why you’ve been waiting to level up? You are working on some evil plot while I wonder if you are unwell?! It’s diabolical.”

He whispered, “So it’s totally what’s happening.” I shook my head. Oden said, “Fang actually asked if that’s it.” My dad shouted, “DYLAN, FOR FUCK’S SAKE! You know I’m not evil.” Dylan hummed, “I mean to humans you are.”

My dad retorted, “We are NOT human.” He snorted, “I know. We’d all be in jail if we were. Which would be sad because I’d have to watch everyone want to be YOUR butt buddy, ignoring my delicious, sexy bodacious bod.” My dad groaned, “Goddesses above, not this again.”

Phil chimed in, “She’s going to charm the minions to life and everything. The pups are going to plan something with them.” Dylan squealed, “I AM IN THE WRONG GROUP! I must help plan this party and then mirror it. I must set my wind up toys in action! PRECIOUS WATER FAIRY PRETTY LUNA OF MINE!” He took off chasing down Cousin Emmaline.

My dad handed Phil a hundred dollar bill. Phil laughed and took it. My dad sighed, “So, what’s up with the minion party?” Jeffery answer, “They were distracting her from some answer they didn’t want to give.” My dad looked and felt sad in the bond as our gaze met. He said, “I see.”

Jeffery clapped, “He knows too. Interesting. I so have to get on the team that knows stuff.” He told my dad, “They are having secret linking conversations and H has theories about hacking that don’t make sense.” My dad frowned and asked, “What theories?”

He said, “He thinks someone took credit for something they didn’t do.” My dad tilted his head and seemed to think about everything. The idea it was Melanie clearly came to him. Oden grumbled, “Just like everyone else he thinks mate couldn’t fool Uncle Gunner.” I replied, “Because she can’t.” I’d be lying if the errant thought that she could didn’t run through me.

That had my dad raising an eyebrow. Oden boasted, “AH HA! I knew it. You know and I know she could do it.” I admitted, “Ok, maybe I do. I just never heard anyone say she could hack.” I told everyone, “I’m going to head home.” My dad nodded, “Get some sleep then we can handle your debrief.” I nodded and popped out.

I grabbed my phone off my bed and called Jason McAlister. He answered, “Hey, I heard you were pretty damn busy tonight. Are you ok? That alert went out on my dad’s phone and everyone panicked. We even left Mel alone after she threw up.”

I asked, “She threw up?” He said, “It’s normal. Or so the pack doctor said. She looked physically ill reading my dad’s phone though.” He muttered, “And pissed.” Holy shit. Oden howled happily. I asked, “Is she any good with computers?”

He snorted, “She’s been better than me and T at computers since she was one and half. I swear she could work tablets better than us. Why?” I said, “You know my Uncle Gunner is always looking for talent.” He laughed, “She doesn’t hack.” Oden practically sang, “I think she does.”

I actually agreed with him. I told him, “Well, I’m fine. My mom healed me, and I just called up my Hackura side. Some asshole rogue thought they could come up on MY mom.” He snorted, “You’re right. Only assholes go for mom’s that have done nothing wrong. Your mom is practically a goddess.”

I agreed, “I know. Hey, you know I really would heal your mom and Melanie.” He replied, “Thanks for saying that, man.” He was about to say more when I heard someone quietly call, “Jase, I need help… looking at my computer screen was not a good call.” That was Melanie.

Oden snarled, “MATE IS HURT!” I knew that. I linked Phil, “Melanie is sick now because she was looking at her computer screen.” He shouted, “OH MY GOD SHE DID IT! You got hurt and she took all his money for YOUR charities." I reasoned, "We don't know that but I'd say it's suspect." Which made me peacock proud.

Jason said to me, "I gotta go help Ladybug get to the bathroom. She begged my parents not to withdraw her from her competition yet. She seems to think she can get better through sheer will." I said, "I would…"

He interrupted, "I've got to go. Melanie Jane, don't you think I didn't hear your feet hit the damn floor! Don't you dare try to get the bathroom, I'm coming. Then you can explain why the damn hell you had computer." He hung up.

Oden whimpered, "Mate needs us." She did and it cut me deep that I couldn't be there. I told him, "At least she's a suspect for who could've hacked into donate all that money. She was alone and with a computer." He puffed up, "That's right. She did it for us."

Now, I just needed to meet her and find out if she was good at hacking. Then I'd know. I grabbed a cookie off the plate in my room and instantly felt better. It was probably a coincidence Melanie had her computer. She couldn't hack.

Earth Shifting

Melanie is Fourteen Years Old

Melanie woke up ready to face the day. Tomorrow was Elise's Luna Ceremony, and I was ready. I walked downstairs and froze. The evil cookie lady was here, and she grinned smugly at me. I linked Tristan, "How do none of you know this lady is evil? She is looking at me like she wants to kill me." He growled, "Who?"

He came running down the stairs and growled at the woman who jolted. Mom gasped, "T!" He said, "She was looking at Melanie like…." Mom interrupted, "Melanie is never nice to her. No one is required to like anyone."

Tristan replied, "I'll growl at anyone who looks at Melanie like that and so should you." She jolted as if he slapped her, but it wasn't her fault. She'd eaten the cookies. Tristan grabbed my arm and led me outside.

He took me to my dancing area and asked, "What the fuck was that?" I said, "The standard… well… what do you mean? I told you the cookie lady was evil." He replied, "And mom didn't care. That's weird. Sugar should be ripping out of her to protect you."

I admitted, "I really don't know what you want me to say here. Like at all. Because I've told you all so many times about the mom monster cookies… and the evil lady who delivers them." He blinked several times as if that was new information.

He ran a hand through his hair saying, "Yeah, well that was weird though." I agreed, "It's always weird… like always. But no covens answer me about the cookies." He asked, "What about Ryan?" I asked, "Bishop? He didn't answer either."

He frowned questioning, "Didn't you just text him? Or call?" I said, "He doesn't answer their house phone when I call, and I don't have his number." He snorted, "You've met him…" I cut him off, "Umm what? I've literally never met him. I told you that."

He gaped at me before saying, "Surely you have." I stared at him, "Nope." He sighed, "I'll look into this harder than I have been." I shrugged, "Ok… but it would probably be better to just kill the evil cookie lady." He snorted.

I insisted, "It would be. If she stops bringing the cookies, my projection says it's over a ninety-nine percent chance of improvement." He laughed, "The store sells them, Ladybug." I shot back, "What store? Because I've never seen them in stores, or online… they literally only exist here."

He snorted, "Ladybug, that's not true. I've had them other places." Awesome. They'd infected more than this pack. I muttered, "They still don't sell them anywhere else." He reiterated, "I'll look into it. Why don't you dance?" We'd been planning to come here so I could.

I put my dancing playlist on and began to dance away all my problems. The evil cookie lady was here, but Tristan was onto her now too. She got overly confident and cocky. Elise's ceremony was tomorrow, and I could actually talk to Ryan Bishop in person… or Xander's cousins that were partial Warlocks. Corbin could help then his uncle would have to answer me. That was just logical.

Tristan called, "Ok, it's been several hours, and I've gotten everything I needed to finished. Let's get you home." I stopped dancing and asked, "What if we go to a training class?" He snorted, "I'll drop you off at one and let you terrorize the pack while I see if there's any paperwork to help out with there."

I muttered, "I don't terrorize people… or the pack." He snorted, "You beat them no matter the level of class you join. You do terrorize them, but the trainers love it." We walked to the gym while I told him all about the statistics of a pack that trained as hard as ours does.

He laughed until when we came in the current class groaned. Zane shouted, "Shut up!" He turned to me and smiled, "Hello, Melanie. This will be a fun class." That was probably true since his classes were always fun.

He paired me up with a Warrior looking to level up. I beat him in a few minutes which he grumbled about. I said, “You drop your left hand when you are about to throw a punch so… don’t do that.” He stared at me then started laughing. He ruffled my hair, “Thanks, pup. Take on your next victim.” I muttered, “It’s just practice.” He winked at me.

I went through the whole class, but none of them really gave me a challenge. All my fights were under two minutes on average. Zane called, “T, take Rocky on home.” Tristan came out laughing. He urged, “Come on Ladybug.” I sighed but decided to leave because I wanted to get home and plug in my new data.

The cookie lady was gone so that was nice. I saw some sitting on the table and threw them away then went upstairs to my computer. I plugged in all my new training data and sent it to Nick Kyle. He helped train me and he thought my tables were intriguing.

My dad came in announcing, “Dinner is ready. What’s that?” I answered, “My statistics on training in the classes I drop in on, with my win rate versus the level of Warrior.” He grinned asking, “Oh really?” I nodded. He came over and looked over it.

He kissed the side of my head, “You’re an amazing fighter, pup.” I replied, “Thanks, Pepper.” My dad took back over saying, “I’m very proud of you. This is impressive and I need to have a chat with Zane. Let’s eat.” Because my stats weren’t possible but they were true.

I went downstairs with him. Once we sat down my mom warned, “I expect you all to treat everyone who comes into this house with respect.” Tristan cut in, “Melanie had nothing to do with me growling at that woman.” My dad asked, “What now?” Tristan said, “That lady who delivers mom’s cookies was glaring at Melanie like she wanted to kill her, so I growled.”

Mom sighed, “You’re being overly dramatic. She is my friend.” They were not friends. I innocently said, “I didn’t realize she’d hung out with you, Valerie, and Momma Chelsea.” Mom replied, “She hasn’t.” I asked, “Has she met them?” She admitted, “No.”

I said, “Statistically speaking even when friends aren’t the same groups, they’ve met each other. I don’t even know the evil cookie lady’s name.” Mom frowned, “Sure you do.” Dad admitted, “I actually only know her as the evil cookie lady or the cookie deliverer.”

Mom rolled her eyes, “You guys are so dramatic. I swear sometimes you never listen to me.” I asked, “So, her name is….?” I trailed off intentionally. Mom snorted, “If you don’t listen to me, you don’t get to know.” I sighed in annoyance.

Dad put a hand on her thigh, “Come on Sam, tell us. I’m sorry I never heard it before.” Mom stood so quickly her chair hit the ground. She scoffed, “I do so much, and no one even listens to me talk about my friends.” I muttered, “She’s not your friend.” Mom pointed at me shouting, “ENOUGH!” I quickly stopped talking and she took off outside and shifted.

I deflated and whispered, “I’m sorry.” Dad frowned, “Something else must be going on. That wasn’t like your mom at all. Sometimes, life is chaotic and messy and sometimes things are overwhelming, and people lash out. It wasn’t nice of us that we never listened to your mom talk about her friend.”

I replied, “She has never told us her name and that’s weird.” He rubbed his temples admitting, “I actually can’t recall ever hearing her name. I’ll go talk to your mom.” He got up and went outside and shifted too.

Jason asked, “Man, why did family dinner have to go that way?” Tristan said, “I think our sister might be onto something about the evil cookie lady.” I jolted, “What? You’re going to listen to me? Like really listen because… I mean… you should.”

Jason sighed, “T…” Tristan interrupted, “That was weird, Jase. We are Beta bloods. We don’t just forget people’s names yet none of us recall the name of mom’s supposed friend? I can name ALL her other friends and acquaintances.” Jason admitted, “I can too.” I thought cheering would be inappropriate, so I excused myself and went upstairs.

I read the most recent Fairy book Jared had brought me. Once I finished that, I wrapped my present for Elise for her mating ceremony. I grabbed Xander’s present for his Alpha Ceremony. I hadn’t gotten to give it to him because I’d gotten grounded for something I didn’t do. Again.

I heard doors slamming and sighing. I winced because this was my fault. Until we fixed the mom monster cookie situation, mom couldn't help it. Now, she was mad at everyone, which had to be the cookie talking. I quickly thought of plan and went downstairs and moved all the furniture around.

I yelled, "FAMILY DANCE PARTY!" I began to play my music and danced while singing. Tristan laughed and joined me seconds before Jason. Dad came up from downstairs and smiled at us. Mom cracked their bedroom door open.

I called, "Come on mom!" I belted out the lyrics to *Home* by Nick Jonas. She laughed but didn't come down. I did a dance move up the stairs and grabbed her. I slid down the banister like I always did. She shook her head at me, but she was smiling.

Dad called, "Come on Sammy girl." She laughed and slid down the banister and we jumped onto the main floor singing. We were dancing and spinning around when I saw an angry face outside our window. I rolled my eyes and stuck my tongue out at Robert. He pointed two fingers at his eyes the one at me. Saying he was watching me.

I looked around noting no one was watching me. I acted like my middle finger was lipstick, uncapped the top and put it on my lips before putting the cap back on and sticking my tongue out at him. He glared then took off. I turned and spotted Tristan still dancing but watching with narrowed eyes.

We danced well into the morning hours and everything was fine again. We did a big family group hug before we were ushered off to bed. I checked over my outfit for the Luna ceremony tomorrow. I slept in because my whole plan revolved around being here, at home.

I spent my afternoon on the phone with Elise. I wished I was there, but it was as close to in person as I'd been seeing Black Mountain. I laughed with her and Momma Chelsea until I had to jump in the shower and put on my makeup.

I was vibrating with energy and could admit I was eager with anticipation. I'd stayed inside all day so no one could say I was anywhere I shouldn't have been. I was finally going to meet my Xander. Everyone always laughed when I called him that, but I knew it was true.

He was mine and I'd always known it. He was mine. All I had to do was meet him, and everyone would know what I did instead of thinking I was a cute pup with a crush. Xander would know the second he saw me, just like with EJ did even before Elise was born.

I knew he'd take me into his handsome arms, then nothing could keep us apart. I just had to go to Elise's ceremony. It was crazy that there was this foreboding feeling inside of me that it seemed like something that wouldn't happen. To be fair, but I'd been burned before. Literally steps away from the car sometimes.

Out of nowhere the Warriors would say I'd crossed the border. My mom would be waffling until she ate a cookie. Then it was like she was possessed. The same thing happened with my dad. No one found it weird but me until lately. Tristan was finally listening to me and onto the evil cookie lady now more than he ever had been before.

My brothers both believed me in truth. I knew deep down my parents actually believed me. They'd always apologize when it happened when they got back. I'd be devastated for days, and they'd feel awful, but the pattern always repeated. The probability of it happening was over ninety-eight percent.

I shook those thoughts off. I just wanted to meet my Xander. Why wouldn't the Moon Goddess let me meet him? The one time I'd gotten out of the pack EJ and Elise's mating ceremony. I actually got into the car with my mom.

The headlights halfway there still flashed in my mind. I closed my eyes trying to remember it, because I swore I'd seen someone's face. They looked familiar, but I couldn't remember. The pieces never came back after that accident.

Because of that injury Xander got hurt. A Rouge Pack Alpha, I would've caught, hurt him. He threw wolfsbane at MY Xander and injured him. I'd stolen all his money though. Well, I gave it to charities Xander owned because that was fair. It was restitution and went to a good cause.

Our pack still didn't have any leads or suspects still to this day on who had caused my mom and my accident. It pissed dad and Peter off. The human cops stopped looking a long time ago, but my dad had never closed the case. I knew he wouldn't until he knew who did it. I just felt like I had the answer somewhere in my head.

I still hated that I didn't get to meet my Xander that night, and I'd missed Elise's big day. I wasn't missing today though. This was happening. I smoothed out my dress with my hands. I did a spin and twirled in the mirror. I looked perfect and I giggled a little at my reflection.

I was meeting my Xander. Everyone would finally know I wasn't just some crazy pup and would stop telling me it was a crush. Xander really was mine. I picked up my toy Xander wolf. I told him, "I'm going to meet the actual you tonight. You'll still be my favorite toy though. You're still my Xander wolf, just the toy version." I set him down when I heard people downstairs.

I skipped down to join them ready for my future to begin. My mom came in looking pretty upset. I stalled slightly but I knew I hadn't done anything. My dad was right behind her with my brothers. Tristan and Jason both looked mad.

My heart stopped when I saw the Warriors behind them. No. Not today. They couldn't lie today! It was Elise's Luna Ceremony. My dad sighed, "Ladybug, do you have anything you want to tell us?" Tears filled my eyes, "No! Don't you say it! I didn't even leave the house today!"

My mom sighed, "Ladybug, they said they saw you." I shouted, "LIARS! I have been here ALL DAY! I haven't left. T, Jase, I didn't leave! I didn't!" My mom grabbed a cookie. I screamed, "NO! DON'T EAT THAT!" She frowned, "I need a snack."

I snorted, "Now you'll transform into the mom monster who doesn't EVER believe me!" My mom frowned but still took a bite. I looked around wondering if anyone else noticed it was like her hand was moving when her brain didn't tell her to.

I asked, "Does no one else find that weird?!" The Warriors were all looking at each other. Traitors! My mom ordered, "Go to your room, Melanie Jane. You can't come tonight." My dad turned to her surprised.

I gasped, "You CANNOT be serious! It's Elise's Luna ceremony! I have to go!" My mom shrugged, "You shouldn't have crossed the border then. You know the rules. Do you not care about us? The council sets these rules Melanie Jane. You are not to cross the border."

I insisted, "Just call Momma Chelsea! I was on the phone with them all afternoon!" My mom scoffed, "Don't you even try to involve them in your lie." I remained calm, "I'm not lying, just ask her. Link, call, text, whatever. She will tell you I was on the phone with them."

She wasn't near the cookies, and they didn't seem to make people lie, just act irrationally and indifferent. Well, that wasn't true, they made people angry. She handed my dad the cookie. I begged, "Daddy, don't eat it! Please! Just ask Momma Chelsea, please!"

My mom clearly linked him, and he ate the cookie. Almost against his will too. I turned to the Warriors shouting, "WHAT IS WRONG WITH YOU PEOPLE?!" Their Beta and Beta Female where clearly being forced to eat cookies. Then seemed fine. It was weird.

My dad sighed, "Mel, don't get mad at them. It's their job to report unsanctioned crossing to Peter and myself." I snorted, "I know what their job is, and they should be ashamed that they aren't doing it. They may ACT like it's their job to lie about me but it's really not. Their job is to protect the pack. I state this because… I think they forgot that tiny detail!"

My mom chastised me, "Don't raise your voice. You are the one who messed up here." I yelled, "NO I DIDN'T! Not that you'll listen because you ate the stupid mom monster cookie, but I was talking to Elise and Momma Chelsea ALL AFTERNOON!"

My mom nodded, "Except when you slipped out." I groaned, "I didn't slip out. It was a video call… they obviously would've seen if I slipped out. What kind of logic is this?! Why don't you EVER just believe me?! You always say I'm a bad liar… and I'm working on it… but it's true! Annoyingly so. I didn't do this!"

My dad rubbed his head, and the Warriors looked at each other. Everyone in the room was acknowledging my words were true. I added, "You always believe me later. After said stupid evil mom monster cookie is digested! Do you know I've asked the kitchen workers about said cookies…. NONE OF THEM MAKE THOSE! Not one."

I continued, "They aren't sold in store, the evil cookie lady brings them and suddenly they are all over the pack. Which is weird since she ONLY ever comes into this house! She shows up at the house and turns my normal parents into weirdos with her EVIL cookies. You want to know what's weird? THE WARRIORS DOING NOTHING ABOUT THAT! Protecting the Beta family IS their ACTUAL job!"

My brothers frowned. My dad warned, "Don't talk to us like that." I shrugged, "Why not? You NEVER remember later. You'll be like... it's fuzzy but we should've let you come. I might as well say what I want." My mom ordered, "Go to your room. I'm so disappointed in you."

This refusal hurt more than all the others because it was about Elise. I missed her and the cookies prevented me from being in her wedding, then the accident, and now I was missing her big moment. It wasn't fair.

I snorted, "You're disappointed in me for not leaving the house? Yeah, how dare I do exactly what I'm told. You know what's ironic? I've NEVER crossed the border. Not once. I should. I can outrun ALL of you. I should go cross the border."

"I keep getting accused of it… I might as well. I might as well do something to prove if I WANTED to cross that border the ONLY way you would EVER know is if I wanted you to… BECAUSE I AM THAT SMART!"

My dad growled, "MELANIE JANE, do NOT joke about that! Crossing the border is dangerous! We don't want you to get hurt." I sighed, "Or maybe it's that you don't want me to finally have a life outside this pack. I'm the ONLY one who hasn't met all of the Conners... or the Lyons… Bartlett's… Thomas'… Or LITERALLY ANYONE OUTSIDE THIS PACK! Yet I keep crossing the border... to do what?"

I stared at the Warriors mocking, "Come on, tell what I cross for. You enjoy lying so make it up… like you ALWAYS do. Is it that I cross for fun? That doesn't make ANY sense though… not that it matters but it doesn't even sound like me. The only times I've left our borders are for dance competitions. Because you and those WEIRD COOKIES are determined to keep me here."

My mom rolled her eyes, "Ok fine. Blame the cookies. Don't accept responsibility for your actions." I growled, "Everyone in this room knows it's weird you're not letting me go. Elise is like my big sister. It's her LUNA CEREMONY."

"You could ground me tomorrow. You could tell me I can't leave your sight, but you're keeping me here. AGAIN! What are you two and your weird cookies so afraid of if I leave?! Or the better question is what is SOMEONE ELSE afraid of? That's the question the Warriors should be asking SINCE IT IS THEIR JOB!" Now they looked nervous because they knew I was right.

My dad said, "Melanie Jane, don't talk to your mom like that." I rolled my eyes. My mom warned, "Don't roll your eyes at your dad." I looked at my brothers who had been silent. I appealed to them, "I didn't do this."

Tristan interceded, "Dad…" My dad interrupted him, "She broke the rules." I interjected, "I didn't." Jason tried not to smile. My dad sighed, "And she's lying." I retorted, "I'm not." My mom yelled, "MELANIE JANE!" I shouted, "MOM!" My dad angrily raised his voice, "MELANIE, don't talk to your mom like that!"

I frowned asking, "Why? She did it. I was simply matching her energy… I have read that in a losing fight there is no reason not to do so. You only keep your cool when it matters, and it clearly doesn't here. You are determined not to believe me because of a cookie. The Warriors are determined to not do their job and go against their oath not finding a thing about this odd." I shot them a glare and several were now flushed.

My mom ordered, "Go to your room. You're not leaving with us. I'll tell Elise you are the reason you're not at her ceremony. You couldn't just stay out of trouble for her." Tears filled my eyes. It was really happening again.

I turned to the warriors, "I HATE YOU! YOU ARE A BUNCH OF LIARS AND I HATE YOU! I have NEVER done anything to any of you. Is it because I beat you in training?" Tristan winced. I wiped my tears, "That's it isn't it? You call act like you don't care… but you just get back at me by keeping me confined here… never letting me meet other packs… I hate you!"

All of them flinched. They should be upset. They sucked. My dad gasped, "Melanie!" I turned to him asking, "What? I DO HATE THEM! They lie about me, and you believe them! You NEVER believe me and I'm your daughter!"

"I've NEVER even crossed the stupid border without permission ever! I'm so tired of this ridiculous argument. I'm a genius… and you know it! Do you know how insulting it is you think I'd get caught? YOU MAKE THE PATROLS, DAD! Sometimes in my presence. You made these patrols in my presence, but you think I got caught… what kind of logic is that?" He looked confused.

They all stared at each other looking like they had no idea what to say. I whispered, "I'm asking you to believe me… even though you ate the mom monster cookies. Just once… please… someone believe in me." I saw the pain on their faces, but they still said nothing.

I scoffed, "You know what? I'm GOING to New York! I'm going to win that competition and I'm not coming back! I'm going to find people who actually believe in me. I'm going to find my REAL people who know when I tell them something is wrong LIKE EVIL COOKIES they look into it."

"I have told you FOR YEARS something is wrong here and you don't listen. I'm always punished for things I don't do. I'm done with no one letting me help or listening to me! You say I will change the world all the time, but you don't ever let me show you I can." I ran up to my room and slammed the door shut.

I held onto my Xander wolf and cried, "I didn't leave. I just want to meet my Xander." I squeezed him tightly. I whispered, "I just want to meet Xander. Who doesn't want me to? Is that it? Or is this the Warriors way of punishing me?" I'd never considered that before because it was ridiculous, but I didn't see another option today.

After ten minutes someone knocked on my door. I yelled, "Go away!" Tristan called, "It's me." I said, "Fine. You can come in." I clutched my wolf to my chest. He sighed, "Aww, Ladybug." I cried, "I didn't want to yell at them! They eat those cookies, and they never believe me."

Tristan sighed, "I'll figure out where the cookies come from Ladybug. If there's anything off with them, and I agree things are weird lately especially, people will suffer." I cried, "I'll never get to meet him, and I'm missing Elise's big night."

Tristan assured me, "You'll meet Alexander. It's only a matter of time. I AM really sorry about you missing tonight. Mom and Dad won't listen to me or Jase." I snorted, "Of course they won't. They ate the mom monster cookies."

I told him, "I didn't leave the house, T. I didn't. I stayed here all day. I was on the phone with Elise and Momma Chelsea. I picked out the perfect dress and I…." I burst into tears. Tristan held me consoling, "Don't cry, Ladybug." I sobbed, "Why can't I ever just meet him? I miss him."

Tristan rubbed his face, "You'll meet him when you're supposed to." I snorted, "At this point, the Moon Goddess hates me and is just blocking my path to him. Everyone has met him. It's weird that I haven't. I'll never meet him." Even though he promised we would when the Charline fiasco happened. That would hurt him and it wasn't fair. He didn't mean to lie.

Tristan conceded, "You might have a point, but you'll meet him." I snorted, "I always have a point. Everyone does when they talk… they are just usually incorrect. Mine aren't." He chuckled out a laugh, "I see we are more bug than lady right now." Probably.

I got up and got the presents I'd bought then crafted with my special security devices. I sighed and put Alexander in Elise's before I walked back out of my closet. I gave it to him. I asked, "Can you give this to Elise for me?" Tristan closed his eyes then agreed, "Of course I can."

I cried, "Can I just ride with you? I won't leave the car… I just want to watch." Tristan hugged me, "I would if I could, Ladybug. I'll figure the whole thing out. There must be a pup in a different pack that looks like you."

I nodded, "Ok. I love you T." Tristan replied, "I love you too, Ladybug. You'll meet Alexander one day. I promise." I wiped my eyes, "Ok." Tristan pleaded, "Don't leave and never come back." I flushed and remembered yelling that.

I admitted, "I didn't mean it." He hugged me, "I hope not." I cried, "I just want them to believe me." He assured me, "I do, little sister." I hugged him tightly. He sighed, "I hate leaving you this upset." I shrugged saying, "It's fine. Go be there for Elise. She's family." Tristan hugged me again and begrudgingly left.

I cried holding my Xander wolf and my pillow. Eventually I got up and packed everything for my trip to New York in my purple backpack. It was time to admit that the moment to enact Plan Z was now. I'd win the competition and then... I'd call Alexander with an emergency.

He could pop to me, and then we could come home together. I loved dancing and it was my passion. It was just that though, a passion. I wanted to be with my family and my Xander more. I was meant to be here. For something. I just knew it.

I threw in Alexander's hoodie with my dancing outfit. I was still annoyed it had gone through laundry and lost his scent by the time I spotted it. I would've known how he smelled if it hadn't. I hugged my wolf and packed it too. I threw in a few other things.

I realized I needed to call Elise. I tried to gather myself. I picked up the phone and started crying when it went to voicemail. I tried to explain. "I.... stayed.... home... all... day.... those... jerks... I mean they are nice… normally… Jerk may be harsh… but it's not! They lied. I'm... I'm so sorry Elise. I wanted to be there for your big day. It's not fair! I didn't do it, Elise. I wouldn't. Not today. It's such an important day for you. You're the big sister I never had, but always had… you know?" The tone cut me off.

I snorted, "That was hardly enough time when one is crying! Why don't providers think about that?" I made a note to work on that some other time and called back. I told her, "I sent your present with T. There's an extra present if you could deliver it for me. All those projects I was working on are under my bed. I was going to surprise everyone, and I'll just never get to." I broke off crying.

All the jewelry I'd been working on. I had them all under my bed. I was going to surprise them. I'd tried to perfect the multiple element piece, but it was tricky. My parents would be proud of me. I just wanted to show my Xander. I wanted him to know I was protecting both our families.

I asked, "Why can't I be there for you? Why can't I meet my Xander? He promised me we'd meet one day. Why can't that day be today? I wanted it to be today so bad…" Xander had promised we would meet when I texted him about Charline. His mom called her Charlooney. It was the best nickname ever.

My Xander believed in me at least. I knew his promise meant that we would meet one day, but I wanted it to be today. I wanted to be there for Elise. Why couldn't I have that? I couldn't stop my tears. Suddenly, I heard something being knocked over downstairs.

Oh gosh… I wasn't supposed to be here the last time people broke in. Did they target the pack because they knew everyone would be at Black Mountain? That would make this the logical time to attack. I looked at my phone noting the time.

Elise and EJ would be on their run. I whispered, "What the heck was that?" Then realized I was still talking to her voicemail and hung up my phone. I slowly opened my door. My eyes widened at what I saw. There were two Warriors down.

Protectiveness hummed in me. They may be liars about me crossing the border, but they were MY pack members. I was a Beta blood, and this was the current Beta's home. No one had a right to hurt anyone in this house.

I saw the man leading the group and nearly gasped. He was a Hunter. They specifically hunted Werewolves, but they didn't enter pack lands. I personally speculated that maybe they were supposed to hunt rogues and got confused on their purpose. Because they were Supernatural's themselves. It didn't make sense their purpose would be to kill us for existing when they did.

I frowned realizing he was with a few coven members. I wasn't familiar with the coven from the mark on their necks, which meant they weren't from around here. I still couldn't believe a Hunter was working with Witches.

They hated all other Supernatural's and claimed they weren't supernatural themselves. They hated themselves and anything that proved Supernatural's existed. So, what were they doing? The Witches were chanting over the Warriors and dragging them out of the house. Why would they do that?

I turned back and burned the man's face into my memory. He was tall with dark hair. He had a scar in the shape of a crescent moon on his face. He rolled up his sleeves and I saw that he had chosen to have two Hunters marks on each arm. That was a weird choice.

He had some injuries, along with the Witches, that indicated the Warriors clearly fought them. The living room was a mess. I went into my closet and brought a bat out. I had decided to learn how to play baseball one day and kept it as a weapon in case Robert and his friends tried to come into my room like they threatened to.

I turned off the lights and hid in the corner. I'd catch them as they came through the door. Hunters nor Witches had the eyesight like wolves to see in the dark. I'd use that to my advantage. I knocked the first one out easily. The second gave me more of a fight.

The man called out, "SLADE! HELP!" So, the Hunter was Slade. I slammed the bat into the guy's face ending the fight. I had to make it to the stairs. I ran out of my room and pushed Slade, who had been waiting outside the door, over the banister. He was groaning, so he wasn't dead.

I ran down the stairs and a mist surrounded me. What was that? It had to be a spell, right? When it cleared, I looked around. I saw Slade grinning victoriously with a gun pointed at my head. How did he get off the floor? Standing I was an easy target, but if I moved that made it harder for him to hit me. I just had to decide which way to go.

Tristan yelled, "MELANIE, NO!" My focused shifted and the gun went off. I had to move, but I'd picked the wrong way. I hit my knees as the pain seared through me. What was Tristan doing home already? I curled onto the landing and whispered, "Xander… save me Xander." I coughed up blood.

Another shot rang out, but I didn't feel pain. Horror filled me as Tristan dropped to the floor beside me. I screamed, "T, NO! HELP SOMEONE HELP ME! HELP US!" I tried to link the pack, "WE ARE UNDER ATTACK! HELP US!" I felt that it was stagnant in the link. I jolted realizing they were working with Earth Fairies too. Why?

I couldn't focus on that because my brother was gasping for air. I took my shirt off and put pressure on his wound. I cried, "T, don't leave me please!" Tristan gasped, "I love you, Ladybug." I cried, "What are you even doing here? You're supposed to be with Elise. It's safe there. Why aren't you there?!" He gurgled and his chest stopped moving.

I screamed, "NO! HELP! SOMEONE HELP US PLEASE!" I heard my mom scream, "TRISTAN! MELANIE! OH MY GOD! MY BABIES!" Something prickled in my mind, that that was a very human way to refer to us. She'd usually say pups.

I turned to see her get shot in the head and all thoughts of her word choice left my mind. Her brain matter spattered onto my face. I shrieked so loud they should've heard it all the way in Black Mountain. I ran over to her.

I cried, "Mommy! NO! I'm so sorry mommy! I didn't mean it! I'll stay here. Please come back. Please! I don't care about the mom monster cookies. I'll make them for you to eat… just come back." I tried to find the pieces of her skull… they looked like a jigsaw puzzle, but I was good at those. I could put her back together.

I heard an angry howl and saw my dad. I frowned knowing that was wrong too. He should've done two howls. The mate bond dying howl and protecting his pup's howl. Pepper sounded weird too. What was going on?

He attacked several people in the room. Where did they come from? How wasn't he down from pain with my mom dying? Where was everyone else? He reached me and I was about to ask when he was shot in the chest. It was getting hard to breathe. I wasted time thinking about my dumb questions and now he was dying.

I crawled between my parents. I cried as I hugged my dad. I said, "Daddy… please don't go daddy… don't leave me." He whispered, "I love you, Ladybug." He shuddered his last breath. I looked around the living room seeing that Tristan and my mom weren't breathing either. My last conscious thought was, "Thank god Jase isn't here to die with us."

I heard a river running. I slowly opened my eyes. I frowned, "You're not the Moon Goddess. Where's my family?" He was in all white. From what I'd read I was thinking he might be Life. In the books Jared lent me from Faerie I knew that Life and Death were brothers. Two sides of the same coin and I was certain I should be seeing the other brother given what just happened to me.

He smiled sadly at me saying, "I can't keep you long. All I can tell you is not everything is as it seems. Please just think about that. You had good questions you should ponder." He faded. Ok, so he was definitely cryptic, like the writings of Life and Death were.

Death was more the rule breaker and direct. Which wasn't surprising. He still skirting the balance of power when he appeared unless he had a loophole. Which was why the Fairies found the brothers so fascinating.

What questions? Did anything matter anymore? The answer was a resounding no. I'd yelled at Warriors, that were probably dead now. I'd yelled at my parents, and they were definitely dead. Even Tristan.

What if those cookies got him killed? He was going to look into them for me and now everyone was dead. Maybe it was just a bad dream. A really bad dream. Nightmare level, really. I heard a beeping sound. That didn't seem like something that should be in the afterlife. It was very annoying.

I opened my eyes noting quickly that I was in a hospital. What the hell? I looked around easily recognizing this was not our pack hospital. Based on the instruments and machines they had it was a human hospital. We didn't share all our technology with them, so it was easy to realize when it wasn't ours.

Great. I had such fond memories of the last human hospital I'd been in. My gaze landed on a woman I'd literally never seen in my entire life, but she wasn't a nurse or a doctor. She was sitting there as if she was waiting for me to wake up. Why? I didn't know her.

She noticed me watching her and put her phone down. She sighed, "You're finally awake." As if someone breaking into my home and my getting shot personally annoyed her. I frowned asking, "Where's my family?"

The woman rolled her eyes, "You saw them die. Or so I was told. I guess if you didn't know then I'll tell you they didn't make it." I flinched then cried, "No, they can't be dead! Where's Jase? Where's Grandpa and Grandma McAlister?"

The woman sighed, "Look, here's the deal. Jason met his mate. Everly." I jolted physically as if she'd slapped me. Was that why Tristan came home? I'd heard him say he liked her on the phone… ok I was eavesdropping. Everly and Tristan were talking all the time. They flirted and the moon goddess mated her to our brother? Jason knew Tristan liked her too. That was so mean!

The woman continued, "He's focused on her now. He's going to have to be the Beta which he wasn't expecting." I argued, "That's not true… he knows he'll be Christopher's Beta. They've just worked out how he can be the Male Lead Warrior and take that role. But he was always going to a Beta… too… he just planned on using the Male Lead Warrior title… which Christopher is fine with."

She corrected, "Alpha Christopher." I retorted, "He's practically my uncle and I've always… literally always… called him Christopher." She gripped my hand, "You will use all their titles per their request." Yeah, ok lady.

If we weren't in a human hospital, I'd break her face and hand for touching me. I had already mentally calculated that I was a better fighter than her. She didn't look like she'd trained a single day in her life. She continued, "Anyway, Beta Jason is basically training full time now."

I interrupted, "He's been full time training this entire time so…" She gripped my hand harder. She warned, "Stop interrupting me." I shot back, "Could you start making sense then? Jase has been training…" She cut me off, "BETA Jason." I stared at her.

I said, "Ummm you do know he's my brother… so…." She snarled, "He can't take care of you. Your grandparents are too distraught over the loss of their son and oldest grandpup." That didn't sound right either, but grief did often have people making snap decisions they later felt remorse over. This was just an odd one for a pack, let alone blood relations.

I questioned, "What about the Kyle's? They are my guardians if anything happens to my parents." It was literally in their will. My dad had told me, Tristan, and Jason that ever since we were old enough to understand everything. So, why weren't they here? Where was here?

The woman sighed, "They are upset. They lost their friends." I tried to sit up and gasped in pain. I asked, "Who are you? Where are my other grandparents? My mom's parents will take me." She sighed, "I was getting there. I'm your mother's sister."

I interrupted, "Excuse me? Like what? Her what? What? Just… I know it's coming out squeaking and confused… but I have no other way to ask… WHAT?!" She warned, "STOP interrupting." I reiterated, "Please start making sense! My mom is an only child."

She ignored me, "Your other grandparents called me. They can't bear to look at you as a constant reminder of the precious daughter they loved so much. I have no pups, so I'm stuck with you." I stared at her. Was I supposed to believe that? She didn't look like either of my grandparents or my mom.

She sighed, "Look, I get it. Saint Sam was always the golden one. I was adopted." Ok, that was the first thing she'd said that made sense. She waved, "Then they had their miracle pup, and I was forgotten." That literally didn't sound like my grandparents at all. Why had no one ever mentioned this woman? Other than the fact that she clearly had no empathy.

I told her, "Jase won't let you keep me." She snorted, "Keep up. He already agreed. He even sent you a letter. Look, you're already here. This is where I live. Nashville." Nashville?! My dad hated it here and so did my mom. They literally wouldn't even let me compete here. There was no way this was happening.

I cried, "NO! I want JASE! I want Grandpa Ben! I want Momma Chelsea! I don't even know you!" The woman stood and grabbed my arm tightly, "Look here little girl, my name is Stephanie McCann, and I'm your aunt."

I repeated, "My mom doesn't have a sister adopted or not. I don't know who you are, but I do NOT know you! Stop touching me or you'll need a hospital bed yourself." She glared at me, but I saw the fear in her eyes.

She released my arm saying, "That bitch would tell you pups she didn't have a sister." I growled, "Don't you EVER call my mom that!" She waved dismissively, "My mate was not popular before he died. It was NOT approved of that I went with him, even though he was my mate." Literally every word out of her mouth was more confusing than the last.

I questioned "Was?" Mentally I ran through memos wondering if I'd seen the name McCann on them but I wasn't recalling them at the moment. I could looking into archives though. Stephanie nodded, "He died. I have a new husband. You'll meet him when we go to the pack. He's a warlock. You can call him Uncle Ajax."

I sucked in a painful breath because that was Jason's wolf's name. I wanted to see my Ajax, not some Uncle I didn't know. I asked, "Can't I call Jase?" Stephanie sighed, "It's Beta Jason." I glared at her. She rolled her eyes saying, "I'm trying to help you pup. He doesn't want to talk to you."

I cried, "Why not?" Stephanie rolled her eyes, "Because you killed your family." I shouted, "I did not!" She repeated slowly like I was stupid, "Sam, Drake, and Tristan came back for you." I growled, "Beta Female Sam and Beta Drake."

Stephanie retorted, "You don't get titles when you are dead." I flinched again but said, "That's not true. You always have the title once you have it, dead or not." Hot tears rolled down my cheeks. I didn't want it to be true, but I'd seen it.

Stephanie continued, "They left Elise's Luna Ceremony early because you were upset. They shouldn't have been there, but they came back for you." I cried, "Coming home early suggests they would've gotten there! They didn't get popped in so they wouldn't even have made it there by the time our house was attacked. This doesn't make sense! T was supposed to spend the night! He shouldn't have been there!"

Stephanie growled, "They said you were smart. He WAS there. You saw him." I stared at her before I said, "I would have to lose over twenty I.Q. points to be smart. I'm pointing out a fact." She retorted, "Well they turned around because of your tantrum." I flinched as if she slapped me. I had yelled at them like never before and threatened to leave. She was right, this was my fault.

I whispered, "What about Uncle Duncan?" She answered, "As far as I know, he's not aware. He's out on some mission." She snorted, "Hopefully, he will want you and then I'll be rid of you. I don't like pups." Hope bubbled in my chest. I wanted anyone else to have custody of me over her. Her story was literally insane and maybe she was too. She threw an envelope at me. I opened it. There were two notes inside.

Melanie,

I have to look out for the pack right now. You know how loved your parents and Tristan were around here. Everyone is devastated. We can talk about you returning after you've shifted.

Until then, I Alpha Command you not to link anyone in the pack. Respect the fact we need to heal and not hear the rambling facts you have to offer. This is a devastating time for us all.

Alpha Peter Kyle

I gasped. He called me Melanie and signed with his Alpha title? He was like a second dad to me. Why did he write Tristan's name instead of T? He always called him T unless he was in trouble. Peter should be holding me.

Chelsea and Peter should BE here. Why aren't they here? I'm a pack member too! Why isn't Peter protecting me? Wait? After I shift? I can't come home for two years? Or link anyone?! I didn't feel the command take hold, but he was my Alpha. It probably had to be said out loud. Why would he say that?

Did that mean Jase wasn't planning on being there for my shift? Elise wasn't coming? Did she know what happened? Was Chelsea not coming? My heart broke, but Stephanie said Uncle Duncan didn't know. I could just stay with him, even if his pack was annoying and borderline terrible. I reached for the second letter.

Melanie,

I know you're confused, but this is how everything has to be for now. It's best this way. All of us are too hurt at the moment. After you shift everything could be different. Mom and Dad may never forgive me in the afterlife, but I'm doing what's best for me.

You know my dreams were to be the Lead Warrior. That went up in smoke tonight, along with our family. I sent your bag with you and everything you use in your room like your books and binders. I just can't be there for you right now. I met my mate, and she's my priority, along with the pack.

I can't raise you, Melanie. I can't. I can't deal with the fact that mom, dad, and Tristan are dead and see your face every day. I'll write and keep in touch. Aunt Stephanie will look after you. Do as she says. I don't want to hear about you misbehaving and crossing the border. We will talk soon.

Beta Jason

I sobbed. Not one ladybug? He always called me Mel or Ladybug. I wouldn't get in his way at home. I'd be good. What was with his signature line? This letter didn't even sound like him. I cried, "Please… let me call Jase… I'll tell him... I won't get in his or Everly's way… I just want to go home."

Stephanie slapped me across the face. I stared at her in shock. She went to slap me again, but I grabbed her hand. I saw her fear before I twisted it behind her back. I told her, "You'll never touch me like that again. I AM a Beta's daughter, and I can and will defend myself." She whimpered in pain.

It was like my memory came back online and I remembered the name McCann. Hell, I knew her name. She was a former Gamma's mate, but I could best her easily. Her mate died because he came to kill Luna Reagan Daniels. I'd briefly looked at an old memo about that.

I let her go and she whipped around like I'd done something she hadn't expected. There were rumors that the Nashville packs barely trained their lower ranked members and pups, but I was thinking they didn't train them at all based on her reaction.

She rubbed her arm as if she was waiting for an apology. I crossed my arms and glared at her. She frowned, "Look, you're not going home. This is your home now." I snored, "This will NEVER be my home." Stephanie grinned evilly, "We will see about that. Let's go."

I frowned pointing out, "I didn't get discharged." Or see a single medical professional. Stephanie retorted, "I'm your guardian and I'm signing you out. You'll have to earn your keep once you heal." I frowned, "What does that mean? Also, there's literally no way you're my Guardian. That would take days, given how the human system works." Her eye twitched.

I continued, "There would have been refusals and signatures from the Kyle's to dismiss my parents' wishes. A lot of lawyers and there are more people listed as guardian options. You are not one. Which means the Werewolf Council would step in to find a suitable home, and it would definitely not be here."

Stephanie ignored all that saying, "You'll be doing chores." I shrugged, "Ok... I did chores at home." Stephine said, "It's more like a day job." I looked at her before explaining, "Ummm I'm fourteen. I have to go to school." Stephanie shrugged, "I say you don't, and what I say goes."

My jaw dropped, "That's… beyond not legal." Stephanie snorted, "We are supernatural's, sweetie. We get away with murder. I don't think anyone will make a stink about you missing high school." I stared at her.

Eventually I said, "Umm the humans care about kids going to school and we live in their realm. The Werewolf Council cares about all of us getting a high school degree." She retorted, "My pack is overseen by the Supernatural Council."

I scoffed, "They definitely care about packs not drawing the attention of human authorities… like you seem dead set on doing… which is strange…" She stared at me. I muttered, "Fine. I'll get a GED." Stephanie waved her hands saying, "Problem solved. On the car ride home pick a new name."

I wanted to go back to bed and transport myself back to a time I'd never met her. I asked, "What?" Stephanie was clearly annoyed, but I didn't care.

She answered, "Your pack doesn't want to hear news about you around their allies. I personally doubt they will hear anything, but it was INSISTED upon that you pick a new name. So, you'll pick one. My pack will obviously know who you are, but in public they will call you by your chosen name." They took me from my home, family, and pack. Now they wanted my name?!

She continued, "You should be happy. I hate my name. Plus, my pack is even going to get you documentation for said name." I asked, "What pack?" She answered, "Black Path." Jason and Peter sent me to BLACK PATH?! They hated it here! They talked about how crappy it was, literally ALL the time. Dad and mom abhorred this pack!

Stephanie signed me out while I held my tears back. The nurses and doctors were not ok with her signing me out. I didn't see a single Supernatural on duty, but I saw several harsh looks going her way. Stephanie rushed us off before they could call CPS, which one nurse was doing as we left.

My side burned with pain, and I felt lightheaded. Logically, I must have lost a lot of blood. Was I flown here? What hospital would agree to make the flight when there was a level one trauma center in Black Mountain's territory? The human hospital and the pack one.

Alpha Eric was determined his area would provide the best care no matter if it was a Supernatural or Human. Was I driven here? Surely, they got me medical attention before I got to Nashville. We got into her car in a tense silence that grated my nerves.

I hated silence, but I'd never felt more alone in my life. Alpha Peter's note, in his handwriting, said not to link anyone. I just wanted to hear their voices, even if they yelled. I needed them.

Stephanie said, "As I said, during the day you'll do chores for the pack." She hadn't said it was for the pack. Which was against Werewolf law because that was a job. The Supernatural Council was not doing a good job monitoring the packs that didn't want to be overseen by the Werewolf Council then.

Especially if they were getting away with that. Which wasn't actually that surprising and I mentally chided myself for not realizing they were doing it to get away with doing shady things.

She continued, "Once you are recovered, I have another activity you'll be enrolled in." I didn't reply which she clearly wanted and to be honest it physically pained me to stay quiet. I didn't want to talk to her though. It was utterly clear to me she was a bad person with no empathy.

She angrily said, "Your brother said you are a good fighter." Jason had said good? I mean… at least he'd said something nice. Although he'd used different adjectives before I'd gotten our family killed. He often called me a brilliant fighter. Once he said I was the talent for my generation, and I was pretty sure I grew taller.

I acknowledged, "I'm good." Stephanie smirked smarmily saying, "We will see." Well, I had just gotten the best of her when injured so she knew I was at least decent. She added, "You'll be fighting with a special group called the Undergrounds."

I snorted, "That sounds illegal. They should've come up with a less obvious name… plus you said special group… be more obvious it's illegal… especially if you're forcing pups to fight… so… be better." Stephanie laughed hollowly, "Welcome to Nashville little girl. We get away with the obvious." Then the Supernatural Council was in a lot of trouble.

I studied Stephanie conceding we might be related, but I could see why my mom hated her. I studied her profile. The only common trait her and my mom had was their hair color. Which wasn't surprising since Stephanie was supposedly adopted.

Why would Jase send me here with strangers? When we got out of the car, I heard people whispering. Stephanie loudly said, "Don't be shy. People know who Melanie the family killer is." My eyes filled with tears, but I refused to give her the satisfaction of actually crying.

I didn't kill them like she was saying. I'd never hurt them! I got mad and they came home. Slade killed them. I wanted to scream that at her. Instead I just glared at her letting her know with eyes I could easily kill her.

A woman walked over admonishing her, "Stephanie McCann, how dare you! That was a horrible thing to say, and I heard what happened to this poor pup! A Hunter killed her family. Have some empathy, you horrid shrew!" I liked her a lot better than Stephanie.

Stephanie turned red with anger. The woman turned to me and knelt down. She cooed, "Sweetie, I'm Luna Elena Davis. This is my daughter, Addison." She waved a man over. She added, "And my son Caine, he's the future Alpha. I'm so sorry we aren't prepared for your arrival. We would've baked you cookies, but the pack doctor didn't think you would be released until later this week."

That didn't explain why I wasn't here in the first place. Why did they let me go the human hospital first? I explained, "She signed me out." The Luna looked at Stephanie. She sighed, "Honestly Stephanie, I cannot understand you. Why don't you let her stay with us? You don't know anything about pups, and they annoy you. She's not ready to be out of the hospital. To the pack hospital you go, little miss."

Stephanie angrily retorted, "The Alpha was fine with it." She was really saying that to the Alpha's Luna? Peter would have someone by the throat if they spoke to Chelsea like that. I knew my eyes were wide as I looked between them.

I glanced around noting there were several Warriors, but they weren't doing anything. What was wrong with them? No one should disrespect their Luna like this. They seemed confused by my confusion which made it weirder.

Luna Elena said, "But I am NOT. She's going to the pack doctor. She has been traumatized by the loss of her family. She's in a new place. Then you show up with your abrasiveness. When did she wake up?" Stephanie didn't answer.

The Luna demanded, "ANSWER ME STEPHANIE!" Someone said, "Lighten up, Elena." I actually gasped and waited for that person to get dressed down, but instead everyone looked at me like I was crazy. Stephanie sighed answering, "About an hour and a half ago."

Luna Elena said, "Get out of my sight before I slap you. Honestly. Taking a pup out of the hospital against medical advice." The Alpha walked up with the Beta. I didn't need an introduction to know who they were.

The Alpha said, "Elena, she's not our charge." Luna Elena looked at him snarking, "Did I ask you? No, I did not. She is a pup, and you agreed long ago pups were under my care. Well, I have decided that she needs care." I gaped at them. I'd never heard Chelsea speak to Peter that way. Luna Elena clearly didn't like her husband. The Beta and Alpha turned away without saying anything.

I called, "Alpha, wait please." He turned around. I said, "Umm a bunch of people were just disrespecting your Luna." He stared at me. He asked, "And?" Caine growled. I said, "Umm… that's… you're supposed to… well… be mad."

"No one is supposed to talk to a Luna like that… it's a bylaw in every single pack. Section Three code B. Treating a Luna disrespectfully has never been allowed since the beginning of Werewolf society. So much so, they literally had it be in one of the first five sections… so… umm… what is going on here?"

Stephanie snorted, "You don't know our pack bylaws." I agreed, "No, I don't…obviously…. since I just got here… but I know that is one because as I said, it's in every pack bylaw. It's a literally a law. So…"

Luna Elena interrupted asking, "It is?" I answered, "Yes." She whirled and stared at her mate and Beta. The Beta said, "I'll look into it." I said, "Ok… it's Section Three Code B… like I said… Wait… you don't know your own pack bylaws? As a Beta blood? Wait… just… what?" Stephanie growled, "Shut up, pup." I stared at everyone here who was now interested in me. I was used to that look though.

Luna Elena held out her hand saying, "Come with me dear. Caine, get her things please." I had never been so confused in my entire life. What was wrong with this pack? The Alpha still didn't say anything about the disrespectful way his mate was treated, but he watched her every move.

I saw that Caine had gotten my purple backpack out of Stephanie's car. At least, my Xander wolf was in there. We walked into the pack hospital. The doctor was visibly nervous upon our arrival. A nurse shoved him out of the way, clearly annoyed.

She glanced at me saying, "You need more fluids. You were shot in the lung. You can't do anything too jarring. Your healing rate is fast, so you won't be out of commission too long. I'm Cecila by the way." I asked, "What's the pack doctor's name?" He scurried away and I frowned.

Ceclia snorted, "He's not going to treat you because the Alpha didn't give him express permission." I blinked, "Umm what? That's not legal either. He has an oath… just… what is going on here? I'm so confused." Addison and Caine exchanged glances that said they were the ones that were confused.

Luna Elena sighed, "I'm sorry for the way things are around here, Melanie." The Alpha stormed in, and I was certain I was the only one who noticed his longing glance at his mate. Why was he being so weird with her when he clearly cared about her? What did he do to make her so mad? Other than not doing his job. Which he clearly did not. I guess that made sense she was so mad.

He asked me, "What name did you pick?" Luna Elena said, "Honestly Edward, she's just gotten here. Let her breathe." I would prefer not to, since breathing hurt quite a lot right now. Alpha Edward retorted, "I'm not starting a fight with Red Run. That would bring Blue Moon and Black Mountain against us. I'm not doing that for their cast away." That hurt more than the bullet had.

My eyes filled with tears and the Luna slapped him on the arm. She growled, "Edward, be the man I first met for five seconds. She's our daughter's age. If, god forbid, something happened to us would you want her treated this way?"

Based on his actions, he would not care…but this was definitely one of those moments Tristan would tell me not to say that. My eyes filled with tears again as I thought of my big brother. Honestly, Luna Elena should be worried about how he'd treat his daughter if she was gone.

Luna Elena continued, "By that horrible Stephanie woman then by a bullying Alpha?" She called her own mate a bully?! I rubbed my temples. She begged, "Please just have some compassion." The Alpha's jaw ticked. It looked like he considered it.

Then his eyes turned pitch black. His wolf whispered, "I can't fight him long, mate. I love you." Fight him? Why would his wolf fight him? His wolf should be more powerful than he was given his actions. He shook his head and looked at me. I noted his eyes were no longer black.

He'd taken back over from his wolf that easily when his wolf didn't want to give it? Something was very wrong here. He asked me, "What is your new name?" I thought about it quickly since he clearly wasn't going to leave without an answer.

I wanted Jason to know any news he heard, even hearing the new name, was me. If I was staying here, I'd become their Female Lead Warrior the second I shifted. Then he'd be proud of me and let me come home.

Until then, he'd hear about how I was helping figure out what was going on down here. I'd get them following the bylaws and help. I could do that. People would know my name. Plus, I was getting a GED anyway.

I'd have a lot of time to dedicate to the purpose of getting Red Run and the allies to know my new name. They'd be proud of me because I wasn't going to fail. I picked my favorite book character. I'd just spell it differently. Jason would know it was me though.

I answered, "Ashley Griffen." Alpha Edward nodded, "Good. You report to the kitchen tomorrow." Holy literally illegal by human and Supernatural laws. Did they do anything legal here? Luna Elena gasped, "Absolutely not Edward! I said have compassion, not be a bullying abrasive abusive Alpha!"

I glanced between them noting the entire staff was on edge, but that actually made sense. The pack was not at ease when the ruling Alpha and Luna weren't in harmony with each other. This was clearly deeply rooted and not some random fight. I'd seen Chelsea and Peter have fights, and my own parents. Nothing like this though.

They were both undermining the others authority, and it pained me to admit in this case the Alpha was wrong. My blood literally hated that though, but the Luna was the one who was right here. I whispered, "I can go. I don't want to cause you trouble."

Luna Elena said, "You're not. He is." Alpha Edward told me, "You have nowhere else to go." I frowned, "Stephanie said Uncle Duncan didn't know yet. I could go to…" He cut me off, "Duncan McAlister was informed and his pack refused to take in a problem pup." Luna Elena's eyes filled with tears.

I said, "One, I am not a problem pup. Two, my uncle would've told them to stick it where the sun don't shine." He shrugged, "His mate convinced him this was the best way." I snorted, "Umm what? She likes me." Even though I didn't like her pack my Aunt still found me amusing.

He said, "Well, they don't want you. You have nowhere else to go, and I'm not going to war with the allies over you." That was the first thing he'd said he said that I believed. This pack would absolutely never go to war with Red Run and all their allies.

He sighed, "Fine, Elena. You win. Two days." She gasped, "That's not enough…" He cut her off, "She can have two days." He stormed out. What was this place? Because it was like nothing I knew. Luna Elena glared after him and it hit me. She hated him.

Not that I blamed her, but the mate bond would make that practically impossible. What on earth had he done so that she was able to go against it? Why didn't she reject him? Rejections with marked mates was rare, but not unheard of. Maybe she didn't know that.

She told me, "He didn't used to be this way. My son will NOT be like his father as a leader." She looked past me as if she was remembering the past. "Edward had such dreams and plans. He was going to be a better Alpha than his father. We were going to change everything here. It was going to better than it ever was."

She scoffed, "Now he's worse. I'm so sorry. You don't need to hear about my problems. My daughter, Addison and the Beta's daughter, Sierra, will come keep you company tomorrow. I'm sure you all will be fast friends."

She paused then added softly, "I'm sure Stephanie didn't say this to you, but I am so very sorry about your family, Melanie. It was a tragic event, and despite what Stephanie or anyone says, it was not your fault. Ok sweetie?" I nodded and she left.

Somewhere along the way Addison and Caine had left. It had to hurt them their parents fought that way. Caine's blood literally had to demand he put his dad in his place. He wasn't developed like other future Alpha's his age from my estimate. Was he not training? Addison didn't have any muscle definition like a Female Alpha. That was weird.

I grabbed my bag and pulled out Xander's hoodie along with my Xander wolf. I cried, "I wish you could make my Xander come to me. I need him. What are we going to do Xander? Jase doesn't want us at home. Why doesn't he want me? I was just mad earlier. I didn't mean it. I didn't. I love them. I don't care if they eat the stupid weird cookies for the rest of time. I just want them back."

I cried myself out of tears, but when they dried up, I was resolved. I had to make Jason proud enough of me that he'd want me back. I was going to get my GED. Then I was going to train. I'd be the first Female Lead Warrior at sixteen. I'd make them all proud and they'd let me come home.

Grief felt like it was going to choke me. I missed my parents and my brothers. I just wanted to go home. A male staff member growled. I muttered, "I do not have the energy for you to tell me my wolf is the wrong color… it's not… leave me alone."

Cecila guided him away, but it looked like he didn't want go. Did no one in this pack train? That was dangerous. I fell asleep crying against my wolf. I woke up to arguing. The Luna and Alpha were outside my room.

He ordered, "Move, Elena." She whispered, "Why are you so determined to be the worst man you can be? What happened to the man I fell in love with? The one with dreams and love in his heart." He answered, "He grew up and found out what that life could mean." Umm… did he mean being happy?

She scoffed, "Oh yes, I forgot the world according to Booker and your father. What did that ever get them, huh? Do either of the men you emulate your life after seem happy? Are you happy?" He replied, "I'm alive." So, no he was not happy.

She whispered, "You were happy once. WE were happy. You, me, Eden, and James had plan to change things here. Then you went off and changed them without me and Eden." He retorted, "I'm the Alpha, not you." She was quiet for a minute.

I interjected, "A wise Alpha listens to the guidance of his Luna." He snarled, "Shut up, pup! Go make breakfast." Umm what? I admitted, "So, while I understand the concept of cooking… and I can make cookies… I've never actually made breakfast… well that's not true. I can microwave stuff. I mean I could probably figure it out."

He threw a sack at me. Luna Elena gasped, "EDWARD!" He told me, "That's your wardrobe, slave." I raised an eyebrow, "Slaves were abolished in packs centuries ago. I'm a Beta." He snarled, "Not here." I hummed, "No, I am a Beta blood… everywhere. That's just a fact."

He snarled, "Get used to life here, slave." I repeated, "The Supernatural Council and Werewolf Council abolished those long before either of us were born…. So again… Pack slaves are not a thing." He said, "They are here." He left.

I told Luna Elena, "That's illegal." She sighed sadly, "It's not the only illegal thing he does. I'm so sorry." I shrugged, "You might be sorrier when you eat breakfast. Unless I can microwave it. My cousin almost burned down the house cooking once… so I'm better than her." Thinking about MaryBeth hurt because I wanted to see her, but I couldn't help but remember that day.

Flashback

Melanie skipped into Grandma Esther and Grandpa Ben's house. Marybeth shouted, "No, no, no, no!" I ran into the kitchen and found the microwave on fire. She'd opened the microwave door, but I wished she hadn't. You were supposed to unplug it.

I quickly did that and turned to see she had a bucket of water. I shouted, "NO! Don't do that." I gently pushed her back to safety and went and grabbed the fire extinguisher. I popped the pin and sprayed it.

My dad, Grandpa, and Uncle Duncan burst into the room with Peter a second behind them. MaryBeth whispered, "I might have linked that I caught the house on fire. Why didn't you let me throw water on it?"

I answered, "Because that can spread the fire, and it's an electrical shock hazard. So… no water and stuff." She asked, "How the heck did you know where the fire extinguisher was?" I muttered, "I know where all of them are… for reasons…" I'd looked at the blueprints for every house because I'd been curious.

Grandpa Ben asked, "Sweetie, what happened?" He walked over and hugged her tightly. She whispered, "I just wanted something to eat between classes. I forgot to pack my lunch for school." I asked, "Is that the box it came in?" She answered, "Uhh yeah." My dad snickered and Uncle Duncan joined him. I told her, "Yeah, you're supposed to take it out of the box."

She retorted with a smile, "Well, not everyone can be as smart as you." I pointed out, "People that are not as smart as me eat meals like this all the time without things catching on fire." She stuck her tongue out at me and then we busted up laughing.

Dad said, "Well, I linked the fire chief that's in our pack. So, he'll come check this…." He trailed off. Uncle Duncan snorted, "This what, big brother?" He rubbed his face, "Uhh attempt at cooking." MaryBeth huffed.

Dane ran into the house like it was on fire. He screamed, "MARYBETH!" She groaned, "Who linked him?" Peter chuckled, "Guilty as charged." She blushed, "It's fine. I was just hungry." He growled, "I would've given you my lunch, or bought you some." She muttered, "The chicken parmesan meal sounded really good." He hugged her and I couldn't help but smile at them.

My dad hugged me then asked, "What are you doing out of school?" I answered, "Uhh well… through… umm…." He stared at me. I groaned, "It's so boring and the teacher got mad at me because she asked a silly question… that I answered."

He snorted, "Oh boy." Grandpa Ben laughed, "This is karma my boy. You used to do that all the time." I said, "She kicked me out…so…" Uncle Duncan growled, "SHE WHAT?!" Peter pointed at him, 'What he said. What do you mean your teacher kicked you out?" Dad growled, "Do you mean from class?"

I answered, "Well, yes…but she said the school…" They stared at me. I said, "It happens a lot so… it's not really a big deal." Grandpa Ben shouted, "THEY WHAT?" I hummed, "Yup." MaryBeth snorted, "They just hate that you are smarter than them." I agreed, "They do."

Peter snarled, "And they think they can just KICK a pup out of the BUILDING?!" I answered, "Well, they do at least once a week….so yes?" My dad growled, "What do you do during the day?" I answered, "Dance or think of inventions."

He was fuming mad and on the phone with the school cursing out the principal. I nudged MaryBeth, "I totally got you off the hook for almost burning the house down." She laughed, "You did and the best part is you don't even get how." I didn't. I simply followed the instructions of the adult in charge. I didn't do anything wrong.

Flashback Ends

Melanie sighed and got out of bed. I put on the sack. Then reached for my cell. I called Jason but he didn't answer. I said, "Jase, can you call me back? I just… I want to talk to you. I miss you… and no one mentioned when the funerals are and I…" I wanted to go. I hung up and called Peter, but he didn't answer either. I sighed and went to go make breakfast.

It was a disaster. Apparently trying to eat was a crime around here. I was locked in the cupboard. Where there were mice and spiders. I heard a man call, "Melanie." I whispered, "Hello." He said, "The name is Mason King. I'm sliding a granola bar under the door. Can you eat it for me?"

I cried, "Can't I come out?" He admitted, "I don't have the key. The door is altered so you can't get out from the inside." I'd noticed because I was going to pick the lock. He slid the food under the door. I whispered, "Thank you."

He gently said, "We'll get you out of here. Ok?" I admitted, "I don't understand why I'm in here." He sighed, "I know you don't. To be honest, we are confused too. Everyone gets told the rules and all of us know you weren't. I'll teach you at my diner how to cook once you're on your feet. Cecelia gave me some cream for your burn I'm putting that under now." My hand the Alpha had put on the stove.

I flinched because that thought hurt. I nearly opened the pack link to Jason, but Alpha Peter's words had stopped me. I wanted to go home. I asked, "Do you know when my family's funerals are? No one said." He answered, "They were yesterday." I cried, "What? No!" He apologized, "I'm so sorry." I took the burn ointment and rubbed it on my hand.

I let my tears come. What had I done to deserve this? I know I was mad when they left the house, but… I still deserved to say goodbye, didn't I? Mason came several more times before I was let out. Aunt Stephanie was waiting. She said, "Come on, you have to get ready." I asked, "Ready for what?" She went to backhand me, but I grabbed her hand.

Mason called, "Stephanie, she has a fight to get to. You don't want to hurt her." Aunt Stephanie growled, "It's Gamma Stephanie." A man stepped up beside him and put his hand on him. He said, "If you insist, it would be Former Gamma Female Stephanie." She growled at him, "Pervert."

He laughed, "I think that's reserved for your man friend." She shot back, "He's my husband." He replied, "Sure." Umm, ok. He told me, "I'm Hendrick. Mason's mate." I grinned, "Finally… a mated couple that acts like it… I…" I grabbed Stephanie's hand when she went to hit me again.

I warned, "Stop doing that, or I'll break your arm." She gasped, "You can't do that." I pinned her in a second. I assured her, "I can." I got off her greeting, "Hello Mason and Hendrick." Mason said, "I'll be seeing you after your fight at the diner. We are going to work on your cooking skills." I asked, "What fight?"

Aunt Stephanie growled, "If you could listen then you'd know." I replied, "I can listen. I just get bored when people say dumb things." Hendrick tried to cover his laugh as a cough. She demanded, "Go inside and take a shower you reek." True.

She frowned at me. I said, "If you are waiting for me to disagree about me smelling bad…you will be waiting a long time. For the first time since I met you, you're right." She growled, "Shower and then get dressed." I asked, "Am I fighting in this lovely sack?" She growled, "Probably." That wasn't ideal but doable.

I asked, "Is this like a fight to stay here? Because I gotta say… I might throw that match." Mason snorted now. She warned, "You freaks shut up." I asked, "Why do you call them freaks? Do they also unlawfully throw pups into the cupboard after not allowing them to heal and trying to hurt them?" She glared at me.

I grinned, "So, no. Why are they freaks?" She scoffed, "They mated each other." I asked, "And?" Hendrick said, "They don't like gay couples down here." I blinked, "Uhh what?" She sneered, "They are fated and didn't reject each other."

I asked, "And you're jealous because your fated mate rejected you? I mean I guess that makes sense…but…you weren't officially rejected…but this pack not filing the correct paperwork wouldn't really be shocking at this point so…"

She growled, "It's because they are gay." I admitted, "I don't understand… I'm pretty sure it's because they seem happy and you're… well… not." Mason put a hand over his mouth. Aunt Stephanie said, "Just because I'm not happy about you…"

I cut her off, "It's definitely not me. I mean I probably have a little to do with it but your general disposition is… bad." She growled, "And you wonder why your old pack wanted you gone." I acknowledged, "I do… the vast majority like me." She scoffed, "Not anymore, family killer."

Instantly, I thought of twenty different ways to kill her. I replied, "Slade Carter killed my family. In case you were curious… it was not me. I would've died before I hurt them, but something tells me you wouldn't know anything about that kind of loyalty."

She raised her hand, and I lifted an eyebrow. She glared at me and put the hand down. She repeated, "Shower and I'll drop you off at your fight." I asked, "Is the gym not somewhere we could run to… or walk?" She snorted, "It's not on pack lands."

I hummed, "Ummmm it's not legal for a pup not a part of any pack to fight in a ring without parental permission." She retorted, "I'm your permission." I said, "False. The Kyle's are or my grandparents." She growled, "I told you…"

I cut her off, "And I told you it would take a lawyer time to sort all that out. You are absolutely not my guardian in any legal capacity. A Werewolf Council representative would have…" She cut me off, "You're in a pack that is under review of the Supernatural Council." I blinked at her.

I asked, “Do you think that was a point of any kind? Because I am physically present in your pack you believe I’m under the Supernatural Council’s purview. I’m still from, and in, a pack that’s governed by the Werewolf Council… so… you’re point is wrong… or superfluous.”

She stomped her foot, and I was pretty sure she never grew up and was possible a pup in women’s clothing. She snarled, “I’m an older woman.” I said, “Umm… ok.” Hendrick supplied, “You called her a toddler.” I said thought out loud? I shrugged because I wasn’t really sorry. She was horrible and had no empathy. I was somewhat certain she was a narcissistic sociopath.

I waved, “Well, it was nice to meet you Mason and Hendrick. I’ll find your diner after… some fight… I’m in… that is definitely illegal…” Mason smirked and Hendrick chuckled. Stephanie dragged me into her house.

She said, “Other than cooking you’ll have nothing to do with those freaks.” I replied, “So, I’m not sure why you think I care about your opinion… but those two men are the closest to normal people I’ve seen in this pack. So… I’ll probably talk to them the most.”

She pushed me further into her house. She waved, “This is your Uncle Ajax.” He was a Warlock. A creepy one at that. He kissed my hand, and I jerked it back. He chuckled, “Let’s not be rude to Uncle Ajax.” My heart pinged because I wanted Ajax, my brother’s wolf, not this man.

She showed me to the bathroom. I turned the water on and felt the hair on the back of my neck prickle. There was no one here though. I got in the shower and rinsed off. I saw an eyeball staring at me and screamed. I poked his eye knowing it was Ajax. He screamed bloody murder. I jumped out and pulled on what MAY have been a clean sack and ran outside.

The Alpha and Beta were there. I gasped, “He watched me shower!” The Beta raised an eyebrow. Alpha Edward asked, “Who could blame him?” I blinked, “Umm you? Everyone… with a pulse…” Aunt Stephanie came out.

She shouted, “You hurt Ajax!” I replied, “He was watching me shower so I poked him in the eye. Logically… if he wasn’t a creep… he..” She went to hit me again, but the Beta stopped her. He said, “She can report to the punishing fields later. She has a fight to get us to.” WHAT?!

He continued, “We all have money on her and while you run around doing what you want more often than you don’t, we aren’t letting you risk losing us money.” Uh what? That was definitely illegal then. I said, “Honestly, you saved her the broken arm I told her she’d get if she raised her hand to me again.”

I stared at the Alpha. He asked, “What?” I questioned, “What’s the matter with you? Your wolf should be furious a non-pack member just spied on a pup’s shower. I’m even a visiting pup. That’s really bad.” He said nothing.

I continued, “You punished me for no reason and plan to do it again. It’s against all the laws and ordinances for visitors to your pack to be treated this way… You don’t make any sense. You’re standing against the blood running through your veins. So is he.” I pointed at the Beta.

Which hurt. It physically felt like it hurt my veins. Alpha Edward warned, “You don’t know me, little girl.” I retorted, “Of course I don’t. We never really even met, and I just got here. I do know that most of the things since have been illegal and you’re not doing anything about it but being a bad leader.” He glared at me.

I added, “And I know your wolf agrees with me because you didn’t growl.” Aunt Stephanie shouted, “I’ll whip you.” I asked, “For what?” She answered, “Disrespecting your Alpha.” Was she high? He wasn’t my Alpha, Peter was.

I shot back, “Supernatural Council Edit 854125 21b section five says any Alpha who does not make others respect his Luna is subject to the same kind of treatment and tolerance from the pack. You can’t whip me either, I’m not in this pack.”

She retorted, “Your Alpha gave us permission to punish you.” That hurt. I replied, “That doesn’t mean you can whip me. That’s for traitors and I’m not one.” She snorted, “We do things differently here.” Alpha Edward said, “You will be at the punishing fields after your fight for calling Beta Jason and Alpha Peter.”

I asked, "What? You're saying I can't call my brother?" Hendrick said, "Alpha, you can't…" Alpha Edward snarled, "I can and will. You're nothing here." I argued, "He's a Warrior and business owner. So, he actually is something here… which means you're wrong…again…it's a pattern that's weird…"

Hendrick shot me a look. Alpha Edward said, "His business makes us money." I reasoned, "And him." Alpha Edward sorted, "Jean, enlighten the pup." The Beta told me, "No, just us." Beta Jean. Got it. I gasped, "What? That's not fair! You can't do that. It's his business."

Alpha Edward said, "Yet I do." I was going to fix that, and I had plenty of blackmail material already to get it done. Beta Jean continued, "And he's not a Warrior." I hummed, "False. He's literally a Warrior. I can sense it."

Beta Jean explained, "No one that's into the same sex can hold a position here." I stared at him. Alpha Edward sneered, "We usually just say no homo's allowed." My jaw dropped at his incredibly offensive language.

I asked, "Would you like to know the Werewolf Supernatural Laws and Supernatural Council Laws you're breaking? Because yes, it's plural for both. Technically it's five for the Werewolf and three for the Supernatural Council."

A crowd had gathered, and people began to whisper like they didn't know that. Alpha Edward said, "Pup, you're cute." He didn't mean it though, he was sweating and turning red. I shrugged, "Umm ok? That's inappropriate for you to say as a mated… Alpha… no person… since I'm visiting and a pup… but I'm still right and I can prove it…. so… he's a Warrior and you're…." A terrible Alpha. I just couldn't say that part.

Alpha Edward growled, "Go!" Everyone bowed their heads but me. He blinked questioning, "What's wrong with you?" I snorted, "You can't be serious? Is he serious?" I looked around and found Caine grinning ear to ear at me.

So, Alpha Edward's son didn't like him. Interesting… and weird. It meant Caine was smart though. It also meant this behavior was normal. I could see why he didn't like him. I'd be mad if anyone in our pack disrespected my mom the way his was.

Hendrick ground out, "He's serious." I scoffed, "He can't be. He asked what was wrong with me? I'm not the one breaking over twenty laws… in like under forty eight house of being here I've discovered over twenty… so… logically he's breaking more… and he's asking what's wrong with ME?! Are you for real?"

The Alpha took several steps towards me and promptly shoved me at Stephanie. He ordered, "Give her the letters." I asked, "What letters?" Aunt Stephanie shoved me towards her car. She demanded, "Get in." I replied, "I have zero desire to go anywhere with you."

Alpha Edward growled, "It's an order." I pointed out, "Umm… you're not my Alpha… visiting Alpha's…" He snarled, "Can tell visiting pack members to leave the grounds." I agreed, "That's true… so I'll just go to a bus stop and go somewhere else." Anywhere was better.

He got in my face breathing heavily. He declared, "You will go with your aunt, fight, and return." I blinked asking, "Or… what?" He put his hands around my throat. I was actually shocked that he did. He said, "Or I'll beat my mate until you return."

I gasped, "You can't do that. Article…" He cut me off, "We don't abide by those rules down here. So, you return or know Elena will be suffering until you do." I looked around when he stepped back. I asked Beta Jean, "What is wrong with you? With all of you? Is no one going to move to protect your Luna besides her son?"

Alpha Edward snorted, "He's never been trained and he knows he can't beat me." I was beginning to think I could. It could require a goddesses help, but Selene should back me up here. Aunt Stephanie snarled, "GET IT THE CAR!" I didn't even look at her.

I said, "Mates are gifts from the gods and goddesses. To treat one as you're suggesting is a spit in their face. It would also mean you are an extreme deviant if you are capable of causing your mate physical harm. Does that scare you… for… obvious reasons?" He replied, "I get away with it, so no." His eyes twitched. I frowned at him because he was a bad Alpha.

I admitted, “I don’t understand.” He replied, “Shocking.” I agreed, “It is. I’m a genius… so….” A few people snickered. Luna Elena said, “You’ve never raised a physical hand to me, Edward.” So, he was just an emotional abuser.

Alpha Edward ordered, “AJAX!” A pain rippled through my chest because I glanced to the side hoping I would see my brother’s wolf, but it was the Warlock. He chanted and smirked at me. I asked, “Is something supposed to be happening right now?” He gaped at me.

I continued, “Or am I supposed to wait for him to come over here? I’m pretty sure I can take him… no, I’m positive I can… the probability is…” I turned and caught the Gamma’s fist when he tried to punch me. Then kicked a guy who was likely his son in the ribs. He smelled like a wet dog. Literally. His son smelled like a dirty, wet dog. That is an unfortunate scent to have.

Now several people actually bent over laughing. Mason being one of them. I flushed, “I said that out loud… didn’t I?” Caine answered, “Yup, you did. To be fair, it’s an accurate description of his scent.” Darn. Ok… getting in the car. Alpha Edward growled, “Finally.” Man, I’d said that out loud too.

I got in the car and Aunt Stephanie started it. She growled, “You embarrassed me.” I asked, “Why do you think I care? I don’t know you… you’re not even kind of nice… so… it doesn’t matter to me if you’re embarrassed. You don’t care what I think of you. It stands to reason I do not care about what you think of me. My mom didn’t like you enough to mention you and I see why.”

If my mom didn’t like her, that was good enough for me. Plus, my grandparents were very nice people. Pains stabbed my heart again. She handed me a stack of letters. I’d ask what they were, but I recognized the handwriting. They were from family. I ripped open the one from Grandpa Ben.

Melanie,

You need to be where you are right now while we heal. Do what you’re told. We all deserve to heal from this tragedy.

Grandpa Ben

I stared at it as if more words would appear. That was all he had to stay? Why wasn’t I with them? Melinda and Marybeth wrote letters, so I quickly glanced at theirs.

Melanie,

I can’t believe you did this to our family. You stole my brother from me, and I’ll never forgive you. I wish you were dead.

MaryBeth

Tears filled my eyes, and I let them fall. It wasn’t my fault. I tried to save them. Why would she say that to me? With shaking hands, I opened Melinda’s.

Melanie,

I can’t believe we are being forced to write these letters. If I ever see you again, I’ll rip you to pieces for making us lose T, Sam, and my brother. Your selfish bitchfit caused their deaths. They came back for you when they should’ve been with us. If you had just not crossed the border none of this would’ve happened.

You’re the most selfish person I’ve ever met, and I hope you get everything you deserve. I hope that pack does awful things to you. The fact you were the one who lived isn’t fair. I wish you had died, they lived instead.

YOU ARE SUCH A BITCH!

Melinda

My tears fell before I realized I was crying. They blamed me. They still didn't believe that I hadn't crossed the border. I went for the letter I didn't recognize the handwriting on.

Melanie,

My mating isn't starting how I wanted. Planning the funerals of my mate's family while he drinks all the alcohol in sight and mourns them was not on my list of things to do when I found my mate. I'm living with a man who smells more like a distillery every day instead of his natural scent.

All because you couldn't stay in your borders. Or, not get caught. I'm honestly flabbergasted. All teenagers are selfish, but you take the cake.

I have to take care of Jason and focus on him. I can't have you and your grief to handle as well. Especially considering this is all your fault. Leave us alone and allow Jason to heal and take over the spot he never wanted.

You took his dreams from him with your selfishness. I honestly can't with that or you. You should've died with them.

Fuck off,

Everly Bond

Indignation filled my veins. She didn't know me, and I didn't do this. Besides I knew she really wanted Tristan to be her mate. What the heck had happened? Selene really paired the woman our brother wanted with Jason?! That was messed up.

Wait, Jason was getting that drunk? He only drank socially. Hold up, why was she calling him Jason in this letter? Shouldn't she be calling him Jase? She didn't even know me. This was rudest introduction letter as my new sister in law.

Honestly, she was nothing like Tristan described her. He said she was kind, caring, and sweet. She was none of those things. I still couldn't believe she was Jason's. That was just wrong. That had to be why Tristan came home. He would've left but they couldn't have arrived in Black Mountain yet. I was so confused.

I grabbed Chelsea's next. A necklace toppled onto my lap. I picked it up and clutched them it my hand. She'd sent me my parents' wedding rings on a chain. The fact that someone was showing they knew I lost people too sent warmth through me. Of course, it was Chelsea, she was the Luna.

Melanie,

I know things must be confusing to you. I did a few things to get your parents rings. I think you can tell, if anyone finds out I sent them to you it would not be taken well. You should wear them every day to honor that since I'm going against my mate doing so.

It might be hard for you to understand this is all for the best, but it is. The pack has been ripped at the seams and your hands were there to cause it. Listen and stay out of trouble down there. We do not need reports of you acting up. Keep your head down.

Luna Chelsea

That was not what I'd been expecting to read. I put the necklace on anyway, grasping for any chance at feeling closer to my parents. I grabbed Grandma Esther's letter. It had to be the one filled with understanding.

Melanie,

Losing a pup is something I'd never wish on anyone. I need some time and space. Please respect that.

Grandma Esther

It cut deeper than I wished seeing how short it was. No one was concerned about me and my pain. No one cared that I saw those horrible things happen. Not ONE person called me Ladybug or wished me well. Not one. Who were these people?! I grabbed the letter from my Grandma Haskins.

Aunt Stephanie snorted, "Whatever she said will be vicious." I muttered, "You don't know her." She's not vicious. Aunt Stephanie mocked, "I know her better than you. You'll see." Whatever. I still didn't really buy her story fully.

I just didn't understand her angle here. It made no sense. She didn't know me. Sure, her pack wouldn't like Yellow Hills but I wasn't from there. Plus, her mate got what he deserved for attacking Luna Lexi Daniels intending to hurt Luna Reagan Daniels.

Melanie,

You AWFUL, SELFISH, UNGRATEFUL BRAT! How dare you get my daughter, son in law, and grandson killed! Stay inside your borders. What is so hard about that? You knew how Sam suffered, and you selfishly didn't care!

They asked us if we'd take you and I scoffed. I don't have time for selfish brats.

You and Stephanie deserve each other. Sam was the good pup, and you took her from me. I hope you starve to death and live a horrible life while you do.

Helena Haskins (You do not have the right to call me Grandma.)

Sobs wracked my body. Aunt Stephanie mocked, "Told you. Get inside." She shoved me out of the car. I went to the door. A big guy grabbed me, "Hey, you can't just come in here." Another shoved him flirting, "Hey, pretty lady. What's got you down?"

I wiped my tears, "I'm here to fight." One snorted, "In a sack? Are they for real right now?" Someone showed up saying, "She's Black Path's new fighter." I muttered, "I don't belong to their pack so I can't be their fighter and…"

He cut me off, "Don't talk back to me. I run this Undergrounds fighting area. You've got the last fight of the night. Hopefully, someone has…." He trailed off looking at me disdainfully, "clothes for you to wear."

The guy at the door said, "I'll help her find something." He introduced himself, "I'm Crush. You get a sense for people who enjoy this and are like us." I asked, "Like us?" He replied, "Not asked to be here but required." I clutched my necklace as he led me to the locker room.

He called, "Lydia, we need some clothes." She gasped, "Who put a pup in a sack?" She jolted, "I'm sorry that was insensitive. Are you homeless?" She told Crush, "This really isn't the place for her. You know that." He said, "She's Black Path's new fighter." It clicked for me.

I asked, "What happened to their old one?" They winced. Lydia warned, "We don't ask questions here." I couldn't help it, I laughed. I shrugged, "Well, everyone's going to hate me more than they do… I can't seem to stop asking questions. It goes with being a Beta blood and all."

The leader stalked back up, "You won't ask any." I replied, "I absolutely, without literally any doubt, will." He went to hit me, and anger welled inside me. I blocked it and hit him square in the nose. He squealed like a stuck pig while Crush tried to cover his laugh.

He screamed, "You hit me." I retorted, "You run an Underground illegal fighting ring, I'm positive me hitting you is the least of your problems… and by positive, I mean…" He cut me off, "You don't talk about this Ring to anyone. Got me?"

I answered, "Not really. I don't understand the half of what's been going on since I woke up in this town. Which is honestly hard for me… because I understand a lot and…" Lydia gasped, "They didn't explain the rules to you?"

I asked, "Why does everyone seem to have rules that aren't actually rules? They also ignore the Werewolf and Supernatural Council rules. You are breaking ten. No underage fighting is allowed for any Supernatural's. For Werewolves that is until they are sixteen. I'm fourteen."

Lydia covered her face with her hands gasping. The guy running the place snapped, "I don't pay you to gasp. Get her dressed. She's fighting Alpha Alan." I jolted, "Mueller?" My dad's reports had an Alpha Alan Mueller in them. He'd been trying to prove the guy was bad news with Peter. He was clearly right.

He answered, "Yes." Crush asked, "Her first fight is against an Alpha? She's an unshifted pup. The audience won't like that." He replied, "They like what I sell them. Get her ready." He stormed out. I told Crush, "It's ok. People don't tend to like someone who breaks their nose."

I paused then added, "Admittedly, he will like me less when he realizes since he didn't reset it immediately if he doesn't want it to be crooked for… well forever, someone will have to rebreak it." Crush stared at me and busted up laughing. He asked, "What's your name?"

Lydia replied, "Our new fighter's name is Ashley Griffen." I made a face that had Crush raising an eyebrow at me. Lydia dragged me away and found a sports bra and spandex shorts. I put them on replying, "Thanks." She left and I opened the next letter because apparently losing my parents and brother had turned me into a masochist.

Melanie,

You took them me. From us. I hate you so much that I can barely breathe. You stole my dreams and now my mate probably thinks I'm insane.

Why aren't you dead? Why are you around to torment me with your presence? Why didn't you just die with them like you deserve?

You'd better listen to Alpha Edward and do everything he says because I don't want to hear about you. Even Alexander is disappointed in you. I know that hurts you, and that's why I wrote it. Maybe I'll get him to write you a letter all about how horrible he thinks you are.

He thinks you're a joke. A pathetic loser just like all of us do. The girl who got her parents and older brother killed. Don't make me have to deal with anything about you not listening down there or I will make you regret it.

Beta Jason McAlister

A sob choked up out of me. He didn't mean it. He didn't. He was grieving. He would be sorry one day that he'd ever said this to me. I'd read Princess Luna Haley's papers about grief and how things are said in anger. They were clearly going through it with the ones they were sending to me. I wasn't even replying and they were still writing vile things.

This wasn't fair. They hated me. Was it really all my fault? What did I do wrong? I didn't cross the border! I never had. Was Jason feeling guilty because he was mated to Everly? I wasn't the only one that knew Tristan liked her.

Lydia told me, "You're up in an hour." I nodded and reached for Peter's letter. It was going to hurt because he was supposed to stop all this. It was his job. The job he would do for anyone. He told me I was like a daughter to him, and he let them discard me. I was supposed to be with him and Chelsea. He was being so mean to me, and I didn't understand why. He was never mean.

Melanie,

Behave for Alpha Edward and follow their rules. I have told them that they can punish you if you get out of line. I probably should've since you've always been a daredevil crossing the border. I wasn't firm like I should have been and you certainly paid me back for being lenient. You took my best friend and my mate's best friend along with my son's Beta.

You deserve to be where you are. We deserve to heal the hole you put into our pack. Be on your best behavior while you're there. Do what you are told and as I said do NOT link anyone in our pack for anything. I'll banish you if you do. I'm so disappointed in you.

Alpha Peter

It felt like everything around me shattered. My brother wished I was dead. Everyone that I loved did. Uncle Duncan didn't even send a letter. Aunt Allison's was in here, so I grabbed it.

Melanie,

I'll talk to them. I can't have you because I'm raising my pups, and a rebellious teen isn't needed in our house. Honestly, Drake rebelled and so did Duncan. Not quite to your extreme but it's not like you meant for any of this to happen.

Actions have consequences, I know these probably seem harsh to you though. Maybe the selfishness you've always carried around will diminish in the face of what you've caused. You've always thought you were better and smarter than everyone else. Now, I think you see you aren't.

Regardless, I will talk to them. Sending you to an unknown relative, the only one willing to take you, seems extreme. Drake wouldn't like it and that's what should matter to them. You were his little girl. He treasured you and you got him killed. Try not to kill anyone else while I work on them being insane.

Aunt Allison

I didn't kill them. Slade did. Did they actually think I killed everyone? Were they even going after Slade? He couldn't get away with this! He had to pay. He just had to. Pain beat on me like a drum. Did people really think I thought I was better than them? My family thought that? I didn't. I must… I… well…. Clearly, I didn't express it well enough to them.

I whispered, "I didn't kill them. I didn't." Crush cleared his throat. He walked over then told me, "This is your locker. Don't put anything you like in it because people take shit around here." I nodded, "Ok… How… umm… have you been here long?" He winced, "Nope. Just go down easy, kid. That Alpha is vicious, and he's killed more than one fighter."

I deserved the hits. My actions killed my family, clearly. Everyone thought so. They were just wrong about the facts. That didn't make them wrong though. My reaction was why they'd come home. I didn't cross the border, but if I'd just taken the punishment and gone upstairs, they would've stayed at the party. This was my fault. Everyone was right, just not in the way they thought they were.

I asked, "Why is a Demon in a Werewolf fighting ring?" He answered, "The Undergrounds include all Supernatural's, not just wolves." That was definitely why the Werewolf Council was struggling to lock onto the Undergrounds. They were looking for just wolves.

A plan devised in my mind of how to help them and get the guy running this on my side. By making him more money. I stepped into the Ring surprised to see Alpha Edward, Beta Jean, and Gamma Booker McCann here.

His wet dog smelling son was next to him looking at me like I was dirt under his shoe. What was his problem? I'd never done anything to him before he attacked me. I wondered why he wasn't in my dad's files. I knew who the leadership was because of them. I just needed a minute to recall after getting shot.

A man stepped into the Ring. He sneered at me before taking me in. He winked, "I think I'll keep you as a sex slave." I replied, "Pass." He chuckled, "Who said you get a choice?" I answered, "Literally everyone." He stared at me.

I replied, "My Alpha, visiting Alpha… well I don't know him really… and he does break rules… like a lot of rules… but umm… slaves were abolished a long time ago in packs… and selling underage pups is a crime that even humans punish people for… their ways are like… a lot nicer too. Jail is nicer than what any Supernatural group does for selling people… especially underage people. Soo…."

He chuckled, "You talk too much." I admitted, "That's the going theory." Which probably had merit. He said, "I'll enjoy taming you. Maybe I'll make you mine." Wet dog boy growled, and his dad backhanded him. Umm what?

I emphatically stated, "I'm not yours." He argued, "You are if I decide you are." I shook my head and the bell rang. He charged and I raised my hands. Then all my family's hate poured into me from the letters. I could hear it in my head. I deserved the hit. I lowered my hands.

Alpha Edward shouted, "PUT YOUR DAMN HANDS BACK UP!" Nope. I took the hit and staggered a step. The place gasped. Alpha Alan growled, "You should be on your ass." I shrugged, "You hit like a third year Warrior in my pack…. You should probably train more and…." He cut me off with an upper cut I could've stopped but didn't.

With each hit I saw Tristan when he laughed. My parents together dancing in the moonlight. Our family dancing in the living room. All those moments were gone, and I was here. I forced myself to stay on my feet as he beat me up. I swore I saw Tristan standing behind him at one point looking worried.

I reached out, "T." I took a kick to the ribs and went down, but Tristan wasn't there. My brother was gone. He was dead and it was all my fault. He wasn't worried about me. I'd stolen his life from him. Slade killed him, but my brother came home to take care of me. He never should've been there.

I cried, "He wasn't supposed to be home. He wasn't." Alpha Alan snarled, "I'm going to make you mine." I jolted back to the present and screamed seeing his teeth elongated. Alpha Edward didn't even make a move. Gamma Booker did though. He shouted, "NO!"

Fury filled me and I heard a growl from deep within me. I threw my right arm around my neck then screamed in pain when his teeth sank down onto my forearm. Rage filled me and I kneed him in the balls. He crumpled and I threw him off me. I rolled onto my stomach and got to my feet.

Blood was dripping down into my eyes. Every single part of me was in pain, but I didn't care. Alpha Alan growled, "You'll pay." I replied, "No, you will." The crowd was dead silent. He threw a punch I dodged.

I mocked him, "Sloppy." I countered and he staggered. He came again. I mocked him again, "Slow." I kicked out his legs. I jumped on him and began to hit him over and over. I screamed, "THEY WEREN'T SUPPOSED TO BE THERE! THEY WEREN'T!" He growled, "You'll be mine."

I declared, "I WLL NEVER BE YOURS!" I hit him long after he stopped responding. I was grabbed around the waist and hauled off him. A man declared, "And our new winner is Ashley Griffen. She certainly wiped the floor with our reigning champ. What's her fighting name?"

That guy was their reining champ? This was not a good fighting ring. Also, why did they get to decide MY fighting name? He answered, "The crowd decides after your first fight. It's tradition." I really needed to stop talking out loud without meaning to.

They began to chant, "Swiffer, Swiffer, Swiffer." Someone must have talked into his ear peace. He said, "For making the floor drip with blood then cleaning it all up and wiping the floor with her opponent the crowd has dubbed her SWIFFER!" He held up my hands and they cheered.

I stared at them bewildered. They were loving this, but they knew I was underage. They knew I had no business fighting an Alpha. I was shoved out of the ring while medics were working on Alpha Alan who was still unconscious. His Beta raised an eyebrow at me but said nothing.

What was wrong with everyone down here? If someone hurt Peter like that my dad would've been going at them. Did his Beta understand this was all wrong? Crush led me back to the locker room. Someone clapped my back, "Damn new girl! Beating an Alpha is a hell of a way to join our fighting ranks!"

Someone shoved him and I reached so he didn't fall. I asked, "Why are you in chains?" Wet dog barked, "Stop asking questions." He went to hit me, but I'd had enough. I hit him back, dropping him to the ground. He shouted, "You will pay for that." I muttered, "Add it to my tab… I guess."

The guy I'd helped laughed, "The new girl is funny. I'm chained because I live down in what they call the fighters quarters. It's a nice name for cell." I gasped, "What?" Wet dog sneered, "Behave or you'll join them."

I rubbed my temples, "I'm not in your pack… you literally can't have me thrown into a cell… or people will ask where I am." The guy laughed, "Tough luck, Trevor." I preferred wet dog. The guy laughed and I turned red. He bumped me, "See you around new girl."

Trevor mocked, "If you live." I frowned asking, "Why wouldn't he live? He's a fighter." Trevor growled, "He's won some, but all the fighters die eventually." Horror filled me. I watched the guy leave. He threw me a wink and I realized I didn't get his name.

Determination filled me. I'd save him. I would. I didn't save Tristan, dad, or mom but I could save that guy. Crush announced, "You'll have to be seen by the doc." I shrugged, "Ok." After two hours Lydia came in with the guy who ran this fighting ring. They jolted.

Lydia gasped, "The doctor didn't come in yet?" I replied, "Nope. It's not like I have anything to do… so…" She ran off to get a doctor. The leader said, "You did good tonight." I hummed, "I'm operating under the assumption you paid someone for me to fight… right? There's no one way someone isn't getting paid."

He agreed, "I did. You were worth every penny. By your next fight, I'll have earned it all back." Good. I nodded, "I'd like to talk to you about an opportunity after that fight." He laughed, "Sure, kid." I was going to convince him, I was certain. It was going to work.

The Doctor came in while Lydia berated him. He said, "I was told to make sure I saw her last." He stalled then his eyes widened. He shouted, "A PUP! A FREAKING WEREWOLF PUP! You people are DISGUSTING! There isn't supposed to anyone underaged in these fights." That was definitely good to know.

The guy in charge shrugged, "Her Aunt signed the waiver." The doctor pointed at him, "There are lines even for those without many morals. You do NOT allow anyone underaged to fight. Why are you making an exception after all these years?" I was an exception again. Yay. They all looked at me.

The doctor asked, "You allow biting now?" I replied, "The Alpha I fought tried to mark me." He snarled and snapped his jaw at the guy running the place.

The man in charge questioned, "What I supposed to do? She's not marked, and she won her fight." He evaluated me with care which told me Crush was right. I would know who was here against their will or not. He told me to go. I went outside but no one was waiting to take me back. I grumbled, "Jerks."

I began walking. I was about five miles away from the pack when I heard someone screaming in pain. What the heck? I ignored the pain and began to run. Dread filled me as I realized I was getting closer and closer to the pack grounds.

I pushed people out of my way. Several stared at me in shock. I screamed, "NO!" When the horror that was happening before me came into view. Alpha Edward was hitting his own daughter with a whip. I knocked Beta Jean to the ground when he tried to stop me and threw myself on Addison Davis.

I felt the sting of the whip and cried out. The intensity increased. Luna Elena shouted, "Edward, no." I held onto Addison tightly as twenty-five lashes came down on my back. He stopped and Addison scrambled out from under me and helped me to my feet looking at me like I was the crazy one here.

She whispered, "No one has ever…" She trailed off but I could guess what she was going to say. I replied, "No pack worth anything watches as anyone is hurt. Let alone the Alpha's daughter. Their wolves must hate all of them. Or they were Alpha Commanded to do nothing, which is against the laws… that people down here clearly do not care about."

She said, "A few are Alpha Commanded." I shrugged, "Then a lot of these people's wolves don't like them." No one growled, which meant I was right. Alpha Edward growled, "It was your fault. I warned you not to be late." So, he'd just lied about who he'd hurt.

I pointed out, "One cannot be late if one was not given a time to be back by. Plus, I was doing as instructed waiting for the doctor who was told to treat me last… probably by you… then no one was waiting to drive me back, so I walked… then ran when I heard your daughter screaming."

Luna Elena gasped, "You…" I turned and her eyes filled with tears as she looked at Edward. He took a step towards her. She backed up, "You told them to treat her last so you could hit our daughter." I hummed, "It's likely so that he could make me see he was serious. He gave her five lashes, so it was on a timetable of one every twenty-five minutes."

Alpha Edward snarled, "Shut up." Luna Elena asked, "Is she right?" Yes. This wasn't about her. It was about me. He said, "We can discuss that inside." He told me, "You'll be cooking again with Mason." Caine and Luna Elena had surrounded Addison.

I said, "I'd like to speak to you in private, Alpha Edward." I hadn't planned to do it now, but it was going to have to work. Luna Elena needed time to get Addison away. Logically, Caine was one of the ones Alpha Edward used his Alpha Command on.

He snarled, "Fine." Beta Jean followed us. He said, "You will stay in line." I shrugged, "Probably not." I observed his office and the filing method. I easily found the one on Mason and Hendrick King. He sputtered, "You can't…" Beta Jean moved, and I kicked him in the balls and kept reading.

I put the file down. I said, "You are going to reimburse the King's for the profits that they give you." He laughed, "No, I won't." I grinned, "But you will…. Wanna know why?" He scoffed, "Sure." I said, "Because you clearly don't want anyone to actually know what you're doing in this pack."

Beta Jean snorted, "And you'll tell them?" I answered, "I have the numbers of every Werewolf Council memorized. Allowing a pup from a visiting pack to be beaten means they'd visit. The Supernatural Council would be required to investigate as well, and you're abusing your family's." He snarled, "Watch it."

I said, "You'd be killed for what happened to me tonight. The Werewolf Council would make you accept your mate's rejection if she chose that path, but the Supernatural Council would recommend therapy. Not even they could let it go what you just allowed to happen to me. Plus, the Werewolf Council has lonnnggggg since wanted information about the Undergrounds."

Beta Jean snorted, "So you can talk in complete sentences." I replied, "Obviously. I just talk through my thoughts sometimes… well, ok it's a lot. It's a simple thing… you have the capitol to pay them back now. You owe them twenty million dollars and then you can take the standard five percent cut of profits." He snarled, "I will not give them twenty million dollars."

I disagreed, "You will because you want to live… and now it's twenty-five million dollars in back pay. I find it very odd that you are actually quite rich, but your pack looks like a pigsty…. which… ummm… no offense….no, actually all offense because you're the Alpha and you should take pride in how your pack looks."

He stared at me for several seconds. Beta Jean got to doing something on his computer and Mason and Hendrick came in after a while. Mason again offered, "I'll teach Melanie how to cook." Alpha Edward glared at me saying, "Be sure that you do. I'll whip her every chance I get." Illegal. So very illegal. He winked, "Unless you'd rather sleep with me."

I jolted up, "Huh…? I… you…. me…. what?" I glanced at Beta Jean who licked his lips. Umm gross. Hendrick and Mason flinched. Alpha Edward said, "I'll give you the option sometimes, Melanie. You can sleep with me or take the lashes of your punishment."

I stammered, "You are mated… and… um… I'm not interested…. because… like you're not…. someone…. Well, a specific someone… and… just… well…. no." Mason bit his lip trying not to smile. Alpha Edward growled, "You'll change your mind, they all do."

I gasped, "You sleep with other people?! But… Luna Elena… it hurts you both. Why would you do that? I mean… you seem kind of horrible… but she's so nice… and…" He growled, "There's a way I don't feel pain. She has to be taught her place."

I asked, "Why not reject her because you're being….?" His eyes flickered black and he roared at me. I asked, "Why are you letting your human treat her so horribly if you care? Are you ok?" He shook and Alpha Edward was back. He said, "Elena is mine."

I muttered, "But you're not hers… that's hardly fair." He replied, "I don't give a damn about being fair. Your packs hang around Fairies too much." Beta Jean cleared his throat. Alpha Edward said, "Twenty-five million dollars has been transferred to your account, Hendrick." He paused.

I added, "And Mason. Because… you can't transfer that much at once, so you'd have used both their joint accounts and separate ones. Plus… their business one obviously." Mason said, "We were not allowed to open a joint account." I rubbed my temples because I was getting a pounding headache.

Hendrick asked, "Why are we getting twenty-five million dollars?" I answered, "It's what you're owed from you profits that they stole…." Alpha Edward argued, "We didn't steal it. It's owed to us." I shook my head, "That they UNLAWFULLY stole from you that I… obtained… well via blackmail. You will have to pay the standard five percent to the pack… which is somehow only the Alpha since they have more than enough to maintain the pack grounds and do not."

Mason grabbed me by the shoulders and led me out. I jolted seeing Alpha Alan standing there. Mason nodded, "Alpha." Alpha Alan growled, "Faggot." I gasped, "You…" Mason put a hand over my mouth. I spoke through it, "Horrible person… you're just… awful." It was muffled but Alpha Alan laughed.

He shook his head, "No one in my pack will stop me from hurting you." Huh? Gamma Booker showed up and glared at me. What? What did I do? Other than blackmail his Alpha… Ok, maybe I did earn that glare, but… they deserved it! They were being bad at their jobs and stealing money people earned. That was wrong… so blackmail was ok in this instance. Right? It totally was.

Gamma Booker asked, "Alpha Alan, what are you doing here?" He answered, "I'm here with a request to buy Ashley." I said, "You cannot buy people… I already explained that." It was muffled again because of Mason's hand. Gamma Booker said, "We aren't selling, but I'll take you to see Edward." I raised an eyebrow at him.

Mason took me outside and took me to a house I assumed was his and Hendricks. Addison, Sierra, Dax, and Caine were all here. I greeted, "Umm hi… so… I know I've been rude… to your dad's but… like they are horrible and…"

Dax interrupted, "We know." I nodded, "Right and… wait what?" Dax asked, "Is it true that you beat an Alpha tonight?" Sierra whispered, "Alpha Alan?" I answered, "Uhh yeah… I mean he's not that good at fighting honestly… not like the Alpha's that were training me. I could've… well…."

I could've beaten him without taking more than a couple hits, but my body didn't look like that. Embarrassment filled me that I'd let it happen, but then I dismissed it. I needed the pain. Every breath reminded me that Tristan, dad, and mom were gone.

Caine asked, "Can you train us?" I jolted, "Uhhh well… yes… obviously… but Alpha's are trained by their dad's for a reason and…" Caine cut me off, "My dad doesn't train me. He refuses because I don't like the direction he wants to take this pack in. He's worried I'll get stronger and challenge him." I nodded, "Odds are he is correct for once… but…"

Dax interjected, "My dad doesn't train me either. Trevor is the one that gets lessons." I gasped, "The wet dog gets trained? Really? He… umm… he's not toned enough… like normal future Gamma's… I mean… Caine has more definition… which obviously Alpha blood… but you must at least do cardio… are you sure he trains?" Addison giggled, "Wet dog?" I winced, "Well… he smells like one." Sierra agreed, "That's a great way to describe it." Caine said, "That's what I said."

Hendrick came in and shook his head at me. I said, "Umm you're welcome." Mason laughed and handed me a compress. Maybe it was for my face. He agreed, "It is." Stop talking out loud, Melanie.

He got everyone drinks. Caine asked, "Why did my dad call you guys in this time? You're walking fine this time, Hendrick." Why wouldn't he be? Hendrick sat down, "Melanie here blackmailed him into giving us the money he owes us. Money that I didn't know he owed us."

I snorted, "He's not allowed to take all your profits, that's…" They looked at me like they didn't know that. I winced, "Don't you know that?" Sierra answered, "Nope. Let's have a lesson in what we should know." This was going to be a LONG conversation.

I'd been right. They were shocked by the things I'd told them which surprised me. They knew nothing about how pack life was really supposed to work. I set up times to train Dax and Caine and I worked with Mason and Hendrick in their diner. Things were not even remotely close to normal. Everything here was wrong.

I'd stopped the Alpha from beating pack members for minor infractions. Some weren't even infractions. The Alpha, Beta, and Gamma, that were all mated, constantly wanted me to sleep with them. My creepy Uncle Ajax had me on edge every second of every day.

My calls with Jason and Peter were pointless and got me beaten. The worst so far was after Jason had sent all of my things to me. Walking into Mason and Hendrick's house and finding all my belongings in the loungeroom was painful.

I was so grateful they'd manage to save them from Aunt Stephanie, who'd been dragging them to the trash cans. My home pack couldn't know that though. They kept insisting I use their titles, and it hurt. Today, I was going to have a good day though. I'd found a plot of land and purchased it to use as a commemorative spot for my family. I didn't get to go to their funerals, and I couldn't' go on pack lands… so here I was.

The guy who'd brought everything, including the stones with their names, asked, "Does it look how you want it to?" I nodded, "Yes, thank you." He left and I sank to the ground. I apologized, "I'm so sorry. You shouldn't be here….well you aren't here….but you shouldn't be in the ground somewhere. It's all my fault." I laid down on the ground and sobbed.

I stood, "I'll find the man who did this. I will avenge you if Alpha Peter won't listen." It physically pained me to say it. The words burned. I added, "It's not his fault really. They just don't want to talk to me. He didn't ask so he doesn't know what happened." I was the only one being punished for their death. I stood, "I have somewhere I have to be, but I'll be back." I touched each stone and went to my meeting.

The man there stood asking, "Are you sure about this? It's a lot of money." I shrugged, "I don't need it." I was starting several charities with the money I'd earned from investing. I was giving away most of what I had to other charities. Once it was all done, I left. I'd tied up what I had left in some stocks. I knew I'd get a good return and could put the money back into everything.

I went to a field I'd found and let myself loose it to the music. Eventually Caine shouted, "MELANIE!" I turned, "Oh, hi Caine…umm…we don't have a training…" He winced, "No, my dad is sending you to a meeting with Addison and Sierra tonight." I breathed a sigh of relief.

Maybe the Alpha wasn't all bad then. He was giving responsibility to women which seemed to contradict everything else he'd done. Caine told me, "You'll get through it." I asked, "Huh?" He squeezed my shoulder and took me where Sierra and Addison were waiting.

They drove off and pulled into a place that set my teeth on edge. There was enough silver to kill us all. My bracelet turned brown too. Wolfsbane. I whispered, "We shouldn't be here. We need to go." Sierra told me, "We can't go."

A man laughed, "Our newest recruit." Say what now? I grabbed Addison and Sierra and put them behind me. I shouted, "He's a Hunter! RUN!" Addison told me, "We know." I whirled, "You what?"

Someone cleared their throat, “Dante, this is my group. You shouldn’t be here.” The person called Dante laughed, “I wanted to see her join us. How’s it feel?”

I asked, “Excuse me?” He grinned, “We killed your family and here you are, to join us.” I screamed and ran at him. I smashed my fist into his face over and over. I felt myself get shot with something, but I didn’t care.

Alpha Edward’s voice boomed, “Get off him.” I heard the Alpha Command behind it, but he wasn’t my Alpha. That wasn’t going to work. It took ten of them to get me off him. I screamed, “I WILL KILL YOU!”

Alpha Edward said, “Then Addison and Sierra die.” I jolted, “Excuse me?! SHE IS YOUR DAUGHTER!” He hummed while Addison choked out a cry. I stared at Alpha Edward and shook my head. Pain filled my entire being as he stood against his oaths.

Dante moaned and someone loaded him in a car and took off. I told Alpha Edward, “I will not work with people that killed my family.” He laughed, “You will.” I got away from those who had held me back. I noted the man who said he ran this group had Fairy blood. Interesting.

Trevor McCann showed up with fifteen pups. Sierra screamed, “DAD!” Beta Jean growled, “Shut up.” I asked, “What’s going on?” Trevor shot one pup. I screamed and ran for them to get tackled by ten people.

Alpha Edward asked, “Will another pup die for your insolence?” I shouted, “MY INSOLENCE?! YOU… YOU…” I stared at Beta Jean and Gamma McCann. I screamed at them, “Do something! This is your oath and blood on the line.”

I stared at Alpha Edward, “Especially yours! They fight against us. They KILL us!” He said, “They don’t do that with us. Our unshifted pups work with them. You will as well, or I’ll gather up more pups to shoot.” I pushed people off me and threw a knife that hit Trevor square in the wrist.

He screamed like a stuck pig. I warned, “You’d better get him to the doctor, or he’ll never regain full use of his hand.” They all stared at me. Gamma McCann snarled, “You bitch.” I replied, “Your son killed a pup in cold blood… of the pack he’s supposed to take over. You’re working with Hunters…. and you’re calling me names?!”

Sierra said, “Dad, you knew better than to blindside her.” Alpha Edward said, “She needs to do things the right way.” I shouted in my head, “No, you do.” Hurt built inside me like a physical ache I didn’t understand. I stared at him waiting for the Alpha in him to do the right thing, but he walked away.

He turned back saying, “Every time you are asked to come here, you will. Or the death of a pup will be on your head. That one’s family will be told this was your fault.” I snorted, “Even your backwards thinking pack will blame Trevor. I don’t understand how you…”

He cut me off, “There we agree. You don’t understand. You could make things better for yourself, but you don’t.” The man running things cleared his throat, “This is my meeting, and I need to speak to my new recruit.” If not for the Fairy blood running through him, I’d kill him. Xander wouldn’t like that though. I needed to flip this guy for the allies instead.

Beta Jean asked, “Why didn’t the wolfsbane and silver hurt her?” I stared at him like he was insane. Alpha Edward answered, “Adrenaline.” I scoffed, “Adrenaline doesn’t affect any Werewolf getting hit with silver, let alone wolfsbane. I clearly didn’t get hit with that…” I trailed off noting the darts sticking out of my skin. I plucked them out.

The leader grabbed me and ordered, “All of you get inside.” He led me into a room that had my instincts screaming at me to run. He led me to an office. He announced, “You’ll work on missions with us.” I replied, “I’ll kill every single person you put me with.” He chuckled, “That’s not the smart way to do it.” I frowned at him.

He said, “This room is soundproofed.” I rubbed my temples, “I don’t understand why wolves would even work with…” He cut me off, “I’m not a wolf.” I agreed, “No, but you….” I trailed off then studied him. I admitted, “I’m pretty sure you’re in a pack… not like mine… but you have a pack… so what the hell… Plus… you have other stuff…”

He replied, “Fairy blood. I am aware. The Ring took my sisters. A Werewolf pack adopted me and Hunters with the Ring took my sisters away. I came back during a school break and found the ashes they left behind. The survivors told me what happened. I got them help and I joined the Hunters." I jolted, "You're a mole… and you're telling me… what you're doing? You don't even know me… that's… a horrible plan on your part."

He admitted, "I've never been as hopeful in my search for my sister's until I heard your name." I asked, "Uhhh what? Why? That's…" He cut me off, "We come from packs where we know this shit isn't normal. We know it's wrong. What that Alpha did was appalling." I scrunched up my nose. A pup was dead on his orders. The Alpha. I nearly crumpled with the pain.

He offered, "We can work together. You can't kill the Hunters in this sect, but we work with others that are smaller. I can get you on those missions and we can save people. I just don't know where we will put them."

I answered, " That's actually easy. We send them to the allies… because… well… obviously." He frowned, "I don't have that kind of money." I waved, "Leave it to me. I'm good at making money… I did kind of give a lot away today… but that's fine. I'll make it again and… I'll do this with you." He nodded and our alliance was formed.

I went back to the pack and was beaten and thrown into the hole. They covered the top of it, and I began to panic. I tried to climb the walls, but I'd slide back down. I lost track of time, but a water bottle was hurled down and hit me in the head. I drank it slowly. I was going to go crazy down here.

I was pulled up and whipped by Gamma Booker. He thought I was passed out and said, "Our people are moving. Alpha Alexander is as good as dead. They left our territory five minutes ago." He kicked me and left. What people? I stood up gingerly, shook it off and took off running.

How was I going to find people after Xander? I could just call and warn him if I couldn't find them. Then I spotted a camp. Ok…that was oddly easy. Maybe Selene was FINALLY watching out for me. These were lone wolves working together.

I quickly climbed a tree. One asked, "Do you smell that?" One waved, "Who cares? We need to focus. Taking out Alpha Alexander is going to be tough." I jumped down offering, "Impossible even." They jumped.

One frowned asking, "Pup, what are you doing here?" I answered, "Stopping you. Or… just… leave. Don't do this. It's silly." One took out a knife, "Killing her would be a kindness. Look what they did to her." Another said, "Or she can join us. She's clever."

I replied, "I won't let anyone hurt Xander." A woman laughed, "Oh, a pup with a crush. Honey, he's dead whether we do it or not." I screamed, "NO!" I jumped on her and snapped her neck and they came at me.

I was stunned when Hendrick's wolf jumped in and helped me. He shifted back, "Melanie, what are you doing?" I blinked answering, "I think I just found my purpose. I can honor Mom, Dad, and T by… stopping this… I already have a deal with the Hunter guy…."

My brain wasn't working but I knew that was from lack of food and water. I explained, "This will help." He asked, "This what? Let's get you to my place." I argued, "We need to set them on fire… so…" We pushed the bodies on their campfire. He ended up carrying me to his place where Celia was waiting. She gasped, "These cuts are infected. Get her inside."

Addison's eyes widened when she saw me. Dax and Caine growled. Sierra ran over and took me into the bathroom. She called, "Ads, come on." Addison whispered, "They are so mean to her." They had to drain the tub four times before I was clean.

It was a haze but when I came out of it, I got to work. Because I had a new purpose. I whispered, "I'll make the world my dance floor for you guys." I was going to change everything.

I started my plan by bugging Alpha Edward's office. It was very easy actually. Bugging his, Beta Jean's, and Gamma Bookers phones were also really easy. I followed all of Prince Gunner's tips to the letter then went to Mason and Hendrick.

Honestly, I hadn't been here that long, but it really felt like an eternity. I knew this idea I had was crazy, but I could do it. I had the plans drawn up for Hendrick and Mason. I just needed some start up cash since I'd given up most of my money.

I planned to show them how quickly I could return the loan. I'd started my new investment profile. I just needed some cash to get everything going. I even had a symbol for our group. It was quite clear what our name was too.

It was a ring with a slash through it. Obviously, we would be the Ring Resistance, but we could just call it the Resistance for short. People could remember it either way, but studies showed shorter names were more memorable.

Hendrick and Mason walked into their office in the diner. Mason said, "Caine is standing guard with Dax, but he doesn't know why." I took a deep breath, "So, I have a plan… and it's just that I need your help to put it in motion."

"I mean I could wait… but then people could get hurt… being here I've got intel that I can act on… People need the Ring to fall…. But they can't do that because they are in the light… if we move in the shadows like they do… then…"

Mason asked, "You want to stop the Ring?" I nodded and showed him the logo design. I explained, "This is the simple logo I chose for the group… there were some more complicated ones, but they aren't as easy for everyone to draw as these…"

Hendrix chuckled, "Circles are easy to draw." I frowned, "It's a ring… which is a circle, but it's supposed to be a ring with the slash through it. So obviously everyone would know our name is the Ring Resistance. But we can drop the Ring and be The Resistance since the logo obviously shows a ring so that's implied."

Mason grinned, "Obviously." I continued, "The thing is I just need some start up capital." I handed them everything I'd prepared. I said, "I can pay you back in a few months. I know it's a large loan, but I can guarantee the returns with interest in…"

Hendrick said, "We don't need all of this." He put my plans down. Mason agreed, "We don't. We will give you anything you want. You are family to us." It was a lance to my heart while simultaneously being the healing balm I needed. We'd forged a quick bond, and it felt like a betrayal to my family, but they'd abandoned me.

He continued, "We honestly want you to live with us instead of your wretched Aunt. Who I CANNOT believe never lorded it over everyone her sister was a Beta Female of a famous allied pack with Black Mountain." I cringed.

Hendrick said, "Of course we will give you the money with one condition." Mason raised an eyebrow. I asked, "What's the condition?" He answered, "That you include us. We want to be a part of your group. We need to know what's going on and how to help you."

I muttered, "Well... I already planned to ask you because you guys are a great fit and good shots. We definitely need snipers and stuff. You know how to fight, and you need to see what your investment is for. So logically… like that's not really a condition then since I was already going to do that. Do you want something else?"

Hendrick replied, "No, we just want to be a part of it. It shouldn't take a fourteen year old pup to stand up and let us know we can too." I argued, "I mean you've been fighting this your whole life. The fact you are together proves that. I'm sure there are many who gave up a fated mate and are miserable because they are now marked to a man or woman they don't love."

I continued, "Actually… I know that's the problem a lot of people have with you. They are rude because you were brave where they were not. That's hard to do. You guys are reminders that they didn't do what they should've… which makes them mean and hateful to you… which is obviously wrong." Mason interrupted, "Who do you think feels that way?"

I answered, "Well obviously Avery's dad." Hendrick snorted, "I'm sorry obviously?" I nodded, "Sure… when you aren't watching he looks at you guys with such jealousy… I asked around. Buck and Avery's mom isn't his fated mate."

Mason agreed, "She's not but I never heard about him finding his. He didn't date though. He is incredibly hateful toward and about us." I shrugged, "Kind of proves my point. Most wolves don't care if wolves of rank aren't gay. I mean allied packs don't care about rank, well not anymore, but down here they clearly do… and it's confusing because Buck's dad didn't have a rank…"

Mason interrupted, "He used to. He was the Lead Warrior once upon a time." I nodded because that made sense to me. I was also excited because now the Ring Resistance could truly start. Dax and Caine came in.

Caine declared, "We're in." I grinned, "Really? Are… you sure? Because we are going against your dad's and…" Dax cut me off, "You're training us and doing more than anyone ever has." I hummed, "And you're great! Have you been watching Xander's videos?" They confirmed that they were. That was good. It would be better for Caine to learn from him as an Alpha, but he was stuck with me.

Addison and Sierra joined us. They said, "Obviously we are in too." Dax and Caine made a face. Addison looked at her brother whispering, "Please." He nodded, "We all need to fight back." I grinned, "All it takes to start a Resistance… is one person. We are going to do this. We will take them down."

Mason asked, "Do we have a first assignment?" I answered, "Hendrick and I … well… we kind of did one… because they were going after my Xander." Hendrick declared, "I stepped in because you were in danger. I tracked you, not them."

I shrugged, "We killed a group after Xander. Which… the Hackura will probably get wind of. So… that could get fun." Caine said, "I mean I'm not brought into things, but I know we don't want to be on the Hackura's radar."

I hummed, "Not exactly….We as the Resistance do… we just have to do it right. We need to get to the point where we can be a secret source for them. It would provide a layer of protection… and then they'd want us to keep working with them."

Dax argued, "They would want in on missions and then they'd would take over it." I winked, "Only if they figured it out and I've got a pl for that." Caine asked, "Don't you mean a plan?" I admitted, "No… well… kind of. It's not a full plan yet. I'm working on it but I've studied every single paper Prince Gunner Cambridge has put out. That should give us a starting base. Plus, I've got some inventions that will help us."

I pulled out my scent cancelling spray. I said, "I need Mason to order some things from his supplier so I can make more but this will make us smell like nothing. We'll get tactical gear from humans and…" Sierra asked, "How do we do that?" I grinned, "They have sales for old equipment…and maybe I know of one happening tomorrow."

Caine asked, "So, what's our big statement?" I answered, "The allies are meeting with the Drug Ring." Caine winced, "They can't do that. They don't know the right words to say." I asked, "What's the right word?"

Hendrick answered, "It's a phrase." I prodded, "And it is?" Dax said, "We don't know it. We just know there is one." I hummed, "I'll look into that." Addison asked, "Who is going?" I answered, "Me." Caine snorted, "She means who is going to the drug buy for the allies?"

I answered, "It hasn't been determined. It's going to be someone from Black Mountain and Red…" I choked on emotion and put my head between my legs. I answered, "Run." Dax snorted, "Fuck them." I shook my head, "I'll go."

Hendrick asked, "Why you?" I explained, "Because I'm an excellent shot. We'll need to assign titles. I'm thinking Bravo's. So… I'll be one." Caine said, "I like the number six." Dax winced. I nodded, "Sure… not going in numerical order is… totally fine." They snorted.

Dax said, "We'll have to save you if you ever get caught because you can't lie for shit." I frowned, "I can evade. Plus, I don't get caught when I do things… oh gosh that was braggy but…" Dax said, "We believe you."

Hendrick offered, "I'll be Bravo two." Mason jumped in, "Three." Addison shouted, "I call five!" Everyone looked at her. She shrugged, "It's my favorite number." Dax grumbled, "Fuck it, I'll be seven." Caine asked, "Why?" He replied, "If you're six, I'm seven. You're my Alpha."

I clutched my chest feeling something prickle inside me. I didn't understand what it was, but maybe it was because an Alpha and Beta were acting like they should. Sierra said, "I'll be eleven." Dax groaned, "Why?" She said, "Because Melanie is one and I'm going for double one's since two is taken."

I wrote all of that down. We went to the range, and I began to train them to shoot with Hendrick. He'd been in the army and was a good shot along with Mason.

I'd taken more beatings for other pack members and useless things I'd "done" according to the Alpha, Beta, and Gamma. Pack members spit at me when I walked by, and I felt pieces of my soul being chipped away. Their hatred was all consuming, but I was helping. They couldn't see it right now, but they would one day.

I was at Mason and Hendrick's reviewing the tape from Alpha Edward's office when they declared who was going to the meeting we were going to be protecting. I threw the headphones off and ran out of the house as if I was on fire.

I went to my dancing spot, put on music, and lost myself to it. Jason and Grandpa Ben were going. How could Alpha Peter do this? Did he not understand he was sending them to die? Logically, that answer was no, but my anger didn't seem to care about that.

The Alpha's down here went against their oath, and he'd made me believe in true Alpha's. He was a true Alpha to everyone except me. He was the reason I was seeing this side of everything. I couldn't live with the rose colored glasses they did anymore and it hurt. I screamed in anger going through my movements.

I heard people talking, but I didn't care and danced until the playlist ran down. Dax asked, "Are you good now?" I turned, "Not really." He winked, "Well, come on." Right… I was training them. Dax walked me to where we trained in secret. Caine said, "We did our cardio." I nodded and we went through fighting paces.

Satisfied I urged, "Shift." They both looked at me. I explained, "You have to know how to fight in wolf form. Let's go." Dax cringed, "Uhhh that's a no." I snorted, "It's a yes… because… I'm the trainer and I said so… so… shift." They stared at me.

I groaned, "Come on. It's not like it's the first time I've fought a wolf in wolf form… with highly trained wolves even…..let's go." They did and we worked together. I pinned Dax and warned, "Never underestimate a human form just because you shift." His wolf nodded at me, and we worked for several more hours.

We went home when it was pitch black. Not that it made a difference to us. We could see perfectly. I walked into Aunt Stephanie's house. I had a sleeping bag in the hall closet to sleep on. I opened my door and found letters on my sleeping bag. I quickly shut the door and reached for them. I cried seeing Jason's handwriting. I tore it open.

Melanie,

Everly cries most nights because I can't be the man she needs. All because of you.

I've got something coming up. Something I wouldn't be doing if not for you. If I don't make it, don't come for my funeral. I don't want you there and it would just upset Everly.

Beta Jason

Well, he wasn't going to die because I wasn't going to let him. He was going to be just fine. He may hate me, but I'd have his back. I would never let Jason get hurt and deep down he had to know that. It had to be why he'd sent me the letter. I was choosing to believe that.

The next one was from Grandpa Ben. I opened it and a note slipped out before his. I picked it up.

Melanie,

If dad dies, it's on you. I hate you.

MaryBeth

Tears fells and I opened the letter from Grandpa Ben with shaking hands. Part of me wanted to shove them into my backpack and never read it. The other part hoped he said something nice. Just one thing because my heart ached. I missed them. The homesickness I suffered felt ever prevalent here. I took a deep breath and flipped open the page.

Melanie,

Jason and I are doing something dangerous. He shouldn't be going. It should be T, but we know he can't be here. I find that hole in me growing wider every day without seeing his smiling face. I can't hear his laugh nor my son's ever again.

Drake always found the good but without him there isn't any. I used to hate when he listened to his sad ass country music, but now I just want my son back. I can't have him, and I can't reconcile that you took him from us.

You took Sam, Drake, and T from us and now there is no more laughter. It died with them. Don't come home if something happens to me. I don't want to see you. None of us do.

Former Beta Ben McAlister

P.S. That is how you should refer to me from now on.

I bolted out of the house as if I was being chased. I ran all the way to where I'd had stones placed for my family. I threw up and kept dry heaving. I sobbed, "They hate me. They will always hate me. I can't do this… I need you back. Please come back."

I screamed at the sky, "Give them back! I'll do anything." Not even the wind answered my pleas. I cried, "Please!" I laid on the ground not caring that the sun rose. Not caring that I would be punished for not starting breakfast. I whispered, "What if I just laid here until I died? Who would care?"

Images of Mason, Hendrick, Sierra, Dax, Caine, and Addison flickered into my mind. They needed me to keep it together. Caine and Dax were the future of this pack and they needed to be trained. Which probably meant other packs that were allies of Black Path needed it too.

I went back and took my punishment. My friends were worried. Caine whispered, "Let Hendrick or Mason go." I shook my head, "No. We don't know the level of danger we are up against and…" He cut me off, "Exactly. More than one of us should go."

I disagreed even though it pained me, "No, you are the future of this pack and their hope…so you can't go… and Mason and Hendrick have a love that should be protected…. and Dax… well he can't come for the same reason as you…" He grimaced because I was right.

Sierra stood declaring, "I'll go." I disagreed, "You're not trained enough yet… and neither is Addison. She's actually a very… um… she has room for…. well…. improvement…. in the shooting…. area." Addison snorted, "I'm a hopeless case and we all know it." I quickly said, "No… you hit the targets… so… you do have promise… and you just started. It's not like everyone is amazing right away."

Addison asked, "And what about you? How were your first shots?" I admitted, "I got it right away… but I get a lot right away and… like my Grandma Esther is…" I gulped down the sob that wanted to bubble up, "a great shot. I've had a gun in my hand since I was a very young pup… so… my cover is intact anyway. I was whipped…so spray me down." They used my scent concealer.

Dax gasped. Sierra's face lit up while Caine and Addison looked stunned. Mason whispered, "It worked." I winked, "Of course it did." I'd worked really hard on it. I'd wanted to talk to Levi about it, but it stood to reason he hated me now too. I put on my gear gingerly and took the rifle, running my hands over it.

Mason asked, "And how will you get away?" I answered, "I won't. Well... I mean... I will...but I'll just wait them out..." Dax asked, "And if they look into the tree?" I snorted, "Werewolves don't search trees for people. It's a risk... but a very low one... I've calculated..." They waved, "We know." They chorused. They chuckled.

I left and got in the car. In theory, I knew how to drive. I wasn't going to crash this old beat up truck I'd purchased in cash. I drove until I was twenty miles out, then hiked. I found the spot based on the communications Alpha Edward had and scoped it out.

I found my perch and the tree I'd go to once I'd made sure no one died. I set up and waited for hours. I knew when other people got here. The hair on my arms began to rise. I willed my tears away when I saw Grandpa Ben with Jason and Julian Conners.

I looked at them both and felt a multitude of emotions. They looked fine, the same even. I didn't. I'd lost weight, my wounds were still bleeding, and they looked fine. I looked through the scope trying to see Jason's mark, but his collar was too high. Caine sent me a text.

<u>Caine:</u> Got to see Nate and asked about the code phrase. It's Bless the Goddess for such a good day. No matter what the question is.

The group coming to meet them arrived. I watched my brother square up to them. I nearly called out to him but stopped myself. It started off wrong and I could see that quite clearly. They knew who they were before a single word was spoken.

My finger hovered over the trigger. I was not going to watch a member of my family be shot ever again. I pledged it here and now between me and the gods and goddesses. The guy they were meeting called, "Nice weather today, isn't it?" Grandpa Ben agreed, "It's a nice day."

My stomach tightened knowing that wasn't the right answer. One took out the drugs. Julian Conners was instantly suspicious. He asked, "You're not going to name your price?" The one guys snorted, "No, I just thought you'd like to know what you're dying for." I saw the man in front of Jason reach for a gun and rage filled me.

I fired three shots before anyone could react. All head shots then hit them for a total of six shots each because I had their six. That had been my plan. I wanted them to think the Hackura did this... or at least have the Hackura as suspects. It would peak their interest in us too. It was all a part of my pl to be their secret source.

Logically, I had to throw everyone, allies included, off my trail. The problem was I wanted to fire more than six at each of them. I fired at the other side's snipers. Jason shouted, "GRANDPA BEN!" I could see them all in my scope. They were fine.

I was a little surprised Julian didn't pop to me, but that was ok. I fired another shot to keep them distracted. Jason called, "Julian!" He replied, "I got nothing! I can't..." He trailed off and I set everything up. All my shell casings and drew the Resistance circle.

I fired another round to keep them thinking someone was out there then ran to my tree and climbed. Grandpa Ben asked, "Do you hear any heart beats Julian?" I quickly pulled out the eerie emitter I'd been working on.

I prayed it would work, and they wouldn't hear my heartbeat. Running away was my fall back plan. I was always faster than Grandpa Ben and Jason. Julian admitted, "I did but now I don't." They fanned out and I nearly groaned when they went in the wrong direction.

Jason ended up right below me. Part of me screamed down at him silently in my head begging him to look up. To see me again, but he didn't. Which wasn't really that surprising at this point. He didn't want to see me.

Grandpa Ben said, "We need to find some clue, but we also need to get back. Everyone will be getting worried." Julian replied, "They already are." I bit my lip hard, so I didn't say anything. My Xander was worried about his brother and probably mine. Jason and Xander were best friends.

Finally, they'd found what I'd left for them. I saw pride in all their eyes. Tears filled mine. Jason and Grandpa Ben were proud of me again. Then Julian popped them out. I waited a beat then got down. I called Sierra.

She answered, "Yeah." I told her, "Have a message thrown across Red Run's border with the code word." Nate gave us the names of some good Hunters and they'd agreed to help us if they could. She replied, "It's done and addressed to the Beta no name because they were being weird. Are you on your way back?" I answered, "Yup."

When I got in the truck my scent came back, and I quickly wrote down the times. I needed to get my watch program done. It was close, but not perfect yet. I drove back and parked. I told myself, "Pretty good for never having driven before."

Hendrick shouted, "YOU HAVE NEVER DRIVEN BEFORE?!" I jolted admitting, "I didn't know you'd be here." He snorted, "We are teaching you how to drive. I cannot believe you didn't tell us you didn't know how to drive."

I pointed out, "Umm you would've insisted on going and…" He cut me off, "I know." He took me back to their house and I changed. I left and felt the air still. What the hell? Why did everything suddenly feel wrong?

I hid in a bush and tried to figure it out. I heard screams and people began to come outside. Someone cried, "Oh no. Who is it this time?" Somone replied, "A pack from Virigina came." A woman gripped her husband's hand. She whispered, "Are they coming for our pup?" His eyes showed devastation and defeat. He said, "We don't know." Huh?

I heard Dax scream, "NO!" I started running before I saw who it was. Caine was being held down and so was Dax. Addison, Beta Female Eden and Luna Elena were as well. My heart stopped. That meant this was about Sierra.

A man was dragging her by her hair. She screamed, "Leave me alone!" He hit her and I saw red. Beta Jean urged, "Sierra, don't fight him. He won't hurt you. Clay will be a good mate." Clay actually laughed. Yeah, no….Beta jean was wrong… that was not the laugh of a sane person.

Beta Female Eden screamed, "YOU CAN'T GIVE OUR PUP TO HIM! SHE'S NOT EVEN EIGHTEEN! SHE COULD HAVE HER FATED!" He replied, "He has Alpha blood. It's a good match." Sierra tried to fight back.

Clay snarled "You're MINE! Clearly you lack discipline, so I'll mark you now." Dax roared in anger and shifted into his wolf and was promptly shot with a dart which forced him to shift back. Caine shouted, "NO!" He shifted too and was shot.

I hadn't stopped running to watch. People gasped at me as I flew by them. Alpha Edward finally saw me. He ordered, "Do not interfere!" The Alpha Command yet again did nothing. Sierra was pinned to the ground.

I dove and got my arm between her neck and his teeth. He sank his canines to the bone, and I screamed in pain. Sierra gasped, "Ashley." Right. Because that's what outside packs could know about my name.

I kicked Clay so hard I heard his ribs crack. Someone grabbed me from behind and I took him down with a simple move. I stood over Sierra and took them down as they came. They stared at me in shock. I screamed, "Is that all you got?" They said nothing.

I shouted, "PATHETIC! All of you! Come on! LET'S GO!" I had all the rage I could ever need on my side and nowhere and no one to take it out on until they showed up. One man said, "We are taking Sierra with us."

I mocked him, "Then come get her… jerk. Oh wait, you tried that didn't you? You will NEVER get past me." Alpha Edward said, "They bought her." I replied, "Then give the money back! She's not going anywhere, and you can't just sell pack member! Ordinance 124…"

He shouted, "I don't care! That's how it works here." I replied, "No, it's not… because if it is then every Supernatural will come down here and SLAUGHTER you all. If you're left standing which is questionable at this point… because… I think you know that I know… I can take you all." I didn't know why I felt that way, but I did. It was true and I knew it.

I told him, "You will NOT let him take Sierra. You WILL BE the Alpha you are supposed to be! Marking an unshifted pup is AGAINST THE LAW! All of them… BE AN ALPHA!" I was begging him. I needed him to be one right here and now.

I would fight to the death for Sierra. She wasn't going with Clay. She was there for me when I was abandoned. We were friends and I wouldn't have stood by even if we weren't. Clay asked, "Who the fuck do you think you are?"

Addison replied, "She's Ashley Griffen." I added, "Fighter for those who can't fight back… be that training or drugged… apparently." He snarled and shifted. Gamma Booker yelled, "DO NOT KILL HER!" Huh. That was shocking. More than actually… I was pretty sure he hated me.

I stared down the wolf with black markings. Sierra whispered, "Ashley, it's…" I told her, "Go get behind your mom." Beta Jean growled, "Sierra." I shouted, "NOW!" Clay's wolf jumped and I moved. I ran full force and slammed him into the ground, broke his front leg, took a knife from my shoe, and held it to his throat.

The shocked gasps that went around the pack didn't phase me. I stared at the group that came with Clay. I demanded, "Shift back." He did and screamed in pain. I looked at them, "You leave here… or he dies. Then you never… EVER come back…. Sierra Kiern is NOTHING to any of you."

One snorted, "And when we come back, what are you going to do?" I warned, "If you ever come back to this state, I'll kill each and every one of you." I jabbed Clay in the neck. He shouted, "Ok! Ok, Jesus! You crazy bitch."

I said, "I'm not the one with Alpha blood trying to mark an unshifted pup. Or running around taking her from her home in the middle of the night… gosh you people are something else." He replied, "I win." I was shot with a dart and simply dug the knife in harder.

Alpha Edward shouted, "Hit her again." It felt like yet another crack inside me. The Alpha was ordering me to be shot for protecting someone he should. I felt ten more darts hit and decided to stab Clay in the thigh. He screamed, "GOD!"

I heard the next dart coming because it was closer. Trevor McCann wore an evil smile, and I moved so it hit Clay instead. He screamed in agony. His pack winced. One said, "Ok, we'll go." I reiterated, "If you come back to this state, I'll kill all of you… I heard you're from Virgina…. So, stay there… or find out just what I can do when prepared." That scared them and it made me happy.

They urged, "Give him back to us." I replied, "No….not a single chance. Do I look dumb to you? I mean… I'm a genius… so… I'm not dumb. I'll give him back at the border. So… move it." Alpha Edward growled, "You don't give orders here." Yet I was and it still hurt. His distain and hatred hurt, but I ignored it because I wasn't wrong; he was.

I dragged Clay with me to the border then threw him in their SUV. I took a dart to the chest that only hurt because of the proximity and close range of the shot. Gamma Booker snarled, "You stupid girl!" He punched me.

I asked, "What is WRONG with all of you? But especially YOU!" I pointed at Beta Jean. I said, "She's your daughter! She was terrified and you just…." I looked at him shaking my head sadly. He flinched.

I turned Alpha Edward, "You… what happened to you? You shouldn't allow this! It has to hurt your blood as it does mine…" I saw him flinch too but Gamma Booker hit me again. He asked, "Are you going to take your punishment?"

I shot back, "Are you going to answer what's wrong with all of you?! Why are you hurting yourselves and your wolves this way? It doesn't make sense and…" Gamma Booker yelled, "LIFE DOESN'T MAKE SENSE! Now, you can either be whipped and thrown in the hole."

I shivered not wanting to go back in there. He grinned evilly and I knew whatever was coming meant I was going to take getting whipped and thrown in the hole. "Or you can sleep with all of us here and now."

I whispered, "You're all mated and…" He replied, "And our mates were relieved when you stood up for Seirra. They must be punished." I jolted as if he'd smacked me, "Punished… for being human? For being the blood in their veins? Do you… do you hear yourself? Why would you punish yourself that way…you seem arrogant and conceited?" He replied, "We have ways it doesn't hurt us."

I replied, "I belong to someone else… and I'm not having sex with married, mated men. I'm not going to be party to ruining a bond… fated or chosen… you…. what are you doing to your wolves? How could you? HOW?!" I had to know. They were ranked wolves.

Gamma Booker grabbed me around the neck, "You don't get to ask questions here." He carried me to the punishing fields. I gripped the boulder I was slung over as he whipped me. Eventually Beta Jean said, "You'll kill her if you don't stop." Did I care? Not really. He kicked me into the hole.

I woke up and saw my parents laughing at a picnic. I screamed, "MOM! DAD!" I ran to them, but I went right through them. I cried, "No." Then I watched myself run up to them. It was last year. Tristan howled happily and led our pack on a run. I sobbed watching it all.

Jason spun me around in a circle then threw me on his shoulders. He boasted, "My sister is the national dance champion! WHOOHOOOO!" He'd had that same pride earlier when I had his six. I gasped and woke up feeling pain in the dark. Right. I was in the hole.

I was never going to see the happiness in Red Run like I'd dreamed of. Even when I went back, everything would be different. I knew everything had changed. I was changed. Actually… I was changing and I could feel it. Each crack in me was growing and my loss of faith in Alpha's… wasn't good.

By the time they came to get me and pull me up from the hole I'd resolved to make sure no one was stolen from their homes again. I would make sure word went around to the packs. I would be the voice and fighter for them. Sierra ran to me the second I was closer to the pack.

Beta Jean sighed, "Sierra…" She cut him off, "Don't you ever speak to me again. Come on to Hendrick's house, Mel." Uncle Ajax argued, "She's coming to our house." Sierra winced. I said, "I'm not." I walked off leaving them behind me.

Sierra whispered, "That's not how things are done here." I replied, "I'm kind of past caring. Really… really… so far beyond caring. Everything here is messed up and wrong." Celia groaned, "Really pup?" I shrugged, "I guess you didn't see what I did."

She replied, "Everyone saw it. Even the people who hide away when people come in the night to take someone. You had the entire pack watching you and hope rippled through the pack afterwards. Which, was not cared for by some." Yeah, I'm sure. I'm also sure I didn't care.

She treated what was left of my wounds. She hummed, "Thank whatever or whoever you believe in that you heal faster than any pup I've ever treated." I asked, "Don't you mean Selene?" She snorted, "Down here in the forgotten packs, we don't worship her. She turned her back on us, so we've turned our backs on her." I could see the logic on that and was honestly with her on it.

Sierra hugged me tightly and sobbed. I told her, "We will start working on self-defense… I… I didn't realize you didn't know any moves and…" She cried, "He was going to mark me, and I couldn't stop him. I knew what my future was in those terrifying moments, and you stopped it all. I'll follow you into Hell itself if necessary."

That was kind of like a pack getting a new Alpha. Umm… weird… but… nice. Dax hugged me next. He whispered, "I couldn't get to her." Addison replied, "They drugged us and you still got outside." I admitted, "That is impressive."

Caine asked, "And why doesn't silver or wolfsbane affect you?" I replied, "It affects every Werewolf. I'm going to guess the ones that were shot at me… had operators with some sort of moral… compass? Which seems weird… but it's the answer. Because like anyone with Werewolf blood gets hurt from wolfsbane or silver." They all nodded, and we spent some time together.

Weeks went by. Trevor and his friends tormented me. They screamed at me and threw sticks. I took my GED and the beating that followed when my results of passing came to Aunt Stephanie's house. I did all the chores and took all their abuse but noticed the shift in the pack.

When things started to go wrong, they looked at me. I was pretty sure it was driving Alpha Edward insane… Well… more insane…than he currently was because he clearly had already lost it.

I was cleaning outside the office when I overheard Edward say there was a shipment of Demons was coming in. I'd been slowly saving people from him and his dirty deeds. This one was bigger than him though because based on what he said this was the Ring.

I listened and got the details. The Demons were being held in a warehouse. The Ring was holding them there until they were transferred for experimentation. These people were just sick. How could they do this? It was unfathomable to me.

No matter how much I saw, I could not make it make sense. I honestly didn't understand how they could sleep at night. I researched the place and came up with a plan. I went to meet with Hendrick, Mason, Dax and Addison.

Caine couldn't make it tonight since he was on patrol duty. I walked into the diner and explained everything. Mason asked worriedly, "Are you sure you want to do this, Mel?" I replied, "We have to." Dax sighed, "You're only fourteen."

I said, "Age is just a number. I know right from wrong. No one deserves to be experimented on until they die… it's sick." Mason commented, "No one is arguing that point with you." I told them, "I've studied the warehouse. Mason, Hendrick and Addison can create a diversion. Dax, you can fill Caine in when you join him for your patrol. Edward is making him pull double duty. So, make sure you take him some coffee..."

Dax grumbled, "Damn patrol schedule." Mason warned, "He suspects you two are doing something, that's why he's doing it." I grinned saying, "And now he won't because this will happen while they are on patrol. Sierra is cooking and Edward thinks Addison and I are here with you two." Hendrick nodded.

Dax got up and grabbed two thermoses of coffee and left to go see Caine. We waited twenty minutes until we put our plan into action. We geared up and put on our masks with our voice modulators. I had assigned myself to go in and be the rescue team because if something happened to me… no one would care.

Mason, Hendrick and Addison could all get away. I'd already lost most of my family. Beta Jason hated me, and he made that very clear every chance he got. Maybe if I died saving people, he'd be proud of me again like he'd been when I had his six.

I shook those thoughts. I was going to do good things. I had a whole plan. I was going to make the world my dance floor, just like my family had said to. In truth, my hacking skills needed improvement. I could take some courses. I was running on less and less sleep as time went by.

If I took courses, I could meet some people in that community and learn. So far, I'd kept the Resistance to all local inside Tennessee missions. Getting around was hard since, even though I could run really fast, getting to a bordering state was complicated.

I had thwarted another attempt to kill Xander already. It wasn't my best plan, but there was no way I was letting them get to him. I'd overheard Edward talking about their assassination attempt. I couldn't do nothing. I had to protect my mate. I left the Resistance circle and knew the Hackura came and saw it. I'd left a camera that they found. So, my plans had room for improvement.

I cleared my mind as I approached the warehouse. I needed to get in and out. There was a busted window I was going to go through. I jumped to the ledge and shimmied my way through it. I had a few pieces of glass stuck to me, but I welcomed the pain like I always did these days.

Pain reminded me of all I'd lost and how it was taken from me. How I was blamed. I deserved the blame, but Slade would get his one day. I jumped down and texted Mason.

Me: I'm in.
Mason: One diversion coming up.

I heard a loud bang. Several people jumped up in the warehouse and took off. I snorted, "Amateurs." I ran to the first room and kicked the door open. I grabbed the keys and took the bindings off the group of prisoners. They stared at me. I commented, "Now would be when you shimmer away and keep running… that's a thing… that's… common sense right now." Several looked at me and nodded.

One stayed behind. I said, "I need to keep moving so…" He looked at me introducing himself, "I'm Virgil. They separated me from my sister. We have to find her." I agreed, "Alright. Let's go then." We'd cleared three more rooms, but Virgil's sister wasn't in any of them.

I heard muffled screaming from below us. What the hell? What warehouse had a basement? I ran down and found a trap door. I opened it and jumped down into the dark. I saw a girl tied to a bed, trying to get away and completely incapable of doing so from her position.

A man, for lack of a better word, had the clear and obvious intent to rape her. I grabbed him and threw him off her and jumped on top of him quickly slitting his throat. Virgil yelled, "Valentina! Oh god! Oh god! Did they hurt you?"

Valentina whispered, "She saved me. He was going to rape me. He said it was the start of my training, but she saved me." I shivered knowing from the papers I'd read from Princess Luna Haley Holloran, my Xander's mom, exactly what the Ring meant when they talked about someone's training.

I heard people upstairs again. I sighed and decided to press my luck. Demons didn't often trust anyone who wasn't a Demon but… I had saved them so… they should trust me a little. I whispered, "Any chance you could shimmer us outside? This took longer than I'd planned."

Virgil grabbed me and shimmered us all outside. I started to jog to the getaway truck. To my surprise, they were following me. I turned asking, "Can I help you?" Valentina replied, "Where you go, I go. You saved my life. Both our lives. I swear an oath that I will protect you and serve you."

I took of my mask. I told her, "I don't need people to serve me… don't say that." Virgil laughed, "I go where Val goes. Plus, you don't seem boring. I like it." This went further than them shimmering me out and trusting me. Oaths… those were serious to all Supernatural's.

I sighed, knowing I wasn't going to get them to leave. I waved my hands, "Fine. No oaths though. We can just… be friends or something. Let's go." We got in the truck. I guess I had two new members in the Resistance. That was good. Shimmering was helpful. That meant we could take things out of state.

I changed before sneaking back into the diner. I spotted Gamma Booker getting out of an SUV. I winced, "Crap." Virgil asked, "What's wrong?" I admitted, "I need to get inside… and…" He shimmered me inside then left. I sat down at the desk.

Hendrick shouted, "Gamma McCann, how…" I heard a hit and opened the door to the office. I gasped, "Hendrick!" I ran and touched his face. Gamma McCann ground out, "You were just in the office?" I replied, "Umm obviously… that's the door I came out of…" He rolled his eyes and left.

Hendrick asked, "How the hell did you do that? You didn't get back with Mason and Addison." I replied, "So… I kind of have two people you guys should meet." Virgil and Valentina shimmered in. Hendrick asked, "You added two Demons to our group?" Virgil answered, "We kind of added ourselves."

I snorted, "Then you have to pick Bravo Names. I'm one." Valetina giggled, "Is anyone four?" I admitted, "Nope." She nodded, "Cool. I'll be Bravo Four." Virgil said, "I'll be twenty." Mason snorted, "Dax will lose his mind." Virgil grinned, "Sounds fun." They melded seamlessly into our group.

I sold enough stocks and bought an apartment building, and they moved in there. It amused them because they thought they'd continue to live in the diner. Before I knew it, I was back at the Undergrounds. Crush wasn't there tonight, but I saw pity on several faces.

One fighter whispered, "They will die tonight." I asked, "Who?" They turned and winced. I snorted, "So, you think I'm part of this 'they' because… obviously…" The guy in charge shouted, "Go see the prisoners, Swiffer. Feed them." I asked, "Uhh what?" Another fighter said, "I'll take you." He drove me to another facility and handed me some fast food.

I was let inside and nearly threw up. They snorted, "You're new." A guard said, "She's Swiffer." They all stared at me like I was crazy. Well… they weren't wrong. I immediately saw there was a girl and boy who were on their last leg. It was the guy from my first night that I swore to get out and save.

I left and told the guy driving I need a minute. He replied, "Everyone does their first time here… it's… yeah." I took off running then grabbed my phone. I called Virgil. He answered, "I need two bodies. One male and Female." He shimmered to me grinning asking, "What are we doing?" I said, "They are going to take two fighters tonight. We need to get them out… or… well…. no or… they will die." He nodded, "We are faking deaths. I'm into it."

I admitted, "You'll need to kill whoever is driving the car…so..." He laughed, "Goodie." I thought about the schedules and told him, "Bring Caine, Sierra, and Mason." He winked and shimmered away. I ran back and I was driven back to the fighting grounds.

I went and found the guy who ran everything. He asked, "What are you doing back here?" I said, "I want to make you an offer." He snorted, "This will be good." I said, "I want a percentage of what I win here." He laughed, "Why would I give that to you?"

I answered, "For my silence. I saw Werewolf fighters I think the Werewolf Council would be interested in… investigating. Plus, the Supernatural Council would find you forcing fighters to fight to the death…. well… I could bring down at least five Supernatural groups on you."

He stared at me. He admitted, "I did earn what your Aunt was paid from one fight. Should you survive tonight, you have a deal." So, they really thought I was dying tonight. I nodded to him and went to get ready.

I left a phone we hoped they would steal. I waited until the guy who'd driven me walked in. The doctor was right behind him. I stood to leave but He grabbed my wrist. He urged, "Try tonight, pup. Ok?" I replied, "I'm not going to lose." He winced and I left hearing them introducing me as the Swiffer.

Everyone roared and cheered. To my shock Alpha Edward, Beta Jean, and Gamma Booker were here. Trevor and his friends were too. I got in the ring. They announced, "The twin Alpha Terrors." Oh good. They shouted, "The Kings of the cage." Cage? Two of the biggest men I'd seen in my entire life got into the ring and a literal cage came down around us.

The crowd noise for them was deafening. I stared at them watching as they raised their fists. The one on the right had clear indicators. One had a weak knee, the other had a week elbow. Probably from a previous dislocation. Both had been drinking. They weren't drunk but I could use that.

They turned to me, grinning. One asked, "Do you know what happens to our opponent?" I answered, "Uh huh… yup… I got it." The other looked disappointed in my answer. He replied, "No, you don't." I snorted, "They die… right? I mean… I know I'm right." They grinned, "And now it's your turn." I shrugged, "Ok." They blinked, staring at me in shock.

I asked, "Is this how you usually fight? Because it's not really…" They jumped into action. I took their hits while staying on my feet. One shouted, "Put your hands up!" I shrugged at him, and he hit me hard. They kicked and went at me. I went to a knee and took an uppercut. I glanced at a woman in the crowd, then did a double take. It looked like my mom. She screamed, "FIGHT BACK!" I whispered, "Mom."

I caught one of the twin's legs and pulled him upwards until he fell. I ran at the other and hooked my leg up around his neck and squeezed my thighs together. He gasped and hit my stomach. I punched him in the balls, and he went down.

When he fell unconscious, I looked for the other one. The crowd was screaming, and I felt a whoosh of air. I moved on instinct. The other roared and looked at his twin. He wasn't dead though. His eyes fixed on me. He said, "I'll rape in you this cage before I RIP YOUR BEATING HEART OUT!"

I replied, "Umm hard pass…. Very much hard pass…. On any of that." His eyes were now pitch black and he'd partially shifted. He came at me claws out. I backed up deciding to use the cage against him. His claws would get caught. When my back hit it, I waited.

He snarled, "You're dead." I replied, "Not quite… I mean… not even close really…" He swung and I ducked at the last second and put all my weight into the kick on his knee and heard it dislocate. I pinned him and the supposed ref ran into the cage and counted them both down.

He shouted, "Your winner, continuing her winning streak, is SWWWWIIIFFFFFEEERRRRR!" The cage lifted and I jumped out. I called, "Mom!" I ran to the woman I'd thought was her and jolted back. I apologized, "Sorry." She shrugged, "You've got a concussion and blood in your eyes. Maybe don't let people kick your ass when you can fight as well as you do." She didn't get it.

Trevor snorted, "She's a weak ass bitch." The woman laughed, "You need your eyes checked young man. This here is a bad ass fighting bitch." She nodded to me and left. I walked to the back and was seen by the doctor. I hobbled to the leaders office afterwards. He shouted, "A damn accident and they blew up a damn car and cost me two fights tonight! You're lucky the Twin Terrors went down to our new fighter. Everyone was enthralled." I cleared my throat, and he hung up.

He told me, "I'll give you a percentage IF you bring in a certain dollar amount." I replied, "You'll give it to me anyway… because… well… I'm blackmailing you… so…" He pulled a gun and pointed it at me. I didn't move.

He realized, "Good god pup, don't you fear death?" I answered, "Nope… which makes me very dangerous." He jolted, "Huh?" I said, "The person that's the most dangerous… in most situations… is the person with nothing to lose. Everyone around me wants me to fear death… but I don't. My family wishes me dead with every conversation we have… so…" He put the gun away, "Fine. Get out of here." Gladly.

I headed back to the back. Aunt Stephanie saw me and screeched, "You're alive?" I replied, "Obviously… though I could see why you think I'd haunt you if I died… I so would…" She screamed, "EDWARD!" She stomped off.

Lead Warrior Buck said, "Here, pup." He handed me a towel and walked off. He went and swung his sister, Avery, around. She shot me an unimpressed look. She animatedly told Buck all about her day. He looked at her how Jason used to look at me. I turned away because it hurt. I was happy she had though. I didn't see many siblings' bonds other than my friends.

I went to Hendrick's house. Mason was there waiting with Celia. They both gasped. Celia groaned, "Pup, what on earth…" I answered, "I fought twin Alpha's." They stared at me in horror. I winked, "You should see them. I mean they lost, and they have Alpha blood so… they are definitely pissed…we can safely assume they did not join the Melanie fan club." Celia treated me and everyone joined us.

Hendrick dropped his coffee when he saw me. Addison screamed. Dax growled, "Who did this?" I answered, "Uhh… well… through a series of events… they didn't give their names… but they called them Alpha Terrors." Addison flinched.

Caine snarled, "Good." I asked, "Do you know them?" Addison replied, "They want me to be their shared mate." I pointed out, "No Werewolf has ever shared a mate… like… ever. I actually think it's because wolves are too possessive and…"

Caine interrupted, "They've had multiple shared mates." I blinked asking, "They have a harem? That's weird for wolves… and…" Dax said, "No their mates are dead. Everyone thinks it's them that's killing them." I considered it, "Was anyone a fated mate?" Dax answered, "No."

I nodded, "Then they probably can share while together but having separate time leads to the other killing the mate… which would probably be why no fated Werewolf pair has ever had more than two people in it." Addison wiped tears away.

I told her, "They won't touch you. I'll keep you safe… like I did Sierra." Hendrick said, "They are actual Alpha's. Not just an Alpha blood." I asked, "Yeah, how did Clay have Alpha blood but he's not all black? Like the Conners don't… but that's…" They cut me off, "He's the Alpha's son but not the Luna's." I nodded, "Like Future Alpha Lux Bar…"

Mason jumped in, "No, Clay is the son of the Alpha but not the Luna. She's alive. He's the product of him raping a she wolf in heat." I gasped, "What?" They nodded and I rubbed my temples. I waved, "Well, they won't touch you Ads. I took them down tonight… I'll do it again if necessary."

Dax whispered, "You're so awesome." Caine agreed, "I'm jealous." I said, "We'll get you there… you guys are doing really well… and it's not your fault you were never trained. It's really irresponsible of…" Their dads.

Caine waved, "We know it is. They don't like that we have, and I quote, dreamer plans of how to change things." I reasoned, "You already are. What happened with the fighters?" Caine answered, "Virgil got the bodies you needed. He delights in setting things on fire."

I hummed, "He is a Demon so…that makes complete sense." Cain chuckled, "I caused a diversion which had them crashing. We got the fighters out and up it went. They are on a bus going to their cousins pack they swear will hide them." I nodded, "Ok… that's fine… hopefully they are right."

Life got into a routine. I would save people, get whipped, beaten, bullied, and thrown in the hole. Honestly, I'd prefer it all to the hole. I spent time with my friends. Mason taught me to ride a motorcycle. I trained with Dax and Caine and danced in the field.

I'd become the whispered voice of the forgotten. I'd stopped three girls in our pack from being forcibly mated since Sierra. I'd stopped four more at the Underground fights from other packs. It had been a while since I'd been hit though. I knew that was changing today based on a tip I was acting on.

I didn't want to go into the Nashville coven today. I'd actually rather chew nails, but I'd received a tip that someone was being held against their will. It wasn't a solid tip, but it was enough to bother me. People knew that I would help people out, so tips came in often.

It bothered a lot of people, and I walked into a lot of traps. The coven in question, Shadow Vice, was no fan of mine. I'd kicked a few of their coven members' butts a few months ago. It wasn't my fault they didn't understand that they should learn more than spells. Self-defense for example would be handy for them to learn but they didn't.

The ones I'd come against were horrible with their magic. Not one of their spells did anything to me. It was sad, honestly. Then they couldn't even attempt to block a hit. I tapped my fingers on my desk in Mason's office, then I groaned and hit it.

I knew I couldn't ignore the darn tip. I walked over and knocked on the closet in a particular way to cause it to open. I strapped myself down with weapons. Someone in their coven probably wasn't completely crap… which meant the tip could be correct.

I sent a text to Addison and Caine telling them to get eyes on the coven. We had done recon on them before, so we had their highest traffic times. I'd like to avoid that if I could. Obviously, if it wasn't possible then I'd just be going in whenever. I wasn't going to let someone suffer.

I stared at the tip. It was vague. It just said 'someone.' Not even a clue as to who. If it was true, it would be clear. It would be the person tied up. I left and met up with Caine and Addison. Caine announced, "It's a lighter time of day, but the best time to do this would be in the morning."

I sighed, "Well, my tip says it has to be done by tonight." Addison hummed, "Then in the next thirty minutes would be the best time." I instructed, "Try and keep more people from coming inside." I'd already looked at the schematics. I was going to go in through the roof.

If there was someone there… I'd have to fight for them to get out. Technically speaking. I'd just get whoever it was out and come back tonight for the fight. I'd get punished because the coven leader would cry to Edward when I kicked their butts. Happy day to me. I'd been on such a good streak.

I went around the back and up the ladder, then in through the skylight and dropped to the ground. Thankfully, Witches didn't have superior hearing. I slowly started clearing the rooms. I was fairly certain I knew where they would keep someone here.

I used the heat signatures on my watch to determine if people were in rooms. I was close to having it the way I wanted to give to the team, but for now it was still just me. My readings so far, only showed people that were standing up. Someone who had been taken would likely be sitting tied up or laying down with other people standing up.

I got to the room where I suspected they would keep someone against their will. I wanted to curse. There was someone seated in the middle of the room, with ten people around them. Why ten? How powerful was the person sitting there? Was this a trap? Ten Warlocks or Witches seemed excessive. I had to know though.

I pulled out my lock picking kit and quickly got to work. When I heard the lock click, I took out my tranquilizer gun. I'd rather kick their butts, but I needed to think about the prisoner. I opened the door and entered the room. I had four people down before everyone caught on. Someone came up behind me. I turned and used more force than I intended with my kick.

I quickly shot the warlock with a tranquilizer. I'd feel bad that I broke his leg, but he was clearly a jerk, so… it wasn't that bad when you thought about it. People started chanting. I turned, "I hope you guys are better than the other people in this coven I've come up against." Nothing happened when they finished their chant.

I sighed, "You guys kind of suck at magic. Maybe give up… or practice more… both of those seem to be valid options." I shot them all quickly and pulled out my knife. I turned to see a girl sitting in a chair, staring at me with wide eyes.

I frowned, "How does a Witch get ten guards when they did something to your magic?" The girl snorted, "I'm way better than them. How did you know something was wrong with my magic?" I admitted, "I don't know, I just do….but gosh, I hope you're better than them. These guys really suck. What did they do to your magic?"

She winced, "It's bound for another seven hours." My jaw dropped. I said, "But… but doesn't that hurt you? Like a lot?" She nodded answering, "Yes. It does." I frowned, cut her loose, and took out a piece of paper and wrote a note that I'd be back to fight them for… Crap.

I didn't know her name. She whispered, "Paige… I'm Paige." I quickly wrote her name and took her back towards the room I'd entered in. She was moving really slowly, which told me she must really be in a lot of pain.

I threw her over my shoulder. She gasped as I lifted her with ease. I got back to the room with the skylight and got us out. I climbed down the ladder with her. She snickered, "How much do you work out? Jeez. Werewolf strength is no joke." I nearly faltered.

I was stunned because she knew I was a Werewolf without her powers. She really was a powerful Witch then. I reached where Addison was waiting. She told me, "Caine has a car. Let's go." Paige commented, "I can walk."

I disagreed, "You are in pain, and I'm guessing you need food… so… you don't get to walk." I felt such an intense need to take care of her it didn't make sense. If I was back home, I'd say she should meet Dalton. They'd be cute together.

I called Sierra. She answered, "Hey." I asked, "Can you grab some soup and bread and meet me at Valetina's place?" Sierra agreed, "I'm on it." We reached the SUV Caine was sitting in. Addison got in the front. She handed Paige a Gatorade and some water, which she opened and sipped slowly.

Paige asked, "Who are you guys?" I answered, "My name is Melanie McAlister. People around here often call me Ashley Griffen." Paige snorted and laughed, spitting out some water. Well, it wasn't that funny.

She asked, "Really?" I nodded. She commented wryly, "They really don't like you back there." I shrugged, "The feeling is mutual." Paige smiled saying, "I think we will be good friends." I shrugged. I didn't really make friends often anymore… but at the same time, she felt right. I had my close group of friends.

I asked Caine, "Can you come back with me tonight for the fight? Or should I ask Dax to come?" Caine said, "I'll come." Paige crossed her arms saying, "I'll come with you." I disagreed, "No, without your magic that wouldn't be a good idea. Do you have any self-defense training?" She shook her head.

I asked, "How did you get here?" She sighed, "My foster family sold me." I wished that was the worst thing I'd heard. I muttered, "Things like that used to surprise me… I kind of miss those days. Were they going to have a Warlock mark you?" She nodded. Then he's who I'd be fighting then.

I told her, "You can relax now. I'll sort everything tonight, and you'll be free. They won't bother you again." She snorted, "I'll curse the shit out of them once my magic is back." She had fire. That was good. I sat back and closed my eyes. It was going to be an interesting few days.

I had been correct. I'd fought for Paige been punished and when I got out of the hole and showered, I went to see her. She was in the apartment complex I owned. She opened the door and gasped. She yanked me in.

She asked, "The Warlocks did this to you?" I snorted, "No. I get in a lot of fights…. to be honest… I'm not really popular here… people actually hate me so… Anyway, I handled the Warlocks with ease. That Coven is awful at spell casting." She raised an eyebrow.

I looked around surmising, "You're cramped and uncomfortable here." She insisted, "I really appreciate you giving me this place. I'm glad you're here though because I want in." I questioned, "In on… what, exactly? Because I mean…" She waved, "You know exactly what. You're in that circle group." I groaned, "The Ring Resistance. The Resistance for short. How is it not obvious?"

She admitted, "Actually now that you say it, it is." Was I going to have to tell everyone the name for them to get it? She laughed, "Maybe." Dang it… I hadn't meant to say that out loud. She asked, "So, what Bravo can I be?"

I shrugged, "Which one do you want to be?" She jolted, "Just like that?" I replied, "You were vetted while I was… umm… detained. I don't have an alert so you're fine… and…" She hummed, "I'll be eight."

I nodded "That happens to be open so you're good… and I'll find you another place." She told me, "That's not necessary." I replied, "I want you to be comfortable. Did they take your spell book? I don't see one and…"

She winced, "My foster family did. I'm starting a new one." I asked, "What happened to your biological family?" She answered, "They died." I'd look into that some more. I went down to a different apartment that had a bunch of my stuff. I needed somewhere bigger, but it was going to do for now.

I stared at the picture, with Slade in the middle. I vowed, "I will get you." I pinned up more pictures and set up the things I'd taken from the Hunter missions Nate gave me. I'd saved fifteen Omegas so far and sent them away.

For those missions, I was Red One. I ordered, "ILYX, look for properties with a remote location, small cottage type feel for sale in this area." ILYX answered, "Working." I heard the door open and turned to see Dax. He stared at the board.

He commented, "One might say you're collecting names. I heard your fighting name the other day." I bit my lip and picked at my sleeve, "Umm well… I didn't pick that one so…" He snorted, "Yeah, I've heard rumors of how you got it."

I looked down. He told me, "You know, they didn't actually take your name from you." He hit at the heart of the issue without trying. I disagreed, "They definitely did. They don't want to hear my name so I made others… ones they will be proud of."

He growled, "Fuck them and their pride. YOU did NOTHING wrong. You're out here doing jobs you have no business doing. You're teaching how packs should be. You have bigger plans for everyone." I agreed, "I do. Did Caine… umm… get my message to other Alpha and Beta heirs?" He answered, "Yes." He didn't continue.

I pressed, "And?" He sighed, "They want to meet and train with you. This is dangerous." I shrugged, "We have two Demons and a Witch on our team now. The risk has significantly decreased. Plus… I think I have a pla if I'm still here when I'm sixteen… ya know after I shift and…"

Dax snorted, "So now there's an A in your plan. What's the N?" I shrugged, "I'll figure it out." He asked, "What's the pla?" I explained, "If I'm still here after I shift, then I'll challenge for the Lead Female Warrior position."

He jolted, "You can't. You're not a pack member." I grinned, "But I'm not supposed to be here either… and technically speaking, Ashley Griffen IS a member of this pack. I saw my name on the pack census. So I actually joined…when you think about it."

He snorted, "Idiots. I swear my dad gets worse every damn day." I asked, "Was he always like this?" He answered, "No. That's the hardest part to reconcile. I remember being little and back then he adored Sierra. Him and my mom were happy but…" I asked, "What?"

He sighed, "Him and Edward were really close and good friends. Booker had the job of Gamma, since his uncle died, and they were close until he distanced himself. Then they got close again and everything changed. My dad turned into a monster I don't recognize." He stood to leave.

He turned, "Thank you for protecting Sierra that night. For all the girls and boys you have protected. I wish I could have." I reasoned, "They drugged you." He said, "And they talk about how they can't do it to you. You scare them."

I snorted, "I told you… that's not possible." I needed to test my own blood at this point. He left and I worked on my watch program. With Paige here I could use some spells on them. I asked, "ILYX, can you locate Xander?" He answered, "Xander's GPS location is in Black Mountain."

I jumped and cheered for myself. I'd sync with Paige and get the spells on the watches, and they'd be ready. ILYX asked, "Is that all you require, Melanie Jane?" Paige asked from behind me, "Is that Alpha Alexander Conners?! Damn. You guys are deep into this if he's in too."

I squeaked, "Huh? What? No… that's not… him… it's ILYX… which is not him… at all." She snorted, "I've heard his voice and that was it." I questioned, "Umm what are you doing… ummm here?" She shrugged, "I saw Dax leave and wandered in."

I nodded, "Uh huh… wandering that's…" ILYX announced, "Melanie Jane, I have found three cottages that match your criteria." I blushed. Paige asked, "And what does ILYX stand for?" I squeaked, "Stand for? Umm… it doesn't have to stand for anything. Nothing… yup nothing." She laughed, "You're a terrible liar." I grumbled, "So I've heard."

She stared at me. Finally, I blurted out, "It's I Love You Xander… ok? So…." She nodded, "So Alpha Alexander doesn't know you're using his voice." I squeaked, "It's… ummm just a programmed voice… like lots of other software." She threw an arm around me, "You and me are going to be great friends." In a different life maybe. I was broken now.

She stared at me, "You are far from broken." I groaned, "I have to stop talking about loud… this is a skill that I require." She laughed, "Probably." ILYX said, "Code Red alert, Melanie Jane. Four bounty Hunters are going after Xander."

I grumbled, "It's like they just don't get my messages." I geared up. Paige declared, "I'm coming." I hummed, "You can be on comms on the computer… since... well… I haven't evaluated your skills… so… computer. ILYX, give Paige the same access as Sierra." ILYX replied, "Adding Paige to the system."

I parked her in front of the laptop. I told her, "ILYX will tell you if you need to tell me something." She grumbled, "I could curse the shit out of people." I agreed, "That will be very helpful… I also kind of need holoports set up… but again… I haven't evaluated your skills."

I called Valentina. She answered, "Hey girl." I told her, "I need you to shimmer me to no man's land." She shimmered in and stared at Paige. I asked, "Have you two not met?" Paige snorted, "We met but she's being a typical Demon about new people. I'll wear her down." She winked, "You'll be my friend too, Val." Valentina shot me a disbelieving look and shimmered me out.

She declared, "The new girl is bright and shiny." I snorted, "She's got her way of coping… and I think it's nice. She seems like a good person. She's definitely powerful, but I did rescue her… and let me say the guy I fought for her was… umm… horrible. So, I wouldn't say her life has been roses." Valentina asked, "What are we doing?"

I hit the buttons on my watch hoping this worked. I was having ILYX scan for heat signatures. A map projected with four of them. I pulled my gun and shot at three before return fire came. I shot him down. I walked over to him while he gasped for breath.

I asked, "Why don't you all listen to my warnings? LEAVE HIM ALONE!" I shot him five more times. Then I walked over the other bodies and did the same. When I was done, I arranged them in our symbol and painted it on the middle one's shirt.

I told Valentina, "Shimmer us back." She did. Paige jolted, "You're already back?!" I nodded, "Yup… I'm… kind of really good at killing people at this point." She snorted, "I'll say." I got undressed and started to work on my file.

Paige asked, "What's this?" I explained, "I plan to go the Supernatural Council for help… so… I'm working to perfect this file." She began poking around. She said, "You know, I think we could develop a lot this stuff together." I turned to see what she was talking about.

Valentina groaned, "You're going to talk to her about her science projects? Oh, Asmodeus give me strength. You two have fun." She shimmered out but it turned out that Paige and I did have fun. We managed to accomplish a lot.

I was working on developing my counter agent to iron poisoning, but it was going slower than I wanted. I wanted to protect Xander. I was thinking about it when I walked into the coffee shop to get Edwards' freaking coffee order.

A woman laughed, "Alexander Conners can go all night." What? I turned and looked at her. My heart dropped because she was stunning. She might even be perfect. From her blonde hair to her model like look. She was stylish too.

One woman with her asked, "Huh? You met Alpha Alexander?" She answered, "Yeah, that's where I was the whole weekend." Male Lead Warrior Buck cleared his throat beside me. I blinked up at him with tears in my eyes. He said, "Don't listen to her." If only I could take that advice.

Another woman laughed, "Tell me how you got to him because…" She trailed off then continued, "I'm impressed and want a turn." The first woman answered, "Don't be the pathetic pup they are worried is his fated mate." A knife to the heart would've hurt less.

The barista called, "Alpha Edward's order is up." I rushed forward and grabbed it, threw a tip on the counter, and ran out as the tears fell. Lead Warrior Buck shouted, "Ashley, wait." Right, me. Because in public I was Ashley.

I turned and he sighed. He said loudly, "Make sure that gets back without you spilling it." Several people snickered and my heart dropped. I thought he was going to say something nice. He got in his truck and drove off.

I started to walk back. Once I was out of sight of the town Buck called, "Get in the truck." I jolted, "Lead Warrior Buck…" He rolled his eyes jabbing his thumb, "Get in the truck." I did as he said. I asked, "Why are you giving me a ride?" He answered, "Because."

I asked, "Well… why didn't you offer in town? Because…" He cut me off, "You ask too many questions, pup. Keep your head down here because you're painting a massive target on your back." I argued, "I'm doing what's right… that's more important than…"

He disagreed, "It's not. Keep your head down pup and survive." He stopped and told me, "Get out and keep walking." I frowned, "So you'll only help when no one is looking but…" He added, "And don't listen to the gossip about Alpha Alexander. Maybe make it less obvious you're in love with him."

I blushed, "I… that's… he…. you…" He snorted, "Good god. Your stuffed wolf everyone hates looks just like his and it's obvious you love him. Get back to the Alpha." I got out of the truck, and he took off. He confused me.

He knew what was going on was wrong. Did that make it worse than those that thought everything was right? He was strong enough to help people… he kind of helped me… Those thoughts swirled in my mind.

I put Alpha Edward's order in his office and left. I smelled Trevor lurking and ducked so his fist went through a wall. I commented, "That was really sloppy… you should go to the gym." He snarled, "A gym you're not allowed into because you're unworthy…"

I snorted, "Ok… I could beat you in a fight. Literally anytime, anywhere…. my genitalia barring me from a gym is against code…" He swung a knife that I dodged. He shouted, "Women are meant to be on their backs and in the kitchen. You have no place in the gym! We don't care about codes and rules! We make our own."

I admitted, "So I have seen… it's…. against basic human decency… you know it's bad when Humans would call you out on what you're doing… but I also know you don't care." His friend, Mark, urged, "Let's just go."

Trevor sneered, "You'll be whipped for talking back to me. You're a curse and family killer." He slammed his shoulder into me. Francis sighed, "Just do yourself a favor and stop making him mad." I asked, "How do I do that?" He sighed.

I pointed out, "My mere presence caused him to take a swing… .so… your advice is terrible unless you'd like me to die." He replied, "No one wants that." I busted up laughing. He looked at me like I was crazy until Trevor shouted, "FRANCIS!" He took off running like the good lap dog he was.

I left and called Alpha Peter. He answered, "What?" I said, "Umm… I just… was…" He growled, "Spit it out. I don't have all day." I stammered, "Can I come… just… home?" He growled, "No, stop asking." He hung up on me. I stared at the phone and cried. He'd never talked to me that way in my entire life.

I went to where I danced and let everything go. Tears coursed down my cheeks. Everyone wanted me to accept this was my life now, but part of me just couldn't. I left the field and took off running for the plot of land where my parents and Tristan were to me.

I cried, "I can't do anything right for them anymore. They hate me and it hurts." I begged yet again, "Come back to me. Please. Just come back. I'm sorry." I stayed there and cried until I had to go back to the pack I was staying in. Maybe everything would be ok once my file for the Supernatural Council was perfected. Black Path was under their purview. They could make everything ok.

The Mundane

Alexander is Nineteen Years Old

Alexander was furious. I hit the heavy bag wishing I could hit someone in New York. Melanie left and I'd never to meet her. Oden growled, "Just go to New York." I might just do that. Cassie's emotions slammed into me, and I popped to her.

I growled, "Who the FUCK made you cry?" She sniffled and I gathered her into my arms. I asked, "What happened?" She whispered, "Promise me that you won't retaliate." I agreed, "I promise that I won't for now."

She chuckled humorlessly, "I guess that's all I'll get." She sighed, "Cayden's ex is being awful." I reasoned, "Then kill her." Oden growled, "Rain said this ex said our sister couldn't have his pup!" What?! She told me, "She's started all these ugly rumors about her that me, Milana, Aiylee, and Bea shut down. I've gotten her ass back but…" She trailed off.

I asked, "Why did you show up at the sex dungeon Cayden and I were in?" She winced and the pain she felt had me pulling her into my lap. I told her, "I'll fix it all, just tell me." She whispered, "Cora showed up in our bed, naked." Fury overtook me.

EJ linked, "What is going on?" My dad linked, "Are you ok?" Mom linked, "I'm ready to kill whoever." That made me laugh because it was just like her to say. I asked my sister, "And is she still alive? Or do I need to bury a body?" I hadn't heard about her dying but Cassie was incredibly stealthy.

Cassie snorted, "She appears to be recovering." I said, "Then I'll kill her." She smacked me across the chest reminding me, "You promised not to retaliate." I reasoned, "I also said I'd fix this." I conjured us drinks until Beagan showed up.

She waved, "Hey, Alexander." I kissed the top of her head, "Cousin. Take care of Cass." Cassie asked, "Where are you going?" I answered, "To the gym where I do my best thinking." I winked at her, and she chuckled.

I shifted into Oden. He growled angrily as we ran to the gym. That fucking bitch better hope she didn't cross my path right now. I shifted back and grabbed shorts and went into the gym. She'd come onto me when we'd come home from that mission too.

Right in front of my brother in law, who didn't even care. I flicked her off, but she now coming after Cassie. I was sick of women coming onto me when they didn't actually like me. Oden growled as our thoughts trailed back to our birthday party when I got as drunk as a I could and someone kissed me.

Flashback

Alexander was hurt. Melanie had been grounded from coming to an event again. Oden whined in my head. I was tired of being kept away from her. I was tired of being kept in the limbo of whether she was mine or not. Oden declared, "She IS ours." I took another drink.

Jason McAlister asked, "You good man?" I didn't answer and conjured ten more drinks and slammed them. My cousin, Cory, asked, "Alexander, are you ok?" I didn't answer him either and kept drinking. I was never going to meet her.

They kept her away from me because they questioned my character. Oden growled, "We are a good person." I reasoned, "They don't mind you. It's clearly me." He said, "Then they are dumb." I wasn't going to say he was wrong.

Jason snorted, "You have a fan club over there." I asked, "And?" I drank several more whiskeys. I saw Hastein fade in with a worried look on his face. Jason repeated, "Seriously dude, are you ok?" I turned to him, "You know what? No, I'm not because…"

Someone shouted, "ALEXANDER!" Oden grumbled, "We were about to tell him why we were upset. It felt like a breakthrough so obviously someone ruined it." I turned and my collar was grabbed and before I could process it lips were on mine. It felt wrong. Nothing about it was right because it wasn't Melanie.

I pulled her off me and felt like I stared at her letting my eyes blaze for hours, but I knew it was barely a second. Her face seared into my brain. She'd stolen my first kiss, the one I'd been saving for Melanie. It was just gone because I couldn't meet her. I stalked off.

Cory popped beside me and wisely said nothing. I stormed into the gym then shouted, "Get out!" to everyone here then hit the heavy bag with all my strength I could. It flew off and I went to the next one. I raged and screamed.

I heard a pop and knew it was my mom. She popped in front of me and blocked my hits. I didn't go hard at her though. I never could. I looked in her eyes and just knew she knew what happened. She might not understand my feelings that it was stolen from Melanie and I, but she understood. She was pissed off too.

Hastein called, "I've got this, Aunt Haley." She kissed my temple, "I love you, Alexander." I whispered, "It was supposed to be my mate." She squeezed my arm, "Then your next one can be. I'm so fucking sorry that was taken from you."

She walked over to my dad, who was here too now, kissed him then left. Hastein came at me, and we went round after round. Jason commented, "This is not a very festive birthday." It wasn't because Melanie didn't come, and I was as tipsy as I could get. Which allowed someone to steal what I'd been saving all this time for Melanie.

I was so sick of the people who couldn't respect my boundaries. I didn't mind people who flirted with me that respected me. Both women and men seemed interested in determining my sexual preference, but the ones who were rude and tried to take things from my mate pissed me off.

Hastein said, "It's ok." I growled, "NO, IT'S NOT!" We fought until Uncle Evin jumped in. Then I fought him until my dad jumped in. He pinned me after an hour. He linked, "Pup, it's ok." I replied, "I was tipsy, and she put her lips on mine. I wanted my first kiss to be with my mate." He said, "And your mom had a lot of things to say to that she bitch most of which involved her fists." Of course she did.

He told me, "You didn't kiss her back." I had not. He reasoned, "So, that doesn't count." I snorted, "That's not really how it works." He argued, "If someone kisses you but you don't kiss them it definitely means it's not your first kiss." Maybe, but it seemed like semantics.

Oden was sulking and I didn't blame him. I said, "Well, I won't be doing anything with anyone else until I meet my mate." He nodded, "Fair enough. I respect your choice." He hugged me whispering, "I'm proud of you." He wouldn't be if he knew I was sulking because they were lying about Melanie crossing the border to keep her from me. Oden whined in my head. Happy fucking birthday to me.

Flashback Ends

Nothing had changed on that front either. I wasn't going to do anything with anyone who wasn't Melanie. It might not be official, but she was my mate to my wolf and myself. Being with someone else wouldn't change that. I stormed into the gym and got into the ring.

A few people joined me, and we went at it. I fought for hours yet again as the plans formed in my head. I had over hundred ways to kill Cora but that wasn't what Cassie needed which left me with one option. I nodded to the guys I'd been fighting and walked into Cayden's office.

Silas had been in there with Jed. I glared at the latter who wisely left without a word. Silas asked, "Did Jed piss you off?" I answered, "No." Silas teased, "Do you want to tell your face that?" I replied, "No." He nudged me saying, "He's so verbose." Cayden ordered, "Give us the room, Silas." He left.

Cayden asked, "Would you care to tell me why you're beating up everyone in the gym?" I answered, "I was thinking through the best solution for something." He replied, "I live with a Fairy now." I shot back, "I am aware since that Fairy is my sister." He grinned, "Yes, well I know you're being evasive."

I called EJ. He answered, "What on EARTH is going on with you? Cassie's so nervous about your reaction to something I'm on edge." Cayden chimed in, "I'd like to know the same answer since it's my mate who is on edge. Your brother is being evasive."

I told them both, "We need to work out how I'll remain as an Alpha, EJ's Enforcer, and a be Squadron Leader here." Cayden's eyes met mine. He jolted, "You're serious. You're finally going to take me up on that offer?" I answered, "Yes."

I linked EJ, "I need to be here more to protect Cass. Shit is going down and it would be harder for someone to keep doing that if I'm here more." I wasn't going to delude myself into thinking it would stop, it wouldn't. Cassie was going to have to handle this how she determined was right for her, but me being here more often would put Cora on notice.

EJ replied out loud, "I have no problem with this as I've said many that before. I'm proud of you, Alexander." Cayden eyes narrowed. He said, "I am too, but I know this move is about my mate." I agreed, "It is. I want to be closer to her." EJ linked, "Evasive." I replied, "Yet true."

Cayden rubbed his temples, "For fuck's sake. I already told you I recognize the evasions but fine. Just tell me she's safe." I snorted, "You know she is." She could kill Cora easily even without Fairy powers. He studied me, "Do I need her Guard around her?" I shrugged, "It couldn't hurt if they were around a little bit more." He nodded, "Alright. Let's figure this out."

It only took an hour since we'd all been thinking about it prior to me officially agreeing. Cayden nodded, "We will have the ceremony here in a few hours." I laughed, "You'd better let me have my mom plan it." He rubbed his temples again, "This will be a squadron leader ceremony for the ages, but I'm not dumb enough to deny my mother in law that honor."

I left and headed back to Cayden and Cassie's home since the bond told me Cassie was there. I called my mom. She answered, "Alexander." I teased, "Aren't you in a session?" I knew she was. Oden snorted, "Mom always answers us." She did. She replied, "I just finished one, but I will always answer when you all call. What's going on?"

I answered, "I accepted a position in the Hackura realm from Cayden as a squadron leader. My ceremony is in a few hours here. I thought you'd like to plan it." She screamed, "I am so fucking proud of you! I'll plan everything and get your dad." She hung up.

I linked dad, "Mom is very excited and coming in hot." He replied, "I can feel that and now she's here. Congratulations on the position, son. I'm proud of you." I replied, "Thanks." He said, "If you'd want to share why you finally accepted, let me know." I chuckled, "You always know everything." He snorted, "Now, if you pups would just keep that in mind and tell me shit that would be great."

I walked into Cassie and Cayden's home. My sister evaluated me. She said, "Well, everyone is excited about whatever you did. Mom seems to plotting some party." I laughed, "I'm going to accept the squadron position your mate has wanted me to. I'll be here more often." She raised an eyebrow.

I snorted, "I do that better than you. Everyone will think twice about messing with you if I'm around more. It sucks but it's true. I'm the sibling that's very in your face and knocking teeth out." She grumbled, "So being stealthy makes them think they can walk all over me."

I crossed the room and hugged my sister. I answered, "No, but it does seem to make these women think they can get away with hurting you. I'm going to show my face around more often and make sure they know it's not true. Everything is going to be."

She hugged me tightly and whispered, "Thank you, brother." I told her, "I will always have your six." Oden told me, "I told Rain the same." Good. I felt a tug on my bond before Uncle Bjourn linked, "I think we need to talk."

I kissed the top of Cassie's head, "I have to go talk to Uncle Bjourn. I'll see you at my ceremony." She checked her phone and laughed, "Yeah, you will." Mom was going to go all out, but that was fine. If it made her happy that was what I cared about.

I portaled to my uncle's office. His secretary smirked at me. I chuckled, "So, mom already told you." Uncle Bjourn snorted, "Yes, along with a prepared argument about why a Duke being given the title of squadron leader should be a bigger celebration." I admitted, "I'd say I'm surprised but that would be a lie, and I can't do that."

Uncle Bjourn laughed, "Yes, I let her present the whole argument even though I know she knows that I was going to let her do whatever she wanted." I replied, "I'd like to invite some of my friends." He nodded, "Go ahead." I winked at him and left.

I called Jason McAlister. He answered, "Hey, Alexander." I told him, "There's a party going down in the Hackura realm. If you can tell your pack and have the partial Fairies bring you if they want to join." He asked, "What's the party for?" I answered, "Me. I'm becoming a Squadron leader."

He shouted, "Congrats, man! That's awesome." I said, "Your whole family is welcome." He snorted, "Maybe that would get Mel to text me back." Oden howled excitedly. I offered, "She's welcome to come." Jason replied, "I wouldn't get your hopes up." I would because I had promised Melanie that I would meet her right before I went to confirm her intel with my family.

That train of thought reminded me of when I killed Charlene and our conversation before I killed her. I didn't kill her for myself really. Someone else would've done it, but I protected Melanie from that awful bitch.

Flashback

Alexander waited until everyone left. I turned to Charlene and asked, "Do you have any idea how you got caught?" Charlene frowned asking, "Didn't Alpha Peter or your uncle tell you?" I shook my head, "No. I do have to thank you before I kill you because for the first time, I got to talk to someone via text."

I winked, "In fact, it's someone that I've been wanting to interact with for quite some time." Oden snorted, "Since she was born. We have wanted to mate since she was born." That was true. Charlene questioned, "Who?"

I snorted, "You know exactly who it is if you're half as smart as you want to claim to be." Charlene's nose wrinkled up smarting, "If you like that little Beta bitch…." I grabbed her by the throat and squeezed. Oden growled, "RIP HER HEAD OFF!" I planned to kill her, just not yet.

I warned, "Speak of Melanie that way ever again, and I'll take you to the Hackura realm to torture for decades. Why didn't you just leave Melanie alone? I don't like you, and I never did. I never gave you any indication that I did either."

I questioned, "Do you think my brother's and I are oblivious to people who just want to use us for our name? News flash, you are in an allied pack of ours. I've known since the dance you didn't want me for me. I'm best fucking friends with Jason for god's sake." I released her from my hold.

She coughed, "Yeah, well I have noticed your best friend doesn't know you like his little sister. Go for someone your own age. She's a pup." I tilted my head, "Since you're going to die, I'll let you in on a secret."

She pleaded, "No, don't tell me. I want to live." Oden scoffed, "She's delusional." I replied, "We knew that." He huffed his agreement. I ignored her saying, "My secret is that I'm fairly certain Melanie McAlister is my mate." Oden growled, "Sure. We are sure."

Charline snorted, "Of course you are. Some bitches get all the luck. She's so in love with you she can't see straight. No matter how many times I tried to get her off that path." I growled, "What does that mean?" I used my pushing power.

I heard steps and briefly saw Charlene and her friends were talking. When they started talking the picture faded and I only heard voices. One spoke, "Shh, let's just go. This is crazy, Charlene. She's just a pup. The Beta's daughter to be exact. You know T comes out here with her sometimes now. We need to go."

Charlene growled, "No, she needs to understand." One sighed, "Maybe you need to understand. She's a pup with a crush. Most pups have those. Alexander may have gone crazy on two peaks, but we ALL know it wasn't for you. There's no point in telling the smartest pup in this pack it was. She'll find out it's a lie."

Another added, "She's right. Alexander probably lost it because that's his best friend's little sister. If anything, I'm beginning to think Melanie isn't the only one with a crush. Which means this is a BAD idea. Goddess above, what am I doing here?" Several people sucked in a breath.

That same voice announced, "I'm not going to die because you can't stand the fact Alexander might like her too. They both fight like insane people. It would make sense that they gravitate towards each other. I'm out of here."

I heard steps then the same person said, "Don't call me anymore. Hell don't talk to me until you get over this crazy idea of making Melanie pay for Alexander not liking you. You did that all on your own. You openly talk about him taking you as a chosen mate. You even loudly proclaim how things will run when you are a Luna of Black Mountain and getting the respect you deserve."

She paused then added, "Around us, you talk about how Alexander will penalize Alpha Peter for giving you punishments. It was already crazy, but now you've gone delusional. I don't know where the girl I grew up with went, but this is bizarre."

She muttered, "I'm also really fucking tired of getting my ass kicked by a pup five years younger than me. It's embarrassing and I hate it. Melanie will never agree to work with me on training so I can get better if I keep hanging around with you guys."

She snorted, "You have gone off the deep end and I don't see how this doesn't end without you dying. I, personally, don't want to die. I want to meet my mate and have a family. I want to be a Warrior in our pack. You know what? I just can't do this anymore. If you guys are smart, you'll follow me."

"The last time you tried to jump her about this Alexander Two Peak situation Elise and Ray were there. Isn't that a big enough sign this has to end? Melanie didn't even know what Alexander had done. Which means she didn't think it was about her. You put that thought into her head. She's a freaking genius. Morons, all of you."

I heard the leaves crunching as if someone was walking away. Charlene growled, "Kristin, come back! Your point isn't valid because Melanie does think it was about her now. We are helping her." Kristin snorted, "I repeat, she thinks that because YOU told her about it."

She admitted, "Hell, I even think she's right to think it was about her because it's the logical conclusion. She's the one who was attacked, and Alexander had no other reason to be pissed. Could that be because she's Jason's little sister? Yes. Could it also be because Alexander likes her too? Also yes. Meaning this path leads to death and I'm off it."

Charlene snarled, "I'll kill her! He's mine." Kristin laughed, "First, that's treason so shut up. Second, you'll never beat Melanie in a fight, Charlene. You'd also never have Alexander if you killed her. If anything happens to Melanie McAlister, I'll tell the Alpha it was you."

She stated emphatically, "I will not be part of the witch hunt if the Beta's daughter gets hurt. I'd be under suspicion because I associate with you. Because I was looking for the girl I used to know, but she's clearly gone. Melanie is a member of our pack. She's just a pup."

She urged, "Stop being so crazy and jealous over a pup. Alexander isn't your mate, but the signs that she could be his are certainly there. Stop ignoring them before you are killed for a man who was never yours and gives no shits about you."

"He finds you annoying which is clear as day on his face. Elise doesn't even like you anymore. Alexander is quiet around most people, but he loves Elise like a sister. If she tells him to stay away from you that's exactly what he will do. You dug your own grave. You could've been friends with him. Leave our Beta's daughter and Alexander alone. Your obsession will be the end of you."

Charlene snorted, "Who needs you anyway? Fake friends are the worst." Kristin sighed, "You would know. You're the fakest of them all. There's no way you know anything about what's going on with any of us in our lives because you're so self-involved."

She sounded near tears, "You're just so wrapped up in your delusions of you and Alexander that it's all you can think about. Tell me one thing going on in my life and I'll keep looking for the girl I once knew. There's even a big one that the whole pack knows about."

Charlene was quiet for several minutes. I heard shuffling feet indicating the others with her were nervous. Maybe listening to her sage advice. Kristen was obviously the smart one of the bunch. Kristin snorted, "Exactly. My brother is in the pack hospital. He was hurt on a scouting mission. Thanks for caring so much about me. Bye."

Charlene yelled, “I’m sorry! I just have a lot in my life going on.” Kristen called, “Wanting Alexander to be yours and plotting how to bully the Beta’s daughter is not more important than my brother suffering from silver poisoning. Princess Luna Haley and Alexander are off on missions so they can’t be called to heal him yet. We hope he can hang on.”

She added, “Oh, and do you know who comes every day to read to him and his scouting group? Melanie McAlister. She even sent all the family’s a care package separate from the Luna’s and her mom’s. It was catered to every member of our family.”

“I’ve stood back while you bullied her, and she sent me all of my favorite things and a book she thought I would like. Hell, I do like it and I bet you can’t name a single thing in that care package. Like my favorite candy.” Charlene didn’t say anything again. Kristen shouted, “BITCH! I know every goddamn thing about you.” I heard someone running away now.

I snarled, “You ambushed Melanie?!” Charlene whined in pain. Oden took over, “My human asked you a question!” She sighed, “Well, that pushing thing hurts a lot!” I growled, “Answer me!” She finally replied, “We ambushed her fairly often. We never won a fight against her though. I just wanted to beat her once then you would know I was worthy.”

I snarled, “You are not worthy to wash her damn socks! She is so far above you it’s crazy. Your friend, Kristin, was right. I attacked Two Peaks with everything I had because they wanted to take Melanie and SHE IS MINE!”

I vowed, “When I meet her that will be clear. Anyone who has hurt her will know my wrath.” I used my pushing power this time not to see anything, but to kill her. Her head exploded. I snapped her body away and took several deep breaths.

Oden snorted, “Welcome to team mate is ours.” I calmed down and answered, “Yes, well we will see.” Oden sighed, “And he’s back to his normal state of being. So close and yet so far. I could almost taste your lack of doubt fading.” I sat down in the corner trying to gather myself.

This proved people were already after Melanie because of me. I needed to protect her better. I just didn’t know how. I’d have to come with something that I could do. I just didn’t know what, because Melanie clearly didn’t tell people when she was ambushed.

To be honest, I couldn’t blame her. She thought those in charge wouldn’t believe her, but she did reach out to me. For the first time tonight, I texted with Melanie McAlister from Tristan’s phone. I had to hope she’d text me if she needed help. I smiled and spoke aloud, “I’ll meet you one day, Melanie McAlister. I already promised.” It made me feel at ease because a promise was something I couldn’t break.

Flashback Ends

Jason asked, “Hello? Are you still there?” I shook off the past answering, “Yeah, just know your family is invited.” He laughed, “I’ll see you there and I’m excited for you. I know that you were toying with this idea for a while. What decided it for you?”

I replied, “I want my presence here more often to deter people from thinking they can start rumors about my sister without consequences.” He growled, “Someone is trying to hurt Cass?” I replied, “Yes, and her subtle ways aren’t making them back down.”

He chuckled, “And here I was worried for a solid second. You’re as subtle as a two by four to the head.” I saw Jed walking by. I replied loudly, “I’m more like a mallet to the head than a two by four. You’ve seen the mess I create when I explode someone’s head. The damage would be more consistent with a mallet as a weapon.” Jed slowed his walk and paled.

Jason asked, “And who are we trying to capture the attention of because you almost blew out my ears? I can hear you just fine.” I replied, “Someone who knows exactly what I’m referring to and should probably pass along that information.” Jed subtly inclined his head. I told Jason, “I’ll see you later.” He agreed, “Yeah, you will.”

I called my Beta and Gamma on a conference call. Gage, my Gamma, answered first, “Hey, Alexander. I’m not totally cool with the chain of information dissemination about you today. Fair warning, Phil is even more so not cool with said chain of information." I heard the beep indicating that Phil joined. I snorted, "I'm calling you now."

Phil snarked, "Oh, now. Now you call me. I've known about this development for quite some time. I can understand Cayden and EJ knowing before me. Even your parents but JASON MCALISTER texted to say he was going because you invited him."

I replied, "Well, I just got off the phone with him so that was fast." Gage jumped in, "Come on, Phil. We know why he called Jason." Phil retorted, "And I'll forgive him if our future Luna shows up." Gage laughed. I sighed, "You know that…" Oden grumbled, "Here we go."

Phil interrupted me, "I know that you have your reasons for not wanting to admit what you and Oden know. I even understand them. I just think that they are…" Gage cut in, "Since he won't say it the way he should I will."

Phil warned, "Gage." Gage retorted, "You're the Beta who waters shit down. That's your role to guide the Alpha to water. I'm not as subtle." I asked, "My reasons are what?" Oden warned, "Youa are a glutton for punishment is what you are."

Gage answered, "Bullshit." I scoffed, "No, it's not. People are…" He jumped in, "You are NOT fucking people. You are Alpha Alexander Marcus Nathan Conners. You are a healer, which makes you more sensitive than any other fucking Alpha out there. You would NOT hurt Melanie McAlister. You're not capable even if she somehow led a group of our enemies against us, you wouldn't hurt her."

I growled, "She would never do that!" Phil quickly said, "We know that. Hell, everyone knows that. Melanie is good person. It's just that we know our Alpha. We believe you and Oden. I understand why you want to meet her. I know you wouldn't this way if so many people hadn't been possessive of her as a pup." Oden snarled and it came out.

Gage groaned, "Dude, you're not like them." I reasoned, "I know. I'm more powerful than all of them combined." He groaned "Good god. I'm going to find a wall to slam my head into." Phil sighed, "Don't do that. I'll have to hunt up a partial Fairy to fix it and they are all excited about the parade."

I snorted, "Why don't you guys have Phil portal the both of you here and find someone who wants to fuck you." Gage admitted, "That does sound more productive and less hurtful to one of my heads than the wall." Phil and I busted up laughing. I added, "Plus, I see my cousin." I winked at Jeffery who was walking towards me.

Gage asked, "Which one? You have a million." I answered, "Jeffery is here." I saw a portal begin to open. Jeffrey laughed, "I was going to surprise my brother when he showed up." Phil ran through the portal that Gage stepped through.

Phil hugged Jeffrey. He said, "I missed you, big bro." Jeffrey replied, "I missed you too." Egres faded in and shot me a look. I grinned at him and wiggled my eyebrows. Gage said, "Uhh he does look amused." Phil snorted, "Because I usually tell him things, but after Jason texted, Alexander called. He's lower on Alexander's information wrung than we are."

I replied, "He usually knows things before all of us and he doesn't share." Egres replied, "I do things for your safety. It would be nice to know that you're going to come here more often before Blade tells me. Do you know how he tells me things?" Gage answered, "In Latin."

We all glanced at him, and I busted up laughing. Egres retorted, "While laughing. He tells me things while laughing." Gage replied, "Good for him. The guy needs things to laugh about. Think about how hard his job is. You think your job is hard and he's got Haley to Guard." I snorted, "I'm practically the easiest one to guard in my family. Now, it will be easier because I'll spend more time here."

Phil said, "Point of reference, you are not easy to be a Guard for. People are coming after you that you haven't even met. Egres is a busy bee." I replied, "Which is hardly fair. I haven't met them, so I didn't piss them off." Gage snorted, "You piss a lot of people off when you do meet them." Oden chuckled.

I winked, "Exactly, they should give me a chance to upset them in person." Phil said, "You'd kill them." I grinned, "I know that." Egres commented, "Yes, well those threats seem to be handled lately." I asked, "What does that mean?" He replied, "I am going to discuss that with your uncle."

Oden asked, "Did our Uncle cut our Guard out of something involving us?" He wouldn't. Egres walked out. Phil groaned, "UGH! REALLY EGRES?! You get back here and you answer the questions my brain now has!" Egres kept walking.

Phil said, "I'll catch up with you later, brother." Jeffery laughed, "I'm coming to find out what's going on with that. I have questions too." They took off and my Guard turned his head back over his shoulder, smirked, and took off running.

Phil shouted, "HEY! YOU CAN'T OUTRUN ME! I KNOW WHERE YOU ARE GOING!" Gage laughed, "Poor guy. You know he hates it when his questions aren't answered." I shrugged, "We all had the same question."

Gage hummed, "I have a different thought about it than you do, but that's what I do. I'll go see if I can help Phil solve things while I think crazy things." I asked, "What crazy things?" He said, "Why after certain people have left the general area, Egres is late to threats." I snorted, "Melanie has nothing to do with it." He hummed and walked away.

Oden agreed with me, "It's a coincidence and they don't like those, but it would be sweet if mate had something to do with it." I agreed with that. My cousin, Kade, commented, "That was weird." I turned, "Hey, man." I gave him a hug. I inhaled then said, "That's a smell, cousin."

He shut down, "Yeah, I'm going to take a shower." I laughed, "Why would you do that? Who smells like expensive champagne, and did you sew your skin to hers? Is that where you've been? I haven't seen you in a hot second."

He asked, "Can we keep that between us?" I agreed, "Of course. Uncle Drake doesn't know you're sewing your skin to the woman that smells like champagne?" He admitted, "Only your mom does." I snorted, "Ok, I won't say anything. Why am I not saying anything?"

He replied, "It's complicated to explain." I urged, "Try." He said, "Your family would be the only one not worried about it." I questioned, "Why?" He admitted, "There are things you don't know about rules and such."

I prodded, "Tell me then." He shrugged, "I need to shower before the parade." I hummed, "I'll guess the champagne smelling woman will not be there." He shook his head. I replied, "Well, I'd love to meet her whenever you're ready. Congratulations, cousin." I wasn't sure why he didn't say anything, but based on his feelings in the bond the woman was his mate.

He said, "I wouldn't plan on meeting her anytime soon, cousin." Oden said, "She must not be a Supernatural then. Or she's not aware she is." Yeah. Was this about the no Royal Hackura having a child with a human thing? No, it couldn't be. That was for off period kids, not mates.

Oden agreed, "It can't be that. Maybe the human wants things to move slowly." I smelled Uncle Drake coming. I urged, "You'd better portal to that shower. Your dad is coming." Kade sent me his gratitude down the bond then portaled away.

I walked towards town and ran into my Uncle Drake. I greeted, "Hey." He nodded, "Hi. Have you seen Kade?" I replied, "Yeah, he was heading to shower." He sighed and nodded. He turned to go and asked, "Did you talk to him?" I answered, "Yup." He snorted, "For fuck's sake you are as verbose as Kade is lately." Weird shit was definitely afoot.

I went and found my mom in her office in this realm. I commented, "So, Kade." She glanced up when I didn't continue. She said, "Is my fucking nephew. I am aware." I chuckled, "He has secrets." She evaded, "Everyone does." I winked, "Is she pretty?" She answered, "You would know the answer to that question as you've seen who he dates." I nodded, "Fair enough. What's going on?"

She admitted, "I don't fucking know. I know it's pretty damn weird and maybe people won't listen to my goddamn hints. It's maddening." So, she'd tried to tell Uncle Drake and Aunt Heather. Interesting. I asked, "What's this about rules?" She shrugged, "I don't fucking know. What are you talking about?" I sighed, "I'm not sure."

She changed the subject, "I've got your ceremony and parade ready to go." She snapped me into black pants that looked like leather but were far more comfortable. They looked exactly like Squadron Leader pants, but I'd heard they were not comfortable.

I had a belt with a fur coat that had no buttons. I asked, "What's this?" She replied, "The Squadron leader ceremony outfit. Your dad insisted I keep it simple. Those are the new squadron leader pants. I can't befuckinglieve they were trying to walk around in leather pants and fighting." I replied, "Hood members and you do that."

She snorted, "I don't have fucking balls though. Your dad admitted they were not exactly comfortable. I'm practically doing everyone a favor changing them." I grinned, "That you are." She snapped herself into a corset crop top and some type of skirt that had a belt with green and red material and arms guards. I asked, "And that is?" Oden snorted, "Something to make dad lose his mind."

She answered, "The outfits the women are going to wear to the ceremony. Well, not the same fucking thing, but you get the point." I laughed, "I love you mom." She hugged me, "As I love you." Uncle Bjourn came in, "Hales, it's time to…" He trailed off and took in her outfit.

He grinned asking, "Is Astrid wearing that too?" I replied, "Not the same thing but similar." He grinned, "I do love the moments when you do things like this, little sister." I felt the full force of how happy that made my mom. Uncle Bjourn and I actually a took a step.

Mom winced, "Sorry, I…" I cut her off, "No, I liked it." Uncle Bjourn agreed, "You know I love it when I feel the full force of your emotions, little sister. It wouldn't shock us all so much if you'd do it all the time." My mom grumbled, "I'm fucking working on it." Uncle Bjourn conceded, "And you are much better at it now than before."

Uncle Bjourn added, "The McAlister's are here. They said you invited them, Alexander." Before I could say anything, mom gasped, "You mean the fucking prank is here?! Holy shit. I'm wrong? Really? She's real? I have a lot fucking things to say if she is actually real about the shit going on since she left." I felt myself let my hope fall when I saw my Uncle Bjourn's face. Melanie wasn't here.

Mom called, "Alexander?" Uncle Bjourn said, "Melanie couldn't get away from class." Mom snorted, "Of fucking course not. Son, what's wrong?" I shrugged, "I was kind of hoping that…" I stopped talking when TJ popped in.

He hugged me and then mom. He asked, "What's going on?" Angela popped in looking annoyed. I asked, "What's wrong?" TJ sighed, "She told me to wait." I laughed and picked her up and spun her around. She beamed at me and popped us outside.

I linked my mom, "Is the whole ass realm out here?" She replied, "Most of the Capitol is." I spotted the Manning's in the crowd. I waved at Grammy Veronica's grandparents. I knew they saw me as one of theirs. I claimed them as grandparents over Cassandra.

Oden growled, "I disliked that woman so much." Yeah, I did too but my wolf knew that. We never trusted her, and I definitely wasn't sad when she died. I felt bad about that, but it was how I felt. My family joined us on stage. I felt the jolt of lust from my dad when he spotted my mom. I felt hers back for him. I glanced back noting he was shirtless and in the same outfit my uncles were.

EJ and Cassie sent me their pride. Cayden joined my Uncle Bjourn on stage. Uncle Bjourn called, "Hello, today we make history." Oh, for the love of god. My Mom linked, "You ARE making history and I will fucking brag about my kids any fucking time I want." I nearly laughed.

My dad linked, "I can tell you don't agree, but this has never been done. No Duke has ever been a Squadron Leader. I'm so proud of you." I felt my family's pride thrum through me and my grandpa shot his at me.

Uncle Bjourn continued, "My nephew, Duke Alpha Alexander, has put in the time and effort into learning our ways and meeting all the requirements for additional positions here. He has gone out on missions, and he has been selected by your Commander to be a Squadron Leader. It's been something our Commander has wanted since before he took the post. They have worked together to find a way to do this." Cheers erupted from the crowd.

I spotted Jason in the crowd whistling. He was with Gage who winked at me, his arm around a woman. I chuckled and grinned back at him. He linked, "Even though I wasn't told first, I'm proud of my Alpha. I'm damn lucky to be your Gamma." I replied, "You are also my friend." He laughed back, "I know."

Uncle Bjourn inclined his head over to me. I walked over and joined him at the front of the stage. His voice boomed, "Alexander, do you accept the position of Squad Leader?" I answered, "I do." He nodded to Cayden.

Cayden asked, "Do you swear to your Commander and King that you will uphold your Squad to their standards of our army?" I answered, "I do." He dipped his hand into the paint. I linked, "You're painting me?" He replied, "Evidently." I knew if my mate was here, she'd do it.

He painted the symbol for squadron leaders on my arm. He declared, "Dux tuus novus Squadron, Dux Alpha Alexander (Your new Squadron Leader, Duke Alpha Alexander)." The crowd erupted into cheers and the parade started.

The crowd was already raunchy. My own family was getting into the mood. Elise and EJ were making out. I scooped up Angela and TJ, popped them inside, and conjured ice cream. TJ asked, "Aren't you going outside?" I replied, "And give up this moment with my youngest siblings? Nope."

Angela replied, "He goes to gym after we eat ice cream. Dad convinces him to put in some face time at the parade before he goes back to the gym." I laughed, "Do I eat cake?" She replied, "That's how dad gets you to show up for a bit."

I winked, "Well, I think we all know what dad's busy doing right now. So, we should eat our ice cream." Angela wrinkled her face, "I'm sorry you're disappointed someone wasn't here." TJ asked, "Who?" Angela grumbled, "The blur." I told her, "It's fine."

Her feelings told me she did not agree. TJ grumbled, "I want to know." Preston popped to us and conjured his own ice cream. We ate in silence. I asked, "So, what trouble are you two going to get up to?" Angela gasped innocently asking, "Me?" I snorted, "Yeah, you."

TJ grumbled, "I should be the one to gasp. It's me who gets taken along for the ride all the time." Angela rolled her eyes before she said, "You love my type of trouble." I told her, "Maybe you should focus on Kade." She shrugged, "Mom and I talked about that already."

I asked, "So, what's the problem?" She admitted, "I don't know but I know that the way that's solved are blurry. It's very annoying." I ruffled her hair, "You'll figure it out." She made a face, and I felt how much the blurry visions annoyed her in the bond.

Preston asked, "Can I talk to you, Alexander?" I agreed, "Of course." Angela looked sad. I linked TJ, "I know her blurry visions upset her so do whatever crazy thing she wants to cheer her up." He laughed, "I was going to." I knew that and sent him my love.

I walked off with Preston and he popped us to his wing. I asked, "What's up?" He replied, "I don't understand something." I pressed, "What would that be?" He said, "Your deepest fear changed, and I don't get why." Oden grumbled, "I do."

I questioned, "What's my greatest fear?" He answered, "That people you love will see you as a monster. You know that's not true." My heart sank into my feet. I evaded, "Fears don't always make sense, little brother." He shot me a measured look.

I asked, "What? They don't." He pointed, "I am a Fairy too." I grinned, "Gosh, I'm so glad you told me that. I missed it." He growled, "You're being sarcastic with me." I grabbed him, "Hey, let's go for a run. You can let Bernard out with Oden." Oden perked up, "Yes, a run would be nice."

Preston sighed, "Fine but I still don't understand." I admitted, "Some days, little brother, neither do I. Actually, more often than not I feel like I don't." He paused then I felt him accept that answer for the truth it was. He popped us to the Manning's area. We shifted and ran around.

I popped us back to the gym and grabbed shorts. A woman came up, "Duke Squadron Leader Alexander, I would gladly service you." Preston snorted, "Service him? Jesus Christ." I declined, "Thanks for the offer, but I'm good."

She frowned, "You have to have excess energy. We all get raunchy." Yes, but she wasn't the right person, and I had three sides to myself. I told her, "I plan to let off that feeling in the gym." She sighed but walked away. Preston snorted, "Service you."

I replied, "People say shit like that all the time to us." He pointed out, "But you never engage. Who exactly are you waiting for? Because I have figured out based on the bond you are waiting." I winked, "I'll know the second I see her." He nodded, "Your mate then." I confirmed with a nod.

He shrugged, “Fair enough.” Oden snorted, “If only he held onto the bond a second longer to know that there was a specific person we were waiting on. Mate.” It’s not that I didn’t find other women attractive, I did. The woman who came up to me was attractive, but it all felt like cheating on Melanie.

Oden grumbled, “Because she is ours.” I sighed, “We will see.” He groaned, “We get so close to break throughs and then they stall out. I am right.” We’d know when we met her, but he knew that’s how I felt. I didn’t doubt him. It was me that I wasn’t certain about.

Egres joined us in the gym. I commented, “Those clothes look new.” He snorted, “Shut up.” I asked, “And who did you enjoy the parade with?” He laughed, “Another Guard.” I asked, “Any mate or chosen on the horizon?” He replied, “I have not met my mate yet. I would tell you if I did.”

I nodded, “Good because I want you to take the mate bonding time when you do.” He laughed, “I will be sure to do that.” We fought. I felt Preston sneaking up behind me and took out his legs. He grumbled, “It’s so damn impossible to surprise you.”

Eventually my whole Guard trickled in. They always knew where to find me during the orgies that followed any event here. I didn’t get my energy out the same way because Melanie wasn’t here. Something I think they knew, but didn’t acknowledge because we didn’t talk about.

Oden said, “Because you’re trying to kill me.” I snorted, “You’ve been with me my entire life. There is no me without you. I’m not trying to kill you, and you know it.” He agreed, “I do know that, but I don’t think the situation with mate needs to be so complicated.”

I reasoned, “Well, Elise lives with us now. When Melanie comes home, they will do whatever she wants because she’s done this whole thing.” I already knew the McAlister’s were ready to give her whatever she wanted if she’d come home. Oden said, “I wonder if she’s talking to other people in her family more than she was.” Jason had mentioned she wasn’t really talking to him.

I felt bad for him on the one hand, but I felt worse for Melanie. I couldn’t imagine having one of my siblings as upset at me as Melanie was with Jason. Oden grumbled, “They shouldn’t have made her feel that way. Plus, their pack disobeyed protocol.” That part of it still pissed me off. They let a pup leave without talking to the parents.

Oden scoffed, “After not letting her leave without Warriors since her birth they thought Pepper found some damn chill and was letting her go to New York by herself. That’s just madness.” It really was. I still didn’t understand how that happened.

I knew that when they told Drake he’d rightfully lost his shit in front of everyone in our pack. The McAlister’s were all inconsolable the night of Elise’s Luna Ceremony. Drake got so drunk Ethan had to monitor him for a bit.

Egres landed a shot. He asked, “What’s got your distracted?” Preston grumbled, “Who is distracted?” Egres replied, “Him.” I shook myself and focused back on our fight. He urged, “Come on, tell us.” Preston popped in front of me, and I blocked his punch.

He told Egres, “The bond says he’s not going to say which means he was distracted. Why can’t you be a normal distracted person, brother? You can fight better than normal people when you’re distracted.” I laughed, “We have never been normal, brother.” He conceded, “That is true.”

My dad agreed, “You all are better than normal. Why don’t you boys come join us? It would mean a lot to your mom and there’s cake. None of us can have any until you do, son.” He was looking at me. I snorted, “Didn’t you tell mom it’s not a wedding or my birthday?”

He shot me a look. “Do you think I can convince your mom that person of honor for an event or parade shouldn’t have the first bite of cake?” I answered, “Let me guess, she believes it’s a tradition.” Egres commented, “Since you love being fair, it’s kind of a tradition.” I snorted, “This is the first time we’ve ever celebrated a Squadron Leader like this.”

Dad commented, “The precedent is still set. Come on, the cake looks and smells delicious.” I winked, “Anything for you, dad.” He chuckled knowing I was dead serious but teasing him right now. He replied, “I don’t know why I bothered to have this conversation. Angela told me I just had to show up and say the word cake. I guess you talked to her.”

I laughed, "TJ, Angela, me, and Preston had ice cream together after the ceremony." He hugged me and linked, "You are such a good brother and man. I'm so proud of you." I threw my arm around him, and we walked outside.

People literally parted for us and started cheering. I linked my dad, "How damn good does this cake smell?" He answered, "It's mouthwatering." Then the scent hit me. Strawberry. I spotted the giant ass cake in question. Oden purred, "I am on a layer of that cake." He was. It looked like he was running around the bottom tier. That was cool.

There were swords and shields on another. It would actually probably feed the whole realm, it was that big. My mom popped to me. She asked, "What do you think?" I could feel some nerves in the bond but not like I could with every other bond I had.

I told her, "That this is the most amazing cake I've ever seen." She beamed at me saying, "I hope it tastes really fucking good. Isabella did the top of the cake for me." She grabbed me and flew to the top with her wings. I linked, "Your wings are still really fucking cool." She smiled at me.

I spotted Chase and Lexi Daniels in the crowd. I waved at them, and they waved back. My mom landed us on a cloud that was waiting for us at the top. I laughed asking, "Why didn't you have the cloud bring us up here?" She shrugged, "Your dad thought me flying you would be more fucking fun."

I agreed, "It is." I conjured a knife and cut the cake while people cheered. I cut myself a slice and conjured a plate and at it. I moaned, "Damn this is good." I heard someone mutter, "I wish I could hear him groan like that while naked." Preston growled which had my family paying attention to my bond.

I linked Preston, "It's fine." He retorted, "It irritates you." I chuckled, "Sometimes feeling like a piece of meat grates." Oden grumbled, "Especially at an event mate didn't come to." That was true. I usually didn't mind.

Mom asked, "What's going on?" I replied, "The usual." She snorted, "This party is brand fucking new so I doubt that." I cut her a piece of cake and the cloud floated us back down. She spoke in Fealish, "Cut yourself Den send pieces Ze those yuiopl wish Ze Wer cake (Cut yourself and send pieces to those who wish to have cake)."

Everyone cheered as knives began to cut the cake and pieces flew on plates to the people with forks. I told mom, "You're amazing." She blushed. She pointed, "Don't think that will distract me. What had Preston growling? Did someone say something? Not having your hearing pisses me the fuck off." I laughed, "I know."

I told her, "Sometimes hearing people make sexual reference to me gets old." She growled, "Who the fuck did that?" I admitted, "I don't know. It's ok." She replied, "No, it's not. You have good hearing. So, unless they meant to say it your face, they can keep it to themselves. Or say it when you can't hear them. No one deserves to be objectified if they don't want to be. Everyone here knows that."

I told her, "People will say what they do. It's not their fault I can hear them." She replied, "So long as there is breath in my body people will fucking respect my kids and this family. I have killed people for less." I asked, "You have?" She winked at me, and we landed on the ground.

I wondered why my uncle's didn't ask questions about her statement. When we landed back on the platform, I realized they weren't close enough. EJ linked, "What the fuck did that mean? Does mom have some secret killing crusade thing going on? We are FUCKED if that's true."

I replied, "I think she does… or did." Uncle Aiden popped to me, and I felt the wind at my back knowing Uncle Arion was here. Uncle Aiden hugged me, "Your Aunt Lucinda and I were here for your ceremony. We are so proud of you. I seem to have lost Aiylee and Exsis. I will be busy continuing not to think about where they went to."

I chuckled. He added, "Za Er Dinko proud Fren Zu. Zu Sintra if Zu Sepl Tem position in Uise fae army Op Uy yours yuz (I am so proud of you. You know if you want a position in the Fae army it is yours too)."

I replied, "Let's see deft Freetra siblings Trew end oolo. Za will Kent anything Ze protect them. Dinko, if Za need Tem position in Uise fae army Ze Kent Dinko, Za will take Op (Let's see where my siblings all end up. I will do anything to protect them. So, if I need a position in the Fae army to do so, I will take it)."

Uncle Aiden raised an eyebrow. My mom linked, "Is someone trying to hurt my fucking daughter?! You did this for Cassie?" I replied, "Not physically." She practically growled, "It's that BITCH, isn't it? I knew I should've killed her as a child. I really fucking considered it, but she was a child. She was so damn weird and obsessed with Cayden it was fucking creepy." Interesting. I'd not known that.

I told her, "I'm here now. You and Cassie are more subtle sometimes." My mom gasped, "You think I'm fucking subtle?! I am in people's faces with Fairy Hijinks and fuckery! They ALL know it's me and they know why."

I replied, "Yet you just told me you killed people and I'm certain you mean ones I don't know about. Maybe even other people, like my uncles who have never mentioned it, don't know about it." She winked again.

I reasoned, "See? Subtle. I am NOT subtle. I will make sure whatever is going on doesn't go too far. I will have Cassie's six, always." She replied, "You'd better pull me into anything that needs my special brand of justice."

I agreed, "I will if it's necessary. Cassie has her own way of doing things that mirrors yours. She idolizes you, we all do." She blushed. Uncle Aiden hummed, "What are we linking about?" My dad joined us asking, "Yes, what would that be?"

Mom answered, "Our brands of justice." Dad threw his head back and laughed. He asked, "And who is getting hit with this brand of justice?" Mom grumbled, "Apparently we are waiting on mine." Dad nuzzled her neck, "I feel how intensely that annoys you. You want to kill someone badly."

The wind howled around us. I was pretty certain that was Uncle Arion being annoyed that we were waiting. Mom grumbled, "Letting your kids be grownups sucks ass." My dad's gaze narrowed on mine. He told my mom, "It definitely can."

He linked me, "I know you decided to do this for your sister. If you need to make a statement, I'll be there beside you." I agreed, "Of course. You know I go big with my statements. I think my increased presence will calm things down." He nodded and I felt he agreed.

I may not have my mate yet, but I would be the best damn big brother I could. Meanwhile I'd count down the days until Melanie was in my arms.

New Connections

Melanie is Fifteen Years Old

Melanie was waiting. I'd started the Resistance, but I'd been perfecting this filing at the Supernatural Council's building for a while. A wolf came out, "Let's go, Melanie." I stammered, "Umm I said Ashley... uhh Griffen… that's a thing…"

He snorted, "My name is Thurston." I muttered, "I didn't ask but ok… I still said that…" Thurston cut me off, "I am aware of what you said. I'm also aware of who you are. So is the Supernatural Council." I wasn't sure if that would be good or bad. I walked in with my file.

Herman, a Vampire and head of the Supernatural Council, was waiting. He said, "We will not hear your case, Melanie McAlister." I faltered, "Umm but…" He waved, "We read it." I pointed out, "I have several cases and folders."

He hummed, "And we read them all. No one can pay for the death of your parents." It was as if he sucked the air out of the room. Several people looked uncomfortable. He added, "Black Path passes our checks." I said, "Umm but like I proved they are paying for that and…"

He interrupted, "Our people are above reproach." I frowned saying, "Clearly not since…" He hissed, "You will show respect." I wanted to cower down to him, I did. The things was, he was lying and he was wrong. He was yet another leader letting me down and it fueled my rage.

I said, "I see that the Supernatural Council is just a corrupt bunch of figureheads who will nothing about the suffering of people. You have a duty and you're ignoring it. I will get justice for these people and my family. With or without your help." He snorted, "What's a pup going to do?" Everything. I was going to do everything.

I ran out of the room before I blurted out that I ran the Resistance. I needed to get back to my computer. I'd planted a bug while I was here in case… ok, I was going to use it either way. That's a thing I was going to do. Now, I could get into their files. I still read Prince Gunner's papers and followed them religiously.

I went through the holoport Paige had set up and let myself cry for five minutes. I jogged and went to the place I'd bought and put my parents and brother's headstones. I told them, "It didn't go well… that's kind of putting it nicely. I will get you guys justice, I will. Alpha Peter just won't…" I choked up then admitted, "talk to me about it. Everyone hates me and I miss you so much." I touched their headstone.

I whispered, "I'm making the world my dance floor. I hope you'd be proud… well not of all the stuff I do… I do beat Alpha's in fights… you just wouldn't… approve… but everyone says I deserve it… not my friends… but… they don't know how real packs work."

"Or maybe our pack was the façade… I don't know anymore, ya know? Everything is wrong all the time… but I'm fixing it. I help train future Alpha's and Beta's… I'm doing this." I kissed the stones and left for King's diner.

I walked in and noticed everyone was tense. Mason greeted, "Hey, Melanie." I sat at a booth with my friends. I said, "It didn't go…" Sierra whispered, "SHH!" I looked around then asked, "Why?" Addison nudged me and looked in the direction of another booth.

I gasped, "A visiting Vampire." I swore I saw a hint of smile on the man's face. I got up and Sierra tugged on my sleeve. I shook her off and moved over to him, then sat in his booth. He glanced up, "Can I help you, pup?" I answered, "Probably… definitely. I mean… with a lot." Dax growled, "Ashley." I waved, "Don't mind them… they don't know how things go."

He asked, "And how do things go?" I said, "I was wondering how old you are." Several people growled, "ASHLEY!" The Vampire chuckled, "I am quite old." I pushed, "Like a century or two?" He grinned, "Maybe." That was a yes. He snorted, "Aren't you fun?"

I groaned, "Did I say that out loud?" He answered, "You did. My name is Charles." I gasped, "Lennox? Stop… no… shut up… wait… hold on… I'm fine. Everything is fine. You're probably not Charles Lennox. There are other people and Vampires named Charles… that's a fact. I'm calm."

He asked, "Are you aware you are a terrible liar?" I muttered, "I evade pretty well." He snickered, "I see. Do you spend time around Fairies?" I answered, "Well, I used to… in my old pack…." He asked, "And you know me how?" I choked on my own spit.

I gasped, "You are… like you're Charles Lennox? Like THE Charles Lennox? Are you sure? I mean, of course you are. Hold on. DO NOT MOVE!" He tilted his head and watched as I ran around the counter and poured myself coffee.

Hendrix whispered, "You might not want to…" I cut him off, "Do you have ANY idea how much history Charles Lennox has seen? He knows it all. He could tell us SO much. Plus… he hates O'Toole's." Charles hissed and barred his fangs. I inclined my head, "See? Totally helpful." I ran back and sat down.

He asked, "And how do you know that surname among the Fae? It's long since not been spoken." I snorted, "Uhh I used to have a deal in my old pack about homework and Fairy books." He hummed, "And how does someone from a pack in Missouri with no partial Fairies make a deal for books only Royal Fairies have access to?" Everyone was quiet.

Caine growled, "And how would you know her former pack?" I waved, "He's like a world renowned hacker. He's also a recluse. We are literally in the presence of basically hacking Royalty. Prince Gunner rivals Charles reputation… which totally impresses Charles because of Prince Gunner's age and…"

He agreed, "It does impress me. It also impresses me you know that." Caine warned, "Ashley." Charles laughed, "Do cease using that name. I can tell it's not hers. Her eye twitches when you say it and there is no way she'd have access to those books in the pack your files claims she's from."

I grinned, "Gosh… it's like meeting one of your heroes in person and…it being better than you thought… like people say don't meet your hero's but this is going SO well." He hummed, "So, you are the one copying some of my code then." My jaw dropped. He'd come here to meet me?

I shrieked, "YOU CAME TO MEET ME?! That sounded braggy… but you totally did. You didn't just end up in this diner. I'm fine. This fine… everything is fine… I'm totally fine." He snorted, "As your voice is currently in a completely different octave, I do not think that is true."

I admitted, "I have so many questions for you and… Do you think you could train me? Like… on hacking and…" Caine sighed, "Seriously?" I asked, "What? He totally knows so much of the dark web. He basically invented it. He's a vigilante on the web for all intents and purposes. He was a Knight… technically he still is…."

Dax warned, "Stop talking." I asked, "Uhh why? He totally knows his reputation." Caine groaned, "You called him a vigilante and he's a Vampire." I reasoned, "He knows both of those things are true." Charles agreed, "I do." I pointed, "See? It's fine."

Charles chuckled, "Aren't you fascinating? What is your real name?" Caine warned, "Don't." I answered, "It's Melanie… McAlister… I'm not popular around here." Charles replied, "I could take you plenty of places you would quite popular." Caine snarled, "Watch it, Vamp."

I ignored that, "So, about the whole training me thing. You're also rumored to be good at street driving. Like evasive maneuvers. Can you teach me?" He grinned, "I could teach you many things." Dax snarled, "Watch it. She's in love with someone else."

I said, "Uhh he didn't need to know I love my Xander… that's not a thing he needed to know." He asked, "Xander? How unique." Caine spat out, "She means Alpha Alexander Conners." Charles hummed, "The young Alpha Enforcer. I see."

I squeaked, "You could totally help me perfect the software on my watch. I would give you one… if you did." Caine warned, "That's a bad idea." I waved, "If he wanted to know who's behind our group… he would know. I used his code for that… so he already knows. It's why he's here… but he probably didn't think it was me."

Charles agreed, "I did not think it was you. I thought it was someone far more well known and older. I cannot say I have been this pleasantly surprised in quite some time." They all froze. Caine asked, "You know what we do?" He hummed, "I have since about two weeks after you started."

Dax questioned, "Then why did you just come now?" I replied, "He's a recluse… obviously… I said that already… and he was waiting to see what we'd do and then he waited to see if we'd get away with it." He chuckled, "And I am quite intrigued you have, given that you cannot lie."

I pointed out, "I'm not really a suspect." He snorted, "Yes, well your pack is run by morons then." He glanced at Caine and Dax. When they didn't growl, he chuckled, "Fascinating. The Ring is getting less intelligent as time goes on." Yes and no.

He asked, "What's your story, Melanie McAlister? Because I do know that last name and you are not in a place one with your name should be." I sighed and explained most of it leaving out quite a bit. I couldn't exactly tell him about the Undergrounds, the beatings, and the punishing fields.

He offered, "I could speak to your brother and old Alpha." I gasped, "Umm no… don't do that… that's not…" Caine said, "I mean, he could." Charles laughed, "Easily." I panicked, "No… don't… that's just… can you like leave them alone? I'll be your protégé… I mean you haven't had one in almost a century… so like… umm…. just leave them alone. Please."

He hummed, "I'll consider it once you show me this watch." I took him into the office then opened up the bunker that no one knew was there besides me and my friends. He came down and looked at the setup. He commented, "Impressive."

I showed him the watch. He asked, "And what does it do?" I admitted, "Umm kind of everything. I'm working on the biometrics, but I can't quite get it right." He sat beside me. He chuckled, "This is going to be fun. What's the programs name?" I whispered, "Umm… name… what…?" He threw his head back and laughed. He said, "I do hope you didn't name it Xander."

I blushed, "It's ILYX." Saying the name brought the system online. It answered, "Yes, Melanie Jane?" Charles tilted his head asking, "Is that the young enforcer?" I squeaked, "Huh? No… it's obviously not… him… because he's not here and…" He snorted, "That is his voice though." I shrugged, "So… it's… uhhh…."

He laughed, "This is amazing. What does ILYX stand for?" I squeaked, "Stand for? Why would it…?" He cut me off, "I'll help you and say that you can't lie. So, let us cut to the chase where you just tell what it means." I muttered, "It could mean I love you Xander… that's a thing it could mean." He chuckled and got back to work.

We actually got a lot done. He helped me finalize the watch. We loaded the software onto it and got them ready for everyone. I quickly programmed one for him. He said, "This is quite impressive what you have done."

I blushed, "Gosh… really? You… wow…" He grinned, "I will be around for a few days. I would like to teach you things. I float around, which you clearly know. I'd like to see you when I do." I agreed, "Umm yes… Obviously… that's like a serious honor."

Sierra groaned, "Are you serious?! He's a Vampire." I replied, "I know that. He's Charles Lennox." She sighed, "Melanie, he's a Vampire and we are Werewolves." Charles chuckled, "She's not from a pack that cares about that. Her Xander is quite close with Vampires." Related to a partial one in fact.

Sierra glared at him, "Look Charles, if there's something to know about Melanie's Xander we already know it. I know all about his relatives." He replied, "I'd imagine so, since you do protect them quite fiercely. Which now I understand. I'll see you later, Melanie." He flashed away.

Sierra waved, "Come on." We went up into the diner. Hendrick said, "No way." I asked, "No way what?" Caine growled, "You CANNOT run around with a Vampire who could drain you." I reasoned, "If he wanted to drain any of us… well… he would've already."

"Mostly his way of killing isn't draining. He's old. Draining us all would've made him feel sick… not sick… but super full. He doesn't need that much blood… he's old… like old old. Gosh… I need to sit down and write new questions." They all groaned, and I ran to get my notebook.

True to his word Charles was around the next few days and I learned so much. I didn't sleep much anyway, and I needed to soak up all I could while he was here. Plus, Edward and Booker were gone so Jean was in charge. Other than constantly trying to get me to sleep with him, he left me alone.

Charles and I talked a lot about the O'Toole's, and I'd set him in the Resistance system so he could use what we had. Mostly because he could do it himself. I spotted him waiting and he smiled at me. I greeted, "Hi Charles!" I gave him a hug and heard Caine growl. He'd insisted on coming.

Charles instructed, "Get in the car. Today I'm going to teach you how to drive, my dear." I admitted, "I do know how to drive… so you mean…" He cut me off, "You do not know how to drive like I drive. You need to learn more than evasive maneuvers."

Yes! He was going to teach me everything I'd asked about. He got in the car, and so did I before he could change his mind. I noted it was a manual. I admitted, "I don't know how to drive a stick shift, but I've read about it." He replied, "You'll learn my driving techniques in a stick shift first, then an automatic."

I asked, "What are your techniques?" He smirked and revved the engine. I watched the dashboard, noting he let off the gas once the rpm's were at six. He used the emergency break to fly around a cone. I realized he'd set up a course to teach me.

I could sense his attention on me, but I couldn't get over the thrill. I watched every single move he made and noted when he made it. This was basically an equation. I had mapped out the angles and everything as he drove. I could do this. I would keep impressing Charles… then he'd keep coming around.

It was a little sad that he reminded me the most of home. He was a vigilante but so was I. He was a lost soul, and so was I. He knew how life really should be. He knew what was going on here wasn't normal pack life because he'd seen it. He also knew that bad things happened and was disillusioned with the good façade life showed, with people in good places.

We were kindred spirits, and I hoped he sensed it like I did. He made me feel more normal. Before I knew it, Charles pulled over. I pointed out the obvious, "You really don't drive like other people. You drive like the fast and furious." Easily like he was being chased.

He laughed, "I was driving that way before those movies made it popular. I'm surprised you've seen them." Pain lanced through my heart. I'd watched them all because my brother loved them. I whispered, "T loved those movies."

I nearly jolted when I felt his hand on my shoulder. He didn't touch people a lot. In fact, from what I'd read about him, he made a point not to touch people. He defiantly knew we were kindred spirits. His tone was emphatic, "He would be proud of you."

He was right and wrong. Tristan would be proud of what I was doing with the Resistance. He would be proud of every invention I had created. He would be proud I'd gone to the Supernatural Council. He would not be proud that I was in the Undergrounds.

He would also be terrified that I lead the Resistance. He would be furious that I was basically undercover with Hunters as Red One. Werewolves and Hunters shouldn't mix. He would also scream at me to fight back when I took whippings and beatings without trying to stop them.

I realized I hadn't said anything and quickly offered a halfhearted, "Maybe." Charles argued, "There is no 'maybe' about it. You've started an organization that goes against evil at such a young age. You amassed your investments with little input from me." He'd offered tidbits over the last several days. His tone implied he was going to do more. Which meant continued contact.

I snorted, "That's not true. I asked for your opinions on all my investment options yesterday." He chuckled, "Yes, and that's a wise decision. However, you found the investments on your own. You didn't just ask me to do it for you." Well, that wouldn't be nice of me not to do my due diligence.

He continued, "I would've because I like you, but you continue to fascinate me and simply asked for my opinion. Now, I want to see what you picked up." He liked me? This was better than I expected. People never liked me anymore. I was the least popular person in Black Path. Maybe he would be my actual friend.

He got out of the car and indicated I should drive. I managed ok. I didn't stall the car but I knew my shifting gears was choppy. He did it so effortlessly. I just needed to figure out the formula here. Then I'd do better. I hit several cones and wanted to groan. I was messing this up and Charles would go away because of it. I always ruined every good thing I got anymore.

I huffed and pulled over. He complimented me, "You did really well for your first try." I argued, "I messed up." He teased, "You are such the perfectionist. It was your first try." I was a perfectionist. I had to do this well because I needed to help my people.

I was the voice of the forgotten and the Resistance leader. People counted on me, and I needed to do my best for them. I pulled my hair back into a ponytail. I declared, "I'll do better this time." He admitted, "Of that I have no doubt." We practiced again and again.

He declared, "I'm beyond impressed." I nearly let out a breath of relief which he caught. He said, "I do have to leave, but I will see you again. I'll keep in contact. Email me if you need anything." I said, "Umm I could just talk to you on the watch." He laughed, "Yes, do use ILYX to contact me." ILYX said, "Charles, I cannot put you in contact with yourself." That amused him.

Charles instructed me on where to drive. I asked, "Do you have a contact coming to drive you? Or… well I can run back." He snorted, "You'll take the car back." I saw a shimmer start and nodded, "Naturally, you have a Demon friend… you probably have several." He replied, "I have few friends." Umm ok.

A woman appeared, and I gasped, "YOU HAVE A VAMPIRE CHILD THAT SHIMMERS?! Former Demons retain their power to shimmer?! That's so cool… and helpful… and…" He asked, "And why would you assume she is my child?" His child evaluated me.

I reasoned, "Only a child would reveal that to a maker. I mean you could be siblings… but you're totally her maker." She laughed, "I see why my maker is so amused lately." Charles winked, "Do keep my secrets."

I agreed, "Of course! I mean… even if I didn't want you to like me… which I do… I'm aware you're into mutually assured destruction. What you have on me is way bigger… than this… so… which you know so... I don't know why I keep saying so." He snorted, "Take care, my dear."

He paused then added, "Maybe find something to do for yourself." I asked, "Huh?" He said, "It could even help with your cause, but you do so much for other people. Find something you enjoy and do it." I waved and they shimmered out.

I thought about his words the whole drive back. I loved to dance, but Beta Jason would throw a fit and Edward would never allow me to dance competitively. I had applied to Julliard but that went over poorly. Aunt Stephanie declined my spot before I knew I'd been accepted, and I was beaten within an inch of my life and shoved in the hole. I shivered just thinking about it.

Flashback

Melanie finished her chores. I walked out of the pack house and saw everyone looking nervous. Aunt Stephanie screamed, "YOU HORRID PUP!" I asked, "What now?" She waved a bunch of papers around. Lead Warrior Buck said, "Stephanie, I don't see the problem. She'd be gone. It's what you want."

Aunt Stephanie growled, "She did it behind my back." I grabbed the papers and gasped, "I got in. I GOT INTO JULLIARD! OH MY GOSH!" Luna Elena said, "That's very impressive, Melanie." Aunt Stephanie snarled, "I already declined her spot."

I asked, "But…why? Lead Warrior Buck is right…I'd be gone. You say that's what you want… I actually thought this would make you happy…but I should've known you're literally never happy." Gamma Booker snarled, "You think you get to go live the high life?"

I said, "I don't think you know much about dancing….or Julliard….it's hard work.. and a lot of practicing….they push you really hard. I'm sure you'd be a fan of my grueling schedule." Trevor snarled, "You're not leaving! Get rid of that stuffed wolf too!" I sighed, "Pick a struggle, Trevor." People snarled. Alpha Edward drove up and got out with Beta Jean.

The part of me that grew up in my old pack wanted my Alpha to be proud, but the part of me that knew this one understood he wasn't going to be. He demanded, "Get to the punishing fields." I stared at him. I questioned, "For what?" Aunt Stephanie said, "Applying to this school."

Beta Female Eden said, "That's not a punishable offense." I agreed, "It's not." Aunt Stephanie sneered, "Where did you get the money? You obviously stole it." I laughed, "Are you serious? I did not steal it. I have money." She screamed, "YOU STOLE MY MONEY!"

I asked, "What money? You're the one who is broke between us." She screamed, "EDWARD!" Alpha Edwards sighed, "Go to the punishing fields, Melanie." I shook my head at him but started walking. Aunt Stephanie tried to take the papers from me, but I yanked them back.

She sneered, "I told you I declined your spot already." I said, "Ok. This is still proof I got in. It's a pretty big deal and you'd throw them away." I handed them to Hendrick and Mason. I didn't know how the letter was addressed to Aunt Stephanie's house instead of theirs but I'd guess it was because Selene had it out for me.

End of Flashback

I was still proud I'd gotten into Julliard. My parents would've been so proud. Tristan would've bragged for months on end about it. I just thought it was my way out of Black Path and that they'd be happy to have me gone.

In fact, everyone had agreed it was a good idea, but it was not. Clearly. Even though Lead Warrior Buck pointed out that they should be happy. He got it and their reaction to my acceptance confused the pack as a whole.

A store caught my eye, and I slammed on the breaks. I stared at the electric guitar letting it take me back to better days.

Flashback

Melanie was studying Tristan through the crack in his door where he couldn't see me. He snorted, "I can smell you, Ladybug." I really needed to work on my scent spray. He called, "Come on in." I scampered into his room.

He grinned teasingly admonishing, "You are supposed to be doing your homework." I groaned, "I finished it before school and it's boring." He chuckled and waved me over. He handed me an electric guitar.

I admitted, "I don't understand why you have this one now. You love your acoustic guitar." He replied, "I play both. I like the different sounds. Would you like me to teach you?" I squealed, "Yes! I love learning new things." He gasped, "What? I never knew this about you."

I hummed, "Umm yes you did." He chuckled, "Sarcasm, Ladybug." I grumbled, "I need to get better at recognizing that. My Xander and his siblings are sarcastic." He agreed, "Yes, the Conners are quite sarcastic." He'd figured out a while ago I liked Xander. He called it a crush, but he was my mate. I knew he was.

He took me through the cords and laughed. He said, "You're such a natural." He took it back and switched between guitars going through different songs. He was better at playing that I was, but I didn't care. I just loved playing with him.

Flashback End

Melanie jolted and parked the car before running inside. I bought guitars and ordered a drum set, keyboard, and microphones. I ordered a bass and several other instruments letting the idea form. We could be a band.

I knew some of my friends could sing and play instruments. Having gigs near where we needed to be gave us a natural cover. Plus, it was something for us; just like Charles suggested. I even knew what our name should be: The Rebels.

Black Path would all think it was about how we acted with them. It was yet another act of defiance and I couldn't keep the grin off my face. It was perfect.

I burst back into the diner with all the stuff. Caine asked, "Um did you start a band?" I squealed, "YES! How did you know?" He blinked several times dryly commenting, "I was joking." I clapped, "We are going to be a band. It's called The Rebels!" His jaw dropped.

I explained, "It's perfect. It gives us a reason to be together more… and…" Valentina agreed, "I'm in." She was always in. Any time I suggested things she was all about it. Virgil agreed, "Me too." Paige laughed, "What the hell? It sounds fun." They all quickly agreed, and we mapped everything out.

As time passed, we got pretty popular. I used Charles' tips to help myself get the information I wanted. I was currently hunkered down in the bunker reading through Former King Ragor Cambridge's files. I had to be super careful with the Hackura, but it's not like anyone was monitoring his files. I jolted realizing there was a Hackura in the human realm.

Benny Cambridge wasn't dead, he was alive. There was a massive cover up going on with how the line of his father, Prince Magnus, had died. Benny was definitely looking into that. I pivoted and set up runs to look for. I needed to find out everything I could about Prince Jeremiah Cambridge.

I was deep into looking for Benny when I heard a ping. ILYX said, "I have got on a probability of Prince Jeremiah's son." I gasped, "What? They wouldn't leave a partial Hackura and…" ILYX added, "Probability is eighty percent. There is an uncle listed as a case of emergency on Jeremiah Junior's school files. It is likely an alias for Benny. Jeremiah Junior also goes by JJ."

I hummed, "There's no way he's in school. He'd be too old." ILYX replied, "I have all his files." ILYX added, "I have found him on traffic cameras. He appears to be being chased." I gasped, "Like right now?" ILYX answered, "Yes."

I groaned, "Give me his location. I swear anyone of Cambridge blood just like to challenge me to protect them….and I didn't even know about this one." ILYX showed me where Jeremiah Junior was and I got my gear on. I grabbed my sniper riffle and sniffled at the memories it brought back.

Flashback

Grandma Esther stood behind me. She chuckled, "You look where you want to hit. Line the bead up and squeeze the trigger." I took the shot and felt the recoil. I admitted, "That wasn't as bad as I thought it would be."

She winked at me, "You're a natural shot, Melanie Jane. Possibly the best of all my pups and grandpups. Let's keep that as our secret." I beamed at her. I asked, "Won't daddy know?" She replied, "He will easily figure it out. Your Uncle Duncan already knows SINCE HE IS SPYING!"

Uncle Duncan laughed and came into view. He came over and hugged Grandma Esther. He greeted, "Hey, momma." He hugged me, "Hello, sure shot." I grinned, "Hi, Uncle Duncan. Can you shoot?" He winked and took the gun.

He shot all the cans Grandma Esther had set up. I clapped, "You're so good!" He winked, "There's a reason I got out and do things for the pack." Grandma Esther snorted, "Yes, because you are a daredevil and you have been since you were two." I laughed while they bickered and set up more cans.

I came back and lined up just like Grandma Esther showed me and hit every single can just like Uncle Duncan. I turned to face them and they both gaped at me. I asked, "What?" Uncle Duncan laughed, "You're a regular Annie Oakley." I blushed and they both laughed.

Flashback Ends

I shoved all those memories back because I needed to protect Xander's family right now. I didn't need to remember how much my Grandma Esther used to love me. It was now all replaced with hate for getting her son, daughter in law, and grandpup killed. I did that. My hands shook.

ILYX commented, "You'll need to move quickly, Melanie Jane." It pulled me out of those thoughts. I put on my Resistance mask and left. I clicked onto the coms. I called, "Bravo Twenty, I need you." Virgil shimmered to me.

I projected the location we needed to be at on my watch. He shimmered me in and I quickly took up my spot on the nearby rock. I quickly fired in succession. Jeremiah Junior used the fact I was on his side to get the hell out.

He'd been fighting and he was impressive. Benny would've trained him. I drew our circle once everyone after Jeremiah Junior was dead and he was long gone. Virgil shimmered us out and back to our home base.

He hummed, "That was a Cambridge but not one in your file." I grumbled, "I need more files. They have secrets… and secret family members. That's going to be so unhelpful! I need to have all the information to protect them and…" He chuckled, "I look forward to the new files."

Paige showed up hours later. She tapped my shoulder, "You told me to come to work on our project about making something for the women and men whose mate's cheat." I grumbled, "Well, the cheater uses a Witches spell, so they don't feel pain and I just thought… it's not really fair the mate who did nothing feels all the pain."

We got to work and within hours had come with how to combat it. I tapped my chin, "We need a way to get it to them that they won't suspect. I'd say vitamins but they'd throw that away… everything down here is just…"

Paige jumped in, "Wrong. I know. We need something they won't want but something they won't throw away." I hummed, "Caine just got here… so he might have an idea." Caine snorted, "You are so hyper aware it's maddening. Do them in Sweethearts form. It's the candy pups and women are allowed."

I grumbled, "Allowed. I hate that word…." He added, "And the men don't eat them because of the name." I sighed, "Toxic masculinity at its finest and…" Paige jumped in, "But it works for our purposes." I agreed, "It does." She got to work on that, and I went back to figuring out how to contact Duke Benny.

Between my chores, monitoring the Ring via the Resistance, and the Undergrounds it took me two weeks to figure out where in Arizona was the likely spot for Queen Veronica and Duke Benny's drop. She clearly had one and he frequented it the most.

I'd found out a lot in those two weeks though. I knew practically everything about Duke Benny, his brother Duke Alastair the partial Hackura Selkie, their kids, and Jeremiah Junior.

I was also pretty sure I'd nailed down that Duke Benny's mate was a Valkyrie. I was pretty sure I knew who it was too. I had met one before. I'd actually met several Supernatural's that, as a whole, had been thought to have died out.

It helped that he was looking into a coven the Resistance was also investigating. It was how I'd backtracked the hack to the Valkyrie. Which led me to believe that's what his mate was. Because I could easily see a Hackura and a Valkyrie together. It just made sense because once upon those realms were quite close.

So now I was in that spot waiting. I began to get nervous. I was pretty sure this was Queen Veronica's drop with Benny. He came here the most, so I was going to find him. Hopefully. When I felt a Hackura here I nearly cheered. Sierra shot me a look.

I called, "Umm Duke Benny? So… hi… I…" He faded in a few feet from me. I said, "Gosh, well umm… hi." He asked, "How do you know me?" I said, "Well, so… from your uncle's…well and your cousins files… for reasons…. and things."

He questioned, "And you are?" Sierra came up by my side saying, "She's Ashley Griffen." He snorted, "Is that name supposed to mean something to me?" I admitted, "Probably not, since your mate is a Valkyrie, so you don't know about the forgotten packs… I just… well… I thought I could help you…"

He asked, "How could you help me? And how did you find me?" I gasped "Find you? What….? You were here and we were here…." He cut me off, "Jesus, kid. You're a terrible liar. Do you mean me or anyone in my family harm?" I shouted, "What? No! Why would you ask…?" He cut me off, "I believe you." Well, that was helpful.

I said, "Well, you're looking into a coven… that I am also… ok I plan to kill them…. all… which sounds bad…. but I was just wondering why you were looking…. at them." He ignored that question, "How do you know I am?"

I shrugged, "Knowing things is kind of what I do… I'm just confused on why you don't go home." He stared at me, but I wasn't backing down. It's one thing to have a long mission but this was beyond all reason. He'd never been home since he left from what I found.

He answered, "I'm on a special mission." Obviously. I nodded, "I mean… I did kind of figure that was the reason. Since no member of the Royal family would stay out so long…. I think it has to be about your family." He questioned, "What would a Werewolf know about my family?"

I answered, "Well it's clearly a cover up. I feel like you're out here trying to find the right people… but it's been forever and…" Sierra elbowed me. I asked, "What?" She whisper yelled, "You can't insult the Hackura." I knew that.

I replied, "I didn't… I stated a fact… several… well, some of it is supposition… but it makes sense." Duke Benny commented, "I believe she's referring to the fact that you said it's been forever since my family died and I haven't avenged them."

I clapped and pointed at Sierra, "I totally told you that was his mission! The probability…" I stalled when I felt another Hackura. I asked, "Is the person with you your guard, Duke Alastair, JJ, or one of your kids?" Sierra grabbed my arm when his eyes blazed.

He asked, "You know JJ?" I replied, "Well, he didn't shoot those Demons that surrounded him two weeks ago… Now did he?" His guard, Otto, faded in. Duke Benny asked, "Why did you help my nephew?"

I squeaked, "Why? I mean… don't you mean thank you? Because like… I did help… helping is a thing that I do… for people… and reasons…" Otto said, "Duke Benny, she's something." Benny nodded agreeing, "She is." This was going well. I could tell. Sierra still seemed nervous, but there was no reason for that.

Duke Benny asked, "Which of my cousins do you like?" Sierra said, "She doesn't like any of your cousins." I muttered, "He says cousins like… including them all…like literally he means…." She shot me a look.

I frowned explaining, "I mean he doesn't say second, third, twice removed or…" She put a hand over my mouth. Duke Benny asked, "So, which one is it? Because I watch over them all. None of them have mentioned an Ashley Griffen." That stung and I hung my head.

Sierra whispered, "They don't know your name, Mel." I admitted, "I was hoping they'd figured it out." It's why I picked the name after all. I wanted them to know I was me. People did talk about me by name. Especially after starting The Rebels. We were basically the most popular Supernatural Band in the surrounding area.

Benny apologized, "I didn't mean to hurt your feelings." I whispered, "You didn't." I wiped tears away. He sighed, "If you'd come home with me and meet my wife and kids, we'll have a meal. We can figure out a way for us to help each other."

I nodded, "I mean… I hope you'll trust me over time… I'm young… so I know you won't like… let me fully help… but if you would, we could totally get you home sooner… rather than later." He shook his head and chuckled. We followed him and Otto to the portal near here the Valkyries had.

We walked though and took it all in. Sierra gasped, "Wow." I admitted, "I have a list started of Supernatural's I've met that you'd find interesting." Otto and Duke Benny looked at me. I picked at my sleeve, "Well it's just that King Titus… I mean former, because Bjourn…. I mean King Bjourn… is King now… and you knew who I meant."

He agreed, "I did." I continued, "Well, he was going to appoint you liaison for hidden Supernatural's … which is why I know that you'd find my list interesting… because… well… yeah. By the way, I think if you told your cousin your pen name he'd read your books too." Otto choked.

Benny asked, “My pen name?” Sierra whisper yelled, “Stop talking.” Benny laughed, “Please do not.” I pointed out, “Umm you write romantic fantasy books… under a pen name… that I found…” He snorted, “Do come inside.” He opened the door.

He called, “Mist, we have company.” I gasped, “I KNEW IT! I totally called that Si! I knew it was her and him. I said that.” She groaned. I asked, “What? I did. It makes sense. He’s a Duke and she’s related to the crown of this realm.”

Duke Benny said, “You get more interesting the longer you are here.” I reasoned, “That doesn’t make sense. I’m either interesting or not… the location is basically irrelevant.” He snorted. His mate walked into the room and their kids followed behind her.

Jeremiah Junior asked from behind us asking, “So, who is she?” I asked, “Is Duke Alastair coming too?” Sierra smacked her own head. Jeremiah Junior laughed, “I’m going to like her.” Benny replied, “She had your six the other day.”

He hummed, “You found the circle group, Uncle. Nice.” I groaned, “First, it’s the Ring Resistance. Or the Resistance for short and I cannot believe I have to explain that to people. Two, I found him… if we are being technical.” They all laughed, and we sat down. Duke Alastair did join us. Duke Benny seemed really resistant to our help, which was disappointing.

After we left Sierra bumped me. I asked, “What?” She said, “He’s not going to fully let you in.” I shrugged, “I knew that coming here. It’s just that I need to help have his back. That cover story is horrible though… like… truly bad.”

She shrugged, “I wouldn’t question it coming from my dad. Their family is good, so people are going to say anything. They haven’t all this time.” I hummed, “It seems like there is more there… I should…” She cut me off, “You can have his back and when things cross, we will help. Let him have this.”

I argued, “I could help more and…” She interrupted, “This is his family. You understand what your vengeance means.” I grumbled, “He’s not telling me everything.” She pointed out, “You don’t tell everyone everything about anything you do either.” That was true. I wouldn’t push Benny on his vengeance because I wanted my own.

More time passed. I was basically in a groove of inventing new things, never sleeping, cooking, cleaning, Underground fights, getting whipped, beaten, and working on Resistance things. Currently I could feel my friends eyes on me. They were incredulous I was actually thinking of following up on the Hunter lead.

Caine warned, “This is a bad idea.” He wasn’t exactly wrong. I reasoned, “It’s a change to bring…” He growled, “You don’t know this isn’t a trap for Red One.” I told him, “The probability is…” He cut me off, “I don’t give a damn what a computer program, and your mind, says is going on here. This is dangerous.” He was right, it was.

I whispered, “But if a member of the Knakonechny’s starts working WITH us we can bring their family back to their rightful place… and that’s…” He reasoned, “They got pushed to the background of their OWN supernatural race. THAT HUNTS US.” I argued, “But this note says Hunters weren’t meant to hunt us.”

He snorted, “They could be lying.” That was also true. I told him, “My gut says it’s true.” He growled, “No.” I winced and looked down. He was using an Alpha aura and everything in me wanted to let this go. He was a good Alpha, but I was teaching him about how things worked. Xander would meet with this person.

Ultimately, I let my friends think I let it go. Which was mean, but I had to know. Once they left, I went to the bunker, like normal. I just geared up then used a holoport Paige set up and left. I called over the coms knowing whose was on. “Bravo Twenty and Bravo Four, I need you.” They shimmered in.

Virgil grinned at me. He said, “You are never boring.” I shrugged, “I guess not.” I showed him where we were going. He grinned again, “I love this so much. To Russia.” He shimmered me in. I ordered, “Stay back here and if it goes bad, leave.”

He snorted, "There is not a single chance I'll do that, Bravo One." Valentina replied, "We will get out with you." I left them behind and went to the meeting place specified in the email that had been sent to me.

I called, "I know you're here. I can sense you." A woman came out and I felt an instant kinship with her. She revealed her face lowering her hood. I realized, "You are Princess Anastasia Knakonechny, the youngest one in your family."

She agreed, "I am. The Hunters have turned from us leading and our purpose." I replied, "It had to be a very long time ago that they did that. Most supernatural's do not know you have Royals. You mentioned you're not meant to hunt Werewolves." She handed me torn pages from a book.

She said, "I found a journal of my ancestor's that had proof. I want to join you and turn our people back to our true purpose. I want to save them and those we are meant to protect. I feel it in my blood this is the right path."

It would blow the Supernatural world's mind that Hunters were meant to protect us. I held out my hand, "You're in then." I took off my hood. I introduced myself, "Many call me Ashley Griffen." She hummed, "The voice of the forgotten." I agreed, "Yes." She grinned, "Well, my family agrees with me, but Slade has them scared. He's got some type of collateral or blackmail I'm not sure."

I growled, "He will go down." She nodded, "Good. You hate him as I do." I admitted, "You speak English very well." I'd been prepared to speak Russian. She nodded, "Yes, well I spend a lot of time secluded to be kept from my purpose. So, I know many languages." We exchanged information and I went back to Virgil and Valentina.

They shimmered me back to the bunker. Caine growled, "Goddamn it, Mel!" I reasoned, "It worked out." He retorted, "That's not the point!" I hummed, "It feels like the point." He groaned, "You are IMPOSSIBLE!" I was. It had been a problem all my life.

He softened, "Hey, that's not what I meant." UGH! Talking out loud when I meant to be in my head was a problem. Ignoring Alpha bloods was actually new for me, and it really hurt…I was just right here… so… that had to count for something even if my very blood felt like I was aching for doing it.

Caine sighed, "I wanted to try linking you. It's why I came back." I reasoned, "I'm not in your pack." He argued, "But my dad made Ashley join. He made Paige join while you were in Russia." What? Why? She could've cursed him and said no so she must have wanted to be able to link the group.

I replied, "But I'm Melanie and…" He waved, "Let's just try." I nodded pretty certain it wasn't going to work. He linked, "Can you hear me?" I jolted and tears filled my eyes. I hadn't heard a link in a while, and it hit me how much I'd missed it.

A sob bubbled up inside me and I let it go. He quickly grabbed me and whispered, "I'm so sorry. We could've been in your head all this time. I imagine it was so quiet." It was. Alpha Peter's command was hard to stick to when all I wanted was to talk to them. To hear them again.

Caine had given that back to me. I could hear them in my head, and it meant the world to me. I'd come to see him like my brother, and I knew he saw me as a sister. I'd never say it out loud because I'd gotten my oldest brother killed and I couldn't let anything happen to Caine.

Weeks passed and I met with Anastasia again. Paige had set up a holoport for me. So, I found myself in Russia in our Resistance gear. Anastasia admitted, "Wearing this black mask is fun, yeah?" I admitted, "I mean… it … well… yes. Because…"

She laughed, "I don't need a reason. This feels like a very tangible thing to do to help that I'm doing. I was in the shadows helping and doing what I could, but with you and your organization it's actually helping my people and others. I cannot thank you enough for it."

I nodded, "Sure… and OH MY GOD!" I saw a deer-like creature with a horse's head, a unicorn horn, feathers, and deer legs, with Rhino-like snout. I squeaked, "It's an Indrik. INDRIK'S ARE REAL!" Anastasia laughed, "I would question how you know our lore, but you are you." I whispered, "They are considered to be the King of all animals!" She teased, "Again with you knowing our lore."

I heard someone order, “Kill it.” I gasped and quickly shot the group that came in. The Indrik turned to us. Anastasia offered, “By the way, their hearing is great.” I admitted, “I did know that… because I read about them… but like… it’s an Indrik. That deserves to be shouted about. Do you think they want to be on my list for… like… those that no one knows about?”

She told me, “I would like a peek at that list.” I admitted, “Well… it’s kind of only for other races that are hidden… which the Hunters purpose is hidden… but like… I’m trying to get the hidden groups in touch with each other… and form their communities…” She nudged me.

I continued, “It’s just that all of us are meant to be connected and…” A Female voice asked, “Are we now?” I turned to see a woman standing there. I took out my phone and noted that Female and male Indrik’s have antlers. Interesting. I would’ve guessed only males did.

I looked back up and realized both the Indrik and Anastasia were looking at me. I squeaked, “Umm… yes… we are all creatures of… well… some animals want solitude... but like not really… they need their groups… so by uniting the groups that no one knows about… they stay secret, but they feel connected… being isolated is dangerous….” Anastasia giggled.

I asked, “What? It is. She would’ve died and no one would’ve known who did it. We came because we heard rumblings of a threat in this area… it’s to them… obviously… but others would’ve come to help if they weren’t so… secretive.”

The woman ordered, “Come with me.” I got up and put my sniper rifle on my back. Anastasia grabbed my arm. She said, “I can’t go with them.” I asked, “Why not? They probably have some cool Shroud type deal they live in… and you should totally…” The woman interrupted, “Because she is a Huntress and they have been hunting us.”

I pointed out, “Umm she isn’t hunting you… obviously since she’s here with me… and we totally saved you.” She agreed, “That you did. You are welcome to come with us, Huntress. No one will harm you.” Anastasia took a deep breath then agreed, “да, I’ll come (Yes).”

I grinned, “It will be fun… well it usually is… it’s fairly standard that I’m given food.” The woman asked, “You do this often then?” I answered, “Pretty much… it’s kind of our thing.” She hummed, “Yes, the group in black.”

I sighed, “The Resistance… we are the Ring Resistance. How is that not obvious? We draw rings with lines through them.” The woman chuckled, “We thought it was a circle.” I clapped, “Semantics! I need to study why no one guesses our name… it’s weird…. Because… it’s obvious.”

She agreed, “Now that you say it, it is.” Anastasia asked, “What’s your name?” She answered, “Queen Tatiana Petrov.” I pulled out a notebook and wrote that down. I asked, “Do you run your area?” She answered, “I do with my husband, but I am the ruling line. Which I feel was your question.”

I agreed, “It was… the question is did the Hunters coming out here to try and kill you know that… or are they just killing you off as they can? Is this a common occurrence? Are your numbers dwindling?” Queen Tatiana laughed, “You ask many questions.”

I agreed, “I do… it’s kind of my thing.” She grinned at me and led us further into the wooded areas. This was going to be fun. I was right, it was fun and there was food. I added them to my list and got them in touch with other people.

More time went by and I continued my work. Currently, I was monitoring a group of Hunters going after my Xander. They had a literal death wish and it needed to be studied. Sierra offered, “I’ll go track them with you.” I snorted, “I didn’t say I was going…” She gave me a look.

I continued, “The group said no.” She stared at me I grumbled, “Fine. I already know where they are. It’s a secluded area but you’re on the dinner shift. I got this. They will totally pay for thinking they can go after my Xander.”

She snorted, “That I know, but first they were getting information on him.” Which was also not allowed in my mind. Because he was MINE and I was the one allowed to gather information about him because….he was mine and that was fair….Plus, I did it to keep him safe and they were trying to hurt him. There were clear differences.

She left, and I got all my gear on and went through a holoport. I easily found them. Heck, a pup could've. Which technically I still was, but I felt like a grown up. I'd had to shed the pup mentality quickly down here and that's really all there was to it.

I knew something else was out here. Something calling to me. Which was silly… neither things nor people called to me… they kind of did though. It's how I kept finding other secret Supernatural groups. Well, some were accidental.

I set up my scope to scout the area and see if I could spot a new one and nearly screamed. There was DRAGON! A real Dragon. A purple one. I was fine. Normal even. Caine linked, "Are you all good? I know you hate it when the group disagrees with you."

I squeaked, "Me? What? I'm so good. Normal and…" He groaned, "God, what did you do?" I answered, "Nothing yet." He snorted, "Do not tell me you went where I think you did." Well, he said not to tell him, so I didn't reply.

One of the bounty Hunters yelled, "A Dragon?! Are you fucking kidding me?! There are Dragons!" Good plan, draw the Dragon's attention to you by shouting. Darwinism at its finest. Dragon's breathed FIRE. People were so dumb it hurt my brain.

One said, "Let's skin it." The other retorted, "Are you insane? It's a dragon! We should keep it!" He had me thinking he was the smart one for a second with his first comment then he ruined it. KEEP A DRAGON?! Just casually. They did realize that was technically a WereDragon? Because I did. A royal one even.

The dumb one replied, "We can't keep it! Look how big it is." The less dumb one snorted, "Oh, but you think we can kill it." He had a point, but it was moot since they were both going to die. Then I'd have to make sure I didn't upset the WereDragon like they had.

I needed to get on that, so I quickly shot them both. The Dragon wasn't happy. Which did not make sense. I'd saved her, but maybe it was because she didn't know if I was going to shoot her. I made a snap decision to be in front of the Dragon.

I walked down slowly and took out a spray can and drew our symbol on both guys chest. I considered the fact I wasn't on fire to be a good sign. I took a deep breath and turned to the Dragon. We were staring at each other, but she hadn't shifted back.

Well, I still wearing my mask. So, I'd give some leeway there. I quickly took it off and studied her more. The Dragon seemed to smile at me. I whispered, "Wow… I didn't know Dragons still existed and you're… beautiful." The Dragon definitely liked the compliment.

I continued, "That's a unique color of purple, two horns on top with four down each side for a total of ten. A silvery white chest and some on your wings and a horned tail." Stop describing the Dragon, Melanie.

I admitted, "Dang… you probably didn't need me to shoot the Hunters, but I was kinda awestruck I mean… look at you! It's so cool and… I mean you know that. You're a Dragon. Are you the only one? You should be in their realm… I mean everyone thought they died off, but clearly they did not… because you are here… and you can't be the only one… because biology."

I tapped my chin, "Gosh, it must be hard for you to find some place to fly. Poor Dragon… I know wolves like to run but people are used to seeing wolves… not dragons though. I have a Witch friend… I have a lot of buildings too."

I thought about adding, "If I asked her to spell the inside of one to look like the sky that might be nice for you. She could put up a holoport so you could get to it if you needed to shift. It's not ideal or perfect because it's not actually being outside, but maybe your Dragon side would feel less restless if she had a space where she knew she could come fly without fear of Hunters." She still didn't shift back. Ok.

I started asking questions, "Do you breathe fire? Because that would be so cool." Now the Dragon looked amused. I was still not on fire so that was still good. She turned and roasted the bodies. She was showing off. YES! She liked me.

I gasped, "Wow… you do breathe fire! That's so cool. Purple is a royal color. Are you royalty? I bet you are. Even if you're not, it's so cool." That got her to shift back. She was stunning. I was pretty sure

Prince Hastein Cambridge would agree. Maybe I could get them to meet. The Hackura realm would be safe for her. Her hair was partially purple at the bottom. I wondered if she dyed it that was or not.

When she turned around, I said, "Wow… your hair is so cool! Is that natural?" Good going Melanie. Keep saying the word wow. She's not going to believe us if we tell her we are a genius. She answered, "Yes, it is natural. It matches my Dragon. I can't dye my hair either. It doesn't change color."

Well, she couldn't but I could prove I was genius even though I couldn't stop saying wow around her. I told her, "I bet I could figure it out. Or get you a nice wig that no one could tell the difference if you wanted. I'm Melanie by the way. People call me Ashley too… but it's really Melanie. Melanie McAlister."

She hummed, "Sounds like your story is complicated." I sighed, "Most people around here have complicated stories." She questioned, "Why were you following these guys?" I sat down by her and tried to let go of my anger since they were dead.

I explained, "They were going to gather information on my Xander." She made that smile people did when I said that right before they decided I had a crush. It was annoying. She asked, "Your Xander? Who might that be?"

I explained, "My mate." I could see her confusion, but I just really couldn't hear ONE more person call it a crush. Eventually she said, "I didn't know Werewolves knew before eighteen who their mate was." I admitted, "I've known since I was three."

She pressed, "Why did your mate let you come alone? Is your mate not a Werewolf? They seem to be possessive even when they are assholes." They did not from what I'd seen down here. This pack and the ones around here were not at all really. Well, not in a way that protected their mates… more in a way that made it seem like they owned them.

Alpha Peter and my dad were… Even Garrett was. He didn't write to me though. He just closed the door on our relationship as if I meant nothing to him. He used to run and play with me. He'd even tried to dance with me once when I showed him a move. I pushed that sadness away harshly.

I told her about Xander, "We've never met. He's my brother's best friend." She seemed to be arguing with her Dragon about something. Eventually she said, "My name is Kingsley." I responded, "That's a pretty name."

She grinned saying, "Thanks. Why don't you tell me more about this Xander? I'm sure we can get the two of you together." I whispered, "I can't get to him. He doesn't want me." Yet. I was working on getting him to be open to the idea.

The Resistance making Beta Jason proud was my best shot. The Rebels couldn't hurt either. We were popular. I was also Red One. So, I had a chance I was giving myself. She asked me, "Why do you think that?"

I explained, "My brother told me." She pointed out, "Your brother could be lying. What is Xander's full name?" Beta Jason wouldn't lie to me. If he was going to, he'd tone down how much he hated me after all this time.

I answered her, "Alpha Duke Alexander Marcus Nathan Conners." She snorted, "Honestly, your brother is likely lying. If even a fraction of the rumors about Princess Luna Haley Conners are true, she'd kick her son's ass if he rejected his mate over something like that."

My brother didn't lie, and I wasn't sure where Princess Luna Haley would come down on this. Ultimately, he was her son, and she wanted him to be happy. Which was what I wanted. I admitted, "I trust you for some reason. Plus, I'm pretty sure you could breathe fire and kill me easily. I guess I might as well tell you my story."

She replied, "I won't set you on fire. My Dragon and I both like you. That's rare for her. She doesn't tend to like people; however, I'll tell you what; you tell me your story and I'll tell you mine." Ok, Melanie no screaming about a Dragon liking you. That's not normal and she might think you are mostly normal. I agreed, "Ok."

I tried to tell her a short version of my story but blurted the whole thing out. She breathed out smoke a few times during it, but she didn't seem to notice. When I finished, she asked, "So, you're fifteen?" I answered, “Yup. I have a lot of plans for my sixteenth birthday… since Beta Jason will let me come home and… getting Xander to be open to us is one of them.”

I should probably acknowledge I had another plan if my brother didn’t let me come home. I didn’t like to think about that plan because it upset me… but every plan needed other factors. I liked having other plans ready to go. I didn’t do well when taken by surprise.

I asked her, “So, what’s your story?” She laid it out for and I nearly cried. She had people who cared about her, but they clearly hurt her. She was so lonely. I admitted, “King Aiden Holloran could tell you more about yourself… but… I do… I could… do some research… and…” I might lose my new friend before our friendship really started, but she should know about who she was.

She cut me off, “You can do that. I don’t know King Aiden and I don’t trust him.” He would definitely let her come to Faerie, but she didn’t look like she wanted that. I could get her somewhere to fly though. I called Paige.

She answered, “Hello, Melanie.” I greeted, “Hi, yeah…” She asked, “Do you need to rant about the group not agreeing to kill those Hunters?” I snorted, “No…” She snorted, “Because Sierra seemed to think you were going to do it anyway.” Well, Caine did link me already so they knew I’d gone anyway.

I admitted, “I did go kill them….” She sighed, “What’s the point of us saying we don’t think we need to kill people if you do it anyway? We agreed…” I cut her off, “Well, I did NOT agree… I don’t really care about the group consensus…”

She groaned, “Your Xander could deal with them.” I snorted, “I know he could handle it… that wasn’t the point. THEY IGNORE MY MESSAGES…” Paige snorted, “You’ve to be kidding. They don’t know it’s you.” They should. I leave the Resistance symbol….therefore, they are ignoring the Resistance and that’s irritating.

I groaned, “Look… I did not call you to argue… I need you to go to the new building I acquired…” She asked, “The most recent one?” I answered, “Yes that one…” She snorted, “You know when you say the new building it’s not exactly a small selection of buildings.”

I replied, “I know there are several… but you literally knew which one I meant. Anyway, if you could use a spell to make it look like the sky inside…” Paige snorted, “The sky? Why would you need that? This request makes no sense.”

I groaned, “I know that doesn’t make sense, but… well it does…” Paige laughed, “Fine. I’ll go now.” I let out a breath saying, “Ok, thanks.” Sometimes I was pretty sure she just liked to give me crap when she’d planned to do what I asked all along.

I explained to Kingsley, “She’s going to get that done. Then you can fly inside. I mean… I know it’s not outside but…” She quickly cut me off, “It’s more than I’ve had in sixteen years. I don’t remember ever flying.” That was really sad. Apollo, Ajax, Sugar, Pepper, and literally every wolf I knew loved running. If they couldn’t remember doing so it would be sad.

I rambled, “It’s a big building too so…” She quickly said, “I appreciate it.” I asked, “So…I remember reading Dragons eat people… Does Kayda want to eat those guys?” Her eyes flickered and became purple. So cool. She stepped further away than a wolf would to shift, but that made sense since she was so big.

I shirked, “Oh my gosh. This might the coolest moment of my entire day…. no life. A Dragon. I saw you shift into a Dragon.” She ate them and shifted back. Out of nowhere she gasped like she was in pain. Uhh what? Did she have indigestion?

I asked, “Uhh what’s wrong?” She questioned, “When did your family die? The exact date?” Not a topic I liked discussing but I could give her an event that would tell her the date. I was also proud of Elise and all she accomplished. I was proud everyone knew the date she took over.

I explained, “You’d probably know it best by the Luna Ceremony that happened that day. Everyone… I mean… I was supposed to be there.” I wanted to be there more than anything. I ruined my whole life that night. I should’ve just stayed with my dad all day. Just like I had for Elise and EJ’s Luna Ceremony. The odds of being in a car crash twice like that were practically non-existent.

Kingsley whispered, “It was you. All this time it was you.” That didn’t make sense. I asked, “Huh? What was me? I didn’t… I’m not a Luna.” She snorted, “You belong to Alpha Alexander Conners therefore you are a Luna. I just mean that day I had this overwhelming feeling that something bad happened. It was you. I am somehow connected to you. My Dragon keeps referring to you as our pet."

That was easily a nicer name that I got around the pack. I shrugged, "I could be a Dragon pet… since … well, you don't drink blood or anything… I mean… I have given some Vampire's blood… to save them…" Charles. I'd saved Charles.

He'd come into town to surprise me and happened to be where a group of Hunters were. I'd killed them and waited for his bloodline to get to him. Another time I'd had two of his Vampire children out with me and they'd gotten hurt.

So, I had to give them blood to heal. I put it in a cup and everything, which had amused them all. It wasn't like they bit me, I cut myself for them. Which…apparently made their makers interest in me abundantly clear to them…which still didn't make sense.

Paige sent out the all clear to my phone and that she was heading out. I grabbed Kingsley saying, "Come on." I stepped through the holoport and frowned. Paige had not left. I commented, "You said you were leaving and…"

Paige cut me off, "Yes, I possess the ability to lie. Unlike some of us." I was working on it. Paige warned Kingsley, "Don't hurt her or I will curse you." Uhh, don't threaten a Dragon. That was clearly a bad idea.

Kingsley laughed, "I won't hurt her." Paige studied her for a long moment. I was practically begging her with my eyes to stop it. Paige offered, "I don't know what you are, but Melanie rescues people. If she trusts you then I will as well. I hope you enjoy the scenery inside. If you want me to change it and you turn out not to be an asshole I could change it for you."

Kingsley replied, "Thank you for doing this." Paige finally caught my eye and left but everything about her told me she was serious. She just casually threatened a Dragon without knowing it. That was no good.

Once Paige left, I took Kingsley to the door. I instructed, "ILYX, I need to set up Kingsley on the system. Only Paige, Kingsley, and I should have access to this building." ILYX answered, "Of course, Melanie Jane. Put her hand on the palm scanner."

Kingsley asked, "Was that Alpha Alexander Conners voice?" Gosh, I was hoping she didn't know that since she was off grid, but then again, we were talking about Xander. I replied, "Huh? What? That… Xander… No?" Maybe I pulled off lying this time since she looked startled. Then she busted up laughing.

Caine linked, "YOU FOUND ANOTHER PERSON YOU JUST BROUGHT INTO THE RESISTANCE?!" I admitted, "I mean… technically haven't brought her in. I did tell her about it… but to be fair, I shot two people to help her." He groaned, "For fuck's sake, Mel."

Kingsley brought me back to the present, "You really are a bad liar." Yeah, I'd heard that. I grabbed her hand and got her set up. I admitted, "Ok, I might have borrowed his voice… for reasons… and…" She jumped in, "Why isn't the system named Xander then?" Because that was too obvious.

I explained, "It's an acronym." She snorted, "So the X is Xander. ILY. Oh my god. It stands for I love you Xander. That's adorable." How did she figure it out so fast? I replied, "What? Huh? That's… a random group of words… you threw together… not me…. I did not say that…"

She laughed, "Please quit while you are behind. How is the Resistance leader the worst liar ever?" I admitted, "I'm pretty good at evading… I studied a lot about Fairies when I was younger." The pang that reminded me of Jared nearly sent me to my knees. I missed him so much. He'd always smile at me. He was my friend. No, he was family and now I was nothing to him.

I got everything set up in the system for Kingsley and took her inside. She took off into the skies. I watched her in shock for several seconds before I got on setting things up for her. I had to help her. It was a thing I needed to do. No one could argue that.

When she came down, I was worried. This wasn't big enough for Dragon. She had to do so many loops, and it wasn't the actual sky. I apologized, "I'm sorry… I know it's not much… but …" She hugged me tight and started to cry. Great. Good job. You made the Dragon cry.

She whispered, "I've flown for the first time today. I don't know if I ever did before, but I know that today I was in the skies. Even if they were an illusion." She started to sob, and I understood that it was coming from her very soul because I had this moment myself sometimes. So, I held her while she cried it out.

When she stopped, she pulled back without looking at me. She apologized, "I'm sorry. I have been emotional lately." I admitted, "I get it… I'm emotional a lot myself…. and Paige said it's good to cry it out… they just get me drunk to do it."

She snorted, "You don't strike me as someone who gets drunk a lot." That was wrong. I laughed humorlessly, "I drink a lot… like a lot. It's easier… especially on letter days." It was coming up too, but I saw the question on her face.

I explained, "My family… well… and people I consider family… they send me letters. They are so angry… especially Jason. I used to call him Jase… but he doesn't let me now. Anyway… we can get Paige to set up Holoports for you back here in other places. She likes setting them up… and based on what you do, and I do… I feel like we can help each other out… like a lot."

She agreed, "Probably. I'll eventually run out of money and…" I interrupted, "I can set up a diversified investment portfolio for you." I did it for all my friends. Caine's was the most expansive because he was going to have to invest a lot into fixing Black Path.

She agreed, "I'll get everything to you." Everything. All her money? Oh gosh. I replied, "Well, not everything… you should set up a few CD's and a Roth IRA…." She cut me off, "What would a CD do? I don't need to buy music." They really sent her out here with no knowledge of the human realm. That was mean.

I explained, "No… no… it's a Certificate of deposit. It's a savings account that holds a fixed amount of money for set periods of time. Usually, six months or twelve. You leave the money in the account and the bank pays you a fixed rate interest. So, you literally earn money for it sitting in an account… which is why most people have savings accounts with money sitting there. CD's just earn more than savings accounts… for the same thing… and you can just keep earning interest on it."

She questioned, "What if you need the money?" I explained, "You pay a penalty, and you get it back." She nodded, "Ok. You are officially in charge of my finances." That would be fun. After we nailed everything down, I took her to a place I had in Arizona.

Her voice changed and she asked, "How much money do you have?" I admitted, "A lot. I'm a billionaire." Twice over now. I'd earned it faster than I had my first that I mostly gave away. My foundation was doing great things though.

Kingsley snorted, "Then you are definitely beyond in charge of my finances." I assured her, "I promise I'll turn you a good profit and…" She interrupted, "I'm sure you will." I called Paige again. She answered, "Caine is going to lose his mind, and you keep calling me."

I said, "Well, I need you to go through our holoport to the Arizona house and set up our new friend." She showed up within moments and everything was done. I showed Kingsley around, thinking it was the best house for her really.

I told her, "It's ok if you don't like it… we have other places…" Paige snorted, "She likes it, Mel. Take a breath." I continued, "You can change anything you like. There's a card in the safe, which…" I handed her a file I'd worked on while she flew around the warehouse.

"We give this to everyone… and you could have people here to host before they leave… for your stuff and mine… like combining our stuff…" She smirked saying, "Sounds good. I'll look over this." I sighed in relief before I left her there.

Paige snorted, "To the firing squad." I grumbled, "They will be fine." We walked through the holoport and into King's diner. Mason shot me a look while Hendrick shook his head. Caine growled, "Are you for real? Why do we vote if you just do things regardless of what we say?" I winced, "They were going to…"

He cut me off, "And you brought someone else in." I explained, "She does the Underground abuse group. It's called Operation Saint Rita." He rubbed his temples before telling me, "You'll give me gray hair. You know that, right?" I reasoned, "It is highly unlikely you'd get gray hair until you're like… seventy." He snorted, "Well, you're trying to give me it DECADES ahead of time." I was not.

More time went by, and it was time to go to a Hunters meeting. I was late because Edward had stalled me. I pulled up outside the den. I found it INCREDIBLY ironic they called it a den since wolves... the real ones tended to live in dens.

These people hunted wolves… but only some wolves. I couldn't believe their own stupidity. They basically worked for the bad wolves. The ones they hate. The ones that attack humans and crap like that. They were too blinded by their hatred to realize they are run by awful wolf packs.

They got around it saying, 'oh well we make them work for us' … but what do the bad wolves get? They send wolves, who are not harmed unless they act out, and Hunters avoid their packs. What packs get hit? The good ones that were not hurting anyone.

Honestly. It was just sad how easily manipulated these people are. They had no idea they were going against their true purpose. Anastasia was working to restore it, but it was a slow process. At least she could realize they were dead in the water once they started incorporating other wolves into their schemes.

The larger group did not realize it yet. They thought they were safe because they had silver. Yet every single wolf in there could snap their neck before they reached for a weapon. We are faster than they are. Which is why they should hone their hunting skills, but they were lazy.

My musings were interrupted by Addison. She linked, "Mel, where are you? Dante is here and he seems to think this new guy is a Conners mate. I don't know what all of the mates look like because I didn't look at the mate files you have on them. That family has a lot of people so I've never seen Micah." He was in the folder for Max…so she should've seen him….he had a separate folder too.

I questioned, "His name is Micah?!" Addison answered, "Yes." I snorted, "Sure, why change his name? It's probably not him. It could be him… CRAP! Does Dante want him to take off his shirt?" Addison groaned, "He does."

I grabbed a concealer I'd been working on. It was for the Hackura and I'd perfected it last week. I got out of my car and palmed it. I ran into the house, my mind racing with solutions. If Micah was here… who came with him?

Was it Max? There had to be someone else here with them. Tristan said Levi told him that they always went places like this with at least one other person. That rang true from the files I'd looked at for the Hackura. What if…? That thought stalled me.

What if Xander was here? I shoved that from my mind because I needed to help Micah. I could hear them downstairs. Micah was trying to leave. Oh my gosh. Did they try to stop him? Idiots! He could kill them so easily. I came down the stairs quickly. Micah wasn't facing me, but I knew who he was. I recognized him instantly.

I quickly said his name. "Micah? Is that you?" He turned and I smiled because I felt at ease despite the situation. It really was him. He was my mate's brother in law. Why the HELL would they send him in of all people? They couldn't have changed his name at least? Come on.

I replied, "Oh my gosh… it is!" I ran over and touched his arm putting the concealer on him. I saw his questioning gaze. I continued, "It really IS you! How are you? Is Dante being dumb? I mean… he usually is… so I'll just consider that question answered. Ignore him."

Dante asked, "You know this guy, Ashley?" I hated that Micah was going to call me Ashley. It literally felt like my soul may die if he did. I replied, "Obviously, since I said his name." Honestly, it was a little insane they didn't know this was Micah Percival.

Anyone who paid attention… which was DEFINITELY not Dante… would know who he was. He somewhat paid attention though because Micah's name must have caught his eye. It was a little insulting that these guys thought they could stop him. Maybe I should've just let it go and let Micah and whoever was here kill them all.

They would've left Addison and Sierra alone… the problem was me. What would they do to me? They definitely call former Alpha Eric about Addison and Sierra. I was coming anyway so me too. Then all hell would break loose.

I commented to Micah, "Saying your name makes it obvious… I'd say don't judge on his lack of intelligence, but you kind of should… so… take that how you will. Anyway, Micah's fierce. What's your kill count up to Micah? I feel like it's got to be in the thirties.... maybe forties.... it's upper thirties for sure." It easily was.

I bragged about my should be brother in law, "He's impressive you guys, and you KNOW I'm not often impressed... since not one of you has EVER impressed me. He could beat ALL your butts, so easily... it's kind of sad... you should work out more... not that it would help... he'd still beat you, but it could be less tragic for you."

I asked, "What are you doing here, Micah?" Micah said, "Hey, Ashley." I was right. It felt like a piece of my soul crumbled and died when he said Ashley and I barely kept my gasp of pain internal. He continued, "I was thinking about joining your cause, then shit got weird."

I grumbled, "Dante, what did you do? Why are you even here? Where's Nate? You know we hate it when you show up. Well.... 'We' could be strong word... I mean me. I definitely do, but I'm pretty sure I'm not alone in that."

Dante answered, "I heard we had a new recruit, and wanted to meet him personally. Especially when I heard his name was Micah. There's a Micah mated to one of the Conners brothers." Everyone stiffened. I muttered, "Yeah, sure Dante that's logical. Like a mate of the Conners would just stroll on up in here."

I shot Micah an annoyed looked adding, "That's like the WORST idea of all time. Also, Micah is near the eighty-seventh most popular name for boys dating back to biblical times... so... that's a horrible reason to be weird about a name. There are over three thousand boys and two hundred girls born who are named Micah every year ON AVERAGE. Do you know how many people are named Ashley?"

He cut me off, "Spare me your statistics." I waved, "Seriously, Dante, you are paranoid. Go back to Nashville and whatever hole you crawled out of. No one here likes seeing your rat face. You're surprisingly unattractive for a supernatural." Dante grunted, "You can't speak to me like that."

I replied, "I think I just did... so I'm pretty sure that I can." I acted like I was going to punch him while asking, "What are you going to do about it? Oh yeah, that's right... nothing." He jumped back in fright knowing I could take him down.

Addison linked, "Umm whatcha doing? He's going to push it." I replied, "He's might, but it's fine. My concealers work now. Or he'll take it out on me." She reasoned, "Everything you've mentioned about the Hackura says Micah won't let him." That was true, which meant Dante would die sooner than I planned. I was ok with that though.

Dante sputtered, "I'm not leaving until he takes off his shirt." I knew it was too much to ask that he just leave. I turned to Micah and blinked twice. That was a sign to any Hackura that the person had their six. He'd know it and trust me because we were meant to be family. I'd put the concealer on him, and I knew it worked. I'd had Luna Elena test it for me.

Micah stared at me. Come on. I encouraged, "Go on Micah. If he tries to make a move on you, we can both kick his butt. Easily. I mean I've done it... like thirty seven times... not like, actually thirty seven times. Ok... it's actually forty-five... I was lowballing it for some reason...To be fair, I've had to."

I pointed at Dante, "He's a bit of a pervert. Though... most guys are. I mean I swear, what's up with the grabby 'I'll own you' or 'let me fuck you' crap? Honestly. Oh, I can't forget the time honored 'I'll possess and tame you' rhetoric. It's like people forget women have standards."

Micah's jaw clenched. Sierra linked, "Are you trying to get Dante killed? Because I think Micah might kill him." I was not opposed to that idea, but I was just trying to get Micah to trust me. His jaw could clench for several reasons. One being these people wanted to kill his mate...which offended him for obvious reasons.

I continued, "I've had to ask a few of these guys if their pick up lines actually work for them. I mean obviously, they have some reason to think they would. It's not like any of them are god's gift to women or anything so... I don't understand how it wor...."

Dante interrupted, "ASHLEY GRIFFEN WILL YOU STOP RAMBLING FOR ONCE IN YOUR LIFE!" I was surprised he didn't just say shut up. Micah tapped his thigh letting me know he trusted me and just like that an old feeling burst into my chest.

An emotion so sharp I nearly went down again. He trusted and believed in me. He was a good guy who knew how life was supposed to be, and he was trusting me. It meant more than he could ever know. Micah took off his shirt.

The guys who brought him in hit each other smugly. Dirk grunted, "See? I told you he was cool, Dante." I muttered, "If we are being technical, I believe I said he was cool. He's killed more Werewolves than you've ever thought about killing. He could also snap you all like twigs. Seriously, you all want to fight Werewolves, and you can't lift twenty pounds... it's sad... honestly..." He'd killed rogues, but they didn't need to know that.

Dante yelled, "SHUT UP, ASHLEY!" I glared at him, wishing I could kill him here and now. I warned Dante as I moved in front of Micah, "I'll drop you like a sack of potatoes if you try anything weird, Dante. I just told Micah you wouldn't, and I meant it. Which you totally know because you laugh when I lie to you…" Several people snickered.

I grumbled, "You don't even like guys." Dante complained, "You rarely stick up for anyone. You barely have friends of the male persuasion. You hate most of the guys here. We have a pool about whether or not you're a lesbian." I had male friends! That wasn't a remotely true comment.

I snorted, "I totally have male friends… that's a thing… that I have… just not here, because you suck! As far as you are concerned on my sexual preference... let's go with that. It's simpler. There's one man I'd ever let touch me in the way you all want to, and one man alone."

"So keep on dreaming. You all with your grabby hands have NOTHING that I want. I don't want to be touched by ANY of you jerks, and you INSIST on trying knowing that… and that I can beat you. There's a definition you should look up. Insanity."

I pointed at the man who should be my brother in law, "Micah here does swing the other way which means I don't have to worry he's going to try and cop a feel. He's actually a good guy, unlike you tools. Come on Micah. Let's go get some food and catch up."

Sierra linked, "Maybe don't tell them he has something else in common with the Micah related to the Conners." Yeah, that would've been good advice a second ago. I asked, "Samantha and Cindy do you guys want to join?"

Addison answered, "Yeah, we're coming. Dante, you know if you keep treating the new people like this they won't join." Several people made noises of agreement. They were so easily led it was a little sad. They were all riled up and on Dante's side a second ago.

Dante cleared his throat, "We'd welcome you, Micah. I don't lead this group. A man named Nate does and he will be back tonight." Micah said, "I was prepared to join, but after whatever the hell this was, I'll have to think about it." The answer was no because I wasn't going to let it happen. This was an in I could take and protect Micah all at the same time.

Dante offered, "Ashley, do tell him he could work with you if he joined, since you two know each other." I scoffed, "Because he doesn't have ears and can't hear you himself? This isn't kindergarten. Tell him yourself… which you did, so… I'm not your telephone. I swear you all are a bunch of pups with grabby hands."

When we got outside Micah asked, "Uhh have we met? Because I don't think I was there." I lead him to my car without answering. Addison groaned over link, "Do not geek out about meeting him." Yeah, that was going to be hard. I admired him and his dad. His dad was my tech idol and mentor without knowing he was.

I managed to not answer Micah as everyone got in the car. Addison linked me, "You ok?" I sighed, "Let's just get to the diner. He won't be alone." Addison replied, "And if he's with his mate? Or his mate's brother?"

I sighed, "We will find out. It's not Xander though. He'd have been in front of me declaring me his and I'd have passed the hell out because… when he finds out who I really am…. We'll have a lot to talk about." Addison frowned but didn't say anything as I started the car. This could be a long night.

It turned out in my favor really. We got everything we wanted and something I never thought I'd get; an in with the Hackura. I knew their inspection of everything was going to go just fine, but I was still nervous. Virgil called me.

I answered, “Hey.” He declared, “They got everything and left. No one was hurt.” I replied, “Thanks! Get out of there.” He chuckled, “Got it.” He hung up and I got back to work. Black Path members came in, including Trevor McCann. He lived to torment me.

Normally they left me alone in King’s Diner. I knew I spent a lot of time here, but I liked it. Mason and Hendrick kept the whispers to a minimum. I could also work without the pack people bothering me.

I had narrowed down a spot for The Resistance headquarters away from here. I just needed to win another fight, and I could buy the building. I needed my other money for my inventions. I’d set up a shell corporation. Manford at Modd. It was just a silly antigram but putting a shell corporation that spelled out ‘For T, mom, and Dad’ was too obvious.

Only Fairies would guess the real name, and they’d have to look really hard. I doubted the Ring would ever figure it out. It would have to be an allied Fairy for Red Run. Or the Fairies in Red Run themselves. They’d taught me Fealish and worked with me on making antigrams.

It hit me again how much I missed being back home. I missed dancing at my spot in the woods. I had to close my eyes and imagine I was back home sometimes to dance. I’d found a place to dance here, but this place sucked the creativity out of everything, including nature. I sighed.

Everything would be different once I had my wolf. Beta Jason would see… they said after my shift... maybe I could come home. I’d talk to Elise. She’d help my friends, and we could continue our work. I was positive nobody in Red Run would want to see much of me, so it was perfect.

I’d even picked out a spot for a new King’s diner in Red Run. I just needed them to come with me. Without Hendrick and Mason… without my friends… I don’t know what would’ve happened to me here. These people believed in me. I had to stand up for what was right.

People were whispering, “There’s the family killer.” I didn’t let them see my hurt and despair over their words. Trevor whispered, “Even her own brother doesn't want her. Why do we have to have her here?” I’d tried to leave and go to college but they didn’t let me so that was on them.

One snickered, “I asked the Alpha if she could clean the sixth floor in the pack house tomorrow. We wrecked it. Let’s see how the do-gooder slave feels after that.” I yawned, “Just fine. I can clean all day long. You know that. You’re wrecking the floor routine is getting old and tired. Pick a new line, guys.”

Mason brought out my burger and growled at them. They went back to glaring and talking quieter. I could still hear them. Everyone here who wasn’t human could. Jerks. I hated it here, I really did. Slaves weren’t allowed but they called me one still. It hurt more than I wanted to admit.

I heard the bell ring indicating someone else walked in, but I was working on an old idea trying to map it all out. I wanted to give all supernatural’s a special antidote that would counteract silver, iron, and other things. I almost had that equation worked out.

I felt the booth I was in move. I glanced up startled then quickly shut my notebook, “Uhh Mic... M. Let’s just go with M. No one around needs your name… that’s not a thing people need. So umm... you’re here. I did not expect you here...Why are you here? Where’s Ca… I mean C? What’s going on? Did everything not go ok? Oh gosh... Did C get hurt?”

Virgil said everything went fine, but the thought of getting the men that were supposed to be in my family hurt made me panic. Micah snorted, “Everything went perfectly fine. C did not get hurt. I’m actually here because C got you something.” I frowned, “Me? Why would he do that?”

Micah answered, “Because we do things for people. We saw that you have something glaring we could fix, and as you did a phenomenal job, beyond all our expectations, we have something for you.” I replied, “You didn’t need to do that. I don’t really need things…”

Someone coughed, “Family killers don’t deserve nice things.” My eyes dropped. Micah stood and walked over to the table. He crossed his arms saying, “I’m sorry. Did you have something to say? Or were you going to continue to pussy foot around it pretending you’re a big tough guy picking on someone whose family died tragically?” My jaw dropped.

He added, “I sure do hope nothing happens to your family. One never knows who could be lurking around the shadows. I’d hope everyone would be nice to you if someone were to break into your home and kill everyone except you. That is definitely something that I hope for you.” He slapped the guy's cheek twice lightly and let his eyes blaze gold briefly.

Micah came back to sit down across from me. Before his butt hit the booth cushion the pack members had scurried out of the diner, including Trevor who shot me an angry look, but I didn't really care. He wasn't scary because he never trained. He was just an angry hateful guy, and he hated me probably more than was rational. I'd never done anything to him.

Micah pulled my attention back, "Anyway. This is for you." He took out a backpack, both light and dark purple blended together and handed it to me. Tears welled in my eyes. The last time someone bought me a backpack was when my mom and I went shopping for school. My dad even came the last time before… for high school. Tears filled my eyes, and I couldn't stop them from falling.

It was such a simple gesture, but it reminded me of being cared for. Of being home. I missed it so much. My heart ached at not being home. I'd gotten physically ill from how homesick I'd gotten. I didn't understand why Beta Jason was doing this to me. He knew how I got if I was away too long.

Micah spoke, "If you don't like it…." I shook my head shouting, "NO! I love it. It's perfect. Thank you!" I got up and hugged him on his side of the booth. I walked back over to my side. Micah asked, "Why didn't you buy a new backpack? That one is on it's... no, it's past its final leg. It needs to be retired."

I shrugged, "My money goes to more important things." Like saving for the headquarters and my experiments. My heart tugged as I remembered my Grandpa Ben called them tinkering's. He said I liked to tinker. Like "Tinkerbell" from the human story *Peter Pan.*

Micah nodded, "I've got to get going. Are you going to be ok?" I shrugged noncommittally. Micah reached across the booth and took my hand, "Call or text me if you need help. I'll come with Cay… C… or some other backup."

I whispered, "Thanks M." Micah laughed, "You're welcome." He clearly didn't know why he felt so compelled to help me, but I did. I was his sister in law. It was also probably why they felt the need to get me a gift.

When he left I quickly checked out my new backpack. It was really nice. I transferred all my stuff over to it. Mason came out and sat down. He offered, "So, they seem nice." I nodded agreeing, "They are." Mason snorted, "You know how they behave towards you is not unlike I've seen other mates of siblings behave. They had an instant connection to you."

I told him, "They are my Xander's siblings' mates." Mason nodded, "I know who they are, I'm just saying you could be right. Your Xander could be your mate." I frowned, "I am right." He laughed, "I'm beginning to think you are." I sighed because no one understood.

They thought I was a pup with a crush, but Xander WAS mine and I was his. I just knew. I always had. I knew it was strange, but I did know. Mason walked away. I smiled at my backpack. I couldn't throw the old one away though.

I'd keep at Mason and Hendrick's house or someone would ruin it. I touched the backpack my parents had bought me. I couldn't get rid of it, but I could use a new backpack. I closed my eyes and breathed deeply then got back to my notebook.

Before I knew it the next problem was on me. Bounty Hunters. AGAIN. This time I was leaving them a clearer message. I grumbled, "Not that they listen to my messages." I left a message in BOLD, red letters to leave Xander alone. Ok, I put Alpha Duke Alexander but still. They would only guess at who I meant if I put Xander.

The message was at their main hub where they gathered to get assignments. The warning came with multiple heads on pikes. They'd think it was the Hackura, and if the Hackura knew they were headquartered here they might just give me a second with their taking bounties on Xander deal.

I was about to leave when I decided to spy on the meeting. What's the harm? I moved closer and heard them groan, "Is that girl not dead yet?" Who me? Well, that was prideful. They didn't know me, so it definitely wasn't me. They didn't know I was a girl. Or the one leaving them messages because I was that good. That was a prideful thought too.

Someone snorted, "Where is the last group that went after the Demon/Angel girl? Do we have a name?" One guy stood, "I'll take her out, that's too much money to pass out. Where is she?" Seriously? He wanted someone to do his job?

The man with the assignment answered, "She's in Arizona." He put up the coordinates up on a screen. We had a safe house near there. It was where I'd put Kingsley a few weeks ago. I left and went through our holoports.

I found the place she was staying easily enough. I called, "Umm, hello? We need to go because there's a Bounty Hunter who will shimmer in at any time and…" I trailed off when the shimmer started. I groaned, "Great. He's here. Ok, just stay where you are, and I'll kill him first."

The man appeared and he stared at me. He said, "You're not a hybrid." I answered, "I mean… no. So that's an odd statement." He frowned, "Do you live here?" I snorted, "No… who could live here? It's a decrepit old shack. Seriously, this is not an inhabitable building."

He cut me off saying, "Leave wolf, I have business here." I sighed, "So, that's a problem. I'm just going to give you the one chance to leave. Which is SUPER nice on my part so…" He rolled his eyes and drew on his power.

I pulled my dagger from my shoe and stabbed him in the heart, twisting it. He gasped, "Why?" I answered, "You came here to kill someone who didn't deserve it. I gave you a chance to leave. It was all very fair." He scoffed, "You're no Fairy." I agreed, "I know that. Obviously."

A voice called, "Step away from him, she wolf." I grumbled, "It's Melanie but ok…" I saw a woman throw a fireball at the bounty Hunter. I asked, "Did you get Angel powers too?" She tilted her head, "Yes, why did you help me?"

I grinned admitting, "It's kind of what I do. I think you'll like my friends. What's your name?" She raised an eyebrow, "I'm not meeting your friends, but I'm Angelique." I bartered, "How about one who also doesn't like people? K would like you and I have a house around here she's staying in for a little bit. No offense to your decrepit shack… but my house is nicer, and I'll throw in a car… plus..."

She asked, "How do you have a house with a car? You're like fifteen." I replied, "I mean I am fifteen, not like fifteen, and I'm a billionaire so that's how." She gasped, "WHAT? Are you serious?"

I nodded, "So, would you like to meet K? She bought new furniture for the house and everything is VERY comfy. I doubt this place has a bed and K imported one for all the guest rooms. You could even pick a room. Then rotate through the safe houses if the bounty Hunters catch on. You could also join us."

She asked, "Join you? Oh my god, are you the blue circle drawing people?" I huffed, "Why doesn't anyone know our name? We are the Ring Resistance." She chuckled, "I'm kind of off grid." I nodded, "Right. That's fair then."

She laughed, "Alright, let's go meet this K. I have always wanted a roomie, as they say." I asked, "How do you know that?" She answered, "I log into my siblings accounts to watch television on this." She held up a device. I grabbed it and stomped on it.

She yelled, "HEY!" I said, "That's how they know where you are. I'm not saying your siblings did that but… someone found out they got it for you. I'll get you a new one and set it up with an alias for your apps and television watching."

She grinned asking, "Could you get me Netflix?" I snorted, "I can get you all of them." She squealed, "AND A BED?" I didn't like her family at all. I nodded. She admitted, "I don't know why I'm trusting you, but I feel like I can. Don't make me regret that." I promised, "I won't." I liked and trusted her too.

She and Kingsley hit it off like I thought they would. I went back to the diner and worked on my plan for what I'd do if Beta Jason didn't let me come home when I shifted.

Dax sat down next to me. He faltered, "The Female Lead Warrior of our pack. What is this?" I explained, "If Beta Jason doesn't let me come home, I'll challenge for it here." He frowned, "You don't belong here while the pack is like this. You're supposed to get home, and we all keep working. Addison and Si will end up with you." That was the plan. I nodded, "I know I just need to cover all my bases." He hummed and watched as I worked.

My sixteenth birthday was inching closer and closer, and I had to get the timing perfect. I wanted to have my serums ready to go when I went home. Currently, I was working on the serum for Fairies. I was using my beakers and conducting my experiments. I was close, I knew I was.

This combination was going to be the winner. I announced, "Test one-hundred and sixty-five. I am about to test the serum. I dropped a drop into a vial of Fairy blood that I'd dropped Iron into. I watched the reaction.

I screamed and pumped my fist into the air when the serum separated the iron from the blood then disappeared. I screamed, "I DID IT! I DID IT!" I looked around for someone to high five, but no one was here. Tears filled my eyes, and I sat on my workbench.

I whispered, "I did it, dad. Now, I can do ones for other Supernatural's. It should be quite simple." I wiped away my tears and looked at my serum. I grinned saying, "I really did it." I should've had my family and Xander by my side when I did.

I was putting everything away when my friends came in. Addison declared, "It's intervention time. You need to shower and wow. You look like a mad scientist with your dirty hair and…" Sierra nudged her in the side. Addison asked, "What? She does and she's been crying. Oh no, it didn't work."

I grinned admitting, "I got the right combination. The Fairy Serum is ready." Sierra asked, "Have you decided what to call it?" I wanted to name it Xander, but that was too obvious. I made it for him though, so it had to have him in the name that was just reasonable.

I told them, "I don't want them to know it's from me, so they'll use it." Addison snorted, "Unless they are stupid, which based on everything you've said, they aren't, Alpha Eric would probably cut off his right arm for something like this. King Aiden definitely would. They wouldn't care if it came from you."

I shook my head saying, "I can't take that risk. They might not believe us. I have the perfect way to deliver it to them." Sierra waved, "We know how you plan to do that. We want to know what name you landed on. It's got to be unique. Like its creator." I blushed.

Paige said, "Girl, you made a revolutionary serum. You should be screaming from the rooftops. You should be celebrated by the whole supernatural community at large. Everyone should clamor to work with the brilliant Melanie McAlister." I replied, "But they wouldn't."

Paige sighed, "That's just your fear talking. I know it's hard to rise above it all with asshole relatives, but I think you should. This is amazing." I couldn't do that. I said, "We had a lot of good times. We had all the love in the world." My tears fell even though I tried to hold them back.

Sierra whispered, "Mel." I cried, "I miss them all so much. I didn't just lose my parents and T. I lost everyone and I miss them so much….but they hate me and it hurts all the time. There's this constant ache and…" I faltered when they held me while I cried.

Eventually I shook it off. I apologized, "Sorry." Paige said, "You are not the one who needs to be sorry." Addison nodded, "Agreed." I shrugged, "Anyway, I did pick a name." Paige encouraged, "And it is…?" She trailed off intentionally.

I answered, "Laxenread." Addison asked, "Laxen what? Is that Fealish? It doesn't sound Latin." I explained, "It's neither. It's an anagram for Alexander." Sierra frowned, "They will figure that out." I nodded, "And Fairies will assume it's another Fairy. They love anagrams. Princess Luna Haley or King Aiden will figure it out first, but they won't look for me. I'm a wolf."

Paige sighed, "It's brilliant but it's sad. You should take credit. Make your mark on the supernatural world in a light shining way. Your Resistance network is beyond impressive, but that has to be in the shadows. This could be your moment to reclaim everything you lost. You could have everything you deserve."

I shook my head, "I can't take the risk Xander's family wouldn't use it because it came from me. I can't do that." They all sighed but let it go.

I locked everything up knowing tomorrow I'd be back, producing this in mass so I could flood the allies with Laxenread. Well, as much as I could, given the materials I had on hand. I'd get it to them on my sixteenth birthday if they let me come home. If not, I'd give them the building in Yellow Hills we'd gone in and cleared out. It wasn't my first choice on giving it to them, but everything would change after my birthday. It was going to be different now. I was going home.

Haunting Movements

Alexander is Twenty Years Old

Alexander was annoyed. I punched a bag, and it fell onto the ground. Angela popped to me. I turned right away greeting my sister. "Hey, Ang." TJ popped to her a second later. I laughed, "You guys look like you are up to something." Klaus smirked.

Angela nodded telling me, "We are and we want your help." I asked, "Me?" TJ laughed. I asked, "Why are you laughing?" He shrugged, "I said the same thing when she told me we were coming to you." I would argue, but I had to be last on the list of people to help.

Cassie was a shoe in for sure. We were still reeling from the attack on her, organized by Cora after her tournament. My sister got shot and it still pissed me off.

I asked, "So, why me?" Angela huffed, "Because I said so." I felt her feelings in our bond. I knelt down assuring her, "Ang, it's not your fault." She stomped her foot, "It's just blurry and I can't get it right. Now, you're upset, and I decided you're going to help us today. You have fun on this path. Please."

I admitted, "You know I can't say no to you." She beamed and happiness flooded our bond. She acknowledged, "I do know that." TJ concurred, "We are all such saps for the women in our lives." I sighed, "Why must you say shit like that around me?" TJ just laughed.

I was going to ignore the fact that my little sister was growing up as long as humanly possible. Angela was always going to be my baby sister, and that meant I would look at her as such. So, if she could've just helped me out by aging at a human rate I'd have been happy. It was completely irrational, but it's how I felt.

I changed the subject, "What are we doing?" Angela giggled, "We are going to get Dad and EJ." I smirked admitting, "I love it already. How? And what do I do?" She answered, "Well, it's really easy. I need you to get them to the war room."

I asked, "Aren't they there?" She grinned replying, "Dad isn't." I chuckled, "Alright, I'm on it." She kissed my cheek, "Thanks!" I jogged inside and went to my dad's office. I knocked on the door before I entered. Both he and Caleb looked up.

I asked, "Hey dad, can you come to the war room?" He answered, "Of course." He followed me there where EJ looked up.

EJ commented, "I can't believe you're out of the gym." I shrugged muttering, "I leave the gym." Oden snorted, "I could still be in the gym." I reasoned, "It's for Angela." He grunted. EJ chuckled, "Not on gym days you don't." My dad asked, "Why are we here?"

I sat down and they followed suit. Before I could say anything, we were hit with water balloons. Water balloon launching guns appeared in front of us. EJ popped up yelling, "WHAT THE HELL?" My dad laughed and grabbed his gun. He said, "You can't get them to stop. Just join the fun, son." I grabbed my gun and popped us outside.

All my siblings and my mom were in an all out war. I laughed and quickly joined in. My dad linked, "You were supposed to get us together, weren't you?" I admitted, "Yup, apparently I need to have fun." He laughed and we launched ourselves into the war that mom, Cassie, TJ, and Angela were winning.

Cayden portaled in running through. He asked me, "What the hell is going on? Cass pulled me so hard I…" Cassie nailed him with a balloon and yelled, "SUCKER!" I tossed him my gun and conjured a new one.

He loaded his and yelled, "You're in for it now!" Cassie giggled, "Promises, promises." We all yelled, "NO!" Cayden simply smirked and faded back. Cassie yelled, "CHEATER!" I retorted, "You've been popping! It's not cheating when you use what you've got." That sparked a debate of what was cheating.

I linked Angela, "You were right, this is fun." She giggled, "I know. You guys are always so serious. It's why I'm around." I replied, "You are around because mom and dad can't stop having sex and you were everything all the realms needed." I saw her blush from here.

Our parents having sex and even the topic of it wasn't weird to us. I didn't want to hear about my sisters having sex, but that was mostly because I wanted to keep them in a box where they were little and needed my protection.

I watched all my siblings firing and taking aim. I chuckled and shot Tim and Brady. Both gasped in surprise. I laughed and ran off with both of them hot on my tail. I popped out of the way of a shot from Bryce. He growled and I threw my head back laughing.

Phil linked, "The Warriors don't know if they should hide or join." I replied, "Everyone should join, this is fun." Phil scoffed, "See here's the thing, I already knew that. I am already out here in the trenches with Gage." I was about to ask where, when I got hit on the shoulder.

I rolled my eyes knowing exactly who hit me. My cousin who happened to be my Beta. Gage linked, "I didn't do it." I replied, "I knew that." Oden growled, "Now it's on." Angela was even getting him out of his sullen mood. That was good.

Phil howled in laughter, and I just raised my eyebrow. He called, "All in family and Beta love and fun!" I replied, "I'll give you some family love." I was going to nail him in the face for that. I winked at Angela, who grinned back at me as I took off after Phil.

She easily caught him, and rapid fire shot him water balloons. Gage came up next to me. He said, "There is strength in numbers." I laughed, "Let's go then." I portaled behind Phil while Angela grinned. Phil tussled her hair before saying, "I could never get mad at you." Oden snorted.

He turned and groaned, "Et tu, Gage." I glanced at my Gamma, smirked, then fired in succession with him. Phil shouted, "You try to help a guy!" We laughed and he took off running with us following him. Cassie joined us which led to Cayden coming over.

Phil shouted, "THIS IS HIGHLY UNFAIR!" I replied, "You started it, therefore it's fair." Phil shouted, "Someone be on team Phil!" Dylan shouted, "I AM HERE FOR YOU MY BETA BROTHER!" He launched a balloon at Gage who snorted and took off after him. Dylan yelled, "The things I do for the younger Beta generation." He ran and ducked behind Buttercup.

Gage snorted, "Hell to the fuck no. I'm not getting into this with Wesley. That's insane." Dylan retorted, "You are no fun. Who could've predicted such a reaction?" Buttercup laughed and Wesley popped beside her.

Cassie bumped me asking, "How are you doing?" I replied, "I think that's my line." She was freshly engaged and had been betrayed by our people. She shrugged, "I'm really happy." I gave her a look and popped her to one of our shared treehouses with EJ.

Cayden linked, "What the hell?" I replied, "I'm sure you will find us." I asked, "Cass?" She groaned, "Bonds and all." I nodded, "Yes, bonds and all. I feel that pain inside you." She whispered, "One of our people betrayed me. Plus, I also know you feel some type of something about that day too." I admitted, "I do. I felt weird there." Oden howled in my head.

It felt like a piece of my soul was in that field briefly before the feeling went away. Oden had been sad ever since. I told him, "Melanie wasn't there." It didn't make sense for her to have been. I asked, "So, what was the word on Cayden's source?" I knew one of his had gotten him word about the attack.

She told me, "I can't really talk about that." I replied, "Ok. You can tell me it hurts that Cora betrayed you." She snorted, "It's not that it's even surprising." I disagreed, "Doesn't mean it doesn't hurt. Besides, the level of which she betrayed you and our people is surprising."

Cayden agreed, "Yes, it was." EJ and Elise were with him. Cassie snorted, "Yeah, well I should've seen it coming." I argued, "There is literally no way you could've." She retorted, "I should've asked Angela to look into it with her sight. She could've seen it sooner and then she wouldn't feel bad."

I replied, "We don't ask Angela to look into every little thing. We would never take advantage of her sight like that. Plus, if we asked about every jealous and catty bitch or dick she'd do nothing else." Cassie asked, "And how many do you have?" Cayden snorted.

I said, "I don't have someone they are jealous of so less than those of my siblings with mates, or partners." Cassie said, "I hear there's another crazy chick running around about you." I asked, "Huh?" She laughed.

EJ said, "Brother, Lomax and Cheyenne came for a visit." I grinned, "Really?" Oden huffed, "I guess that's something." Cassie warned, "Watch it, brother." I asked, "Why?" She rolled her eyes but didn't continue that statement.

I told Cayden, "I'll see you tomorrow at formation." I had my squadron practicing. He nodded to me and his eyes said he wanted to say something, but he didn't.

I popped to Lomax. He greeted, "Hey, Alexander." I gave him a hug and turned to Cheyenne. I inclined my head, "Hey, Chey." She squealed, "Alexander!" She jumped into my arms, and I gave her a hug.

I asked, "What brings you by?" Cheyenne answered, "It's been too long, and I wanted to see you." I nodded, "Alright. What are we doing?" She replied, "I'm famished." Oden grumbled, "I thought we were getting back into the gym." I reasoned, "We will later."

I told them, "Let's head up front. We will go to my mom's pizza place. I'll drive." We walked around to the front of the house. I spotted Chason and Fowler, two men in my pack. I nodded to them. Both blew out a breath but waved to me.

I linked, "Are you guys good?" Chason replied, "Of course, Alpha." Fowler asked, "How long are your friends in town?" I admitted, "I don't know. They just dropped by." He replied, "Yay." I snorted, "I sense sarcasm." He hummed. Honestly, I wasn't sure what that was about.

Oden told me, "Their wolves are annoyed and say their humans are too. Chey likes certain accommodations and only fights you in the gym which throws off our schedule." I'm sure they just didn't see her fighting other people. She loved sparring.

We got to the pizza place and filed out. I walked in and waved to the workers. Our waiter came by. He asked, "The usual?" I agreed, "Yup!" Cheyenne chimed in, "But make sure the black olives aren't on one side of the pizza. Last time they were." The waiter nodded and left.

He came back with beers and Cheyenne's wine. She asked, "So, what's new?" I replied, "I'm a squadron leader in the Hackura realm." Lomax whistled, "Damn, man. That's awesome." Cheyenne looked sad.

I asked, "What's wrong?" She shrugged, "I can't believe you didn't tell us that." I told her, "I kind of thought my mom sent an announcement about it." Lomax snorted, "I linked my dad, and he said the Alpha got the announcement."

Cheyenne gasped, "I can't believe they didn't say anything. You could've texted us though." I agreed, "You're right." It just hadn't occurred to me, but they were my friends. I replied, "It was a while ago and I did it to be closer to Cass."

She nodded, "I heard she got hurt. I'm sorry, I know that must be hard on you." That was a massive understatement. Oden growled, "I still want to know what the HELL that wench was thinking." He meant Cora and she was thinking something insane and psychotic. She thought she could have Cayden if something happened to Cassie and that was the definition of insanity.

Our pizza came and they caught me up on their lives. When we got back to the pack I spotted my cousin, Kade and knew something was wrong. I waved, "Hey, guys I'll catch up with you at the gym." Cheyenne huffed, "Oh come on. We need to work off that pizza." I said, "I'll be right there. Probably." She groaned and Lomax dragged her off.

I jogged over to Kade. I asked, "What's wrong?" He looked up, "I have a problem, but I told Aunt Haley about it. She's helping." I pointed out, "That didn't tell me what was wrong." He looked around then opened a portal and took me through it.

We were now in a secluded area in the Hackura realm. I admitted, "Ok, I'm officially worried." He ran a hand through his hair, "I think I spotted someone I don't want near a specific person, but I can't be sure." I asked, "Who?"

He stared at me and I realized I wasn't specific enough. I clarified, "Who is the person you don't want near the person we aren't talking about?" Oden told me, "I have a headache from the riddles you are speaking in right now." Well, my cousin was clearly keeping things close to the vest.

He admitted, “I think…” He trailed off. I prodded, “Yes?” He sighed, “I think I saw Ariena.” My eyes widened. I said, “We need whoever it is you’re not talking about in a safe house, right fucking now.” He sighed, “She’s stubborn and fiery.” My jaw dropped seeing the stupid dopey smile on his face.

I whispered, “You love her.” He replied, “Aunt Haley went to talk to her.” I hummed, “Alright. Let’s go see where you think you saw Ariena then.” He nodded, “That’s a good call.” I snorted, “I know that. I’m an enforcer.” He asked, “What about your friends?” I replied, “I’ll see them later.”

I linked EJ, “I need you to let Cheyenne and Lomax know something came up. I’ll be back as soon as I can.” He asked, “What’s going on?” I replied, “I’m helping out Kade.” He questioned, “Do you guys need anything else? His bond is weird.” He’d have pulled on it the second I mentioned his name. I assured him, “I’ll let you know if we do. Right now, we are good.”

I asked Kade, “Does the woman you’re in love with have Fairy blood?” He answered, “Not a drop.” I frowned, “Then what the fuck would Ariena be doing around her? God, I’m so sick of her bullshit.” He took me to a downtown area.

I asked, “Are we in Milwaukee?” He answered, “Yes. That’s the building my woman works in.” He paused and I felt in the bond that there was more he wanted to say. I shifted through his feelings and decided to ease his fears.

I told him, “I won’t tell anyone about this unless you are in danger, but Ariena wouldn’t have anything to do with you.” It would be something about that woman. I asked, “What does your woman do?” He answered, “She works in marketing at a lingerie company.”

I laughed, “And do you get to help her with customer research on new designs?” He shoved me and laughed. He admitted, “Maybe.” I asked, “Do we have the customer list?” He handed it to me and dread filled me.

I asked, “And your woman has access to this list?” He nodded, “Yeah, why?” I answered, “There are a lot of partial Fairies on this goddamn list.” He ran a hand through his hair. He winced, “I should’ve noticed.” I replied, “You wouldn’t but I’ve met them. Ariena is going after partials. I’ll assume your woman is high up in this company?” He nodded, “Yes, and she’s one of the few with the actual names.”

I admitted, “I’m convinced you saw her. Did she see you?” He snorted, “Don’t insult me.” I replied, “Might I suggest letting her and letting your eyes blaze.” He jolted and looked at me. He reasoned, “She’ll rabbit, and you want to catch her.”

I agreed, “I do but not at the cost of your heart or woman. You’re clearly not ready to tell everyone about her. If she gets taken, we come for her. No questions asked.” He admitted, “I don’t know if the whole family would.” He really didn’t based on the bond.

I punched his shoulder, “We would come.” He replied, “Your family, the Conners would. I’m not sure about the rest.” I asked, “What the fuck is going on? Why wouldn’t they?” He sighed, “It’s a long story.” I replied, “I have a fuck ton of time at the moment.” He didn’t say anything.

I asked, “Oden?” He replied, “He doesn’t have a wolf or counterpart for me to talk to. I know what you do.” His phone rang. He answered, “Aunt Haley.” He sighed in relief, “Thank you.” He hung up.

I surmised, “Mom got her to agree on the safehouse.” He chuckled, “Aunt Haley went a step further and got her job to agree to remote work for now. She presented a credible threat and the money my woman brings in is worth keeping her.”

I could feel how relieved and happy he was in the bond. I told him, “No matter what, I will always come if you ask. Ok?” He nodded, “I know that.” Then why the fuck didn’t he believe his parents, brothers, cousins, Aunt’s, Uncle’s, and our grandparents wouldn’t?

He warned, “You won’t figure it out.” I replied, “Then just tell me.” He wasn’t going to, and his face and our bond told me that. What the hell was going on? Our family was very understanding and always came for those we loved. Kane knew that.

I sighed, “Let’s see what we can do tracking wise. Which direction did she go?” He inclined his head, “She got in a car and tried to follow us.” I laughed, “That’s hilarious. I hope your woman didn’t freak out about your evasive driving.” He sighed, “She said I’m paranoid and watch too many movies.”

I asked, “Does she not know what you are?” He replied, “She knows.” Ok then. I asked, “Where did you lose Ariena?” He got into a car, and I did too. He drove off and we drove into an alley. He said, “She got dropped off here. I came out and peeled left right around onto the other side and turned off the car. When she came out, they stopped and then drove back through this alley. I had to get my woman out of there."

I replied, "I understand. Just pull me next time, I'll come follow Ariena while you get your woman to safety." I got out and looked all around. I knelt on the ground and found a pulsing piece of jewelry. Kade asked, "What's that?" I conjured it to myself. I answered, "Something…" I trailed off when a couple walking by ran up to us.

I asked, "Can we help you?" The woman blushed, "Uhh no. I just had to come see this." I covered it up and they looked at each other confused then left. Kade admitted, "Ariena was wearing that." I hummed, "She was going to use it to get your woman to come to her. I must not be drawn to it because I'm a Fairy. It's not a charm so she's working with other people."

I linked my mom, "Has Ariena been trying to get your database of partial Fairies?" She asked, "Are you with Kade?" I answered, "I am." She replied, "Ariena can't break into my goddamn fucking database because your Uncle coded the shit out of it and I charmed it."

I hummed, "So, she has tried." Mom answered, "Yes because she's a fucking bitch." I said, "Well, she's now targeting businesses that have pretty things partial Fairies would be drawn too." She admitted, "I thought as much. Aiden and I will work on this."

I said, "Then I'll conjure this to my Uncle Aiden." I conjured the jewelry piece away. She replied, "Thanks. Tell Kade it's under fucking control." I hummed, "Will do." I stopped linking her and stared at my cousin.

I asked, "Do you need me to ask the local pack to look out for your woman?" He replied, "Your dad already did." I asked, "And when can I meet her?" He sighed, "It's complicated." I snorted, "I got that, but if she needs to be guarded let me know." He hugged me, "Thanks, man."

I assured him, "Ariena isn't going to get your woman." He snorted, "No, she won't because I'll kill her if she tries." I asked, "Is there any way this could be about more than partial Fairies?" He stiffened, "You mean me? It would be crazy of her to go after my woman."

I agreed, "I know that, but Ariena isn't exactly stable." He nodded, "I'll make sure my woman is safe." I reiterated, "You call me if you need anything." He asked, "What are you thinking?" I admitted, "That there's something more here." He questioned, "Why?"

I explained, "She went after your woman who just happens to have a connection to possible partial Fairies? I mean sure, I know their names. I train with them, but Ariena doesn't. She's not exactly the worker bee who is going to track these names down. She couldn't have counted on you seeing her. My instincts say something more is here. Like the list is a bonus, but I don't know why."

Kade assured me, "That's good enough for me. I'll protect her." I warned, "Watch your six too, cousin." He nodded, "I will." I'd be making moves to make sure someone else did as well. I popped him back to our pack. He left and I went in search of who I needed.

I found my dad in his office. He said, "Your mom told me Kade brought you in on certain things." I snorted, "I pushed him and I still didn't get to meet his woman. You need to do what you do and cover Kade's six." He put his papers down and sat back in chair studying me. He pulled our bond close to him.

He said, "You genuinely think Ariena is going after his woman and him?" Oden chimed in, "The bond says the woman in question is Kade's mate." Sure, but why the hell couldn't I meet her then? Oden retorted, "Why can't we meet our mate? These are questions I cannot answer." He was still in a mood.

I told my dad, "I don't buy that Ariena just happened upon Kade's woman. It's too coincidental. Ariena is purposeful. The longer we went on this, the less it felt like that's how it went down. I think the hitch in Ariena's plan was Kade seeing her." That could not have been her plan.

My dad nodded, "As it happens, I now own the business she works for." I laughed, "Damn. It's still yours and mom's world and we all live in it." He hummed, "I'll be talking with the local pack about security and as with all our businesses Ariena won't get in." I nodded and gave him a hug.

I left and shifted. I found Lomax out on my run and felt bad. I'd ditched them. I was surprised Cheyenne didn't come out to run with him. When we got back and shifted, I apologized, "Sorry, man. My cousin needed me." Lomax dismissed me, "It's ok. Family comes first."

Cheyenne called, “Alexander!” She ran over and gave me a hug. I greeted, “Hey, sorry about earlier.” She giggled, “Make it up to me in the gym.” Oden grumbled, “Maybe we could hang out with them and our mate if you would just meet her.” I asked him, “And how am I supposed to do that?”

I’d tried to buy tickets to her recitals but by the time I got off the online queue the tickets were sold out. It’s not like they sold them on a secondary market for me to buy. Oden grunted, “Ask our uncle Gunner to get us the ticket.” Then he’d ask why.

Oden sighed, “So?” It wasn’t like I hadn’t thought about it. I really had. It wasn’t like I possessed the hacking skills to get the damn ticket myself. I’d knew because I’d tried. I’d gone to a damn class in the Hackura realm on hacking, but I still didn’t get a god damn ticket.

Cheyenne nudged me, “Where did you go?” New York. Oden huffed, “I wish.” Me too. I told her, “Just thinking over some things.” She urged, “Then let’s get on the mats. You always do your best thinking there.” She wasn’t wrong. I walked into the gym with her and stepped into the ring.

Lomax called, “Hey Fowler, do you have some time for me?” I was a little worried since he hadn’t seemed thrilled they were visiting. Fowler agreed, “Yeah, man. Let’s go.” I exhaled and sparred with Cheyenne. I went through the motions.

Oden said, “We could spar with mate if you’d meet her.” I replied, “Tell me how to meet her. I’ve been trying. We try to get tickets to her dances.” He admitted, “I don’t know. Just go to New York.” I replied, “I can’t just go to meet her. I need a reason to give everyone else.”

He asked, “And what would the reason be if you got a ticket?” I argued, “You know what it would be.” I dodged a punch and landed one. I saw Cheyenne wince and felt bad. Oden asked, “Who cares? We don’t pull punches. We are helping our friend. If we go to mate’s dance to talk to her about coming home to see Jase, then we can just go to New York and do that.”

There was something that stopped me with that though. A scent reached me that I knew, and I turned. I told Cheyenne, “Let’s break. I love those cookies. Do you want one?” She replied, “Nah, I’m good.” I shrugged my shoulder and grabbed some of Karina’s cookies. Damn. They were so good.

I ate it and calmed down. I told Oden, “We’ll get a ticket or something. She’ll come home one day. Everything is fine.” He agreed, “You’re right. I’m just impatient.” I chuckled, “Me too, buddy.” Cheyenne pouted, “You really are out of it this visit.”

I admitted, “I’ve got a lot on my mind.” She grinned saying, “I’m a good listener.” Gage and Phil appeared. Phil said, “I am also an excellent listener.” Plus, he and Gage knew it was likely Melanie on my mind. Gage said, “Me too. As it is, we need our Alpha.”

Cheyenne sighed, “Everyone is taking you away from me this visit.” I asked, “How long are you staying?” She admitted, “We leave tomorrow afternoon. Lomax has things he needs to get back for.” I winced saying, “I’ll make it up to you next time.”

She beamed, “I know you will. You could always visit our pack.” Gage replied, “Sure he can. With all his spare time.” She giggled and touched his shoulder before cutting a glance at me. Were they a thing? Oden hummed, “Good for them.” I agreed.

She sighed then walked over to Lomax and I went into my office in the gym. I asked, “What’s up guys?” Phil nudged Gage saying, “He asks what’s up as if he did not disappear earlier.” I reasoned, “You could’ve linked me.” Phil snorted, “You are supposed to tell me things.”

I tapped my chin, “I think I did.” Phil grumbled, “What did Kade need?” I replied, “My help.” Gage grumbled, “You’re not going to tell us what for.” I agreed, “I’m not. My parents know more than I do, and they are all over the problem.”

Phil waved dismissively, “Know that it pains me not to have answers, but I’m changing the subject. You have your I’m pouting over Melanie face on. Not to be buzzkill, but if Cheyenne ever figures out that’s what that face is life will NOT be worth living.” I frowned, “I thought she liked Gage based on that touching less than sixty seconds ago.”

Gage groaned, “I told you he was helpless, Phil.” Phil hummed, “Not helpless, just clueless. She wanted you to be jealous. Which you were not, hence her pout.” I waved him off, “We are just friends.” Gage laughed, “Good one.” I replied, “We are.”

Phil sighed, "To you." I confirmed, "Yes, to me. Which makes us just friends. Chey has never made a move." Gage admitted, "That's true, but that woman wants you. There is no denying that." I argued, "There is absolutely an argument that she wants me. She doesn't. We are just friends. I want Melanie." Gage grinned, "Lovely. We got to the Melanie of it all. Can we tell people that yet?"

I growled, "No." Phil told me, "You know we agree she's yours." Gage nodded, "Definitely. I personally can't wait to see the Luna spar with you. It will be show stopping. Speaking of fighting." I growled, "Were we?" My pants were getting tight thinking of sparring with Melanie.

Oden purred, "We could show off for mate and pin her under us. I bet she'd feel amazing." I shouted, "You are NOT helping." He purred back at me, undeterred. Gage said, "I heard rumblings of a great fighter." He stopped talking.

I rubbed my temples, "Was that the end of that sentence?" He replied, "I'm trying to get in better with the contacts because the chatter shut down. I passed it on your Uncle Gunner, but it was like they sensed me there. It was very annoying."

I jolted, "You mean a good fighter in the Undergrounds? The real ones." He agreed, "I do. I got into a chatroom for all of thirty seconds before it was shut down. There was someone they called a sure thing. A Female fighter."

I asked, "Did you get anything else?" He hummed, "Said fight is a Werewolf. Possibly unshifted." I shouted, "A PUP?!" He nodded. I snarled, "How fucking dare they! Did you pull missing pups from packs?"

Phil jumped in, "We both did. No one matches. I looked over the messages before it all got shut down and your Uncle is trying to recover it all but they crashed it hard." I had no idea what that meant but if anyone could uncover it, it was Uncle Gunner.

I asked, "How can you narrow down the age?" Gage said, "We both got the sense this she wolf was close to sixteen." I snorted, "So, what? They think it's perfectly fine to have unshifted pups fighting?" He said, "Well, not like a pup pup. She's almost shifting age." I growled because not only was I fuming Oden was furious.

He snarled, "How dare they do this!" I said, "I'll go talk to EJ about this." Phil handed me what they had. I popped to my older brother. He said, "Fancy seeing you here." I sat the file down. He flipped it open and snarled, "Son of a bitch!" I agreed, "I feel that sentiment wholeheartedly."

He grabbed my hand and popped to Uncle Gunner. He was heads down typing and cursing. I asked, "Uncle Gunner?" He held up his hand, "Just a second." He typed some more then shouted, "GOT YOU FUCKER!" I asked, "You got in the chatroom?" He snorted, "They shut down the chat, but I got some more of the logs."

We came around and read the screen. I rubbed my face saying, "This is bad." EJ said, "We knew the Undergrounds were." I snarled, "But pups?!" Uncle Gunner said, "She's almost sixteen." I growled, "And? We don't know how long she's been fighting. Someone able to beat up older people should flag for us. How do we NOT know who she is?"

Uncle Gunner admitted, "I don't know. With the level of training she has to have, we should." Exactly. I ground out, "Do we have anything?" He replied, "Well, I have a tip for an old Underground site."

I asked, "Tip from whom?" He asked, "Isn't that the question? Information has been funneled to your dad, me, your Hackura Uncles, your grandpa, and even your Uncle Aiden. More so in the last year and half, almost two years, than ever before."

I asked, "Who is doing it?" He said, "I think it's the same person." I jolted, "How? Is it coming from the same place?" He admitted, "No. They are doing it how I would. It's coming from different locations all over the world. I've tracked them back and it's not someone hiding in a central location. I actually wrote a paper almost ten years ago about this."

I said, "Then it's someone who knows a Fairy, Demon, or Hackura." EJ argued, "A Hackura would just tell us." I pointed out, "Telling our Uncles, Grandpa…" I trailed off, "Wait, what about the women of the family?" He stood and shut his door quickly.

He told us both, "You didn't hear it from me but all the women in the family have gotten information too." I asked, "Why didn't we hear that from you?" EJ said, "Because mom has gone off and killed people without telling people who her source is. All of them have." I shrugged because I didn't give a shit about bad people dying. Also, they clearly told Uncle Gunner. So, someone knew.

I said, "Not to mention the people coming off the buses." Uncle Gunner said, "Your mom has gotten several coordinates herself. The worst of what we've seen ALWAYS goes to your mom." I reasoned, "Someone knows us well." Which grated since we didn't know them.

I asked, "Who could copy you so well?" He snorted, "If I knew that, I'd know who it was. They have my attention that's for sure." I asked, "What has been given to Uncle Aiden?" He said, "I'm sure that's something you should ask him." He wouldn't tell me, but I had a dead Uncle who just might.

I questioned, "Does this go as far as Uncle Lief?" Uncle Gunner snorted, "Yeah, it does. He's gotten a few tips and thinks it's hilarious." I knew where I was going then. I nodded to my brother who sat down to talk to Uncle Gunner more.

I popped to Uncle Lief's house. He greeted, "Alexander, what a surprise." I admitted, "My day has been somewhat of an anomaly. I came to ask about the tips you've been given." He grinned, "And what interesting tips they are. You know they originate in places I cultivated sources."

I replied, "I did not know that." He chuckled, "Everyone's do. Giving the appearance that they are different people." I prodded, "But you don't think so." He winked, "I know it's the same person. The language of the messages are the same. I argue it's similar to a message we got four years ago."

I asked, "What about?" He grinned, "Good question. I've been told it's crazy and not possible, but this old crazy man thinks it just might be. I'd bet your mother would agree." He should tell her then. I snorted, "Since when do you talk in riddles?"

He grinned answering, "When you get to be my age you have to make your own fun, nephew. If I could prove it, you'd be my first call." I clarified, "Me?" He nodded. I questioned, "Of all people, I'm who you'd call first?" He winked.

Oden asked me, "Does he think Melanie is doing this?" She wasn't a hacker. Oden argued, "She could be." I retorted, "In what spare time? Even if she was, could she be good enough Uncle Gunner couldn't nail her down?"

Even as I said it, it rang true. Melanie was a genius. She could absolutely do anything she wanted, but she was super busy with school. I had thought about it once after her accident but ultimately dismissed the idea. Oden agreed, "We are being silly."

Uncle Lief cleared his throat, "Yes, you. Often the tips are about you." I asked, "Me? What about me?" He shrugged, "All different types of things. Maybe look into some clean up missions we've done in the last year and half. See if you notice a pattern."

I pointed out, "Uncle Bjourn would ask me to look at them if he wanted." He chuckled, "Yes, well sometimes the younger folks don't listen to those of us that have been around the block." I shot back, "Maybe come around more often. You guys keep to yourselves a lot."

He sighed, "I never thought I'd live this long without my brothers. They were both older. I was the miracle baby, you know?" I did. He was sixty years younger than Magnus. Even more so than my Grandpa Ragor.

I asked, "What was Uncle Magnus like?" No one talked about him or his family really. He laughed, "He was the one who got stuff done. He'd tell you all about the cleanups. Hell, he'd probably jump on my thoughts and come back with an answer in hours. He was such a lady's man. Gods, I miss him."

I reached out and squeezed his hand. He smiled at me, "I wish I was more like him. We need him. Now, with all this Fairy light sharing mojo I'll be around even longer."

I asked, "Don't you want to be?" He chuckled, "I do. I love seeing the new generations and I still have my role in our family." He advised Uncle Bjourn. He admitted, "I just miss my brothers. If your Aunt Myla goes, I'll follow." They'd been together so long that was understandable.

I conjured us whiskey. He chuckled, "Strongly consider digging into the files." I nodded, "I will." He chuckled, "Your Uncle Magnus would've slapped you on the back head with the files and ordered you to read them." That would be helpful since I didn't even get a direction on the files other than 'clean up.' Which was a shit ton.

I left him and went to the gym. I was there where my squadron arrived, so I ran with them. I put them through drills before Cayden arrived. We worked on formation before I dismissed them for the day. Cayden said, "I hear you missed Cheyenne leaving?" I groaned, "Fuck. I forgot. I'm a bad friend."

He said, "You are not. They came by unexpectedly." They had. Normally, if they scheduled a visit, I was better about being around. I told him, "I have a lot on my mind." He asked, "Anything you want to talk about?" I admitted, "I don't know."

I turned to leave then asked, "Did you hear about that chat room?" His eyes narrowed, "Yeah, I had some interesting conversations about it before they were cut off." I asked, "With?" He answered, "A source of mine." I asked, "How was the conversation cut off?" He replied, "By her friends."

I jolted, "You think you know the fighter in question?" He hummed, "I don't have any proof." I urged, "Take Cassie and talk to your source then you'd have proof." He inclined his head, "Maybe said source is incredibly jumpy about your family."

I frowned, "Why?" He shrugged, "I do not know. It's weird." I replied, "At this point everything is weird." Oden sighed, "I miss mate." I did too. I wanted to go home and watch her dance. I waved to Cayden and popped to my room. I locked the door then opened my laptop.

Since Micah had put a backdoor into Jason's computer for me, when I needed to see Melanie I could. I didn't watch their calls because they seemed off. She was stiff and not like herself. Besides, he deserved the privacy.

When she danced though, she came alive. It was like she was a whole other person. Oden agreed, "She is. In the videos she's stiff and robotic. Her moves are nothing like that when she dances." I joked, "Yeah, she like two different people."

Once I'd thought they were different people, but I was being crazy. I'd had some cookies and calmed down before I made a fool of myself telling anyone that. Oden snorted, "Yeah, we would've had to explain how we knew that and how we got the videos."

I would evade because I wasn't giving Micah up. He'd been nice enough to do this for me and I was certain he knew what, rather who, I was watching at this point.

I queued up the new video and watched Melanie dance. It took my breath away every time. I touched the screen, "She seems sad and angry." Her movements told me she was too. I got up and followed her movements pretending we were dancing together.

Her anger came through loud and clear. I wondered if class had gone poorly that day or something. I touched the screen again saying, "I would destroy anyone who upset you." Oden growled, "Her movements have been sad or angry a lot lately."

To be honest, most of the dances were hauntingly heartbreaking. It was as if she was being driven by sadness. I told him, "You know we think she misses home." He agreed, "Yes, but not coming home now is no longer proving a point. She's hurting herself. We have to do something." I asked, "What can we do?" He growled, "Something." I closed my eyes and rubbed my face.

I took out my phone and called Jason. He answered, "Hey, Alexander." I greeted, "Hey, how's your day going?" He replied, "Fine, I guess. My call with Melanie was…" He trailed off. I asked, "Was what?" He snorted, "Cut off. Again. I haven't talked to her more than five minutes at a time since she left." Oden growled.

EJ linked, "Why are you mad?" I replied, "I'm fine." He snorted, "Gosh, if only that was what I'd asked. You were concerned and now you're raving pissed." I grunted, "I'm on the phone." He growled back but didn't reply.

I asked, "Do you think she's sad? I'm worried since you said she got homesick a lot. I mean, I know we all think she's proving a point staying away. I just worry that she's hurting herself more in the process." He sighed, "Yeah, her dances lately. Gosh, since she's left… they're sorrowful." I knew that but I couldn't exactly say so.

I offered, "I could send you money for a surprise ticket for her home." He snorted, "I can pay for her ticket. You know what? It's a good idea. I'll send her a ticket with no dates. She can come when it works in her schedule. She needs to come back and it's clear in her dances. She was never this sad before. T went with her the most to dance in the fields here and he said that." She never danced in fields now, that I saw. She was always in the practice rooms or the auditorium at her school.

He admitted, "It's breaking all of us down, Alexander. Dad gets sick." I asked, "He what?" He snorted, "Yeah, we just brought him home from the pack hospital. He was throwing up." I growled, "Jase, what the fuck?! I would've healed him."

He admitted, "I didn't know about it. Mom and dad kept it under wraps." I asked, "What's wrong with him?" He replied, "The doctors think the grief of thinking he ruined our family is getting to him because there's nothing actually wrong with him."

I argued, "He didn't ruin your family." Jason snorted, "I agree with you. He just believes it's his fault Melanie won't come home or be normal with us. She's so brief when we do get to talk to her that it cuts us all. I think it's because she'd run home if she stayed on the calls talking to us longer. Plus, that damn school, I swear it's evil."

I growled, "Why?" He snorted, "Because they've changed her entire personality. Got her some damn manners coach or whatever. They didn't like her rambling. They didn't like this or that. They hang Julliard over her head. It's like they know the minions in her brain can't handle rejection. She has to be the best at everything she does." Oden purred, "She's amazing."

He quickly growled, "But we can kill all those teachers." Yes, I could. Jason continued, "She's just so busy and I worry they've taken the joy out of it for her. There used to be a lot of happy dances. Her movements held hope I just don't see anymore. You know?" I did but I couldn't tell him that.

I urged, "Send her the ticket then." He agreed, "I definitely will. Thanks for calling man." I replied, "You are one of my best friends." He agreed, "And you're mine. If she shows back up, I'll bring her to you." I jolted asking, "Really?" Oden declared victory, "YES!"

Jason agreed, "Of course. It's your idea." I heard Tristan yell, "Jason!" He muttered, "And that just might get her home. I gotta go." He hung up. I asked my wolf, "What might get her home?" He puffed up feeling ten feet tall, "Maybe it's meeting us." I snorted, "Sure." He hummed, "It could be." I went to argue but he was right.

Logically, most people wanted to meet someone in our family. Oden grumbled, "Except Cayden's source." Yeah, except her. Back to Melanie, though. Our family was popular. I was her brother's best friend and a good fighter. Oden snorted, "We are a world renowned fighter." It's true.

My mom popped into my room and squealed, "You signed up to do the cage fights this year!" I asked, "I what?" She snorted, "I'm in charge of the signups for the Hackura games. Here is your schedule for tomorrow." I had not signed up for this. I took it and smiled at her. She said, "I know you'll win!" She hugged me and popped away.

I linked my Uncle Darrin, "Hey, did you sign me up for cage fighting?" He replied, "I got signed up for boxing the first year the games were held after we met your mom and she didn't ask. I figured that was the rule."

I snorted, "I can't do it." He disagreed, "You can, and you will. I'm going to win boxing again this year, and you'll win cage fighting." I reasoned, "It's not fair if I fight." He argued, "No, it's not fair that you haven't so far because of your last name. I went through this kid, and I'm not letting my nephew shirk away like I did."

I asked, "Huh?" He said, "I felt the weight of my last name and felt I was hindrance to it. I know you don't feel that way, but you're not competing because of your name. I noticed last games that you wanted to compete because you watched all the games. Your mom has always hoped you'd join in. Besides, Angela is excited."

I groaned, "Oh come on." He snorted, "Yeah, I went for the Achilles heel. I know. Which is why I told her and your mom that you were competing." I asked, "And you filled it out with my signature how?" He snorted, "Figure it out, kid." I chuckled, "Thanks, Uncle Darrin." He replied, "Any time."

I opened a portal and saw the games being prepped because of where I'd portaled to. I cleared my throat. Grammy Veronica turned around and smiled. She hugged me, "Hello, grandson of mine." I hummed, "I have been bamboozled by someone who can fake my signature." She winked, "I'm sure I have no idea what you're talking about."

I teased, "Sure you don't." She laughed, "I'll be having a minor heart attack, but I will be front row cheering you on. I hear there's a section reserved for our family at all your fights." I laughed, "Mom always coordinates everything so we can watch everyone compete." We always had sections there too. She winked, "I know you'll win."

Oden agreed, "We definitely will." I hugged her and whispered, "I won't let you down." She replied, "You could never let me down, even if you go down in five seconds." I snorted, "I'm not going down." She laughed, "No, I don't think you will." I hugged her again and waved then went back to my room.

Phil linked, "I didn't do it. I should have but I didn't." I snorted, "Yeah, I know." He said, "You're going to decimate them." I was getting pumped up just thinking about it. I faded off into sleep thinking about Melanie's haunting dance moves.

I woke up ready to go. Oden gently asked, "Can we watch mate dance first? One of the old ones?" Jason had dances from her competitions when she was here. God, I was such a sap. I quickly fired up my laptop and pulled the video from her competition in California when she was eleven.

Just like always, I was captivated by her dancing. These movements were full of love and light. It shone through her eyes. It nagged at me how haunted and sad her eyes looked now. What was I doing? I had to get her home.

A knock came on my door. I opened it and found a plate of cookies. Oden urged, "Eat the cookie. They always make us feel calmer." I quickly gobbled them down and snorted. What the hell had I just been thinking?

Melanie wasn't haunted or sad. It was probably just a mode she got into for the dances she put together now. She was living her dream, and I was being selfish. Oden whined, "We could pop her back and forth. She could still dance." I agreed, "The second we meet her, that's what's going to happen."

I popped downstairs and found my dad waiting with my siblings. I didn't need to ask where my mom was. She'd be in the Hackura realm already. Dad hugged me then linked, "We can't wait to watch you fight." I snorted, "You see me fight every damn day." He winked, "Not like this."

My dad's former Gamma, Marshall, his mate Riley, and their kids joined us. Gage jumped around me. I snorted, "Calm down." He growled, "Nope! My Alpha is finally going to dominate in the cage." I linked him, "Do you think when Melanie joins us, she'll sign up for the fighting competitions?"

Oden growled, "I both like that and don't." Gage snorted, "I think you two will take home the gold if she kept her fighting training like she did when she was here." True. She might not like fighting as much anymore. I didn't hear about it, but I didn't hear much.

EJ linked, "What's up?" I replied, "I was just wondering if Melanie still fights." He answered, "She does. Apparently, she's as fierce as ever, but she doesn't train as much as she did here. They had to argue to get her to agree to keep going in for training. She's hard to argue with because she's better than everyone else there at fighting." She'd been good here too so that couldn't be the reason she argued.

I nodded and we portaled to the games. Uncle Benjamin was up first throwing rocks. He won, like he always did. Watching Aunt Ariel greet him was everything I wanted with my mate when I was their age. We went to the spear throwing to watch Uncle Lief. Oden linked, "We are up." We were. It was our first fight today.

I popped to the arena for the fights. I got ready and found Phil and Gage waiting in the locker room. I snorted, "Are you guys my pit team?" Gage snorted, "Who else would be on your pit team?" I asked, "Which of you is the coach?" Oden said, "Thor is here."

Dad answered, "I am." I laughed, "Of course you are." He had taught me to fight. He warned, "They are going to be gunning for you." I replied, "I can beat Thadius in a fight." Phil snarled, "If you need more motivation that asshole made my mom cry when she was younger."

I growled, "What?" Oden growled, "We could rip him apart." Phil growled, "Yeah, he made her cry. I hate that guy." Gage fist pumped into the air, "Team we hate Thadius." My dad supplied, "Your mom made him oink like a pig if he tried to kiss someone."

I snarled, "Did he cheat on Cousin Miley?" Dad shrugged, "Your mom seemed to feel he did. I didn't actually ask if they were dating. I know he kissed Miley and then kissed someone else." I questioned, "Why the hell is he still walking around?"

He answered, "It's my understanding your uncles and cousins don't know it happened. Ase comes to mind as someone who would kill him for that." Cousin Ase would absolutely kill someone for making Cousin Miley cry.

I snorted, "I'm taking him down in under a minute. Book it, Phil." Phil started to clap then punched me in the chest. Gage shouted, "LET'S FUCKING GO!" I linked Cousin Miley, "This is for you." She asked, "Huh?" I walked out into the area and heard her go, "Oh no." When she saw who I was fighting.

I linked mom, "How badly did he hurt Cousin Miley?" She answered, "She really liked him, and I've been charming the shit out of him since that day." I nearly laughed.

Thadius and I tapped hands. He said, "Hey kid, no hard feelings." I disagreed, "There are definitely hard feelings." He gulped and the look on his face was priceless. He knew exactly what I was pissed about and he was stunned I knew what he'd done.

Uncle Bjourn linked, "When did you meet him?" Hastein threw confusion at me. Kade linked, "The fuck? Since when do you know him?" I shot back, "Since when did you join the pack?" He answered, "Six months ago. What's going on?" I replied, "This fucker hurt Cousin Miley." I felt his shock in the bond.

Thadius lowered his voice, but he knew I could hear him. "It was long ago and your mom has never let me forget it." My dad and siblings all snarled. That set my whole family off. I replied, "No one hurts my family." The ref groaned, "Fuck my life." He shouted, "FIGHT!"

Oden said, "I could bite him." I snorted, "That's not allowed." He argued, "It's not not allowed." I replied, "Maybe he'd piss his pants if we shifted after we take him down." He came at me swinging hard. I normally would've just dodged the hit and observed him. Instead, I tackled him full on and took him down.

He grunted trying to kick out so I dislocated his hip. It was a legal move and everything. Everyone gasped. Thadius groaned but stayed down. The ref yelled, "PINNED!" I got off him. Dad linked, "Forty-five seconds. I'm proud son." I backed up and shifted into Oden.

The ref stared at me. Oden snapped his jaws at Thadius. He shouted, "Jesus Christ, I'm fucking sorry, ok?!" I shifted back and snapped my pants back on. I winked at him and popped outside to my crew. My mom was standing on her chair cheering waving the sign she'd made for me.

Cassie simply raised an eyebrow which had me raising mine right back. Cassie linked, "Is there a reason I should charm him?" I answered, "Yes. Get Aiylee and Bea in on it too." She laughed, "Consider it done."

My dad announced, "You have twenty minutes, give or take, until the next round." Phil jumped on my back. Gage commented, "You took him down hard." Phil shouted, "I know that's right!" I snorted and carried him into the locker room.

I reasoned, "I really feel this should be the other way around since I just fought." He snorted, "A Beta carrying their uninjured Alpha? Are you insane? I'd get my ass kicked by you and that doesn't sound like any fun." I threw my head back and laughed.

Gage said, "Don't worry, if you were hurt, we'd carry your ass anywhere." I rolled my eyes at both of them. I admitted, "I do know that but I don't plan on you ever having to do that. One, I don't get hurt. Two, you'd never stop mentioning it." They fist bumped.

Uncle Bjourn came in and simply crossed his arms. Oden grumbled, "What did we do?" I asked, "What?" He snorted, "You did not just say what. What the hell was that out there?" He glanced at my dad. I said, "Hey, I just found out why I needed to be mad at him. Go talk to mom and Cousin Miley. They know exactly what just happened." He growled.

I complimented, "Good one." He said, "Yeah, well we hang out with wolves a lot." He stormed out of the locker room. I commented, "I think Thadius is soon to be grateful I broke his hip and sicced Cassie, Aiylee, and Bea on his ass." My dad spit out his water and choked a little.

He asked, "You did what? Jesus, you pups keep me on my toes. Because I would've just thought Cassie would prank him alone. You added Aiylee and Bea? YOU?!" I asked, "What? I'm fun." Phil said, "Yeah, that's we call you the super fun Alpha." I rolled my eyes at him because I knew he didn't call me that.

My dad groaned, "That's what Julian usually does. He's the shit stirrer, not you." I winked, "That you know of dad." He grumbled, "God damn pups trying to keep me young, changing their dynamics and shit." I laughed, "Well, you and mom stopped having pups so we gotta keep you young another way." He said, "We may have more." I was pretty sure they were going to.

I won my next three fights and had two more to the finals. We watched Julian surf before my next fight though. I teased him, "For a non-water Fairy you surf so well." He punched my shoulder, and I put him into a headlock and messed with his hair. He groaned, "Alexander." I chuckled and let him up.

I ended up winning all my fights. Uncle Darrin was on top of his chair waving a towel around cheering when I was given my medal. My mom was cheering holding her sign. I linked Gage, "It's your sister's fault she found Hobby Lobby." He agreed, "It definitely is Gia's fault. There is nowhere else to place the blame." There was fucking glitter glue everywhere now.

I still smiled at my mom and sent her all my love and her pride and love bounced back to me. My dad had his hands over his head clapping and cheering. So did all my siblings. Angela and TJ had a sign. I blew them all a kiss.

A few women fainted for some reason. There was just one thing missing form this moment: My mate. Melanie being here would've made everything perfect. I went back to the locker room to change and conjured my computer. I quickly noted there was a new dance.

I watched it and was captivated. It was a dance of longing. Oden snorted, "We'd definitely know that emotion." We would. It felt like the dance was directed to me, but that didn't make sense. Oden reasoned, "Maybe she wants to meet us, just like we want to meet her." Then she should come home.

To be fair to her, the past indicated we still wouldn't meet if she did. The truth of the matter was that I didn't know who this dance was for, but in this moment I imagined it was for me. I whispered, "I promised you that we'd meet one day, and we will."

I still went over that text conversation and how she'd rambled. Everyone said she didn't do that anymore, but I believed the second she got away from people judging her she'd be back to doing just that. She was around people who wanted her change, but one day she'd come to people who loved her.

EJ popped in and I conjured the computer away. He hugged me, "Congratulations, little brother." I asked, "Who is up next?" He answered, "Mom's jumping competition on Pirate." They were going to win. They had every year I'd been alive. Hell, they won before then. Ever since mom first competed and Pirate LOVED to win. It seemed he had the competitive Hackura spirit.

We popped to the event where we had an entire section because we were a big ass family. Uncle Lief made his way over and gave me hug. He whispered, "Consider pouring over the cleanup files." I nodded. He said, "I know that look you had at your event. I had it watching my brothers with their mates. I wanted mine. Listen to me now and believe me later."

I linked Phil, "Get me the cleanup files for the last year and half." He asked, "Whose? That was broad. The pack?" I replied, "No, the Hackura." He snorted, "Do you know how many files that will be?" I admitted, "I do. It's not a priority. We can go through them as we have time." He snorted, "So, never."

He wasn't wrong in thinking that would be when we got to it. I was pretty sure Uncle Lief was being a shit stirrer. There was no way Melanie had anything to do with those clean ups because she was living her dream. If she was out there protecting me, she'd come meet me.

I shook myself, "Melanie is living her dream." Oden agreed, "She is." Uncle Lief hummed, "Yes, well she's young and dreams change. Speaking as someone who was the youngest sibling. When you find out the things you are being kept out of, you can act irrationally." He walked away muttering, "And alone."

Oden growled, "Mate better not be doing anything alone." I reasoned, "She wouldn't. She's a pack wolf, not a lone wolf." He agreed, "That is true." She'd know that any member of this family would help her. Hell, the Hackura would. Melanie was living her dream, but one day we'd share this day together and I was really looking forward to it.

Crumbling

Melanie is Sixteen Years Old

Melanie felt numb. I knew I was I was in the pack hospital. Which was only because Caine forced them to treat me. They normally wouldn't. I wanted it to all be a dream. Everything went by me in flashes.

My friends were all forced out of town the night before my birthday. I rubbed my head because I swore I heard my wolf at midnight on my birthday. She told me to fight, and I did. Then I woke up in Alpha Edwards office.

They said I didn't have a wolf, and Slade Carter was my father. It had to be a lie, but I still couldn't contact my wolf. There was just nothing. It felt like my entire reality was distorted. Beta Jason and Alpha Peter requested they punish me for Slade killing my family since apparently he came to get me. They claimed I was his daughter and not my dad's and my lack of wolf proved it.

Alpha Kyle banished me from Red Run. In a note. He didn't even do it in person. I wasn't sure if that was worse or better. I was too numb and in pain to feel the pack link break, so that's one thing to be grateful for apparently. It was probably a phantom feeling in my mind that I still had it. I was deluding myself to keep the pain away.

I was dragged out in silver chains to the punishing fields. Booker nearly choked me to death with the silver chain, and I would've let him, because I didn't care anymore. Silver should affect me, but it didn't. That's what caused my heart to break.

They'd sent me down that hole again and everything that happened after was something else I was trying to block from my mind. I could still feel the knife on my back. Trevor had come out there to beat and whip me for refusing to sleep with him.

I still don't understand why he was so upset. It wasn't like I hadn't declined before. All the time actually. I closed my eyes hoping that when I opened them it wouldn't be real. I felt Caine's calloused hand in mine.

He whispered, "Mel, we've kept Edward, Jean, Booker, and Trevor away. The doctors are adamant you leave soon though. It's not right." Normally he called Edward dad, but when he saw me I saw the Alpha in him snap. He'd found me and Trevor.

I whispered, "Did you kill him?" He growled, "No, I had to get you here but I wish I had." I cried, "Was it all true?" He grimaced, "I am so sorry Melanie." I sobbed, "I look like my dad, Caine. I do." He held me as I cried.

We were family and everything in me cried out for his arms to be Jason's arms. I screamed for my brother, Alpha Peter, Dalton, Dakota, Elise, and Xander. No one came during my torment except for Caine. It wasn't fair to expect Elise or Xander to show up because they had no idea what happened or what Beta Jason or Alpha Peter requested.

To be fair, what Beta Jason and Alpha Peter were asking for wasn't for me to be tortured. Pack punishments are bad patrols and more work. Not that I could be given more work. For two years all I did was chores.

Caine was forced to leave. I heard a doctor whisper, "It's weird. All the packs around went down." Huh? Someone snorted, "Everyone did." I needed to get out of here and check my alerts. My whole body seized, and Celia ran into the room. She gasped, "Melanie!"

I felt myself seizing and forgetting the conversation that just happened. I tried to hold onto it, but it left. Celia held me saying, "You're ok." The doctor said, "She is and she can't be here any longer." Celia growled, "She just had a seizure." He replied, "And she's fine now. Know your place, woman. Don't you growl at me."

I whispered, "Her place is above yours. She's a better doctor than you and if your pack followed the rules… that you are supposed to, because all packs are… she'd be the Head Doctor here." He stared at me. I replied, “Yeah, well I’m right and you know it.” I told Celia, “You’re better than him and he’s just jealous. You should know that.” She stared at me.

The doctor left and I pulled the sheets back. Celia grabbed my hand. I turned to face her. She ordered, “Don’t you do anything you’ll regret.” You can’t regret anything if you’re dead. She growled, “Melanie Jane.” I asked, “What?” She replied, “You said that out loud. I will have your friends sit on top of you. You are someone this world needs.”

I had nothing to live for at this point. The words Beta Jason wrote ripped out what was left of my heart. He wanted nothing to do with me for real, and he said Xander promised to reject me. I just needed to let the allies know about Laxenread.

I had everything for the Resistance set to be transferred to Kingsley. She could run it. What did I have left to do since she could? My life meant nothing. They said I had no wolf, but deep down I think I failed her. She told me fight and they killed her. Or I didn’t fight hard enough, and Selene took my wolf away from me. That seemed more likely. She was the worst.

Celia told me, “I’m serious. We need you.” She might have a point there. Kingsley might not be able to work as heavily in the packs as I was. Well… might not… was the wrong word. She wouldn’t. They’d be too curious about her. I told Celia, “I’ll consider it.” She pursed her lips as I went into the bathroom.

I took a deep breath and took off the hospital gown. I turned around and a sob bubbled out of me. Celia stormed into the room. Sympathy filled her eyes. I went to touch my back, but she grabbed my hand. She said, “I need to apply the salve.” I shrugged and let her.

My eyes trailed down the words Trevor had carved into me. Each one was a dagger to my chest. Curse, Family Killer, Freak, Ice Queen, Unwanted, and Trevor. I was a curse to those I knew. I shouldn’t be here. I could get my friends killed.

She put the salve on my back and gave me a loose fitting shirt. I put it on scenting it was Hendrick’s. I whispered, “Is he here?” She answered, “He’s waiting outside.” Why couldn’t he be my long lost relative? He never would’ve laughed like Aunt Stephanie did over the news I got. He never would’ve agreed to let me be hurt. Why wasn’t he my family?

I closed my eyes. You know what? He is my family. The family that I choose. I put on loose fitting shorts and left. Hendrick and Mason were waiting outside. Mason’s eyes were filled with tears. He cried, “Oh my girl.” He wanted to hug me, but he knew it would hurt. He squeezed my hand, and I squeezed his back.

Hendrick linked me, “Everything is going to be ok.” I asked, “Where is Caine?” He replied, “Waiting with the keys to your new place.” I whispered, “Charles moved forward with it?” I’d given Charles access to my financials, and he was going to purchase the new Resistance building under my alias we’d set up: Estella Mia McNair. He’d cautioned against it since a Fairy could put it together, but I wanted to.

Mason answered, “He did and sent Caine all the information as a birthday present.” I laughed humorlessly then groaned, “Ow.” It wasn’t fair to laugh. Charles didn’t know what had happened to me on my birthday or after. Everyone here would be dead if he did.

I glanced at my watch and noted how long I’d been allowed to be in the hospital. It was a pittance and not long at all. This pack was a travesty. Alpha Eric should know that before I left it all behind. He could fix it. Charles would burn the town to the ground if I did nothing. Probably.

I walked into the new building that was supposed to be our entire base of operations. I felt my plans crumbling around me as a fresh set of tears spilled down my cheeks. I was supposed to bring everyone to Red Run. I was supposed to be home.

I tried to link my wolf, “Please be there.” She didn’t answer and nothing happened. Hendrick hugged me, “Melanie.” I whispered, “How can he not be my dad?” He replied, “I don’t know. It reeks of bullshit.” I cried, “Where is my wolf?” He consoled me, “I’m so sorry, Melanie. I’m so damn sorry.” Selene was a sadistic goddess, and I hated her.

I walked further inside and found my friends. I whispered, “You set up my computers.” Sierra nodded, “I did it just like the sketch, but we can change it.” I asked, “Why does everyone look like you’ve swallowed something sour?”

Dax replied, "Because we have some news and we made an executive decision while you were in the hole without us knowing where you were. It cemented while you were in the hospital and we don't think you'll like it."

I snorted, "What do I like? Currently? Nothing… not a whole lot so… that tracks." They winced. Goodie. I was just a barrel of fun. Sierra told me, "No one expects you to be fun right now." Dang it. I hadn't meant to say that out loud.

Dax said, "While you were being treated, Nick Kyle and Cameron Daniels went to a drug buy meeting." I took several deep breaths trying not to cry. I missed Nick. He was like my second grandpa. He used to smile at me and train me. He'd joke around and now he hated me.

I whispered, "What happened?" Mason said, "I went but…" I should've. It should've been me out there, but Trevor was busy tormenting me. Mason replied, "I got the guys after them, but Nick was shot." I gasped, "Is he ok?" I needed him to be ok.

Dax snorted, "It was a flesh wound, he was healed." I pushed, "Is that confirmed because I can look up pack hospital records and…" Hendrick said, "It's confirmed." I squeezed Mason's hand, "Thanks for having their six."

He snorted, "They called me the B team. Little do they know I'm the C. The B would Hendrick." Hendrick was actually on the A team with me. He was who I sent when Xander was out because I knew he'd have their back.

I replied, "You're not the C team. You did a good job… so they shouldn't have said that… it's rude." Caine agreed, "It is." Addison snorted, "Yeah, they could say thank you." Mason replied, "They did say thank you." Well, that was good then.

Dax added, "Your Xander put out a lot of inquires after that." I went over the computer and opened his email since I'd hacked it. He wanted to know all about the Resistance. I quickly typed out the answers to everything he wanted to know.

I told Sierra, "Go put this in the place where Laxenread is." Dax asked, "We're still giving them that?" I answered, "Uhh of course… it's for them. Why wouldn't we give it to them?" Sierra sighed, "One second." She left and went through our holoports and came back minutes later. She announced, "Done." I smiled at her.

I stood, "Well, I have something to do." I hobbled out of the room. Hendrick asked, "Uh Mel? Don't you want to hear about the other thing? It's just a possibility. We just decided how to respond in case it happens." I replied, "Later." I went through our holoport to the pack, and they followed me.

I saw Male Lead Warrior Buck Lavant. He was talking to Avery, his little sister. She glanced at me and pity filled her eyes before she looked down. I stood straight, despite the pain, and stalked up to Buck. He asked, "Can I help you?"

I declared, "I challenge Female Lead Warrior Aimee Dunlap for her position." Avery gasped. Buck stared at me in shock. He asked, "Are you serious?" I asked, "Do I look serious? I feel like I do… because I am… so…"

He rubbed his face sighing, "Melanie, you're hurt. That's a thing you have noticed right?" I replied, "I am aware that Trevor is a deviant… and so is everyone else now. This is the thing… that should have been obvious." He growled, "It is." Ok, so…

Edward growled, "You can't challenge for the position." I asked, "Why? Because I promise you I can… so…" He said, "You're too young." I replied, "There is no law, bylaw, or council decree that states the age of a wolf challenging. Just that they have to have a high school diploma or the equivalent of one. I have a GED. So, I can in fact challenge for…"

Edward snorted, "Then you have to fight everyone who signs up, beat Aimee, then all the pack leadership and future leadership in human and wolf form." I replied, "I mean… the future isn't stipulated anymore but it is your right to demand that so…"

He grinned, "I do demand that. Buck, get the tournament together. It will be in an hour." Buck's jaw clenched and Avery gasped again. Caine snarled, "Edward!" Edward turned, "I am your father!" Caine snorted, "Donating sperm doesn't make you father. What you allowed to happen here is disgusting! I can't even look at you. She's hurt. Make the tournament next week at least."

Sierra linked, "Are you insane?" I replied, "Nope. Genius, remember? It's been tested and everything." She reasoned, "Then you knew when Edward heard you challenged for this that you'd fight tonight." I did. I just didn't care.

Bring on the pain. Beta Jason hated me. Alpha Peter and Luna Chelsea hated me. My grandparents disowned me. Mom's parents stopped talking to me and sending letters and I was their blood. I had no wolf and Xander didn't want me.

I replied, "I told you this was plan if Beta Jason didn't let me come home." She groaned. Edward laughed, "Just wait until you see her fight, son. She's certainly got a style." Buck interjected, "Melanie, I have to ask if you really want to do this?"

I knew he hoped I'd say no. Hell, Avery's eyes were practically pleading with me to say no and weren't even friends. I wanted to be, but I was loud about her brother needing to do more and she adored him. I understood why she didn't want to be my friend, even if I felt she should be mine.

I replied, "I want to do this." He sighed, "Fine. I'll get everything ready." Celia rushed over and dragged me to Mason and Hendrick's house. Mason exploded, "What the fuck are you thinking right now?"

I answered, "That this pack is about to see how bad everyone is at fighting… since they should be able to beat me… but they won't." Celia growled, "You should be laying down on your stomach in a bed with nothing on your back. God damn it, pup. You'll give me gray hair."

I replied, "I'm not a pup anymore… and well… it's very likely that you will not get gray hair for a long time." She snorted ordering, "Lie down. I need to do what I can here." She got out medicine. I snorted, "You know drugs don't affect me." It was something we learned early on.

She said, "Well, I'm making it a high dose." I shrugged, "I guess if it makes you feel better… that's fine." She put some medicine on my back and the burning went away so at least that was nice. The drug she injected me with did nothing. She taped up my ankle then put a big bandage on my back.

Mason was crying. When I glanced up and realized everyone was. Addison had thrown up seeing my back. Caine grimaced, "Melanie, he will Alpha Command us to go hard at you." I replied, "It's ok. I knew he would. Because he knows you'd just let me pin you. It's fine." I could beat them.

Maybe not his wolf. His wolf had picked up fighting easily along with his human counterpart. Caine just needed more practice. His wolf was not on his first human, so it came back to him the more we trained.

His wolf, Spear, came forward, "I do not want to hurt you." I replied, "It's ok if you do. I'll be fine. I mean honestly, you won't kill me. So at this point that's all that's left for them to do." He growled, "I will not let anyone kill you." I reasoned, "I know that… it's ok… this was the plan."

Caine took back over, "The plan was NOT for Trevor to…" He trailed off. I snorted, "Yeah, it wasn't even your dad's plan. Pretty sure I heard you yelling at him." Caine agreed, "You did. I nearly took over the pack." He wasn't ready but running on the fury he'd had, he'd have won.

He grinned, "Thank you for saying that." I asked, "Saying what?" He replied, "That I'd win." I groaned "How does one have thoughts that stay in their head?" Addison laughed a little, "You wouldn't be you if you didn't blurt things out." That didn't sound so bad right now.

Someone pounded on the door. Mason went to it. Sierra helped me into my sports bra and shirt. Celia tapped my hand for some reason.

Buck walked in and stared at me. He practically begged, "Take it back, Melanie. Just challenge in a month." I stood taller announcing, "Someone needs to protect people, and I can do more as the Female Lead Warrior."

He rubbed his temples arguing, "That will be true next goddamn month too. Can you just take a fucking beat?" I answered, "No… I can't… because…" I trailed off. He groaned, "Why?" I didn't answer him, but I had to bite my tongue not to do so.

He asked, "Guys, can we have the room?" Caine growled, "Don't hurt her." Buck asked, "When have I ever hurt her?" Dax muttered, "You do nothing when she's hurt." Because Buck kept his head down… which I understood… and didn't. They all left.

He asked, "Why? You tell me why it has to be right now." I whispered, "They will announce Ashley Griffen as the Lead Warrior." He stared at me. He asked, "And?" I replied, "Maybe Beta Jason will finally figure out my name here… and he could be proud… maybe he'd forgive me one day."

Buck's mouth parted slightly. He rubbed his face with his hand. He told me, "Maybe some people don't need or deserve to be proud of you. Look, you're hurting and that's beyond fair. Maybe just look into what happened on your birthday."

I asked, "What are you talking about?" He frowned, "You don't know? Didn't you go down too?" I asked, "Go down?" He sighed, "Look, I'm saying if you figure THAT out then the whole Werewolf community would talk about it. It's a looking up information job, and you like doing that. Just do that instead of fighting."

I admitted, "I have no idea what you're talking about. Who went down?" He answered, "Everyone. Literally everyone is talking about it." I hadn't heard anyone talk about it. The harder I thought about it, the more I felt sick to my stomach. I ran for the trashcan and threw up.

Buck tried again, "Just look into that and have the Werewolf world talking about how goddamn smart you are. Don't do this challenge until next month." I stood, "I still don't know what you're talking about and I'm doing this." He groaned, "Come on!"

I agreed, "Ok. Are we going to gym?" He grumbled, "That's not what I meant. Goddamn it, kid. You're going to make me lose my fucking mind." I replied, "I have no idea why… so…" He muttered, "You really don't. Let's go."

I asked, "How many people am I fighting?" He snorted, "Two before the pack leadership." I laughed, "How mad is Edward?" He answered, "Very. I'm sure that bodes well for you." I snorted, "It bodes fine." He stopped, "Yeah I am on the leadership memos and what not, Melanie Jane. I know how you fight as Swiffer. It's not a good thing."

I winked, "Aww, are you worried about me? That's ok… it's really fine. I don't plan to fight like Swiffer tonight." He sighed in relief, "Thank god. Because if Caine or Dax find out I know, they might kill me."

I snorted, "No they wouldn't. They have no one to take your spot… no one is anywhere decent enough at fighting. I'm so curious how you got so well trained…but my guess is it involved providing a layer of protection to Avery so…." He shot me an incredulous look, but I was right.

Buck wasn't my favorite person, but he was a good fighter. I'm certain he could take on Booker and win. I doubt he knew that. It's why I didn't understand why he took Edward, Jean, and Booker's crap. He clearly didn't see how good he was…I guess I could tell him.

Buck whispered, "You don't need to fight Trevor or see him." I laughed, "He won't fight. One, there's no way Caine is going to make him his future Gamma." Buck's jaw dropped. I added, "Two, he's hurt. They will excuse him by saying something about it being Caine's fault he can't fight. So… they might say I have to fight you… which would be more of a challenge than fighting Trevor." He groaned, "Fuck my life. Just go inside." I skipped inside letting adrenaline fill me.

I saw my first opponent and snorted. I was actually stunned, "Aunt Stephanie. You really want to fight me?" She snarled, "I'll beat you now that you're hurt." I saw a lot of eye rolls. I finally smiled because I had something to be happy about.

Edward stood, "We have a stupid challenge that will be easily lost. It's the only challenge this she wolf can make." I hummed, "False. I could make it again if I lose… so…" He growled, "Shut up." I blew out my breath, annoyed that he was getting in on my happy moment.

I was going to beat the ever loving snot out of my Aunt. I'd wanted to do that since I met her. He continued, "If she wins these two fights, then she has to fight the current pack leadership in human and wolf form." Several people winced.

He grinned evilly then added, "And the future pack leadership. I've Alpha Commanded everyone to go their hardest." I snorted, "Which will make it more embarrassing when you lose. Who is the future Gamma I'm fighting? Because I think everyone knows Trevor doesn't cut it… and he hides with you when people attack. He's definitely not fighting injured… so…"

Booker snarled, "You fucking bitch!" I replied, "I didn't hurt him. I would have… but… you know what? No but. He deserved everything he got. He's lucky he's alive." I turned to Edward, "Any CURRENT Alpha would've ended him for what he did. You are a stain on the title of Alpha, and I won't call you that ever again." I stared at him letting him see how serious I was.

His cheeks flushed, "I know you are hurting because…" I cut him off, "You are a stain on the title of Alpha, and you have been since I got here. I'm looking forward to fighting you… more than you could imagine. The question remains who is the future Gamma I'm fighting?"

He replied, "Buck La…" I cut him off, "Is not allowed to participate as the Male Lead Warrior. He's not allowed to harm his counterpart or those challenging for it. You should really read the laws that people put out… because Alpha Prince Consort Eric Conners made that VERY clear in the law his mate Princess Luna Haley Holloran Cambridge Conners formulated."

Buck linked me, "You couldn't have mentioned that when we were walking here?" I replied, "I mean… I could have. I'm in a mood… sue me." He snorted. Alpha Edward turned red. He said, "Then I'll figure someone out."

I cooed, "Aww… does Trevor not want to fight me when I can fight back? Shocking. I'm shocked. This is my shocked face." I pointed at my completely unshocked face. Several people snickered or ducked their heads.

Jean snarled, "You are being…" I asked, "What? Don't you like the new version of me? You're also not worthy of your title. You are a literal disgrace to the position of Beta." I would know. My dad, Tristan, and Jason were all better than him. Jason didn't even want to be the lead Beta and he was better. He'd wanted to be the Male Lead Warrior.

This move was for him. I'd make them all proud of me. Alpha Peter would know. He'd HAVE to. I would be the youngest Female Lead Warrior ever. Hell, Lead Warrior of either gender. This would make them proud of me again. It would change everything. It had to.

Edward sighed, "Let the Female Lead Warrior tournament commence." He told me, "I Alpha Commanded all but the unshifted to come watch you fail." I winked, "Get ready to make everyone leave then. You won't want them to see what I'm about to do." He looked stunned and walked off the mat.

Booker stood and snarled, "Fight." Aunt Stephanie grinned at me. She said, "I've watched you fight. I know everything about it." I laughed humorlessly, "You'd better know something… but I doubt you can claim to know anything about me." She growled and ran at me.

I went down and swiped her legs out from under her. I was on her before she hit the mat with a deafening thud. I hit her and knocked out one of her teeth. She screamed and I slammed her head down on the mat. I hit her over and over until Buck grabbed my hand.

He declared, "You won." I hit her with my left hand, and he glared at me. I smiled back and stood. Booker snarled, "Melanie wins the first round." I mock bowed at him. I saw Trevor's friend, Francis, collecting money off other people. Mark, also Trevor's friend, stared at me like I was an alien he'd never seen before.

Female Lead Warrior Aimee looked beyond nervous, which was fair. She'd never had a day of training and the only reason she was named to the position was because Edward had to put someone down.

I spotted my friends in a group. Mason was squeezing Hendrick's hand so hard I worried he could break it. Luna Elena and Beta Female Eden were holding hands. I really liked Eden Kiern. I knew those women had Alpha Commands on them so they couldn't act like a true Luna or Beta Female.

I hated that it bothered them because they were good people. Seeing them was a stark reminder that not everyone down here was a disgrace to their title and a flat out deplorable human being. I was fighting for people like them.

Booker announced, "Lead Female Warrior Aimee, finish her." I laughed, "You wish. You really do, don't you? Gosh… I never did anything to you, and you've always hated me. It's really not shocking that your son is a horrid deviant. He never stood a chance with a father like you. It's too bad for your mate. She's a good person."

He snarled, “Don’t you speak about my mate!” I grinned asking, “What? You don’t know we talk? I love her. She’s the best. Selene is a horrid goddess for pairing such a good person with you.” He warned, “I will make you pay for that even after you lose this fight.” I laughed, “I’m looking forward to our fight… which is next. Yes?” He glared at me.

Caine linked, “Focus.” I replied, “I am SO focused.” I had goals. This would make my family proud again. Beta Jason wouldn’t hate me so much. We could have some type of relationship. It would work. Everyone would know the name Ashley Griffen, but those important to me would know it was really me. They had to.

Aimee raised her fists but didn’t move. I sighed and walked over to her. She threw the world’s sloppiest punch that I blocked then hit her. She went down in a heap. I mocked Booker, “I think your champion has a problem… also how did you not pick someone who could at least throw a punch? Like… was no one else available for the fake position of Female Lead Warrior?”

I grumbled, “You’re actually going to make me feel sorry for Male Lead Warrior Buck?! Does anyone help you, Buck? She clearly doesn’t even do the gym schedule because if she did… she might have seen someone throw a punch… at some point in her life.”

Buck made a face that told me she did not help him with anything. Dang it! Did I feel bad for him? I did….and I didn’t like that. Not one bit. Was he running the whole damn pack? He didn’t hide when we were attacked. He was fighting. Oh my gosh…he was deny his blood just like I was when the Alpha let him down. Dang it. I really did feel bad for him now.

Especially since I’d helped his mate run away right before my sixteenth birthday. Paisley rejected him and cut ties to the pack before I sent her to Black Mountain. She had to get out though…now I was thinking he’d set that up. But why?

I didn’t understand Buck. He didn’t mark Paisely, which many did forcefully. I usually had to stop that, but he didn’t do it. He’d even kept her in his house, but she’d left it for something… and his men were going to hurt her. He was there and looked pained… it’s why I got her out.

I was marginally worried because Micah had seen Paisley from a distance and heard people talking about her. She was an Omega, but we changed her hair before she left so I hoped he didn’t notice her in Black Mountain.

What was Buck’s deal? I stared at him as if he was a puzzle, but he just gave me a blank look back. Booker snarled, “My fight is next.” I clapped, “YAY!” He snarled and charged at me. I dodged him, to his surprise. I mocked, “Sloppy.” I kicked at his knee and watched delightedly as he went down.

See, I might not be able to come in the doors, but I watched the gym like a hawk. I knew he had hurt his knee before my birthday and his wolf never really seemed to heal him fast. Not that I blamed his wolf… his human sucked. I elbowed him in the cheek and locked him in a headlock until he passed out.

I asked Edward, “So… do I fight Jean next, until he comes Booker here comes to? Because you said I had to fight his wolf too. I’m just not sure on the order… since you didn’t say… because for some reason you thought those two women could take me.”

“Which is sad considering you’ve seen me fight. One could say you set all these people up. I’ve beaten Alpha’s while injured worse than I am now. At least they landed some hits. This is probably boring for everyone…”

He ordered, “Buck, get your Gamma off the mat. Jean, take her down.” I laughed, “Yeah, Jean. Let’s see your feeble attempt to take me on. Do you think you know all my fighting secrets too?” Jean asked, “What the hell is wrong with you today?”

I snorted, “You cannot be serious. You just can’t…” I turned towards Sierra and Dax. I asked, “Is he?” I winked at them both knowing their dad would attack while I was looking at them. In fact, I was planning on it.

The second he was close enough I bent down and grabbed his arm throwing him over my shoulder and pinning him on the mat. I warned, “If you move, you’ll break your shoulder. I’d tap out if I were you… since you want me to fight your wolf… and that would be hard for him with a limb out of socket. Well… not that you care about your wolf… at least I don’t think you do… because…”

He cut me off with black eyes saying, "I concede the human lost the fight." Edward snarled, "You can't do that! You're the wolf!" Jean's wolf replied, "And he lost." Edward growled, "Jean has to say that." The wolf mocked him, "Jean's not here right now." Interesting. His wolf didn't like Edward either.

He tapped out and I got off him. He shifted and linked me, "I have Jean blocked out. There is so much I cannot tell you that I wish I could. All I can say is look into things because they aren't as you think. You do not deserve this." I replied, "It's ok." He added, "I was Alpha Commanded to fight you." I again assured him, "It's ok."

He ran at me, and I matched his speed. He jumped and I went under him and jumped on his back, then put him in a headlock. When he passed out, he shifted back to Jean. I called, "Ohhhh Buckkkkkkk, there's someone else for you carry off the mat." He did but when he grabbed Jean, he subtly pointed to my left with his index finger.

I heard the snarl and snorted. I turned, "Booker, Booker, Booker. You just can't help yourself… you had the element of surprise and gave it away because you're horrible at your job… and at being a person… and wolf apparently." I guess his wolf wasn't like Jean's.

His wolf snapped his jaws at me. I punched him in the mouth with an upper cut. He tackled me and I quickly wrapped my legs around his middle and squeezed. He whined in pain and flipped us. I put my elbow roughly across his windpipe. He scratched my side, but I barely felt it. Vindication was flowing through my veins.

I asked Edward, "Does this make me your Gamma? Because historically… oh no… I could be either your Beta or Gamma and…" He snarled, "You don't have Gamma or Beta blood!" I replied, "But I beat them both… and…"

He cut me off, "Your challenge was for Lead Warrior." I hummed, "True… plus I don't want to be your Beta or Gamma. I dislike you." Which hurt. He was supposed to be a true Alpha, and he wasn't.

Dax linked, "Let's just ease up there, killer." I asked, "On what? I'm already off Booker." He replied, "The snark." Yeah, I didn't care about that anymore. That was the old Melanie's problem, she cared. Currently, she was crushed inside me right now and new snarky Melanie didn't care.

Edward stood, "I'll end this." I hummed, "Doubtful." He came at me, and I put all my anger into my swing. I hit him and he swayed. I screamed and launched myself at him. I hit him over and over, "You're supposed to protect people! YOU ARE SUPPOED TO BE GOOD!" At some point his face turned into Alpha Peter's and I hit him with all the hurt I felt.

Caine grabbed me around the waist and pulled me off him and tears streamed down my face. He linked, "I'll be the Alpha one day. I believe you. I'll be the good one who does what's right. I will protect my people. His reign will end and that will be that. Honestly, I'd let you kill him but he Alpha Commanded me to stop you if it got close."

Sadly, there were others like Caine out there. Sons who hadn't been trained. Alpha Peter let me believe the lie that Alpha's were good people. That they had a duty to protect. I never knew in the shadows under the Supernatural Council that wasn't the cases in packs.

Everyone let me believe a lie then dumped me here to let my perception of reality completely warp. It felt like the floor beneath me fell out and I was all alone. They had their façade going in their packs, but mine was shattered and nothing was the same anymore.

Edward came around and he shifted. His wolf said, "I blocked him out. Like my Beta there is much I cannot tell you. Please tell my pup to move and I love him." I linked Caine, "Your dad's wolf asked you to move. He also said he loves you. I think something is wrong with your dad's wolf." He didn't look right. Actually, neither did Jean's. Maybe that's what they wanted me to look into.

Caine raised an eyebrow but moved. Edward's wolf linked, "He didn't Alpha Command me to fight you and I will not." He stood there as I went over and gently pinned him. Booker snarled, "FIGHT!" The wolf snarled at him until he bowed in submission. The pack watched in awe.

Edward's wolf linked, "I'm going to lose control to him again, but thank you for everything you've done. I'm sorry. You need to move." Buck announced, "Melanie won." I got away from him and Edward shifted back.

He growled "What did he say to you?" I asked, "Why doesn't anyone know their Alpha's wolf's name?" He replied, "Several people do." I replied, "But the pack doesn't… and that's weird." He shouted, "I don't care about what you think is weird!" Ok.

Edward snarled, "Francis, get in here." He gasped and groaned, swaying on his feet. He asked, "Do I have to?" Booker answered, "Your Future Gamma isn't here because of your future Alpha." Caine snarled.

I replied, "Please. He's so not the future Gamma…. he doesn't even train. He's not coming because he knows I'd kill him." I would too. Today especially. Booker growled, "As if you could." I replied, "I could've killed all of you so far. Caine only stopped me from killing Edward because… well…. his dad made him and….I'm not an Alpha blood. I can't actually be an Alpha and that's what killing the Alpha makes me… though I suppose…"

Booker snarled, "You cannot be an Alpha." I wasn't going to say I could be one permanently. Obviously. I snorted, "I'd be better at than him…if we are being honest." Everyone gasped. I asked, "What? Is that news? I don't think it is… a REAL wolf with no human would be a better Alpha than Edward."

Francis sighed, "Fine. I'll get my ass kicked next." He barely swung before I knocked him out. Booker snarled, "Dax." That fight was actually a challenge because I'd been training him. I linked, "I'm sorry." He replied, "Do it." I took him down using a move Xander put out in his workout videos.

Francis came back in wolf form. I asked, "Uhh is his wolf ok? Or is he drunk?" His wolf was stumbling around. I shot Dax a look and he shrugged. I took his wolf down. Francis shifted back, but I didn't smell any alcohol on his breath.

I asked, "Hey… umm… is your wolf ok? Do you need…?" He groaned "Stop talking." He took his seat. I pointed out, "That's not really my forte and I'm pretty sure something is wrong and…" He shouted, "SHUT UP!" I sighed, "I was just trying to help you."

Dax shifted into Torst. Torst told me, "I want to fight the Alpha Command for you." I replied, "You don't have to. Just come at me like we've practiced." He emphatically stated, "You don't deserve this. You are a good person. My human wants to challenge for the Beta position."

I gently said, "But Caine and Dax aren't ready. That's not their fault. We just started working together two years ago." He hummed and I knew he agreed. Torst and I fought. I pretended it was practice, so when it ended, I was really proud of him.

Edward snarled. Booker demanded, "Caine." I laughed, "Edward, isn't funny you're relying on the son you insisted wasn't trained yet?" Booker glared at me. I asked, "What? It's funny… no… it's ironic… that's the right word."

Caine got on the mats. Edward said, "You have to fight her." Little did he know I fought Caine all the time. Another way he wasn't like Alpha Peter. The only thing that ever got by him was people bullying me and I that's because hid it from him. He always knew what was going on around the pack. He would've known if Dalton, Dakota, or Cooper were training with someone else.

I linked my wolf, "Some Alpha he is, right? It hurts to think… but it's true." I stalled remembering I didn't have a wolf and yet again no answer came. Because I was wolf less. Caine came at me as tears filled my eyes.

We fought for hours. I was so proud of him. Buck called, "According to the rules, this is a draw." Edward growled. He said, "There, you failed the challenge." I snorted, "Good lord… read a book… any book. Draws don't count against me. Only losing. Plus… fighting the future pack leadership doesn't count against me… so really, I've already won. But you just continue on…knowing nothing… I guess." He turned red in the face.

He asked, "Jean?" Jean was looking something up. I sighed loudly. Caine linked, "You are due for a break." I replied, "I'd rather keep fighting. If my adrenaline fades… I'm kind of screwed… well…. no… I'd be fine." I would not. He stared at me and sighed, "You suck at lying." Yeah, I knew that.

He shifted into Spear. Spear linked me, "I don't like this." I reasoned, "Just pretend like we are training." We fought each other for hours. Pride was swelling in my chest. Caine and Spear could fight like this because of me. Buck eventually announced, "This is a draw as well." Caine shifted back and Addison brought him clothes.

Buck announced, "Black Path, your new Female Lead Warrior is Melanie McAlister." I nearly choked with emotion because he'd used my real name. Edward snarled, "To outsiders it will be Ashley Griffen." Buck inclined his head. Sierra, Mason, Hendrick, Addison, Dax, and Caine cheered but no one else did. Which wasn't that surprising.

Edward snarled, "I cannot believe she won." I retorted, "Because you don't pay attention." He stalked out and left. Sierra ran over to me. Buck told me, "We will meet up to discuss how this works now." I asked, "Can't you just give me the schedule… and…?" He cut me off, "I could if there was one. I did her job and mine." I hummed, "Yeah, ok… we can meet up tomorrow and…"

He cut me off, "Next week. I'll send out the announcement that you've won to the local packs. I'll get the paperwork ready for the Supernatural and Werewolf Council. You need to heal." I blew out a breath, "Fine. That is… nice. It's weird… but it's nice." He snorted, "I have never been mean to you." He walked off grumbling about how I needed to learn how to survive down here.

I sagged and nearly dropped but Dax and Caine caught me. Caine sighed, "Melanie, I'm carrying you to Hendrick and Mason's." I agreed, "Ok." He carried me gently and when we got inside, he took me to a bedroom and laid me down on my side.

I looked around and asked, "What's this?" Hendrick said, "It's your room." I started to cry, and they both laid down on the bed holding me like I was their pup. I didn't feel like anyone's anymore. I was in a fog, healing, and I could admit it. It was taking time, but the wounds were healing.

The words remained though. I was drinking a lot. I'd seen Kingsley and Angelique. They were worried but I did recall them being there while very drunk. Kingsley and Kayda took care of me. My friends were worried to leave me alone for even a second and it wasn't unfounded really.

Buck was still putting me off because I wasn't fully healed but he let me look at some of the paperwork. So, I was doing something. I'd been watching my emails, but Beta Jason hadn't commented on the name Ashley Griffen or the news of a new Female Lead Warrior.

Caine hadn't really let me near my other place. He was practically sitting on top of me, and I was nearly going insane from inactivity. We were all meeting today to discuss whatever they'd wanted to when I'd challenged for the Female Lead Warrior spot.

Caine cleared his throat, "You know how you've speculated that if the Ring gets someone of importance, they will throw a party?" Horror filled me. I ran to my computer asking, "Is it Xander? Did they hurt him? How could you just…?"

Caine cut me off, "We could because he'd deserve it for promising to reject you." Dax nudged him and I burst into tears as fresh pain sliced through my entire being. Caine added, "It's not him." I cried, "Ok… who?" He answered, "Julianna and maybe Everly." Everly.

I gasped, "Jason's mate?! You can't…" He replied, "We took a vote." I snorted, "This isn't a democracy! I run this… I started it and…" He cut me off, "Yeah, and you can't go. You know that." That was not a thing I knew.

He replied, "I've barely left your side since I found you." I know that… because it's how this plan got by me and I didn't send anyone body parts to warn them! He growled, "You didn't see how you looked and…." I whispered, "I was there, so… I do know what he did."

He snarled, "Well, I should've stopped it! No one has ever been that hurt here. No one but YOU has ever been hurt that much. They always come after you, but not even they were this sick and twisted! It's disgusting and vile."

His first clenched, "I told my dad I'd kill him and Trevor if I saw them that day. I have never felt like more of a failure than when I found you guys. I was too slow to stop him from branding you with his name." I shrugged, "You didn't do anything wrong… you couldn't have gotten there."

He said, "Well, that doesn't mean jack shit to me or my wolf. You had the idea about the Ring having a party and planned to expose and destroy that syndicate when they do. We can get them now that we are letting this happen."

I argued, "Not at the expense of Everly and Julianna." Caine retorted, "Well, none of us care for the fact that you probably plan to be the person caught by the Ring. Especially now." I flushed red because he was right. He snorted, "Yeah, that's what we all thought. You don't deserve this."

I whispered, "Slade killed my family because he was coming for me." Pain lanced through me again. Caine asked, "Then why aren't you with him? This story doesn't make sense. My dad is a liar, cheat, and dirty rotten person. I don't know the story, but I know it's not the bullshit he told you." I wanted that to be true more than I could say.

Mason said, "It's not like they will really get hurt either. We will move in when the Ring hosts the party." I reasoned, "You don't know they won't hurt them and…" Dax replied, "Sure we do. It's too fast and they'd want to mock the allies." Yes. They'd mock Jason and Xander and I didn't like that.

Caine snorted, "Beta Jason deserves to be mocked and so does your Xander." I winced, "That's not true. They…" Dax replied, "Turned their back on you two years ago. They deserve this for that alone." I cringed, "Everly and Julianna didn't…"

Sierra replied, "Everly absolutely deserves to get kidnapped for the shit she said to you. She blamed you for her mating going a certain way. She refused to invite you to their mating ceremony. I maintain it was because you would've mentioned that she and T liked each other. She didn't talk to her mate about you attending the funerals. She deserves to be kidnapped. They aren't going to hurt her."

I disagreed, "Out of those prisoner options, Everly is more likely to get hurt. Julianna is part of the…" Hendrick sighed, "Promised Siblings Family, we know." I asked, "ILYX, what's the probability of Everly being hurt in this plan?" ILYX answered, "Ninety-Eight percent." I choked out a sob.

Addison offered, "Maybe we change the voice of ILYX." I cried, "No." Caine said, "Like we said, we took a vote and this is our decision. We can implement the plan you've put forth." They talked around me, but I was busy planning.

Addison came over, "We have to go. My dad called and I know you weren't listening to what we were saying. Paige is going to come sit with you. Ok? I'm going to put this salve on your back like Celia told us to." I snorted, "She shouldn't be a nurse… it's literally insane." She agreed, "We know." Caine added, "I will make her the lead doctor when I take over." I nodded because that was good.

They left, which was helpful. I had a lot of thinking to do. Why was I even still here? The Moon Goddess couldn't even take enough pity on me to let me die. Beta Jason hadn't even commented on my Female Lead Warrior status. Beta Dylan had emailed me, but I hadn't read it. So had Alpha Eric.

I carefully removed the gauze Addison had put on me to see my back again. I broke down sobbing when I caught my reflection in the mirror. It was so ugly. All the words he'd put on my back… his name and family killer cut the deepest. Literally and figuratively. I told the mirror, "I'm Xander's. Not Trevor's. I am." The pain of knowing he didn't want me hit again and I hoped it killed me this time.

My computer alarm started going off. I quickly threw some gauze back on and hobbled over to my desk. At least here I could give in to the pain. I didn't need to pretend to be ok. My blood ran cold when I saw my friends were right. Julianna and Everly had been kidnapped.

They got Everly first, and they used her phone to get Julianna. She had her first and last name as the contact. ARE YOU FOR REAL?! Red Run refused to be even moderately helpful anymore. I thought I had more time to stop this. I didn't realize it was happening NOW.

I thought Julianna was the main target. This was directed at Everly. Why? No, you know what? I didn't agree with my friends' plan. We couldn't let this happen. Beta Jason couldn't lose Everly too. Despite everything he'd said and done to me… I couldn't let him lose anyone else.

Julianna hadn't done anything to me ever. She was a nice person and everyone knew that. I couldn't just leave her there. I grabbed my mask and drafted a text for Mason and Hendrick. I'd send it when I got there.

I'd already found where they were, or ILYX had. Dante had them kidnapped, so they'd be in Kentucky at the main Hunters headquarters. I quickly geared up and put in my colored contacts. I couldn't have them see my eye color. It was too unique.

I went through to our holoport there, shoving the pain to the back of my mind. I needed a distraction to get everyone outside. Dante would have to order it and the perfect tool to get him to do that was practically staring at me. His favorite car was here. I sent my text.

Me: I can't let Beta Jason lose anyone else. Julianna Lyons is completely innocent, and we protect those that are. I can't do nothing. I'm going in and if you want to come have my back, I'd appreciate it. I understand if you don't though. I know this wasn't the group decision. I'll take their place if all else fails, and you can enact the plan if the Hunters capture me.
Mason: The fuck we won't come. God damn it, Mel. You fight to get out of there because we are gearing up and coming. If they take you, they will have to take us too.

Well, I wasn't going to let that happen at all. It made me entirely too happy when I hotwired one of the cars outside and crash it into Dante's. He loved that car so he'd definitely come outside for it, and I could get in. Easily. Thank goodness I had the foresight to pack a go bag. They contained everything I needed, but even if I hadn't ILYX and my watch could produce it.

I moved inside the second that the crash happened. I heard them argue, "I don't want to tell him." I nearly snorted because of course they didn't. Everyone moved out and I found the room they were holding Everly and Julianna in easily.

Seeing Everly sitting there had my anger mounting. She was supposed to be safe. Betrayal etched its way into my soul. She was supposed to be my sister, and she turned her back on me. She still wasn't supposed to be here though.

EJ asked, "Who was that?" I quickly ordered, "SHUSH! Or they will hear us!" I ignored the jolt of pain I felt talking to EJ that way. One, he was my brother in law. Two, he was a good Alpha but it just all felt fake now.

They were tricking people… me. I was tricked and I didn't like that. My whole life was one big lie after another. I wasn't a full blooded Werewolf. I wasn't Drake McAlister's daughter. I wasn't anything.

Everly asked me, "Who are you?" I'd have preferred it if she'd stabbed me in the heart. She should know me. This wasn't fair. I quickly took her silver chains off ignoring her question.

She should feel like we were on the same team. She was my sister in law. Didn't she feel the connection we shared? Was that too much to ask? I turned my attention to Julianna because she couldn't hurt my feelings by not knowing me.

She had on iron, snake like bracelets. They were Hunters designs for partials. They weren't supposed to be ready yet. I was going to steal them before they could use them.

I grumbled, "Seriously?! I can never get a break… and I really think I should… I'm pretty sure I've earned it… when you think about all the things I did to get here… and previously… I am a GOOD PERSON!"

Everly didn't even try not to laugh. Hope pinged inside me, but I shut it down. She wouldn't laugh if she knew who I was… she wouldn't. Do not feel a kinship with her right now. Don't do it Melanie… but as hard I tried not to, I did.

I glanced at my watch. It was taking too long to get out. We were going to be in a shootout. I gave my vest to Everly. I commanded, "Put this on." Everly did so without question. Because we were related by marriage. We were supposed to work well together. Why didn't she feel it?!

I kneeled beside Julianna. I felt bad when I told her, "This is going to hurt, but when I get these off… and I'm sorry about that… the whole perfection process wasn't perfected… Hunters suck… along with their timing… right? That's a thing that you think too… because… well… yeah. You just pop Everly and yourself the heck out of here Julianna."

I'd have to give her the element that allowed them to pass through the Hunters barriers which would hurt… because it wasn't ready to give to the allies yet. It still hurt people. Not me… for some weird reason… probably because I had Hunter blood. I didn't feel like any partial Hunters I knew though. I shoved those thoughts aside.

Everly whispered, "Who are you? How did you get here? How do you know us?" She needed to stop asking questions because I was going to cry. I got everything ready for Julianna. She was key to my plan. Julianna admitted, "I can't pop."

It was fair that she thought that. I told her, "You'll be able to shortly." The look on her face told me she didn't believe me… which was also fair. Laxenread was revolutionary…and they didn't know about it yet, but they would once I got them home.

I quickly injected Julianna with the first dose of my newest creation for the allies. I cringed when Julianna choked in pain. It wasn't ready but this was an emergency. The iron bracelets fell off her. Julianna cursed, "Shit."

I knew she was feeling the kick of her powers return. My watch beeped letting me know Hunters had re-entered the house. Dang it. Well, I could still get out. I'd just have to go through the window, rather than the door. Anastasia and I were behind their remodel. These windows broke easily and that was in case we needed to escape.

I complained, "Oh come on! I asked for ONE measly break!" I addressed Selene, "I think we know you owe me a break… bitch." I didn't usually curse but this was a necessary one. She was the worst.

I gave Julianna the next dose so she could get through the shields, which would feel like her power on steroids. I heard the stampede coming up the stairs and got ready to fight.

Caine linked, "Tell me you didn't." I replied, "Busy." He growled, "MELANIE JANE!" It was odd that it was nice to hear. It sounded like my brothers being mad at me for something. Caine and Dax were my family by choice now though, so I guess my brother WAS mad at me.

I pushed Julianna and Everly down and took great delight in kicking over Dante's desk. He loathed disorganization. He had everything on his desk 'just so' and knowing it would ruin his whole day made it all better. I began to fire at everyone coming through the door.

Everly asked, "What the hell is going on? Was this the plan? Where's your backup?" Was she for real? I didn't get to plan this! I was busy being kept away from my computer healing from the request from her mate to punish me.

Which I knew Jason thought would be bad patrols and dish duty but STIILL. I grumbled, "Well… my plan is better than yours now, isn't it? I didn't have a lot of time to come up with a plan. I had to come save both of you… with their last minute… I think we talked about their timing already."

I waved saying, "You know what? Save people in your phone with code names… that's annoying but you should do it for me… I feel like that's something you owe me. They texted people from your phone because you put their first AND LAST NAME in it. Don't do that… please… No. Actually, no please just don't do it." My watch blinked a code sixty-sixty. Dante had called in more backup.

I handed Everly a card with the coordinates to Laxenread. I ordered Julianna, "Pop her out now!" I shoved Julianna and Everly away from me and turned to shoot. Julianna popped. Sierra linked, "ILYX is giving fifty percent on you being captured. I will not be alone in kicking your ass if you get captured." I replied, "Ask ILYX what the probability is with the new window replacements."

She shouted, "YOU ARE GOING TO JUMP OUT THE WINDOW?!" I reasoned, "There's a lake below the window." She shouted, "Are you serious?! God, you are. ILYX gives you eighty percent on escaping with the window data. It's also a ninety percent chance of injury."

She paused then added, "No, one hundred with your injuries already." I snorted, "There is nothing that has a one hundred percent probability." She growled back. I greeted, "Hi Tori." Tori, Sierra's wolf, growled, "You need to get back here unharmed." I reasoned, "That's the plan." I still had to make Alpha Peter and Beta Jason proud. They didn't know what I'd done yet with the Female Lead Warrior position.

I was taking down a massive chunk of Dante's most loyal followers. I didn't feel bad about that. They knew the true Hunter purpose. They were hiding it from those they recruited. So, they totally deserve to get shot… that had logic to it.

I switched to my knife that Charles had gifted to me. I still didn't feel bad about taking them out. Some of these people had decided to come after Xander and his mom. Someone shouted outside, "Dante, stop worrying about the car and get back in here." Aww poor baby… his car was ruined.

Dante filled the doorway looking enraged. He was going to burst a blood vessel or have an aneurysm. That would be a little funny. He told me, "You are outmanned and outgunned. Surrender or die." I would be killed if I surrendered eventually. The allies weren't going to come for me. Beta Jason would convince them not to.

I replied laughing, "Not a chance… to both. No to the dying… and definitely no on surrendering... that's a lot of no…" Dante cut me off, "You came alone. That was foolish and arrogant. Now we finally have one circle group member in our grasp. I kept telling people you'd fuck up. Your little blue circles and your line drawing days are over." Seriously? The circle group. IT WAS A RING!

Sierra linked, "DO NOT RANT ABOUT THE NAME!" I asked, "Are you in the cameras?" She snorted, "Yes, ILYX gave them to us." Well, I kind of wanted to rant about the name. Caine ordered, "Evade your ass off right now. He doesn't need to know you're alone." I could evade.

I asked, "Who said I came alone?" Exactly like I thought they would, they turned to door ready to take the people coming at them from behind. Except no one was coming. Mason and Hendrick would be outside. Mason on his motorcycle and Hendrick behind a scope.

I threw the gun at the window, shattering it just like Anastasia and I planned. I took off running. Dante and his men sputtered. "STOP!" Uh huh. Ok. Why would I listen to them? I jumped. I flipped midair so I was ready to dive into the water. Please be deep. Please be deep. Hitting the water felt like hitting lead. I felt several of my ribs crack, but at least the water was deep. I hit my ankle on the bottom and nearly screamed in pain.

I swam the length of the lake. My lungs screamed for air, but I'd trained with Tristan on outdoor tactics. I could hold my breath for a long time. I nearly inhaled but I swore I saw Tristan waving to me. I could reach him. He was right there. I swam harder, but just as I reached him he disappeared. Because he was never there Melanie. He's dead.

I surfaced drawing in air I desperately needed. Dax linked, "SWIM!" I shook myself and followed his instruction. I got out and took off running. Pain radiated from my ankle. It might actually be broken. The Hunters were running after me. Which was insane. I was faster than they were.

They started firing tranquilizers at me. Well, the joke was on them. That wasn't going to do anything to me. Something that had been proven over and over. Most missed me, but one landed. Addison linked, "Did that do anything? Are you ok?" I replied, "You know I'm fine."

Mason linked, "On your six." I heard the revving of a motorcycle. He came charging towards me. Hendrick linked, "I'm on BOTH your sixes. Get to Mason." I changed direction and ran for Mason with everything I had left.

He held his elbow out and we locked both of ours and I swung up behind him. My ribs screamed in protest when he quickly executed a turn to get us out of there. Hendrick shouted, "Get in the front of Mason. They are shooting!" His return fire was coming but I flipped around Mason and began to cover his shots, so they didn't suspect a sniper.

Mason drove through our holoport and Hendrick jumped through after him. Mason ripped off his helmet. He yelled, "WHAT WERE YOU THINKING?!" I replied, "That I couldn't just… sit there and let something like this happen… and it didn't make sense. Julianna should've been the target… but it was Everly and…"

Hendrick sighed, "God damn, kid. You can't do stuff like this. Especially right now." It wasn't the first time I had, and likely would not be the last. We went back and found the group. Caine growled, "We decided not to interfere!"

I disagreed, "No… you did. I did not. Definitely not me…" Dax raised an eyebrow looking at me. It made my skin itch to go against Caine, but I was right. It was the right call. ILYX announced, "Black Mountain and their allies have entered the building you wanted, Melanie Jane. They read the note."

I sighed in relief. They had Laxenread now. They would be ok. Caine said, "Let's listen to the group vote next time. Ok?" I shrugged because I was absolutely not going to do that. ILYX told me, "Micah is calling." Oh gosh… did he know?

I answered, "Uh hi." He chuckled, "Hello. I have a request." I asked, "What is it?" He chuckled, "My sister in law wants your email. The one I have, not your lead Warrior one. Congratulations on that, by the way. Are you doing ok?"

I sighed, "That seems like a veiled way to ask about how I'm dealing with not having a wolf… and probably like you'd imagine… or worse and no on the email. Wait. Which sister in law? Actually just no. No is good answer." He ignored me, "Elise."

I shrieked, "ELISE WANTS TO TALK TO ME?!" Addison grabbed the phone ordering, "Ashley, calm down." I whispered, "She wants to talk to me… well… .no probably not…. no… because no. Right? Like… Elise though."

Micah said, "So, it's still a yes on Elise being the one who wants your email. The personal one. Actually, Former Beta Dylan Frost is literally begging and pleading with me to give it to him too." I said, "He emailed me… not on my personal email though."

Micah hummed, "Well, Elise, Eric, and Dylan want it." Caine covered my mouth when I screamed. Micah said, "I still heard that whoever muffled it." I replied, "Umm no. So…no… but maybe… no. Former Beta Dylan Frost… I mean…. ok. I'm curious… umm Alpha Eric could get it anyway and…. umm sure… but Elise… no… but then…."

Dax groaned, "For the love of god." I declared, "I need coffee." They simultaneously shouted, "NO!" I frowned at them all. Micah asked, "So, yes to Eric and Dylan. No on Elise." All my friends nodded. I winced, "Umm that would probably hurt her feelings… so just yes. Fine. Ok bye." I hung up before I could say anything else. They all groaned but when she emailed me, I actually screamed.

Caine stiffened, "We have to go. Virgil, shimmer us near the pack." He did then grabbed my arm and said, "She'll catch up." Caine sighed, "Fine." He took off. He said, "I will always be on your side and go with you. Val too."

I admitted, "I know that…it's just…I was panicked." He said, "I understand more than they do. My brother betrayed me and Val. I want to hate him with every fiber of my being, but I can't." I hugged him and he hugged me back.

I took off running to catch up with everyone. We walked in a group and I nearly fell over when we reached the pack ground. I stammered, "Alpha Theo…and technically already an Alpha Lux…" They both stared at me.

Edward said, "He's not the Alpha." I disagreed, "He had his Alpha Ceremony and he can link other Alpha's he just didn't take the title yet because his younger brother hasn't and he wants to do it together. Read a memo for ONCE in your life."

Alpha Theo Barlett raised his eyebrow. Lux said, "Oh, I like her." Booker snorted, "That's ill advised." I snarked, "So is you breathing, but you keep doing it." Lux's jaw dropped. Alpha Theo said, "I feel we have a lot to discuss."

Edward said, "With us." Alpha Theo laughed, "I'm good. I do know how to talk to women. Come on, Lead Warrior Ashley. The entire Werewolf Council is intrigued by you. Caine linked, "Don't." I squeaked, "Really? Everyone?" Was Alpha Peter proud of me again?

Lux said, "Yup. Let's take a walk." I shrugged, "Ok." Edward said, "We have a conference room you can use." Honestly, I'd prefer that option with my injuries. Alpha Theo declined politely, "Thanks, but it's a nice day." They started to walk off with me.

Lux said, "So, beautiful lady tell us everything." I chuckled, "About?" Alpha Theo said, "You're the youngest Female Lead Warrior. Why?" I answered, "Umm because I won the tournament?" Lux laughed, "Awww, she's adorable. Let's keep her." I blushed furiously.

Alpha Theo said, "If she wants to come with us, she can." I gasped, "What? Umm…that's… you can't do that." He replied, "I can. Back to why you have a GED." I disagreed, "You didn't mention that at all… so we can't really get back to it."

He pressed, "What's the answer?" I said, "Well, I wanted to get it…" He questioned, "But why aren't you in school?" I replied, "It wasn't really an option….school has always been boring to me anyway." He asked, "Are you ok here?" I laughed, I couldn't help it.

Lux said, “I don’t like that laugh at all.” That was fair. Alpha Theo asked, “Did you get some injuries against the wolves you fought?” I said, “Booker got a shot in on me in his wolf form, but I still won.” Lux asked, “Don’t you mean Gamma Booker?” I answered, “No, I mean Booker.”

Alpha Theo said, “If you want to tell us about something going on, I’ll listen.” I asked, “Have you ever had your entire belief structure shattered?” He answered, “No.” I said, “Mine was.” Lux offered, “We really will take you back to our pack.” Except they couldn’t.

Edward asked, “Are you trying to poach my Female Lead Warrior? I’ll complain to the Supernatural Council.” I scoffed, “Oh please, you pathetic sack of bones just shut up.” Alpha Theo’s jaw dropped. Lux said, “Please, dad. Can’t we keep her? She’s so amazing.”

Edward said, “I think you’ve stayed long enough Alpha Theo.” I scoffed, “Yeah, they knew they could beat you in a fight before word went out that I beat you in human and wolf form. Now, they know they could pummel you into the ground.” He glared at me.

Alpha Theo said, “Well, this is interesting.” He told me, “We came to make sure you were ok and we’ll be here tomorrow too. Just know every single member of the Werewolf Council is impressed by you. The ones officially on it and the ones slated to come on.” Which meant Nick AND Alpha Peter were impressed by me. It felt like a balm to my soul even if it was going to be short lived.

Life kept on going. We’d stopped an attack on Elise and EJ. Which was honestly insane. But tonight, I was watching the allies but mostly Xander, come up with ideas for who came up with Laxenread. I watched on his computer in the document I was hacked into.

I was drunk with Sierra. I was so annoyed as the names on the list mounted while I drank. Sierra winced as I took another drink from the third vodka bottle. She tried to appease me, “Mel, you wanted them to think you were a Fairy. That’s why you named it Laxenread. They took the bait. It was a genius plan.”

I wiped my mouth and lamented, “Over ONE HUNDRED suspects, Si. ONE HUNDRED! I’m not even on the list. Do you know how INSULTING that is?” She huffed, “Yes, because you’ve told me repeatedly for the last three hours.”

I scoffed, “OVER ONE HUNDRED! How can I not make the list? They KNOW how smart I am.” Sierra pointed out, “They didn’t meet you though.” I rolled my eyes, “They still know I’m a literal gosh darn genius. That they don’t even CONSIDER me a suspect is just so….”

She interrupted, “Exactly what you wanted. They did exactly what you thought. They think it’s a Fairy because of the note you left. You’re so good at evading.” I grumbled, “Don’t patronize me. They did what I wanted, yes. That’s true. I wanted them to think I was a Fairy.”

I added, “But I also want to be CONSIDERED! NONE of the people on their damn list is HALF as smart as I am. I mean come on…. HALF. I did something AMAZING!” Sierra snorted, “I’m glad you can actually admit that. We try to tell you that and you blush. All I needed was bottles of vodka and you admit how smart you are.”

I ignored that, continuing. “Yet my Xander is out here with a list of HUNDREDS OF SUSPECTS…” Sierra huffed, “A little over one hundred.” I ranted, “AND I AM NOT ON IT! That’s just…” Sierra supplied, “Insulting.” I clapped, “YES!”

Caine came in, “Sierra, you’re needed in the kitchen. I’ve got our little hacking drunk Melanie.” I grumbled, “How annoying.” Caine told me, “The Luna in Clarksville died.” I asked, “And? No… she was friends with Cassandra…right?” He nodded, “Yes.” He looked at his watch then groaned, “I have to go. Don’t do anything crazy.” I shrugged and kept drinking. Then I hacked and found I had things to do.

The Clarksville Luna had recordings in her possession that would hurt Xander if he knew them about his grandma. She bragged about recording their conversations all the time. Both women were awful. I couldn’t have that. Could I? Nope. Not my mate. Cassandra didn’t get to hurt him anymore. She was mean when she was alive, so I would not allow her to be mean in death.

I linked Addison, “Going to break into the Clarksville main house to steal the dead Luna’s things.” She groaned, “No you are not!” I replied, “Uhh can’t have her being mean to my Xander in death… so yes." She asked, "Why would the Clarksville Luna be mean to your Xander?! She's dead as you clearly know." I said, "Uhh Cassandra... not the Clarksville Luna. Obviously."

Sierra linked, "Don't you dare do it!" I gasped, "What?" She huffed. Dax growled, "Melanie, I will be right there. Don't leave and don't break and enter when you are drunk into a house in a different pack!" I asked, "When would I do it then? I don't know if you've noticed… but I drink a lot now." He groaned, "We noticed." Ok, then this wasn't surprising.

Technically, I knew this was a bad idea. My friends said that I didn't need to do this, but I knew that someone would send these recordings to Black Mountain. They would infuriate Xander and hurt a lot of the Conners. I couldn't let that happen.

Really, if the Luna in Clarksville hadn't just died it wouldn't be urgent. Caine told me so he clearly, deep down, wanted me to do this…when you thought about it. Plus, the Clarksville Luna's mate was vile. He'd send this to Eric to torture him.

I knew that and I hadn't even lived here long. I'd been here for a whole seventy-two hours before I found out the Luna liked to spread around the things Cassandra said. Everyone around here hoped they got a Conners family member alone to make some jab about it. As if I would let that happen.

Ok, they didn't know that but still. I wasn't going to let it happen. I winced when I jumped through the window. My knee wasn't fully healed, but that was ok. This was for Xander. I quickly stole everything the Luna had in all her hides. The thing about her having loose lips that was helpful to me was that I knew where she kept everything. I didn't even need to look very hard.

I left quickly and got back to our holoport. I walked into my secondary place. I needed to call Charles and thank him for helping me get this place. I couldn't stay with creepy Uncle Ajax all the time. Sometimes a girl needed a shower without someone staring at her. I shivered, still feeling gross about that.

I should've just moved in with Mason and Hendrick. I just thought it would be too hard to leave when I turned sixteen and Beta Jason let me come home. I took a deep breath because he was never going to do that now.

I looked around and snorted, "I beat Dax back. Look at me go. He thought I couldn't break and enter drunk. He's so silly." I plugged in the tapes and played the first one. The Luna said, "Cassandra, how nice to hear from you. How are you?"

Cassandra huffed, "That wretched Fairy keeps ruining everything. My boys have never been closer. It used to be Eric and Jackson Then Darrin and Harold. I had them segregated. They of course hung out altogether, but Jackson and Eric were always the closet."

She tisked, "Now, that blasted Fairy has them go on monthly brother retreats. Well, that's not what she calls it. The girls always join them on the last day, now they are thick as thieves." I had no idea what was bad about that.

The Clarksville Luna sighed and replied, "Well, maybe if you explained their purpose to them they'd listen." Huh? Cassandra snorted, "They would take it wrong. Harold has always accused me of loving Eric the most."

"The boys just wouldn't understand. I don't want anything to happen to my pups, I love them. It's just their destiny to be lines of defense for Eric." My blood boiled and I threw my headphones off. I screamed in anger. How DARE she!

My mom loved me and my brothers equally. She didn't raise any of us to live but be ready to be a lamb to the slaughter for the others. How could she? I didn't have pups, and if Xander rejected me I never would. Pain ripped through me and stole my breath.

I took several deep ones before I acknowledged that I'd imagined our pups in my head. Our family was beautiful, and I already loved them. I would love them with everything in me if I somehow that dream became a reality. How could she say these things about her sons?! Nathan would be furious if he found out.

Addison came in, "Hey, ok you're still here. Dax got pulled into something. Look I know you're upset that we don't think you should steal those…" She trailed off seeing me surrounded by the evidence I had in fact stolen.

She groaned, "Oh my god! You went anyway." I snorted, "And they are worse than you think. She was the biggest snake of all time." Addison replied, "You've always said that. You didn't like her even when you were three years old." I snorted but she was right, and she knew that because I'd told them.

I hated Cassandra even though I had never met her. I harbored a lot of anger and bitterness from the stories I'd heard. Plus, my mom said she'd visit when I was pup so Cassandra might have met me but I couldn't be sure. My mom was also convinced Valerie Bishop met me and I knew she hadn't. There was no picture.

I explained, "I heard Jason talking about how Xander offered to heal Cassandra so she could have a pup she didn't want." Addison winced. It wasn't a secret down here that Cassandra had not been trying to have a pup.

I told her, "I didn't know that last part at the time, but I DID know it would hurt any Healer's feelings to have their healing denied over and over again. They are sensitive, and she didn't care. She never thought of anyone but herself."

"I never bought that she wasn't the world's most selfish person. I've listened to two minutes. TWO! Which is how I already know I'm right. She fooled so many people, and maybe most of all herself. She was a horrible person, but she couldn't see that about herself. She thought she was just great."

Addison snorted, "Yeah, well delusional people are everywhere. My dad and Beta Jean think they are great. They seem to think that their actions make them good Alpha's, and maybe that is because until we met you, we didn't know Alpha's behaved differently."

I frowned, "But your dad definitely does." She nodded, "He has to, which makes it weird. He thinks showing my mom affection would show his weakness, but according to you; the most powerful werewolf in the world adores his mate. Basic logic dictates my dad is wrong." He was about so much.

I huffed, "Alright, well I'm going to get back to those tapes. Don't mind my screams of fury." Addison snorted, "Just play them out loud so I can understand how awful she is." It would be normal to her though. It was just annoying for me because this would hurt Xander and the people he loved, and I couldn't have that.

I ended up screaming more than once. Even Addison agreed that Cassandra was awful. I didn't understand why she seemed to believe her sons purpose was to die if Alpha Eric needed them to. It was weird because he'd never let it happen. It was on my list of things to figure out.

One day after the other kept going. I was in the office with Buck when Edward came in. He announced, "Your brother is the Beta and a father." I jolted, "What? He's what? Did you say a father? He said that right…you heard that?" Buck said, "He did say that." How was that possible? Everly didn't look pregnant when I saw her.

He hummed, "Yes, well apparently Everly was kidnapped and healed. It sped up her pregnancy." He started to leave. I stood asking, "What's his or her name? When did Everly give birth?" He replied, "I couldn't be bothered to care about either of those things." He left me behind utterly shocked.

I left the office and went to my closet… they said office, but it was a closet. I could barely be in here because of the lack of space. I called Beta Jason. He answered, "What?" I said, "Umm... I just…I heard that…" He growled, "Spit it out."

I rushed, "Congratulations… I heard that I have a niece… or nephew." He said, "Nephew. His name is Kai." I touched my chest. I whispered, "Kai. Can I come meet him? Just once… I just…" He cut me off with a harsh laugh.

Tears filled my eyes. He said, "I will NEVER let you within one hundred yards of my son. He will never even know about you. If he does, it will be as the person who killed his grandparents and Uncle." I cried, "Jase…" He shouted, "BETA JASON!" Then hung up.

I quickly called Everly. She sighed, "You have some nerve calling me after upsetting my mate." I explained, "I just want to see Kai and…" She cut me off, "Are you insane? No." I pleaded, "Can I just have a picture of him?" She sighed, "No. Stop being such a selfish brat. This is such an amazing time for us, and you ruined it. Again." She hung up.

I stared at the phone. Melinda called. I answered "Aunt Melin…" She cut me off, "You stupid SELFISH bitch! HOW DARE YOU CALL AND RUIN EVERYTHIGN AGAIN! God, why can't you just die!" I heard voices I knew in the background, yelling, "Die! Murderer! Family Killer!" That was Grandpa Ben, Grandma Esther, and MaryBeth.

Jason snarled, "Leave us the fuck alone! No one wants you, not even Alexander." I sobbed, "I just wanted to see Kai's picture… I'm sorry… I…" He cut me off, "Yeah, you're always sorry. If only you could just die." I gasped for breath, "Jason…" He shouted again, "BETA JASON!" He hung up.

I couldn't breathe. I ran to my second place and got Jason's watch. I ran through our holoports and tossed it over the border. The note was brief but it's what he'd want. ILYX had biometric monitoring. It would keep him safe.

I ran back to my place and started drinking. Caine linked, "Buck is worried about you. Which worries me." I didn't answer him. I ordered, "ILYX, lock everyone out." He replied, "Ok, Melanie Jane." I cried listening to my mate's voice. I pulled up his workout videos and watched him.

I drank more and touched the screen, "I would be the best mate. I would." Edward called me. I answered, "What?" He said, "Pick up our order from the coffee shop." He hung up and I dragged myself out of the building and ran there.

I walked in and hiccupped. I went to the counter, "Edward Davis's order." She nodded, "Coming up." I heard someone say, "Alexander Conners is a TIGER in bed." Her friends whipped their heads to her but mine did too. She was gorgeous like the others.

She wasn't the first to come down here and talk about him in bed. They were all gorgeous blondes. There were SO many of them too and each other took a piece of my soul with them when they left. I wasn't sure I had any pieces of my soul left if I was honest.

One of the blonde's friends asked, "You met Alpha Alexander? Is that why you called? Why didn't we meet in Black Mountain then?" She dismissed them, "You guys were nearby this cute place so I came to see you. He popped me in." He had been here? He'd been here and I missed him? My heartbeat felt like it was in my feet. That wasn't surprising really. Missing Xander was the literal story of my freaking life.

She said, "Yeah, he said we could stay in touch maybe be more than fuck buddies. Possibly even his Chosen." I would rather die than listen to this. I really would. Strike me dead here and now if you exist Selene. I stared at the ceiling but nothing happened.

One of the girls said, "I mean that's kind of crazy. Why would he take a chosen Luna already? Because that's really fast and you both have fated out there. He's only twenty one and you're twenty-five."

The blonde glared at her replying, "There's some girl who is the sister of one of his good friends. She likes him and thinks they are mates. He's desperate for her not to be his because she's a weak little brat that got her family killed." A choked sob bubbled up.

The girl behind the counter said, "Get out of here, Ashley. You don't need to listen to that drivel." It wasn't a secret to Black Path I loved Xander. I shot a glance back over at the woman my mate wanted over me. She winked at me and I saw in that moment she knew exactly who I was.

My heart felt like it was breaking. I saw Buck who did a double take. He asked, "Why do you smell like a distillery?" I handed him the coffee order, "Here." I took off running. He shouted, "MELANIE!" I ignored him and went back to my place. Everyone's voices screaming at me to die filled my head.

I would never meet Kai. My nephew would hate me just like everyone else. Xander wanted a blonde and I wasn't one. He even showed those women what I looked like and was probably sending them down her to taunt me personally.

I was holding them all back. I drank more. Dax linked, "Melanie, let us in. ILYX said you locked us out." I didn't answer. I grabbed my nine millimeter and stared at it. Jason would be thrilled if he got the call that I was dead. I stared in the mirror at my face.

I cried, "Why do I look like Drake McAlister if I'm not his daughter? WHY?!" I punched it and it shattered. ILYX announced, "Paige is calling." I answered, "Hello." She ordered, "You let me in this place, or I will do something drastic."

I replied, "Tell K she can keep everything going." She shouted, "WHAT?! No! No, don't talk like that." I stared at the gun unsure what I'd do. Caine snarled, "Melanie, don't you dare!" I cried, "They called me a murderer. They won't even send me a picture of my nephew."

I screamed, "I saved Everly. ME! She had him because of me. I saved her and… and I won't ever meet him. They want me to die. I should've died that night… I should've." He argued, "No, you shouldn't have. You survived because you are going to make the world your dance floor." I whispered, "I can't anymore."

Caine snarled, "Beta Jason is a disgrace to his name, pack, your parents, and older brother. They wanted you to live and you know it." I cried harder. I said, "He doesn't want me." Dax said, "Yeah, Buck linked me. He said that woman was lying her ass off and even her friend said so." Why did she know who I was then?

Caine demanded, "Let us in." I ended the call. I took out some of the many letters I'd received from my family since I'd been here.

Melanie,

Since the moment my son died, I felt you'd be Slade's. I knew you wouldn't shift and that's why we couldn't have you here.

My son, daughter in law, and oldest grandson died for you. You're how the Hunters got into the pack. Your blood. You killed them and I hope you suffer every day for it.

Ben McAlister

That wasn't really how it worked either. Anyone could get into the pack, but the patrol's should've spotted them. Which Grandpa Ben knew deep down. He wasn't thinking when he wrote this, but he really did want me to suffer and it gutted me. I read the next one knowing my already shattered heart would break so loud I'd hear it this time.

Melanie,

You may be my half-sister, but I wish we'd never met. You ruined my life.

Beta Jason McAlister

I couldn't read the rest again. I put them all away and pulled up a picture of Xander. He didn't want me. He really didn't. She said he was considering a chosen because he didn't want to be with me so badly. The elevator dinged and I glanced over.

The relief I felt at seeing Charles told me I didn't really want to kill myself. He flashed in front of me and took the gun. I cried, "Charles." He held me like a child. I sobbed, "They won't let me meet Kai." He said, "I don't know who that is."

I explained, "My nephew. They want me to die. Xander doesn't want me and…" He cut me off, "That seems unlikely as the Alpha Enforcer is not stupid." I hiccupped, "The blonde that he slept with… she… said … he didn't want me… so badly he was… considering a chosen."

He hummed, "As someone who has looked deeply into the Alpha Enforcer, I would say she's lying." I sniffled, "Everyone wants me to die." He replied, "That is hardly true. You just took a position to make a real difference in the inordinately horrible pack you insist you have to stay in. I will take you away from it all. You could come with me, my dear."

I held onto him, "I don't have a wolf and…" He patted my head, "I am sure you are a late bloomer." I whispered, "Have you ever heard of that?" He answered, "Not for a full blooded Werewolf, but that is what is going with you. I know it." I admitted, "Everything hurts all the time… everything is wrong… and so am I."

He disagreed, "There is nothing wrong with you. There is something wrong with plenty of people, but you are not one of them. I have met many people in my life over the centuries. None hold a candle to you."

I asked, "What are you doing here?" He answered, "Paige called. She was very worried, so I had my child that retained her shimmering power bring me here." I whispered, "For me?" He cupped my face, "My dear, I would do anything for you."

I replied, "You are a good friend." He chuckled, "I don't think anyone has called me that in a long time." I questioned, "Friend?" He hummed, "Yes. One did once upon a time. He is now a King." I surmised, "King Arthur."

He laughed, "Yes. Do you see how the world needs you? You figured that out so quickly." I sobbed, "I just wanted to meet Kai." He said, "Then you will make it so one day. Think of this, who would protect that young babe if you died?" I jolted, "The pack would…"

He cut me off, "The same pack that has done this to you? So, they'd protect him unless he happened to be in the wrong place at the wrong time like you were. They could blame him for something and he could become the new scapegoat they have as you are. Would you want him to be all alone? Or would you want to be able to bring him to the pack you, Caine, and Dax plan to change?"

I admitted, "I'd want him with me, but they wouldn't do that to him." He snorted, "They clearly would." He stayed with me until I fell asleep. I dreamed of my life, but Kai was living it instead. Booker was going to whip him when I woke up screaming, "NO!" Caine grabbed me, "It's ok. We are here."

I panted, "You guys are supposed to be…" Paige cut me off, "No one has left. Look, your asshole family can fall off a cliff. You get to stay with us." I whispered, "Ok." Dax demanded, "Promise us you'll never think about this again."

I snorted, "I mean… thinking… and having a loaded gun in my lap are very different." Caine growled, "Then don't ever do that again." I felt my tears fall. Sierra wiped them away. I cried, "They'll never let me meet him. I have a nephew."

Addison hugged me saying, "And that's great. When he's older we'll just find a way to meet him. Ok?" I shook my head, "He will hate me." Dax said, "Buck said they told you he'd never know about you. Just meet Kai as Ashley." Buck heard that whole demeaning call?

Caine said, "He did and I've never seen him look so disgusted with anyone before. Being a good brother is his one redeeming quality." He was disgusted with Jason? He wasn't disgusted with me? That was new.

Caine growled, "My dad wants to see us." Great. That was going to be good. We went to the pack where everyone was gathered, including pups. Edward announced, "It's time for the hunt." That sounded bad. I asked, "What hunt?" He grinned, "First, you need to meet Dante at Nate's building. We will prepare for the Hunt here."

I repeated, "What's the hunt?" Aunt Stephanie sneered, "Where we hunt the wolf less." I stared at her. She snarled, "You. We are hunting you." I snorted, "For what purpose?" Trevor snarled, "To show you your place." I glared at him, "And if I show you yours? Then what? I get punished, I'm guessing? That's definitely it."

Booker shouted, "We will defeat you." I nodded, "Sure, ok… that's a thing you'll do." Jean sighed, "You're a bad liar, but we will hunt you down." I shrugged, "Sure, Jean… I think I showed you all your place the other day." They growled at me, but it wasn't their wolves.

I called them out, "Those are weak human growls. Your wolves don't like the hunt, do they? No, they wouldn't… except Booker's. His totally would… and Trevor's… so…" Caine interrupted, "Dad, she's the Female Lead Warrior. You can't do this."

I laughed, "Let them try… this will be fun." All my friends looked worried, but I wasn't. Trevor winked, "And you can't wear a shirt. Everyone will see my masterpiece." I replied, "I mean art is… subjective… but it makes you look like a sycophant deviant so…by all means…advertise that." He snarled at me.

Edward ordered, "Leave. Go meet up with Dante then come back." I left the pack grounds and saw Paige waiting. I asked, "Are you coming with me?" She replied, "I'm driving you." I hugged her. I whispered, "Thanks for calling Charles." She punched me in the tit. I shouted, "OW!" She pointed at me, "Don't you ever lock me out of any place you are in ever again or I will hex you."

I laughed and got in the car. We drove to the local Hunters base. Paige said, "I don't like this. The air feels charged with evil." I agreed, "It does." I got out and told her, "Stay out here." I walked inside. Dante flicked on a flashlight in front of his face.

I asked, "Is this supposed to be scary? Because you'll have to work on it. I'm not sure how close you and Edward are but… Trevor stole the scary corner market going all evil psychotic…" Dante cut me off, "Tonight you join the Hunters." I asked, "Uhh what? Umm…. no… so…"

He said, "We were going to give you our mark but that was overruled. Harshly." I reasoned, "Because it's a choice…. so…" Anastasia had probably tried to call me. I checked my watch and noted she'd contacted me several times, but I was busy feeling sorry for myself… so I missed it.

He asked, "Do you, Melanie McAlister, swear to the Hunter oaths?" I replied, "That's a no." He continued, "Do you pledge to follow me and…?" I interrupted, "Double no… very much no." A few people snickered. He acted like I wasn't talking, "Do you accept your position in the Hunters?" I hummed, "I think you have a hearing problem."

He clicked on a screen. I shouted, "STOP!" There was a sniper rifle trained on Paige. He demanded, "Accept or she gets shot." I agreed, "Fine." He hummed, "It's lackluster but here's your outfit, Huntress McAlister." I grabbed it in a huff. Honestly, it was pretty cute.

He snapped his fingers, "Do her hair." They did it pretty fast and I stood. He ordered, "Put on the outfit." I sighed and went to the bathroom and changed. It was a black pleather one piece with a brown corset that had a pouch on one side for notes and amor cuffs on the sleeves with a place for a Huntress dagger. I put the hood up and walked out.

He took my picture smirking at me. He waved, "Go back for your hunt." I hummed, "I thought they were hunting me because I'm wolf less… Am I supposed to be hunting them? Since you all having me join? Which… is so dumb… by the way." Several people looked like they agreed.

The amount of access I had now as opposed to before I walked in was immense. They were going to pay for pointing a gun at Paige. I needed to get my head back in the game. Dante was never going to take me by surprise again. I was here. I didn't die and I was going to do right by Mom, Dad, and Tristan.

Dante said, "No, you're being hunted and this is the best move we've made in a long time." I repeated, "Worst idea ever. You're such a hypocrite it's not even funny. Plus, you have no morals which is why you send Nate away when you do this crap. Everyone knows you're not leader." I turned and left while he sputtered indignantly behind me.

I stalked outside and Paige's jaw dropped. She got out demanding, "Did they make you join?" I answered, "Yes… but it's fine." She blinked realizing, "You're not freaking out." I agreed, "Nope. I need you to take me to my parents and T." She nodded and drove us to the spot I'd had commemorated for them.

I got out and touched the stones. I whispered, "I'm sorry I almost gave up. I'll never quit on getting you justice again. I'm going to keep making the world my dance floor. I'm going to do this hunt and show them… I will show them the mistakes they just made. I promise." I got up and played some music and began to dance.

When I stopped Paige was crying and clapping. I walked back over. She hugged me, "That was so hauntingly beautiful." I nodded without saying anything. She asked, "Why aren't you freaking out about being forced to join the Hunters?"

I answered, "I'm going to make them pay. As a Huntress I have more access than I did before. I'll get this hunt done then have a password to their network." She snorted, "Oh lord… they really did just mess up big time."

I agreed, "They did, and I will MAKE them pay for it. They don't get to threaten the people I love. This is my stand… now it's time to show them they can't hunt me. T taught me about hiding in the wild. They don't train… I'm going to make them wish they'd never uttered the word hunt."

I added, "I need you to monitor everything. This clearly should've been done after my non-shift… or before now. Something is going to go down they don't want me to find out about… so… I need to find out." She snorted, "I'm not you, but I will do my best." I added, "It's weird they didn't mention Slade being my dad as why I didn't have to join."

She said, "Honestly, that's bullshit Melanie. You look nothing like the man and you've been around partial Hunters. I know the pack all thinks it's true, but deep down you know it's wrong. Just like you know so much is wrong here, you know it's wrong. You know who you are even if they tried to bury her deep down. I understand your denial and your identity crisis, but I'm firm in exactly who you are Melanie McAlister." Tears filled my eye and I nodded and we got back in the car. It was time to show the twisted members of Black Path who was really being hunted.

Thirst Traps

Alexander is Twenty One Years Old

Alexander was on a mission. I was waiting in the shadows, so I had a lot of time to think about all the shit that had gone down this year. Jason had nearly died. It took me and my mom to heal him. The Resistance saved him, and I nearly tried to get him to let Uncle Gunner look at his watch. He was so adamant it shorted, but I thought it was something else.

Thankfully, I'd taken a beat before I went to Uncle Gunner. Karina had come in with cookies, then Theo had popped in to chat and by the time we were done I knew it was nothing important and I was glad I hadn't wasted Uncle Gunner's time.

Laxenread was a huge thing for all of Faerie. If administered in time it could help prevent full blooded Fairy from dying. I knew because we'd used it. Mom had to heal them the rest of the way, but it was incredible.

I just couldn't figure out who was smart enough with Fairy blood to come up with it. Oden said, "Because we don't know them." I asked, "Then why the FUCK would they create a counteragent TO IRON POISONING with MY NAME!" He said, "I mean, our family's pictures are all over Faerie." He had a point.

I reasoned, "It seems like they know us though. It's a big fucking deal and they don't even want credit. Why? Why does our sniper think we will hate them?" We stalled when Goblins showed up. They were not supposed to be here.

My dad was practically holding on our bond so I knew he would know but he wouldn't act unless I pulled him. He was probably pacing with Uncle Bjourn based on the bond. The Goblin declared, "Princess Haley will be…." Shots were fired and all they died. But not six shots. Mother fucker!

I shouted, "We want to talk to you!" I ran towards where the shots came from. I yanked Uncle Logan to me. He was the closest person to my location. He opened a portal in a second. He shouted, "ALEXANDER!" I pointed, "Shots fired from this direction." He caught up to me and shoved me behind a tree.

He demanded, "Explain!" I said, "It's the Resistance!" He nodded and we started off again. We found the hide. I punched a tree. I yelled, "God damn it! They set up a FUCKING blind! They knew I was coming. Why doesn't our sniper come out with me?"

He answered, "I'm not a psychologist, but our sniper likely had a hand in creating or naming Laxenread. They are probably worried they'd mess up if they came out into the field with you." EJ linked me, "You've calmed down and didn't link me so WHAT THE FUCK?!" I demanded, "Pop to me."

My dad linked, "Are you ok?" I pulled him and Uncle Bjourn with my mom. She popped in and hugged me then Uncle Logan. EJ popped in right when Uncle Bjourn and dad came through a portal. My dad walked over and hugged me.

I said, "Goblins were talking about hurting mom. They didn't finish their sentence before the sniper that comes when I'm out fired." Uncle Bjourn sighed, "Then they likely already know the threat to Haley." I asked, "And we can't get a clue on what it is?" My dad growled, "Clearly not."

Mom said, "It's obviously not going to be a problem. If they thought they couldn't handle it, they'd tell us. They clearly want to give us every advantage they can." Dad growled, "How can you be so calm about this?" Mom replied, "Goblins have been trying to hurt or kill me since I was born. This is practically a boring ass day for me. It's tedious. They bore me and I'm not worried."

She inclined her head to Uncle Bjourn, "Bjourn has ALFUCKINGWAYS gone hard after Goblins because they are fucking dickheads about Astrid and my nephews. For reasons I cannot understand, and it irks me. I have studied them and have concluded they are just infuckingsane." I snorted.

She continued, "They would never get a threat past my brother. Not one. He has too many sources who are more than happy to deliver Goblin plots to him. It's asinine to believe they could. Between Bjourn and the Resistance whatever their plan was won't happen. I'm not worried and you shouldn't be either."

I agreed, "We should work on tracking it down though." My mom sent me her pride in the bond. EJ hummed. I said, "We should. Maybe we can track where their information came from that way." Uncle Bjourn agreed, "It's worth a shot."

I added, "Then maybe we can figure out how they knew I was going to be here. I didn't tell anyone, and it was only in my mission file as far as I know." My dad said, "It's in my email and your mothers." EJ said, "We would've detected a hack or break in."

Uncle Logan said, "It could be Alexander's sniper was scoping this place out." Except that was wrong. Mom asked, "What do your instincts say, son?" I answered, "That it's me. They are following me, but this hide says they were here when I got here. The question is how they figured out I'd have this mission. Or be in this area."

Mom asked, "And what are you doing here?" I sighed, "We had a lead on Ariena I was running down." She tilted her head. She said, "Then I would guess that is what the sniper that goes out with you was doing here. You are running leads down on her and they probably are too."

EJ asked, "Why would they care?" My mom stared at me. She answered, "Because Alexander cares. Someone who named Laxenread after him would probably know everything about everyone in his life. I would imagine they are hunting her too. Because they probably did know about the Goblin plot, I wasn't here. They were here because Alexander was."

I muttered, "You nor Ariena was here." I'd been waiting for three days. My mom popped and hugged me. She said, "We will get her." I snorted, "Or they will." She admitted, "That does seem like a very likely scenario." I stared at the blue circle.

I asked, "Do you think it annoyed the person who came up with the Ring Resistance that we called them the blue circle group when it's a ring and not a circle?" My dad laughed. My mom answered, "Yes, it probably did. They didn't bother to correct us until you asked about it though."

I snorted, "It seems really obvious now." Oden chuckled, "Mate would've figured it out." Melanie could probably solve all of this for us. I needed to call Jason and ask if he told her about the Hunters hurting him. He was experiencing nightmares and PTSD after it all. I think he'd feel better if he was honest with her about what happened, but as far as I knew they'd lied to her.

She'd come see him if he told her, and then this insanity would all stop. I hadn't heard his exact nightmares, but I knew she was in them. He thought she saved him, but that just told me someone with black hair was in the Resistance. Which was not super helpful.

Uncle Bjourn opened a portal and we went back through. Cassie jumped on me. I teased, "How's wedding planning going?" She snorted, "Fine. You were under fire." Cayden was right behind her. I corrected her, "No, the Goblins were under fire. I was present." She asked, "The Resistance?" I nodded.

She glanced at Cayden who stepped out with a phone to his ear. I had my own call to make after this debrief. Cassie hugged me and they all left. Uncle Bjourn sat behind his desk. I admitted, "Until the Goblins showed up it was boring." He chuckled, "I knew that from your feelings."

I asked, "Do you know the threat the Goblins were referring to?" He answered, "Yes, and I know that all that were involved were those that are now lying dead in that field." I asked, "Were you already moving on them?"

Spencer opened a portal and sat down. He said, "They took my kills." I snorted, "You seem upset about that." He lamented, "I had it all planned. I was LYING in wait for them. Then they took a stroll and got capped by the Resistance for being near you. I was all keyed up to kill and now there is no one for me to get that energy out on."

I disagreed, "There is often always someone that needs to be killed. If Uncle Bjourn doesn't have one Heath Scott does." Uncle Bjourn snorted and tossed a file down for Spencer. He snatched it up saying, "This is really best for everyone. You can't key up a Hackura to kill and not have him kill. That's literally madness."

Aunt Torvi knocked, “Bjourn, you…” She trailed off and clapped, “I knew I felt you in here, Spence! I thought I was crazy you’re not supposed to be here until tonight.” Spencer hugged her, “Hi momma. I’ll see you later.” She shouted, “Take Oligar with you. He just got back too.” He waved, “Sure thing.”

Aunt Torvi asked, “Am I interrupting?” I admitted, “Not really. There’s nothing to debrief. I was in a field for three days without my target then because of random Goblins I found out the Resistance was out there.” I paused then Oden growled.

I asked, “How are they doing that?! I didn’t smell or sense their presence! I should’ve heard a steady, consistent heartbeat.” Uncle Bjourn replied, “They have ways to block it out.” Aunt Torvi said, “Which will be very cool when we finally pin one down. Drake and Heather want to lock them in a lab with them and see what they will show them.”

I rolled my eyes. Oden growled, “I don’t like that. We can’t let them lock our sniper up.” Yeah, we didn’t like that our sniper wasn’t technically ours. I had a different one. Oden retorted, “She’s OUR sniper and that’s the end of that story.” Maverick popped in agitated.

I asked, “Mav?” He sighed, “I just feel keyed up. I was walking around town. This random Frost Giant was there but when I walked by he died of a heart attack. I was keyed up before that.” Uncle Bjourn asked, “A random heart attack?” He nodded.

I asked, “Isn’t that like the fourth person to randomly die of a heart attack near you? Because I’m thinking the Resistance might be more subtle than gunshots sometimes. They’ve upgraded to poison.” Maverick’s jaw dropped.

He asked, “Are you serious?” I replied, “You feel me. I am very serious.” Uncle Bjourn agreed, “That’s a big coincidence.” He called Uncle Gunner, “We need you in my office.” He showed up in seconds.

We explained my theory and he pulled cameras from the area. Maverick said, “No one touched his drink.” I pointed, “Right there. On the chair. Son of a bitch.” I opened a portal to where Maverick had been. I walked around the corner where they were already doing CPR on the Frost Giant.

Not that the humans would know what she was. She looked like a normal person right now. She could transform into her giant though. I conjured a hood and kept my head down and swiped her purse then got into an alley. I portaled back to Uncle Bjourn’s office.

I dumped the purse. Uncle Gunner said, “There was a smaller framed person that sat in that chair two hours prior. It’s subtle but watching the chair you can see them subtly place something there.” Uncle Bjourn said, “We are having someone get the chair.”

I snarled and yanked my parents to me. Mom popped them in half dressed. I threw pictures of Maverick over to my uncle’s desk. Dad snarled, “What the fuck is this?” I replied, “They were going to kidnap him.” I held up written instructions.

Uncle Bjourn answered his phone, “Evin, what did you find?” Uncle Evin said, “There’s nothing on the chair to suggest anything was here. No adhesion, nothing left behind, not a single fucking clue. I sent Brody to the hospital to bring the body to our realm. I’m going to see if I can collect the others from the locations Gunner sent. It might’ve been too long though.”

Uncle Bjourn snorted, “If they are gone get who took the bodies.” Uncle Evin agreed, “On that. Gunner, put something in there that I’m family.” He agreed, “Doing that.” Uncle Evin hung up. Mom asked, “What the fuck is going on?”

I said, “Maverick saw another person die from a heart attack near him and I found it odd.” Uncle Bjourn offered, “Poison is often a woman’s game.” Dad snorted, “How do you boys keep getting women obsessed with you?”

“They are also helpful. None of the women obsessed with me have ever even ONCE thought about being helpful. Yours kill people that are threats to you.” Mom agreed, “He’s right. The ones obsessed with him are the fucking worst even if they have damn good taste.” She popped and wrapped her arms around my dad’s neck and kissed him.

When she pulled back she said, “How our sons get women obsessed with them is an easy answer. Have you seen them? They look JUST like you. You’re all handsome. Honestly, this type of obsession is preferable." We all turned to look at her. She warned, "Don't give me that damn look. I far prefer the women who goes to every length to protect you than the psychotic fucking crazy one."

Uncle Gunner turned his computer around. There was split screen of the places where Maverick had seen those dying of heart attacks. We raised an eyebrow at the same person there placing something on a chair.

Mom ordered, "Play it forward." Other people sat in the chair but thirty minutes before Maverick showed up the people who sat down in that seat were the ones who died. I asked, "How the fuck did they target those people directly and not get every single damn person who sat in that chair?"

Dad answered, "They are really smart. Scarily so even. It's going to be some type of device." I asked, "Who the hell are these people?" Oden snorted, "Mate could go undercover with them." That was true. She was smart enough they'd want her in.

Mom asked, "What was that feeling son?" Everyone raised an eyebrow at me. I carefully said, "We know someone smart enough that could go in undercover trying to get into that group. They'd drool over the prospect a genius like her." Oden perked up, "And we could meet her then. It would be our mission." That was true.

Dad said, "They'd never agree." I shrugged, "Ask." Mom questioned, "Are we talking about the prank? Because I did suggest her involvement on creating Laxenread and you all acted like I was fucking crazy." Dad said, "She's living her dream." Mom groaned but dropped it.

I thought through everything while my dad worked on talking to Red Run. Uncle Bjourn asked, "What are you thinking?" I replied, "Maverick has had a sniper previously. This change was four months ago. Did someone new join the Resistance? Does he have a new person assigned to his threats? The only reason they would change their MO would be a different person is handling it."

Uncle Bjourn nodded, "I agree. It does sound like he got someone permanent. It must be someone our sniper trusts because you are the only person that appears to have a permanent person on you. Our sniper covers everyone else they can, otherwise it's sporadic on the coverage."

Mom agreed, "Someone probably proved they had a knack for figuring our threats against Mav. What do we have on these assholes that died?" Uncle Gunner admitted, "We were watching them. Whoever is on Maverick doesn't like anyone watching him. Today was not going to be the kidnapping attempt. They were observing him to see if he had a pattern."

Mom shrugged, "Like I said, I'll take this type of obsession over the crazy ass women. They are protecting my sons from harm with superior technology has me ready to conjure them the world. Maybe she'll end up being mated to Maverick then we could meet them."

Maverick snorted, "Nothing in the area smelled good." Oden commented, "They don't have a scent and he did feel weird." That was true but I wasn't going to get his hopes up in case it was wrong. Mom said, "Well, that's the type of woman or man I'd hope for my kids to find. Someone willing to go to any length to protect them." Dad agreed, "It is really helpful."

Caesar came in with files on the people who had died. Uncle Bjourn agreed, "We were aware of them, and they had plans to make moves, but this one just made a derogative comment about wishing Maverick dead." You have got to be fucking kidding me.

Mom snorted, "I love these people so much. Where are we at on the theory someone with Hackura blood is involved?" My head jolted over to hers, but I had to admit it made a lot of sense. Uncle Bjourn replied, "We cannot find anyone involved. Dad had a lead he went to handle personally."

She asked, "Where?" He answered, "He was talking to a Selkie source. They have nothing to do with it, but they have been helped by the Resistance." Mom pointed out, "This is someone who doesn't like disrespect. Particularly to Alexander, but anyone who is important to him as well."

Uncle Bjourn said, "Yes, the people who threaten Alexander die as well. One might say harshly." Mom rolled her eyes replying, "Then they are very busy, and our sniper never sleeps. Which isn't possible. Even Vampires sleep. All Supernatural's need time to rest."

I said, "There are periods of time where our sniper isn't around. What if they run themselves into the ground then sleep for a week." My mom sighed and I reached for our bond. I asked, "Why are your walls up?" My dad put a hand on her shoulder.

He answered, "Because she doesn't think you will like the theory she came up with." It was likely not a theory then since Mom studied people. I gently said, "Mom, it's ok. You can tell me. I probably won't like it, but I believe in you and your theories."

She rubbed her face, "I had Keaton confirm through an assessment, but it is more likely the times our sniper isn't around, it's due to injury. When she saved Everly and Julianna they smelled a salve." I asked, "Do we have anything on their missions where injuries occur?"

Uncle Bjourn commented, "You know the answer." I snarled, "Then who the fuck would hurt her?" Dad replied, "A lot of people would if they got ahold of her." I snorted, "But they don't know who she is. So, that doesn't really work as an explanation." Mom sighed, "It is possible that this group is operating from inside the Ring to some degree. The Ring could be who is hurting her."

Oden roared in anger, and I knew my eyes blazed. I said, "I'll be back. I'm taking a walk." I stormed out of the office as my mom sent me love. I sent the need to do something for this woman back to her. She agreed with that sentiment and my dad just sent me understanding.

I popped to the hill overlooking the castle. I conjured my phone and dialed the sniper's number. I got the beep for the message again. I said, "I am STILL worried about you. I need you to know if the Ring is hurting you, we will handle it."

I sighed, "I'd also like to know what type of poison your people are using to cause heart attacks. You somehow directed that at people who are after my brother. I don't know why you don't think I'll like you. I do like you. You're saving the people I love. Uncle Bjourn was aware of those threats to Maverick but you're taking them out before plans get too far."

I reasoned, "You know all about my Supernatural sides. You have to know that means something to every single part of me. I want to help you. Hell, we want to meet you. Please just let me protect you at least." The beep cutting me off signaled again.

I threw my phone, and it shattered on a tree. I snapped my fingers, and it was repaired. Hastein commented, "That has to be handy for your Beta." I snorted, "And you care because my Beta is our cousin." He hummed, "How often do you call that number?" I grumbled, "I'm sure you know."

He reasoned, "They might not check it." I asked, "Do you want to know how I know they do?" He answered, "Yes." I said, "The voicemail would be full if they didn't. They check it, listen to my messages, and then they don't reply."

He nudged me saying, "They just might answer some of the things you asked about." I snorted, "Probably not." He didn't agree. We sat there overlooking the Kingdom in silence for about an hour.

Kade portaled to us. He announced, "We are needed in Uncle Bjourn's office." I admitted, "I was going to shift and run." Hastein offered, "I'll go. If you're needed, we can pull you." I nodded to him and shifted into Oden. He could have control while I had time to think.

He took over and ran for thirty minutes before my dad and Hastein pulled me. I shifted back, snapped myself clothes, and popped to Uncle Bjourn's office. I asked, "Where did mom go?" Dad answered, "She's with your Uncle Benjamin questioning people with Blade and Javi faded back."

I asked, "Questioning people about what?" The showed me a black and white box. Oden purred, "It's the color of me." Well, that was true but so were Oreos. He snorted at me, The Oreo BOX is not black and white just the Oreo themselves." True.

I lifted the lid and tilted my head. Hastein chimed in, "I told you they might answer some of your questions." I lifted up a mini jar with small needle like devices attached to some type of adhesive. The one I had was labeled Goblins. I glanced over at Hastein and he nodded.

Uncle Bjourn said, "The Frost Giant's body basically turned to Lava on the inside. Marcus is currently studying it." My eyes widened. Oden said, "That's smart." I said, "They used their cold temperature against them by burning them alive from the inside out." It wasn't a question, it was what they did.

Grandpa Titus joined us and looked at them. I asked, "Where did the box come from?" Dad answered, "It was placed over our border with a card on it for your mother." I snorted, "She's going to use that and say they are hers."

Uncle Bjourn agreed, "She will and I think the Resistance knows that." I glanced at all the doses in the box. Uncle Marcus portaled in with Aunt Katie and Uncle Logan. She announced, "There's a spell, a very powerful one, on those. The humans obviously would not see someone insides turned to Lava. They see a heart attack."

Uncle Evin came in reporting, "There was one body that hadn't been there long enough to be claimed yet. Gunner's fabrication I was family let me pull the Warlock's body here." Dad groaned, "Of course it's a Warlock." Mom would go off about that.

Uncle Evin replied, "The other bodies were claimed by research facilities after so long." I asked, "Will the spell hold?" Uncle Evin chuckled, "I'm not done. It's a Supernatural facility but they never got the bodies. Nor did they know they existed."

Pride filled me for some strange reason. The Resistance really had a way of getting around red tape. He added, "I did get everyone's personal affects." He tossed them down and we searched through them. Their phones were missing, which told me the Resistance took them.

I admitted, "I think it's weird the Resistance left the pictures of Maverick." Aunt Katie said, "Because there is a spell on that picture. It alters someone's face so humans wouldn't see Maverick." I pulled Brenton to me. He came through in a second.

I handed him the pictures, "Go ask Caius's mom what she sees in those pictures." He nodded and left. When he returned, he said, "She sees four different people. One young guy, one older, and two middle-aged men."

I asked, "Seriously, how powerful are these guys? We already knew the Witch working with them was. Can we tell if it's a coven or one person?" Aunt Katie said, "Me, Dustin, Ryan, and Charlie Rose all believe it's the same person. The magic feels the same."

I asked, "Who is this strong?" She shrugged, "I don't know but we all want to meet them." I snorted, "We want to meet a lot of people we can't meet. This is such a strange feeling. Normally, I'm annoyed about people wanting to meet me. Now, I'm irritated people don't want to me meet me."

Oden whined in my head because it was us. Maybe without us as a factor, they would meet someone. Dad replied, "No, Alexander. Without you, they wouldn't even talk to us. Hastein told us about your call. We have this box because of you." Oden told me, "That's true."

Phil portaled in. He looked around saying, "This looks fun. I clearly need to get caught up, which the bond told me. How Beta's survive without a bond with their Alpha like I have with my cousin, I just don't know. It makes NO sense to me."

I asked, "What's going on?" He hummed, "I kind of don't want to tell you but I'm going to." I snorted, "So, you have more good news?" Dad offered, "Everything we've learned today is good news." I muttered, "It's super great that my voicemails are being listened to, and they will answer my questions if they want. Yet they will not call me back."

Phil winced, "Oh good. This will cheer you right up then. Female Lead Warrior Ashley Griffen is putting on workshops for smaller packs and their Warriors." Hope filled me. I reasoned, "That's great! We can see if she'd come…" He made a face and I trailed off.

I surmised, "You already asked her about it." He said, "My source in Nashville said it's only a few packs but I looked up the criteria. Neither us nor our allies meet them, we are too big. Also, our defenses are too good." Oden muttered annoyed in my head, "Why is everything good always a deterrent with this group that doesn't want to meet us?"

I actually saw a bright side here. I waved, "This is good. She's just starting out. When you start something like workshops they grow naturally. She can get this going and then we can offer to host or something. Or do a joint workshop. That can actually work for us."

He admitted, "Ok, you took that better than thought. What's going on here?" We caught him up and he whistled. He nudged me, "You have squadron practice." I portaled out ready to run. Phil came with me. I asked, "What are you doing?" He said, "Someone has to get film for your social media. You do the workouts and instructional videos. I do all the other posts with footage I get."

I told him, "We are working on cardio today." He clapped, "Great! You don't have a program for cardio out yet. So, we can get the footage, and you can put out the plan. I'll promote with the footage, and we will get more money while helping people. Everyone wins."

I went over to my squadron. I told them, "Don't mind Phil filming." He shouted, "They literally never do." One of my men smirked. I asked, "What was that smirk for, Kolton?" He said, "Well, the whole realm watches your workout videos. We have been in some of them and the result is awesome."

They all nodded. I snorted, "So you guys are swimming in pussy and dick from the workout videos." Kolton winked, "So much." I shook my head but smiled. I ordered, "Let's run." I put them through their paces. I had an obstacle course out too, but we kept moving the whole time.

Phil came over, "I got great stuff." Nadia shouted, "Please post the thirst traps you have from all the sweating." I asked, "The what?" Phil waved, "Nothing for you to worry about. I post what I post, and I get a lot of engagement. Leave it me." I looked at all of them but shrugged.

I walked away but heard Nadia talking to Phil. She said, "The one where you see Alexander with the guys in the background jump roping would be good with a music background. Then you could have another one with the women of the group doing…" I popped back and she stopped talking.

I said, "Phil, we should hire her." He asked, "Huh?" I said, "She can help you free up some time. She can edit the posts together and you can approve them. That way you're not going through hours of film." He gaped at me. I asked, "What?"

He smacked my arm, "I told you we needed to hire someone, and you said we were doing fine." I shrugged, "I didn't realize how much time you were spending on it. Hire Nadia to manage…" I trailed off. Phil snorted, "You don't even know what to call it." I winked, "But you do." He prodded, "And if Nadia has a job?" I said, "I know what her job is. Steal her away with a good offer."

I turned to her, "You don't have to take the job if the offer isn't competitive. There's no retaliation here and Phil can find other candidates." She admitted, "I'm kind of pigeon holed at my job now. It's not a challenge anymore. This could be fun." Phil threw her arm around her, "Let's talk details." They left.

I walked into Cayden's office. He glanced up, "I hear you've had a morning." I asked, "What the fuck is a thirst trap?" Now, I had his full attention. He dropped his pen and sat back in his chair. He admitted, "I don't know, but I asked your sister and she's laughing hysterically." I nodded and popped to her.

She was sitting with Aiylee and Beagan cackling. I asked, "What's so funny?" Beagan managed to answer first, "Cayden didn't know what a thirst trap was." Cassie's eyes jolted to mine. She screamed, "Oh my god he asked for you! You felt annoyed in the bond and like you didn't want to tell us! IT WAS YOU!"

I reasoned, "Cayden doesn't know either." Aiylee popped over to me and showed me a clip on her phone. I said, "Phil had me do that push up deal for a video." Beagan said, "It's a challenge." I asked, "What challenge? It was quite easy." Aiylee explained, "It's the Sea Shanty push-up challenge. Your video went viral."

I asked, "Huh?" Cassie groaned, "No, stop it right now." Beagan cackled, "Your belt flick when lifting is really popular too." I asked, "What the fuck are you talking about?" Aiylee snickered and showed me a video flicking my weight belt off after I dead lift. Then there was a woman staring at the screen and licking her lips.

I asked, "What the fuck? Those were different workout days." Beagan hummed, "Yes, it's popular in this realm. The belt click to the music is…" She kissed her fingertips." Cassie groaned, "No. We are all related to him." Beagan snorted, "I made JP do his own video. Alexander's videos are such good challenges for the men here and make those of us who like men swim in the thirst trap content. I appreciate my cousin for that."

I snorted, "It's Phil doing that, apparently." Aiylee hummed, "We know." I muttered, "I can't believe Dylan Frost hasn't told me about this." I popped to him, and he squealed, "My show has come to me. I asked, "Why the fuck haven't you told me about thirst traps."

He gasped dramatically, "SOMEONE TOLD YOU ABOUT PHIL'S VIDEOS! NOOOOOO! I had the perfect moment to tell you about the REALMS thirsting after you! You were going to blush, and it was going to be glorious! I was going to film it and post it and go viral. How dare someone take this moment from me!"

I asked, “Is my dad in these? I work out with him too.” He snickered, “Don’t you take that from me! Just imagine your mom’s reaction.” I groaned, “Mom doesn’t know?” He winked, “Maybe your dad has a thirst trap account.”

I linked my dad, “Do you know what a thirst trap is?” He answered, “Something about being thirsty. Is that a business we want to buy or run for people to get drinks? Is it a bar?” That was worse than me and Cayden. I told him, “You should link Cassie you think a thirst trap is a bar.” He felt like that was a trap but my bond with my sister told me he had said that her.

She linked me, “I AM NOT EXPLAINING THIRST TRAPS TO DAD! Did you tell him it was a bar?” I replied, “No, I asked what he thought it was. He came up with the bar all by himself.” She linked me back laughing.

Dylan grumbled, “How rude you are Mini Moody. No private links.” I explained, “I asked my dad if he knew about thirst traps. He thought it was a bar.” Dylan threw his head back and howled with laughter. I said, “So, I know he doesn’t know his content is a thirst trap.”

Dylan snorted, “Please. He doesn’t know the account exists. I run it and I hired someone to film content for it. I piece it together and post it. I’ve gotten him to do challenges he has NO IDEA about.” I asked, “Are you in this with Phil? Because apparently, I do them too.” He winked, “I know. You guys have gone viral so much. The comments are VERY thirsty for you and your dad.”

I asked, “Huh?” He winked, “I post some of you together. Phil and I do joint videos sometimes.” I gaped at him. I asked, “Are you trying to piss my mom off?” He snorted, “Never. I am making you all money. I simply sell the equipment you use and profit that way.” I rubbed my temples.

He warned, “Don’t you take my thirst trap moment with SGAP from me.” I snorted, “I wouldn’t dream of it, but he’s probably going to open a bar named Thirst Trap.” Dylan squealed, “It’s brilliant! They could just play videos from content creators. You could have them come in too. If you showed up it would be crazy!” I shook my head and popped away from him.

Oden told me, “He’s very excited about it.” I opened my personal Instagram. It was private and I barely posted on it. I found my business one and stared at the content. Oden purred, “What if mate watches?” That gave me an idea.

I called Uncle Gunner. He answered, “Hey, Alexander. Do you have another killer for me to run down?” I snorted, “No, I want to know who the top viewers on my work Instagram account are.” He laughed, “Why?” I muttered, “Reasons.” He snorted, “Alright. I’ll get that quickly.” He hung up.

I got a workout in and for the first time, I noted the cameras set up. I didn’t know if they were Dylan’s or Phil’s. Oden offered, “There have to be other pack members that get in on this too. Fang said it makes a lot of money with sponsorships and stuff.” I rolled my eyes.

I went at the heavy bag until my phone rang. I answered, “Uncle Gunner.” He was laughing. I asked, “What?” He said, “Your top accounts that react and view your videos never comment on them. They also tried to cover their tracks.” I asked, “Huh?”

He chuckled, “Your top viewers are Melanie McAlister and Ashley Griffen. Ashley has nine different accounts that view yours under different names.” I asked, “Melanie watches them?” He hummed, “Repeatedly. It’s odd she doesn’t post on her account anymore, but she logs in to view your content and Jason’s.” I asked, “What about T’s?”

Gunner replied, “Tristan doesn’t have an account and Jason’s is for one of his businesses. He doesn’t have a personal one for her to follow. Melanie used to post her friends and dance competitions. She posted several dancing videos that are still popular, but she doesn’t anymore.”

I muttered, “She’s busy living her dream.” Ugh. I asked, “What does Ashley post?” He answered, “Nothing. She just has the accounts.” I asked, “Can you send me the videos Melanie has watched the most?” He replied, “I already did.” He was laughing as he hung up.

I went into my office and viewed her most watched videos. One was of me running my hands over my sweaty stomach in slow motion. If she hadn’t watched this so much, I’d kill my Beta for posting it. Gage came in and groaned. He said, “I warned Phil not to post that one.”

I waved, “It’s fine.” He looked suspicious he asked, “Why?” I shrugged and he came around and looked at my screen. He laughed, “I see. Melanie watched the video, so you don’t care.” She’d watched the weight belt videos and the jump rope ones too. She watched the weight belt click videos the most out of those two. Who knew taking a weight belt off on different days set to music together would get her attention.

I snorted, "Phil told me to mess around with the jump rope." Gage said, "Well, she watched it." Those videos were what she watched most but she also watched the serious work out ones where I hit a new weight lifting goal.

I told Gage, "Tell Phil to keep posting the content she likes to watch." He snorted, "I can do that." I called Uncle Gunner back. He laughed, "What now?" I asked, "Does Melanie watch any other accounts that posts content like this?"

He snorted, "One might find it strange that question came to you. I happened to dig into it. Yours and Jason's business accounts are literally all she views on that account." He paused then added, "You didn't ask but you are also all Ashley Griffen views." That made me feel things I did not understand.

I instructed, "Keep this between us." He agreed, "Of course." He was good at keeping confidences. I hung up. Oden preened, "Mate likes our videos. Mate thinks we are hot." That was highly likely. Gage warned, "Your cheeks are going to hurt from smiling that wide." I said, "She watches my videos."

He winked, "That you had nothing to do with." I gasped, "I did too! I'm in them." He reasoned, "But Phil edited and created them." I agreed, "You're right. We need to something for Phil." He shrugged, "Ask Aria who his mate is." I clapped him on the shoulder, "Be right back."

I popped to my cousin. Aria greeted, "Hello, Alexander." I hugged her, "I was wondering if you know who Phil's mate is." She scrunched up her face then shook her head, "No, but I sense she's a busy woman maybe…" She trailed off.

I asked, "Maybe what?" She told me, "It's silly." I kissed her head, "Nothing you think is silly." She said, "It's probably nothing. I do know his mate is a Werewolf." I winked, "Handy. Thank you." I popped back to my office.

I told Gage, "She doesn't know." He snapped his fingers, "Damn." We worked on a different surprise. Phil came into my office announcing, "Here is your schedule for tomorrow and…" He trailed off, "What's that face you're making? You feel very happy in the bond."

I turned my screen around revealing the video of my sweaty abs in the frame in slow motion. He said, "Ok, this is getting weirder. Gage and I both thought you'd be pissed if you saw that, but you seem happy. Gage is nearing a conniption fit with his silent laughing. Why aren't you mad?"

I turned around my other monitor. He shouted, "God damn! I am a GENIUS! People say Melanie is but it's me. Also, you might be right about Ashley agreeing to a joint workshop later. She's watching your workout videos. More importantly, Melanie is."

I hummed, "Yes. She likes the jump rope and weight belt content. So, keep doing things like that." He laughed, "She'll love the content Nadia is putting together." I asked, "That worked out? You hired her?" He nodded, "Yes, and it is going to free up my time. I'll just go ahead and have Gunner set up something for me to monitor her favorites and have Nadia create that content."

I nodded, "Yes, do that." He warned, "Then you'll have to cooperate with Nadia if she has you do challenges." I shrugged, "Fine. Are you aware that Dylan has a thirst trap account for my dad? I assume you are since he mentioned doing joint videos."

He hummed, "I am aware." I asked, "Is your grandpa?" He snorted, "Grandpa Caleb? No. Grandpa Zader of course. He has his own account. It's also popular." I groaned, "Good god. What is going on right now?" He winked, "Our family is hot. Supernatural's are in general so get used to it."

They left and I cleared my monitors and found my dad's account. I pulled my mom to me. She came in her underwear and bra. I snorted, "So, dad will be hunting you down." She winked, "Won't that be fun? What's going on?" I asked, "Are you aware of this account?"

She fanned her face, "It's so good, right?" I blinked asking, "You know about it?" She snorted, "Harper's boytoy lover alerted me when Dylan created it." I asked, "Are you aware dad doesn't know about it?"

She frowned, "There are cameras filming his workouts and he does these challenges. He definitely fucking knows." I asked, "Are you sure? Because he doesn't know what thirst traps are." I felt her utter confusion as she stared at me. She questioned, "You're saying there people out there trapping those who are thirsty?" I bit my lip so I wouldn't laugh.

I explained, "These videos are called thirst traps." She hummed, "They are called fucking challenges and workout videos." I agreed, "That they are. Dylan plans to tell dad about it someday." She raised an eyebrow and I winked.

I teased, "I do that better." She agreed, "You all do but your dad definitely knows about this. There is literally no way he doesn't." She kissed me on the cheek. She told me, "I love you for being concerned about me and my feelings. You are an amazing man and I'm very proud of you. Your mate will be incredible."

I snorted, "Thanks, mom." She said, "I am very serious. I know your mate will be an amazing woman with a kind heart." She paused adding, "Always follow your heart, Alexander. Yours is so big and open to all. Never lose that." She squeezed my arm.

She added, "Oh, and if you ever need an ego boost read the comments on your posts. I personally stopped since you are my son and the comments on your dad's account had me tracking a few down and beating the ever loving fuck out of them. As the person in the videos who is single, you might enjoy reading them." I snorted, "I'm good." Melanie didn't comment so I didn't care.

Her words got me thinking though. I popped to Uncle Gunner. He chuckled greeting, "Hello." I asked, "Have any of my other top viewers been beat up?" He hummed, "You mean like your dad's?" I nodded. He pulled up some runs and we both blinked.

A few went to jail and some were beat up. He laughed, "Well, Ashley or Melanie might have done that. It looks like the ones in jail were previously under investigation for different things. A few I'll put on my own watch list if they get out. They were stalking people so badly even the human authorities put them in jail."

Oden purred, "I bet mate is watching out for us." I asked, "Would it be hard to see these people in the comments?" He snorted, "No, these are their comments." He put them up and I blinked. I said, "Wow." They were deeply concerning and clearly unhinged.

He put up other comments explaining, "These are the normal thirsty comments." I looked at them and laughed, "Those are amusing." Mom was right it was an ego boost. He said, "I'll run a program on all the accounts now."

He clapped me on the back, "Thanks, Alexander. You alerted me to a potential security threat. It's safer on our realm's social media accounts, so I wasn't really thinking about monitoring such things on the human ones."

I asked, "Do you monitor the ones in Faerie?" He said, "Yes. Aiden has killed a few people that way because I pass them off to him directly sometimes. Others I go to Bjourn." Aunt Calista came skipping in. She winked, "I have things set up in our sanctuary, so you have to stop working." He laughed, "Let me go verbally tell Bjourn about a report I'll be running then I'll be there." He portaled away.

Aunt Calista's kissed my cheek. She asked, "How are you? I heard that you found out about your thirst traps. All my friends talk about them." I asked, "Does it bother you?" She snorted, "Of course not. I'm aware that my nephew is attractive. All of you are. As long as it's kept out of the realm of being disrespectful, I can hardly blame them for having eyes. Plus, Harper does some of those challenges for me."

She winked adding, "Then Gunner does them with him." I laughed, "As long as everyone is happy." She hugged me tightly then whispered, "Your mate is coming." I replied, "I know." She was about to say something when Uncle Logan walked in. She waved to us both then portaled out.

I warned, "If you're looking for Uncle Gunner, he's not here or coming back. Aunt Cali had a thing set up." He replied, "I'm not. Your mom pushed all her feelings at me to come find you and linked I'd better not ignore her."

I questioned, "Why?" He opened a portal to one of his favorite places. I walked through with him. He said, "I came here a lot to look out over the cliffs wondering where my mate was. At one point all my siblings, even your mom, were mated. She never expected to be, and in truth I thought my dad would have to tell her he arranged the marriage to your dad."

He chuckled, "Your dad was who we wanted for her, and she adamantly believed she would not get a mate. It annoyed us all. I won't lie, I thought I'd have my mate before she had hers. I was so happy for her, but it hurts being of age and not finding yours."

I snorted, "Yeah, it does." He said, "A lot of people seem to know things about your thoughts on your mate. I won't push you to talk about that, but waiting is difficult. We are patient people, but when you are surrounded by the type of love that you crave yourself the lonely nights are hard."

He paused then added, "You know, your mate isn't going to be upset if you have sex with other people." Oden growled, "No. We know it's her!" I told him, "I can't. It's not that I don't find women attractive. I know people talk about me being asexual but I'm not."

He replied, "I know." I admitted, "It would feel like cheating to me and Oden. He would probably take over and I couldn't go through with it. I was kissed when I was as tipsy as I could get, and I still feel bad about it to this day. I feel like I let her down."

He offered, "That's not even remotely true." I sighed, "I just want to be with her." He put a hand on my shoulder, "Then that's what you'll do and fuck all the noise. If anyone makes you uncomfortable, you let me know and I'll take care of it."

I snorted, "I don't need people to die for thinking I'm asexual." He winked, "No, but I could set my wife and kids loose on them. They enjoy cursing or hexing people. Maximus might just start a few fires." I threw my head back and laughed. He added, "You feel free to use this spot anytime you want." He hugged me and left.

I pulled out my phone and found Melanie's account. Uncle Gunner said it was private, but I could see her content. He must have done something techy so I could see it. I watched all her videos. Oden purred, "She's a beautiful dancer." He was right.

I was a little sad she hadn't posted any content since she'd left. Something prickled at the base of my spine, that it was weird. I checked how regularly she used to post. I checked her comments and saw people asking where she was. They wondered if she was ok. She hadn't replied but she clearly was on the account because she viewed my stuff.

I popped home ready to have someone look into this. I spotted Karina's cookies on a platter in the main room and ate a few. I sighed and sat down. I told Oden, "I'm seeing connections where there are none. So, she doesn't want to post. I was ready to launch an investigation into her social media activity. What is wrong with us?"

He reasoned, "It's normal to be worried about our mate. We calmed down but I agreed with you or I would've said something." Theo came and sat down by me a grabbed a cookie. He asked, "So, what's up?" I snorted, "Are you aware I'm a popular thirst trap with dad?" He spit out his cookie.

He asked, "I'm sorry, what?!" I showed him my account and dad's. He threw his head back and laughed. He admitted, "I've seen these videos with dad because I've caught mom watching them. I thought she made them for herself. This is too good." He handed me my phone and popped out.

Angela and TJ popped next to me. Both ate cookies. I asked, "Are you guys ok? You had this sense of urgency but now you don't." Angela snorted, "It's silly." I asked, "How does dad react to finding out he's lusted after by the internet?" She snorted, "He knows but he's letting Dylan think he doesn't."

I asked, "Does he tell Dylan he knows?" She grinned, "No, that's no fun! Dad likes to say he never had fun until us but he's always giving Dylan the reaction he wants." I snorted, "So, he yells at Dylan and acts like he didn't know." Angela winked at me.

She shrugged, "It's their dynamic. It's pretty funny and it happens at a picnic. Everyone laughs." I asked, "Does Dylan know that dad does actually know about this account?" She hummed, "I think he doesn't want to know to be honest." I laughed, "Good to know."

She muttered, "Thanks for actually asking." I told her, "You don't need to take on the weight of the world just yet, little one. We may not ask because we want you to be able to be little as long as you can. The weight of your power and our name will come, but there is no need to rush into that destiny before you have to."

She made a face, "EJ went to a meeting that was a trap without asking me and it hurts my feelings." I admitted, "I could easily see why that would hurt your feelings. You need to talk to him about it again. He thinks it's all settled but it still hurts you."

She grumbled, "I'd help you find Ariena if she wasn't blurry too." I ruffled her hair saying, "I know you'd help if you could. I'll get her. Do you have any advice on her?" She said, "I think she's going to get hurt, but she's around later. It just looks like if she gets hurt, she goes dark for a few years."

I asked, "Hurt how?" She groaned, "It's blurry but I think it's the Resistance." Which would make sense if they were following me around. I nodded to her and hugged TJ. He was quiet but I could understand that. People said it about me as well.

I asked, "How's training with Breanna going, TJ?" He answered, "Good. Dad insists it's done here but that doesn't feel fair to Breanna." I offered a solution, "Maybe ask if Faerie is a reasonable alternative to taking turns and being in the Vampire's mansion. That way after your practice there, you'd both be happy visiting Uncle Aiden and Aunt Lucinda."

He grinned at me, "I'll ask. I like that. I feel bad she's always coming here." I assured him, "You know she doesn't mind. She loves coming here, but training in Faerie would be good for you both." He hugged me and they popped out.

I linked Uncle Bjourn, "Are you awake?" He answered, "I am." I popped to him. He was drinking whiskey in the main area of his wing. I conjured myself a drink. I sat down then said, "Angela thinks Ariena is going to get hurt. I'm guessing the Resistance has a hand it. Maybe we can monitor chatter for her." He nodded, "Of course we can. We do but we can focus on her getting injured." I nodded.

He added, "I know that's why you're not here. I would know without a bond, but I do have one." I asked, "Where is Aunt Astrid?" He answered, "She's with Kashe. I'll join her with Dawson later." I admitted, "Melanie watches my Instagram videos, and I really like that." He snorted, "If I was you, I would like that too."

I snorted, "I nearly launched an investigation into her social media activity." He shrugged, "You did to a degree if you know she's watching your videos." I admitted, "I had Uncle Gunner find the accounts that viewed my business accounts videos the most."

He laughed, "What videos does she watch?" I showed him and he winked, "I guess we will see more content like that." I told him, "Phil hired Nadia today and I did mention it to him." He laughed, "I do believe Phil has been worried about your reaction to those types of videos."

I snorted, "Yet he made them anyway." He replied, "He's doing a good job of getting your content out there. A lot of those that watch them engage on your workout videos. They are a really good thing for the Supernatural Community. I'm really proud of you." I didn't know that I would go that far.

Oden said, "It is a good thing because mate watches." That I could agree with. I would post all that type of content to engage with my mate in any way. I asked, "Does it make me weird that I enjoy getting some type of interaction with her? I didn't post the content or film it."

Oden growled, "We ARE the content." Uncle Bjourn snorted, "You are the featured person in the content. Phil has a clear talent for the editing and all that. You're the star of it though. He doesn't have something like this to post without you. She's not complimenting the editing. She's watching you."

He admitted, "I would be peacock proud knowing Astrid was the person viewing my content if I was doing this. Maybe I'll get one of my kids on it." I laughed, "I'm sure you're featured on dad's. You work out in our gym and the cameras are set up here too."

He shook his head. He muttered, "I doubt it." I reasoned, "Aunt Astrid would know. Or you are on Uncle's Zader's." He threw his head back and laughed. He said, "I'm sure my cousins are on that. So far, your Grandpa Titus hasn't gotten into it." I prodded, "But?"

He grinned, "Uncle Zader is trying to get him to do it. Uncle Lief is too. He's popular as well and dad has been in his videos. People want Uncle Lief to tag his account." I pointed out, "He doesn't have one." He laughed, "Yet."

I shrugged, "They should get Grammy Veronica on their side. Then he'd do it." He chuckled, "That would be the way to do it." I felt the bond. I said, "You're not going to create an account." He said, "As the King of this realm, I could do our social media but not in the human realm."

I asked, "Are we putting our family at risk with these accounts?" I'd shut them down if they were. He answered, "No, you are a public figure in the human realm. If it was a danger, I'd have talked to everyone. It's not a big deal, it's just not something I can do right now. Your Grandpa could since he's no longer King." I laughed, "I can't believe our family has somehow morphed into a bunch of thirst trap content creators."

He admitted, "I would not have guessed that either. The point remains, it's not a problem to be excited that your mate likes you showing off." I snorted, "I wasn't showing off." He smiled "Which makes it better. She's interested in watching you." Oden purred.

I told him, "I'll let you get to your evening." I hugged him and snapped myself more whiskey. His phone dinged. He said, "Your new content just dropped." I asked, "You have my account on an alert?" He answered, "Of course I do. You are my nephew, and I love you." I hugged him again and he left.

I opened the video of me and my men jump roping that cut to the women slow motion jumping over the cones then back to us on the rope. The song was catchy too. I liked it. Oden asked, "Do you think mate already saw it?"

I popped back to my Uncle Gunner's office. He had my account activity up and monitored. I saw Melanie's name. She watched it the second it posted, and Ashley watched it after her. Oden said, "That makes me happier than I can explain."

I agreed smiling as I watching my own damn video again watching how many times Melanie was watching it in real time. Oden purred, "She has notifications turned on for our account." That was the only way she would've been able to see it.

I wondered if she'd ever comment. Oden excitedly shouted, "She could talk to us! That would be great! Mate would talk to us again!" I wished she'd text me again like she had that one time. I would take any scraps from her.

Oden reasoned, "This is scraps. She's engaged with our content and no one else's besides Ajax." That was Jason's wolf. I pulled up the videos she'd watched the most again. I could do more things like that. Oden snorted, "Rocket edited us in slow motion. Mate likes it." Yeah, she clearly did. I could work with that.

I clicked back on her page wishing there were more recent videos. I popped to my room and pulled up my computer to watch her dance. I watched her one from four months ago. It was a dance that was filled with so many emotions. She really connected with the music.

There was anger, despondency, hopelessness, but it ended with resolution. Her determined moves that felt like she was owning the room she was dancing in. Oden grumbled, "Why doesn't she ever dance in a room with mirrors?"

I snorted, "I don't know why she doesn't ever film her dances outside. Jase says she did her best choreography there. Inside, she's always sad and angry." There had been a gap in the videos after she turned sixteen.

It was like she got her wolf and stopped dancing. I rolled my eyes at myself saying, "She was just busy running and getting to know Ember." That's the only thing it could have been even if the McAlister's found it weird too.

The conclusion we came to was that she was just enjoying being a wolf and everything was fine. It clearly was since she was back to dancing regularly now. Everything was fine and she was interested in my content. Now, I could gear it towards getting her to comment.

Walking Around Broken Hearted

Melanie is Seventeen Years Old

Melanie was dreaming. The fact that I knew it was dream, didn't help keep me from remembering my dramatic return to Black Path's territory to be hunted. I heard Trevor mocking me, "We're after that bitch now. It's the hunt to end all hunts. The wolf less Melanie McAlister is on the run and hiding from us. I can't wait to kick her ass." Please. He wishes he could.

Mark groaned, "You've never been able to kick her ass. You've only been able to hurt her when she lets you." Trevor yelled, "DUDE! Shut up! I'm recording us because people want to see Swiffer's takedown. We brought in extra people to take her down. It's like fifty on one." Like I didn't already know that. He was pathetic.

Francis mumbled, "There's more. You can't count, and I still don't like our odds. That look in her eyes was like she was taunting us and saying she'd take no prisoners." That was true. I wasn't. I was going for blood. Which they'd find out soon, because they were about to run into the group I'd left unconscious on the lawn.

Trevor spotted them first and yelled, "YOU FUCKING BITCH! When we find you, I'll give you the beating of your life! Maybe I'll carve a new word on your back." I shivered and nearly gave myself away from anger.

Caine linked, "Tell me you're hiding well. Because I was just linked you left bodies on the front lawn." I replied, "They are alive… so… bodies… is a word. Probably the wrong one, because that implies they are dead. They aren't… they are unconscious. There is a difference."

He snorted, "You're doing great." I knew he was still worried. They all were, but I was doing this my way. I told him, "You should know by now, I play to win…so…they are going down so hard. This is a barbaric and wholly illegal thing that will NEVER happen when I'm through with them." He said, "Just stay safe." Safe wasn't something I was anymore.

Someone shook me awake. I gasped and startled staring at Hendrick. I apologized, "I'm sorry. Was I screaming?" He replied, "You were tossing and turning and muttering about killing people. I just wanted to make sure you are ok."

I answered, "Peachy… well…" He snorted, "I know that's a lie. Was it about finding your brother with Hunters or the Hunt?" I answered, "The Hunt." I still shivered thinking about finding out a Hunter group had my brother.

I only thought about that in my dreams, so I shoved it from my head. I got up slowly and Hendrick sighed, "I wish you wouldn't let them hurt you." I shrugged, "I'm going to run to the diner. I've got some stuff to work on." He just tilted his head knowing arguing wasn't going to do anything for him.

I got dressed and found Hendrick waiting in his car. He gestured me over. I asked, "What's up?" He said, "Let's compromise. You ride with me and run back." I'd planned to run both ways, but this would make everyone happy, so I nodded. He sighed in relief.

He drove us to the diner where I was immediately under scrutiny. I sighed knowing it was because I'd been punished a few days ago. I sat down in my booth and pulled out my laptop. I started checking all my programs.

Addison said, "You don't have to be on twenty-four seven, Ash." We were in public, so they often referred to me by Ashley because they weren't allowed to say Melanie. My brother and old Alpha, actually the whole pack, didn't want to hear about me.

Honestly, that hurt worse because when I lived in Red Run we never heard things about Nashville, which was where they sent me. So why did they think they'd hear my name? if I had a wolf, she'd probably point out the entire Werewolf community was talking about Ashley Griffen so they would've heard my name if they didn't make me change it. I shoved that aside.

I reasoned, "I was not on for two days." Caine snorted, "Recovering from a beating doesn't really count as being off. I still don't understand how that Alpha got a single hit on you. He came to our training, and I beat him. You train me." I'd fought in the Undergrounds before I got punished.

The workshops I put on helped a lot of future leadership get training they were denied. That Alpha's son was forced to fight in the Undergrounds because he refused to be a bad person, and it irked me. A lot. He hated it and it wasn't right.

I picked at my sleeve saying, "You have Alpha blood… And… well I don't… which you know… so.. how he got a hit…is answered with his blood." Caine told me, "That's bullshit, Ash. You taught me and I can't beat you yet. Also, you can't lie for shit, so stop." I immediately countered, "You're getting so much better though!"

Caine leaned forward, "I know. Dax and I both are. My point is unless you let him, that Alpha couldn't have hurt you." I shrugged and looked away. Caine instructed, "Give us a second here, Addison." She nodded and went to the back.

I told him, "I'm fine." Caine retorted, "Being fine isn't letting people beat the shit out of you because your shit piece of brother and old Alpha told you to do so." I frowned, "I mean… Beta Jason isn't a bad brother… we have really good memories for fourteen years and…"

Caine interrupted, "It doesn't matter. When you needed him, he abandoned you and let you think you deserve all the punishments you get down here. When in reality he has no idea how our pack runs or does anything. He doesn't know what he's asking for."

He paused adding, "In my opinion, that doesn't matter much. You're his little sister and he should protect you. You're letting people beat you up before you win." I picked at my sleeve again. I muttered, "I didn't say that…"

Caine whispered, "You didn't have to. I have half a mind to just tell Cayden you're fighting in the Undergrounds." I gasped and looked up, "You can't! They… it could mess up everything." Caine frowned, "You seem to think I care about messing up everything and I don't. I care about you. I care about my mom, sister, friends and pack."

"My wolf and I are protective of you, Mel. I'm getting closer to being ready to challenge my dad. I want to make you my Gamma when that happens, but I can't have you letting yourself be beaten to a pulp. I won't be popular with my dad's friends when I take over."

He reached over and took my hand saying, "I need you. I need you to be at one hundred percent. That might not be fair, but I will need you. I also don't care about being fair like the partial Fairies you befriend." Tears filled my eyes.

I whispered, "You're going to make me your Gamma? I don't have a wolf, Caine." Caine rolled his eyes, "I don't give a shit if you have a wolf or not. I won't have anyone named McCann be my Gamma. I also don't care if your old pack wants to hear your name or not. I'm listing Melanie McAlister as my Gamma."

I gasped, "You can't do that." Caine shrugged, "I'll be the Alpha. Which I've been told many times means I can do that. I will too. Now, let's go meet the gang at Paige's place so everyone can see you and know you're ok." I nodded.

I told him, "If you make me your Gamma; I won't let you down. It's an honor you'd even think of doing that." Caine said, "I wouldn't dream of having anyone else. Plus, I think that would bring certain people to our pack borders."

He winked adding, "Along with the fact that I'd keep you as Female Lead Warrior because lord knows you get bored doing just one job. I'll have Ashley Griffen listed as my Female Lead Warrior, and Melanie McAlister as the Gamma." I'd say I couldn't do both, but that would be a lie. I easily could.

He continued, "If anyone wanted to say anything about that; well, they'd just have to come say it to my face, wouldn't they?" I snorted, "You're being very Alpha blood-like today." Caine winked, "And it feels so good." I would imagine it really did.

We got in his car where Addison was already waiting. I didn't know where his plan to make me the Gamma would play into being Xander's mate. I'd have to let Xander reject me so he could move on. I just didn't know when that could happen. I'd have to figure it all out because I wouldn't let Caine down.

I also didn't know if Xander's rejection would kill me or not. The projections weren't solid one way or the other. I didn't have a wolf, so it was possible. Would it even work now since I wasn't eighteen? It wasn't like Caine was taking over tomorrow… so… this would be fine.

Caine snorted, "Your mind is thinking far too hard over there." That was not possible. My phone rang and I answered, "Tao, how's…" He cut me off, "Don't ask how I am! I hurt you." I hummed, "I still beat you in the fight… so…technically I hurt you…when you think about it." He growled, "What the hell was that fight?" I got out the car at Paige's and walked away.

I told him, "It's how…" Tao growled, "Yeah, I asked around. You fight that way all the time. Why?" I whispered, "I can't really talk about this right now and…" He disagreed, "You are in fact going to talk about it right now because it doesn't make sense to me. You come here and you help us. You're training me to take over from Alpha Ezra." He didn't call him dad, which was fair.

Alpha Ezra raped his mom on her heat while her mate was sedated. He tried to make Tao bad like him, but it wasn't working because his mom taught him the right way to do things. Her mate, his father in every way that mattered, did as well.

I admitted, "Getting something over on Alpha Ezra and making him mad… kind of makes me happy …and by kind of I mean it's literally one of the things I look forward to the most so…." He cut me off, "You'd do it even if he wasn't my dad." I would, that was very true.

He snorted, "He's trying to push me to take a chosen mate already." I hummed, "You just turned nineteen… so that's really fast and…" He interrupted, "I'm not going to do it. I think I know who it is." I knew that too. They were cute together.

I asked, "Isn't she on the list? She's a Warrior's daughter and… they don't really care about age." He snorted, "She's headstrong." I reasoned, "As most Luna's are… they care about the pack… which Talia does… and…" He snorted, "And Alpha Ezra hates that. There's nothing he can do though when she's eighteen."

That wasn't true, but I had plans just in case. I would be listening for chatter next year when Talia turned eighteen. Ok, I was actually already working on them now because it's possible Alpha Ezra suspected they were mates. He'd have to stop being a self-centered egotistical jerk for five seconds, but anything was possible even if the probability was in the negatives.

Tao said, "I've been told I'm done fighting in the undergrounds. They won't accept any more fighters from dad anymore. Do you know why that is?" I answered, "Uhh… well… logically speaking…" He cut me off, "You did something."

I admitted, "Maybe… I mean… I fight for money. They have to keep me happy… since I make them the most by far….so maybe I used that and made sure you don't have to fight… because you don't want to and…" He growled, "The conversation about the way you were fighting is not over."

I grumbled, "Isn't it though?" He snorted, "No." Avery waved at me, and I waved back. She'd joined our group and moved in with Mason and Hendrick after the debacle that happened after she shifted went down.

I still didn't get that. Buck clearly rode my motorcycle around to run it out of gas, so I'd have to run and stumble upon Avery. He loved her. So, I didn't understand why he didn't act instead of having me do it. He made no sense to me….even though we worked together. I had a better sense of him but still…

He was happy Avery was with me under my Warriors, and I saw his pride when she fought now. He was perplexing….and that irked me…. but Cayden seemed to have more information about the situation with him and Avery somehow.

Cayden was now married to Cassie. I should've been at the wedding as Xander's mate, but I did get him a watch like my friends had. I would know if he was ever in trouble. Cassie wore her earrings I'd given her. Which wasn't surprising, I knew what she liked and purchased accordingly. Then added extras to them so I could track her and stuff.

I told Tao, "I have to go, but I'll see you for training in a month." He agreed, "Good. Then we will discuss this the next time I see you." I hummed, "Keep up your training and your cardio." He snorted, "Your Xander is insane with this regiment. He is aware he has Hackura blood and the rest of us are mere wolves, right?"

I defended him, "It's a good program… because other wolves won't follow it and…" He snorted, "Yes, I know the man walks on water to you. He just needs to be good enough for you." I reasoned, "He's more than…"

He cut me off, "He has to prove that. I'll withhold judgement for now, but he has to earn the right to be yours. Not the other way around." I argued, "I mean he's not the one with a black stain on his name." He said, "If he blames you for a single thing that happened, then he is." He hung up before I could say anything else.

I walked back over to where Paige's protection for her place was. She gasped and hugged me the second she spotted me. I winced but hugged her back. She sighed, "You're ok. I haven't seen you and no one would let me come take a peek at you to settle myself."

That was because I looked bad the other day. I said, "I'm fine. Where's your vodka?" She stared at me. I drank a lot more ever since I'd turned sixteen. Avery asked, "Is Drunk Melanie coming out?" I snorted, "No, I have things to do later."

Paige considered then offered, "I will make you ONE drink." I shrugged, "Fine by me. I've got something to do then K said she wanted me to meet people so… I'm sure you've noticed people don't really like me and…"

Addison snorted, "People love you." I asked, "Do you live in the same place I do? I mean… I know you do, so that statement makes NO sense." She rolled her eyes at me and Paige put a drink in my hand. I asked, "How did you make this so fast?" She replied, "I've met you so I had the drink ready to go." It was a vodka cranberry drink.

We walked inside and sat down. Paige studied me. She said, "I know something is wrong." I was better though. I shrugged, "I mean… we've got Alpha's cheating on their mates to cause pain…" She cut me off, "But we fixed that." I hummed, "I mean they still do it so…"

She interrupted, "We came up with the candy, so they don't feel pain." That was true. I continued, "So cheating mates trying to hurt their mate… which is… sadistic. Alpha's who would let pack members be forcibly marked… I have to fight so they aren't… and it makes me less popular. I've got Trevor SHOOTING ME IN THE BACK DURING PACK ATTACKS…" I took a deep breaths.

Paige gasped, "HE WHAT?!" Caine snarled, "And I took him down for that." Addison explained, "She was rescuing pups." She shouted, "You got SHOT in the back and no one called me?!" I replied, "It was in the vest I got bruised ribs… which is just… I was doing my job. Like WHAT is his problem?! The fact he smells LIKE A WET DOG is NOT my fault!"

She agreed, "It's not. Don't worry, I will curse him." I shrugged because I didn't care. I finished my drink and sighed, "I need to go blow up a building…. and RUIN Dante's day." Caine asked, "Are you going to be mad at him forever?"

I grumbled, "He got one over on me… TWICE… in succession. He had guns trained on Paige AND HE GOT MY BROTHER! MY BROTHER! Hunters killed MY FAMILY, and he thinks he can TORTURE MY REMAINING BROTHER?! No… it's a no."

Caine reasoned, "The only way he was able to do that is because you were being hunted when it happened." And they weren't monitoring Resistance things because they were worried about me. Paige shrugged, "I get it. I cursed and hexed Dante too. Use me against my friends? I don't think so." I leaned my heads towards her. I didn't fall down on the job now.

I geared up then left them and went through several holoports. I got the building the Hunters sold to the Ring. I was kind of hoping since Dante was personally involved the Ring would take him out for double crossing them. They probably weren't even going to consider it though.

I set the charges and got back to my spot when I heard some teenagers talking. I groaned, "UGH!" I looked out from behind the boulder I was hidden behind. I quickly noted they were not human, but I'd never seen them before.

They stiffened as if sensing my presence. I watched as they shifted into… holy crap. I gasped, "Big Foot is real?" They ran towards me now, but I didn't even care. This was amazing. Former Beta Dylan Frost would DIE for this knowledge.

Maybe I could barter with him to keep me alive if I got captured. Because I know about supernatural's he would want to know about. That was something to keep in mind. Because he would easily convince Alpha Eric he needed to let me keep breathing to talk to me. That was an option if I was caught I filed away for further consideration.

They approached me cautiously. I asked, "What are you even doing out here? Besides keeping me from blowing up bad people's stuff." I was in all black so they couldn't see me or my face. They shifted back and grabbed shorts.

One explained, "These guys built this on our lands, so we steal their stuff sometimes and smoke the weed. Are you really going to blow it up?" I nodded, "Yes, I really am. What are you guys?" They looked at each other clearly wondering if they should answer.

One girl told me, "Most people say Bigfoot." I smirked, "But that's totally not your name… I mean I guess it could be. People call us Werewolves, and we have wolf halves. Well, not me for some reason… well people give me a reason all the time I just…"

The one who was the talker interrupted, "We are Quatchiees." I blinked asking, "Like the combination of the name Sasquatch and wookiees? That is the COOLEST THING EVER!" They laughed. She confided, "Actually one of us helped with the wookiee design. It's a big joke with us. A fun, lovable version of us in case people ever discovered us. Our failsafe is to look like a lovable character."

I asked, "Do you make the noise the wookiees do in the movies? Because that's amazing… and…" One cut me off making the noise. I squealed, "This is SO cool!" The other girl asked, "How old are you?" I answered, "Seventeen. How old are you?" They replied simultaneously, "Thirteen." I nodded because I knew they were younger.

I pulled them behind the boulder then blew the charges. I said, "So, I'd come with you to meet your people if you let me." I took off my mask. I explained, "People have usually heard about me. Oh gosh… that sounded like I'm bragging. I mean it's usually true though… I should introduce myself. I'm, well two people… but you'd know me as Ashley Griffen… if you know me. It's fine if you don't."

The more talkative one surmised, "The voice of the forgotten. We know you. We aren't exactly forgotten though, just not known." I frowned reasoning, "There's a desire to be known if you put yourself in a movie." They looked at each and nodded.

The talkative one instructed, "Follow us. Let's see how fast you are." I was ridiculously fast for having no wolf. I kept up with them. I could've run faster, but I didn't know where they were going. I ran through to a society that had filmy quality to it like the Shroud. It wasn't visible from the outside. It was like the Shroud.

Several people stopped when we entered. The man, that was clearly in charge, was in front of me in seconds. I greeted him, "Hi, I'm… well that's complicated but again you'd know me Ashley Griffen… well they did so… you probably do. Don't worry about that explosion it was me. I'm an ally if you didn't recognize the name."

He scoffed, "I did worry about the explosion until you showed up. I see you met my daughter. One of them anyway. Her and her best friend are always running off." The girl kicked the dirt with her shoe. So, he was worried because she was out. He answered, "Yes, I was." Oh…dang it. I really had to work on not talking out loud.

I shrugged, "Well, she's fine…she was with me…. Also, I'm kind of a fan because knowing Quatchiees exist is cool. I could put you in touch with other supernatural groups that aren't known to the… well everyone except themselves and me. The ones that don't mind others reaching out. There's kind of this whole community of unknown's I've formed…."

He laughed, "Why don't you come have dinner with my family? We can discuss these unknown's you've found." I frowned, "You probably don't want that. I get told I talk too much… and I'm annoying … by a very large group of people."

He chuckled, “Nonsense. We don’t get visitors outside our own kind. I’ll be fascinated at what you could tell me. You seem to know quite a bit. My wife would castrate me if I let a young woman leave without a meal. She’s cooking up a storm or she’d have been out here.”

I looked at my watch admitting, “I have time for dinner.” Barely. He smiled saying, “Good.” I was going to have to add Quatchiees to my growing list of unknown’s. There were so many. He asked, “So, you not only are the voice of the forgotten you find unknown Supernatural’s?”

I hummed, “I mean…it’s more like I run into them…out and about.” His daughter I’d met said, “We felt like we should come talk to you the second we heard you.” Interesting… weird… but interesting. I shrugged, “I get that a lot. I’m theorizing I have a comforting voice… or something…”

A woman, I was guessing was his older daughter groaned, “Belina, what did you do now?” Belina, my talkative girl, answered, “I found Ashley Griffen.” Her sister snorted, “Sure you did.” I chimed in, “I mean… found is a strong word… but…”

She shouted, “Wait, you’re actually Ashley Griffen?” I answered, “That is what some people call me.” She put her hand out introducing herself, “I’m Lyric.” I inclined my head, and we went to dinner. I met all her siblings and deduced they were the Royal family.

After dinner Lyric jumped up and started dancing the cha-cha. I giggled and joined her. She gasped, “Another dance lover!” I winked, “You have no idea… literally…” I’d gotten into Julliard. She hummed and we danced.

I told her, “I’ll call you Cha-Cha.” Her brothers threw their heads back laughing and her sisters snickered. My watched beeped. I said, “I have to head off. I will come see you all another time.” I handed her dad my card.

I asked, “Do you want the list of people who would talk to you and form alliances?” He chuckled, “I do.” I handed it to him and ran off. Someone said, “Damn. She’s fast. Like really fast.” Another said, “Ashley Griffen has to be fast. I’ve never heard of someone being so many places.”

I was fast but Demons shimmered us around. Partial Fairies I’d helped train that could pop, and we had holoports. So, it wasn’t surprising at all that we got around so fast. I smacked my own head, “They were talking about the workshops.” Not the Resistance.

I went through several holoports and saw Kingsley waiting. She stared at her watch and started to leave. I whisper yelled, “Wait! I’m here… I’m totally here. I’m late… and I’m sorry. I met the Quatchiees!”

She asked, “You met who now?” I answered, “Big Foot Wookie’s. Their real name is Quatchiees.” She threw her head back and laughed. She said, “Oh my god I miss you when we aren’t together.” I shrugged, “They’d probably talk to you… so…” She hummed, “Let’s rescue these women first.”

We were rescuing a group of women Kingsley’s group: Operation Saint Rita. I asked, “How many?” She said, “I know there are four.” I hummed, “That’s too big of a building for four people… too many escape options. The risks are too high. ILYX, scan the building.”

ILYX replied, “Scanning, Melanie Jane.” I shivered. Kingsley chuckled, “So, how many new videos has your Xander posted?” I admitted, “He’s done an uptick in the challenges he does… so Phil probably told him… and his Hackura side likes the challenges… and the lifting belt click videos… the jump rope ones… well and…”

She cut me off, “So basically all the ones you drool over. Have you considered the fact that he might just monitor who watches those videos?” I snorted, “He’s an Alpha…. So…. No. Maybe Phil does… or Prince Gunner Cambridge… but if I looked into it and found that, then I’d stop watching and…”

She actually scoffed, “You couldn’t stop watching if you tried.” I grumbled, “Well, you all told me to relieve myself after watching them… then when I do… they STORM in on me….” She gasped, “They did not!”

I hummed, “Yeah… they did…I watched a slow motion hand down his chest then the belt click with the sea shanty challenge and they BURST in…for no reason… so…” Kayda took over asking, “Do you want me to eat and regurgitate them for that, my pet?” I snorted, “No, but thanks.” She hummed.

Kingsley shrugged, “Try it again but lock the door.” I grumbled, “I do that now. I’m actually working on a study about why the weight lifting belt click is so hot… I think it’s his smirk… he winks now too.” I pretended that was for me since he's looking at the camera…even though it definitely wasn't….in my head it was. Kingsley chuckled.

ILYX said, "Scan complete. There are one-hundred heartbeats in this building." I hummed, "That is…" Kingsley screeched in anger. I asked, "How is it guarded?" She'd been here doing the intel gathering. She answered pointing to the men leaving. "Once they leave, we have twenty minutes, but they aren't far away. There's a Guard house five miles out."

I snorted, "That's so much time between rounds… I mean it makes it easy for us… but jeez.. talk about a lack of security." She called in more of her people that could shimmer in and out. They nodded to me. My face was pretty common for them to see these days.

Kinglsey and I walked up to the building. She said, "I haven't been able to get the code for the door." I snorted, "There would be nothing for me to do if you had." She chuckled and I broke into the door system easily.

I winked, "This is actually the company I just bought." She shook her head. We went in and heard guards inside. Kingsley and I both stopped. Someone grumbled, "I don't know what this intel about this location getting hit by those dumb ass circle or women's group, but clearly they aren't coming."

Kingsley pulled her lighter out of her watch. I tapped several buttons and my broadsword came out. Xander trained it with most often. We went in stealthily. We were behind them before they noticed. I cut the first guy's head off.

A woman came at Kingsley. She screeched and knocked her out. We killed the rest. Kingsley scoffed, "A WOMAN is helping do this to OTHER women?! I'll have someone take her to my flying building so I can HUNT HER!"

I agreed, "Sure thing Kayda." We walked over and I bent down to pick the lock on the trap door. Kingsley asked, "Whatcha doing?" I answered, "Picking the lock on the trap door. Which… Feels kind of obvious… and…" She hummed, "Trap door?" I pointed, "This one." She made a face I couldn't interpret.

I picked it and opened it up, and her eyes widened. People screamed, "Help us!" I inclined my head to Kingsley and her other people shimmered in. I went and placed charges all around the building while they took care of that. It felt fair since this building had been used for evil that I turn around and blow it sky high.

When everyone was out, Kingsley and I walked back to the spot we'd met in. I hit the detonator and the building went down. Kingsley snorted, "I see you were just as mad as I was. Come on, I'm going to introduce you to the Yule Cats." Uhh what? She really liked them…and people did not like me.

That made me very nervous. Kingsley said, "They will love you and we need to get out of sight. They have a Shroud type deal." We were covered in blood, and we had killed a bunch of people. Loudly.

I whispered, "I probably shouldn't have detonated the building." She scoffed, "I would've if you didn't." It had been an evil building they used to traffic women and young girls. That was definitely reason to kill them and blow up the whole place.

She said, "I have brought people here before so don't worry, it's fine." Don't worry and Melanie didn't really belong in the same sentence… Worrying was basically my job. She called, "LUCA!" A Hawk flew down, but I knew he was a shifter.

He shifted back, commenting, "This is a larger group than normal." We'd brought some of the women with us because she thought they'd do well here. Kingsley said, "We need to get inside quickly." He chuckled, "That explosion was you then."

I winced, "Umm it… was me… well… no it was just me… I got mad and…" Luca cackled. He said, "You have such interesting friends that you keep, Katla." Kingsley shrugged. He took us inside and a woman I knew was powerful squealed, "K!"

She ran over, "Oh my grandkitten is covered in blood. Stefan, get her to your shower and take care of her." She gave him a look while wiggling her eyebrows. She cooed, "Grandma wouldn't mind a grandkitten in the oven." My mouth dropped open.

Kingsley laughed as a man came over. I gripped her hand tightly. She squeezed mine back saying, "I will leave you in grandma's capable hands, Ashley." She told Grandma, "This is Ashley Griffen." I said, "Uhhh… that's … well…"

I whispered, "People don't like me, usually… so…" Grandma hummed, "Well, then I already like you." I blurted out, "Can I see your Cat?" She grinned. I continued, "I've just never seen a Yule Cat and I have a list…. of lesser known Supernatural's…. Which… like, Yule Cats are more well known than most people on it since you meet with the Hackura… which I totally don't know about… for reasons…"

She laughed, "Oh my adorable new Grandkitten I love you so." She waved calling out, "Get these women and children showers, clothes, and anything they need. I'll be taking my new grandkitten around to find who she likes. I have yet to succeed with getting K knocked up. Let's find your taste in my available brood."

I faltered, "I… umm… that's… just… no?" She snorted, "What man has stolen my grandkitten's heart then?" I winced, "One that doesn't want me." She tisked, "Then he is a fool. The best way over a man is under a new one." I sputtered, "Umm… that's… I've never… I mean … I just… no…. I'm good."

She chuckled, "Do you still want to see my Cat?" I answered, "I really do." She walked away from me and shifted. I gasped, "Wow." She bowed down. I squeaked, "I get a ride?" Her cat chuckled. She waited for me to get on then took off.

I laughed, enjoying the ride. The man that was clearly her mate was standing there shaking his head at her with a smile on his face. It tugged at my heart because it had been a while since I'd seen that look outside Hendrick and Mason.

I saw it all the time at home in Red Run, but not anymore. Today, I'd seen it with the Quatchiees and now the Yule cats. All I saw now was tragic love stories or heartless non-existent love stories. I never saw this anymore and my heart pinged with sadness over it.

Grandma knelt down and I got off. I told her mate, "Umm she said I could ride so…" He cut me off, "My mate does what she wants. You are most welcome here, Ashley." Grandma shifted back announcing, "Kristian, meet our newest grandkitten. K said her name was Ashley Griffen."

He hummed, "The voice of the forgotten. Really?" I blushed, "Umm… well… that is what they say… they say a lot… all the time actually." Kristian grinned, "You're also in a popular band. Our Clouder would love it if you played for us sometime."

Grandma squealed, "We have one of our grandkitten's birthday's coming up!" They had heard of us? Cayden said practically no one Black Mountain or their allies had. How did they not know when the Yule Cats did? We were in Europe for goodness sake.

I offered, "We'll play. I mean… if you want." She grinned, "I do." She winked at Kristian, "She's my favorite grandkitten." He told me, "It changes minute to minute, but K is usually always in the top spot." I agreed, "She should be… she needs people around her because she's been alone too long. But me and our friends help with that… though you probably helped first… you probably kept her sane… which is good… everyone likes…. sanity." Good gosh, stop talking.

Grandma laughed, "She talks to herself out loud thinking she's not. She's adorable and I love her, Kristian." He cooed, "Of course you do." She added, "She needs a new man to get under since she's lovestruck by one before they've even done the deed." He snorted at her.

Tears pricked my eyes. I realized I desperately missed seeing their type of love. The love I grew up around. Grandma gasped, "Are you alright?" I waved, "Totally fine and…" Kristian interrupted, "Has anyone mentioned you're a bad liar?" I grunted, "A lot of people… all the time, actually." He chuckled.

I admitted, "It's just that I've seen a lot of the love I grew up around today… and I see it few and far between these days. I make sure marked mates don't feel the pain of cheating… and make sure forced markings don't happen… so… seeing you guys is like a breath of fresh air." They looked sad.

Grandma took me to a room where I got to shower. I spent several hours with them, and I could admit that I really missed this. I felt lighter here. Grandma pulled me aside, "You can stay here. I gave this same offer to K and she comes around often. I wish she'd stay." I did too.

She laughed, "You talk out loud still when you don't mean to. It's quite endearing." I winced, "It's problematic at times." She nodded, "Like when you go out for your circle group." I sighed, "It's the Resistance… I mean…. so I've heard… from people…"

She snorted, "I can already tell you are in it. We will help if you need." I reasoned, "The Hackura would want that knowledge." She shrugged, "Then they can piece it together as I have. If you need us, we will help." I asked, "What's your proof?" She answered, "Kingsley has come here in all black and now she brought you. You are aware you also came in all black."

I shrugged, "Black is standard mission garb for like… well, everyone." She laughed, "Maybe a certain King of the Quatchiees called my husband. My mate is curious why he's on the list when you haven't met us. I'm no longer curious. It's because K knows us."

I conceded, "Fine. That's actually… sort of proof." She chuckled, "We will assist you if you need it." My watch beeped and I touched it. I stood straight up. I shouted, "I need to go… so… tell K to have fun with your grandkitten… she needs some fun… she's said she's had bad experiences… recently and she never says that after spending time with him."

She snorted, "No one would, I taught my grandkitten's right. One must be a generous lover in bed." I blushed, "Umm ok… sure. That sounds…. reasonable…" She chuckled, "Come back and I'll find someone you like." I shook my head, "No… I'm just… kind of a one man woman… so…" She winked at me and I took off running.

I left and found our holoports and ran all the way back to my second place. I quickly changed and ran to the pack. I flew into the gym and grabbed my weapons. Buck asked, "Are we being attacked again? We were just challenged last week!"

I waved, "No, bad people are coming… but you won't help with me that. Even though you know it's wrong. So… I'll just be gathering weapons." He whispered, "Are they coming for Avery? Just get her out of the pack like you have others."

I muttered, "Others? That's… you say weird things…sometimes." He sighed, "Please don't try to lie." I waved, "It's not Avery. I stopped that already." He whispered, "Thank you." I grumbled "Will you just go talk to your sister and stop moping around? Because… I don't get you." He replied, "I know you don't." He walked away.

I linked Caine, "Where are you?" He answered, "At a neighboring pack on an errand with Dax. Why?" I ordered, "Get back! There's a group coming to try to take Addison!" He snarled. I linked Addison, "Where are you?" She replied, "Getting bad vibes. My clothes are all packed."

I warned, "Get out of sight." She replied, "I don't hide anymore." I groaned, "I get that… really, I do.. because…well you know I do…but this works better if I just challenge them, and they leave… tail tucked…" She hummed back.

I linked Sierra, "Get Addison out of here. Drag her if you must." She snorted, "I'm a Beta blood so that's not going to work. For some strange reason you can drag Alpha blood around, but I cannot." I blew out my breath.

Three trucks came to a screeching stop, and I took off. Edward was standing with Jean, Booker, and Trevor. Just waiting. Edward nodded, "Regus Kliner, nice to see you." WHAT?! The guy who had killed his last FIVE mates?! No.

Addison linked, "Isn't that the guy you are considering killing?" I snorted, "He tipped the scales in my favor… hard. Actually, just like… completely in my favor…so…considering is a word." She replied, "You can't kill him here!" I could… and I was probably going to.

Edward said, "Addison is inside." I called, "And she's not leaving. She doesn't like him." He growled, "That doesn't matter, and they haven't met." I shrugged, "Well, we've all discussed Mr. Kliner here. He has a reputation for…"

Regus snarled, "Who are you?" I answered, "I'm…" Booker cut in, "Lead Female Warrior Ashley Griffen and she's leaving." I rolled my eyes. He warned, "I'll whip you until you're barely breathing." I waved, "That was so last week… come up with a new threat please and thank you." He growled at me.

I asked, "What? I said please… and thank you. You're just never happy." I waved, "Anyway Regus, you won't take Addison. Or see her. I'll challenge you… and you really don't want to do that." He snorted, "I can kill some wolf less bitch."

I linked Sierra, "I didn't even have to goad him into a challenge to the death… man I'm good ….Maybe I should give a class on how to annoy people in ten seconds or less." She sighed, "Just do it fast. Ads is freaking out because she pulled his reptation off ILYX. Which by the way, is WORSE than you mentioned." Ok, so maybe I hadn't mentioned how the mates died when I briefed them on him being a possibility of someone we killed.

Edward asked, "What reputation do you think he has?" I snorted, "You cannot be serious! Why do I feel like you're serious?" Caine pulled in, crashing into the back of Regus' truck. He shouted, "What the fuck?" He got out and snarled, "Get the FUCK out of these lands!"

Edward growled, "Son, you aren't the Alpha." Caine was breathing hard and ready to challenge Edward here and now. I told Caine, "It's fine. Regus challenged me to a battle… and he even said to the death." Caine blinked and glanced at me.

Jean sighed, "Regus, let's not make it to the death." Regus snarled, "You clearly can't teach this wolf less bitch her place. She'll learn it, then lose her life before I take my mate home." Caine roared in anger. Everyone in the pack glanced at him in shock.

I tisked, "Making an Alpha wolf mad… is dumb. To be clear, Addison could kick your butt. Her backwards thinking dad won't let her hold a position she should… so she's just my Warrior." He scoffed, "She'll be popping out pups shortly." I hummed, "No. She wants her fated."

He snarled and shifted. I pulled out a gun and winked, "You never said no weapons." His wolf paused. Edward shouted, "No weapons." I replied, "You don't get to say that. He has to because HE issued the challenge. I swear it would hurt your brain to look up the LAWS."

Regus shifted back, "No weapons." I shrugged, "Ok." I holstered my gun while running at him. I took him down and snapped his neck. His group screamed. I wiped off my hands, "Done." Booker snarled, "PUNISHING FIELDS!" I asked, "For what?"

He shouted, "You killed our ally!" I reasoned, "He is the one who made it a fight to the death. Which by the way Edward, is what he does to all his mates. Every single last one of his past mates were beaten to death." Edward paled and looked at Booker.

Booker demanded again, "PUNISHING FIELDS!" He threw a letter at my feet. It was from my brother. I opened it.

Melanie,

I'm getting reports you aren't behaving. Peter, Sebastian, Christopher, Dane, Dalton, and Dakota are FURIOUS. I'm furious. I should've had mom and MY dad send you away when you wouldn't stop crossing the border. Will you just LISTEN for ONCE in your life!

Is it not enough for you that T and mom died? You killed MY dad, and I hear that you still say he's yours. STOP! He is MY father and yours KILLED HIM! BEHAVE FOR GOD'S SAKE!

I've told Gamma Booker he can punish you like MY DAD should have when you refused to admit you crossed the border.

Beta Jason

I clenched my jaw and walked towards the punishing fields. I took off my shirt. Jean said, "I convinced Booker to let Edward give you the lashes." I snorted, "So, you got me more… am I supposed to thank you?" He asked, "Huh?"

I scoffed, "If you'd stop denying the Beta blood running in your veins you'd know exactly what I'm talking about. Honestly, it's just pathetic you don't know." He demanded, "What don't I know?" I answered, "Booker will just show up when Edward is done… and somewhere, probably deep down in your pinky toe, you know that." He frowned and seemed to be thinking about it.

Edward said, "Assume the position." I asked, "Do I look like I'm dancing a jig? I'm not. Also, you're welcome for saving YOUR daughter's life. Probably yours too…not that I care about that." I knelt down and braced myself for the pain I deserved. I thought back to when I sent my appeal to Dalton and Dakota when the whip came down.

Flashback

Melanie had read through the appeal a million times. I was at the UPS store to send it expedited back to my home pack. I clutched the document into in my arms and waited in the long line. People were complaining but I didn't mind.

When it was my turn, the guy up front asked, "Where is it going?" I gave him Dalton and Dakota's address. He held his arms out for the package after he printed the label. I took the label and put it on and tried to hand it to him.

He asked, "Are you ok? It will be one hundred and ten dollars to overnight it." I felt the walls closing in. I told him, "I'll come back." He warned, "We will be closing shortly, just give it to me." I winced telling myself, "It's as good as it will get." I slowly went towards him.

A pack member in line behind me snarled, "Just do it for god's sake. We have things to do." He snatched it from me and handed it to the guy behind the counter. He frowned, "Umm it wasn't that big of deal. Please do not touch packages from other customers." The pack member grumbled and went back to his spot.

I left and went to my secondary place and went to sleep. I woke up to Caine linking, "You need to get to the pack." I drove my motorcycle and parked where a group had gathered. Aunt Stephanie screamed, "HOW DARE YOU!" I asked, "Huh?" She went to slap me, and I punched her in the face. She dropped to the ground unconscious.

I muttered, "One of these days, she'll learn." Booker snarled, "When will you?" He tossed my unopened appeal at my feet. They didn't even open it?! Now THEY were ignoring pack laws and Werewolf Council decrees?! They were good people! They couldn't do that! Yet they had.

Edward threw letters at me, all in handwriting I recognized. Former Alpha Peter, Former Luna Chelsea, Jason, Melinda, Marybeth, Cooper, and Dane. Wow, Dane even said something. I faltered realizing Fromer Alpha Nick was in there too with Alpha Sebastian and Alpha Chistopher.

I actually jolted seeing Grandma Esther and Grandpa Ben in the mix. They hadn't written to me since my sixteenth birthday when they disowned me for not being their blood. I gathered them all up with my appeal and ran away.

They yelled after me, but I was going to read these notes in my secondary place. I'd be punished later. I got back and emailed Buck the schedule for everyone then took a deep breath. I knew these letters would be mean, but in a way, it showed they still cared. They were handwritten. You don't handwrite letters when you don't care.

You just didn't engage or interact just like my ACTUAL BLOOD GRANDPARENTS. My mom's parents had sent their letters and then never said another word. Not one and I'd called. I left messages but they blocked my number after three months.

I shoved that hurt away while preparing for the new one. I just took it as signs that forgiveness could happen one day. I muttered, "You're a masochist now, Melanie." Knowing that wasn't going to stop me from reading them.

Flashback Ends

Caine shouting brought me back to the present. "What are you doing?" He picked me up. He growled at them all. He warned, "The day I challenge you gets closer and closer, Edward." He replied, "I am your father."

Caine replied, "Sperm doesn't make a father. I can't beat you today, but I might have been able to earlier. Do you know what that man would've tried to do to Addison?!" Edward replied, "Booker arranged it all. Regus would've been good for…"

Caine growled, "Get your damn head out of Booker's ass for five seconds. He thinks Trevor is a good person. LOOK AT MELANIE'S BACK!" Jean jumped in, "His mate died and…" Caine snorted, "And what, Jean? He got off the floor from her death and CARVED words into a she wolf who he has bullied and abused since she got here. Then he used magic on it so it wouldn't be able to be removed or altered. When I tell you if you'd found them, you would know how evil he was."

Edward asked, "Son, are you ok? There aren't any words on her back." Caine snorted, "Ask ANYONE else in the pack. Ask ANYONE about Trevor's masterpiece. Surely you've heard them discuss it."

He sneered at them, "Even Trevor knew you'd see him for the deviant he is if you could see it. So, the magic doesn't allow you to. Just know I'm fully aware you won't ask a damn soul because you're shitty ass people."

He began to carry me away then added, "Oh and don't call me son." I whimpered as he walked away. He whispered, "I know." He linked, "Celia is waiting at Mason and Hendrick's place." I replied, "I'm sure this will make her love me more. I'm her favorite patient… obviously." He snorted, "You are certainly her most frequent flier."

I swore I saw Buck's worried face in my peripheral but when I managed to turn my head he wasn't there. Avery shrieked, "Oh goodness! What did they do?" Ceilia sighed, "I swear someone needs to get our Gamma into anger management."

Addison screamed, "Melanie!" I waved, "It's fine… I've had worse… literally." Celia sighed, "I hate to agree with her, but she's right." Addison cried, "This was for me." I muttered, "Over my literal dead body would that guy have gotten near you."

Caine chimed in, "Her dead body and mine." I added, "I'd have taken him out with me… but it wasn't even really a fight. I'd studied him and how he fought… so…" I winced when Celia began to wash out my cuts.

I gripped the sofa cushion, and she gave me a strap of leather to bite down on, so I didn't scream too loud. I really needed to study the science behind not screaming during the whipping but during the aftercare. It was quite annoying.

More time passed in a flash of punishments, mean letters, and saving the pack from take overs. Alpha Theo had visited with his son Lux again. He was an odd duck. He was a partial Alpha, and he'd also had his Alpha Ceremony… but in private… and he did the job of the Alpha but he refused to completely take over until his younger brother, Harrison, was eighteen. So, he wasn't the official Alpha, but he was.

Honestly, Lux was funny and a flirt, but a nice one. That was new for me. Literally. He asked me on dates which was weird. I'd never been asked on one before. I got told I'd be in someone's bed… or possessed…but never a date. I'd attempted to go do a dance as Addison's date once and that was a disaster.

Flashback

Melanie spun around. Addison said, "I can't believe you found that dress at a second hand store." I smoothed out the light pink dress. It wasn't my usual color or style, but it had been a good find. Addison admitted, "I don't understand why you didn't just go to a store or order a designer dress."

I said, "Well, for one I don't need your dad knowing I have the money to do that." She scrunched up her face, "Fair point." I said, "And two…" I trailed of and forced myself not to cry. She squeezed my hands, "Mel?"

I admitted, "I was supposed to do this with my mom and momma Chelsea. We talked about it… all the time…about how much fun we'd have. Momma Chelsea even promised to try to get my mom to agree to shopping in Black Mountain…which probably wouldn't have happened but…I can't go to some dress shop without my mom." She nodded, "I get it."

We walked out and Mason and Hendrick fanned their faces. Mason took several pictures and squeezed us both. He said, "You look beautiful. I'm so sorry we can't drive you." In the back of my mind, I knew this was a trap but I didn't want it to be.

Hendrick sighed, “Yeah, Edward pulled us into a border patrol run.” Definite trap. No. I was GOING to this dance. Addison waved, “It’s fine. I’m driving us.” Edward wouldn’t do anything or have it planned for the car since that was the plan.

We left and got in the car. I asked, “Are Si and Paige there?” I’d had us stagger our arrival. Paige was Sierra’s date. Addison nodded, “Yup. Sierra said plenty of guy want to be on your dancing card.” I laughed, “That’s…actually oddly familiar…people used to clamor to be my partner at dance competitions.” She grinned and we took off.

I knew it was going to hell the second we got out of the car. I whispered, “Go inside, Ads.” She asked, “What’s wrong?” Trevor and his friends plus some others came out of the shadows. They had paintball guns. I told her, “Go.”

Addison said, “This was approved.” Trevor laughed, “For this reason.” He took a shot at her but I pushed her aside and took the paintball right in the gut. It was green and splattered all over my light pink dress. I took shot after shot.

Trevor said, “You can leave or we can ruin Addison’s pretty dress next.” She’d gone shopping with her mom for hers. Addison growled, “You son of a bitch!” I told her, “It’s ok. We knew this was a long shot…just go have fun with Sierra and Paige. Ok?”

She whispered, “I can’t…” I interrupted, “You can.” I linked her, “I’ll just go be with my family in the way I can and dance.” She clenched her jaw. I continued, “Dances like this are a wright of passage according to my mom. Go on, have your fun.” She turned and stomped away.

I took off running while they laughed behind me. Tears burned my eyes. I’d just wanted to go to a school dance. Just one. I went to where my commemorative headstones were for my family and danced my pain away.

Flashback Ends

I shook off the past and looked around at my friends. My eighteenth birthday was coming up. I already knew Xander was mine, but next week… it was official. I could find my mate. I lifted the bottle of vodka to my lips and drank.

Paige asked, “Is drunk Melanie making an appearance?” Addison snorted, “Making? She’s already had five bottles.” I pulled up my laptop and opened the camera for Black Mountain’s gym. I sighed, “Isn’t he just… handsome?”

Avery questioned, “Umm did she hack into Black Mountain?” I did it a long time ago, so I giggled. I squealed, “And there’s Elise! That’s EJ… Oh and Wesley! Hey, Micah and Max are there! We should call him.”

Paige disagreed, “Uhh no… I don't think you should.” Addison muttered, “Why not?” Paige snorted, “Are you kidding me?” While they argued I took out my phone and called Micah, but he didn’t answer. Which was rude… when you thought about it.

I sighed and left a message, “MICAH! Why didn’t you answer the phone? This is no fun… you could answer and maybe things could be different. You didn’t though… so that’s sad… Call me back!” I frowned and hung up.

Avery said, “It’s ok.” I sighed, “He didn’t even look at his phone. Probably because he’s with his mate. Look how cute and happy they look. They are so smooshy in love.” Paige groaned, “Dear god… smooshy? She’s making up words again. Do NOT hack Webster to put your words in them again.”

I ignored that saying, “Look at how their faces smoosh together. They are smooshy. OHHH Let’s call Cayden!” Paige sighed while Addison encouraged me, “Yes, call Cayden.” Paige sighed, “Addison?” Addison shrugged, “You’d agree if you knew about certain things. She’s having fun and she deserves it.” I so did.

Cayden’s phone rang three times before someone picked up. “This is Cayden’s phone.” I sighed, “You’re not Cayden.” He laughed, “What gave me away?” I answered, “Several things. Your voice being one then the fact that you said Cayden’s phone. No one answers their own phone that way.”

He laughed again, “Cayden stepped away for a moment.” I sighed, “He’s probably with Cassie being adorably mated.” He asked, “Do you not like Cassie?” I answered quickly, “Oh no, I think she’s great. I’m happy for him… and her. Because mates… yay… I’m just bored. I hate being bored. Who is this?” Paige smacked her own head.

The guy laughed, “My name is Spencer.” I surmised, “Prince Marcus’ and Princess Torvi’s son.” Addison winced. What was their deal? Spencer said, “Now how would you know that?” I answered, “Uhhh… well you’re answering Cayden’s phone, and your name is Spencer. You’re obviously Duke Spencer Cambridge.” I took another drink.

Spencer said, “I don’t know that it was obvious.” I disagreed, “Well… it is to me.” Spencer laughed, “And you are?” I sighed, “You would ask a complicated question.” Paige chimed in saying, “Ashley, her name is Ashley.” I huffed because it wasn’t.

Spencer said, “I’m not sure how that was a complicated question then. That makes this caller Ashley Griffen. Is something wrong?” I answered, “Yes, I’m deeply and utterly BORED! I don’t like being bored.”

Spencer snorted, “Is there a reason you're drinking in excess?” I looked at my phone and asked, “Why do you ask such complicated questions? You’re harshing my buzz.” Spencer said, “I highly doubt that’s possible. It’s also not a hard question.”

I said, “Cept it is a… very hard to answer, given that you’re…. you. Have you ever told your god that he should figure out how to kill an immortal being? WAIT! You’re a Hackura… if anyone could kill an immortal being it would be you.”

Spencer replied, “A stake can kill a vampire.” I snorted, “I meant a goddess. Everyone knows how to kill a Vampire… I suppose I could stab her in her chest where her heart is supposed to be. It would at least hurt… don’t you think?”

Spencer said, “I’m sure that it would. Why would you do that?” I snorted, “Uhh because Selene’s a colossal evil horrid excuse of an immortal being.” Spencer asked, “Are you bitter about your lack of wolf?” Well, that was a word choice.

I cackled, “BITTER?! Bitter, he asks. Guys… the Duke of the Hackura is hilarious. He’s got jokes. Bitter. I’m pissed. No, no, I am infuriated. There’s no reason I shouldn’t have a wolf even if what they say is true.”

Spencer questioned, “And what do they say?” I snorted, “You’re a Duke of the Hackura. If you wanted to find out what they say about me, you could find out. Easily.” Addison linked, “Did you really just challenge a Hackura?!”

I replied, “Uhh no… I stated a fact. A literal fact.” She groaned in reply. Spencer said, “How very true. I’m curious how you know that.” I said, “Uhhh I’m smart. Obviously.” Spencer sounded amused, “Obviously. Oh look, Cayden’s back.”

Cayden asked, “Ashely?” I groaned. Paige hit me. I shouted, “HEY! That hurt.” Cayden cleared his throat, “Ashley, what’s wrong?” I grumbled, “I used to like that name.” Cayden clarified, “Your name?” I sighed, “Yup. Loved it. Now… now I hate it. Can you ask Duke Spencer why he asks such hard questions?”

Cayden said, “I could do that. Why did you call me? Never mind, you’re bored, aren’t you?” I complained, “I AM SO BORED! You just get me. Like a brother would.” Because he was supposed to be my brother in law. That thought hurt and had me drinking more.

Cayden laughed, “Have you tried learning Russian or something?” I considered, “I could do something like that. I learned French the other day… I do know Russian already though… for reasons… I could learn something else. That’s a thing… I could do. There are several languages I don’t know yet.”

Cayden laughed, “I could give you a tour here.” I gasped, “REALLY? OMG YOU GUYS!” Cayden practically shouted, “I’ve offered to do just that several times!” I urged, “GUYS LET’S GO!!!!!” Paige, Addison, and Avery yelled, “NO!” I sighed, “But… I would be so much less bored.”

Avery somewhat demanded, “Hang up the phone, Ash.” I sighed, “Apparently I have to go, Cayden.” Cayden teased, “Should the wardens leave, and you want a tour, call back.” I snickered, “Aye, Aye Commander Captain.” I hung up the phone.

I sighed, "I just want to see the Hackura realm once." Paige consoled me, "You will one day. Do you really want to chance meeting your Xander hammered?" I shrugged, "It could be fun." They all laughed at me but I was serious. Oh well, I guess.

I grabbed a bottle and kept drinking. I shouted, "Let's dance!" Paige said, "That we can do." I smiled. Lots of things went to crap, but I had great friends. This moment reminded me of when I was little and found one of my mom's BAGG day goodie bags.

Flashback

Melanie wandered the house. Tristan had come into my room to let me know he and Jason were going to the Kyle's. Mom would be back once whatever emergency she had come up was settled. Then he'd left.

I was looking for the cookies to send to Ryan Bishop again. I wandered into my parent's room and saw a bag with Mom's name on it. I opened it and giggled. She'd gotten dance costumes. I grabbed the S.W.A.T outfit.

I turned on their stereo and began to choreograph a routine that matched the outfit. I heard my mom coming but the dance was in my head and I wanted to get it out. I knew I wasn't in trouble when she laughed. She asked, "Melanie Jane, what are you doing?"

I squealed, "MOMMY! I found all your costumes! You didn't tell me you used to dance too! Can I use these for my routines?" She shook her head saying, "These are mommy's special outfits." I frowned saying, "Well, some are see through you know?" She snorted and covered her mouth.

I asked, "What's so funny, mommy?" She managed to say, "Well, how very silly of the people who made them to make them see through. I'll have to talk to the person who gave them to me right away."

I agreed, "You definitely should." She told me, "You know daddy wouldn't like this costume." I admitted, "You're right. Would he let you wear it? Because I think it would look good on you. WE COULD DO A MOTHER DAUGHTER ROUTINE!" She covered her hand with her mouth but didn't laugh again. Did she not like the idea?

Eventually she said, "I have two left feet when I dance. I don't know where your abilities came from, but it certainly was not me." I giggled, "Daddy says you just need the right partner to dance with. He said Uncle Duncan, Grandpa Martie, Grandpa Ben, T, and Jase are acceptable partners to dance with but he's the best one. I'm certain he'd say we could dance together though."

She smiled urging, "Why don't you go change and we will learn a routine before you head off to your grandparents." I squealed, "Really?" She answered of course, "Of course." I ran out of my room and took off mommy's costume and put on my clothes.

I yelled, "Mommy I'm ready to dance." She joined me and we danced. I'd made the routine easier for her and we laughed the whole time.

Flashback Ends

I blinked away the tears that had formed. Avery whispered, "Melanie?" I whispered, "We used to have fun and once I found her dance costumes… OH MY GOSH!" Paige asked, "What?" I gasped, "I put on my mom's lingerie, and I JUST REALIZED IT! I hadn't thought about it in so long… and oh gosh… oh no… that was good memory until thirty seconds ago… I need more vodka."

Paige snorted, "I'm going to agree with you there, only because that does sound like something that you should not remember or recall. Remember the fun part because there clearly was one." I hummed, "Are sure you're ok because don't remember your childhood? Maybe it's good you don't remember you WORE YOUR MOM'S LINGERIE AND DANCED IN IT!"

She shrugged, "Most days I've coped with not remembering my family. They died and clearly, I blocked it out." I tapped her nose, "I'm pretty sure Patrick isn't dead… so… there's that." She questioned, "Then where is he?"

I admitted, “Well, there are two options… and… one sucks… which…” Addison cut me off, “Is why we told you not to tell her.” Paige scoffed, “But Drunk Melanie gives ALL the answers.” I tapped her nose again, “You’re so cute. Wanna know who you’d look SO CUTE with?” She replied, “No, I want to know the options on Patrick.”

I clapped, “Oh yeah! His probability of being alive is over ninety-nine percent.” She blinked several times. Avery sighed, “Why is Sierra cooking dinner tonight?” I answered, “Uhh it’s her turn. Duh.” Avery snorted, “Yes, duh.”

I waved, “Anyway, option one is he’s hiding. Which is the one that sucks, but to be fair it’s only like a ten percent probability.” She asked, “What’s the other one?” I hummed, “He’s been captured. Because that would make sense for why you were with those people… and then they stripped your powers and planned to mark you… maybe he tried to escape…so they used your forced marking to keep him in line…which I saved you from so… that’s the one I go with.”

She whispered, “Can we find him? Either way?” I assured her, “Don’t worry. I have scans running… the longer we don’t find him though… the more likely it becomes that he is not hiding. I can find people who are hiding easily. Because they cannot hide from me! I am the master finder.” She agreed, “You are.”

Caine came in, “Melanie, you had a HUMAN arrested for her comments on your Xander’s Instagram page?!” I snorted, “Uhhh no. I started looking into her for her comment on MY MATE’S Instagram. She got arrested because she was stalking multiple people, him included, and stalking is bad.” Paige snorted and covered her mouth.

He groaned, “Dare I point out that YOU stalk people.” I gasped, “I do it to be nice… and helpful! She was crazy. There’s a very clear difference! She had a pattern of behavior of injuring people… and she got away with it… and that’s bad. I didn’t do anything to CHEYENNE and her THIRSTY COMMENTING BUTT!”

Paige groaned, “Caine, why dear god, why would you bring up something that led to Cheyenne!” I muttered, “Chey… and her STUPID online journal. I hate her.” Avery sighed, “We know. Really, we do.” Caine snorted, “There’s a Supernatural she got put in FEDERAL prison too.”

I hummed, “I got a human put there too. If people want to STALK my mate… then they shouldn’t live in glass houses that I can SHATTER. Just like the people who tried to take down Elise and Jase’s businesses. STRAIGHT TO JAIL! Federal jail is when it’s Xander’s… ok and his mom… no… several other people too. Maybe Alpha Peter’s old business with my dad that he kept going… and a few others.”

Paige snorted while Avery and Addison groaned. Caine asked, “How many people have you sent to jail?” I grumbled, “Maybe it’s more than a few… if I could send the MODELS that came down to MOCK ME and say Xander didn’t want me… I’d find whatever law they broke and give it to the feds too. Did you know there are A LOT of federal laws regular people break on the regular? Plus, some states have strange laws.”

I snickered, “You can’t wrestle a bear in Alabama. Why is that a law? Who did it? I have questions. In Arizona, you can’t put donkeys in a bathtub. So… did a THIRTSY STALKING commenter find a donkey in their bathtub WITH the authorities that I called on her after putting a donkey in her bathtub? Yes… yes, she did. I’m equal opportunity though. I’ve gotten men thrown in prison too.”

Paige said, “So, you made her break the law there.” I snorted, “Well, she was building a creepy stalker shrine to Xander. She was planning a trip to Black Mountain to kidnap him… so, when you think about it… I saved her life from the Hackura. Like she would’ve DIED for that. Think of how insulted they would’ve been that she thought she could kidnap him.”

I scoffed, “His Guard would be so mad. I helped people not go golden eyed about the entire thing… when you think about it…and all I did was use a donkey…who is now happily living on a farm. So, a dangerous stalker is off the streets and there’s a happy donkey running around. Everyone wins. Everyone.”

Caine asked, “Dare I ask how you got a man stalking your Xander arrested IN CHURCH?” I admitted, “I’m super impressed you found that one. In Alabama, where the stalker is from, it’s illegal to wear a fake mustache in church that causes laughter.” Caine snorted, “I don’t even want to know how you lined all that up.” Paige laughed, “I do. That’s hilarious.” I grinned at them all.

There were bleak days in this pack, but I had bright spots like today. My family's letters were calling for me to re-read them from the draw I had them in. To remind me I didn't deserve moments like this. What most people knew down here was I walked around with a broken heart twenty-four seven.

To the world outside this, Ashley Griffen was an icon to look up to. Beta Jason might not know it was me, but he knew everyone knew Ashley's name. People were proud of what Ashley Griffen did, which meant they were proud of me, and I held onto that knowledge.

Testing Games

Alexander is Twenty-Two Years Old

Alexander was worried. Everly McAlister was here in our pack with Kai. He was outside with my mom. She whispered, "I shouldn't be here." I replied, "Nonsense you are an ally of ours you are always welcome here."

She admitted, "I went out early this morning to shoot some pictures of the sun rise in the place T told me Melanie used to love dancing in. It sounded perfect for the shot I wanted." Oden purred in my head. I'd visited the spot in question.

In fact, I was in the process of having Phil acquire me a house in Red Run's territory for me and Melanie. Jason used to say she got home sick, so I wanted her to have somewhere to stay in their territory if she needed it. It wasn't in the area where all the pack houses were, but it was still considered their territory.

Oden said, "It does have a nice private area for her to dance into." It was a mansion, and I planned to make updates to it. I thought it would be a good place for us to have our pups run around and until they came along, should she still want them, it was a nice place for us.

Oden said, "Jase said she wanted a big family like ours." Yes, but a lot about her personality had changed in New York according to all of the McAlister's. Oden growled, "Well as soon as she gets away from all those bastards who think she needed to change she'll be herself again. I will not STAND for someone making mate be different." Nor would I.

Everly pulled me back to the conversation. "I went by Jase's place." He'd gotten a cottage after the Hunters tortured him. She sighed, "The therapy isn't helping him. I heard him screaming when I came back by. It's horrible." Tristan had ordered him into therapy when it became clear Jason was struggling.

I told her, "Trauma can take time to get over." She cringed, "He wakes up asking for Ladybug. He's screaming her name and telling her to fight back." I frowned, "But that didn't actually happen. Melanie wasn't there. No one hurt her."

She sighed, "I know that, and you know that. He's pretending to know that, but I don't think he believes it. You should've heard him; it was so sad." I told her, "I'm really sorry." It had to be hard to hear. If I heard one of my in laws going through that I'd be furious.

She sighed, "I just don't get it. I know T and I mated quickly, but I'm shocked she didn't come back for our matin ceremony. I excused it because she was mad and hurt. I did stupid stuff at her age, but she didn't really even try to come to our mating ceremony." Oden growled.

She rubbed her face, "Now, she's never even come to see Kai. I acknowledge she's tried but it's all so weird." She was right. We needed to look into this. Karina came into the room and dropped off cookies. I took one and offered one to Everly.

She chuckled, "I do love these. We have them in our pack too, but Karina's are better." Karina blushed and bowed her head. She said, "Thank you, Beta Female Everly." She took a bite and moaned, "You are welcome. Please open a bakery. I'll make my best effort at gaining weight eating all your creations." She giggled and left.

She sighed, "I swear Robert is bad for her ego." I asked, "Do you see them together a lot?" She answered, "Here I do, but he never brings her to our pack." I questioned, "Never?" She nodded. I linked Gia, "You might need to talk to Karina. Robert has never taken her to Red Run and they've been dating for way too long for that." She replied, "I'll do that, but Cassie has talked to her." I knew that.

I linked Gage, "Is Robert here?" He snorted, "He's lurking." I replied, "Make sure he stops." He chuckled, "Happily. Normally Genevieve gets to have all the fun." She would, as EJ's Gamma. He had a short fuse for Robert being here.

Everly snorted, "I'm being silly. Melanie is living her dream." Oden deflated in my head. I agreed, "She is." She looked out the window watching Kai. She said, "She'll meet him someday." I agreed, "She will." She admitted, "I think she'll get into Julliard." Oden grumbled, "She will."

I replied, "I'm sure she will." She sighed, "Then she'll never come home." Oden growled in my head. I assured her, "She will. She can't stay gone forever." I'd have a limit of bullshit I could deal with. Oden grumbled, "I've been at my limit for quite some time now." He was and he wasn't.

Some days we were in sync ready to just go find her. Then we'd remember that it was selfish, and she was living her dream. It was always the reality slap we needed. I couldn't stop her from living her dreams. She was my mate and I wanted her to have everything she wanted.

I offered, "Why don't you go ask Rissa if she'd come see Jase." She was his ex-girlfriend. They had been on and off dating since he and Cassie decided to just be friends. Rissa was a big help to him with everything Melanie. She beamed at me saying, "That's a brilliant idea." I winked at her, "I've been known to have those." She laughed and left.

I grabbed some food from Nana Blanch. I kissed her cheek, "Love you, Nana Blanch." She grinned at me and pinched my cheek. She said, "You have a heart of gold, young man." I laughed, "I don't know about that." She shrugged, "You go ahead and not know. I'll just be over here knowing."

We walked outside together and heard two pack members whispering, "It was the best damn muffin of MY LIFE!" Nana Blanch stopped and I knew they had her full attention. The girl said, "It was good, but they said they stole them. Plus, we weren't supposed to be down there. They don't sell them regularly and they literally pushed us out when we asked who made them."

I asked, "Where were you?" The girls squeaked. I greeted, "Hannah and Kaia, how are you?" Nana Blanch grumbled, "After eating the best muffin you've ever had." I bit my lip. Oden chuckled in my head, "Now, they've done it." Yeah, because Nana Blanch took pride in her cooking.

Hannah sighed, "Can we not answer that?" I replied, "Not a chance." She groaned, "We took a road trip." I jumped in, "I am aware." She blushed, "Well, we needed supplies and gas." She winced, "Maybe I didn't look at the gas tank to notice how low we were. Which I do know is bad. My dad warned me a million times to check it and keep the music down so I could hear when the ding for the low gas light went off. We were jamming pretty loudly to music the whole time. Please don't tell him."

I reasoned, "So far in this story there is no reason for me to tell him. Just be careful when you road trip. We don't want you stranded." Oden reasoned, "You should tell them what to do if they are." He had a point. I added, "If you do though, link my mom or any of us that can pop. We will come help you. Ok?" They both nodded.

I urged, "Continue." Kaia winced, "Ok, so we noticed we were nearly out of gas when we were going through Nashville. We were close to Franklin, but we didn't think we'd make it gas wise." I wanted to groan.

I linked EJ, "We might get a call from Alpha's in Nashville about pack members being there." He asked, "OUR pack members?" I answered, "Uh huh." He groaned and I understood that. We never enjoyed getting those calls because they were ridiculous. I said, "They had to stop for gas." He snorted, "I better not get a damn call about people needing fucking gas. I will break a phone."

Nana Blanch questioned, "How does this relate to stolen muffins that are the best you've ever had?" I laughed then teased her, "You are stuck on that." She retorted, "And I'll be making muffins today." I grinned at her.

Hannah said, "So we were walking by this bakery, and a wolf was running towards them with a basket. It just smelled so good." I shrugged. She continued, "So we walked in and asked to buy them. It was weird though because people were waiting for them. We heard them whispering about how they stole them from some drunk girl that was making them."

I asked, "Did they say who she was?" They shrugged, "They called her Ash and said that if she found out they stole them she'd kick their ass." Nana Blanch snorted, "So the wolf less Female Lead Warrior ALSO cooks?! My plump behind needs to get to the gym."

I laughed, "I'm sure there is more than one Ashley and you're incredibly fit." Oden was purring. Nana Blanch cooed, "Oh you flatter you." I snorted, "I cannot lie." She winked at me. Hannah said, "Well they were saying she made so much they just knew she wouldn't notice, but several people disagreed. We bought them and they practically shoved us out the door calling us outsiders. We didn't tell them what pack we were from, and we left."

I asked, "Did you pay for the gas with a card or cash?" Kaia admitted, "Cash. We didn't want our parents to know about the whole ordeal, and we had emergency cash." Oden hummed, "Smart." It was. Hannah shrugged, "They were SO good. They had this fudge center."

Nana Blanch gasped, "I can make a fudge center muffin too." They glanced at each other and Nana Blanch left in a huff to go make muffins. They both winced and I could tell they were worried.

I asked, "What's wrong?" Kaia whined, "They were so fluffy and it's not that Mrs. Blanch's muffins aren't amazing, they are. Everyone know that." I agreed, "Yes, they do." She practically whined, "These are just so good!"

Hannah said, "I guess this Ash makes them for her friends, and one of them told her to when she was super drunk. She doesn't make them often, but I tell you that woman could open a bakery I mean it. I also mean it when I say I would drive there specifically to buy them."

I snorted, "No driving to Nashville for baked goods." Kaia admitted, "I would risk the ire of my dad to get them. I would even hire someone to bring them to the boundary line. Beta Phil has his Warrior friend down there. I wonder if they know about the muffins." They walked off and I found myself curious about it.

Oden teased, "You're being such a Beta blood right now." I snorted, "Shut it, Oden." He chuckled in my head. I popped to Phil. He said, "I can sense you have something to ask me." Gage grumbled, "Do ignore my presence. No, no, don't say hi. A Gamma is used to it." I rolled my eyes, "I didn't even say hi to Phil yet. So, hi Gage."

He grinned at me, "It's nice to be noticed." Oden snorted, "We would obviously notice him and Gun." His wolf's name was Gun, but Gage joked it was Top Gun all the time. I asked, "Phil, has your Nashville Warrior friend…"

He interrupted "You know his name is Walker." I huffed, "Does Walker ever mention the best muffins being made down in Nashville?" He snorted, "Uh no. Why?" I answered, "Because two pack members enjoying their road trip had to stop in Nashville and now Nana Blanch is making muffins."

Gage jumped in, "What? That doesn't make sense. What do those two things have to do with each other?" I explained, "Because said pack members said they said they had the best muffins they've ever had." Both groaned.

Gage hit his head on the desk. Phil asked, "Why? Dear Moon Goddess, WHY?!" I shrugged, "We get Nana Blanch muffins I see no problems here for us. Leo will probably see a problem. I'll go talk to him." Phil asked, "And do I need to warn Toby about Nashville Alpha's calling? Or put road tripping girls on bad patrols?"

I snorted, "They are seventeen and they learned their lesson. Sure they got some amazing muffins, but they are very worried about their parents finding out they didn't listen to the lecture about watching the gas tank light." Phil threw his head back and laughed.

Gage hummed, "Good call. They will probably be worried about a visit from me or Phil. Anticipation is always a good deterrent." I nodded, "If it happens again, then we can dole out some extra patrols. I think they learned the lesson though." Oden agreed, "They did. Their wolves were promising me they'd look out better next time."

I popped to Leo and found him in the gym on the weights. I walked over and said, "So, the cooking minions in your mate's mind have been set loose." He dropped the weights. He asked, "What? Why? Who did it? Did someone have a recipe better than hers? Goddess above tell me she's not trying to figure out a recipe."

I snorted, "Some pack members mentioned they'd had the very best muffin they'd ever eaten. I believe the only detail given was a fudge center." He grabbed his head then glared at me. I asked, "What?" He grumbled, "You left out the detail that A DRUNK GIRL made the best muffins they've ever tasted!!" I nodded, "That is what they said." He snorted, "That was VITAL information before I linked my mate about it." Oops.

He grumbled, "I'll see you folks later. Haley and my mate are now drinking and making muffins." I snorted, "My mom has never made a muffin in her life." He shrugged, "She's stirring a batch my mate mixed up. She ranted about the story to YOUR MOTHER who suggested they try their hand AT DRUNK BAKING!" Several people snickered.

I reasoned, "To be fair, that was part of the story." He grumbled, "I don't give a shit about being fair. She could burn her hand or have a kitchen related accident. Now, I'm going to monitor the situation so they don't hurt themselves." I shrugged.

Oden warned, "We should probably tell dad." He had a point. Oden muttered, "I always have a point." I popped to my dad, who was with Dylan Frost. The latter instantly perked up. He practically begged, "Mini Moody, please give me fun news. You so rarely do, and my day needs a pick me up."

I glanced at my dad then questioned, "Dare I ask why? Because what I have to say will absolutely make Dylan's whole day." Dylan squealed, "YAY! I always knew you had that interesting DNA your mom supplied deep down inside you."

I snorted, "Of course you did." Dad told me, "Ashley declined his invitation to do one of her work shops in Blue Moon." Dylan pouted, "It was such a long rambling decline too. She was so worried I'd be offended I have to wonder why she didn't just say yes. She clearly wanted to and talked herself out of it. It was a fascinating email."

I snorted, "Well, I'll turn that frown upside down. Mom and Nana Blanch and drunk baking because some pack members mentioned they had the best muffin they'd ever had and it was made by a drunk girl." He squealed, "I love you so Mini Moody. I don't care what they say about your moods. You're the best."

I snorted, "You're the only person who talks about my moods." He cooed, "Awww, you're so cute when you're wrong. I talk about them with love. Some people are quite upset about them. Especially when you make them run."

He whispered, "Then others complain because other Lead Warriors in other packs talk about how much this pack runs. Which means they then have to run more. They, rightfully, blame you." I rolled my eyes, and he took off.

He shouted over his shoulder, "Don't worry SGAP! I will make sure our precious fun sized Fairy ninja goddess does not get hurt drunk baking." My dad snorted, "Leo is already with them." Dylan replied, "I shall send him away post haste."

I told my dad, "I don't think Leo will leave." Dad agreed, "He won't. So now, there will be Blade, Javi, Dylan, and Leo to make sure that nothing happens during this drunk baking session." I admitted, "I came to warn you about it." He laughed, "I appreciate that, but Blade linked me." Damn it, Blade!

He winked at me, "Next time, just link me." I admitted, "I had to go tell Leo anyway." Dad hummed, "Yes, Blade finds him amusing. Leo told him the baking will last all day because Mrs. Blanch will be determined to make it right and find the right level of drunk to bake the perfect muffin."

I reasoned, "The pack members could just lie to her. Most possess the ability and the two that said it are full blooded Werewolves." Dad rolled his eyes, "Yes, well your Nana Blanch would spot that. Especially if it was about her food."

I admitted, "I'm not sure she's going to able to recreate the recipe. She doesn't have a sample." He waved, "We can get her one." I snorted, "No, we can't. The pack members nearly ran out of gas in Nashville."

He groaned, "Why?" I snorted, "They were teenagers on their first road trip without parents. It was a teaching lesson. Anyway, the muffins in question were stolen from a drunk girl that the bakery then sold." He inhaled deeply before he sighed.

I laughed, "Have fun with that, dad." He snorted, "I'm sure I'll have a sexy baker in here later." Probably. I left as Caleb walked in. I winked, "He's already aware of the drunk baking." He snorted, "Yeah, Leo linked me when he left the gym."

He smacked the back of my head saying, "Something you have the ability to do." I replied, "Leo told me about the drunk baking. I only knew Nana Blanch would be making muffins. I had no idea mom was involved until he told me."

Oden chuckled, "Bork is grumbling that we could've told him that part at least." Bork was Caleb's wolf. I shrugged, "I told Phil." He grumbled, "I swear to god we have got to get the newer generation more into Dylan's Beta chat."

I reasoned, "I'm sure if you pointed that out to Dylan, who is in the kitchen, he would be thrilled." He snorted, "I'll be texting the Beta Chat that. He'll be off to the races." I laughed, "Which he will be happy about because he had a bad start to his morning."

Oden grumbled, "If Ashley won't come to Blue Moon, then she won't come to our pack." That was true. They were smaller than us. I went to the kitchen and caught Dylan's eye. He linked, "I did join the pack so you can link me. You silly young whipper snapper."

I snorted, "Why did Ashley decline your workshop?" He answered, "I mean in the rambling string of thoughts, she said it's because we don't need it. She doesn't get the pack resources that she should, and they are helping much lower caliber fighters than us."

That was solid logic. He grumbled, "Don't make that 'it makes sense' face. I hate that face. Your dad made it too. He was supposed to tell her she had to come." I replied, "Their pack doesn't follow Werewolf Council decree. They are under the Supernatural Council."

He huffed, "Yes, and THOSE FUDDY DUDDIES said I had NO BASIS to order Ashley to give me a workshop." I blinked asking, "You went to the Supernatural Council?" Oden told me, "Fang said they did and he's wound up about it."

Dylan huffed, "The Fairies on the council found my request more than FAIR. Then they were blocked out, like always. My windup toys must be upset about this." I knew my dad and Uncle Aiden would be. Which Dylan also knew.

I popped to my Uncle Aiden. He was red faced pissed on the phone. He shouted, "When Herman rises you tell him that if he continues to disrespect the Fairies this way, we will pull out of the Supernatural Council." He should just do that.

He continued, "You don't let my people in on things. They know you are keeping secrets and at this point, I'll make sure they find them." Oden chuckled, "People never understand our uncle." No, they didn't, but then again he didn't want them to.

The man on the other side of the phone gasped, "You cannot just…" He cut them off, "You would do well to remember I can just. Easily. I can easily bring two Kingdoms down on your head. Remember if I stand against you, my sister does. If my sister does, who else does?" He tapped his chin as if they could see him.

He snapped his fingers, "Oh yes, the Hackura. The ROYAL family even. They would probably declare war. You are no match for the Fairy Army, let alone the Hackura." The man on the phone shouted, "The toilets are overflowing. I have to go."

I snorted, "How very short sighted of him not to realize who did that." Uncle Aiden grumbled, "They should be used to it. One of the two Fairy's sitting on the Supernatural Council as our representatives is a Water Fairy. She just keeps changing their issues when they are blocked out."

I replied, "Then they have to realize at this point a Water Fairy is going off on them." He replied, "If they do, they haven't said." I asked, "What's the other Fairy?" He grinned, "Fire, of course." I questioned, "How does one not notice that they've pissed off a Fire Fairy?"

He winked, "The Fire Fairy is more subtle about it. Nothing at the Supernatural Council building has caught fire. It's the places they are from or have loved ones." I snorted, "I see." He hummed, "What brings you here?" I answered, "Dylan."

He snorted, "Yes, he was most upset." I pointed out, "And you let him 'wind you up' as he says." He winked, "Do you want to know who called the Supernatural Council in the middle of my conversation?" I replied, "I'm certain it was my dad." He winked at me.

I laughed, "We really are his wind-up toys." Uncle Aiden shrugged, "I don't really mind it. He alerts me to things faster than Fairies do. My representatives on the Supernatural council will pop in once they've caused their chaos."

I asked, "Do you think the Supernatural Council should have Ashely come do Dylan's workshop?" He said back, "Yes, because according to Dylan he thought she wanted to but felt she couldn't. Her Alpha isn't providing her with the resources for a booming business for his pack. Ashley doesn't charge people, but Alpha Edward Davis does."

I gasped, "He can't do that." Uncle Aiden replied, "Your dad, me, and Dylan believe that Ashley somehow pays because those packs don't. It didn't come out of their finances." I snorted, "If I was Ashley, I'd find a way to siphon it out of Alpha Edward's accounts."

He grinned at me, "That's brilliant." I shrugged, "I'm petty." He snorted, "Yes, but she watches all your videos. It's possible she's trying to emulate you. Plus, that is amusing and I like it better than some poor teenager paying to make people better. People your dad believes are being held back."

I reasoned, "Then you believe that too." He agreed, "I do because he does, but they are not my people. I make sure no Fairy of any blood ends up with the packs whom your dad doesn't like or approve of. That is all I can do from my end. It annoys your dad he cannot do more." That pissed me off.

I hugged my uncle and popped to Aiylee. She greeted, "Cousin." I hummed, "People are annoying our parents. Do things with our cousins about that. Fig is always willing to set things on fire." She laughed, "Who has upset them?"

I answered, "The Supernatural Council." She sighed, "If they manage to live until I'm Queen, the first time they upset me I'll go all Queen of Hearts in Alice and Wonderland on them." I laughed, "Are you going to yell 'Off with their heads!' Or something like that?"

She winked, "That actually. I will do just that. I'll deploy our cousins and my siblings. I have them thinking of charms for my reign. This would be a great time to test them out." I agreed, "It definitely would. As an enforcer, I say test runs are vital and necessary." She grinned at me.

Exsis popped in and groaned, "When he comes to you it ALWAYS means psychological warfare is about to be waged." Aiylee snorted, "He is a man of action. It could literally be war." Exsis replied, "Then he would've had you pop to me so we could both do it."

I shrugged, "You could get in on it for all I care. I just want them to feel the pain of upsetting our parents. We are the promised family. Our parents are the promised siblings and enough has been taken from them. I'm sick of people upsetting them when Uncle Arion isn't here to be the balance. I can't step up completely like he could, but I CAN make people's lives difficult."

Aiylee clapped, "YES! That's the spirit. I like it. I'm here for the Fairy side of your enforcer blood coming out. This is SUCH a good moment. Keep feeling those feelings. Even if we don't kill people, we can make them suffer."

I laughed, "The Hackura side of me likes drawing out torture, physical or mental, when there is no immediate threat." Which was part of the problem and reason we needed Uncle Arion. I didn't think he would care too much about how long people suffer. He sounded more like a 'see a problem, solve a problem' kind of guy.

I admitted, "Maybe we need to let Jarrod and Fig do what they want more often." Both of them stared at me. Exsis said, "They are extreme in their reactions." I postulated my question, "If Uncle Arion were alive, would we say that about him? Sure. Would we let him do it? Yes. They are his sons. Maybe they can help us with the balance Uncle Arion was to provide."

Aiylee hummed, "I could tell them that's the case for this realm." I nodded, "It's a little less than nothing." She agreed, "It is, but I do think that would make them happy. It would also signal the strength of our family. Our people would love to see Uncle Arion's children acting just like he would've."

Exsis agreed, "They would. It would deeply amuse the Fire and Water Fairies especially." He paused then added, "Actually even the Sky and Earth would." I understood why he paused. Since Fenilton had died the Fire and Water Fae were opposed to the Sky and Earth Fairies and their ideals.

I couldn't say I blamed them, especially after what the Sky and Earth Fairies did to my mother. I would've distanced myself from them too. Oden snorted, "Distance is an interesting word for kill." I snorted, "I would've distanced myself and made a plan to kill them." He conceded, "Fair enough."

I hugged Aiylee then Exsis. He said, "It's always good to see you leaning Fairy. Your cousins love it, Aiylee especially." I laughed, "It is quite fun." Aiylee nudged me, "Remember that because I'll use you for your mind and the strategies that live in it when I am Queen." I laughed, "It's not using me if I agree, cousin." I winked at her then popped out.

Uncle Gunner greeted, "Alexander." I asked, "Can you find out if Alpha Edward is somehow paying himself for the workshops Ashley puts on?" He laughed, "I don't have to find out. I already know the answer. He does."

I snorted, "How did you already know? Did dad have you look?" He answered, "No, he doesn't know that's happening to my knowledge. He probably suspects." I raised an eyebrow, "You didn't tell him?" He shook his head. I hummed, "Interesting." I hugged him and popped to my dad.

He was yelling, "I'll find a way to bring all Werewolves back to my purview." The person sighed, "Former Alpha Eric, you can't do that." He warned, "I will find a way and WHEN I do, you will ALL regret not working with me."

He practically vowed, "I will uncover every shady thing you have done with those packs and then you will not be able to escape the ramifications of those choices." He slammed the phone down. He picked it up and slammed it down several times. Caleb winced, probably ready to jump in to save the phone.

I cleared my throat. Oden snorted, "He knew we were here." I offered, "Alpha Edward pays for the workshops Ashley puts on for other packs." Caleb eye's jolted to me. He asked, "You have proof?" I answered, "Uncle Gunner does. I asked him because I was going to reach out to Ashley or the packs themselves and offer to cover the costs. What she's doing is good and she appears to have an in we don't."

Phil came in shouted, "AH HA! I knew those packs couldn't afford the price he slapped on them. It's probably why they are afraid to agree to having a workshop with us now. They know Ashley is fixing the bill, but they think we wouldn't."

I asked, "Were you lurking outside?" Gage called, "Yes and no. Also, I'm sending an email to those packs that declined our workshops to let them know that there is LITERALLY no charge." Dad ordered, "Caleb, put my seal on those emails so they really know it won't happen."

He ran a hand through his hair. He hummed, "Well, then I'll guess Micah helped Ashley set that up. Otherwise, Gunner probably would've had to look." I asked, "Why wouldn't they just tell us they did that?" Oden grumbled, "You know the answer." I did.

Dad gave me a look. I grumbled, "Fine. I know it's because she's their source who clearly asked for us to be locked out." He sighed, "Which makes no sense. I swear there's something just on the edge of all this that I'm missing. Some days it feels obvious and like it's right there, but I can't grasp it."

I assured him, "If anyone could figure it out, it's you." He laughed, "Your mom has theories, but they lean more towards conspiracy." I asked, "What's her theory?" He replied, "It involves a prank." The bond felt like he'd answered me quite cautiously.

I chuckled, "Surely mom knows no one in Nashville is pulling pranks." He hummed. So, there was more to it. I asked, "Are you going to tell Dylan you called the Supernatural Council?" He snorted, "I'm sure he already knows Aiden and I called."

Phil groaned, "And now we have a memo, a chastising email, and text about how we need to use our Beta Chat. Awesome." His phone rang. He answered, "Hey, T." Then walked away. Gage grinned, "I am not in trouble because we use our Gamma Chat since Alpha's and Beta's keep us out of so much. We are in the know." I rolled my eyes.

I threw an arm around him, "Let's go then, Mr. In the Know." He snorted but followed me. I found Angela. Gage laughed, "I'm having SUCH a good day!" She grinned at me, and I ruffled her hair. I said, "If you and TJ want to go to Faerie and help Fig and company out, I'm sure they enjoy your input."

TJ popped in asking, "Dear god, why Angela?" Gage snorted, "She totally squealed at him to come over link." TJ agreed, "She did. I was even coming because she told me to be here in five minutes." Angela replied, "Alexander was early. We are going to work on pranking charms with Cousin Fig!" He snorted, "Then someone is truly and utterly fucked." They kind of were.

I reasoned, "They deserve it." Gage said, "Agreed and I have NO clue what we are talking about." Angela winked, "The Supernatural Council." Gage snorted, "I see." TJ asked, "Do you still agree?" He replied, "Probably." They left.

I linked Parker, Cole, Calvin, Tim and Brady, "Go to Faerie and watch over Angela and TJ. Should you want to get involved in what they are helping with, do so." They all cheered. Grant, Bryce and

Bradley popped to me arms crossed. I winked, "Don't be mad I didn't link you yet. You guys get to the go the Hackura realm." They looked at each other and I felt their excitement in the bond.

Gage snorted, "You're going back there too. You have squadron practice." I agreed, "I am, but I want them to see if they hear anyone talking about Ashley." Bryce snickered, "We get to spy on Cayden." It wasn't a bad idea. I admitted, "I don't care how you do it, just see if you hear anything." They all nodded.

Gage shook his head then grabbed me when I popped. He called, "I'll see you later. Let's go crazy triplets." He must know where Cayden was. I shouted, "In formation!" My group quickly lined up. I took them out to the obstacle course, and we ran though it multiple times then we went through the mountain path.

I conjured bikes at the top and we rode down. I let loose a cry of excitement. "Decima turmae heus heus (Tenth squadron hey hey hey)." My Squad repeated it back. I added, "Nos laborare sed hodie ludere (We work hard but today we play)." They shouted it back to me then cheered.

We got down the mountain and biked through town. I yelled, "Hey, Tah!" They shouted, "TAH, TAH!" I smirked and several people gasped as we flew by. A few fanned themselves. My squad was rather attractive. Oden scoffed, "It's us." I didn't really care. Which might be mean, but they weren't Melanie.

Oden purred, "Mate finds our videos attractive." Yeah, her views had increased since I started putting out content geared to her. Nadia really took it and ran with the direction. She had me doing more challenge. Which Phil grumbled over the fact that I did them without complaint.

Calvin linked, "Ashley and Micah code together a lot. They have an open chat where they put ideas in. Everyone in the technology building thinks she has a lot more ideas and they are jealous Micah is cultivating her as a source."

I replied, "Good work." He snorted, "We aren't done. Bryce has more." Bryce chimed in, "Some think that he's hoping she'll agree to come to the technical college here." It was a good thing I was coasting, or I might have crashed the bike. I replied, "We don't offer spots in the college to outsiders."

Bryce agreed, "I know that, but they think she's talented enough. Micah's colleagues believe he is building up to that request. They don't understand why she'd turn them down, but they clearly think she would." Bradley chimed in, "Yeah, and they think she sounds hot." I growled, "WHAT?!"

Bradley snorted, "Yeah, they have a bet on who could talk code well enough to get her pants off." I was going to kick their ass. Oden snarled, "LET'S EXPLODE HEADS!" Well, that was an extreme reaction.

I told Bradley, "Go Fairy hijinks on their ass." He asked, "Really?" I answered, "Really, really." He cheered over link. Bryce linked me, "Bradley said…" I cut him off, "You go full hijinks on their ass. I'll deal with Uncle Gunner if he says anything." Which he probably wouldn't. Uncle Harper might though. Bryce cheered, "You're awesome!" I laughed, "Love you little brother."

I pedaled harder and went through the bike course here that led to Hastein and Mom's Dragon themed park. I parked my bike and took my Squad, in nodding to the guy out front. I said, "I'm bringing my Squad in today." He gave us passes.

I turned, "Everything is free for you today. Enjoy." They all shouted and cheered and took off for the rides. Hastein faded in and came up to me. He commented, "I hear the Technology division is having a prank filled day."

I snorted, "Yes, well they shouldn't talk about trying to get into a wolf less girl's pants and take bets on it. That's rude." He hummed. I asked, "What? It is." He said, "It's not great but that seems like an interesting reaction." Whatever.

He tapped me, "Come on, let's go ride the roller coaster together." My Squad was headed there anyway. I snorted, "You just want to because it's a purple dragon." He winked at me. He'd always liked purple Dragons. It's why he and my mom opened this place together. She was sad she never met a Dragon before their realm closed themselves off.

I held onto the dream that one day we might see them again, slight as it was. They could open themselves back up. Uncle Aiden staunchly believed they didn't die off and I held out hope that he was right because it would be awesome.

I asked, "When you meet your mate will this amusement park be your first stop with her?" He snorted, "Cousin, my first stop will be a bed." I threw my head back and laughed. He added, "When we have spare time, I'll bring her here. Lord knows when that will be though. Our lives are quite hectic." I nudged him, "Make the time if she has it. Ok?" He nodded, "You know it."

We got on the front and the roller coaster took off. People were screaming but Hastein and I were holding our arms out. The roller coaster made you feel like you were flying on a Dragon's back. Well, as best we could guess.

Hastein took me to get a drink when we were done. It came in mugs with different colored Dragons with the handle as their tails. I asked, "Do they just know you get the purple one?" Mine was green and gold. He winked at me. I asked, "How are you?" He answered, "Busy as always."

I pressed, "Cousin." He sighed, "Lonely. I am lonely. Some days not having my mate is harder than others." I agreed, "I know what you mean." He winced, "I wish you did not." I laughed, "I think everyone of age yet to find their mate feels that way."

He changed the subject, "Would you like to come test out a new ride your mom and I have been working on?" I answered, "Of course I would." He laughed and slammed his drink, so I did too. Oden snorted, "Those things are strong." They were but I didn't mind. I couldn't get drunk. None of us could.

We jogged across the park to a new building and walked inside. It looked like a cave. We made it to the VR stations where there were different colored dragon statues with riding saddles. Hastein got on the purple one, because of course he did. I chose the black and white one. Oden concurred, "Good choice." I snorted.

I grabbed the VR helmet that mirrored a motorcycle helmet and put it on. I felt the Dragon move beneath me and nearly faltered. Oden snorted, "I would never let you fall." I knew that. I blinked and realized I was in a whole new realm. I looked down and realized I was on the Dragon I'd picked. It screeched excitedly.

A woman appeared in front of me, "A fight is awaiting you, mighty rider. You must go and help those already fighting." I chuckled, "Will do." My Dragon took off and we spotted a charred village. We flew down and helped the villagers put out a fire.

I asked, "What happened here?" One answered, "These Dragons came through with riders! They were evil, but she chased them off." I asked, "Who?" Their heads tilted and I spotted a man in all white. I asked, "Who are you?" He jolted and disappeared into a stream of light. What the fuck?

Someone grabbed my hand. The woman insisted, "You must go and fight with her. She is alone and she needs your help. She is a brave rider, but you are meant to be with her." I agreed, "Ok." I got back on my dragon and flew. I heard a Dragon screech in pain.

I heard someone shout, "NO!" Everything in my body stiffened. I screamed, "MELANIE!" My Dragon flew with urgency towards the sound of her voice. Oden said, "I don't like this game! I don't like hearing mate this upset." Neither did I. We found my mate and I nearly faltered.

Dad linked, "Alexander?" I answered, "I'm testing a Dragon ride at H's and mom's park." I'd get into the charm my mom used to make my mate appear later. Melanie's black hair was in a ponytail. Her Dragon was all white, and her outfit would be something I fantasized about for decades to come.

She had a leather crop top bra with bikini bottoms and a big belt buckle that was a skirt. She had on thigh high brown leather boots and two arm cuffs on her arm. She was fighting with a sword as her Dragon fought with her.

I shouted, "I am coming Lovebug!" I flew all around setting the enemy on fire. I jumped off the saddle and landed behind her to have her six. She said, "I have been waiting a long time for you." I snorted, "I have been waiting longer for you to come home." Oden reasoned, "This is a video game character." I retorted, "Obviously one charmed to be someone I wanted here."

She sadly said, "I'm not allowed home." I asked, "What the fuck? Wait, you mean in the game. I'll get you home." She smiled at me, and I knew I'd do anything to keep that look there. We moved as an impressive team. Her Dragon screamed in pain. She gasped, "NO!"

Oden growled, "What's wrong with her Dragon?" I answered, "Someone must have hit it with a spell. Her Dragon is growing weaker." Melanie ran to her Dragon, but it was encased in glass, and they were cut off from each other. I asked, "What the fuck is going on?"

Oden demanded, "Get that Dragon out! I don't like her being behind that glass." Melanie sobbed, "I need you. Why aren't you here? I'm supposed to have you!" I told her, "It's ok. We will get your Dragon out." She cried in my arms until the helmet was ripped off my head.

I asked, "H?" He asked, "What the hell? It's a ten to fifteen minute game. You've been in it for hours!" Oden snorted, "It did not seem like hours." I said, "Well, it's a little weird but cool the heroine is who you want to see." He asked, "What?"

I answered, "Melanie and her white Dragon were fighting with me." He stared at me for several seconds then pulled me through to the hospital. Uncle Marcus asked, "What's going on?" Hastein insisted, "Check his head." I scoffed, "I'm fine." I was ignored.

Uncle Marcus scanned him and agreed, "He is fine." I knew that already. Hastein then yanked me through a portal to Uncle Bjourn's office. Oden said, "I feel we are being yanked around a lot and I do not understand why." I replied, "You know what I do."

Uncle Bjourn asked, "What's wrong?" I answered, "The hell if I know. I just tested some equipment for H. My mom clearly used charms to have the fighter you rescue be someone you want to fight beside." Hastein replied, "Mmmhmmm except there is no rider to rescue. You're supposed to hunt down the riders that torched the village. The army joins you at the end."

I frowned, "No, I saw the village and the guy in all white that disappears." Hastein questioned, "What guy?" I answered, "He was in a white suit." Hastein shook his head, "There is no guy." I reasoned, "The game talked about how the woman chased the other riders off."

Hastein insisted, "There is no woman. That's not what's supposed to happen and there is no white Dragon in the game." Oden huffed, "But she was so pretty." I told my cousins, "There should be. She was stunning. The Dragon gets cut off though. She's encased in glass. Melanie was distraught."

Uncle Bjourn asked, "Melanie was in the game?" Hastein answered, "No." at the same time I answered, "Yes." He looked between us. I insisted, "She was there. We fought together." Uncle Bjourn rubbed his head, "So the guy wasn't supposed to be there nor was Melanie?"

I said, "But they were both there." Cookies were conjured to his desk. I grabbed some, "Karina cookies! Hot damn!" Phil linked, "You need to come get cookies? Karina was near tears that you weren't here. I think Robert makes her keep you in supply of them and thinks you will be mad at her if you don't get them." I ate several.

I assured him, "Some were conjured here. H, me, and Uncle Bjourn are eating them. If Robert told her I'd be upset to the point she is scared if I don't have these cookies, beat him within an inch of his life if you have proof." He snorted, "I'll just be working on getting proof." Good.

Hastein waved, "I'm being silly. Aunt Haley probably did use a charm." Uncle Bjourn agreed, "She must have." Hastein sighed, "It must be on the helmet he used specifically. I'll have her charm them all. That does make it fun if we get to the pick someone to fight with. We just can't have them be in it as long as Alexnader was."

Oden grumbled, "If that's how I get to spend time with mate, I'll take it." Me too. Sadly, I could not spend all my time in a virtual reality. Oden said, "We could still come and see it sometimes." Yes, we could because that outfit was literally something I wanted to rip off her.

I left Hastein to talk that over and popped back to the gym. My brothers were in there and I took them home with Gage. Bryce assured me, "We went hijinks on their ass!" I winked, "Good." Mom giggled, "I totally agree."

Bradley cheered, "Yay! Tipsy mom! Let's prank the pack." She agreed, "Sure. I just need to ask Alexander something." They nodded and went to get ready to prank the pack. She asked, "So, you had an idea for the new ride in H's amusement part?"

I reasoned, "It's both your park and no. I just told him what happened when I put the helmet on." She hummed, "A partner does make it more fun. He seemed to think yours was a beautiful woman. Are you interested in someone I don't know about?" I snorted, "Go have your fun mom. It's a good game."

She tapped my nose, "I will. You can tell me anything." I nodded, "I know that." I just didn't want to disappoint her. I didn't want her to think I was like those other boys and men obsessed with Melanie. Oden growled, "We aren't! She's ours." I hoped like hell she was.

He insisted, "She IS ours. She's not anyone else's and I expect you explode heads over it." I left my mom and siblings to their pranks. I popped to my shower and closed my eyes thinking about that outfit Melanie was in.

I was rock hard as I fisted my cock. I should've touched her more than holding her. I slapped my hand on the wall and growled, "FUCK, MELANIE!" I came all over the wall then snapped it clean.

Uncle Bjourn linked, "Hastein wants to know if you could draw the outfit you saw Melanie in during the game." I snorted, "Absolutely not." I felt him roll his eyes across the bond. He reasoned, "I asked for the outfit, not her in it." I agreed, "Ok fine. I'm not the best at sketching though." I was decent enough.

I sat down and worked on it for a few hours before I conjured it to Hastein. His laughter poured down the bond. He called me laughing. I asked, "Is there a reason you are cackling like a hyena?" He managed to say, "It explains why you were hard as a rock." I admitted, "I did not notice." He snorted, "Well, I did. I was worried because you were hard for so long."

I rolled my eyes. I asked, "Are you just calling to mock me?" He answered, "No, I was calling to say your imagination is amazing. When you meet Melanie, we should take her and my mate," He paused adding, "You know when I find mine and at some point we should get them wearing those outfits. Everyone would be envious of us." I snorted, "You are aware I might explode heads."

He replied, "Meh, I believe you could keep it to punching." I agreed, "You know what? Let's do that. In a moment, everything is too much for them both, or in a rare lull in our lives." He agreed, "Then it's a date with our mates." I could tell he felt excited about it and to be honest, I was too.

I laid down on my bed, but every time I closed my eyes I kept seeing Melanie with her white Dragon. Sorrow jolted through me when I thought of them being separated. Oden whined in my head too. I smacked myself, "It wasn't real. Melanie doesn't have a Dragon, and she's not separated from it."

I called Uncle Aiden. He answered, "Alexander, you caused all kinds of fun in my Kingdom today." I snorted, "I would say I'm sorry, but I know you don't want me to. I'm also not sorry. I didn't call about that either."

He asked, "Why did you call?" I answered, "I'm just curious about all the Dragon research you did." He hummed, "What about it?" I asked, "Did you ever come across a white Dragon?" He asked, "White? No, they are usually colored."

I pointed out, "There are black ones." He agreed, "Yes. You could ask your brother. He got very into Dragons, and unlike your Hackura cousin who focused on the purple ones your brother looked up everything about them." I agreed, "That's true, thanks." He hummed again and I hung up.

I popped to Bradley. He asked, "Are you taking me away from the pranks?" People were running around the pack. I admitted, "I couldn't care less about whatever this is right now." He grinned, "Good!" I glanced over when mice started chasing people. I shook my head.

I asked, "When you were researching Dragons," His eyes lit up. He loved talking about Dragons. "did you ever run across any mention of a white Dragon?" He snorted, "All white? No." I sighed, "Ok." He offered, "There are black and white Dragons, like you and Oden, though." He thought I was upset there wasn't one like me.

He continued, "There are dragons with white and gold but no all white or gold ones that we have record of." He sensed my disappointment in the bond. He said, "We don't have all their records though. That's just from what Faerie had." I replied, "Yes, but Uncle Aiden has the best records on them."

He agreed, "He does. He speculates that there are WereDragon's and REAL Dragons that aren't humans there. Wouldn't that be exciting?" I answered, "Yes." He winked, "Maybe the real Dragons could be white." I shrugged, "I was just testing out the new ride at H and Mom's park." He jolted, "They put a white Dragon in it? Mom asked me what colors to include."

I snorted, "Apparently there were charms to bring what I wanted to see in." He questioned, "And you wanted a white Dragon?" I admitted, "Well, no." Oden argued, "I would like to point out that now I want a white Dragon. I wish H would've let us break that wall separating them. They were meant to be together."

I calmly said, "It was a game." He shot back, "I feel you, so I know that you also wish we could've gotten to that part." Damn him knowing all my thoughts and feelings. He snorted, "It's been that way our entire life." He was yet again right.

I asked Bradley, "If you could have a Dragon, what color would it be?" His cheeks tinged pink. I felt he didn't think the answer was the macho one. I rolled my eyes, "Brother, I'm out here asking you about a game and Dragons. I am not going to judge you for the color of Dragon you'd like if their realm was still around."

He answered, "Pink." I laughed, "So you want a Duchess? Or a real Dragon?" He kicked the ground with his shoe, "Well, a WereDragon." I squeezed his shoulder, "No one would fault you for wanting a beautiful woman that turns into a Dragon. Do they have saddles like mom's game?"

He answered, "It would depend on the flier. Supernatural's wouldn't need one, but humans would." I asked, "They had human fliers?" He answered, "Yes, there were some famous ones in their realm but obviously they lost out on that when they closed off. I wonder if they still had their games. They sounded fun. I wish they were still around."

I encouraged him, "Uncle Aiden thinks they are." He snorted, "Even if they are, they won't come around. Dad doesn't think they are and neither does Uncle Bjourn. They are more realistic than Uncle Aiden." I agreed, "That's true on most things, but it doesn't make Uncle Aiden wrong." He smiled at me, and I popped back inside.

I shook myself, "It was just a video game." Oden encouraged, "Let's join a patrol." He probably needed to run. I popped to one and shifted. My cousin, Asterine Henderson, linked me, "Are you joining our patrol?" I answered, "Yup."

My other cousin, Ashleigh Henderson, linked, "Could you not run so insanely fast?" I assured her, "You don't need to keep pace with me." She groaned, "That's not true. The group will keep pace with you. You know what? I'm just going to fix this."

Her brothers, and my cousins, Thaddeus and Cory, popped in. I teased Ashleigh, "You didn't link all your brothers?" She answered, "The others were busy." I took off with Cory and Thaddeus. We ran the whole territory before Oden was calmer.

We were winding down when we heard pups screaming. I linked the pack, "ROGUES! GET TO YOUR SAFE PLACES!" EJ linked me, "Where?" I answered, "Southwest side of our border. It's three of them, we've got this." Oden growled, "I've got this."

He snarled and jumped over the frightened pups and ripped the wolves to pieces. I shifted back when EJ and Maverick popped to me. Thaddeus snorted, "You could've left some for us." Cory agreed, "Yeah, there was one each."

I replied, "I've had a weird day." EJ admitted, "We've had a lower number of rogue attacks these last few years." I muttered, "Since the Resistance formed." Cory asked, "Can't we just keep calling them the blue circle group? I mean, I know they have a name, but we called them that for so long and they didn't correct us."

Oden growled, "No." I sighed, "Just call them the Resistance." EJ agreed, "Since mom thinks that it probably annoys the person behind it all that we didn't figure out it was a ring and not a circle; just call them the Resistance. We don't need them to have another reason to avoid us."

Cory groaned, "But it's their fault we didn't know." I laughed, "Somehow I doubt they feel that way." Maverick chimed in, "Yeah, I'm guessing they don't see it as their fault. When you think about it the circle as a ring is kind of obvious since that's who we are fighting."

Cory grumbled, "Then it should've been gold or something. Who wears a blue ring?" EJ shrugged, "It's true." Oden huffed in my head. Cassie popped in with Gia and Tory. Genevieve, Toby, Phil and Gage joined us.

Phil whistled, "A rogue attack, they are so rare these days." He turned, "And what are you pups doing so close the border?" I was surprised they hadn't slunk away yet. Not that it would help since I saw them. Oden agreed, "They probably knew we'd remember their faces." Cory offered, "I'll pop the pups home."

I linked the pack, “The rogues are handled, resume normal duties.” My parents popped in. Cory went over to the pups and popped them away. Elise joined us and admitted, “These always shock me now. I’m so used to never having them.”

Ray called from just behind her, “Because we didn’t have one in Red Run for fourteen years.” That was true. Elise shrugged, “And most avoid this territory.” Our attacks were few and far between, more so in the last three years.

I walked back to the pack house. Phil nudged me, “You need to talk?” I snorted, “I had a weird experience in the game H had me try for the Dragon theme park. It’s super cool but…” I trailed off and linked him, “Melanie was in there fighting with me. She had a white Dragon, but Bradley said there was nothing in the histories he’s read about a white Dragon.”

He replied, “It’s just a game.” I agreed, “Yeah, but they asked Bradley about the Dragons, and you know how accurate my mom is.” I shrugged adding, “But it must just be my imagination or something that worked with the charm.” He asked, “Wait, what?”

Before I could say anything, Nana Blanch shoved a plate of muffins in front of us. She demanded, “Eat them.” Leo grabbed her from behind before she could fall down. He sighed, “Alyssa, I told you all those batches previous were amazing.”

She narrowed her eyes, “Those two girls said they weren’t the best yet.” I asked, “Have you been cooking all day?” She answered, “Yes.” Leo grumbled, “And drinking. She only paused for the lockdown. I thought I had my escape from the kitchen.”

Nana Blanch asked, “Are you not out of the kitchen?” He stared at the sky. I laughed and grabbed a muffin. I moaned, “This is delicious. Honestly, these are your best muffin ever and that is not a low bar.” She grabbed the plate back from Phil who was devouring them.

She shrieked, “Kaia and Hannah, you two get over here!” Leo followed along behind her catching the muffins before they fell. Hannah was hiding but Kaia had been in plain sight and froze. Hannah caught my gaze and put her hands up in prayer form.

She linked, “Please Alpha Alexander, don’t tell her I’m over here. I’ve tasted so many muffins today.” I snorted, “And they aren’t as good as the Nashville muffin?” She replied, “Not even close.” That surprised me.

Kaia told Nana Blanch, “I couldn’t possibly eat anther muffin today.” Phil snorted, “Poor Kaia. Nana Blanch is a shark scenting blood in the water.” Nana Blanch disagreed, “Of course you can. You left the gym thirty minutes ago.” She shoved the muffin under nose. Kaia sighed and took a bite.

She moaned, “This is really good. Wow. Definitely the best batch today.” She gave her a thumbs up and turned to leave. Nana Blanch asked, “Better than the Nashville muffin made by the drunk girl?” Hannah leaned forward from her hiding spot.

Kaia answered, “For sure.” She was lying. Nana Blanch gasped, “LIAR! Leo, back to the kitchens!” He said, “Ok, I’m calling a kitchen hiatus. People have to eat other things besides muffins. Let’s get you…” He trailed off when my mom popped in. She snapped the mated women and the one’s with boyfriends into sexy outfits.

All the men who loved to get dressed up were in sexy outfits too. Mom winked at me yelling, “SCATTER!” She popped away with Nana Blanch. Leo growled, “Are you fucking kidding me right now?” Nana Blanch gasped, “LANGUAGE!” Her voice carried from the mountain.

Dad and Leo shifted and took off running. I laughed and popped inside. I watched from the window while everyone was enjoying themselves. Oden whimpered, “We could play these games with mate.” I snorted, “Sure. If we made sure Red Run was sedated.” He grumbled, “We could do that.”

We could. More than likely if I’d been with Melanie this whole time, they’d be used it. I assured Oden, “Our time is coming. She’ll be home soon enough and then we can play these games with her.” Soon, we wouldn’t be on the outside of the fun we’d be right there with them. I couldn’t wait until that day. I’d been patient and soon it was going to pay off.

On My Own

Melanie is Eighteen Years Old

Melanie was walking around the pack. I had hoped Jason would send me a card or letter for my birthday, but he didn't. No one did. I heard Trevor growl, "Mine!" Oh gosh. His poor mate. He ran and stood in front of me.

I moved the side, but he mirrored me. I saw Buck's jaw drop and his eyes widen in horror. I told Trevor, "By all means, go get your mate. I have a meeting with Buck so… move… and I'll just be thinking positive thoughts for you mate." I'd probably have to get her out of here.

Trevor grabbed my arm, and I put him on his back in a second. I asked, "What do you think you're doing?" He snarled, "You are my mate! We are going to my room, mating, marking, then I'll burn that stuffed wolf of yours." I threw my head back and laughed.

A crowd had gathered. Dax pushed through. He asked, "What's going on here?" I answered, "Trevor is lying for some reason. I'm not really sure why… but he lives in a fantasy land of things that are NEVER happening."

He growled, "You're just mad you had delusions of grandeur. Alpha Alexander isn't yours, you're mine!" I blinked at him. I asked, "Do you think I like the smell of wet dog? I don't." He growled at me, "That doesn't matter! You are mine."

I argued, "It does in fact matter…I am not yours… also I don't feel tingles when I touch you… nor am I drawn to you. I'm pretty sure you're lying because everyone knows if you decided you wanted me as your chosen, you can't forcibly mark me… because I'd kick your butt. Maybe even kill you. It's all a strange turn of events with whatever stunt you're pulling today."

Dax put himself between me and Trevor. Trevor snarled, "Move. She's mine." I scoffed, "Please… literally no one believes that." Booker said, "You will do what fated mates do, Melanie." I sighed, "Of course Booker believes you because he has no brain." He snarled at me.

Aunt Stephanie shouted, "You go mate with that boy right now." I agreed, "He is a boy. Oh my gosh, we agree on something…I honestly never thought a day would come where we did…but you're right. He's not a man… that's for certain." Buck hung and shook his head.

Edward called, "Buck, you'll have to make do without Melanie. We clearly need to talk this through." I called, "I'll be ten minutes late tops, Buck. Because this is easily solved. It's not true and literally everyone but you three…" I paused.

I admitted, "Actually probably even you three, know it. Trevor, come on… dispense with this drama. You hate me. Everyone here knows you hate me. Wanna know how? You tell everyone… a lot… like all the time….at least three times a day…and that's an average."

He snarled, "That doesn't change that you are mine." I warned, "Stop saying that because I am NOT yours nor will I ever be." Dax followed us into the meeting with Booker, Caine, Edward, and Trevor. Edward said, "I linked Buck you wouldn't be joining him."

I disagreed, "I'll join him so fast… like blazingly fast." Jean said, "You just can't feel the mate bond." I snorted, "Are you going to try and gaslight me right now? I feel you are. I really do." Edward, surprisingly gently, said, "You don't have a wolf. So, you have to be marked to feel the bond." Dax tensed but I laughed in all their faces.

Trevor's mom joined us and sat quietly. I started crying I was laughing so hard. I asked, "Is this what you tell all the wolf less members?" I looked at their faces and sobered. I gasped, "You do! Oh my gosh… why do I keep thinking I know how DEPRAVED you are? I clearly don't… you all are on some…"

Booker interrupted, "You will mate my son and like it." I laughed, "I've yet to hear about an encounter a woman enjoyed with him." Trevor snarled at me, "You are my second chance, and you will submit." I said, "I am not yours and you know it."

He argued, "You can't feel…" I cut him off, "I'm not letting you gaslight me. I grew up in a pack with partials. There are Werewolf hybrids that have a QUARTER of wolf blood running in their wolf less veins, and they recognized their mate. A QUARTER!"

Dax's head jolted to mine as if he didn't know that. I scoffed, "I'm not mating Trevor… end of story." I walked out of the room with them following me. Booker demanded, "Alpha Command her, Edward!" I scoffed, "Oh my gosh… try it. Try it and find out what happens. That is ILLEGAL even to the Supernatural council."

Edward grabbed Booker's arm because one of the men that mated to a woman from another pack were outside in the yard. Her jaw dropped and her arms crossed. Edward laughed nervously, "Of course I wouldn't Alpha Command Melanie to do that." He couldn't.

He'd tried before and it didn't work, but that was before Red Run banished me. He hadn't tried since that had happened which was odd now that I thought about it. The woman nodded and the guy shot me a look full of apologies as he rushed her out of the pack. I didn't need an apology. He should get her out. This wasn't true.

Booker snarled, "Mate my son, now." I answered, "No, in fact if anyone wants a lesson in how to know when you're being gaslit... I'm here for you. I'm here for you all the time but none of you listen… which…"

Trevor growled, "You just don't feel the bond yet." I replied, "Chosen mates don't feel a bond until they are marked. FATED mates do… even if they are a partial. I, Melanie Jane McAlister, reject you Trevor McCann as my mate." Nothing happened.

I snorted, "See? LIAR!" Booker stammered, "It didn't work because you don't have a wolf." The rumblings had started around the pack. A lot were indignant. I snorted, "Every single wolf knows that if he had been my mate, it would've hurt him even if he didn't accept. Because while you claim I don't feel the bond… he said he did. Yet he's standing there just fine…"

I paused adding, "And I think we all know he's a wimp when it comes to pain." Trevor snarled, "You can't talk to your mate like that." I shouted, "YOU ARE NOT MY MATE! I AM NOT YOURS!" He warned, "Just because you wanted to be someone else's doesn't make you not mine."

I replied, "The fact you hurt me the way you did does… the fact that you have been NOTHING but a bully, tyrant, evil, sadistic jerk to me since I came does… the fact that you didn't go down IN PAIN when I fake rejected you WITH THE REAL REJECTION WORDS does… AND EVERYONE HERE KNOWS IT!"

I got in his face, "You can't gaslight me about mates. I didn't grow up here with your crap being spewed at me. I was raised with love." He shoved me, "And got sent to us because you're a cursed family killer!" Pain lit through me. Dax snarled at him.

Caine jumped out of a truck. He asked, "What's going on here?" Someone muttered, "They've been lying about how wolf less don't feel the bond with their fated mates until marked. Melanie said she wasn't Trevor's and proved it by rejecting him. He didn't even flinch in pain. They have been LYING all along!" Good. Finally. People were pissed.

Caine snarled, "Trevor, back off." He declared, "She is mine." I scoffed, "I'm not and you know it." Edward Alpha Commanded, "No one will tell Melanie she's not Trevor's. He's said she is, and we believe him. This is just a mate's spat." People stared at him like he was insane. He blinked realizing that he was losing the tentative string he held on this pack.

I shook my head, "You're disgusting. You are a disgrace to your blood. You should have my back… especially considering this is the man who hurt me… and you let that happen. You should've said you'd get a pack approved couple's therapist if you believed him. You should PUNISH him for LYING about me being his mate…" He went to talk, but I wasn't done.

I scoffed, "And not how you punish people. Like normal Alpha's do… though Trevor would be DEAD in any other pack. He shot the Female Lead Warrior in the back while she was saving pups." Trevor growled, "You deserved it."

I scoffed, "For saving pack members? Even if it wasn't MY JOB… no one deserves to be shot by a coward in the back… and…" He cut me off, "You got your family killed! Beta Jason told us we could do whatever we wanted to you."

I scoffed, "No he didn't. If you want to hold onto that though I'll drive to their border with Blue Moon's border and ask. Do you think Alpha Peter and Beta Jason would enjoy your masterpiece and condone it, Trevor?" I knew the answer even if they'd deluded themselves into think they had permission to do that. They all paled.

Booker snarled, "You're not leaving. You are my son's mate." I mocked him, "Just because you keep saying it, doesn't make it true… he's not mine and I'm NOT an idiot. No one here believed he was my mate before he didn't react to my rejection. It's literally unthinkable, even to you dolts, to hurt your mates the way he has PHSYICALLY hurt me."

I sneered, "Only deviants hurt and abuse their mates. Are you finally admitting he is one? Because then he will be taken to the Supernatural Council and…" Edward said, "That's not necessary." I argued, "Under Supernatural Council decrees 149 SSB subsection…"

Trevor shouted, "We don't care about your rules!" I rolled my eyes saying, "You don't care about anyone's rules until they affect you. It's very uneducated of you… unbecoming… there are more adjectives to describe you, but we'd be here all day, and I have a MEETING!"

I took off running and for once, most of the pack covered my escape. Trevor snarled, "You can't escape me, mate." I shouted, "I am NOT your mate… you wet smelly dog…" I grumbled, "He smells so bad and… opfff…" Trevor's mom grabbed me and yanked me behind the gym.

I asked, "Alice, are you ok?" Mentally I pleaded, please don't tell me to be with Trevor to save him… please… I really liked Alice. I actually felt really bad for her. She whispered "You can't mate with him. He'll kill you." I winced, "It's more like the other way around."

She glanced sharply at me then nearly laughed. She waved, "I needed that. Just don't let him convince you to be with him. You don't deserve the things he's done." Tears rolled down her cheeks. She whispered, "I tried so hard with him. He was a sweet boy then…" She trailed off and wiped her face.

I squeezed her hands, "You did what you could." She cried, "It's not enough. He's even more of a monster than his father is. Booker does unkind things, but that candy you gave helps. Booker never hits me. He's never raised a hand outside the bedroom though I wish he would've instead of making our son evil. I wish he'd beat me black and blue and left Trevor alone."

She continued, "He's so focused on Trevor, I've been able to keep the rest of my pups away from him. You know my other pups are so sweet." I agreed, "They are." She shook her head, "The things I've heard him say about this day and how he'd treat you. I'm so glad you're not his. I want to be surprised he lied but I'm not. God, I'm really not. Please stay away from him. I have to go." She ran from me as if her life depended on it. To be fair… it did.

I walked into the gym and found Buck. He sighed in relief when he looked at my neck. He whispered, "Can the wolf less really feel the bond if it's fated?" I answered, "Of course… why wouldn't they? Because they don't have a wolf to growl 'mine'? They still feel everything everyone else does with their fated. Tingles can't be faked."

He asked, "How is Avery?" I answered, "Talk to her and find out… you guys were talking, did something happen?" He replied, "No, it's just different now." I shrugged and we worked out the schedules.

Buck walked out with me where Trevor, Mark, and Francis were waiting. I announced, "I have another meeting so… I can't do this strange thing where you're being cra…" Trevor cut me off, "Get to my room and lay on your back, naked." Buck rubbed his face with his hand.

I answered, "Not only no, but hell to the never gonna happen no." Mark sighed, "I told you to ask her on a date." I hummed, "That's a better way to approach it… if he could go back in time to about four years." Mark winced. Francis sighed, "Will you just get on with mating him?"

I scoffed, "No. It's never happening. I'm not going to be with him. I'd rather die." Francis jolted saying, "You don't mean that." I turned to Buck who looked stunned. I questioned, "Has this pack not established my lying abilities leave something to be desired?" He answered, "Uh huh." I prodded, "So, clearly I'm serious I would rather die than be anything other than his mortal enemy." He nodded, "You are apparently serious." I winked, "There it is."

I ran past them and got my motorcycle from Mason's house. I revved past Edward and Jean who were trying to flag me down to talk. They could wait. I drove to my secondary place where I was meeting with several people.

I walked in and chaos ensued. Avery shouted, "Oh my gosh, are you ok?" I answered, "I'm fine… well… ya know…it's not a great birthday so far…but overall…I'm fine." I went and grabbed some vodka and started drinking it.

I asked, "Olivia, how are poisoning Maverick's threats going?" I'd been working with her on the range. She could switch between the two now. She answered, "Quite well. I do feel bad though. He seems agitated." I told her, "I gave them the poison we were using so he's probably just aware it's us and wondering why he can't catch you."

I asked, "Hendrick, what about Aria?" He answered, "I went out last night and took out several Goblins and a Demon. I swear they go after her with the Frost Giant's the most." I hummed, "Yes, you seem to enjoy killing the Frost Giants." It's why I'd assigned him to them.

I offered, "I went out and offed a whole coven that was going to go after Killian Farmer. Have we figured out why they are after him?" Paige snorted, "No." I hummed, "Is Guster doing it?" I kind of hoped she said yes. Rya Daniels kept going back to dating him and I didn't like it. He sucked.

Paige replied, "He's in a good coven from what I can tell. I met two of the women in it and three men. They are good people practicing the right way. If it's him, he's got another coven involved. Or he's working with someone else." I sighed, "I liked some of those words. So… that's progress… I suppose."

Hendrick added, "I used that device planted with iron set for Ariena." I squealed and kicked my feet. I demanded, "Tell me we got her. Oh gosh… that will turn my birthday around… and…" He cut in, "She didn't die according to the chatter."

I grumbled, "Did she at least get hurt?" He nodded enthusiastically, "Yes, she did. Her new lover took the brunt of the blast." I muttered, "I'll just calibrate it better. Next time, glancing blows also kill." Paige reasoned, "She'll be out of commission for a while though, recovering. She's a full blooded Fairy and she has no access to healers at the moment."

I acknowledged, "That does make me happy… Xander will be happy about that." I drank more and listened to the reports. An alert went off and I quickly checked it. I snorted, "Someone dumped a body on the Resistance?! Who would do that? Hmmm…."

Addison asked, "Is it a cover up?" I looked into it and admitted, "No, we would've killed this person. They were on our watch list. They are obsessed with Luna Alexandria Daniels. It was likely a Hood member. I'll find it."

I threw my hair up and began to hack looking for any type of evidence. I found the frame I wanted and froze it. I admitted, "Wow… I didn't see that coming. Good for him." Caine asked, "Good for who? Are we moving against someone?" Dax replied, "Her tone says we aren't."

I grinned, "We are getting our first honorary member. That's exciting…. and new… I like this a lot. I just need to pull a list together of who he would mostly likely target so we can have his back… from afar… because he's so fast."

Caine leaned over my shoulder. He said, "I remember that outfit. Dax, which one is the Silver Blade?" Sierra gasped, "Keaton Daniels assassinated someone without his family's permission?!" I had already hacked Heath and Joe Scott, so I knew the answer.

I hummed, "He did. Look at him… that's such growth for him…. He's such a cute honorary member of the Resistance." She snorted, "Don't say it like that." I waved, "I'll write him a note and…" Valetina said, "I will shimmer to his room with it." I grumbled, "That's not as fun but fine… we could've had fun."

Addison threw out, "I think we've had enough excitement for the morning." Caine agreed, "It's been a heck of a morning." I waved, "I won't be gaslit about my mate… honestly… no one believed we were mates before threats of Alpha Commands and fake rejections were issued."

My phone rang. I answered, "Beta Jason." Caine growled. He said, "You refused your fated mate?" I answered, "Nope… he's not my fated." I hung up. He called back. I answered, "Uh huh….this is a record of you calling me…so…please say something nicer…like happy birthday for example." My friends gaped at me.

I'd never been rude to my brother when he called before. I'd usually try to explain, but they were NOT going to lie to my brother to try and GASLIGHT me. Not about my mate. It was NOT happening. I was Xander's.

Jason snarled, "Alexander IS NOT YOURS!" I winced, "Even if you think that… it doesn't mean I wouldn't feel the bond with my fated mate. You know that… and I know that. So whether you believe me on who my mate is or not…we both know it's not who they claim it is."

He asked, "Wait, you don't feel the…?" I cut him off, "Oh and Mom would punch you in the FACE for saying otherwise. T would get you too. He'd kick your butt and you know it. So… for once… do what you do and LEAVE ME ALONE! I'm busy!" I hung up.

I wrote out my note for Keaton letting him know it was ok to throw his kills on the Resistance. I handed it Valentina and found everyone staring at me as if I was an alien. I asked, "What? Why are you all looking at me like that?"

Sierra said, "Umm." When she didn't continue I questioned, "Was that the end of the sentence?" Paige said, "Girrlllll! HUG ME!" She jumped up and gave me a hug. She squealed, "I should've known your Xander was the key to getting you to SNAP! I am SO proud of you right now! All of us are!"

Avery said, "Umm we are mostly shocked but proud." Olivia agreed, "I'm newer to the group and I'm mostly shocked. I'll get to proud. I'm working my way out of the shock." I hummed, "But we love you… and it's been like almost two years… so you're not new."

Flashback

Melanie was annoyed. I grumbled, "I can't believe I didn't find…" Paige interrupted, "But we did find this facility. They do move prisoners around a lot. So, this is a good find." Of course now that I'd found it there was only one person inside right now. Caine wanted to wait and hit it when there was more to save.

He wasn't wrong… but I didn't want this person to suffer. Who knows how long she'd been down there? Paige and I got in and she hexed the guards to think there were spiders coming at them. They came running to me where I killed them with my broadsword.

She said, "You are scary with that thing." I bragged, "Xander is too." She rolled her eyes saying, "I know that your Xander prefers his broadsword. We are ALL aware." I huffed and went to the door of the room where the girl was being held. I easily hacked in, and it opened.

She cried, "Please leave me alone today. It still hurts." I told her, "They will never hurt you again." She gasped when she saw us. She whispered, "You're the blue circle group people. Right? You are in all black and have masks on." Paige snickered.

I grumbled, "The Resistance. We are the Ring Resistance. Why isn't that obvious?" I picked her up, "Let's get you out of here." She cried, "I tried once, but I didn't make it." I asked, "Did you even known about Supernatural's when they took you?" She answered, "I didn't." Odd. She was partial wolf and Fairy.

I asked, "Where are your parents?" Paige hit my arm as we got to the elevator. I asked, "Why are you hitting me?" Paige said, "That's not a nice thing to ask." The girl said, "It's fine. I was left at a Fire station." I hummed, "I see." There was no way to know if her mom or dad gave her wolf or Fairy blood. I took her to one of my safe houses then took off our masks.

She gasped, "You guys are like, my age!" I went to answer but she grabbed both my hands. She insisted, "I want in." I asked, "Huh?" Paige said, "She wants to join the Resistance." She reasoned, "I have nothing to go back to. I'm not the girl who was the life of the party anymore. They stole her and I can't do it." Paige said, "You can get her back."

The girl stared at me. She pointed, "I can see in your eyes you know I can't. You feel that ache for your old self that I do, but she's dead. She's changed. Let me do this. I need to fight back." I sighed,

“You’re a partial Were…” She cut me off, “I know now what I am. A Werewolf / Fairy hybrid. They were disappointed I don’t have a wolf.”

Some hybrids with Fairy blood didn’t get their wolf until they were marked. I just wasn’t going to give her false hope. I asked, “What’s your name?” She answered, “Olivia. I’m smart, I swear. I can help! I’m advanced and I studied biological attacks and counters to them.”

I glanced at Paige. She was trying not to laugh. I nudged her, “She can make poison… we are totally missing that element.” Paige snorted, “It’s only missing because you like to shoot people.” I grinned, “But Olivia can add a different facet to the Resistance. I like it. Welcome to the Resistance, Olivia.”

Valentina shimmered in with Celia and the latter gave me a look. I said, “I didn’t do it.” She sighed and got to work. Paige whispered, “Are you sure about this girl?” I was because I felt an instant kinship with Olivia.

I answered, “Yes, she’ll fit right in. She’s a missing piece we didn’t know we needed until now.” She snorted, “Ok, but Caine will be pissed about this.” Yeah, he would be. We were supposed to wait… and as a Beta Blood I should’ve listened to him.

That thought nearly crushed me because I wasn’t a Beta blood. Mom was Warrior blood though… so I should still listen to him. In my defense, it was the wrong call…and I’d made the right one. It still hurt my soul though.

Flashback Ends

Caine said, “She’s not new, but I agree. I’m here for you putting your brother in his place. Because your parents and older brother WOULD be ashamed of him.” I hummed, “It must have worked, because none of the rest of them have called to chastise me….” Tears filled my eyes.

Paige hugged me gently this time whispering, “Mel…” I cried, “He didn’t even say happy birthday. He was just mad at me. He’s always mad…. and it’s so exhausting all the time… he must be so tired.” She snorted, “Well, he deserves that, but you don’t.”

The rest of the night was a haze of alcohol. I was going to sit on Black Mountain’s border to see my REAL mate, but Trevor got in the way. I woke up in my room at Hendrick and Mason’s house. I asked, “How did I get here?”

Mason answered, “Caine found you and brought you here.” I hummed, “Did I fight Trevor?” Hendrick snorted, “According to Caine, you fought Trevor, Francis, and Mark.” I shrugged, “So a normal day.”

Edward banged on their door shouting, “Open up, I know she’s in here!” Hendrick sighed and did so. He growled, “You can’t attack pack members!” I replied, “We all know he attacked me… we also all know you’ll ignore your duty and protect him. So… what’s the point of this conversation?” He snorted, “You have a Huntress duty. Killing more Omegas.” He grinned evilly at me.

Little did he know I’d never a killed a single person that wasn’t bad. They kept bringing in small Hunter groups that I gave the choice to embrace their real purpose, or I killed and pretended to be them. I was easily saving thousands of people my way. Then I was sending those Omegas to the allied packs I came from.

I glanced at the list. I startled, “This is a pack doctor.” Uh oh. I had recently rescued someone from this pack who asked me to save her sister. She said her brother in law was the pack doctor. Why would they move on this pack again so quickly? That was totally against their regular pattern. I hadn’t had time to look up the family and work on getting them out.

Edward winked, “Get moving. You’re meeting the group coming in.” I sighed and went and got into my Huntress gear. I sent a coded message to Anastasia, so she’d know which group we were impersonating next.

I did research on the doctor. His name was Ezekiel, and it had been discovered he was running away because his daughter was going to be auctioned off. It sounded like that was a set up, so I dove further into it. I easily found the answers I was looking for.

His mate's younger sister was someone we rescued recently. His mistake, and his wife's, was trusting her brother. He betrayed them to the Alpha because they'd threatened his pups. Great I was going into a cluster of a situation.

I dove back into Ezekiel's life. He had Gamma blood. I snorted, "Getting too big for our britches there now Dante. A Gamma blood could take Hunters… ugh… stupid." Rescuing him was going to be a problem.

At this point, as the voice of the forgotten, Ashley Griffen was known around here. Ezekiel was going to put it together that Red One was Ashley, but there was nothing I could do about that. I left and got on my motorcycle.

Once I got to the scheduled location, I moved my motorcycle out of sight. I didn't have time to look up the family, but my senses were telling me this was that same woman's family I'd saved previously.

I met up with two of their group. I easily spotted they were mates, and they probably didn't even know. I said, "I'll be in the trees." They snorted, "Whatever. You just have to help with the Gamma blood." Yeah, no.

Once they left me alone, I tapped the buttons on my watch to get my Resistance gear. I climbed the tree and waited. Maybe the brother will have second thoughts… maybe he would do the right thing. I whispered, "Don't show up. Don't show up."

I just needed a happier story than mine. I needed another brother not to betray his sister because, just this once, I was acknowledging Jason betrayed me. My hope vanished when I saw them arrive. How it hurt my soul at this point I wasn't certain. I barely had one left.

The woman was beside herself and the doctor was carrying his daughters. He stopped and glared at the brother in law. He smelled the Hunters, which wasn't surprising. His brother in law asked, "Ezekiel, what are you doing?"

Ezekiel practically snarled, "What have you done?" His wife turned to him in surprise. He growled, "I have Gamma blood, John. I can smell them." John cringed, "They threatened my little girl. I had to. I'm sorry." He fled, leaving them behind.

I muttered to myself, "That's a clear sign not to rescue him… I would've if he stayed, but he left. So, he should think he got them killed… that's a thing… Fairies would say it was fair… Xander is a Fairy… so he'd be proud of my logic. Yup. Going with it."

Ezekiel's wife cried, "Ezekiel." He whispered to her, "Donna, it's going to be ok." Hunters surrounded them, but they were waiting for me because they couldn't take him. Donna cried, "Oh my poor sister. Dorothy went out this way too." Nope. Not true at all.

Dorothy impressed me with her self-defense. She'd watched my Xander's videos and taught herself. I was proud of him like I hoped he was proud of my persona, Ashley. I also acknowledged this was the family Dorothy asked me to get out.

Ezekiel shifted, ready to fight for his family. One Hunter sneered, "I'll take you down first and you'll watch me rape your weak wife and break your pups one by one." I rolled my eyes. Ok, so no chance given for him. He was dying.

Several in the group looked excited, but the two I'd talked to didn't. They looked disgusted and horrified. Ok, I could give them a chance. They could hear the truth and decide what to do from there. If they were a problem, then I'd kill them too.

Ezekiel's wolf snarled as the group mocked him. Had they ever taken on a wolf? He'd get more of them for that comment alone. Donna screamed, "Ezekiel, they have silver weapons!" All Hunters did. It was really the only thing they had because at this point, they were lazy Hunters.

Plus, they weren't meant to Hunt Werewolves, or Supernatural's, at all. I'd had enough. I shot the ones that weren't being given a chance in rapid succession. I left the ones I'd talked to earlier alive to get some answers. I jumped down and entered the field. Ezekiel was hovering around his family.

I was going to send them to Black Mountain. I quickly sent out the orders for Valentina to get a car in the area for them. I just knew they'd fit there, I knew it. I addressed the two I'd spoken to earlier, "I'll give you two a choice, since you weren't out here making horrible comments about the pups and the mate. In fact, you look horrified. It's the only reason you're still breathing. You can turn to your true cause as Hunters or die." Everyone stared at me confused. This always happened.

The woman questioned, "What true cause? We hunt wolves." I scoffed, "No, you don't. First, you're horrible at it… because you're not supposed to do it in the first place. You're Supernatural's yourselves. You're even mates." Donna actually gasped and Ezekiel raised an eyebrow.

The Hunter argued, "She's my wife." I mocked him, "Oh yeah? Is that so? She's just your wife. So, you don't feel sparks when you touch her? You don't feel possessive? Touch my hand." I held it out for him. His wife instantly looked like she wanted to kill me if she possessed the skills.

I explained it to her, "The name's Red One, and you're quite possessive in ways human women aren't. I asked him to touch my hand to prove he feels sparks when he touches you." I had to reach out and touch him, but his wife yanked him back.

Both looked shocked by this revelation. The man said, "I want to know more about what you're saying." I hit the call for Virgil to come to me. He did instantly. I instructed him, "Debrief them." He would take them to Anastasia, and she would explain and determine if they should join the cause.

They would be monitored and if they stepped so much as a toe out of line, I'd kill them. Or one of my people would. Anastasia was very protective of her cause for good reason. Virgil shimmered away with them.

I turned back to the stunned couple. Ezekiel questioned, "Who are you?" I repeated, "Red One." It was the name I'd chosen for operations when I went out with the Hunters. It felt right to have a different name than Bravo One.

I couldn't have them in allied territories letting them link Red One and Bravo One since Cayden knew I was Red One. I gave him information and was his source. So, I had to let him in on this code name. It was reasonable… and logical… plus, he had to help sometimes. That was a thing… and I just really enjoyed seeing the pride in his eyes when I did it. It meant everything to me.

I urged, "Let's go. I have a car waiting to take you to a bus." I tapped the button on my watch for the bus tickets to Black Mountain and handed them to Ezekiel with notes for the Alpha's. I put them on all the watches for everyone. We had bus tickets for all the allies with notes.

Paige wrote Lux and Alpha Theo's notes out since I knew them, and according to my friends it came across in the note. Avery wrote the one's for Red Run because they said it was the same problem. Ezekiel gasped, "You're sending us to Black Mountain?"

I answered, "Yes, I think you will work well with Ethan. Which…makes no sense to you because you don't know Ethan… that didn't explain anything. So, he's their pack doctor. He runs the pack hospital… but he has another hospital that sees other supernatural's and given your papers I think you will fit well there. He'll like you. Again, it's not the pack hospital, but I think you'll…"

Donna interrupted, "Please can I ask you about my sister? Did you save her too? Can I see her? Please." I winked, "She always wanted to go to California." I'd sent her to Everly's home pack. Donna sobbed, "She did always want to go there. She talked about how sunny beaches were her calling."

I added, "She was placed with a good Warrior pack in California, and she asked me to get you out next." I just didn't know they were going to be targeted and hadn't quite looked into them yet. Ezekiel surmised, "You're Ashley Griffen." Crap.

I took off my mask admitting, "I don't usually tell people that, but I assumed you would figure it out." Ezekiel held out his hand graciously saying, "Thank you. I owe you our lives." I assured him, "Our people will make sure you cross the border to Black Mountain through no man's land. If we need to step in, we will."

He held his pups tighter before saying, "Thank you is not enough." I disagreed, "It is. Go live the life you were meant to have. I'll make sure these guys can't track you." He commented, "You're something aren't you?" I shrugged hoping that he might talk about other things I did down here in Black Mountain.

Not this, obviously. He could talk about the challenges I win, or the attacks I make sure people don't die in. Things my brother would be proud of me for.

I tapped my watch issuing a folder to Valentina's with Dorothy's information. Also to supply one of our coded computers to Ezekiel. We could collaborate with him. He was smart and felt indebted to us. He would help and we could make everyone safer. I watched them until they disappeared then went about setting up their deaths to this pack. Once I was done with that I went home.

My days blended together in a strand of monotony, yet different somehow. The Resistance and being Red One changed up my days along with Rebel Concert, but in Black Path I was repeatedly punished. That wasn't new, but lately it was for refusing to mate with Trevor.

The dissention in the pack was at an all time high now. Wolf less that hadn't felt the bond with their mates were pissed. Ones that had felt the bond were happy they were with someone who respected them. Overall, it was probably the worst tension between the pack leadership and the pack itself I'd seen yet.

Which I was also being punished for. Because it was my fault I'd exposed their lie. Not that they called it that. I'd caused 'pack dissention.' The dolts actually thought it was MY fault their gaslighting came to be public knowledge.

I'd supplied Cayden with tips over the years, but this urgent need to check out the drug buy place we'd told him about recently was eating at me. Sierra asked, "What is that face?" I answered, "I want to go by the drug place we gave Cayden… no want to is the wrong word. We HAVE to." Valentina shot up, "I'll come too." She shimmered us there. Everything immediately felt off.

I was trying to be normal, but my eyes kept being drawn to the edge of the forest. Sierra sighed finally asking, "What's up?" I shrugged admitting, "I don't know. Something." We'd been keeping an eye on all the drug rings, but usually when I'd given them to Cayden we let the Hackura handle it.

I still felt the need to be here today, which made no sense. We all heard someone walking towards the building. I turned to see who it was and my jaw dropped. I linked Sierra, "HE SENT CASSIE?! WHAT THE HELL WAS HE THINKING?! THEY KNOW HER!"

Sierra looked at me when she replied, "That's not Cassie." I retorted, "Uhh yes it is." Sierra whispered out loud, "Val, is that Cassie?" Valentina snorted, "No." I gaped at them nearly shrieking, "Yes... it is! That's Cassie Conners! The red hair ...."

Sierra interrupted, "That girl does not have red hair." I rolled my eyes insisting, "YES, she does. Because THAT is Cassie Conners." Sierra gently asked, "Why do you think that?" I sighed, "Because it is. I have eyeballs and I know what she likes… I'm not sure what other answer you are looking for here. She went with my brother to dances… there were pictures of her EVERYWHERE! That is her."

Sierra frowned and Nate popped in. I was proud of him. We'd worked on his distance. I wasn't the best teacher he could have but he didn't want to meet the Conners yet. He had to have a powerful bloodline to do all he was doing. We were still working on where his sisters were.

I was gaining traction into the Hunter files, but I was going slowly like I was with the Ring. Nate smiled saying, "I made it on the first try." I smiled offering, "Good job. What are you doing here?" Sierra inclined her head asking him, "Is that Cassie Conners, Nate?"

Nate studied her before answering, "Well, it could be. That girl has a Fairy charm." I rolled my eyes, "You all need to get your eyes checked. It IS Cassie Conners. As the one who saw her pictures… I'm right. Also, she looks EXACTLY like her mother. I know things about my Xander and his family… all the things."

Nate shrugged, "Sorry Mel, the jury's out on whether that's Cassie Conners or not." He popped out while I rolled my eyes. The jury was NOT out. It was Cassie. They needed their heads examined stat. Ceila could have new patients that weren't me. She'd be thrilled.

Valentina admitted, "She does know everything about her Xander." Sierra snorted, "That woman still looks nothing like Cassie Conners." She looked exactly like her because she was her! I scrunched up my face when Cassie went inside. I didn't like it.

In fact, I was twitching to text Micah and ask what the gosh darn heck Cayden was thinking sending Cassie here. He wasn't thinking….is what he wasn't doing….clearly. Was this a post sex haze assignment he made? That no one thought... 'hey maybe we send…. literally anyone else.' Literally even Micah with his same dang name. ANYONE ELSE.

Honestly, if they'd sent Xander I'd be calling Micah's SO FAST. Maybe I should call them anyway. I started to pace. Sierra sighed, "Potentially Cassie is probably fine. She went to a buying room." We did have eyes inside. Just not in the buying rooms themselves.

I sighed, "If she's not out in five minutes… I'm calling Micah and we are going in. I won't let anything happen to Cassie or let her be ambushed alone. CRAP! She's probably not alone. Someone else is here." Cayden wouldn't send her alone…nor would her family…King Bjourn definitely had back up here.

Valentina nervously said, "We should go then." I shook my head, "No, I won't leave Xander's sister here alone. Cassie is also important to…." I trailed off. Sierra's eyes softened, "Jason." I nodded. They weren't mates, but Jason cared about Cassie.

I knew they were still friends. He would be devastated if something happened to her. Not to mention my Xander. Everyone knew the Conners boys doted on their sisters. If something happened to her, Xander would be greatly affected.

Especially since he was more attuned to his siblings' pain. Particularly Cassie and EJ because they were triplets. I would never let her get hurt. She was meant to be my sister in law. I couldn't leave without knowing she was safe.

Sierra announced, "See, potential Cassie is out of the room. Everyone is all smiles." I argued, "That guy keeps checking his phone. I don't like it." Valentina agreed, "His whole demeanor just changed." I cringed, "I'm going around the side to scale the building. You guys cover the front. Call out if you need help."

Valentina grabbed my arm offering, "I'll shimmer you to the top of the warehouse. You might want to get ready to shoot." I nodded and was watching. This wasn't good. I needed time to think. I watched Cassie and it hit me that I actually missed someone I didn't know.

Now, I was seriously considering just going to Black Mountain to see if I could spot Xander. I wasn't going to go to him… I just wanted to see him. Not just on a computer screen as he talked through fighting moves. Actually see him, in person.

I just didn't know how far away to be so his wolf wouldn't sense me. If he could. I could spray myself and I didn't have a wolf for him to sense... I shook myself. I needed to focus on what happening in front of me. I needed to make sure Cassie was safe.

Sierra called over our coms, "You're right. Something is off." I knew that. Then watched the guy with Cassie pull a knife. Cassie had it handled, but the guy hit a panic button. She took off. I began shooting to cover her. Sierra and Valentina stepped out.

I yelled over the coms, "What are you doing? I've got this!" Valentina whispered, "The Hackura women spotted us. We had to move." I could not get a break. Return fire engaged, but they weren't aiming at us. I shot as many as I could.

Sierra yelled, "Bravo One, I'm pinned down! I'm pinned down!" Fury filled my core because these people thinking they could get one of mine. I scaled down the building quickly and dropped the remaining several feet.

I pulled the gun I'd been working on, that would shoot gel packs of Laxenread to give a Fairy their powers back, out of my watch. Now was as good a time as ever to test if it worked. An idea clicked. I could leave it for her. The Hackura would search the area. I'd worked really hard on it…it was for them.

I'd wanted to give it Xander… with a note, but Cassie needed her powers back. Someone came around the corner. He snorted, "That Fairy charmed chick will go down. We hit her with our paralytic." She wouldn't because they didn't have it tailored to hybrids.

No one paid attention to the papers King Aiden Holloran put out either, except me, because it would've told them that. I shook myself and killed him quickly.

I grabbed the kerosene kit we all carried for emergencies. Most people probably didn't prepare to blow up drug labs but… most people weren't us. I hopped on the bike and revved it letting Sierra know I was coming.

Valentina's voice came over coms, "Cassie's been hit. Not bad but the bullet grazed her." I knew that because the dead guy told me. This was good. The allies would discover the bullets were laced with other things. I grumbled, "People should really read King Aiden's papers and books." He had literally written an entire book about hybrids. I'd managed to get myself a copy. Through bartering…and blackmail.

The same reason the coating on the bullets would not affect Cassie didn't concern me played into part of my fear…. Some days… I thought that maybe I really wasn't Drake McAlister's biological daughter. Drugs didn't affect me right either. I was a possible Hunter hybrid though. I shook myself chiding, "FOCUS!"

I drove quickly towards the window of the building, waving what was basically a lit up stick of dynamite. They began to focus on me. Good. They started chasing me on foot. Seriously? Who ran these things? Because it was not these people. They were so dumb.

Who thought they were going to outrun someone on a motorcycle on foot? Maybe the Werecheetah's I'd met in the Safari realm… but these guys had no cheetah blood. Honestly, it was basic math and common sense.

I looked over my shoulder noting Valentina used the distraction to shimmer Sierra out. I sighed in relief. Valentina had to stay out of the path of those bullets. It affected her more harshly than anyone we'd come across.

I began to shoot to try and cover Cassie's escape. She wasn't moving though. She was standing her ground. Dang it. I should've anticipated that. A Demon started to fight her. I winced when I saw he had hurt her. I quickly shot him in the head… which was fair… since he was a jerk.

Cassie turned to watch me. I quickly switched guns and shot at her arm. The gel pack exploded and was absorbed into her skin. I smiled knowing she'd have her powers back soon. I gunned it to the lake knowing we were running out of time.

I tossed the gun down when Cassie was looking and pointed back to the building, so she'd remember to run. It was going to blow. It was moderately impressive it hadn't. She popped away. In midair, I put my feet on the seat and jumped for the opposite side of the pond. I felt the explosion reverberate around me in the water.

When I surfaced, I closed my eyes and swam to the edge to get out. Once on my feet I ran as fast I could to where the other Hackura women were. I was stunned realizing who they were. Two of them were Xander's aunts. I quickly checked them over and scanned them with ILYX.

ILYX announced, "Xander's relatives are fine, just unconscious. The other woman has a few puncture injuries from shrapnel to the leg, but she is no danger of dying." I ordered, "Give me gauze." It appeared and I quickly dressed her wound and put gauze over it. It helped assure me that she would be fine.

I ran back to Cassie. I demanded, "ILYX, scan her." If Cassie was even vaguely conscious this would be a problem since I'd used Xander's voice for ILYX. ILYX declared, "Alpha Duchess Cassie shows Laxenread recently entered her system. She is unconscious but there is no damage to her head." I whispered, "Thank you, ILYX." He replied, "You are welcome, Melanie Jane."

I needed to go, but I couldn't leave them here like this. I quickly found her phone and turned it on. I looked at the contacts on speed dial. I spotted Cayden's number. I was surprised it wasn't first. Honestly, if I hadn't found her phone, I'd have had ILYX call Xander.

I shook myself and hit Cayden's number. I placed the phone on Cassie's chest. I froze when my head began to pound. I clutched my own head groaning, "Not now." I could not get caught here. What was wrong with me?

I heard a Female voice weakly urging me, "Stay." I looked around asking, "Huh?" No one were here with me that was conscious. It was dead silent. Perfect. I was officially going crazy. Maybe from the fact a man who hated me was trying to gaslight me into believe I was his.

I ran for the holoport hoping I made it. If Cassie regained consciousness, I might not have a choice on leaving. If she wanted to talk to me, she could get that done many ways. She could call the wind or shoot me with her sunlight without the intent to do more than stall me. She wouldn't want to hurt me, but she and her mate wanted to talk to me.

I turned back to see Cassie waking up as I made it. She spotted me, but she couldn't get through the holoport even if she followed. Paige was too good for that. I paused on the other side, catching my breath and wondering when my head would stop hurting.

Sierra sighed in relief, “You took your sweet time.” I snorted, “Oh ya know… I had to make sure the Queen, Princess, Duchess and other Hackura women were all ok. All in a day’s work.” Valentina laughed, “Oh was that all? Saving Queen Astrid and company? Jeez, ya slacker.”

I snorted and punched her arm, “I also had to get Cassie her powers back… but hey, who’s keeping track of all the things I did?” Sierra laughed, “I’d imagine potentially Cassie did.” I rolled my eyes, “It was Cassie you weirdos. She’s not a Beta blood though… so it could be her aunt instead of her… she does lean Hackura. I’ll just have to monitor that… situation.”

Sierra and Valentina shot each other glances like they thought I was on overload and seeing things. Whatever. I knew that was Cassie. I knew it was, and I’d had her back. Just like I’m meant to as her brother’s mate.

I couldn’t help but smile. I loved doing little things like this for Xander. I sighed dreamily thinking about him. Maybe I could just get a glimpse of him… somehow. I’d figure it out one day. I definitely wanted to watch one of his videos he posted again today.

We went back to my secondary place. We were there when alarms went off. I checked them and everything inside me stopped. The targets named stole the breath from my body as pain rocked me. I whispered, “No.”

Caine snorted, “Let them die.” I replied, “I can’t.” Sierra said, “Well, you need more people. The Hunters got their cabin location. They will come in full force and you know they cannot catch you.”

Addison walked in. I clapped, “Perfect! Addison practiced and is great shot now. Sierra and Caine go back to the pack and Valentina will shimmer us there.” Valentina agreed, “Of course.” Caine growled, “Just let them die! Peter and Chelsea Kyle turned their back on you FOUR YEARS AGO! Just do the same to them.”

I winced, “I can’t. Them dying would break my soul. He… she… they were like my second set of parents and…” He sighed, “You’ll do what you want. Take Valentina and Addison and be safe.” Caine and Addison shared a look.

I admitted, “I hate disappointing you.” It physically hurt me. He squeezed my arm, “You are always you and that never changes. They don’t deserve you and I wish you could see that.” He left with Sierra, and we geared up.

Valentina shimmered us near Red Run’s border. I nearly took a step over it but grounded myself then took three steps back. I found us a spot to shoot from. The Hunters were close. Addison linked, “Mel…” I cut her off, “I wouldn’t have known this if I hadn’t joined the Hunters and took all those computers. They could’ve died….if…”

She snorted, “Yes, you would’ve because you’re terrifying with a computer. You are fierce about the people you love.” I let my tears fall. Valentina whispered, “Mel?” I admitted, “We used to come to this cabin. It was a secret with our family, the Kyle’s, and Richards’.”

Valentina asked, “Who are the Richards?” Addison answered, “The Richards are the Gamma family in Red Run. We just use their first names a lot. So Sharon and Garret along with their brood of pups.” Valentina nodded.

I found Peter and Chelsea through the scope. I choked out a sob because I hadn’t seen them in a while. I protected them but from afar. Everything in me demanded I go run to them and beg them to love me again. Addison growled, “I hate them so much.”

The Hunters began to move. I looked back and gasped, “Why aren’t they moving?” They were talking. I growled, “MOVE!” Addison snorted, “Seriously? They haven’t noticed?” I quickly typed a text out to Peter, but he didn’t answer. I groaned, “Come on!” I texted him again and he finally looked. Good.

They were finally moving. They were going to be ok. We were going to cover them. Addison sighed, “Mel, maybe we just…” I declared, “I will not watch another person I love get shot or die. Nothing hits them and these jerks PAY!”

My watch went off and I gasped, “They launched a rogue attack?! SERIOUSLY!” She assured me, “The pack will have it covered.” I had to hope she was right. Without me there to argue and demand my friends come help Red Run, they wouldn’t.

Addison groaned, "Is he really kissing her? We don't have time for this." I wished I was closer so I could hear them. Valentina reasoned, "He probably thinks he's saying goodbye." Addison huffed. They ran outside and fury overtook me.

I fired more rounds than necessary into all my kills. They thought they could take MY FORMER ALPHA! They thought they could take Daddy Peter away and they were WRONG. Elise would be upset… that's why I was doing this.

What the hell was that though even just now? I didn't think of him as Daddy Peter anymore and I hadn't in a long time. He never talked to me how he used to since I left. I see him again in person and mentally I'm back to Daddy Peter? Get a grip, Melanie.

Valentina said, "Uhh Mel, they are dead." I shot them some more then ordered, "Shimmer inside with this note and take pictures. Leave these bugs and get back to us." Addison pointed out, "You don't have a note." I huffed and clicked buttons to type my note then handed it to Valentina.

They read it and Valentina shimmered away. Addison stared at me. I grumbled, "Ok so I was angry… but seeing him is harder than I thought. They acted how they always did with each other and… why are they so normal and I'm not!"

Valentina came back saying, "Note delivered, bugs planted, and Paige communicated that Micah wants to meet you." I ordered, "ILYX, send a text to Micah that I'll be there later." He agreed, "Of course, Melanie Jane."

Valentina shimmered us back to my place. I asked, "Where are the pictures?" She showed me and I broke down. Addison held me and petted my hair. I cried, "It's like a physical representation of myself." She asked, "How?"

I explained, "The cabin used to be such a joyous and fun place and now it's broken and shattered. Just like me." I knew it made them mad, but it was how I felt.

After that, things continued on as they had, for the most part. Xander emailed me now… but me as Ashley, which… I still couldn't believe. It gave me hope for a better future. One thing I couldn't forget was the visual of how that cabin perfectly portrayed how I felt. I put a picture of it in my desk drawer.

My weird schedule of life continued. Time passing by meant very little to me at this point. Days blended together. Charles had just come into town a few weeks ago and it had been nice to see him.

I was pissed that Alpha Peter didn't call after I saved him. That note literally told him who I was, and he didn't even call to yell at me, let alone say thank you. I'd destroyed the gym I bought across the street from my secondary place after that lack of acknowledgement. It upset me on a very high level.

I was trying to calm down, so I was sitting at her computer, doing pack paperwork. I refused to do it in that supply closet that Edward had given as a test to me. Buck was using his office, but Edward wouldn't let me use it with him. Even though it was more convenient. He was still being obnoxious over the Trevor ordeal.

My computer went off and I paused. I groaned, "Of course Ezra can't be a decent human being! AHHHH! Why can't Alpha's do good things anymore?" I called Tao and he answered. "This can't be good. Ezra is being weird about Talia being my fated mate. What's going on?"

I replied, "He just put Talia's name on those he's giving over to Hunters." He snarled, "I'll kill him." I winced, "Umm so maybe you could… your mate will be in danger… but we started training recently and… I sort of… ok I have a backup plan." He growled, "What is the plan?"

I explained, "I'll be there and kill that Hunter group coming in and get Talia to Black Mountain. Ezra will NEVER look for her there. She'll be safe and then when you're ready you'll take over with her at your side." He took several deep breaths.

Talia whispered, "It's a good plan, Tao." I had not realized they were together but her being there would help me. He growled, "MINE! I don't want to be away from you." She soothed him, "It will be a drop in the bucket of the time we'll have together. With you here partial Fairies can be in our pack, just like Ashley said. We can be a pack people want to join."

She paused admitting, "Being away from you will feel like there's no air for me to breathe in, but I won't risk your life. Or the dreams we have for what this pack will look like. You knew your dad didn't like me." Tao growled, "Swear to me that you will save Talia, Ashley." I pledged, "I swear an oath to you no harm will befall her."

I added, "You'll just have to… pretend to be angry… when she doesn't return, and they say she's dead…. Also, be an actor when her pack link break. So, taking a swing at Ezra… would be expected and…" He snorted, "Alright. We are in. Keep her safe." I promised, "I will." We hung up and I began to plan that.

My computer beeped again. I grumbled, "Be nothing. Just be nothing…I do NOT have time for you to be something." I looked up and shoved the paperwork off my desk. I wanted to throw everything I could get my hands on. I heard the elevator ding and smelled Sierra coming.

I growled, "STOP TRYING TO KILL MY MATE! WHEN WILL YOU PEOPLE LEARN! I KILL YOU ALL FIRST EVERY TIME! AHHHHHHHHH!!!!!! YOU ARE SO FREAKING ANNOYING! HOW MANY TIMES MUST I TEACH THIS PARTICULAR LESSON?!"

Sierra said, "The computer can't yell back, Mel." I glared at her. She said, "I'll call everyone." I told her, "Don't bother. I need to beat some people up, and you have a meeting with your dad." Sierra sighed, "Yes, the lovely monthly meeting where he tells me to just accept whoever he wants me to mate with."

I grumbled, "Then punch him in the face, and say eat dirt!" Sierra snorted, "You get so testy when people come for your Xander." I yelled, "Because they always come for him. Do they think I have nothing better to do with my time? I don't… BUT THEY DON'T KNOW THAT!"

Sierra snickered as I got dressed. I put on all my Resistance gear, spraying myself down to hide my scent. I strapped myself down with my guns, knives, and a rifle the came back out. Sierra hummed, "You don't need all that." I glowered, "Yes, I do." Sierra nodded, "It's such a bad day to be a Bounty Hunter." I walked to the elevator and punched the button.

I rambled, "Bad day to be a STUPID Bounty Hunter. I've killed countless of them at this point, thinking they can kill my Xander. As if I'd even let them get close enough. Oh, he's traveling. Let's get him. Because he couldn't pop or portal away. Or melt our brains… no… of course we are smarter. We are so smart we got caught by a teenager…a genius teenager…but still. Freaking morons. Just give up! This is the definition of insanity."

Sierra called as I got in the elevator, "We all know that, Mel." Yeah, well someone should tell the Bounty Hunters that. I called, "Tell everyone to get ready to extract Talia." She huffed, "Ezra just had to be a dick." He really did, but that didn't surprise me.

I muttered, "Someone really needs to tell the Bounty Hunters the definition of insanity." I gasped, "That's it! I can tell them. Yes. Perfect!" I had a whole plan to get my message across because SOMEONE was going to listen to me today. It was happening.

I walked to our holoport and stepped through. I easily found the first soon to be dead Bounty Hunter. He grunted, "Hey, this is my bounty." I snorted, "It's your nothing. Haven't you heard of the Resistance?" He paled and I quickly slit his throat. I ripped off his shirt and in blood wrote: Insanity. On his chest.

I found the next one and snapped her neck. I'd killed several of them when I found a group. Perfect. I tapped the buttons on my watch and scrolled through the weapons list. I picked the grenade and my watch produced it.

I threw said grenade into the building. No one came running out of the building though after it went off. I muttered, "Surely, they weren't all standing in the same place. I went inside and discovered they were in fact gathered in the same spot. They were all blown to pieces. Whatever. I could work with this.

I grabbed some body parts and took them outside. I lined up all the body parts and wrote on them in their own blood. I laid them out in an order, so the blood read: Insanity: defined as repeating the same action over and over and expecting different results. LEAVE HIM ALONE! The last body had a resistance circle.

I sensed a change in the wind. My instincts practically screamed at me that someone was coming. I quickly ran and climbed a tree watching the area. I grabbed my sniper rifle, looked through the scope, and saw the head of Xander's guard, Egres.

I took my finger off the trigger. I watched as another member of Xander's guard, Gordon, appeared. They both looked at each other and got on their phones. I nearly called them tattletales, but they were doing their job.

They were really close on my tail this time, but I was happy they were so good at their jobs. It kept Xander safe… so… we were all the same team, which they clearly knew. Because they were usually the first on scene after I'd killed people for my mate.

King Bjourn came through a portal, along with Alpha Eric. I ached to run to Alpha Eric and practically demand he be an Alpha of worth. I bit my lip hoping to see pride in his eyes. I wanted an Alpha's pride back in my life so badly.

I nearly fell out of the tree leaning forward but saw that he was impressed. That was practically pride, and my blood hummed with recognition. He was supposed to be my father in law and he was an Alpha. It totally counted.

They looked at each other for a while before they started talking. Alpha Eric commented, "So, yet again, it's for Alexander." Everything was for him… obviously. Was that not obvious? I mean Laxenread… I didn't kill Ariena yet, but I was trying… I'm super busy and I did hurt her… so… I'll get her eventually. I killed Bounty Hunters for him… a lot. It was basically a full time job.

King Bjourn said, "This isn't even the first time the Bounty Hunters have been dead when we got here. The Resistance protects Alexander with more ferociousness than anyone else. Why won't they talk to him?" Umm… technically speaking, I do talk to him all the time now… in email, which counts. He just didn't know it was me.

I wiped a tear away that was going to fall. I wanted to tell them that I listened to every single voicemail he left for the sniper… some multiple times. I transferred them to a file on my computer so I could hear his voice. He sounded so sexy… which really helped with forming ILYX… so…

Egres's voice jolted me back to the conversation, "There has to be someone who would do this for the Duke." Plenty of women would want to. A pain filled my heart thinking about all the women that came down to brag about my mate in front of my face.

On the one hand, my mate was the whole package. On the other, he was supposed to be mine. Circumstances just ruined all our chances. Maybe when he figures out all I've done for him, he'll understand and consider giving us a real chance. He liked talking to Ashley… who is me. So, in some ways… when you think about it… he did like me.

Alpha Eric was rubbing his head. I frowned wondering what was wrong with him. Did he have a headache? King Bjourn said, "Let's take this back to our realm. Bring the bodies back with us. Maybe we can get something off them, like a fingerprint." I nearly snorted.

As if I would've been that careless. I was wearing gloves. Gordon grumbled offering, "We never do." King Bjourn reasoned, "Eventually, something has to break our way with this group." No, it didn't. It really didn't.

I waited fifteen minutes after they left. Somehow, I knew someone else was here. I saw another portal open, and Prince Louis Cambridge left. I waited another half hour. I was about to get down when another portal opened.

I grabbed the tree branch so I wouldn't fall. Prince Gabe Cambridge had just left. I was normally better at figuring out people were here. Maybe they'd figured that out and adjusted accordingly. Or they were further back. I'd have ILYX run diagnostics and recalibrate.

After an hour, I got down. I jogged towards our holoport. I rounded the corner of the building when I heard a man yell, "STOP!" My eyes widened when I spotted Crown Prince Hastein Cambridge. Shoot. I turned and ran for all I was worth.

He yelled, "WAIT! I WON'T HURT YOU! STOP! I JUST WANT TO TALK!" Portals started opening but I was already out of sight at our holoport. I went through and ran into our building. I put my hand on the inside of the elevator and took deep breaths. My heart was pounding.

Of course the future King waited the longest. I'd do better next time when I was observing before leaving. Crown Prince Hastein wouldn't come close to catching me again. I grumbled, "Now, I just need to plan to hide another Future Luna… in another pack… gosh I wish I could say it was the first time."

Seeing the Cambridge's reminded me I needed to reach back out to Benny. He was resistant to letting me help him, and the ONLY reason I let him somewhat get away with it was because he's Xander's cousin….plus Sierra pointed out that I did understand his drive to get his vengeance…but I was trying to help him with that.

I could call JJ. He was funny and I was certain he and Alexander got along the best out of everyone. I winced knowing it probably hurt Xander to have JJ in the shadows. Jason would probably like him too. JJ thought I was funny.

So, ultimately when I went to Xander having his cousins like me was good. Alastair and his kids like me too. I should check their trackers and make sure they were all ok. Ugh. Sometimes it was exhausting running everything alone. But for now… it was the way it had to be.

Waiting Impatiently

Alexander is Twenty Three Years Old

Alexander was nervous. I had reached out to Lead Warrior Ashley Griffen. She hadn't replied yet, which was surprising. Everyone else had mentioned she answered quickly. It had been hours. I read through my email again.

Lead Warrior Ashley Griffen,

I think you are the first person from a pack that I've emailed that doesn't use their pack email address. I'm reaching out for some much needed clarification of the events that occurred during a takeover your pack conducted.

Theo Bartlett just explained his visit and I find myself disturbed by most of what he said. Can you tell me what happened and where your counterpart was?

I'd love to discuss it in person at Elise's birthday party. EJ mentioned he'd invited you. We would all love to meet you.

I also would like to hear what this about this boy (yes, I said boy) saying you are his in your own words. Because I have a lot of thoughts about that.

Alexander Conners

Maybe I should've signed it Alpha, but it felt right to use just my name. I kept clicking refresh waiting for her email reply. Gage came in my room asking, "And what are we…?" He trailed off and read over my shoulder.

He hummed, "She hasn't answered yet? From what we have she answers fast." I grumbled, "Forever. She takes forever." He laughed, "Impatient Alpha blood." I shot him a glare and my email dinged.

I turned back to my screen only to groan at the incoming coupon from a local business. Gage said, "A watched egg never hatches." My email dinged again, this time from Ashley.

I shouted, "HA! In your face, Gage!" He snorted, "Yes, only several hours later. Clearly, I'm the one in the wrong." I rolled my eyes and opened her email.

Alpha Duke Conners,

Gosh… ummm this is such an honor… yes…definitely an honor… and… just don't use my title… because you're you… and that's just… so no title… that's a thing. I can't believe YOU are emailing me… like… you… I watch all your workout videos. I've implemented all of them here with my Warriors.

I don't want to bother you… like you're busy… I know that's a thing… that you are… because you release a lot of content… and spend a lot of time… in the gym… which you know… I just… umm… not trying to bother you here… .at all… and I tend to send long emails…

My counterpart… Buck… well… I don't get him… he's… confusing and obnoxious. I don't really like that. He knows right from wrong. He just… keeps his head down and never makes waves… but he was keeping the pack going before I took the position… so…. he does know things…. he's a dichotomy… that annoys me.... particularly today... other days he bothers me a lot less. So... it's not a good day to talk about him.

As far as what happened in the attack... They tested us... because our leadership is awful... which is what grubby wanting more land so called Alpha's want around here. If someone who was worthy of running a pack tried to take over... well... I'd have my Warriors stand down...but those Alpha's never attack.

We made them come at us the long route and in the way that would have them gassed. They retreated but they hurt someone.... well... he's... important to me... he's family... and I was mad... so I pursued them... and me and my group killed them... so... they deserved it... to be fair... which you care about... as a partial Fairy... Fair is thing you care about... so... yeah, fair.

Elise's birthday... gosh... I can't come... because... I can't... for... well... I'm busy? Or... something... yeah ... I'm busy. That's a thing I am... all the time actually. Edward doesn't run this pack... or have anyone around here's respect... so... it's been bad lately... there was a whole thing which leads to your question that really caused dissention in the pack... so... you know what I mean... the whole boy (I agree he's not a man...like even remotely) saying he's my mate thing...

Which leads us into the discussion of said boy, as you called him... accurately. That was so accurate. I can handle him... it's not a big deal. He's not my mate... I don't feel anything towards him, except anger... bitterness... loathing... animosity.... there are lot of bad words I could use... but that would take up more of your time... and I'm not trying to bother you... so...

It's not a big deal really... everyone knows it's not true. Even Edward who says I just need to be marked to feel the bond. He thinks I'm dumb... which is insulting... I'm not... which sounds like I'm bragging... but I really am intelligent... and I refuse to be GASLIT about my mate...which I have told them...repeatedly...I think they may have short term memory loss...it's the only explanation as to why they cannot remember I have said that...

So everything is fine... totally fine...

Ashley Griffen

P.S. It really is fine... no need to do anything... everything is good... you emailing is like gosh... I... I'm sorry it took me so long to reply... but it's you... and gosh... you... ok bye...just...be safe...and you're fine...so...love your videos! OH MY GOSH YOU DID JUST TYPE THAT! WHO SAYS THAT?

Gage snorted, "Holy rambling run on email." I replied, "It's more like a stream of conscious thoughts." Which was exactly how the McAlister's described Melanie before that etiquette and manners coach got ahold of her. Gage handed me a Karina cookie and I quickly ate it.

I typed out my furious reply. Gage snorted, "I mean, we could go down there and remove that Alpha from power." I agreed, "We could." He handed me another cookie and I hit send. He hummed, "She clearly has some hero worship for you so saying you'd spar and put videos up with her will literally send her spiraling."

I winked, "Then maybe she'll come here." Oden agreed, "She needs to be safe and here would be better." I knew that. Now, I just had to wait for this plan to work because it might not be today or next week, but I could feel that she'd be here eventually.

Gage asked, "Are we going to comment on her parting line?" I chuckled, "It's cute." He said, "She could've deleted it." I admitted, "I'm picturing her fingers getting ahead of her and in a pure panic sending the email." He snorted, "Well, hopefully she agrees and we get to meet her." I'd meet Ashley one day, just like I'd meet Melanie.

Flash Forward - Alexander is Twenty-Four Years Old

Flash Forward - Alexander is Twenty-Four Years Old

Alexander looked around his room. I had Melanie McAlister's hoodie, that had long lost its delicious strawberry scent, clutched in my hands. Oden commented, "Mate smells so good. We should go eat some strawberries to remind us of her amazing smell."

I still held out hope he was right about her being our mate. For many reasons one being he was right about Melanie smelling better than anything else I had ever smelled. Even real strawberries. Oden sighed, "I am right. I don't understand why you doubt me sometimes. Melanie McAlister is ours. She's OUR mate."

I replied, "You know most days I agree. I hope you are right. It's just that other wolves are possessive of her." The last part came out as a growl. Oden was growling in my head too. I could smell Phil coming, but I didn't care if he found me holding the hoodie. He was well aware of all things Melanie, along with my Gamma, Gage.

Phil walked in and sighed. He admitted, "At moments like this, I wish that hoodie still had a smell. I've GOT to get my hands on a freshly scented Melanie hoodie. It would make my life so much easier." I frowned saying, "Two things. One, you will forever be my favorite person if you make that happen. Two, why do you need me to be calm?"

Phil answered, "Well, you know you asked me to keep an ear out for anyone who was possibly hurt recently. Which, by the way, IS A BROAD generalization of a category of people to look out for, I'm just saying. It's such a broad directive, Alexander." Gage entered the room silently.

I nodded, "I know it was. I couldn't really narrow it down for you. You guys know Cayden called and possibly needed me to go heal a source of his. He was cagey and I was curious. You have the blood that wants all the answers therefore I tasked you with finding what you could."

Phil said, "Not that I see this as likely, because I don't want it to be true and that is my sole reason. I also don't know why she'd be a source for your brother in law…" I stiffened, "She? Is it Melanie? Is she hurt? Jase didn't say anything! I'll…." I trailed off trying to plan.

I quickly declared, "I'll call Doris! She will go take care of her. If Doris just so happens to bring Melanie back to the Hackura realm and I'm there well. I mean that's something that could easily happen. You and I are part of the royal family and Gage is my Gamma. I take him there a lot. WE go there a lot. Who would find that weird? Literally no one."

Phil sighed, "I actually now wish that's what I had to say. I am a SERIOUS fan of that plan." Gage agreed, "Me too." I frowned, "If it's not Melanie, then who did you find out is hurt that you think I'll be mad about?" Phil winced, "My source in Nashville told me...."

I growled interrupting, "Ashley?! It's Ashley who is hurt?" Phil nodded answering, "Yes, it's Ashley Griffen. The story is that she was in a VERY bad car accident." I raised an eyebrow when he didn't continue. I glanced at Gage who was staring at the ceiling. I prodded, "But obviously that's not what you believe since you used the word story at the beginning of that sentence."

Phil snorted, "Hey, I'm not the only one who doesn't buy it. Literally no one believes the story. Your dad has Theo and Lux Bartlett ready to go visit Ashley when she surfaces." I questioned, "When she surfaces? What are you talking about?" Gage winced while Phil nodded.

I asked, "Isn't she in the hospital? Specifically, the pack hospital since Black Path has one and you used an adjective to describe how bad the car accident was." Phil nodded, "They do have a pack hospital, but she was never in it and has gone off the grid. Avery Lavant is leading all the Warriors' practices in her absence." I felt like my silence spoke volumes. Oden snarled in my head.

Phil added, "How did Walker know about all this, you ask? Well, the day of said accident he discovered his mate was a Warrior in Black Path. Her name is Blair. She was freaked out about their mate status until Ashley told her it was fine."

Gage hummed, "Huh?" I inclined my head, "What he said." Phil nodded, "I said what I said. Anyway, they spent time together with Ashley and her friends. He was, of course, none too happy about that plan but mates and all."

I asked, "Why wasn't he happy about that plan? I'd sell shit to spend time with Ashley at this point." Gage snorted, "I got that one." Phil explained, "Walker wanted to take Blair home and mark her. She wanted to wait until later that night. Anyway, Blair was all a flutter when he got her back later that night." Oden groaned, "I dislike this story." Yeah, it was weird.

He continued, "She brought all her stuff with her. Which he said was a pittance of things. He's buying her more clothes. He thought she'd been crying about leaving her home pack until she got a call. She told him one of her friends, Ashley, was in a bad accident." So, she wasn't sad about leaving? That was a normal reaction even if you were happy. It was an emotional time.

He added, "Now he's not sure if she was crying about leaving her pack at all. Fishy things, Alexander. Very bad smelling fishy things. By the time he got Blair to the hospital to see Ashley, she was gone. She signed all the AMA forms and was just gone."

I clarified, "What was wrong with Ashley then? If she walked out, it couldn't have been that bad. Wait, why don't you think it was a car accident?" Phil answered, "Walker saw the guy who's name you don't want to know outside the hospital. His friends were trying to get him to change. He had blood on his pants. My guy said it was unquestionably Ashley Griffen's based on the smell."

I growled, "I'll fucking KILL him! I told her if he EVER marked her against her will that I'd kill him, and I meant him." Phil urged, "Let's take a beat with the glowing gold eyes. The story is not over." Gage muttered, "Thank god."

Oden was roaring furiously in my head. Phil prattled on, "Blair assured Walker that Ashley was unmarked. She talked to her friends for several hours before he got to mate and mark her. Then ya know, mates and such. Well from what we've seen anyway. We three are the bachelors of our time. Which, you wouldn't be if you'd just go meet Melanie." My head hurt.

I sighed, "She's living her dream, man. I'm not even sure I'm her mate." Oden growled at me, "YES we ARE, and you would know that if you'd find a way to see her. Or get rid of this DAMN headache!" It was getting annoying and bad. My healing light told me I was fine though. It must be stress induced or something.

Phil snorted, "Fine you be weirdly unsure if Melanie McAlister is your mate. Gage and I know she is. Then one day we will figure out what your weird obsession with Ashley Griffen is." I explained, "She reminds me of Melanie with everything I've heard about both of them. Their personalities, and how strong of a fighter she is reminds me of her."

Oden growled, "We are an Alpha, and we need to protect her." I replied, "You know I feel the same way, Oden." Phil held up his hands saying, "I maintain Ashley Griffen is meant to be my bestie. One of these days she'll get worn down by one of you emailing Conners because you are relentless and we love you for it. Then my future bestie will come to Black Mountain and a beautiful friendship will begin."

I sighed, "I still can't figure out why Ashley would be Cayden's source. What would she inform him about that she can't tell the Werewolf Council?" Phil shrugged, "I don't know." Gage hummed, "Off the top of my head, how shitty Black Path is?" I laughed, "Cayden knows that already and the Werewolf Council could actually do more than Cayden on that topic."

Phil said, "Well, one of our cousins up and went missing after speaking to Cassie on the same day of Ashley's accident." I raised an eyebrow surmising, "I'm guessing this would be a cousin that is a doctor." Phil nodded, "That it is. The winner of this game of who went missing is Brody."

I shrugged, "Alright. Where is Ashley now then?" Phil replied, "No one knows. Who could do that I wonder? Ohhhh well, I think Brody and Cayden could." They easily could and they would only lock that down to them and not us if Ashley asked for that. They question is, why would she do that?

I reiterated, "I just don't get why Ashley would be a source for them. We still email back and forth. I know she's friends with Elise. Why would she turn to the Hackura instead of a Werewolf? Why not the Werewolf Council? Cayden said his source is good. Cayden wouldn't give a shit about how crappy Black Path is or consider that good intel."

Phil shrugged, "I'm just telling you what my ear to the ground says. Now, because I DESPERATELY don't want you to blow a gasket at this party, we need to chat." I snorted, "Why on earth would I blow a gasket at my kid siblings' birthday?" Gage laughed, which didn't bode well.

Phil said, "See I have this theory. That little cousin Angela is OH so excited for this party because her mate is coming." I glared at him saying, "Hell to the fuck no." Phil winced, "And this is why we went with a forewarning."

I growled, "She's too little." Gage scoffed and I glared at him. Phil reasoned, "Elise was MUCH younger when EJ realized she was his." I argued, "That was…." I trailed off then admitted, "not different in any way, shape or form. Fuck! He'd better treat her like a queen, or I'll kill him."

Phil smiled, "That's the spirit." Gage commented, "Told you he'd take that better than most." Probably. I warned them, "My dad's about to knock on the door." Phil winked and opened it a second before he knocked. He said, "See you later Cousin Eric." My dad laughed, "See you later Phil and Gage."

My dad walked into my room and closed the door. He asked, "How are you doing, son?" I shrugged answering, "Fine." My dad studied me before saying, "You were quite angry not too long ago." I debated then asked him, "What do you think happened to Ashley Griffen?"

My dad clenched his jaw and I felt his annoyance in the bond. He told me, "It was reported that it was a car accident. The Beta and Alpha's daughters were involved as well. I find it extremely odd that Ashley was egregiously injured whereas the other two are perfectly fine." Egregiously?! Phil didn't mention that. He only said it was a very bad car accident. Oden growled, "I'm talking to Rocket about that now." Good.

Dad continued, "I am insulted that the explanation is that those two girls have wolves. With the injuries Ashley sustained if the other two were in the car, even having wolves, they should've had more than some cuts."

I questioned him, "How bad is it?" My dad shrugged saying, "The records before Ashley signed out against medical advice were not great. She was hurt pretty badly. It's moderately..." He amended, "No, it's just impressive that she was able to get out of the hospital in the first place."

I asked, "Why are you having Theo and Lux" I growled his name out, "go see her?" My dad replied, "Apparently, not unlike you, I don't buy this was a car accident." He was right. Phil didn't believe it because his source didn't so I didn't believe a single word.

Dad continued, "I need Theo and Lux to see if she'll tell them what really happened. Right now, I have no proof that's not what happened. I saw pictures of the car. Which is why it's insulting to say those other two girls were in said car when that happened. The car is totaled."

I asked, "Who supposedly hit them? Were they injured as well?" My dad snorted, "It was a hit and run. They buried the police report through members of their pack that are police officers." I surmised, "Then they suspect supernatural's."

Dad rolled his eyes, "No, I suspect they know exactly who it was. Hell, I think I know who it was." I growled, "That wannabe claiming to be her mate." He nodded, "I do believe so." My mom popped into the room before I could reply.

She announced, "Angela wants both of you downstairs. Right now." I kissed the top of her head and said, "I'll be right there." I popped away leaving them in my room. They popped in a second after I did. I looked around. EJ and TJ were talking but Elise was missing. Shocker.

I would just bet slugger was out there defending her and EJ's relationship. Her and Melanie were going to be feared Luna's when my mate got here. I stopped myself short correcting myself 'if' she gets here. Hell, and if she's mine.

Oden growled, "I swear sometimes you are the most OBNOXIOUS human! She's ours. Stop doubting me, it's insulting." I replied, "Well, they keep her from us so it's not unreasonable to say if she gets here." Oden growled.

I sighed, "I'm just trying not to get my hopes up. They are already pretty damn high about it. You know I want her. I just know others do too." Oden growled, "They can't have her because she's ours and I will RIP their heads off. Not unlike I will to he who will NOT be named that hurt Ashley."

I snorted, "I cannot believe all that bullshit. Still. I can't reconcile how that Alpha didn't go apeshit." Other than Ashley was correct in her assessments of Alpha Edward, he was shit at his job. She used other words but that is what she meant. Oden agreed, “Nor can I. Can we agree that if he is the one who hurt her, and we can prove it, we go stealthy Hackura on his ass? I WILL HEAR HIS SCREAMS before he dies.” I chuckled, “I like the way you think Oden and I agree.” Oden snorted, “Thank you.”

Tristan, Jason, and Everly arrived. I frowned and walked over because my friend looked like hell. I asked, “Jase, do you need some coffee? Or a room to sleep in maybe.” Jason muttered, “Coffee would be good.” I conjured him some.

I looked at Tristan, but his eyes were on his brother. Jason looked truly terrible. I asked, “What’s going on, man?” Jason sighed, “I’m having nightmares so I can’t sleep. I honestly don't even want to sleep anymore. Every damn time I close my eyes, I see horrible things happening to Ladybug.”

I tensed asking, “What?” That was still going on? I tried to sound calm, but it came out as a growl. Everly shot me a look because we’d talk about this. Tristan, clearly unaware I’d discussed it with his mate, explained, “You remember when he was taken and beaten by Hunters before we got him back.”

I nodded, “Yes, I do recall that.” I didn’t want to though. My mom and I had to bring Jason back from near death. We actually didn’t know how he wasn’t dead. It was like something was pumping an antidote into his system for the wolfsbane that was in his veins.

I knew Jason had thought Melanie saved him, but I thought Everly and I agreed he’d be ok. We thought we were being silly. Was that not true? Oden growled, “Mate wasn’t there.” That was true, my Lovebug didn’t save him because at that exact moment she was dancing her heart out.

I still used the backdoor Micah installed on Jason’s computer for me to watch her dance. Then I’d decided they called her Ladybug, but in my head she became my Lovebug. Her dancing still struck me as sad, but she had a purpose in her movements. Most dances were hauntingly sad, and they called to me. I just couldn’t be selfish and take her dream from her. Even if it hurt.

Tristan pulled me back into the conversation saying, “Well, he dreams bad things happen to Ladybug and he can’t help her.” I stated, “You talk to her though, and know she’s fine.” Jason snorted, “Look me in the eyes, my friend, and tell me if you thought you saw your sister beaten, whipped, and shocked with some high powered cattle prod you’d be fine even after you saw them.”

I shivered admitting, “No, probably not.” Gage linked, “Probably?! The answer is you would not be fine. In fact you would destroy the gym on the regular.” I’d never experienced it personally but that did sound fairly accurate on my reaction.

Jason sighed, “It’s haunting me. I tried to drive up to New York today, but my car broke down and T had to come get me.” I offered, “I could pop you to see her, Jase.” I could see Phil and Gage lean in with hopeful expressions.

Jason sounded extremely bitter when he said, “It’s not an emergency.” Oden growled in my head, “He has NO RIGHT to be bitter! It’s their stupid rule. We OFFERED to let him go see her. He’s being an ass.” I gritted my teeth and walked away to stand in the corner.

I wasn’t going to cause a scene on Angela and TJ’s birthday. They were just pups and it would be best if I was the one here when our little sister's mate showed up. I definitely wasn’t going to focus on that though. I was going to ignore it.

TJ linked me, “Why am I here?” I replied, “For starters, it’s your birthday party.” He shot me a pouting look. I knew it was because his mate, Allison Daniels, was already sleep. She'd come by earlier with Aunt Lexi, and they’d played. TJ was only here at this point for Angela.

TJ groaned, “When will this end?” I chuckled, “When Angela decides it’s over or the fact that her mate is coming goes over like a lead ballon.” He huffed but didn’t confirm or deny. Dang it! I really did need to prepare better.

I linked EJ before he left teasing, “Please tell Luna Slugger that I love her.” He retorted, “Karma is swift tonight, little brother. Claire just got here.” Oden growled in my head and guilt lanced through me. I retorted, “She can get out. I’ll tell her so myself.”

I knew I shouldn’t have been so intoxicated at the party she managed to kiss me at. I’d wanted to save my first kiss for my mate. I wouldn’t have been so slow to react if I’d just not drank as much. I’d been so upset that Melanie wasn’t there and Claire had just kissed me. I’d worked ALL the alcohol out of my system in the gym.

Claire needed to leave this party. I had zero faith Melanie would show up, but I didn't want Claire in this house. I didn't want a single rumor to fly around when Melanie came home about Claire and me. Because there WAS no Claire and me.

Oden snorted, "Glad you're jumping on my bandwagon for the time being. Melanie is ours." I rolled my eyes, "Whatever. I won't have Melanie hear that shit. Claire kissed us not the other way around. There was definitely nothing great about it either. She banged into my teeth, and there was no chemistry." Oden replied, "Preaching to the choir Alexander. I felt nothing except annoyance."

Angela popped over to Claire. Oden snarled, "If she upsets Snow I will shift and rip her throat out!" Snow was my little sister's wolf. I added, "If she upsets wolf or human, she's dead." Angela crossed her arms and pointed, "YOU were NOT invited. Leave."

Claire frowned, "But I…" TJ popped over interrupting her, "You heard my little sister. Get to stepping, or I'll tell my mom why Angela wants you to leave. She does not take kindly to crazy she wolves with C names."

He paused for dramatic effect before adding, "In fact, you're lucky she doesn't have our enhanced hearing. Or you'd already be in a world of hurt." He wasn't wrong and everyone that could hear this exchange knew it.

Phil linked me, "GOD I hope your mom sees her. She did a NUMBER on Claire when she kissed you. It's always the best when Cousin Haley goes off." I rolled my eyes, "It will be fine. She'll leave." Claire was arguing with Angela.

Oden scoffed, "She did not say she wasn't crazy." She did. I replied, "She isn't Charlooney crazy, but she kept coming at me like I was honey, and she was a bee." I repeatedly told her I wasn't interested, but she just kept coming.

Claire insisted, "I'm not crazy." Oden grumbled, "I think she is as previously stated." I think she was desperate and obsessed over the idea of me and my name. I wasn't sure that translated to crazy. Oden grumbled, "I am." Well, he was entitled to believe that.

Angela snorted, "Yes, you are. Do something about that before it gets you killed. It might be blurry, but I see a path where someone KICKS your ass. Hard. Now shoo! You won't ruin our birthday this year. I REFUSE to let this happen."

Oden purred, "Mate is going to eviscerate that she wolf." I replied, "Claire isn't known to be a great Warrior, but we've never seen Melanie fight. We've seen her dance, which is amazing, but we've never seen her fight." We heard plenty of rumors about her skills though.

Oden shrugged that off saying, "Elise and EJ have. Both said she was good and that was YEARS ago. TOO MANY GODDAMN YEARS AGO! I want mate." I wanted to smile with that tidbit of knowledge, but I didn't want Claire to take it the wrong way. Instead, I sighed loud enough for everyone to hear.

Claire glanced at me with an expression I was certain she thought was seductive, but she was wrong. The appeal was clear in her eyes for me to intervene, but I just stared back at her. I didn't want her here and I certainly didn't invite her. I'd never led her on. I'd never even hinted I wanted her.

Claire turned in a huff and started to leave with her friends. Several people were snickering. My dad walked over and spun Angela around in a hug. I saw my uncles, both wolf and Hackura, smirking. Uncle Aiden was actually laughing since he'd been close enough to hear.

I heard my mom ask, "What the fuck are you all so amused about?!" EJ snorted, "Good luck with that one, brother." I sent him my annoyance which just made my older brother smile. You keep a secret from a guy for five years and he gets all excited to make you deal with your mom wanting to know what the hell is going on.

I spotted Robert at the back of the party. That guy. Oden snarled, "Why is he even here? So, he's dating a pack member. That does not grant him an invitation to my siblings birthday." I actually agreed with that. I linked Gage, "Why is Robert here? He was absolutely not invited either." He groaned, "Don't worry. I'm on it." Good.

I looked around for Cassie but she wasn't here yet. I hoped everything was ok. It was easy to lose track of time in the Hackura realm. I sent her a quick text.

Me: Are you all good? TJ and Angela's party started. It's dramatic already.

I glanced back up and saw Phil catch Claire right outside the open front door. He handed her a small container. He smiled saying, "For that severe burn you just got from my Alpha. Run along crazy C named she wolf. No need to ever darken our door again."

He leaned closer adding, "I'd eat glass before letting you become Alexander's girlfriend let alone his Luna. We have our sights on a much higher quality of person. She's fabulous." Claire snorted and they walked further away but I could hear them still talking.

Claire said, "Alexander hasn't met his mate and eventually he'll get tired of waiting. I'll make sure you aren't the Beta around here after that. I'm the only girl he's shown interest in." I started towards the door as fury filled my veins. I knew my eyes were blazing gold. Oden was growling in my head too.

Preston linked me, "I got this." I heard a pop. Preston growled in warning, "I know you didn't just threaten a member of the Hackura Royal family, who happens to be one of the Beta's of this pack, Claire. Did it sound like a threat to you Phil?"

Phil hummed, "You know, I can't decide. Even if it was, we both know she's wrong." Gage growled, "I heard a threat to my Beta." I agreed with him. Claire tried to turn on the charm with my brother, "William, you know I'm the only girl Alexander has ever kissed. If he goes with a chosen mate, it would be me." I rolled my eyes.

My mom glanced over at me and sent me her concern and curiosity. She couldn't hear or see the scene outside so she had no idea why several of us, especially me, were pissed the fuck off. Angela drew her attention away from me though. I sent my sister gratitude. I felt several eyes of a lot of family members eyes on me though.

I heard Preston reply, "William is not here. I'm Preston. Am I supposed to be impressed you got the right group of siblings born together? Because I'm not. My siblings' mates can all tell us apart. Elise has never once gotten confused."

"Nor has Buttercup. Hell, not even little Allison has messed up even once. Micah never does either. I could continue but you get my drift. Let's not forget Cayden though that would be remiss of me. To forget the Commander of the Armies of the Hackura."

Phil laughed, "She's turning a strange color, cousin." Good. Preston commented, "Hmmm I wonder why that would be? Is it because I casually slid in Cassie's mate who could and would kill her over the course of several years if I asked him to?" Oden said, "That has promise."

Preston continued, "Hell, we could take the FAR more entertaining route and tell Cassie that you tried to ruin Angela and TJ's birthday party. Angela said so herself that if you stayed, you'd have ruined it. She can't lie."

Gage threw out, "Cassie would be spitting mad." Preston added, "Not only mad. She'd shoot you with her sunlight and then she'd tell Cayden how upset she was. How do you think that would go, Phil?" Phil laughed, "Astonishingly well, for me. Not for Claire though. On second thought, run back inside Claire."

Claire shouted, "You are awful!" Phil snorted, "Now my feelings are hurt. Some random she wolf, not from my pack who is STALKING my Alpha, doesn't like me. Woe to Phil." I snorted. Gage said, "She needs a bigger tube of burn ointment for the burns she keeps taking."

Preston urged, "Run along Claire, or stay and you will die today." She must have left because Preston shouted, "Oh, and I saw that supposed kiss. Let's be clear about something, YOU kissed Alexander. He didn't move his lips to kiss you back. My brother pushed you off him then spent the rest of the night angrily tearing stuff up in the gym." Gage huffed, "Did he ever."

Preston continued, "I hate to break it to you, but you're clearly not a good kisser. When one gets kissed and it's good, or they are into it, they don't spend all night angrily punching a heavy bag. That's just a general FYI for you. My brother is not into you. He's not playing hard to get. He just doesn't want you."

Claire snorted, "He didn't hurt me though." Preston said, "Good lord, is that your threshold? Alexander would never hurt someone who was not a threat. I'd watch it because you're moving into that territory. Also, aim higher in your standards. That's sad. Plus, he might not have but someone that night did. Or don't you remember who kicked your ass?" I thought mom just punched her a few times. Who kicked her ass?

I linked Preston, "Tell Phil that Gage is right, she needs some more aloe vera." I heard Phil laugh out loud. He sighed, "Alas, Claire you'll have to run along. I was only prepared with a small amount of Aloe Vera to coat your burns."

"My cousin Preston over here is just piling on though. You do know Alexander can hear us, and he's not coming out here to defend you. Or stop us." Claire snarled, "He didn't come out here for you either." Oden growled, "I will kill her."

Preston snidely said, "He didn't come out because I told him to stay put. I know the look on his face. For what you said to Phil he might have accidentally exploded your brain." I linked him, "I have control over my powers, and you know that." Preston replied, "I mean, accidents happen, and she doesn't need to know how good you are. She needs a healthy dose of fear." I rolled my eyes.

Angela popped outside so I walked to the door. She announced, "You have thirty seconds to go. If Alexander actually comes out here, you will not like what follows." Claire asked, "Why would he come out here?" Preston laughed, "Do you know anything about us? The answer is obvious." It was.

Angela answered, "Because I came out here. Stop trying to ruin my party!" Claire rolled her eyes saying, "I'm going." Angela warned, "Word to the wise, STAY OUT! Your path is shoring up and let me tell you it's a DOOZY for you." Preston laughed, "Who kicks her ass?"

Angela sighed admitting, "It's blurry but becoming more and more certain. The girl has black hair though." I smiled knowing it was Melanie. I quickly had to shove my anger down knowing Claire was going to upset Melanie. I should just kill her.

Oden chimed in, "I'm on board." Gage linked, "Are we killing her or not? I could go with yes and normally I say no." I didn't answer and walked over to my Hackura uncles to stop myself from running Claire down. We were allies with Theo Bartlett, and Claire was from his pack.

My Uncle Bjourn smiled greeting, "Hello, Alexander. It seems the crazy girl is back. You know if she does something and your mother finds out we didn't tell her about said crazy girl, we are all in trouble." I replied, "Being in trouble can be fun. You just have to smile at her and she gets less mad."

Uncle Marcus said, "At you. You're her son." Uncle Harper laughed, "Good god, do I know something you both don't? I like that a lot." Uncle Bjourn asked, "What do you know?" He winked, "Our little sister has beat that she wolf up." Preston meant mom? It was clearly more than the punches I knew about then.

I quickly changed the subject asking, "Do you know where Cass is?" Uncle Bjourn said, "Cayden was going to see a source and she was trying to wait for him to get back. She did a pretty intense workout today though. She used a lot of energy then she trained on her powers. She might have fallen asleep waiting for him."

I asked, "Is she ok?" Uncle Bjourn nodded, "She's annoyed at the situation Cayden is going through." I could understand that whole heartedly. My dad walked over, and I went back to my corner. Right when I'd gotten there EJ popped in with Elise.

I raised an eyebrow at my older brother. He reeked of sex and his mate. He linked me, "When your mate gets in a fight and defends your bond with her, you'll understand why I couldn't resist her. Plus, with you, we'll have to worry that Melanie will kill someone. She's always been possessive of you."

I couldn't help the pride I felt from those words. At least that makes two of us. I really hoped she was my mate. Oden sighed, "Not to be the broken record in your head, but MELANIE IS OURS! Stop doubting me."

I reasoned, "Oden, you know why I feel that way." Oden grumbled, "Let's go question the scum that is the bullying wolf over there. Ask him how mate smelled to him. WHEN he says she didn't smell overly good THEN you will accept that I am right." I retorted, "I'm not voluntarily talking to Robert, or I will kill him." He huffed, "Fine. That's fair. He's annoying." He really is.

I replied to my brother via link, "Provided she's my mate, and I'm not some creepy weirdo." He sighed, "I know you have days where you think that, but we all know. Ok? You are not some creepy weirdo." I admitted, "I hope I'm not."

EJ asked, "What's been happening? FYI Elise told me her theory. I'm sure it aligns with Phil's." Angela popped over to mom. She whispered, "You invited Farrin and Trixie, right? They were supposed to be here." My mom assured her, "I invited them. I'm sure they will pop in any minute." A Fairy?!

I linked EJ in a panic, "Hell to the FUCK no! Her mate is a damn Fairy? No. NO. NO!" EJ sounded resigned, "I am getting the sense he is, little brother." Fury filled me because I remembered quite vividly the story of what happened to my mom during her childhood in Faerie. She told us when we turned sixteen and I'd be damned if my little sister knew a second of pain.

I snarled at EJ, "After what they did to mom? NO! They can't have Angela. That's a no." He rationalized, "Fairies are different now. Farrin is obviously mated with Trixie and he's different with her. They have children who were raised to respect their mates." He was being LOGICAL? Oden growled, "He's always logical." He was but right now I REALLY didn't like it.

I replied, "Farrin has a nephew who is older than us." I felt his hope that wasn't who her mate was. He replied, "That's not a big deal to supernatural's, but let's hope it's not him. Or dad might kill him." Dad wouldn't kill him because mom wouldn't let him. She'd say they couldn't ride hypocrisy horses since they have an age gap that humans pause at sometimes.

Oden snorted, "Mom found that absurd because she wasn't raised in this realm." She did and she didn't understand the horror on some people's faces when they heard their age gap. She'd joked Vampires could never come out to humans because their age gaps sometimes spanned centuries.

She'd been stunned when she found out humans loved Vampire love stories. She'd muttered about their double standards for months. Especially when she found out it was cool that teenagers with century old Vampires to the humans.

Angela had her far off stare going before she started clapping. My mom smiled at her while my dad felt like he was facing his own funeral. Farrin, Trixie, and their four kids popped in. Their son, Klaus, locked eyes on Angela. Awesome.

Angela blushed and whispered, "Hi, Klaus." Klaus smirked, "Hello, birthday girl. That must make you Duchess Angela Conners." Angela's feelings told me he was hers even before she shyly nodded at him. I looked at the ceiling and silently chastised two goddess and a god, "Really Azoney, Selene, and Aesir?! You want me to be ok with Angela having a Fairy mate?" I got no response.

I continued, "Granted, said Fairy was raised to be a good person. FUCK! I've met the kid. He's a polite, nice kid and rather powerful with the Fire powers. You want me to handle this WITHOUT Melanie beside me? You do know I'm an Enforcer, right?! That did not escape the attention of you all?"

I ranted, "I'm going to need Melanie to walk through that damn door in the next fifteen seconds." Oden hummed, "I approve of this message to the gods and goddesses." Good. We stared at the door but unsurprisingly, that did not happen. I honestly knew it wouldn't. I just hoped one of the three would throw me a damn bone.

Klaus declared, "It also makes you mine." Angela giggled. It was hard seeing my siblings find their mates. Especially when most days I was certain I knew who mine was. I missed her. Oden growled but didn't say anything.

I was happy for Angela though. I just wished Melanie was here to share that with me. She SHOULD be here to share that with me. She was ninefuckingteen years old. She should be moved in here. Goddamn it. Now I was grouchy. Not about me. This is NOT about me. Angela. Focus on Angela.

TJ popped beside Angela looking bored. He'd been prepared for this and did feel bored by it all in the bond. TJ said, "I'm the birthday boy, if you care." Klaus chuckled, "I did before I met the birthday girl. Now, not so much." TJ sighed, "Normally, I appreciate that, but this is going to hell in a handbasket."

I wouldn't quite say that, but dad was leaning towards detonation with my Hackura family. My siblings were ok though and mom was happy. The anger burning through us were from our Hackura Uncles, some cousins, and my dad.

Oden snarled, "I want mate. Go get her." I snorted, "And how do you suggest I do that?" Karina walked by with cookies. Thank god. I snatched one and ate it. Feeling better about everything. Karina was a magical ass baker.

Mom urged, “Angela, introduce us to your mate.” Angela smiled announcing, “This is Klaus, mom. Klaus, this is my mom.” Klaus chuckled, “I have met your mom. Hello, Princess.” She waved him off, “It’s just Haley amongst family.”

Farrin asked, “Son, what is happening?” Trixie squealed and Uncle Aiden was beaming with joy. I couldn’t really blame him honestly. He wanted one of us to be in Faerie more often so badly. We all loved him, but I was honestly shocked that one of us got a Fairy mate.

Dad roared, “ARE YOU FUCKING KIDDING ME?! NO! HELL TO THE FUCK NO! NOT HIS SON! Not the man who tried to fu…” Mom yelled, interrupting him, “ERIC NATHAN CONNERS!” That brought the entire party to a dead quiet halt.

What now? Oden growled, “He was going to say fuck.” It did sound like it. Which told me why my mom didn’t want him to say it. In all my life, I’d NEVER heard my mom yell at my dad like that in front of other people. On occasion when they’d fight, sure. It was the curse of our super hearing. In a setting like this though it was unheard of.

Preston linked, “I can’t look away. It’s like….” He trailed off then admitted, “I don’t even know. Seeing a polar bear fly.” I rolled my eyes replying, “Obviously, Farrin did something dad didn’t like that mom doesn't want Angela to know about.”

Oden told me, “Thor is pissed.” Yeah, I could tell. My parents were obviously linking each other. Uncle Aiden looked deeply amused. Eventually, my mom bent down and spoke to Angela. “Sweetie, why don’t you and TJ go outside with Klaus and his siblings. Parker, Cole, and Calvin will go with you too. You and Klaus should get to know each other.”

Angela wiped away tears whispering, “Daddy?” Dad knelt down apologizing, “I’m sorry I yelled, Princess.” He squeezed her tightly. She told him, “We are so happy together, I promise.” He nodded then kissed her cheek. He shot Klaus a glare and stalked towards his office.

I linked Parker, Cole, Calvin and TJ, “I’m sure Klaus won’t do anything, but be on alert for other Fairies. They could use you all outside as a distraction.” Parker answered, “We will be on alert, big brother.” I smiled at them as they walked out.

My mom said, “Trixie and Farrin, if you’d join whoever the fuck else ends up in my office I’d appreciate it. I’m sure it will be most of my family. Aiden, you’re coming and that’s nonnegotiable.” Uncle Aiden popped over and smiled, “I would truly not miss this for the world, little sister.”

Uncle Aiden hugged Trixie and Farrin. He held up his hand for a high five. I couldn’t help but enjoy his happiness which radiated from his very being. EJ popped out first and I followed, which is when Cassie popped in smiling. She looked at all of us, then frowned. She asked, “What did I miss?”

My mom walked into the room with her hands on her hips. She answered, “Your father losing his goddamn mind that’s what you missed. Eric….” My dad growled interrupting her, “NOT HIS SON! Not a fucking Fairy! NO!”

My mom reasoned, “Eric, you know he won’t hurt her. He wasn’t raised the way Fairies have been in the past. Fegle has never hurt Julianna. It’s not like Angela is moving realms anytime soon either. She’s only ten and Klaus is thirteen. We will just get them together like we did EJ and Elise. You’ll get to know him.”

Dad replied, “HIS FATHER TRIED TO FUCK YOU!” My mom rolled her eyes, “Once, and he didn’t fuck me.” Thor took over, “HE TRIED TO AT OUR WEDDING RECEPTION!” My mom counted out loud, “One, Two, Three, Four.”

She blew out a breath then pointed a finger at him, “Do you know how many people STILL try to fuck you?” He blinked at her. I linked Phil, “Are people really still trying to fuck my dad? My parents have been together for a long ass time.”

He snorted, “You cannot be serious.” He added Gage to our link, “Gage, he’s seriously asking if people try to fuck Cousin Eric.” Gage said, “It’s an oddly high number given he’s been mated for over twenty years.” Oden growled in my head.

Mom questioned, “Do you? Because it’s A REALLY FUCKING HIGH NUMBER! I’m up to the ceiling in crazy ass she wolves. Farrin is happily mated. He didn’t even like me as a person until well after our reception. He was never cruel to me, nor did he hurt me. Can we just take a fucking minute to calm the fuck down?"

Cassie linked me, "Boy, you take a nap wake for a party and hear things one never needs to hear." I replied, "I never got the impression from Farrin he liked mom in that way." Cassie reasoned, "He'd met Trixie by the time we were old enough to have a memory of him."

I linked Oden, "Do you recall that ever being a thing?" Oden answered, "Thor said she went into her concupiscence at their wedding and that Farrin didn't resist her pheromones." I rolled my eyes because I hated that damn excuse. We were not just animals; we could resist a Female in heat.

Farrin didn't even have an animal side. I'd been around Fairies in their concupiscence and she wolves in their heat. In fact, I'd carried one to her mate and defended a few more. It wasn't the easiest thing in the world to do, but I respected the hell out of women and men alike. Taking someone's choice away from them was wrong. I shot Farrin a glare. He actually looked ashamed. Good.

My parents stood, staring at each other. Grandpa Titus threatened, "If he harms one hair on my granddaughter's head, he is a dead man." My mom put her head into her hands saying, "That is true for ALL your grandchildren and ALL their fucking mates. Can we all please pull our heads out of our asses right now?" I was trying.

She sternly said, "This is about Angela, and she is happy about this. You can all feel how excited she is. I understand the fear and trepidation in this room and it's because of me. I get that but I will NOT allow ANY of my children to suffer because of the things that happened to me. Angela will not be punished for what happened to me as a child. By me or anyone else."

She pointed at herself, "My fears are MINE. Not hers or any of my other kids. Aiden is not the same person he was back then. He is King and he ADORES Angela. He would not let that happen to her. Trixie raised her fucking children like a bad ass. They are respectful and kind. They do not harm innocent people. She has taught them to love their mates." That was true. Uncle Aiden would never let anyone hurt my sister.

Mom practically snarled "And FUCK each and every single goddamn one of you for making me say this next sentence." Oden complimented our mom, "She is very good at growling. Much better than Cassandra was before she died." Huh? Kena would've been growling. Thinking back, she did do a human growl more often than the wolf one. Interesting. I shoved those thoughts away.

The emotions my mom was rolling through in the bond intrigued me. Sometimes, at rare moments like this, I was treated to our bond like my others. She didn't want to compliment Farrin, but she was about to. She was pissed she had to state it and was planning to get everyone back via prank for this.

Mom announced, "Farrin has shown his kids how to be a real mate. He leads by example with Trixie. He loves and respects her. He has not been with another person since they met because it's what Trixie wanted. That's respect."

"That's not what he was taught to do either. He does it FOR HER! He's a good man and dad. Will you all calm down so I can stop listing off nice fucking things about Farrin?! FARRIN FOR CHRIST'S SAKE! You know I hate it when you do this shit."

Farrin laughed, "I knew you liked me, Princess." My mom glared at him. She turned to the room, "Do you see what you have done? Now, he's going to talk about that forfuckingever." Trixie giggled. Dad hugged her admitting, "I have no problem with the Trixie part of this situation. It's him." His finger pointed directly at Farrin.

I linked EJ, "Did you know that Farrin tried to take mom at their wedding to have sex with her?" He answered, "I don't think I did know that." He felt a type of way about that because the excuse was 'he couldn't help it' and those that had attacked Elise last year from our pack used the same excuse about her heat. It was bullshit.

I didn't want to make Angela, or any of my siblings, feel bad. Especially about their mate. I linked my little sister, "I didn't get to say congratulations, little one." Angela replied, "I knew you'd come around first."

I snorted, "He'd better treat you like the queen you are." Angela snarked, "As if I would accept anything less. We are very happy. Just like you are happy with your blur eventually. I'm still working on figuring that out." I assured her, "I have faith in you."

My dad was calming down, but he was still upset. Cassie's bond with me told me she was about to deliver an emotional blow. She declared, "I think we learned it's better for us all to know when mates meet. They didn't try to sneak around. Angela could've popped to him without us knowing. She could've been going between realms with only TJ being aware of their relationship. Instead, she included us all. Let's remember that."

Guilt lanced through me again. That was my fault. I'd been teasing Cayden about ditching EJ and me to babysit and Cassie heard it all wrong. Cassie linked me, "For the millionth time, it wasn't your fault. You didn't know and you were just joking around. If I'd listened to your tone, felt our bond, or called Cayden, none of the events that would've happened. It was on me and no one else."

It did though happen though all because of a stupid joke, Cassie was hurt. Angela popped to her because of her vision. I went down from Cassie's pain. It was a whole mess that it didn't need to be. Dad hugged Cassie.

She whispered, "I love you, daddy." He replied, "I love you too, Princess." She popped to Grandpa and kissed his cheek then smoothed her skirt out. She teased, "Now, I'll leave mom to straighten you all out. I'm going to meet this mate of my little sister's." Cassie was going to leave then mischief overtook the bond. She felt she couldn't leave us on such a downer.

She casually added, "I think you guys are worried about the wrong thing here. Angela is mischievous on her own. I've heard the same of Klaus. Just THINK of the trouble those two will get into." No, I didn't want to do that. Not even one little bit. Oden groaned in my head.

EJ linked me, "Fuck us all with that parting line." I admitted, "I already hate it." Cassie winked at me and popped out. We were in trouble. I already didn't like this. They were going to prank the hell out of all of us. It was somehow already annoying. I needed Melanie. Or I needed to smell her sweet strawberry scent.

Blue Moon arrived when I was rubbing my temples. Dylan got up to his usual antics. Preston snorted, "Dad might actually kill Dylan this time." I snorted, "Nope. That would upset Wesley because Buttercup would be distraught. Plus, you feel dad's feelings. He does see Dylan as family." Preston wiggled his eyebrows at me.

My dad had Dylan running out of the room in under five minutes. I was pretty certain that was a record. Logically, Angela could fight, whereas my mother was raised by the pretending to be peaceful whispering Queen. Alania was a bitch who wanted my mom to be meek and passive, but my mother was neither of those things.

Part of me hoped there was a ribbon where my mother just kicked the asses of all the Fairies from her past and popped away from them until my Grandpa Titus or any of my uncles found her. I think that would be nice for my mom to see.

Some of those realities we'd heard about sucked. They all had different circumstances. I might be biased, but I think my mom got the rawest deal of them all. At least other me's had my mom looking out for their version of her. She saved a lot of them and so did my dad. I was proud of both of them.

Dad linked me, "You get on any and all strategies to protect Angela and Klaus from Alania." I agreed, "I will." I linked Phil, "Is Keaton Daniels here?" He snorted, "Are you serious? No." I groaned, "Why?" I needed to talk to him. He replied, "Off the top of my head? His girlfriend is the worst." Great.

I'd get ahold of him and get his opinions on assessments. He was adept at them, and I was going to project my sister. Because anyone who EVER hurt Angela would see a side of me that surpassed the anger they'd seen from my dad.

In fact, they'd think it tame compared to what I would do to those who'd hurt my family or my Lovebug. If anyone EVER hurt my Melanie, then they would quickly find out what Robert did all those years ago. You stayed away from her. Or else.

Before I left the room, I winked and snapped all the women a strawberry martini in honor of my mom. They all raised a glass to me. Uncle Aiden was practically walking on air. He'd been waiting for this moment. I think he thought it would be Julian though. I needed to ask Cassie what her feelings about it were. She was usually right. I faded into the background and went outside.

I found Angela and Klaus easily. I hugged her saying, "I'm happy for you, little sister." Angela smiled boasting, "Klaus said he'd help me in the library try to figure out my blurry visions." I kissed her forehead, "You don't even worry about that today. Ok? It's not only your birthday today, you met your mate. That's a double celebration that has no space to worry about blurry visions."

I held my hand out to the kid I'd met introducing myself, "I'm Alexander." Klaus smiled, "I know. We've met." I admitted, "Most people can't tell us all apart." Klaus replied, "Once I hear all your names with faces, I'll remember. I'll remember them all for my Angela." I nearly gagged.

Parker linked me, "He's been saying sappy shit like that for an hour. For an hour, Alexander. I need to wash my eyes and brain out." I bit back a smile winked at my little brother. I told Klaus and Angela, "I'm sure you'll see a revolving door of us all now that I've started the train."

Klaus nodded, "I'm sure. I will not harm your sister. Ever. I promise." I raised an eyebrow telling him, "I don't doubt you, Klaus. From the moment I saw you looking at Angela, I knew that. I worry about others."

Klaus declared, "I will light them on fire if they so much as upset my Angela." I laughed, "I could get behind that." I hugged Angela again then walked inside. Parker linked, "No, no, no. Go ahead and leave, I insist. I'll be out here trying not to gag." I laughed, "You're the better man for it." He huffed.

I saw Elise sneak off. I grabbed a glass of whiskey and drained it, welcoming the burn. I grabbed two more, slammed the second one, then held onto the third. EJ trickled outside after Elise. No doubt at her direction.

I walked outside and found a freshly showered Cayden. I laughed asking, "Did you beat someone up?" Cayden answered, "Yes." I gasped in mock horror, "And you didn't invite me after the day I had? I thought we were brothers."

Cayden hummed, "I'm terribly sorry. It involved a source." I nodded, "The one you asked if I'd heal. How is said source?" Cayden answered, "Improving. Unconscious but improving." I offered, "If you change your mind, I'll be there."

Mentally I wanted to scream at him asking, "Was it Ashley? Is Ashley unconscious?" I didn't though, which meant Oden was restless. Cayden went inside to find Cassie. I headed towards the gym but instead shifted and ran to Yellow Hills.

I linked Emmett Daniels, "Heads up, I'm crossing your border to find your younger brother." He replied, "I'll assume you mean Keaton." I replied, "Since he's the one not here, yes. I need an assessment and he's the best." If he and I collaborated more I was certain we'd solve a lot of problems that would never have to happen, but he was a little shy.

I shifted back and walked into their house. I called, "Keaton." He flashed in front of me. He questioned, "Uhh what are you doing here?" I answered, "I need you to do an assessment for me. Angela is mated." He snorted, "I know." I asked, "Then what do you think I want?"

He answered, "Probably a smattering of things, but at the top of the list would be someone studying Alania to see what she'd put in their path in case they met when she clearly never planned on Angela doing so."

I nodded, "Got it in one. Uncle Aiden knows you have access to anything you need because of mom, but I'll conjure anything you need on her for this. I need to be prepared." He agreed, "I'll get it done." I hugged him, "Thanks and consider coming to stuff again. Even if you're going without your girlfriend. I'm always going solo myself." He snorted but nodded.

I left, shifted back into Oden, then hit the gym. I'd been hitting the heavy bag for several hours when I heard a throat clear behind me. I turned greeting, "Uncle Bjourn." He asked, "What's going on? Is Melanie ok?" I answered, "Yes. She's fine." She was always fine.

Uncle Bjourn surmised, "So it's something with Ashley that's bothering you." I snorted, "She was hurt. Supposedly, she was in a car accident. She's gone off the grid though. I feel like shit about the whole thing. I am drawn in by everything Ashley, but Melanie…" I trailed off.

I admitted, "hearing her name still makes my heart skip a beat. Ashley's name does something too though. It's just odd. It's the same name as a character in Melanie's favorite book series." Uncle Bjourn offered, "That could be your connection right there. You feel connected to her because of Melanie. They are both strong fighters."

I agreed, "True. I miss her, which sounds crazy. How can I miss someone I haven't met? Hell, I miss both of them because I'm an asshole. Ashley hasn't emailed me back in a while and I miss her ranting little emails. They always make me smile. It makes me worry that she's hurt pretty damn bad."

Uncle Bjourn said, "I do keep tabs on her." I asked, "You do?" Uncle Bjourn nodded, "I can tell you she's hurt, but she's recovering remarkably well." I realized, "Then you know where she is." Uncle Bjourn smiled saying, "There are very few people that can hide from me."

I pointed out, "My dad is trying to find her." Uncle Bjourn sighed, "I think your dad is waiting for her to come back rather than look for her, lest he find something he might not want to know about where she was." I had no idea what that meant, but he left. So, I went back to my workout.

I hit the heavy bag some more before popping into my shower. I put Melanie's hoodie on my second pillow and jumped into bed. Nope, there was nothing remotely creepy about this. Oden tiredly said, "It's not creepy because she's ours. This hoodie is the best I'll get since SOMEONE won't go get her."

The next morning, I ran into the Omega Robert was dating. Karina smiled offering, "Would you like some cookies, Alpha Alexander? I just made them." Her peanut butter cookies were still to die for. I teased her, "It was a bad idea to offer me these. I'll take the whole plate." She laughed, "I'll just go make more. My boyfriend loves watching me bake."

I snarfed the cookies down to avoid thinking about that. I wished they'd break up already. I hated seeing that guy around here because I still remembered what I'd heard him say to Melanie. He'd hurt her feelings and made her cry. He didn't like that her stuffed wolf looked like me.

Oden perked up saying, "Mates toy does look like me. Elise said she calls him her Xander wolf." He purred the name. I hated it when people called me Xander, but for some reason it always made me smile when I thought of Melanie calling me that nickname.

I found my family in the main room and sat down on the couch a moment before Lexi blazed in using her speed. She was on about some band I'd never heard of. How popular could they be? Micah knew about them though.

Oden offered, "Maybe the Hackura like them then and not wolves." It sounded reasonable. Lexi was perplexed by the situation. What shocked me more was that Micah seemed stunned that we didn't know about this band. He said they'd been popular for a few years, and that unless you had a connection; you couldn't get into their shows.

I'd bet any of us could get in if we wanted. Our family was definitely well known, powerful, rich, and popular. People wanted to meet us. Oden snorted, "Except Ashley." Except her. I couldn't figure that out. She did want to meet us, she just also didn't.

Max was startled to realize Micah and Cayden had been to the concerts several times. I leaned forward in my chair when Micah said he couldn't talk about it. That meant he had a source in the band. I was not getting a good feeling about that.

Elise jumped in and said the only person Micah had said that about was Ashley. How did Elise know that?! What the ever loving shit?! Was Ashley truly a consistent source for the Hackura?! Oden growled, "Evidence says she is." It really did and I couldn't figure out why.

Why wouldn't she talk to the Werewolf council instead? That's who she should trust. I mean Cayden and Micah were trustworthy, but she was a wolf. Plus, how did she know that she could ask to keep us locked out? What was going on? My heart stopped as I put it all together.

Ashley was not only their consistent source, she asked for us to boxed out. That's why Uncle Bjourn knew where Ashley was and her status. Brody was with her. I linked Phil, "You were right. Ashley is the source Cayden was going to have me come heal. Damn it! I was so close to meeting her."

Phil replied, "That was my guess honestly. Not that it makes ANY sense WHATSOEVER unless your dad is right and Black Path is doing naughty things." I rolled my eyes replying, "Just come into the room and sit down. There's no need to hide around the corner."

I added, "Plus, my dad is rarely wrong. If she has proof of Black Path being shitty, the Werewolf council would EAT it up. Why would she go to Cayden? HOW did she go to Cayden?" Phil came in and sat on the edge of the couch. He replied, "Those are good questions. I have no answers. I am remiss and adrift without a purpose as a Beta."

I linked Gage, "Are you up?" He groaned, "No, leave me alone." Fine. I linked Phil again, "Seriously though, how the hell is Ashley managing to be a Female Lead Warrior, running a pack, and participate as a lead role in a band?" I had to admit that was a girl who didn't like to sit still. Just like my Lovebug. My head pounded with pain. I shook that thought and sat back.

Phil linked, "I don't know." I felt like an ass for not knowing about this. I should've mentioned Ashley's band in our emails. I jolted hearing that she played acoustic and electric guitar. Melanie played both too. Tristan told me he taught her, and she took to it easily. Plus, Jason had bragged about how Melanie could play both acoustic and electric guitar several times.

I rubbed my head wondering why I always compare them. Probably to feel less like a jerk about the whole thing. Ashley might be the only werewolf around that didn't want to meet our family. I had no idea why that bothered me so damn much, but it really did.

I remained quiet while more details were thrown around. I'd ask Ashley about the band too, but I liked to have our emails remain private, just between us. I wasn't going to share any of it with Lexi. I had no idea why, I just wasn't going to.

Somehow the discussion turned to headaches. My mom got pissed when she realized we'd been getting these headaches for a while now. Oden whimpered, "Always about mate." I winced. Was he right? Why would thinking about Melanie give us all a headache? I nearly threw up when I tried to connect the dots.

I had to stop thinking about this. She was living her dream. I was being possessive and selfish again. I wanted the headaches to be about her so I could go meet her. I shook myself because I wouldn't stand in the way of her dreams.

Was I really though? I could pop her back and forth. She could do both. My head was pounding with pain now. No, I was being selfish that's all it was. Phil ran into the room. I'd been so in my head, I hadn't even noticed he'd stepped out.

He was frantic and that was never good. EJ and I popped into the office. I shoved every other thought out of my head. I needed to focus right now. The McDermont's Beta was on the phone. He said their Luna was dead. WHAT THE FUCK?! EJ popped out.

I linked my men, "GATHER OUTSIDE RIGHT NOW!" I popped to them. Once I'd gathered our men I popped to EJ. I glanced at my watch noting it had taken five minutes. We were running drills again. That was an unacceptable amount of time for my brother to be fighting with his Luna without me and our men. They needed to get it under three before I would be happy.

I shifted and fought with EJ then shifted back once the fight was over. Theo, my brother named after my dad's friend, popped in surprised we'd never met this pack before. EJ and I had met them, we just didn't see them too often.

Oden growled, "This isn't over." It looked over until I spotted the pack's Beta crawling towards the forest. That was not going to be good. I saw his mate trying to get a Warrior out of her way to get to him. I saw his son, but I didn't see his daughter. Oh god no.

The Beta announced someone took his daughter and the Alpha's. Fanfuckingtastic. EJ tried to pop to them and so did I. We were thrown back, but neither of us got hurt. EJ wanted to lead a scouting party. I spotted Theo, who was sniffing the air. I raised an eyebrow at him.

When he asked if we smelled 'that' my heart plummeted. Oh no. Please no. I nearly closed my eyes in frustration when a Warrior walked out with a hoodie. My brother snarled, "MINE!" Oden said, "Hmmm how odd he can tell from a scent on a hoodie. I myself told you the SAME THING when we found a hoodie in the back of an SUV YEARS AGO, yet you doubt me."

I replied, "Now is not the time. That hoodie was brought out to track the girls. Theo's mate is missing. Ours isn't, she's just not here." Oden grumbled but accepted I was right. It ended up being Jane

McDermont's hoodie. She recently turned eighteen. So, when we got her back, she'd be moving in with us at least. She'd be safe.

Theo kept trying to pop to her. I knew I needed to stop him, but I didn't know what to say. I'd do the same thing if I was him. Angela eventually popped in and got him to stop. EJ led the search even though Angela said the girl had gone through a holoport.

While they were gone, I grabbed Theo and pulled him into a hug. I linked him, "We will get her back, little brother. She will be by your side as she's meant to be. Alright?" Theo cried, "I already failed her. I should've protected her."

I reassured him, "You had no way of knowing. You got here when you could. She was gone before we were even called. You couldn't have done anything." Theo didn't feel any differently, and I still couldn't blame him.

Maverick popped in, immediately hugging Theo. He offered, "It will be alright, brother." Theo asked, "How, Mav? They took her. I don't have her or a lead. They have her and she doesn't know I'm coming." Maverick said, "We are the Conners Family. They made a serious mistake taking her and they are going to know that. We protect what is ours, and we will protect Jane."

Theo still didn't calm down. I knew he needed to hit something, but he was waiting for EJ to return. He returned without Jane, which we knew was going to happen. Now, Theo was past reason. I got him to come with me, but it was a fight.

I walked into the gym and ordered, "Everyone out. We have drills starting bright and early tomorrow. You all took five minutes to get to me and that's unacceptable!" Everyone left. Only a few grumbled about tomorrow.

I turned to Theo ordering, "Get in the ring." We stepped up and we fought. It took hours for him to calm down. When we stopped Maverick popped to his side. I linked him, "Mav, it's going to be ok." Maverick argued, "He's devastated." I knew that.

My empathetic connection with my siblings' emotions, be it emotional or physical hurt, was incredibly strong. I knew how upset Theo was and I hated it. I wished I could take every single bad emotion from him and give him only good ones. I couldn't though.

I popped them to the house that was oddly empty. I knew Maverick was staying with Theo in his room tonight. I popped to my room. I couldn't stop myself from writing an email. I needed something to do because Theo's devastation felt so acute it was practically ringing in my ears.

Ashley,

You mischievous little wolf. I hear you are in a VERY popular band. I feel horrible about the fact that I did not know about it. I'd love to come watch you play. Maybe I could buy tickets for Elise at least. I'd love to surprise her with them. She'd die of excitement. She really wants to meet you. Hell, I want to meet you.

The offer of you training our wolf less still stands. I'd love to host you for an event. It would be popular because YOU are popular in the werewolf community. We could swap tips too. I'd still love to spar with you sometime.

I heard you were in a car accident. I'm not sold on that being what happened. That's just based on the rumors my Beta heard. I stand by my emails to you Ashley. If that ass wipe marked you against your will, I'll kill him. I'll find out too.

I truly hope you are ok because I am genuinely worried about you. I don't know what's going on, but I want to help you. No, I NEED to help you. I can't even tell you why, but I know that I do. Please let me help, Ashley. I'll go around the Werewolf council, my brother, and anyone else you want. I just want to help you. Please.

Truthfully, I need to help someone. That's probably selfish to put on you, but I can't do anything to help my little brother at this moment. His mate was kidnapped. He found out tonight that she's his. When we were going to track the two girls taken.

The Luna of Gray Stone pack is dead. Their Alpha is a wreck, and so is my little brother. His mate is going to be devastated when we bring her home because her mom is gone. My brother Theo, his full name is Theodore, but we call him Theo. He's beside himself.

I don't know how to make him feel better other than get him in the gym. My connection with my siblings' emotions make it very hard to process. I want to burn the world down for him.

I hope to talk to you soon, and I wish you a speedy recovery.

Alexander

P.S. I could make it an incredibly fast recovery for you. I'm just saying, I've got healing hands.

I hit send. Then cursed myself, "I have healing hands?! GOD! Oden, why didn't you stop me from saying that?!" Oden snickered, "I liked it and it's true." I closed my eyes and went to sleep. I told myself we'd have everything settled soon.

I was wrong. Weeks passed by with nothing but us being on the kidnappers' tails. I ran drills with our Warriors. We'd gotten our response time where I wanted it. I hadn't heard back from Ashley though, which was putting me on edge.

The only thing that kept me calm was re-watching videos of Melanie dancing. She was truly mesmerizing. The way she moved was incredible. I was so frustrated with our lack of progress on finding Jane. It was clear Theo's mate had been taken into the Undergrounds. The real ones not the ones we had been to.

We'd found her blood at different places. Theo was in the gym more often with me than he ever was before. The only good news was we were finally on their tails. I needed to see Melanie. I locked my door and watched her dance.

As soon as the dance ended. My email dinged. I smiled when I saw Ashley's email address. I read the first line.

Alpha Duke,

I snorted because no matter how many times I told her to call me Alexander. Ashley called me Alpha Duke. I started to get hard and cursed myself. I kept reading.

I am in a band. I thought you knew that. We are kind of popular. Well I mean... pretty popular. Obviously not like crazy popular if you don't know us. I mean you guys know everything. So probably not super popular at all.

We do ok. We sound good.... if I do say so myself. I mean my bandmates are talented. That's what I mean. Not like I sound good. I'm not bragging I swear... My bandmates though... They are great. We are more like family...than just bandmates.

I don't think we'd be Elise's style. I mean we play a broad range of music. I could send you an audio clip of us performing.... I could do that. That's a thing I could do. Does that work as a compromise? Please say it does. I don't want you to be mad.

Honestly....our shows are fairly private, and the band is... particular... me... well... all of us... mostly me. .Just... let's say that. I'm weird. Let's move on.

As far as what happened to me, I don't really remember the accident. I remember there was one, but not the accident itself. It comes to me in weird flashes. My doctor said that was normal. My friend was UNHAPPY... so very unhappy. Said friend wanted more details.

I wished I had them. I'm trying to piece together what happened. None of my other friends are talking about it. So, it's probably bad. I mean it's fine... totally fine... Why would I say bad? I don't know... I'm just talking crazy over here. They probably don't want to push memory issues... Yup that's totally it. Nothing bad.

I'm not marked so there is no need to sharpen your broadsword or anything. Or I mean... any type of sword you want. You could obviously use any type of sword... and that would be fine. You can do whatever you want.

I don't want you to get in trouble for me. I couldn't live with it if you did. You'd hate me once you knew, and I can't do that. I can't... not you. I know you love your brother and your dad. I can't let you do that for me. I'll be ok. I can handle stupid jerks. I've been doing it my whole life. I've got a system.

I'm very sorry about your brother. I cannot imagine his pain or yours. I'm sure you will find the women that were kidnapped. Nothing can stand in your way when you set your mind to it.

Ashley

I was a little sad because normally I got a P.S. I sat back thinking over her email. She'd said broadsword. Did Cayden tell her about me? I did favor a broadsword. My email dinged again.

Alpha Duke,

OH MY GOSH! Stupid computer! I was not done... and it sent... I don't know why it does that. I wasn't ready to hit send. I am VERY good with computers. I'm so nice to them and then it goes and is mean to me.

I am hurt by my computer's actions... .it will go into a time out after this. Gosh... not like a real time out... I'm not a crazy person who puts inanimate objects into a corner... OH my gosh! I swear I'm not a weirdo.

It's so kind of you to offer to heal me. I'm all good now and cleared by an overzealous doctor. I mean seriously... I was fine a few days ago but the doctor and my friends were ALL male about me being 100% or whatever. I mean... Doctors... right?

I mean... they aren't bad or anything. Well, some are. You have bad apples in every profession... that's just a fact. Literally all professions. This guy wasn't a bad doctor... I'm actually grateful to him for helping and everything. It was nice of him. I probably sound ungrateful... dang... I'm really not. It was nice... I was just fine a few days ago... and moving on again.

The training offer. You just have no idea how much it means to me. Maybe someday... we could meet up and talk about it... I don't know when... but someday. Someday is a good time frame. Of course after we meet, you'd probably take it all back, but that's just... umm well yeah. So, it's an incredibly flattering offer. Someday.

Sparring with you... Just wow. I don't know. You're so good and you're distractingly hot like OH MY GOSH! I DID NOT WRITE THAT! BYE!

Ashley

It was just what I needed because I burst into laughter. Oden and I both liked that she thought we were hot. Which made me feel like shit until thirty minutes later when EJ linked me to get to the office. Hopefully, we got a damn break.

I popped to the office. I linked Phil, "Get the allies on a video call." Phil replied, "Roger, what do we have?" I admitted, "I don't know." The distorted voice on our phone told me that our sniper was back. Ashley was back and our sniper was back. Hell no. Do NOT even go there.

Oden pointed out, "You are already there. It's a hell of a coincidence. If it is one." I argued, "It HAS to be. She can't be in a band, the Female Lead Warrior, running a pack, AND in the Resistance." Oden replied, "You forgot to mention a source for Cayden." I snorted, "Exactly. She has no time. The only person with more things to constantly do is Mel."

I rubbed my head and shoved that out of my mind. Ashley had just recovered from an accident. She couldn't be running around saving the world. She needed to heal. Oden chimed back in, "She already is healed." Ugh. He needed to stop coming up with valid points.

I smiled to myself and smugly added she thought I was hot. I mentally slapped myself to focus. The sniper was giving us information. She couldn't do it herself. Well she could, but she wanted to know if we'd go. It didn't really seem like she doubted we would though.

Oden linked, "Almost like someone told her that one of the girls was mated into our family. Weird." I growled, "Shut it. She can't run off into danger like that. She JUST healed." Oden snorted, "I think she is, and so do you." I repeated, "Shut it."

Jason and the sniper snarked at each other. I knew what Jason's problem was, he wasn't sleeping well. The sniper though, that was confusing. The anger in her tone towards Jason didn't make sense. I didn't know what that was. I texted Tristan like EJ ordered.

Me: Get into the meeting room.
T: What's going on?
Me: Jase and sniper are taking shot at each other.
T: On my way. I'll be a few minutes but I'm coming. What the heck is this sniper's deal with us?
Me: Not a clue.

I linked Oden, "See? It can't be Ashley. She wouldn't be that upset with Jase." Oden conceded, "Sure, that has some logic. But so does the fact that Ashley pops back up, then so does the sniper." He was annoyingly right. I got the call back on point.

Oden linked, "See? The sniper even listens to us." I rolled my eyes, but he was right. The sniper was giving us six fighters in the Undergrounds. Damn. This girl was impressive. How did she know all this stuff all the time?

Oden offered, "Maybe she's good with computers unless she hits enter too soon AND SENDS AN EMAIL!" I growled at him. I didn't want to think about that. I'd have to be beyond a hundred percent sure to float that out there to the larger group. Elise loved Ashley.

I nearly growled when Theo got mad and snarked at the sniper. She was kind to him though. The complete opposite of her interaction with Jason. My dad linked me, "That was weird." It was. Oden said, "I feel like a broken record here but it's like someone told her Theo's mate was taken." He had another good point.

Our sniper could've figured that out though if she'd been watching us at all. It was all over the Supernatural and Werewolf community that Jane was Theo's at this point. So was the fact that we were coming for her.

Oden agreed, "You also have a point." The sniper gave us more details but cut the call after her and Jason got into it again. Like siblings. That didn't make sense though. Melanie was Jason's only sister, and she was perfectly fine in New York living her dream.

I was annoyed that the call got cut off because Tristan had texted that he was minutes away. Everyone was always minutes too late lately. Jason said he had a headache, and he'd missed his call with Melanie. Damn it! I wouldn't have anything to play later.

Oden snorted, "We don't watch those unless the dancing videos are scarce. She doesn't sound like mate in them." He was right. She sounded nothing like the Melanie I had heard about, but they all thought she was still mad at them.

I jolted when my mom made excellent points about our sniper. My mom believed the sniper was the seventh fighter. I linked Oden, "Ok, Ashley cannot do all that. That's too much for one person." Oden reasoned, "Not if she has help." I growled, "Ashley JUST healed. She can't be fighting." Oden sighed, "I don't like it any more than you do. I'm just saying it could fit."

Jason left the room visibly upset. I could confer with Uncle Aiden on something to help him sleep. I should've done that when Everly came to me. What was wrong with me? My mom got next level pissed about the fact that they were getting headaches in Red Run too. She popped out.

Now, my dad was in a bad mood. Elise commented the same thing I'd thought about the sniper and Jason went at it like siblings. Which still didn't make sense. Plus, they couldn't be siblings. The sniper thought Jason was the Beta. Melanie knew Tristan was the Beta.

I told everyone I'd talk to Jason. I'd just talk to Uncle Aiden first. There had to be something to help him get some damn sleep that wasn't a pill. Jason hated pills. We spent some time planning. My phone beeped and I walked away.

Alpha Duke Alexander Conners,

When you arrive in Kentucky to save the girls, you'll need to walk in between the two largest trees. Jump three times, and a panel will pop up. Then you can put in the codes below: 44KKDE23DJ! Three times.

Stay Safe,

The Ring Resistance

I sent the email to Micah and linked him, "Try to run down that IP address." Micah replied, "On it. I do love a challenge." EJ rallied the troops on the lawn. We were ready to go bring Theo's mate home. I linked him, "It's going to be ok. She's coming home." He was tense but ready to go.

Once we got there, I followed the instructions I'd been given. Micah came with me to put in the code. Once we were in, I popped down with EJ. EJ tried to hold Theo back, but he left then wailed for our mother. My heart wrenched at the emotional pain my brother felt.

I prayed, "To all the Gods and Goddess please let my mother be able to save Jane. I'll patiently wait for Melanie's arrival if he can just have his mate." We were being shot at, so EJ threw up his shield. Once they stopped shooting, I moved with my men and easily had the situation under control. They were not expecting us at all.

A Hackura took off for Madeline, the Beta's daughter that had been taken, cell. I knew that man in question. He was one of Angus Crawford's best friends, Drier. He was a good guy. Madeline would probably be heading to the Hackura realm. He was likely going to be a Squadron Leader in a few years under Cayden. Something told me Madeline might just feel rather safe in the Hackura realm right now.

Plus, I knew Madeline could fight but she preferred to design dresses. She was quite good too. She worked for one of our businesses. I'd sent her a proposal about opening her own place. That could be done in the Hackura realm easily enough.

I popped in and healed her while Drier held her. It didn't take too long. Mom was still healing Jane when I was done. I was ready to step in if need be. Mom was stronger as a healer than I was, but if she couldn't bring Jane fully back to health, I could jump in from where she'd left off.

The second mom was done healing Jane; she sat up and instantly wrapped herself around Theo. His relief was practically washing over me. I was ridiculously happy for my little brother. Madeline had information and I nearly cheered.

FINALLY, a break! They could tell us who the sniper was. I was excited for a whole minute. They didn't remember details but my Aunt Katie was all over this. They just knew the girl was a fighter named Swiffer. She wiped the floor with her opponents but first let them beat the shit out of her. WHAT?!

Oden and I were enraged to a degree I didn't understand. I linked Gage and Phil, "Who would do that? Who would have that be their thing?! AND WHY?" Gage answered, "I plead the fifth because my thoughts are having thoughts."

Phil agreed, "Phil also pleads the fifth because of the crazy thoughts that will have you roaring in anger. Let's take a beat and discuss the crazy, possibly correct, theories later." Fine. They thought it was about money.

I linked my Gamma and Beta, "That type of fighting style has to be about more than just for money. She could make that by winning. Why is she punishing herself?" Oden whispered, "Maybe her family died." I snapped back, "STOP THAT! This can't be Ashley. She won't meet us or let us help her. I can't. You know I can't handle this being Ashley." Gage and Phil were quiet.

Oden apologized, "I'm sorry, Alexander. I can't either, but you think it if I do." He was right, but I needed to stop. Ashley couldn't be that hurt all the time. She was the Female Lead Warrior of a shitty pack who people LOVED to attack.

Though they didn't attack as much since she turned seventeen. They had attacked a lot when she'd just taken the job, but not since she'd proved herself at every turn. They'd backed off when they realized she had a strategic mind as well as physical strength.

I walked out of the room with Elise following me asking questions. My mind swirled with questions of my own. If this was Ashley, what could I even do? Nothing. I hated that answer. I NEEDED to do something. I just couldn't think of anything.

Elise pointed out that the sniper wasn't trying to die, but that she wanted revenge. Yes, but revenge for what? Oden sighed. I winced realizing the answer: Her family. I needed to look into who killed Ashley's family.

Last I knew it was unsolved, but someone clearly had to have more details. It couldn't just be rogues. They'd have hunted them down by now if Ashley was the sniper. Elise and I both admitted we were worried then she left. Micah walked up announcing, "That IP address no longer exists. I emailed back and it bounced. My dad and I will keep trying." I nodded.

There was one thing I could do. Something I should've thought of earlier. I took out my phone and dialed the number I'd dialed so many times now. The familiar beep came across. I sighed, "I'm officially worried about you. It's not a natural state for me. I tend to be calm and on occasion angry."

I paused admitting, "Very angry. I've been accused of being moody, which is probably true. I learned something about you tonight and it unsettles me. I am scared for you. I'm begging you to let me help you. I have money. More money than I could ever need actually."

"You don't need to let people beat the shit of you before you win a fight. You can set up a drop with me that I won't even use it to find you. I'll find you another way. I'm a partial Fairy so I cannot lie. Please, let me help you. I can't stand this. For Laxenread and what's it done for my family alone I could fund what you're doing.

"You saved my brother's mate and got us here. You've saved my family more times than I can count. You've got someone assigned to threats on Maverick. I think all my siblings have someone assigned, but we know he has one. You've saved my best friend from Hunters. Please just think about it."

"I fully intend to find you. I WANT to meet you. I DO NOT hate you. I don't know what you're fighting routine is about but it needs to stop. It's not healthy for anyone let alone someone doing all the things you're doing. You need to be in top shape at all times."

I cleared my throat, "Your fighting style honestly sounds like you're punishing yourself. Everyone else thinks it's for more money, but I don't. Please stop and just let me fund what you're doing. Keep fighting if you want, but don't let yourself get hurt so badly. For me. I know I mean something to you, and I wish you'd tell me why. Just think about it." The machine cut me off.

Cayden commented, "That was an interesting appeal." I turned to face him saying, "You know I'm right." Cayden agreed, "I believe you are." Oden linked, "Alarm bells are ringing in my head." He was right. I asked, "Do you know who the sniper is?" Cayden shrugged saying, "I don't." I heard the subtext in his tone and saw it on his face.

I snorted, "You think you do though." Cayden titled his head acknowledging, "You're not wrong. I think I do, but I have no proof." I offered, "I can help you get some." Cayden sighed, "I wish you could. I'm working on it."

I stated emphatically, "If you need anything please let me know. It's important to me." Cayden raised an eyebrow saying, "If you get a response to that appeal you just made, will you let me know?" I sighed, "If you heard the response then you heard it. I don't know if I would tell anyone. I promised not to use it to track them down."

I ran my hands through my hair, "I'll find them, Cayden. I can feel it. Or they will find me. I'm not sure which. I just can't think of someone doing this to themselves. Especially when I can help. Maybe I'm an ass for using myself when it's clear they care about me, but I can't think of someone doing that."

Cayden shrugged, "You use what you got. At minimum, you'll make them consider how they do things. It's very clear to everyone you do mean something to her. So, it does have to make her think about it harder if you object." I nodded. He opened a portal and took his group home.

I popped my men home and ran upstairs to write Ashley an email back. I knew I probably shouldn't tease her, but I just might. I knew I was far too excited about our emails. I just couldn't help it. I watched Melanie dance again. She was breathtakingly beautiful. Oden linked, "And ours." I hoped she was.

I minimized the video to type my email back to Ashley. First, I linked Phil, "Quietly look into who killed Ashley's family." Phil replied, "Who do you love? Who's your favorite cousin?" He walked into my room.

I raised an eyebrow answering, "You. Why do I love you?" Phil laughed, "I'm awesome of course. Walker, you remember is now mated to Blair. Who IDOLIZES Ashley Griffen and the ground she walks on. He now has tidbits for me on the elusive and reclusive Ashley. Like what happened to Ashley's family other than they were murdered and people blame her."

I somewhat demanded, "Hit me." Phil said, "Alright." He punched me in the arm and teased, "I gotta take my shots where I can. Ashley Griffen's family was killed by Hunters and Witches. They all blame her because the family was supposed to be at some event. They came home because she was upset, she'd gotten grounded and yelled at them."

I gaped at him for several moments. I shouted, "Her brother BLAMES her because at fourteen she was pissed at her parents for grounding her?" Phil nodded, "It seems that way yeah. Then there's the other rumor." I groaned, "I don't like how that started at all."

Phil sighed, "The Rumor going around is that when she didn't shift at sixteen that confirmed for the pack the wolf dad, wasn't her biological dad. That the Hunter who killed her family is her biological dad."

I snorted, "Bullfuckingshit. I don't know why she doesn't have a wolf, but Hunters are not half as skilled at fighting as Ashley is." Phil hummed, "Which is what Walker told his mate. His Blair got VERY interested in that opinion and peppered him with questions." Why wouldn't another wolf know that?

He continued, "Then she called her friends, and they talked for hours. She kept asking him how he knew that. He told her it was common knowledge. He also added he'd met Hunters and has met Ashley so he knew she didn't have any Hunter blood. His mate was confused about that as well." What?

Phil tapped his chin, "I myself ask why it's not common knowledge in Black Path that Hunters hunt. Hand to hand combat is not their thing. Tranquilizers, shooting, throwing weapons sure. Hand to hand like Ashley? Nah. She can beat an Alpha werewolf. A shitty Alpha, but an Alpha, nonetheless. That woman is a wolf. Why don't Black Path members know they can tell the blood of other Supernaturals if they've met them? I don't know. It seems weird not to teach pups that, but they are weird."

He took a breath, "Then I ponder about Ashley herself. I ask why she doesn't have a wolf? I find myself more curious with each passing day." I frowned reasoning, "Some people just don't get them." Phil shrugged, "I think her old pack just wanted the excuse to kick her out and her not shifting gave them the reason to cut ties."

We both sat in silence for a moment. He clapped saying, "Maybe she's half Hackura. That rings far more accurate than her being fucking Hunter. I'd have gone with that lie instead of Hunter to be honest. Their Beta is truly atrocious. Ashley is a lot like us other Hackura hybrids minus not having a wolf." Holy shit. Was that why she trusted Cayden and Micah? She was half Hackura?

No, because then surely Cayden would take her home. Oden agreed, "He would." My wolf was right, I knew he would. Maybe she had some Hackura blood in her though. It was a thought. Oden snorted, "A thought that fits, but it doesn't." He was right. I stretched my fingers and got ready to type my email to Ashley. She'd said we'd meet some day. I wanted it to be someday soon.

My Stand

Melanie is Nineteen Years Old

Melanie and her friends were sitting in Mason and Hendrick's diner. The Ring was planning something big. I'd tapped into the computers of the Hunters we'd been sent to work with from day one when we were fourteen.

I had a little wand device I'd built. It helped that Nate was actually working with us. He still hadn't agreed to go see Princess Luna Haley yet, but I did help him with what I could power wise. He'd met other Fairies who were trying to bring him into Princess Luna Haley's orbit, but he hadn't quite got there.

I wasn't pushing because I understood his goals. I'd sent plenty of partial Fairies the Conners way and encouraged all I met to go train at Black Mountains partial Fairy Practices. Nate did practice his magic with the partials he'd met though. He learned how to charm the Hunter tattoo on his wrist.

I couldn't fault him for not wanting to stop since he wanted revenge. He'd been abandoned as a child, and a pack took him in. When he went away to college, he'd returned from a break to find the pack was in ruins.

The family who'd raised him was dead. He's been working through the ranks trying to get to Slade Carter ever since. He wanted to find his sisters that had been kidnapped. Working with him, we'd managed to save a lot of people.

Thinking of Slade brought my memories back to my home pack, which made me internally cringe. A man I considered a second dad banished me when I didn't shift. I couldn't think about that though. I just couldn't. I needed to focus on where I was: King's Diner with friends.

Blair gasping pulled me out of those thoughts. Paige whispered, "Oh no." I asked, "What?" Then I heard a man growl, "MINE!" Blair stood and ran to the man. He wasn't from our pack and based on looks I was certain I knew who he was.

This was good. Blair could get out of Black Path. That was my hope for everyone here. Addison looked at me worriedly. She whispered, "You're fighting tonight." I shrugged saying, "I'll be fine." I would be. I'd have to fight Blair's father first before my Underground fight. It would be a quick and easy one. He wasn't a good fighter.

In the wonderfulness that was Black Path, anyone who wanted to leave and be with their fated had to fight to be with them if they weren't in the pack. Non mated pack members were typically sold off as chosen mates before I showed up. I say that loosely because.... the women especially, had no choice. I'd fought countless times since I came here to stop that.

Especially after I became the Female Lead Warrior. Any Warrior under me was a given. I didn't have to argue they deserved me to fight in their place. Sierra nudged me whispering, "Blair is panicking." I told them, "Someone text Olivia.... I'm not going to make it to see her today." Addison immediately took out her phone.

I was monitoring everything I could for the allies and Olivia was working to develop more things to help. We had planned to work on them today. Sometimes, we were suspects for the things we did but despite knowing Paige and Valentina were my friends we weren't suspected that much. For how smart The Ring could be they were also somehow... very dumb.

I guess they had to be though. The Conners and their allies had driven them into the dark. Which made things easier for my group, The Resistance. It was somewhat of a joke with our group that Cayden and Micah wanted a meeting with The Resistance leader.

When you think about the fact the leader is me.... and I meet with them ALL the dang time... it was kind of funny. Addison grunted. I asked, "Is Olivia upset?" She replied, "No, my dad texted telling me to quit the band again." I knew she wouldn't, so I wasn't worried.

The Rebels had become pretty popular. It pissed off Sierra and Addison's dad's that we had the band… which both my friends loved. So, every time they texted them saying they had to quit it just cemented they weren't going to. Heck, Sierra would probably find a venue to play nearby just to spite Edward and Jean.

I stood and walked over to Blair. Her mate was confused. I assured her, "It's fine Blair. Introduce us to your mate." Blair looked at me with wide eyes. She linked me, "You have a fight tonight." I replied, "Now I have two. I won't have you being unhappy. You belong with your mate."

Blair's eyes filled with tears when she replied, "So do you Mel." I wanted to wince as pain filled my heart. My Xander. We emailed now even though I knew I shouldn't answer him. He was going to hate me when he found out it's really me.

One day he'd find out that Ashley Griffen and Melanie McAlister were the same person. At this point, I'd memorized the letter Jason sent me after I didn't shift. He'd told Xander that I thought he was my mate. The thing was, I didn't think he was my mate; I knew he was.

Now, my mate didn't want me. I blinked and replied to Blair, "He doesn't want me." Blair insisted, "He likes you as Ashley. It comes across in his emails. He's willing to kill for you. He never has to know your real name." They'd all read that second email he'd sent when I passed out and Cayden left.

I snorted, "He'd find out when he introduced me to Red Run." Blair argued, "You could find a way around that. Always be gone or something. It worked when you were a pup." I couldn't do that to Xander. He needed a Luna that was able to do her job.

I explained, "He's an Alpha Enforcer. Of course he'd kill for someone. That's not a high bar… when you think about it." Blair shot me a look. She said, "He didn't say it as an enforcer. There was entirely too much passion behind his words, even in email form."

Her mate cleared his throat, "I didn't actually get to introduce myself yet. I'm Walker. I'm a Warrior in Cedars Run." He was exactly who I thought he was then. His brother was the Male Lead Warrior in a good pack. Walker asked, "Do you have a position in your pack, Blair?"

Blair nodded, "I'm a Warrior in Black Path…." She trailed off when Walker made a face. Blair added, "I'll move to your pack." Walker nodded commenting, "You must be a warrior under Ashley Griffen then. I heard Buck still doesn't allow Females to train under him. Not even his sister."

I snorted, "He always follows the rules… in a way… he kind of skirts them… through other people… but he doesn't… technically… break them. Usually, it's me… but he and Avery barely speak… which I'm pretty upsets them both… but that's a whole thing… that…."

Blair jumped in, "This is Ashley Griffen, and I do train with her." I smiled at Walker, whose eyes widened. He gaped at me before saying, "Well, I'll be damned. I was just sent on an errand and saw this place. Then I had to stop when I smelled Blair and now, I've met my mate and Ashley Griffen."

He paused then added, "My brother, the Male Lead Warrior in our pack, will not believe me. He's DYING to meet you. Even our Female Lead Warrior wants to meet you. You're somehow everywhere while simultaneously being a recluse."

I smiled saying, "Well Cedars Run is one of the few packs around here that isn't complete crap. I couldn't part with Blair for anything less. Have you always wanted your mate?" Walker wrapped an arm around Blair before kissing her head. My heart clenched thinking I'd never have that.

He told me, "I have. My parents and my older brother, the Male Lead Warrior I mentioned, all have their mates. I've been looking for mine, but Blair here has been hiding." Not exactly.

Black Path Females weren't allowed to go looking for their mate. At least they weren't right now, but when Caine and Dax took over that would change. It would shake the Ring when that happened. It's why Edward and Jean weren't training them. They knew how their sons felt about their complicity with Hunters and the Ring.

Edward Davis was a pathetic excuse of an Alpha. Having access to his files as the Female Lead Warrior meant I knew that he made a deal to keep his family safe. Not his pack though, his family. He gave over information… hell he'd almost sold an Omega to a Hunter as a chosen mate.

Luna Elena I felt bad for. She was completely disgusted with Edward, and they were fated mates. I'd thought maybe they weren't since that's how things go down here. She talked about how he used to be different and hopeful. I couldn't really see it.

Beta Female Eden felt the same way Luna Elena did. They lived separately from their husbands. They were just as much prisoners here as the rest of the women... even some men. We all knew that Omega they nearly gave to a Hunter would have been tortured to death if I hadn't fought for her.

I'd taken a hell of a punishment afterwards, but I didn't care. I could stop them from punishing me if I wanted to. They could only do it because I let them. All of my friends, Mason, and Hendrick told me to stand up for myself, but they didn't understand that I deserved it.

It still hit me some days my parents and older brother were dead. I should've died with them. Everyone thinks so from my old pack and… most days… I wish I had. I missed what my life had been like before that horrible night every single day of my existence down here.

I was still upset Selene, the Moon Goddess, didn't just let me die. My family was gone. Jason HATED me. Both sets of my grandparents rejected me. My Aunts and Uncles by blood and marriage wished me dead. Peter and Chelsea Kyle abandoned me. All the Kyle's did.

Elise was different… I didn't think she knew. I talked to her... via email. She always told me I reminded her of someone. Sometimes I pretend that the name Ashley Griffen had got her attention. I just hoped it was because deep down, she knew I was me and she wanted me to come home.

It was a silly notion really, but I couldn't help it. I wanted her to know I was me. She didn't though or she'd ask why I was here. She'd be upset with her parents if she knew. Heck, EJ probably knew I was banished from Red Run. He DEFINITELY didn't know I was Ashley though. He wouldn't talk to me, nor would Xander.

My heart filled with pain like usual. Xander. I loved him with everything in me. I still helped him how I could. I had to send Hendrick out as his sniper though. If I saw him through the scope… I'd run to him. I knew I should go let him reject me so he could be happy, but I knew his rejection would likely kill me.

I needed to stay away so I could get the Resistance to a point where everything could keep going without me. Kingsley could run it all, but she had her own thing going on. If something happened to me, ILYX would transfer everything to her with a message about it.

Plus, as things stood I needed to protect Xander, his allies, the innocents from the Ring, and my friends. Once everything could run without me and the plan to take over the forgotten packs was all done then I'd go to him… and let him do what he needed to. Then I'd disappear or be dead. That was the plan.

I felt bad enough that I'd made Xander wait this long. I knew he was probably looking for his mate. He didn't truly believe it was me and all the women he sent down here said how desperately he didn't want to be mine. They'd come over the years and nearly ripped my heart out.

Flashback

Melanie was furious. Buck and I had just stopped another pack trying to attack and take over. I was dealing with the aftermath and was currently late to the Rebels concert. A hairbrained idea from start to finish at the last minute from someone with delusions of grandeur stopped me from being on time.

All because that invading Alpha's Beta was away and didn't make it back in time to stop them. My friends in the band would announce to the supernatural crowd that I was busy and would join if I could. Cayden and Micah were there tonight though. I had information for them, so I needed to get there.

I finished the paperwork and got up to leave. Edward said, "I need you to go pick up my coffee." I sneered, "Why? Doing your job isn't good enough for you now?" He turned saying, "You'll go or Avery will be in the punishing fields tonight."

Buck jerked upright with furious eyes before he clenched his jaw and looked at the ground… but he said nothing. I silently tried to will him to… but it didn't work. Even though I knew he would never let a whip touch Avery.

I huffed asking Edward, "Where's your dang coffee at?" He shrugged, "The usual place." I wanted to hit him. I called as he walked away, "I'll go get your ungrateful turd face your coffee. Even though I just saved you from dying. AGAIN! Maybe next time, I'll let them get to you IN YOUR OFFICE WHILE YOU HIDE!" I stormed outside and got on my motorcycle and took off.

I was surprised when Buck pulled into the spot beside mine at the coffee shop. I asked, "Are you ok?" He replied, "Better than you will be, since Edward is not the only one whose order is waiting. I'm going to help you get the order back to the packhouse."

I gritted my teeth surmising, "He knew I'd take my bike." Buck nodded. I asked, "And you're here because?" He replied, "We both know I'd have come even if they didn't threaten Avery, but I won't risk anything happening to her." I stared at him, my reply dying on my lips. It was true.

Buck helped me out sometimes and it pissed me off because it was in the shadows. He wasn't brave enough to stand up and do what was right, but he did make moves to be a decent person. Which told me he could be one all the time.

I stalked into the coffee shop. I went up to the counter declaring, "I'm here for Edward Davis's order." The staff nodded and started to get it all together. I shook my head and noted they ordered muffins, likely all they had behind that counter. I swear they just liked to upset me after I saved their ungrateful lives.

I heard a fake annoying giggle, "God, Alpha Alexander can go all night." Buck winced and I closed my eyes inhaling deeply. Ignore her, just ignore her. This was a thing I could do. She wasn't the first to come down here and try to hurt me. It was fine. I was totally fine.

Someone gasped in reply, "He keeps everything so discreet though. I had no idea you were seeing each other. Or that he was with anyone at all. I've only heard people guessing which sex he's interested in." She should hang around here then. She'd hear all about the women he was into.

The woman who'd mentioned my mate laughed, "He invited me back to Black Mountain and introduced me to his family. Luna Elise was so sweet. She's looking forward to having another sister in law." Buck's jaw dropped and pain radiated through my entire being.

Was he really taking a chosen mate this time? Others had suggested it but they didn't usually mention his family. I was stunned that if he was taking a chosen it wasn't going to be Cheyenne. The only solace that offered me was knowing she'd be pissed because she was so sure in her online journal it would be them in the end.

Why was he even taking a chosen mate at all? We could be happy. I would be the best mate to him, I really would. I would defeat all his enemies. I would stand in the void between the good and bad. I did it now, I just wanted to be near him while I was doing it. I didn't have to be by his side with the allies. I knew they hated me. I'd be in the background, I could do that now. Heck, I was good at it at this point.

Another woman scoffed, "Please, he's not taking you as a chosen mate." I subtly looked over my shoulder at the woman my mate wanted. My heart sank because like the others, she was beautiful; flawless even.

She had no scars on her body like I did. She was blonde, of course. They all were. It was some sort of joke I was fated to him when I was clearly not his type. She was tall too, she could be a model. Most Werewolves could though.

She chuckled, "Oh, but he's strongly considering it. I made that man see stars." The woman I decided was cool asked, "And what about his fated mate? All the rumors I've heard are he wants his and would wait just like his dad did." That was the rumor? Hope filled me before it was cruelly dashed.

Xander's possible chosen mate shrugged, "Well, there was one girl who thought she was his, but he's not into her though. He's pretty desperate to have a mate in case she's right. He doesn't want her." I'd rather be whipped, beaten, and left for dead than hear this.

Buck linked, "Melanie, don't listen to her." I waved him off and wiped a traitorous tear that fell. The barista sympathetically called, "Edward Davis's order is up." Yeah, she was from Black Path and knew I loved Xander, and that girl was talking about me.

Sadly, that comment got the attention of the group that had been talking about Xander. The she wolf chuckled, "That's her actually. He showed me her picture. Can you imagine her as a Luna? Covered in blood, beaten up, and dirty. God, no wonder he doesn't want her." The theme of these visits were that he didn't want me.

I'd just saved the lives of countless people. The side of me that clung to hope latched onto the fact that Xander had my picture, but I shoved that part of me away. He had it to remind him how desperate he was not to have me. He had it though. I wondered what picture it was.

The cool girl replied, "I mean, he's pretty in the trenches himself. She might actually be perfect for him. Didn't you hear their pack in here earlier? They were attacked, and I'll bet she's the one who stopped their pack from being taken over."

The wannabe with my mate hit her arm, "I'm so much prettier." She was. The cool girl argued, "You are both beautiful. Your attitude is giving her an edge though." I'd be her new best friend. The other girl scoffed, "Well, he wants me. We are going to discuss contracts and I'm moving into his Luna suites while we hammer out the details." I grabbed the order and ran out because I wasn't certain what else you do to a shattered heart, but she was going to try.

I took deep breaths staring at my bike. Buck came up beside me. He bashfully offered, "Hey, he's an idiot. She's an airhead." I wiped my tears, "You think I'm…" Buck interrupted, "You don't know what I think." I admitted, "I could guess. Everyone down here hates me. I'm the enemy."

He replied, "I don't think you're an enemy. I think you're highly intelligent, good at fighting, and the only person who makes my job easier. You know full well the past Female Lead Warrior never did a damn piece of paperwork. I know you judge me for keeping my head down and toeing the company line; however, I was the one doing all that stuff to keep this pack afloat before you came onto the leadership team." I knew that. I was just shocked he was saying all this.

He added, "I think you're very smart about almost everything. The thing you lack is street smarts. Some of us know how to keep on moving so we stay alive." I studied him, "You knew I was taking that route before that concert. You knew they were going to attack Avery and that I'd get to her."

He stared at me for several minutes. I'd said the same thing to him countless times, but he just huffed and changed the subject. I just wanted him to admit that he cared about Avery the way I knew he did. Maybe he could see I needed the answer tonight because he replied, "I also drove your motorcycle around so it would be out of gas, meaning you'd have to run."

I gaped at him, and he grabbed most of the order except the coffee. I whispered, "I knew it… I freaking knew it! That would mean the world to her if you…" He cut me off, "She's safer with you now that she's of age. I did what I had to do to protect her and now she's with the person who can make sure nothing touches her. All I have ever wanted is for Avery to be happy and safe, even if she has to hate me to do it." He drove off before I could reply.

Flashback Ends

Addison pulled me out of my thoughts, "Well, bring Walker over here, Blair. We want to meet him too." Walker frowned saying, "We could get out of here. We could…." Blair cut him off, "I'll have to meet you back here tonight. Then we can go to your pack."

Walker offered, "I could come with you, and meet your family." I jumped in, "Black Path doesn't allow people inside the pack unless they are our pack members or allies. Or members of the Werewolf or Supernatural council."

Walker snorted, "You don't have that many of those. Allies that is." I rolled my eyes, "I'm aware. Who would want to be our ally? Not smart people… that's who." Walker laughed, "Aren't you just..." He trailed off. He was probably going to say rude. He finally finished, "interesting?" I shrugged.

Walker surmised, "You don't like your own pack. That's strangely clear. Yet you are their Female Lead Warrior." I nodded, "Yes, well someone has to do their job in that pack. Lord knows it's not the Alpha, Beta, or the Gamma. They wouldn't know how to do their jobs if it smacked them in the face with a manual... I supposed I could slap them in the face with said manual…that would be funny."

I tapped my chin saying, "It wouldn't help though, but it WOULD make me feel better. That's for sure…" Blair cut me off, "Let's sit down." Walker looked torn. He clearly wanted me to talk more. I went back to the kitchen to avoid doing that.

Mason linked me, "Blair found her mate." I nodded. He looked sad when he replied, "You have a fight tonight already. I wish you'd let Hendrick or I come with you." I couldn't because they'd hate my strategy and talk me out of doing it.

I don't really know what they thought when I came back hurt, but I knew if they saw how I fought they'd be hurt. I didn't want that. I didn't want what I was doing to hurt anyone, but they just didn't understand the drive I had to do it.

They just didn't understand that I deserved the pain from those fights. The Undergrounds had so many people who shouldn't be there, but I wasn't one of them. Honestly, The Undergrounds were bigger than I'd originally thought. We got people out as we could.

Most often by letting people believe a fighter had died. It was not an uncomplicated process, but the more we pulled back at the layers… the more appeared. For all intents and purposes… the Rings were hiding, but they weren't exactly dumb. In some ways, they definitely were. In others they were quite sophisticated.

Hendrick told me, "You know Alpha Ezra is coming tonight to see the McCann's." I rolled my eyes. Alpha Ezra was always visiting them for some reason or another. Honestly that Alpha Ezra frequented this pack was yet another reason I couldn't believe Jason let me come here. Dad hated Alpha Ezra and often talked about avoiding him.

I clutched my chest. Dad…. no matter what they said… Even if he wasn't my biological father… Drake McAlister was my dad. DNA didn't make you a dad. Everything my dad had done for me did. Tears burned in my eyes. It couldn't be true that he wasn't biologically my dad… but I didn't have a wolf.

The thing was some days I swore I did. I swore the night of my sixteenth birthday my wolf told me to fight. That she was going to get us help… then all I could feel was pain. That's all I remembered. Even if I was just my mom's daughter… I should have a wolf.

The Moon Goddess…. was such a terribly cruel goddess. Especially to those down here and she clearly had it out for me… personally. Or at least it felt that way. I'd clearly done something to piss her off.

Mason sighed pulling me out of my thoughts, "You know Alpha Ezra is going to lecture Trevor about you not being marked." He growled out that last part. I snorted, "Trevor McCann is not my mate." Everyone knew that. The sad sack pathetic piece of crap Edward even knew that.

The pack had been in dissention about everything that came out, especially the wolf less, after that ordeal where I declared I wasn't his mate. Edward claimed there was nothing he could do about it because they couldn't prove it… because I didn't have a wolf. It was complete crap and the pack knew it.

I knew who my mate was, and I always had. Whether he wanted me or not, my mate was Xander. Trevor McCann was so far from my mate it was crazy. I had no idea why he even pretended we were fated. He hated me.

To be fair, he wasn't alone with his hatred because I loathed him. Booker kept telling him he needed to get me under control. His latest tirade about being my mate was that I'd have to quit being the Female Lead Warrior and give him pups.

I'd gouge his eyes out and slit his throat then run to my Xander before that happened. I'd let Xander reject me, but I'd also tell him why I ran to him. Whether he wants me or not... an Alpha hearing their mate was almost marked against their will would go poorly.

I'd read extensive research on Alpha's so I knew that someone else wanting to forcibly mark what was theirs… would send any wolf, but especially and Alpha, into a rage. Xander would decimate the McCann family and probably Black Path as a whole. Whether he wanted me in the end or not.

Caine and Dax could take over then though. Caine felt he wasn't ready, but he was getting there. If Trevor tried to push this mate issue… then he'd be meeting Xander and getting his brain exploded… since Xander could do that.

If I could see Xander without running into EJ… I had a chance of him not finding out who I was. Because the picture he had of me was old. Jason didn't get new pictures… so there was a chance it was probably me dancing… those were from far away and I had on a lot of stage make up.

Truth be told, even if I did see EJ… Xander wouldn't be able to help it. His wolf, Oden, would demand that Trevor be punished for that. Xander himself would agree, I knew he would. Maybe even Jason would.

He must have felt bad because once I denied Trevor was my mate on the phone and yelled at him, my brother never brought it up again. He probably thought it was all resolved. Because my brother might hate me, but he would never spit on the grave of our mother and brother like that. Besides, I hadn't told him in our letters it was still a problem.

I knew there was no way in hell that Jason would be ok with some guy trying to mark and rape me. He definitely wouldn't be ok with me being marked by someone that wasn't my mate. It's clearly why he never brought he situation up again.

He may never want to see me, but he was still my brother. Maybe half-brother, but mom and dad would never forgive him in the afterlife if he let that happen. Tristan would probably haunt him. I was certain he haunted me in the Undergrounds. If only he didn't look so sad it would be better.

I shrugged at Mason saying, "Alpha Ezra coming here doesn't matter to me. He's an enemy of my family. I will never be marked by anyone he approves of. Let alone someone who isn't my mate." I walked back out to the group.

I noted that Walker was enamored with Blair, just how he should be. Another reason we all knew Trevor was full of crap. He banged anyone who looked in his direction and I didn't care. I knew that he couldn't do that if I was his mate. Everyone did.

People cheated down here but they felt bad about it. Some thought they had to do it to keep their mate safe. Edward and Jean still gave their mates gifts after they cheated. They never tried to hurt their feelings in public about it, and they were horrible mates.

Trevor often boasted about who he was sleeping with while spitting in my face. I think he actually thought it would hurt my feelings which was astounding. Several mates had said they couldn't imagine acting how he was with their chosen. So, he was proving he was a liar even though I did when I turned eighteen.

I knew that my dad would've walked over glass before hurting my mother. So would Alpha Peter for Luna Chelsea and EJ would make someone's head explode if they'd hurt Elise's feelings. He and Alexander shared the pushing power… so he definitely would kill Trevor for what he did to me. EJ would never hurt her himself, and he'd never cheat.

I stood announcing, "We need to go pack your stuff, Blair." Blair looked at me nervously. Walker reiterated, "I really can come with you back to your pack. I'm certain if Ashley tells her Warriors to stand down, I'd do just fine with Buck's Warriors." He could technically stand at the border but that would be bad since he'd hear what was going to happen.

I snorted, "I believe you could take them…it would not even be close. It's not necessary though. Addison will bring Blair back here in forty minutes tops." Walker laughed, "Are you already packed mate of mine?" Blair quietly said, "No."

The Females in Black Path didn't have much in terms of possession. I was lucky I had Mason and Hendrick. They spoiled me, but most parents down here didn't buy the females anything. Female Warriors were paid well under me what they should be.

I'd brought it to the Supernatural Council since they were whose purview Black Path was under but they refused to hear my case. Again. Like they always did. I took yearly trips about my family, but they still wouldn't step in. I found it interesting the Fairy representatives were never there if I was.

I excluded them in my thoughts of their colleagues being a disgrace to their jobs. Edward didn't want to encourage it, so Female Warriors made three dollars a day. It was pathetic. I assured Walker, "She'll be back." Walker smiled but said quite seriously, "You take even forty one minutes mate, and I'll come after you." Blair almost panicked.

I laughed, "Challenge accepted. Let's go girls." He jolted, "How is it a challenge for you?" I opened my mouth and Addison said, "We have to get going. See you later!" Walker's gaze narrowed on mine. He was suspicious but I didn't really care.

If his Alpha attacked our pack, I'd have our Warriors back down and lead him to Edward. His one of the few down here that I'd gladly let lead Black Path and mentor Caine until he was ready. He really needed an Alpha blood but all he had was me.

We all walked out of the diner. Sierra offered, "I could do the challenge." I snorted, "You'd be punished after you won. Your dad would use that to give you to that pathetic sack of cow dung we are allies with that wants you. Same for you Addison. I can take it. Better to have two fights than three or four." Because I would fight for them. They were not leaving for anyone they didn't want.

Addison vowed, "We won't let Trevor mark you." I snorted, "They already tried to use wolfsbane countless times on me to accomplish that. I'm a freak of nature so it doesn't weaken me like it does you guys." Normal Werewolves couldn't ingest or be hit with Silver and Wolfsbane.

I wasn't normal so they didn't affect me. Not even drugs did. I was a freak. I scoffed inwardly. I was a wolf less freak. No wonder Jason wasn't proud of me. I'd tried my absolute best, but nothing worked. He didn't catch on that I was Ashley Griffen.

One strange letter from him did say that I should train under her. He said she was a good example of a wolf less pack member. Aunt Stephanie had taken it out of my locker at the Undergrounds and ripped that one up. She said he'd been drunk and didn't mean it.

I remembered every word in the letter though. Plus… I'd already put it on my computer system and ILYX had it locked in a special file with all the other letters. Because technically… in a way… he was proud of me. That letter had been the nicest thing he'd said to me in years.

We walked back into Black Path. Several wolves growled when they caught the scent of another pack on us. An unknown male wolf. I rolled my eyes at them. They must have told Edward because he was waiting outside in the yard between the pack house and the main house.

I jolted when I heard a growl I knew. Interesting. Still the human and not the wolf. I wasn't sure why that still shocked me at this point. He demanded to know, "What is the meaning of that smell? That's not a pack members scent! WHO WERE YOU MEETING WITH?!" Blair looked down while I blinked, realizing he looked genuinely afraid. Weird.

I answered, "Blair met her mate. The scent is his." Growls filled the air. Her dad pushed forward and yelled, "NO! She won't be with him!" Her mom started crying. Her mother was her father's fated mate. Blair cried, "Daddy! Please…."

He growled cutting her off, "I said no, and my word is law." I snorted, "Uhh no… not even kind of… Seriously? Your word is law? Are you for real? Unbelievable… I challenge you for the right to decide Blair's fate, McCoy."

McCoy, Blair's dad, growled at me, "You have no say! She's my daughter!" I laughed, "I'm surprised you remember that fact. You haven't been a father to her since I got here. She's also over the age of sixteen and no longer under your roof."

I added, "She's my Warrior so I absolutely have a say here. Ask the twenty men behind you whose butt I've kicked so their daughters could be happy. I have every right. You either accept my challenge or you don't. Either way, I decide what happens with Blair."

Edward sighed, "Melanie…." I whirled around interrupting, "Oh no… no… no… the sad sack excuse of a supposed Alpha blood doesn't get a say. Can I help you with something not pertaining to this particular issue?"

My aunt growled, "Show some respect." I raised an eyebrow, "When someone worth respecting speaks... I'll be sure to do that." Stephanie spat out, "You are in ENOUGH trouble you brat!" I laughed, "For what? What imaginary sin have I committed in your eyes this time?" She threw papers on the ground.

I wanted to ignore it… I really did…. but the blood in my veins made me pick the bundle up… which made no sense because I wasn't a Beta blood like I thought. It was clearly a nature versus nurture thing. I'd read plenty of scientific journals from Supernatural's saying we cannot nurture traits like humans… but clearly we could since I wasn't a Beta blood, but I shared all their tendencies.

I looked at the papers in my hands and gasped. It was another acceptance letter into Juilliard. I raised an eyebrow asking, "They renewed my application?" I couldn't help but be excited. I'd gotten in twice. My Aunt stepped forward and went to smack me.

I rolled my eyes then put her flat on her back and popped her arm out of the socket. I told her, "You think you'd learn." Her husband ran over and glared at me. I glared back advising, "Look at her like that, Ajax. She's the moron who can't learn… not me." Calling him Ajax still hurt my soul. I hated his name because it was Jason's wolf's name. I missed the wolf Ajax so much.

Ajax hissed, "It's Uncle Ajax." I rolled my eyes muttering, "No thanks. That's going to be a pass on my end, Ajax. No Uncle of mine would flirt and leer like you do." Neither Uncle Duncan, nor Uncle Archer definitely never looked at me like he did. Technically Dane was my Uncle too and he certainly didn't spy on my showers. I'd never met Landon Lyons but I'd go ahead and say he'd never leer at me either as my Uncle.

Pain still gripped when I thought of Uncle Duncan and guilt nearly choked me. I'd been punished so I was late when his mate died in a rogue attack. I'd been taken out of the hole and saw the rogue patterns near his pack. It wasn't the Ring, just a group of rogues.

Flashback

Melanie was pulled out of the hole. I rocked myself back and forth. Buck said, "Hey, you're out now." I whispered, "You're not supposed to be back yet… you…" He cut me off, "Yeah, I wrapped up early and found it weird you weren't doing paperwork in either of our offices. There was a pile on my desk which told me you were out here. How long?" He handed me water.

I took a sip. I asked, "What day is it?" He answered, "Friday." I gasped, "I have…to go…back to my place and…" He stared at me clearly confused by my reaction. Which was fair… he didn't know that I'd been trying to catalog a pattern for the rogues that had been attacking the pack Uncle Duncan was in.

I was close, then I'd fought for a male wolf to be able to leave with his fated mate. She wasn't in our pack, and he wanted to leave. That was five days ago. Five days for a mate fight? That seemed like they either forgot about me out here or they told Trevor to come get me and he just didn't.

I left Buck behind yelling, "Thanks" and I ran to my place. I logged back into my computer. ILYX announced, "I kept running your program, Melanie Jane. If all is accurate another attack will occur in five minutes." I squeaked and geared up. I sprayed myself down so I couldn't be scented.

I asked, "ILYX, is Uncle Duncan in the pack today or is he on a mission?" He answered, "His truck is there." I'd put a tracker on his truck years ago. He went out on missions a lot for them and when he was gone, his truck wasn't there. I quickly left and ran through the holoports.

My knee was giving me trouble, but I didn't care. I heard a fight and knew instantly I was on the wrong border. Crazy rogues! Why couldn't they have a pattern that was easy to track? I mean I knew the answer… they were rogues. If this was the Ring I would've been on it. My friends would've followed up.

I got there as the rogues were running away. UGH! Yeah, you'd better run! I heard people coming and climbed a tree. Then nearly fell out. My Aunt was lying there with her throat ripped out among the other bodies. NO!

I saw Uncle Duncan's wolf running and he shifted back. He let out a devastating howl that had me crying. Tears leaked out of my eyes. I was late. I should've saved her. Uncle Duncan begged, "Don't leave me, baby. What were you doing out here?"

The Alpha touched his shoulder, "We need to burn the bodies." What? I nearly jumped out the tree and screamed at that horrible man. I watched as Uncle Duncan cried and screamed in anger. I wanted to run and apologize to him.

Everything in me demanded I go to him, but I couldn't. He'd hate me more knowing I was seconds late… minutes… that cost him everything. My Aunt was dead. Someone else in my family was dead because I wasn't smart enough to figure things out.

I waited while they gathered up their bodies. Uncle Duncan was carried away screaming. My tears knew no end. My heart was breaking seeing him so sad. When they finally left, I got down ready to hunt those rogues down. They'd killed my aunt and I was going to kill them. I would do that for Uncle Duncan then leave them on the border so he'd know they were gone. I could avenge her for him.

Flashback Ends

Alpha Edward yanked me back to the present, "You applied to Julliard again. That's why you are in trouble." I snorted, "That's news to me. Why would I do that? If I did… why the actual hell would I give my address as her house? I'm smarter than that and you know it."

"In fact, when I applied the first time… I didn't send the acceptance letter to her house. I still don't know how she found out. It still confuses me… and it hurts my brain… but that's not the point right now. I have things to do."

My mind drifted back to Uncle Duncan. I'd left the rogues on their border and knew his pack had found them. I left the one that killed my aunt alive for him with a note stapled to his body he'd been the one to kill her. I'd typed it so he didn't know I'd helped him. I knew Uncle Duncan took care of that rogue personally because I made sure he would.

Aunt Stephanie lunged at me, and I punched her, knocking her out. I sighed, "Lord almighty she's annoying. Seriously... when will she learn? I can and will obviously kick her pathetic self's behind. Seriously Ajax… teach your wife some basic fighting moves. It's beyond pathetic. Or tell her to keep herself in check. My patience with her shit is wearing thin." My Warriors chuckled.

I turned back around, "McCoy… are you accepting my challenge or declining?" McCoy growled, "Accepting, little girl." I shrugged, "Big mistake... someone get the worthless pack doctor ready." Blair's brother was suspiciously quiet.

I glanced at him out of the corner of my eye. He'd met his fated mate, but she was in this pack. She was training with me privately. I didn't think Blair's brother knew… now… I wondered if he told her to train with me. The look in his eye told me he might just have done so.

McCoy snarled, "You ruined everything coming here." I rolled my eyes replying, "First, I didn't want to be here… I've offered to leave multiple times…but for some reason I feel we ALL find strange the pack leadership is ADAMANTLY opposed to that. Second, I ruined nothing. Your crappy leadership ruined everything here. I'm trying to fix it."

"I just need to know, as a father… how do you justify trying to sell your daughter to the highest bidder instead of letting her be with her fated mate? Did you forget how strong the pull is? You're standing next to your fated mate. You hypocritical piece of cow du... no, actually that's mean to cows. Cow dung is better than you."

McCoy snarled and lunged at me. I could make the fight end quickly. One punch would end it all… but that would be too easy for him. I flipped him onto his back then checked my nails. I knew from my research Princess Luna Haley and Queen Astrid Cambridge did that… the results were that in a fight it upset their opponent and made them sloppy. Every. Single. Time.

McCoy tried to shift, but his wolf didn't come forward. I laughed, "At least your wolf remembers he's supposed to protect his pup. You've become so ingrained, indoctrinated, and brain washed with this backwards, no class leadership that you forgot. At least your wolf didn't."

McCoy growled, "Blair, don't do this. It will hold your mother back here. If you went with who the Alpha chooses for you then we'd be set." I scoffed, "Held back? What kind of warped sense of life do you have? Her mother can't do anything here anyway. You want her mother to continue living her life of existing?"

I scoffed, "What a prize. Blair, gosh... I just don't know how you choose. I mean your fated mate in a good pack that knows how to be one… or the family who treated you like dirt because you have a female parts... GOSH... Hard choice. Hard choice."

Someone snorted, "Even when she's being sarcastic, she's a bad liar." I wasn't lying! Technically… I was being sarcastic. That shouldn't count! McCoy turned and came at me again. I round house kicked him in the face and jumped on him when he went down and cut off his air supply.

I warned, "Unless your pride is worth dying for… I'd tap out. Personally, I would want to go if I was you… really, you're trying to sell your daughter like some prized horse... and that's just insane. That's me though and I have integrity. Something the VAST majority of this pack has forgotten about."

McCoy glared at me then his eyes flicked black. I eased off his windpipe. The wolves were usually nice to me. His wolf said, "You're right. I submit to you." I smiled saying, "That's always nice to hear." His eyes changed and the fight died out of McCoy's eyes. He tapped his arm out to the side.

I turned and got off him. I ordered my Warriors, "Get Blair home and get her things. Addison choose five Warriors to go with you to drop her off." Edward looked pissed. I stuck my tongue out at him for good measure.

Luna Elena and Beta Female Eden laughed and clapped. That had both their mates looked torn. I didn't get them, because Edward and Jean clearly missed their mates. All of us knew they wouldn't change for them though.

Their logic of keeping their family and mates safe by treating them horribly didn't make sense either. The most powerful pack in the world didn't do that and… they were the most POWERFUL pack IN THE WORLD. I swear logic hurt their brains though.

Trevor glared at me, so I flipped him off. Booker growled, "You dare disrespect your mate." I snorted, "I would never disrespect my mate… we all know Trevor's not my mate." Trevor growled, "You're mine." I laughed, "Not a chance. I've already told you. I feel nothing for you. When you touch me all I feel is revulsion. Not tingles."

Trevor yelled, "I TOLD YOU THAT…" I cut him off, "Yes, we all know your excuse is my lack of a wolf. My real mate would never throw that in my face like you do, and everyone here with a fated mate knows that."

I tossed a glare at the Alpha blood that was a traitor to his purpose. I threw out, "If Edward had a spine... you'd be punished for claiming to be my mate… when we ALL know you're lying. Literally all of us. Even your own siblings and your mother." Trevor growled and came at me.

I smirked because he was so easy to goad into a fight. I put him on his back in a second. I told him, "I'd never be able to put my mate down so easily. I'm holding out for someone who can take me. Or at least make it a fight. We ALL know that's not you."

Blair ran over to me and hugged me. She whispered, "Thank you." I told her, "You're welcome. Get out of here, and don't look back. Go be happy." Blair pulled back crying, but she walked away. Edward cleared his throat, "You know you have to be punished, Melanie."

I grumbled, "I know this backwards messed up pack believes that people deserved to be punished for stupid crap. I also know that you know that I know… you couldn't punish me if I didn't let you." I stormed off walking to the punishment field.

They were truly and utterly pieces of crap. I was punished for doing what should be Edward and Jean's job. Heck, even Booker's. They were traitors to their own blood. I allowed it because it was my penance. Tristan died protecting me. My mom never saw it coming. My dad… we fought together at the end and he died for me too.

I'd give it all back... I'd give my life if it meant it was me who died and not them. The Moon Goddess turned her back on me. Honestly, she could go fly a kite too. I wanted nothing to do with her ridiculous, not caring about her children, self.

She should be fixing packs like this. These girls and boys should not be subjected to thinking this was normal. The only way the allies didn't know about how they treated people was goddess intervention, which put Selene firmly in the 'enemy' column for me.

I took off my shirt just as Luna Elena ran up. She grabbed Edward's arm when he grabbed the whip. She looked into his eyes begging, "Be the man I loved and had pups with for five seconds again. Melanie did nothing wrong. She did YOUR job. STOP hurting her! My wolf is VERY protective of her and so am I. She's one of our daughter's best friends."

Edward snorted, "She turned my daughter against me." Luna Elena laughed, "Do you actually believe that?" He nodded. Luna Elena sadly told him, "You have no one but yourself to blame for losing your pups and me. Melanie had nothing to do with it. You've never even shown your daughter one ounce of love since she was two years old. Do you know how many nights Addison cried about making you proud enough you'd love her before Melanie got here? It was a lot, Edward. You disgust me." She walked away while he flinched.

Jean looked at his mate, Beta Female Eden who'd followed as well. She glared at him, "Don't you look at me like that. You punish this innocent girl for doing things you should do. This place went to hell the SECOND Alpha Ezra came and got his hooks into Booker. You fool's bow down to his will just like your fathers before him to their horrid masters. Know this Jean, if you EVER give my baby away she's not the only one who will leave."

I laughed, "He's tried already…. A lot. You were there… weren't you? I swear I saw you once… is that magic? Did you wipe her memory with Witches? Did I miss that you tried to leave? Huh… I'll look into that." Eden looked at me, shocked.

I added, "They've actually done that with Addison and Sierra. Sierra was almost forcibly marked in the middle of the pack… I swear you were there… I'll have to ask Dax. Anyway… they've had three marriages lined up for Addison and Sierra. They just can't beat me in a fight to ship them off."

Eden snarled, "I HATE you, Jean! I hate you! She's our pup! Dax will NEVER let that stand. At least I know my son will change things here. You repulse me!" She turned and left. Beta Jean looked broken. Did they actually take their memories?

I offered, "You know… you don't have to make them hate you. You can be better people. I realize without one hell of a story about why you are this way… that's difficult….but I'm sure you were once upon a time. I mean... logically you had to be. Those are amazing women you have that you had pups with prove that. Obviously, you didn't suck at one point."

Edward shouted, "Would you just SHUT UP for once! My mate HATES me. My son HATES me! My daughter HATES ME! Is that not enough for you?" I raised an eyebrow replying, "The better question is when it's enough for you, not me. If I could do anything to have my brother in my life and forgive me, I would." They both looked guilty for a brief second.

I shrugged, "You both have the ability to change things with your families. You chose not to. Because despite both of your lack of spines… you hold out from them, even though that should be the hardest thing for you to do. You go against your wolves and your blood itself to not protect your pups and your mates."

Edward snarled, "For the last time, WE ARE PROTECTING THEM!" I sighed sadly, "So you believe. Really what you are doing is pushing away your family. Those men you agreed to marry Sierra and Addison to, to be their chosen mates… Do you know anything about them?"

Alpha Edward said, "We were told they were good, strong men. With Alpha and Beta blood." I laughed, "Did you even look into them? I told you about the guy that came for Sierra. He'd killed his mates." Jean blinked several times.

I asked, "Seriously, what did someone do to your memories? I said that…that night. Anyway, those men barely had Alpha blood… and those men are KNOWN for beating women." Both their faces paled. I nodded, "Yeah… so if you actually do care about your daughters somewhere deep down… you're welcome, for my saving them both from two men in particular who are rumored to have killed their own fated mates, and the two chosen ones after that. Go ahead. Punish me."

I turned and got down on my knees. Neither man moved but I could smell Booker coming. He must have grabbed the whip. I heard him grunting as he beat me with it. I gritted my teeth not letting my cries escape my lips.

Edward eventually shouted, "ENOUGH! Are you crazy?! She's fighting tonight!" I snorted, "Yeah Booker…. Edward won't get his cut if I don't win… which means you don't." Booker growled at me, "Watch your tone."

I laughed, "Or what? You'll do… nothing. Yeah... I know." I heard a laugh I knew well, "I see the feisty Melanie McAlister is still feisty." Alpha Ezra eyed my body up and down. Jean threw me my shirt. I pulled it on.

Alpha Ezra snorted, "You'd better tell Trevor I'm tempted to take her for myself. She needs a stern hand." I rolled my eyes muttering, "You wish. I'd never let you touch me. You're an enemy of my family. Trevor is just an enemy of mine and he's only claiming to be my mate… but we all know that's a lie."

Alpha Ezra growled, "Eventually I will find your disrespect annoying enough I'll do something about it." I shrugged, "Please do. Ask everyone around here how that goes for them." Alpha Ezra snorted, "You actually think you could beat me." I didn't think I could, I knew I could.

I stated as much, "I know I can. Even now… after I've been whipped.... I could take you." Alpha Ezra growled, "Your family has done enough to mine." I retorted, "Yes, how dare the allies of Blue Moon go after a man you didn't even know was your brother. Who happened to be a rapist. A man who was keeping she wolves... PREGNANT she wolves… on wolfsbane. Yeah… their reaction was beyond justified."

"Red Run found MY AUNT there pregnant… and held against her will… while her mate, my uncle, was nearly dead. You're crazy. All of you are. How you don't see the price of what you are doing… I'll never know. You're idiots… heck you're boys playing at the game of life. You should sit down and let the women play. No one can say we don't have spines."

Brooker went to hit me, but I blocked it and broke his nose. I told him, "You can only hit me when I let you. Something you would do well to remember." Alpha Ezra sighed, "I should just take her with me. You all have had years, and she's still spirited and strong willed." I urged, "Try it." I stalked off. Jerks.

Trevor was waiting with his friends. I groaned, "What do you want now?" Trevor smiled mockingly asking, "I can't want to check on my mate? You know if you'd just come to me this would stop." I faked throwing up.

I told him, "I don't know why you're lying about who I am to you, and I honestly don't really care. Stop getting in my way. I have things to do, and they don't involve being anywhere near your wet dog smelling self."

Trevor growled, "You should be happy you're mine! You don't even have a wolf!" I rolled my eyes even though my heart felt like it was twisting in my chest. I told him, "No one should be happy about having you as a mate. Whoever ends up being yours… god help her. We know it's not me so just stop. Everyone also knows it will have to be a chosen since there NO CHANCE you are getting a second chance fated mate."

He growled, "I only hurt you so badly because I was in pain from my mate dying!" I retorted, "Which you wouldn't have done if I was ACTUALLY yours. So… to recap; I'm not yours, and I never will be." My heart had belonged to my Xander since I was three years old. I was immovably in love with him.

Trevor growled, "Alexander Conners will NEVER want you." I punched him in the face. I told him, "First of all... He is an ALPHA DUKE, and you will address him as such. Second, I never said anything about him." Trevor laughed, "Do you think your letters with your brothers are private?"

I looked at him saying, "Do I think anything in this pack anything is private? No. No, I don't. You know my IQ could run circles around yours." Trevor growled, "I know you want that Alpha. Well, guess what? HE HATES YOU!" I refused to cry in front of him.

I told Trevor, "So you think because he doesn't want me, I'd just… what? Jump on you?" I laughed, "Sorry, like I said… I'll hold out for someone whose butt I can't kick." Trevor growled, "I have Alpha blood." The sad thing was he was right.

I snorted, "So you say. Lord knows I haven't seen it around in any situation… you hide in the damn office when people come here. Like I'd EVER be mated to someone who hides while his pack is under attack. When Caine takes over, he probably won't even let you be a Warrior."

Trevor shouted, "I'm the future Gamma!" I laughed mockingly, "I doubt that very seriously. Caine and Dax don't like you. Only these goonies you walk around with do. Caine and Dax fight with the pack while you follow your daddy's lead and hide like the coward you are. Do you actually think Caine will name you Gamma? Oh that's…."

I trailed off and glanced at him, laughing harder, "You do, don't you? You're wrong." One of Trevor's friends, Mark, chimed in, "You used to be so nice when you got here. You were only mean when it was unintentional."

I retorted, "Yes, well when you think about it you can only offer yourselves congratulations. This pack managed to kill my kindness. Now, I just tell you all that you're pieces of crap… which again... is mean to crap. I'll have to come up with something truly awful… yet alarmingly accurate."

Dax came up to us. He nudged me saying, "Mel, you have your fight." Trevor tried to bolster up to Dax, "You know you can't call her that in public." Dax's growl had them all bowing their heads. Dax said, "I am aware of what to call her public, Trevor. We are within our pack borders. I am also aware you do NOT order me to do a damn thing. Leave Mel alone." They scattered.

I commented, "My hero." Dax laughed then sobered when he saw my shirt. He growled, "Damn it! Did my dad do that?! I'll kick his ass!" I grabbed his arm assuring him, "No. I think they were going to let it go. Booker showed up and you know he hates me."

Dax growled, "My dad could take him. I don't know why he doesn't." I shrugged, "Because Booker is your dad's mentor… for some reason." Dax sighed, "I guess. My mom doesn't understand how Alpha Ezra even got involved." I shrugged because it made sense to me. Alpha Ezra was a horrible person. Of course he flocked to other horrible people.

Dax drove me to my fight. He turned to me when he parked. He said, "I'd like to come in and cheer you on." I declined "Sorry, but no… it's not necessary. I've got this." Dax grabbed my hand and drew my attention to him.

He admitted, "I know who you are in there. I asked around. The Swiffer? Mel, when are you going to realize that neither your parents nor Tristan would have wanted this for you? What would your big brother say if he was still alive? I don't even think Beta Jason, and you know I think he's trash, would be ok with this."

I looked out the window and lied, "I make the most money this way. People love it." Dax sighed, "Your voice just squeaked so loud birds cringed. That's not why you do it. You let the pack punish you because of what happened that night. Then you walked into the Undergrounds and punish yourself some more. It's been five years. When will you have suffered enough?"

A tear slid out of my right eye. I whispered, "Never. They are gone." Dax said, "I'd haunt Sierra's ass from the grave if she did something like this. You let them hurt you." I shrugged, arguing weakly, "I'm always ok though… eventually. Plus…I see them in there when I get hit so my brother does haunt me in a way. He's just not mad like I wish he was."

Dax pursed his lips pleading, "Just think about it Mel. I'm tempted to drive to Red Run myself with Caine and give Beta Jason a piece of my mind." I reasoned, "I don't know if they'd let you in." Dax replied, "I could go to someone I know who would listen to what I have to say." I knew who he meant.

I argued, "They kept Elise out of this. She'd have to pick her family over me. I don't really even know if EJ knows either." Dax rolled his eyes muttering, "There is no way the pristine Conners family knows ANY of this. Your Xander would not stand for this. Not for anyone, let alone his mate."

I wiped my tears as they fell freely now. I whispered, "He doesn't want me, Dax." Dax frowned, "According to your brother and random she wolves, who could be lying. Hell, from the rumors Caine and I hear, they are lying."

I looked up asking, "What rumors?" The words from the woman, who was with the woman who claimed she would be in Luna talks with Xander, floated into my mind. Dax told me, "Alpha Alexander doesn't date. He's waiting for his mate. He and his wolf want their fated. Besides, his mom would KICK his ass if he rejected you. You have to know that's true."

I whispered, "He promised Jason." Dax asked, "Did he? Or did Beta Jason just want you to stay away? Did he not want to anger a seriously powerful ally over what they did to you? You don't even know if your brother did that of his own accord. The Alpha could've ordered him to. You've seen that here a million times over."

I winced admitting, "Alpha Peter wouldn't… but I can't chance that. We have too much to do. People count on me. I'll eventually go see Xander." Dax offered, "I can pick you up after your fight." I shook my head, "Nah, Sierra and Addison are coming."

Dax sighed, "I see you three as my sisters even though Sierra is the only by blood. I'm fighting all my instincts to let you walk in there." I acknowledged, "I know. We need the money though." Dax disagreed,

"We don't. You have made more than enough money with your business ventures and in the stock market. You would still get money fighting without just letting them beat you up."

I disagreed, "I have to do it my way." Dax sighed, "Just think about it or I'm going to Alpha Alexander and Luna Elise." I bit my lip agreeing, "I'll think about it." Dax smiled, "Good. I'll hold you to that." I hated that I disappointed him, but I had to do this.

When I walked up the guy on the backdoor grimaced. I raised an eyebrow, "Crush… you're sad to see me? My feelings are hurt. I was excited to see it was you." Crush pursed his lips, "Yes, well, I don't like when you fight. You're better than this Ashley."

I shrugged, "We were all sold to this, and we make the best of it." Crush sighed, "I make the best of it. You punish yourself for your past." I winked adding, "But I win." Crush nodded, "See that you do." I blew him a kiss and walked inside. He was gay… so it wasn't flirting.

The ringleader of the Undergrounds hissed, "What happened to your back?" I answered, "What always happens?" He yelled, "This will not stand! I will call them right now!" I shrugged, "Knock yourself out what's done is done." He stalked off.

I glanced around and easily spotted who I was fighting tonight. His gaze was locked in on me. He grinned. I rolled my eyes at him and everyone else that looked excited. He could grin all he wanted; I was still going to win.

I went to the room designated for me tonight, put on a tight t-shirt, and some shorts. I only had to wait for ten minutes before Crush came in. He announced, "You're up kid. You don't have to let him get so many shots in tonight. I'm just saying."

I teased, "I'll make it entertaining as always… that is popular advice tonight though… so…. You are in good company." Crush sighed, "One day, I'll get ahold of that aunt and brother of yours. Then they will find out why my nickname is Crush."

I countered, "Just the aunt. Leave my brother be." Crush argued, "He doesn't deserve it." I shrugged, "He's still my brother. I know that doesn't mean anything to him, but it used to. For fourteen years… he was one of my biggest protectors."

Crush said, "The past means jack shit. The present is what counts. In the present he's horrible, and he's not here when it counts. You are what he has have left of your parents. He should honor that. He should honor his father who raised you; however, he does not. He spits on the memory of your parents and your older brother. I believe they would be ashamed." I stopped in surprise because he spoke about Tristan with confidence.

Understanding lit in my eyes. I whispered, "You know who I really am." Crush nodded, "I do. I met your older brother once when he was with his Hackura friend. It took me a minute to put it together, but you look like him."

I smiled sadly saying, "Not so much." Crush replied, "Maybe it was an educated guess, and you confirmed it." I laughed, "You are a smart one, Crush." He made a fist, and I nodded. It was our sign so I'd know he'd put something in my bag. Something told me I might be recruiting Crush for the Resistance. I had an instinct about people that had long since told me he was a good guy.

I stepped into the ring which made the crowd roar with applause. I looked out at the people around me. These people funded the Ring by being here and betting. Which made them my enemies. They cheered as they thought people died in this very ring. I just saved them and planned to get the fighters out instead.

I wondered what their expression would look like if they found out they also paid for the Resistance. They would probably never know though. My eyebrows raised when I spotted Trevor and his friends walking in.

He came every so often to see me fight. I could swear he loved and hated watching me take hits. I focused back on my opponent, who was cocky and heavy footed. The crowd cheered for him, but it was louder for me. Little did these people know how much I hated them.

I did need them though, to a degree. To tear this thing apart from the inside out. I shrugged off those feelings. They would all get theirs one day. The Moon Goddess might let me down, but karma would eventually come for them all. They'd deserve it.

My opponent came at me, and I dodged his first swing. The crowd gasped in shock. I had to keep them on their feet. I was still going to let him get several shots in. My opponent whirled and hit me hard. I didn't budge. His next uppercut landed with a crack.

It felt like it hit my soul as I caught a flash in my mind of Tristan jumping in front of me taking a bullet to the chest. I saw Slade's face as he killed my family. The shots kept coming in physical blows from my opponent, but I didn't stop him. I saw my mom die, then my dad.

For some reason I always got a flash of Robert's face. It had to be wrong though since he wasn't there. Everything snapped back into focus. I swung my legs out and dropped my opponent. I did a kip up and roundhouse kicked him in the face. I punched him twice before going for the knockout.

I walked to my corner surprised when the cage began to come down. What the heck? I wasn't the cage match for tonight. No one had one…so…what the actual hell was happening? The ringleader shot me a sheepish look which told me this wasn't the plan but he was letting it happen.

I smelled Trevor's wet dog scent and turned around. He smiled at me and to be honest… I was stunned because he was inside the cage. Was he really going to embarrass himself in front of crowd by losing to me? In the cage? Was he high? His pupils looked fine… but maybe he took something.

The crowd booed as I spotted Crush moving towards us. I hoped my eyes conveyed it was ok that he wasn't going to make it in time to get inside. I faced Trevor and asked, "Can I help you?" Trevor nodded, "You're mine and you'll be mine by the time you leave this cage, officially."

I felt a fierce anger that came up from within me. I gripped my head as I was certain… no… I could swear I heard something snarl. Trevor, of course, used that and hit me. I put my hand up as he went to bite my neck. His canines sank into my palm.

I screamed in pain and anger. I kneed him in the balls and flipped us. I was at a disadvantage, and Trevor knew that. I was hurt… pretty badly this time and I realized this had been his plan. It wasn't a bad one…. Which told me it wasn't his plan….more than likely it was Alpha Ezra's.

It wasn't going to work though. I would only ever have one man's mark on my neck. It was my Xander or it was nothing. I pushed him further away from me, but Trevor just snarled and came at me again. Another glaring sign he wasn't my mate. He was trying to hurt me. A mate would never do that.

He fought me with a ferocity he'd never come at with me before. If I wasn't hurt, I'd have him down already. He was so sloppy because he never worked out. By this point, he'd bitten me several times, but not on my neck or near my marking spot.

I saw an opening to end the fight. I quickly pinned then choked him out. The crowd was clapping but not like they normally would. Not even they approved of this. Several wolves in the crowd looked disgusted. Demons did too and that said something.

Demons had fated mates or their chosen mates. They called their chosen mates, Spears. It was always a choice though. Even the Fairies present had a look of distaste on their faces. Fairies were all about pleasures of the flesh.

I'm sure it was the fact Trevor was trying to mark me that they disagreed with. They wouldn't have cared if he raped me. The crowd here sucked that way. Or they thought things like this should stay in private. Who could really tell?

The cage came up and I stalked over to the ringleader. I told him, "I hope that was worth it." I turned and walked away. Crush grabbed me and helped me back to my area. The ringleader followed behind him as Crush took me to the doctor.

The ringleader wrung his hands saying, "I didn't have a choice. You see they…." I interrupted him, "You double my cut, or you get outed. Specifically you. I have connections you couldn't possibly dream of. Which will it be?" He quickly agreed to double my pay. Too bad. Cayden would've LOVED getting his hands on this guy. He left quickly.

The doctor came in next. He was a wolf too. He frowned muttering, "I have no idea how you are conscious." I answered, "Sheer force of will, doc." He sighed, "That boy, Trevor, is a disgrace to the Moon Goddess herself."

I snorted, "That's not really an insult. She's a horrible goddess who can go die. He's just a disgrace." Crush laughed. The doctor gaped at me. He whispered, "You can't talk about the Moon Goddess that way." I shrugged asking, "Why not?" He replied, "She's our Goddess."

I reasoned, "If she did her job... you and I wouldn't be here. She can't do her job, so she leaves us to suffer. What kind of sick mother is she? It's a goddess's job to do the hard things. She refuses. She's spineless and weak. She allows the suffering of probably millions of her children at the hand of a few sick bastards. She won't get any sympathy from me for her sins."

The doctor sighed, "You always have such a way of looking at things." Crush stopped Trevor's friends from coming in. I snorted, "What else could they possibly want?" The doctor sighed, "Nothing I'd appreciate. No more fighting for you for the evening."

I grumbled, "I only agreed to one fight tonight… well… here. I issued the challenge in my pack… but that was barely a fight when you think about it." He snorted. I told him, "Really, it wasn't…it was a little more than sad on the other fighter's part." He said, "You are an exceptional fighter." True but that didn't McCoy's abilities less sad.

After an hour, he was done. I got up and Crush took me outside. He gave me my bag and put me in Addison's car. Sierra gasped, "WHAT THE SHIT?!" I laughed then I winced. My ribs were killing me. I explained, "Trevor got in the cage tonight after my fight. He tried to mark me."

Addison growled, "Caine will have his BALLS!" I buckled myself in urging, "Just get us home." The second we pulled out there were lights in our rearview. Trevor could not be so butt hurt I choked him out he was going to hit the car. Could he? What was I even saying? Of course he would.

I cringed asking, "Who's car is this, Ads?" Addison shrugged, "Oh umm I'm not sure. I just grabbed one." I closed my eyes realizing, "They don't know you're in the car. Call your dad, they are going to hit us." Addison questioned, "That's Trevor?"

I nodded, "It's going to be, yes." Sierra told us, "Trevor's link is blocked out. I can't get through to tell him we are in the car. So are his friends." UGH. I never thought to use link anymore because my friends were the only ones who linked me.

She took out her phone and called her brother. He answered and she pleaded, "Caine! Caine! HELP US!" She gunned the car. Caine yelled, "What's going on?" I winced explaining, "Call your wannabe horrible excuse for a Gamma, and tell him he's trying to run the Alpha and Beta's daughters off the road."

Caine snarled, "TREVOR IS GOING TO HIT YOUR CAR?! ARE YOU KIDDING ME?! DAX GET HIM ON THE PHONE NOW! HE HAS HIS LINK BLOCKED OUT!" I heard Caine stomp off somewhere before I could tell him his wolf could rip the link open. He was the future Alpha.

He growled, "Did you know Trevor was going after Melanie tonight?" Edward replied, "To the fight? He goes sometimes." Caine roared, "HE'S GOING TO RUN ADDISON OFF THE FUCKING ROAD! SHE PICKED UP MELANIE WITH SIERRA TONIGHT!" Edward yelled, "BOOKER! Your son better not TOUCH MY DAUGHTER!"

I looked behind us and calculated the distance. I announced, "Too late." I threw Addison's door open, unbuckled her and shoved her out of the car, then Sierra. I was just faster than them somehow. I grabbed the wheel. I was thrown through the windshield when I was hit. I could hear yelling and tired squealing before my world faded to black.

It felt like my life was playing out on a screen in my mind. I sobbed when I saw my life in Red Run with Tristan, mom, dad, and Jason. I studied my dad. I cried, "I look like you! How can you not be my dad?!" My heart felt like it broke all over again.

I smiled when I saw one of my first conversations with Addison and Sierra flash in my head. Addison sat down saying, "So you're not from around here. Are we normal?" I tilted my head answering, "Your parents' relationship is odd."

Addison hummed, "She wolves don't train here. We have a Female Lead Warrior, but she can't fight. It's just to say we have one." I gasped, "What? I've been training since I was little to fight." Sierra clapped her hands, "I knew it! Can you train us in secret? Once you're better? You look a lot better already." I agreed, "Of course I can. It will be our secret."

The next moment that flashed was the pup dying at the first Hunters meeting I'd been forced to go to with Addison and Sierra. Tears filled my eyes because they'd killed that innocent pup. The joke was on the bad Hunters, the Ring, and Black Path's pack leadership though.

They never knew we were working against them… well, more to restore the Hunters to their original purpose. It was a slow moving project. I never did what the bad Hunters wanted though.

The moment I woke up in the Alpha's office on my sixteenth birthday played next. I cringed. I watched myself sit up, "What? What happened? My wolf said I needed to fight and god…. my head…." I couldn't hear my wolf anymore. Is she ok?"

Aunt Stephanie spoke, "You didn't shift. You have no wolf." I argued, "That's not possible. I'm a Beta's daughter." Stephanie smiled evilly, "Your father was always up for debate. You not shifting proved Drake McAlister was not your father."

I punched her in the face saying, "Drake McAlister will ALWAYS be my father, you wretched snake!" The Alpha cleared his throat, "We have these for you." It was painful to watch myself get those two letters. I'd memorized them. The weird part was they wrote so many. I guess as they went through a range of emotion they wrote more. The letters I'd read in the office were different from the ones I'd read after the Trevor debacle. The first was from Jason.

Melanie,

I was hoping this didn't happen, but it did. You have no wolf. You're only my half-sister. Your biological father killed mine and my mother. Along with our big brother. I can't look at you. Ever. I never want to see you again.

Before you think about coming back, I told Alexander about your little crush on him. He promised me he'd reject you if you happened to be his. I can't believe you ever thought you'd be his. We joke about it because the Moon Goddess would never give you to him.

You should've died that night. I wish you'd died instead of them. You have Hunter blood in you, and I can't have you be near my family. You endanger us. I no longer recognize you as Melanie McAlister. You'll be known as Melanie Carter around here.

You are to be killed if ever found near us or our allies. Don't come back here. Don't make me see you die. For the memories of our family, just don't. I will send you updates because mom would have wanted that. Never call me Jase again. To you, I am Beta Jason.

Goodbye,

Beta Jason

I felt tears on my face as I watched myself cry. I opened the next letter. A letter I carried with me at all times

Melanie,

With a heavy heart I informed Jason you didn't shift tonight. Our worst fear was realized. Your biological father killed my best friend. I have to protect my people and my pack. My sons, brothers, dad, and I discussed it at length.

You are officially banished from this pack. You are not allowed in any of our allied territories. You will be put in any of our dungeons if you are found. Jason informed me you believe Alexander is your mate. I truly cannot believe you thought that.

The Moon Goddess would never allow a Hunter and Wolf to be together. Especially not Alexander. He's not yours. Give up that silly notion now. I have requested you be punished for the death of my best friend and my son's future Beta. Take it as you deserve. They are dead because of you.

Alpha Kyle

I sobbed seeing his Alpha seal on the letter. Then I cried harder even though I knew what was coming. I didn't want to be there. They had punished me. I'd done nothing wrong. No Alpha should've allowed that to happen, and Edward knew it. His eyes held shame every time he looked at me for what he allowed to happen.

It flashed to when I saved Jason. I saw myself with Valentina standing there staring at my brother who was barely alive. Tears clouded my eyes when I saw Jason. That had been the closest I'd been to him in several years. I'd been the sniper from afar, but I could drop someone from three hundred yards away, so I didn't need to be that close.

I whispered, "This is my fault." Valentina disagreed, "It's really not." I glanced at the Hunters who were on my side. I shouted, "Why didn't you called me sooner?" They replied, "You were being hunted by the pack for the wolf less thing and…" They trailed off. I screamed, "AND WHAT?" One admitted, "So what if he dies? You have a purpose. He's a useless, shitty brother."

Valentina snorted, "Ok, that wasn't a good thing to say at all. Mel, it's not your fault. Everyone makes choices and Beta Jason chose to go undercover with the Hunters. He knew the risks." I shook my head as the options of what to do flew around my mind.

JC, the wolf less pack member here, said, "You've made life bearable around the pack! Before you came there was no hope. YOU are people's hope. Your life is worth twenty of his! He turned his back on you. He's a shit brother."

Valentina sighed, "Please stop saying that." I argued, "That's NONE of your business, JC! He's what I have left of them. He's my brother! I realize that doesn't mean anything… to him… though I think it actually does deep down to him… maybe. If Jason knew what had happened to me… I don't think he would've stood for that."

JC snorted, "None of us know exactly what happened. We just saw how you changed when you came back. I've heard the whispers about your back too. Are they true?" The wolf less hadn't been allowed on pack grounds during the hunt after it was clear I was winning. Which was why he was here with Jason now.

I looked away without answering. I walked over to Jason and sighed in relief when I saw he had his watch on. I asked, "How much wolfsbane did he take on?" JC winced, "Too much." I scanned him visually and could scent JC was right.

I ordered, "ILYX, do a scan and display data." The display came up and I wiped furious at my tears that fell. ILYX offered the dose I should use to keep him alive in the data display. I took out a syringe with MDTJ and injected him twice. I put one in his pocket and wrote a note to Dalton and Dakota. Those jerks.

Who sends their Beta in alone with Hunters… WHO KNOW WHAT THEY LOOK LIKE?! Idiots! I looked at Jason's watch and checked it. It was still pumping the antidote into him. Good. I sighed, "Why would you do this? You have to live…you know? You can't die on me. Not you too."

Jason groaned, "Ladybug?" I gasped and my heart clinched. He'd said he'd never call me that again. He must be delirious from the poison in his veins. His eyes opened and I scrambled away. I tripped and landed on my butt.

He whispered, "You're so beautiful… I miss you Ladybug." Tears filled my eyes. His head drooped back down. I wiped my tears. I whispered, "I miss you too Jason… You big doofus…. seriously… you're an Idiot... you can't do things like this…you have a pup!" I turned around and devised a plan to get him out of here.

Thank goodness I'd given him his watch. MDTJ kept him alive. I would be totally lost if he died. He was close as it was. I shook myself. No, I couldn't let him die. I turned to my people, "I'm going to have to knock you out. We are going to make it look like he was rescued." They sighed in relief. I hit them harder than I needed to.

Valentina snorted, "Oof. That was unnecessary." I countered, "They were going to let him die, and he's what I have left, Val." Valentina disagreed, "You have us too." I nodded acknowledging that was true. I told her, "Get us out of…"

I trailed off seeing that Dante was on his way here personally from the readout on my watch. I groaned, "Just get out of here. I'll have to put him that tree and use our scent spray. I'll take their punishment for letting him 'escape.' Get Dax here to lie, since… well…" I sucked at it.

She snorted, "I got it. I'd stay but I have…" I cut her off, "You have to take that mission. Virgil is out on his own." She nodded then shimmered out.

I ordered, "ILYX, scan him." ILYX told me, "He has time for your punishment if you get him to Xander and his mother after." I could do that. I bent down and told Jason, "I can't keep you alive forever like this… but I can in time to get you to those who can."

I wiped my tears away saying, "If this doesn't make you love me again… nothing will. Don't you dare think about going into any lights." I broke down and cried. I told him, "You hang on, Jase. I love you, big brother. You can't leave me too. I'd rather have you hating my guts than be dead." I sobbed with myself as I quickly got him out of sight seconds before Dante arrived.

Next it flashed to the night I'd called Xander. I'd memorized his number the night I'd texted him from Tristan's phone. I couldn't stand it. I was on a lot of drugs and traumatized. I'd lost everything. Despite it all his pleas to help me and his voice actually helped me.

He still called and left voicemails on that phone. I should let him go. I was being selfish. Part of me clung to Dax's words though. Maybe Jason had lied… he was in shock and grieving… maybe he just made it up to hurt me like he was hurting.

Maybe Xander would want me one day. Or he'd be pissed I was emailing him as Ashley. I really didn't know. I just couldn't help it. He was perfect. Talking to him and Elise…. It was my lifeline. I knew I didn't deserve it, but I couldn't stop. They made me feel normal again. Loved… like I used to be.

Jason told me in his letters I didn't deserve nice things. So did Everly. She was mad at how much Jason hated being the Beta. I couldn't blame her really. I'd saved her when she was kidnapped for Jason though. Then found out she'd been pregnant with Kai. My nephew they'd never allow me to meet.

Peter Kyle was family to me, and he betrayed me as family and an Alpha. What happened wasn't my fault. Maybe it was… but if this situation happened to anyone else… I'd say it wasn't their fault. I'd say that the Alpha was being a jerk.

Peter Kyle WAS being a jerk… when you thought about it… logically. My parents trusted them to take care of me if something happened to them. Instead, he handed me over to our enemies. To the hands of Alpha Ezra's allies no less.

Some days I wondered if Peter had known what they did to me at his request. I wondered if Jason or Grandpa Ben knew. I didn't think they would be ok with it. I didn't even think Peter would be ok with it if he knew what truly happened. I knew Chelsea wouldn't be. Sometimes I wondered if my parents haunted them. Or if Tristan haunted Jason.

I tried to harden my heart against them all again. They left and abandoned me. I was a pup, and they should've protected me. I woke up from that awful night all alone. My family died that day too, and they acted like my pain was nothing. It hurt coming from them.

Everyone else could act like my pain was nothing… but they weren't supposed to. They were supposed to be my family. No, they WERE my family, and they threw me away. Like I was nothing. Maybe I was nothing. They thought I was. They didn't even acknowledge when I saved them.

I heard a whisper, "You have to wake up and keep fighting now." Wasn't it someone else's turn to fight? I'd been fighting my whole life. I'd been fighting to keep my stuffed Xander wolf. I'd been fighting to not be anyone's but Xander's. Men always wanted me to be theirs. I was fighting for the innocents…. Valentina, Virgil, Paige, and Paisley's faces flashed through my mind.

Where would they be if I didn't fight? Trapped. Like so many others I had to fight for. I was their chance and their hope. I couldn't abandon them. I was on the inside of the underbelly of the beast in a way the allies never could be.

It was my place to stand. Between those that hide in the shadows and those they seek to prey upon. I kept Xander safe this way. I kept the allies and everyone I cared about safe my way. It was a lonely life but it was mine.

I heard a beep and nearly threw up. It was too familiar. I opened my eyes then frowned. I had no earthly clue where I was. I groaned saying to myself in my head, "This is an all too familiar feeling… and that didn't end well for me last time."

I spotted a man with his back to me. I easily noted that he was a Hackura. He had the same sense about him Micah, Cayden, and Levi did. I cleared my throat. He turned around and my jaw dropped. He greeted, "Nice to see you officially Ashley." I nodded, "Sure. You too… Duke Brody Cambridge… What is going on?"

He snorted, "I think that's my line. You know me?" I muttered, "People know you… that's a thing that people know. Was Cayden there when I got in the car accident? Car accident… I was in a car accident, right? I swear I was…"

Everything was now a blur. This was not the first time this had happened. The same thing happened after the car accident my mom and I were in. I knew the answers though... Didn't I? Why couldn't I remember what happened?

Duke Brody smiled saying, "You can call me Brody. Do you remember what happened to you?" I frowned and rubbed my head. I went through the events I knew about. Blair found her mate… which means I'd have fought for her… I'd have been punished.

I had a fight for the Undergrounds. I remember flashes of light. There was clearly a car accident. Why couldn't I remember the rest of the day? It had to be there. I couldn't possibly be in two bad accidents and not remember the details. The odds were astronomically bad for even getting in two bad accidents lets alone not remembering the aftermath.

I told him, "I know there was a fight... maybe two. I don't remember them though. I remember there was a car accident… or was that when I was younger? I was in a car accident with my mom once. Gosh... I need to stop getting in cars."

"Maybe I should just run everywhere. Some people go their whole lives without getting into car accidents. Now, I'm fairly certain I've been in two pretty serious car accidents. That's exceptionally bad luck if you think about it, which makes sense."

Brody laughed questioning, "Why do you say that?" I answered, "Because the Moon Goddess is evil and turned her back on me a long time ago." Brody raised an eyebrow, "Hmmm, I see. I did wonder if you were bitter about your lack of wolf."

I rubbed my temples admitting, "I swear I heard my wolf that night… No, that's crazy... right?" Brody asked, "What do you remember from that night?" I winced answering, "Not much. I remember being in pain then waking up in the Alpha's office… but sometimes I think I heard her telling me to fight."

Brody asked, "What about the people with you? It's my understanding wolf less are not in pain on their birthdays. They just don't get a wolf, so there is no pain." I definitely remembered the pain. I shrugged, "I was alone." Brody's jaw dropped.

Eventually he offered, "That's dangerous." I shrugged explaining, "Edward and Jean sent everyone who would've been there for me away. I didn't have anyone. I was hoping… .my brother would come... but he didn't."

Cayden said, "Because he's an ass. I did not know you were alone that night, Ashley. I would've come." Right... Ashley… they thought that was my name. Be Ashley. I turned greeting, "Hi Cayden and Micah."

Cayden said, "You must still be out of it. We've been here the whole time." He was right then. Micah asked, "Why didn't you call me on your sixteenth birthday? I would've come for your shift." I probably would have just to have someone there.

I clarified, "I didn't know they weren't there. I went to the meadow I wanted to shift in to meet everyone. Buck told me they'd all been sent elsewhere then left. It was one minute until midnight when I was told. He was Alpha Ordered to tell me that and leave so he couldn't stay… he did look like he felt bad about it though… I collapsed in pain in the next second. I didn't have time to call anyone."

Cayden studied me. Was there a test I didn't know I needed to pass? He surmised, "You really don't know what happened that landed you here?" I closed my eyes, trying to remember. I knew what had to have happened but… I had nothing.

Brody spoke, "It's normal, Cayden. She suffered serious trauma. She had a bleed on her brain. I'd be more surprised if she did remember." Cayden groaned, "Great." I asked, "Was I in a car accident? Or was that when I was little?"

Robert's face flashed in my mind. I swore he was there, but he'd been at EJ and Elise's mating ceremony. He couldn't have been there. Or here. Because that was back then. Two bad accidents. Gosh, I was a poster child for bad luck.

Cayden sighed, "So I was told. Yet you had canine marks on your hand and sides." I gasped and checked my neck. Cayden assured me, "Not on your neck. If you'd let me tell my father in law you were almost marked against your will, whipped, and you were beaten to hell; then my father in law would protect you."

I whispered, "You looked at my back?" Brody answered, "No, it was already treated." That was a relief, and it made sense because their eyes weren't blazing gold. I knew that Cayden thought he was right about Alpha Eric, but he couldn't protect me. He would have to put me in his dungeons since he was allied with Red Run.

Jason, Everly, and Kai needed Black Mountain to remain their allies. No matter what. Maybe I could file a complaint as Ashley. That had merit. If I never saw Alpha Eric... he'd never piece it together. If he saw me though… it was all over.

I asked, "If I asked my friends… and Trevor did try to mark me… what would happen?" Micah answered, "The Werewolf Council would come down here and collect evidence and deliver a judgement." I whispered, "All of them?" Peter was on the council now. One look at me, and he'd know the name I'd chosen down here.

Cayden said, "Yes, all of them." I sighed, "I don't even know what happened. They'd question me... I'd have to say I have no clue. Trevor would say he didn't do anything. They'd believe him and leave. He's a Gamma with Alpha blood… supposedly. I'm a wolf less girl, that they won't care about."

Micah argued, "That's not true." It was absolutely true. Peter Kyle would make sure they packed up and left as quickly as they could. Alpha Eric could figure out who I was if he stayed long enough. I had no doubt of then. Then…. what if my Xander didn't want me but he wanted me in the dungeons? Where would I go?

I'd be unable to protect the innocent. I shook my head, "I'm fine." Cayden snorted, "If you look up the definition of not fine it's your friends calling me to come save you from being marked while you were unconscious."

I gasped, "They called you?" Cayden nodded, "And they lied to me." I gulped. I'd never actually lied to Cayden. I never told him my name was Ashley, other people did. I asked, "How long was I out?" Brody answered, "It's been a few weeks."

I nearly shrieked, "I have to get back! My friends need me." Brody laughed, "We'll see how you're doing in a few hours." I questioned, "Where are we?" Cayden answered, "South Dakota." I blinked back tears. He'd come and taken care of me.

He helped me, of all people. I hope he didn't regret not letting me die one day when he found out the truth. I whispered, "Thank you Cayden… I'd rather be dead than be marked by Trevor McCann." I meant that too.

Cayden replied dryly, "He'd be dead if he marked you. He's not going to touch you again. He's fully aware of what will happen." My eyes widened as amusement and a little bit of horror shot through me. I asked, "You went to see Trevor? For me? Oh my gosh Cayden I…."

Micah laughed cutting me off, “Of course we did. We both felt awful. Your friends didn’t tell us what happened, but I know who Trevor’s friends are. They will give you a wide berth now. Unless they want to see us again. Two of them pissed themselves. Your wannabe mate actually shit his pants.”

I snorted, “I’d never be his mate. Ever. Seriously... he could be the last man on earth, and I’d just let us all die off. He makes my skin crawl… and… he smells like a WET dog…so…that’s a…” Micah interrupted asking, “What happened between you two? I heard you have a history.”

I looked away, glad that for some reason none of them looked at my back. I was not discussing what he did to me after I didn’t shift. I evasively answered, “He’s a coward and a user. I hate him and that will never change.”

Cayden sighed, “For the record, that’s not an answer. Sadly, we have to go. Brody, let us know how she is.” Brody agreed, “Of course.” I asked, “Do you by chance have my phone?” Cayden shook his head replying, “Nope. Sorry.” He didn’t really seem sorry. I shrugged, “That’s fine.” They both left.

Brody looked at me teasingly saying, “So, I hear you idolize my cousin.” I flushed, “What? Idolize… I mean… I don’t know… that’s… he’s... I’m… he fights so well... and his cardio is so intense… I bet I could keep up with him now and I…”

Brody laughed, “I like that you knew exactly who I was talking about. Alexander would like you.” I nearly started crying. I shrugged, “Why would he like me? I’m nobody and he’s... an Alpha Enforcer.” Brody snorted, “My cousin very much wants to meet you. He’s impressed by you. Well, what he hears of you anyway. I’ll have to keep it a secret if he doesn’t already know that I’ve met you.”

I blushed asking, “How would he know? I mean... did he know you were here?” Brody coyly answered, “He could’ve figured it out. I’m missing and have been for weeks now. I’m a doctor. Cayden had Alexander on call. If you were dying, he was bringing him to you.”

My mouth was suddenly dry. That was so not how I wanted Xander and I to meet. Of all the ways I’d planned it… I was conscious. Brody shrugged adding, “My cousin is very smart.” I bit my lip hiding my smile because I knew that. I’d always known that my Xander was smart.

Brody and I passed the time by talking about other things. Eventually he agreed I could go home. He opened a portal to King’s diner. I waved to him. He told me, “Something tells me I’ll see you again, Ashley Griffen. Stay safe. Should you not be left alone by those Cayden and Micah threatened, do let whoever tries to hurt you know that they will meet the wrath of a Duke of the Hackura. I find I quite like you.”

I gasped, “Really?” It wasn’t that surprising since I was his cousin’s mate, but people so rarely liked me right away… these days anyway… they used to. Brody smiled, “Yup. You remind me of my cousin's mates. I’d never let anyone hurt them, and anyone who hurts you will not get away unscathed.” That was his parting line as the portal closed. Holy crap on a cracker.

I walked into the diner. Mason looked up when the bell rang then yelled. He ran out from the kitchen with Hendrick right behind him. They both collided into me. I whispered, “I’m ok.” Paige shrieked, “ASHLEY!” Someone must be here they didn’t know.

She ran over to me and sobbed. She said, “I thought I was being paranoid putting a holoport in that area. You just happened to go through, and it kept Trevor from marking you.” I asked, “Where exactly did I end up?” Mason answered, “Paige’s house.”

I smiled and hugged her tightly boasting, “My witchy godmother.” Paige cried, “I was so worried.” I assured her, “I’m fine. What’s been going on?” Mason groaned, “You’re not going to like it.” We walked into the back and down to the bunker. It must be bad if we were meeting here instead of my second place.

Paige had long since done a spell, so it was soundproofed. I asked, “What is it?” Mason answered, “Two girls were abducted from the McDermont pack. One of whom, is Alpha Theodore Conners mate.” I shouted, “You’re kidding me! Where are they? Tell me we know their location.”

Paige jumped in, “We do. The Undergrounds have them. Jane McDermont is fighting tonight, but she won’t make it through another one.” Hendrick added, “And she is Alpha Theodore’s mate.” I sighed, “I’ll take her fight. I’ll convince them… Which means I’ll have to go see them. Who’s been talking to them?”

Paige said, “Addison and Sierra when they can get in.” I nodded, “Alright. I’ll talk to them. When is the fight?” Paige practically growled, “When are all the fights when someone could die is.” I acknowledged, "The last fight of the night if I'm not fighting. Alright. I'll check my email… then go see the girls then meet everyone back at our headquarters." We went back up into the office.

Mason sat down in the office with me. He commented, "Trevor got beat to hell." I laughed, "I heard that." Mason winked saying, "The whole pack was walking on air. Except Booker. He was angry and demanding to know who hurt him since everyone knew you were hurt. So badly that you were recovering and laying low to stay safe from his crazy ass."

I sighed, "I mean... we all do what we can. It pays to have Hackura friends." Mason laughed, "Does it ever." I checked my email. I had some from Elise and.... I saw the other name that had my heart skipping a beat. Xander had emailed me.

Mason sighed, "I wish you'd go see that young man. I think he'd surprise you. I don't think he'd ever promise to reject his mate. His parents' story, and love, is legendary. He'd never turn his back on that." I hoped he were right, but I'd stopped all but a very small part of me from hoping long ago.

I answered Elise then Xander. I messed up and told him he was hot. God… why did I do that? I got up and went to the Undergrounds facility. I walked inside and easily found the women in question. They'd get transferred when I took the fight, but we could figure out where they were going. It was likely to be Kentucky.

It was a little easier because this was supposed to be my fighting group. The Conners' were going to have to get them out. I walked down and found Jane first. Paige was right in her earlier assessment. She wasn't going to make it. I pulled a mask over my face and put a card in her pocket.

I whispered, "I'll get you out of here." She weakly asked, "Who are you?" I replied, "Around here they call me the Swiffer." She gasped, "You've been missing." I nodded, "Well, I'm back." She whispered, "You let people hurt you then beat them. Everyone talks about you."

I evaded, "Hmm, people say a lot then. I'm getting you out." She groaned, "You're paid. You're not like us." I agreed, "True…but I once was just told to be here. I use the money to fight against this. I get people out and I'm taking your fight. You'll get transferred, and people will come for you." She cried, "I'm going to die."

I petted her hair gently assuring her, "You won't." She whispered, "Why do I feel so relaxed around you?" Well, that answer wasn't one I could say out loud. She was my sister in law. I told her, "Because I'm going to save you… Alpha Theo's coming." She cried, "Am I really his? Someone said they heard that." I replied, "Yup… so I heard from… people… reliable people…" Xander and my friends told me. I waited until she calmed down and went to find Madeline.

She wasn't as bad off, but she wasn't good either. She asked, "Who are you?" I replied, "I know you heard me talking to Jane." Madeline tried to growl, "If you lied to her…" I held up my hands before I assured her, "I'm not lying. You'll be home tonight."

Madeline cried, "I hope you are right." I told her, "I promise you… you'll be out of here." Madeline asked, "What about you?" I shrugged, "This is my fight. Hell, this is my stand." Madeline whispered, "It's a dangerous stand to take alone. We would help you." I replied, "I'm not alone."

I walked out and found the ringleader. He smiled seeing me, shouting happily, "You're back!" I answered, "And I'm fighting tonight. You've over worked those new fighters, and you owe me." The ringleader agreed, "Of course. That's a great trade. The Swiffer's first fight in weeks. I'm glad you're all better."

I snorted, "I'll just bet you are." I walked out the back and went to the holoport that would take me around the corner from our headquarters. I stepped through, put in the code, and walked in. Everyone made their way over to hug me.

Addison announced, "I've got everything cued up." With a pounding heart, I called the Conners house. Thankfully Addison had typed a script for me, so I didn't ramble. I got off point when Jason got pissy. What was his deal? He sounded angry. He couldn't know I was in the Resistance.

If he did, he could at least acknowledge that I helped them. He would be dead if not for me. Chelsea, Nick, Grandpa Ben, and Peter would be dead if not for me. They should at least be nice to me. They owed me their lives! Couldn't they be nice for one freaking second?

Xander's voice pulled me back on task. I knew Theo's voice the second he spoke. My heart went out to him. In another life… he'd be my brother in law. Plus, his mate was missing and that was stressful. Anyone would be grumpy in his shoes.

I got in a snide comment about Jason and Red Run always being behind me. I'm sure it did annoy them, but they'd better get used to it. I'd never be behind them. It was a personal challenge in my eyes. I hung up in a huff.

Addison said, "You didn't tell them how to get into the facility in Kentucky." I groaned out loud then sent an email to Xander. I set it up to send automatically in thirty minutes. Addison sighed, "Alright, I'll clean up that email. You go take a nap. Right now." I laughed, "What?" She replied, "You're fighting tonight, so go nap. It will make me feel better. Don't think I'm not pissed you threw me out of the car."

I frowned, "You'd have been more hurt in the car than outside of it. I couldn't have you guys getting hurt over me." Addison hugged me, "I'm so glad Cayden came, and he put a serious beating on Trevor. He just got out of the pack hospital yesterday. His friends are still there."

I laughed, "Well... when you upset a Hackura Commander… I mean… you get what you get." Addison shoved me towards the bed. I was oddly tired for someone who'd been unconscious the better part of the last few weeks and fell asleep right away. Addison woke me up an hour before the fight.

I got dressed and walked back through the holoport. Crush was on the door. The second he spotted me; he grabbed me and pulled us back into the forest. His tone held nothing but relief, "You're ok." I assured him, "I'm all good." He frowned and pulled me into a hug.

He said, "I should've driven you home myself." I reiterated, "I'm ok." Crush told me, "I know you're in that circle group. I want in. I've seen what you've all done and watched quietly but now I want in." I studied him before asking, "Why are you here at this facility?"

Crush snorted, "I'm sure you know what I am." I answered, "You are a partial Demon." Crush nodded, "I was worth more here according to those in charge. My mate…." He trailed off and choked up admitting, "he was sold. He didn't even realize we were mates before they closed the door on the can. I was sent here but I've been looking for him. I just don't have the resources…"

I cut him off, "What's his name? Or did you get to find out?" Crush wiped away tears, "I heard them list off his name as they drove away with him. It's Virgil." I snorted, "You have GOT to be kidding me." He frowned, "I'm not." I felt a great sense of satisfaction when I took out my phone.

I shouldn't have doubted myself when I met Crush. I thought he'd be cute with Virgil and brushed it off. Virgil answered, "Boss lady." I replied, "Virgil… I need you to come to me. Right now." He shimmered in, "Here I am…" his voice faded out when he locked eyes with my company.

Crush grabbed him shouting, "She found you!" Virgil hugged him tightly. He pulled back, "I'm sorry, you know me?" Crush explained, "I saw you before they slammed the door shut on that damn van. I couldn't get to you after they put that shock collar on me."

I declared, "Alright. Crush, you're in. We are the Resistance by the way… not the circle group… I don't get why people don't notice it's a ring. Anyway… Virgil, you can come in and watch the fight tonight." Virgil gasped, "I get to watch you fight? You never let us watch you fight." I replied, "Tonight's not a normal night. Tonight… I am PISSED." Crush whispered like a prayer, "Thank all the gods and goddesses."

Virgil was let inside, and I got changed quickly. I ran out into the ring and spotted Trevor. He was still bruised. Dang. Either his wolf was mad at him, or Cayden really put a beating on him. Everyone else roared with applause.

I was fighting a new guy and felt a little bad for him. He was not in for a fun night. He came at me. I dropped low and punched him in the stomach. I messed with him a little before I got in shot after shot. Flashes of Trevor and I fighting in the cage came to me.

The audience seemed just as excited by this way of fighting. Eventually I knocked him out and got out of the ring. The ringleader frowned commenting, "That's not your usual style." He could not be serious.

I snorted, "Do you think I didn't see Trevor over there? You think after that stunt you pulled… which I am hazy on the details of… but I remember him coming into the cage…that I'd fight with my usual style? I had no respect for you in the first place."

"I'm your biggest earner and you threw me to a horrible wolf who abused me and enjoyed it. I know you don't care about that. You should care about the fact that your crowd didn't back you up… Even those who are willing to watch people fight for their lives seemed upset about that fight… I don't fully recall. That should tell you something. You are lower than scum."

I walked outside and found Virgil and Crush were waiting in a car. I got in the back and Crush took off. He used several evasion tactics. They dropped me off at Mason and Hendrick's house. I walked in and went to my room.

I quickly moved my nightstand and tapped on the floor. My safe was under that. I typed in the code and pulled out the phone Xander called and left messages on. A thrill went through me seeing he'd left another voicemail.

I listened and was instantly unable to stop my tears. He was so sad, and I couldn't have that. He wanted to fund us. I didn't need his money. I'd have to talk to the group about changing some things. One thing I knew… was my old fighting style had to stop.

Xander begged me not to keep fighting like I had been. I couldn't ignore that part of his plea. I could hear his heart breaking when he'd made the request. I heard people coming up to the door. I quickly put the phone away.

I walked and opened the front door. I gasped, "Alpha Theo… Alpha Lux… what are you doing here?" Alpha Theo replied, "We have been waiting for you to get here. I want to hear about your car accident." I admitted, "I mean... I'd tell you, but I don't remember. I do remember a fight… maybe a couple… I remember the flashes of light… I KNOW there was a crash cash… the rest... I got nada."

Lux laughed, "Aww come on pretty lady. Let me whisk you away from this horrid place. They don't deserve you. I'll treat you like a queen." I reasoned, "You have a mate out there, Lux." Lux flirted back, "There's nothing wrong with a little fun before she comes along. You'd still be treated like a queen. There would be no attempts to forcibly mark you. I'd bite you but you'd like it." He winked.

I gently told him, "That's a very kind offer but I'm ok. I really don't remember anything other than what I've told you." Alpha Theo hummed, "How odd." I thought about it and could acknowledge he was right because I'd thought the same thing. This was twice now. Maybe I'd have Paige look into it.

I offered, "Tell you what…. if I remember the details, I'll actually call you." Alpha Theo looked surprised before saying "You'll call me and tell me what you remember?" I nodded, "Yup. it's one thing to lie and claim I'm his mate… it's entirely another to try to mark me... if that's what happened. If I remember and can honestly tell you that's what he did…. Well, then I'll call."

Lux jumped in, "Well, there had to be other witnesses. They can tell us and then we can protect you." I told him, "I can protect myself and I have no proof he attacked me with the intent to mark me. So… there really isn't anything you can do."

Alpha Theo snorted, "I'd believe that what's happened based on the pictures in your hospital chart. I doubt anyone on the council would disagree." He was wrong. I nervously offered, "Take it or leave it Alpha Theo... I promise on my honor, if I remember the events of that night… I'll call you and tell you all about them…maybe even given you a written report."

Alpha Theo agreed, "I will take that. I think we are making progress. I think you like us." I was stunned he didn't know that I did like them. I replied, "Liking you is not the problem." Lux threw on his charm again saying, "Aww, come on tell then. Out with it. Tell Lux the problem. I'll fix it all up and then pamper you as you deserve." He was referring to himself in the third person?

I teased, "What fun would that be? You love a challenge, Lux." Lux acknowledged, "I do. I like you, Ashley Griffen. I promise you would have fun with me. I'd take you on dates and show you the world. While cheering you on as you schooled all our Warriors on how to fight. You'd also like me when you were writhing underneath me, screaming in pleasure."

I shook my head, "Sorry. My heart has belonged to one man since I was three." Lux faked a dagger to his heart. He said, "One day, you'll give up on him and I'll be there." I chuckled, "You're a pathological flirt. Are all your siblings that way?"

Lux laughed, "No. My brothers flirt, but obviously I'm the best. I couldn't answer for my sisters." I frowned, because as far as I knew he just had one but he'd said it as in plural. He sighed, "I'm looking for that answer though. Among others." That made no sense whatsoever. I offered, "I'd help if you needed it." Lux smiled, "Now, we've come full circle."

We talked for a few more hours before they ended up leaving. When they left, I went back into my room. I took my Xander wolf out of my safe and Xander's old hoodie. I held onto him and cried.

I admitted, "I miss you Xander. I wish you didn't hate me. Maybe my friends are right. Maybe you would love me too. Or at least give us a chance. All I need is a chance. We could be happy. No matter what, I'll always be yours Xander. Always." I closed my eyes and cried myself to sleep.

Strawberries

Alexander is Twenty-Five Years old

Alexander saw EJ and Elise popped out of Black Mountain to go on their vacation with the Kyle family. I looked over at my brother, Wesley. He smiled at me before joking, "I give EJ an hour before he makes his first call to ask how things are going."

I laughed, "I think you're giving him too much credit, little brother. I'll give him twenty minutes. He's not actually worried though. We both know you and Max have got this." Wesley replied, "You could take off too."

I shrugged asking, "Where would I go?" Wesley answered, "I don't know. Maybe Nashville for fun and stuff." I laughed, "I'll think about it, Wes." Wesley nodded, "I'm just saying, you've got some spare time on your hands." I did. Oden sighed, "Or New York." It wasn't his worst idea.

Wesley continued, "I know you've wanted to convince Ashley to have a training session up here with the Warriors. Who could say no to you in person? You'd have the advantage. I've yet to meet a woman or man who said no to you in person. Plenty you've said no to, but none say no to anything you ask. Even when they are disappointed in the answer."

I laughed, "Plenty of people could say no to me. In fact, Ashley does all the time." Wesley teased, "I know. It makes me like her. People just do what we say all the time, but she's different. I don't know though, I think she'd say yes to you in person, big brother."

I chuckled, "Maybe we will find out. I'm going to the gym if you need me." Wesley gasped in mock shock before saying, "Of course that's where you will be. It's where you usually are. If you want to talk about that, I'm here. Because I know something has been going on and it was before Ashley Griffen came on the scene." I lightly punched his arm and popped to the gym.

I lost myself in the movements of hitting the heavy bag. Maybe Wesley was right. Maybe I should go to Nashville or New York. Heck, I could do both. Oden perked up in my mind, then someone cleared their throat. I knew who it was turned around asking, "Phil?"

Phil sighed, "A certain little sister of yours requests that I get you showered and dressed. It seems she has plans for the both of us. I, myself am freshly showered. Gage is off on some other thing because his sister asked him to do it."

"I just can't help but comment on how all of us are owned by your sisters. They say jump, we all ask: how high? And for how long? I'm worse off because I have my own sisters that I jump through hoops for AND yours. It's not fair for a group of people who CONSTANTLY talk about what's fair."

I laughed and popped us to my room then quickly got into the shower. I came out and a pale green shirt was sitting out with jeans. I raised an eyebrow at my Beta. Honestly, I'd forgotten I even had this shirt.

Phil laughed, "I know what you're thinking. I have lost my marbles and decided that you are my personal Ken Barbie doll, and I get to dress you; however, I had nothing to do with this." I rolled my eyes.

Phil urged, "Go ahead and put it on. We are all the dancing monkeys of Angela. Gage linked me his sister's errand had something with Angela too." I laughed because he was right. My little sister wanted me to get dressed up so I would be.

I linked Gage, "You good?" He snorted, "I feel like I'm on a scavenger hunt. I'm good." I hoped he had fun. I asked, "For what?" He admitted, "I'm not even remotely sure but I'm excited."

My phone rang and I noted it was Angela calling. I frowned asking, "Why would she call me?" I showed Phil my phone. Phil replied, "Who knows? Maybe it's for dramatic effect. Fairies. What can you do? You should be used to it. You are one."

I answered, "Hello Angela…" I trailed off because there was loud music in the background. I growled, "Where are you?" Angela laughed, "I'm in Louisiana. You should come get me." I shouted, "What the HELL are you doing in Louisiana?!" I grabbed Phil.

Angela answered, "Enjoying some music. The band is actually really good! That was the rumor though and it's true. Are you coming to get me? I'm not leaving until you do." I growled, "Do not move. I'll be right there." Angela laughed, "Just get here fast." She hung up.

I threw my phone across the room. Phil complained, "I feel led astray. This was not the type of fun I thought she had in mind." I growled, "Klaus had BETTER be with her or I'll have someone ground her." Phil laughed, "You'd have to ground her, your parents are on vacation. Correction, your mom is the only one who could do it, because your dad is an even worse sap than we are."

I sighed, "You know I can't ground her. AH HA! Loophole! Technically Wesley is in charge, so he'd have to ground her." Phil laughed, "There ya go." I popped us to Angela but heard her pop out as we arrived. I growled, "What the HELL is she playing at?"

Phil pointed out, "You left your phone at home so we can't call and ask. Might I suggest linking her." I could conjure it. Oden told me, "Snow said she was here because we needed to be. We can't upset Snow." God damn it.

I asked Phil, "Where's your phone?" Phil admitted, "It's also at home. Specifically in your room. I didn't think this was a long stop. We are being pranked. Obviously." The music I'd heard had stopped playing. I blew out a breath then inhaled deeply. I got hit strongly with the scent of Strawberries. Oden demanded, "GET MATE NOW!"

My heart stopped for several seconds. I grabbed Phil. He asked, "Do you smell that too?" Oden growled in my head. I questioned, "You smell it too? It's strawberries, Phil. Do you know who smells like Strawberries?"

Phil laughed, "Strawberries? I do know because you've told me and the hoodie you have used to have a scent; however, you need to get your super nose checked out. That smell is CLEARLY peaches." I sighed in relief because he wasn't smelling Melanie strongly like I was. I wasn't some possessive Werewolf. Well, I was but it was because Melanie was mine.

Oden growled at me, "If you don't go get mate RIGHT NOW I will growl at you until we have her in our arms. It WILL annoy you and I won't feel remotely bad about it." The scent was getting stronger. Phil was bouncing back and forth on his feet. Oden purred, "Mate is coming to us."

I could hear voices now. One girl whisper yelled, "Where are you going? We need to get the HELL out of here!" A voice that stopped everything in my world answered her, "Uhh do you not smell the most amazing sugar cookie that is literally wafting its scent?"

She practically moaned, "Wafting… I NEED it. It's practically taunting me….and daring me to come get it. Who says no to a delicious dare like that? Not me…I want to lick it… No, I want to DEVOUR it. It will be mine. You know I LOVE sugar cookies. We can spare a few minutes to track down the delicious sugar cookie then get the heck out of dodge."

Phil linked me, "Is that really who I think it is? You smelled strawberries because Melanie freaking McAlister is here?!" I answered, "It is her and I assure you she can do all those things to me. I even strongly encourage both." He asked, "What the hell is she doing in Louisiana?!" I had no idea and I didn't even kind of care.

I linked Gage, "I'm about to meet Melanie." He shouted, "YOU ARE WHAT?! I'm linking Phil immediately." The girl with Melanie snorted, "I do not smell a sugar cookie. I do smell chocolate pie, and it does smell really good. I guess we can go this way, but then we HAVE to get out of here."

Melanie told her, "When I have my delicious cookie… we can absolutely leave. I don't know anything about a chocolate pie smell though… you might be losing it. I don't currently care…. Because I want my sugar cookie. No, no… I NEED my cookie."

Oden purred, "I want my strawberry smelling mate. Go get her!" They rounded the corner before I could move, and I was instantly captivated. Phil growled, "Mine!" Both girls gasped and jumped apart. Then my mate's beautiful green pale eyes landed on mine.

I growled, "Mine!" Melanie's jaw dropped. For a split second everything was perfect. Her eyes were on mine, and I was lost in hers. Then she started to fall to the ground while screaming in pain. She was clutching her head. I rushed forward and caught her before she hit the ground.

Her friend screamed, "ASHLEY, what's wrong?" I asked, "Umm what? Ashley?" Phil linked me, "What the actual hell? That's Melanie McAlister. I know because you've made me watch those videos of her dancing a bajillion times." I replied, "I am aware of who she is, Phil. I'd know that scent anywhere."

I knew what Melanie smelled like, and I knew what she looked like because of the videos I'd been watching of her dancing. Melanie was better when I was touching her, but she was still screaming in pain. Her friend looked around before saying, "God, we've got to get out of here." I nodded to Phil.

I didn't care why, but I did want to get somewhere safe to help my mate. Phil grabbed his mate, and I popped us away. Gage linked, "What is going on?" I answered, "Something both good and bad. I can't talk, you'll have to link Phil."

Phil's mate sat down and groaned. I actually looked at her and was shocked to realize I knew exactly who she was. How the ever loving hell she knew Melanie was going to be a whole ass fucking story, I could tell. She said, "Whoa popping is a really weird experience."

Sierra Kiern sat down for several moments then jumped up. She shouted, "HOLY SHIT!" She clapped her hands over her mouth. She whispered, "She was right. Oh my god. She was right! She's been right the whole time." Phil asked, "About what? And who might you be?"

I linked him, "You know who she is. She's a Beta's daughter. That's Sierra Kiern." Phil replied, "I am aware of that. I just want her to say her name. They said Melanie's name was Ashley. So, who knows if we are using real names or not."

Sierra answered, "Umm I'm Samantha McLean." I frowned. Phil linked me, "Ok, so that was a no on using real names for our mates. That makes NO sense." Melanie was still screaming. Sierra asked, "Ashley, what's wrong?" Both names clicked for me. Samantha and Ashley.

I asked, "Ashley Griffen?" Phil replied, "No." Sierra nodded. I snorted, "Where's Cindy Blake?" That was the character they were missing from the book series Melanie liked. Sierra told me, "She left the show with everyone else."

Phil linked, "They use the names for the band from the book series I read with you because I saw you reading them so many times." I retorted, "Thanks for that astute observation. By the way, I already figured that out."

I asked out loud, "What's wrong with my mate?" Sierra admitted, "I don't know. She might have hurt her head earlier, but she said it was nothing." I told her, "There is nothing physically wrong with her, or I could heal it." Oden whined in my head.

Sierra winced saying, "I did know that about you." So, she knew me. Phil linked, "So, Melanie told her about you." I replied, "Clearly." He admitted, "It's not surprising really. EJ and Elise said you are her crush." What the hell was going on? Melanie thrashed in my arms. I set her down and she started trying to crawl.

I felt something wet on my face and wiped my face to realize I was crying but I wasn't the only one. Sierra was crying too. Oden howled in my head. I asked, "Buddy?" He said, "I feel like something inside me is repairing and it hurts because it hurts her."

I asked, "What are you talking about?" He said, "Since mate's sixteenth birthday I have felt pain that I kept from you." I shouted, "Why the hell would you do that?" He admitted, "Because it's not a small amount of pain and I love you."

I growled, "I love you too! You shouldn't have done that. I never want you in pain." He admitted, "I didn't know what it was, and all the other wolves said they didn't feel it, but it's getting better." There was pain in his voice though. I whispered, "Oden." He whined again.

Phil said, "She was better when you were touching her." I grabbed Melanie and pulled her into my arms. I'd never felt more useless in my entire life. I whispered, "I've got you. You're ok. I'm here. Please stop crying. It's ok. Just tell me what's hurting. I'll fix it, I swear." She sobbed into my chest.

I whispered the words to grant her peace, but it didn't work. I looked at Phil, panicked. I asked him, "What do I do?" Phil closed his eyes then said, "I'll be back." He left the house and came back with the pack doctor from our allies here.

The pack doctor looked at us all and sighed, "I've been told this is all in the utmost confidence and I'm not to tell even your father about this." I growled, "Help her!" He studied Melanie. He said, "She doesn't have anything physically wrong with her that I can see. You are a better healer than I am since you can just make people better."

I snarled, "If I could help her, I would. My healing light says she's fine but it's clearly on the fritz!" He offered, "She's clutching her head. I supposed I could start there." He took out a needle. I grabbed his arm growling, "You are NOT giving her something when I don't know what that something is."

Phil commented, "Easy their killer. You're going to crush the bones in his arm. He's trying to help her, remember?" The doctor winced and told me, "It's morphine and it should help her." I slowly released his hand, and he administered the drug to Melanie.

I cradled her and played with her hair as her screams died into whimpers. I held her close offering comforting words, "I'm here. I won't leave you. You're ok." I linked, "Oden?" He said, "Everything is getting better. My pain is going away too." What the hell happened to my wolf?!

Phil said, "There's no way that the others in our family didn't feel that. I could practically feel your concern from that. I'm surprised no one has popped in. I sense Angela's influence afoot people." I held Melanie knowing he was right based on the bond, but I couldn't focus on that.

My whole world was in my arms right now. Her eyes eventually fluttered back open which had me smiling because they were so beautiful in person. She subconsciously smelled me. After a moment, she bolted up without ever looking at me. Her eyes instantly found Sierra.

Melanie asked, "Where are we?" Sierra admitted, "I do not actually know the answer to that question." Melanie rubbed her temples asking, "Who said that?" Sierra answered, "Umm I did? You asked where we were I answered."

Phil linked, "What the hell is going on?" I knew what he did. Melanie waved dismissively, "Not that… THAT! Who said that?" Phil joined their conversation, "Umm you did." Melanie whirled around to face him.

Recognition, fear, and confusion flickered on her face. Then hope filled those perfect eyes and her eyes wildly jumped around until she found me. Our eyes locked again. Her jaw dropped then she jumped back onto the couch, screamed, then covered her mouth with her hands.

Oden growled, "Say something! Why is she upset?" I asked him, "Can you reach her wolf?" Oden answered, "I just made contact, but she sounds tired and weak. Before it was like there was a wall." I knew the problem then

I rubbed my temples, "Ashley Griffen is wolf less and that's not possible since she's Melanie." Oden snorted, "Mate is both and she's not wolf less anymore." I asked, "And the pain you felt?" He answered, "Gone." Because my wolf was able to talk to his mate now? What the hell was going on?

I looked into her eyes, letting her see my sincerity. I told her, "It's ok. You're safe. You're in my family home in Switzerland. I know this is probably confusing. My wolf says he can barely sense yours. I'm guessing that's the voice you're hearing." Her eyes widened and I watched every emotion she had play out on her face.

Her eyes widened in shock but I knew the second she asked if the voice in her head if it was her wolf, because her happiness nearly made me cry. I continued, "It scared you when your wolf said mate, didn't it?" Oden said, "It did. Confirmed by mate." So, her wolf was talking to them both now.

Sierra screeched, "WHAT?! HER WOLF?! Ashley, what's going on?" Melanie didn't seem able to look away from me until Sierra got her in her face. Sierra announced, "My wolf said she senses your wolf too. I don't know what's going on, but you have a wolf. You really do." Why the fuck would Melanie think she didn't? It's literally impossible.

Melanie burst into tears. I couldn't stop myself from going to her. I took her back into my arms. I whispered, "I don't like your tears. Not one bit." Phil said, "He's so rude. He didn't introduce himself.

He's Alpha Duke Alexander Conners. I'm Beta Phil Kruthers. My mate is your friend, Samantha." I guess we were going with fake names.

Gage linked, "WHAT THE FUCK IS GOING ON?" I answered, "Make yourself scarce around the pack. Something weird is going on and Phil will probably have you looking into it." He questioned, "Like what? I need an example because I am listening to Theo freak the actual fuck out about your intense feelings." That made me feel bad.

I answered, "Like the fact my mate JUST got her wolf and my own wolf has felt pain that he kept from me since we went down on her birthday." His gasp was exactly how I felt. He questioned, "Oden has felt pain since Melanie was SIXTEEN?!" I answered, "Uh huh." He said, "I'm on it." Good.

Sierra let loose a growl which made Oden snort. Phil raised an eyebrow. I linked, "You know why she's mad." He snorted, "I do but the thing is I said the name she told me to use." Sierra closed her eyes then said, "Don't call me that."

Phil grinned while teasingly asking, "I can't call my mate by her name?" Sierra looked away before answering, "No, you cannot call me that." Phil chuckled, "Am I allowed to call you sugar lips or babe?" Sierra laughed, "Babe will do."

Phil shrugged, "I reserve the right to call you Sugar Lips." Sierra's lips twitched into a smile. Melanie told her, "He lives with Fairies…not giving him permission to use that nickname made it more fun to him. So…. he's absolutely going to call you Sugar Lips… You should just…" She jolted and covered her mouth.

Melanie looked up into my eyes as tears streamed down her face. She whispered, "Hi, Xander." Phil linked me, "Ummm hello giant neon sign as to her real identity. As a Beta blood, I recall the only person I've EVER heard call you that, and not get punched in the face, is Melanie. Ask her what the HELL is going on? How is Melanie McAlister also Ashley Griffen?"

I reasoned, "I don't know the answer to that question and I'm pretty sure it's a long winded detailed answer. So, in short, stop ruining my moment." I answered Melanie out loud, "Hi, Ashley." She growled back. I bit my lip before asking, "I can't call you that, can I?" She frowned then shook her head no.

I smiled saying, "I could call you my Lovebug." Oden snorted, "She's always been Lovebug to us." I knew that, but she did not. Her eyes met mine again as tears swam back into her eyes. She whispered, "I'd like that."

Phil said, "Fun. I want to take Sierra to my room." Sierra disagreed, "I can't leave her right now. This is huge. She's got a wolf now and she's been without one for four years. It's a big deal." Oden linked, "Freya. Her wolf's name is Freya. I can't wait until we can run together."

I shot back, "Why the HELL hasn't she had a wolf this whole time? Why hasn't she shifted?" Oden replied, "Freya is working through Melanie's memories. She's being tight lipped about it. I think I recognize her voice." I had no idea how that was possible.

Melanie touched my face. Sierra sighed, "Our bags are back in my car in Louisiana." I conjured their stuff here. I told her, "Your car is now in the garage, and your bag is in Phil's room." Melanie asked, "Where's my stuff? Because… I have stuff too, and…"

I kissed her forehead then pulled back answering, "My room." Melanie smiled. I tapped her nose, "There's that beautiful smile. Are you ok?" She admitted, "I'm… both wonderful and extremely confused… but… it's good? I think… no, it is… and..." Sierra jumped in, "It's all wonderful."

That was more than fair that her feelings were all over the place. I took her hand saying, "Let's take you two out onto the deck." We walked outside. Melanie squealed, "Oh my gosh! We are ACTUALLY in Switzerland…. which obviously... Xander can't lie but… holy crap on a cracker... Samantha... can you even... Switzerland?!"

Sierra snorted, "Ash, calm down." Melanie squealed, "I WILL NEVER CALM DOWN! LOOK AT THE VIEW! There's a lake! I can see mountains… this is beautiful... I mean really? You actually said the words calm down... how could you even remotely be calm right now?! LOOK AT THIS VIEW!"

I wrapped my arms around and whispered, "The view pales in comparison to you." Melanie snuggled into me and stopped talking. Sierra snorted, "You're hired Alpha Duke Alexander. You made Ashley speechless. That's practically impossible to do."

I kissed the side of Melanie's head then told Sierra, "You can call me Alexander. You're the Beta Female of my pack, and my mate's friend." Phil said, "Uhh Alexander, you need to put in the alarm code before…." The alarm sounded. Phil sighed, "That happens."

I popped Melanie and myself to the keypad and entered my code. I asked her, "Would you like a tour?" Melanie shyly answered, "Yes. I mean... if you want to... you don't have to... or feel like you have to or anything…" I laughed, "I offered, my little Lovebug." She flushed and I grabbed her hand.

Oden linked me, "If you don't kiss her, I'll growl in your head for all of eternity! Also, I TOLD YOU SHE WAS OURS, YOU BIG DOUBTING HUMAN!" I replied, "I'm not going to rush this. I'll kiss her though, just hang on." Oden grumbled in my head.

I took her to the kitchen then to one of the sitting room with a bunch of windows. Melanie gasped, "This is beautiful." She sat down on one of the seats by the window. I sat next to her and wrapped an arm around her, picked her up, and took her to the other side where there were couches.

She whispered, "I can't believe we are here. I can't believe you're… You're really here." I squeezed her hand, "I'm here. I have a mission to take for my uncle soon, but you'll never be alone again Lovebug. I'm here." Tears spilled out of her eyes again that I wiped away.

I took her into the library and watched, deeply amused, as she ran over to the bookshelves. I knowingly asked, "Do you like reading?" Melanie nodded. I admitted, "So do I. I must say I'm an avid reader of the *Thoroughbred* series. Since your name, and your friends, are derived from them I'd say it's safe to assume we both like the series."

Melanie flushed then stammered, "Umm… well... yes... I do like that series. Let's not talk about that." I raised an eyebrow and walked over and caged her between my arms. Her eyes didn't leave mine. I told her, "I've been waiting for you for so long."

I leaned in towards her and waited for her to close the gap. I didn't have to wait long before her lips were on mine. My hands instantly went to her sides, and I pulled her against me. I cupped her face with my hands. Even her lips tasted like strawberries. Everything about her pulled me in. I was so hard it was embarrassing.

I forced myself to pull away from her lips after several minutes. We were both breathing hard. She stared up into my eyes. There was so much love and trust in them. Something I despised was that I could see fear.

I looked into her eyes begging, "Please don't be scared. You have nothing to fear from me." Melanie looked away and whispered, "You could break me." I turned her head back to me. I told her, "I will never break you; I promise. I will not ever physically hurt you."

I added, "I will do my best to never hurt you emotionally. I know we will have fights, but I will never intentionally do something to hurt you. Ever. Please don't be afraid of me. I may be an Alpha Enforcer, but to you I'm like a giant teddy bear. I'll never hurt you."

Melanie wiped tears out of her eyes. She put her head on my chest while I inhaled deeply. Oden growled and I knew he wanted to shift because he was mad. He just knew Melanie needed me right now. I asked, "What's going on in your head?"

Melanie cried, "I don't know. I don't understand. If I have a wolf… then everything is different. We could be different. We could be like this. Everything could be ok. I just want to freeze this moment and never leave it." Oden demanded, "Make her stop crying." Gosh, I was thinking of not doing that. He snorted.

I assured her, "Honestly, I don't care if you have a wolf or not. You're mine either way. I've told you many times I'm impressed by you in our email exchanges. My feelings about you make a lot of sense to me now. Plus, you think I'm hot."

The tips of her ears turned red. She pushed back, "I mean… you know you're hot. Look at you. You like, stepped out of a magazine or something. You're perfect and I'm…." I kissed her again. Oden complimented, "Good job. She stopped crying."

I pulled back before I said, "I'd say sorry, but I wouldn't mean it. I just couldn't help it. You're beautiful and your kisses are addictive. I'm a very lucky man." Oden purred, "Mark mate." I told him, "This is so not the time for that conversation, Oden. She's reeling."

Oden begrudgingly admitted I was right, "Fine. She's so beautiful, Alexander." I replied, "I know." I asked her, "What's going on?" Melanie looked up in my eyes. She frowned admitting, "I really don't know… which is… hard for my brain." Of course it was. She was a Beta wolf.

She continued, "All I know is… I'm really happy to be here with you right now. Can we just… embrace this moment? No matter how long or short it is. I just want to be with you. Let's just have it be you and me and forget everything else."

I sighed knowing that meant I wasn't getting the answers I wanted, but I wouldn't push her. This was her story to tell, and I'd grown up in a house where we didn't push people to tell their stories. I agreed, "If that's what you want." She nodded her head yes saying it was.

She eyed my lips then moved forward again, kissing me tentatively. We lost ourselves in the kiss. I heard and smelled Phil coming with Sierra before they even came into the room. He cleared his throat. Oden told me, "I am berating Rocket for this." Good.

I linked my cousin, "What?" as I slid my tongue back into my mate's mouth. She moaned and gripped me tightly. Phil answered, "My mate wants to see yours." I complained, "You're losing your touch, cousin. Once you've got your lips on a woman, I've never seen them want to talk to another woman until much later." He snorted and I pulled back from Melanie.

She looked confused then stiffened and looked past me. Sierra asked, "Are you ok, Ash?" Melanie blushed, "I'm… I don't know… about... a lot... but I know I'm perfectly fine with Xander." Sierra nodded. She added, "We aren't really packed for… chillier weather."

I commented, "That's easy enough to fix. Let's go to town. Phil and I will take you shopping on us." Melanie argued, "Oh no… you don't have to do that. It's fine. We will be fine." I kissed her then pulled back.

I explained, "I'll either snap all the things you could possibly want, or we can go shopping. My family owns the place. It's free either way." Melanie looked at me and I could see she felt guilty. I told her, "You're my mate. Let me do this. Please."

Sierra chimed in, "He wants to, Ash." Melanie looked at her, clearly frustrated. She turned back to me saying, "I can pay you back." I laughed, "I don't need money, and what's mine is yours." She admitted, "I don't want you to be upset later." I kissed her again.

Oden purred, "I like when you have these ideas. Kissing is good." I knew that. I assured her, "I won't be. Come on. It really would make me happy." She sighed, "Ok." I grabbed her and popped to the shop.

She laughed, "You kind of… left them behind." I smiled saying, "Phil can open a portal, or they can walk. He interrupted us earlier and I wasn't done kissing you." I pulled her back into me which had her instantly melting into my embrace.

I really didn't know how my mated siblings got anything done. Which told me I was in big trouble, since I'd only kissed Melanie so far. The night was young though and there was plenty of time for other things.

I smelled Phil coming again and pulled back. I whispered in her ear, "Your friend is going to steal you to shop now. Phil and I will be right here." Sierra grabbed her the second I stepped back. The desperation in her eyes telling me she clearly didn't want to leave my side almost had me pulling her back. I was about to break when she turned and went with Sierra to shop.

Phil hit me in the arm and hissed, "SPACE UNHEARD!" I quickly whispered the chant. He said, "Thank you." He called Gage. My Gamma answered, "What the hell, guys?" Phil shouted, "WHAT THE FLYING SHIT IS HAPPENING?! My mate isn't telling me her real name. NEITHER is Alexander's." Gage asked, "Huh? I thought this was about Oden feeling pain since we went down."

Phil shouted, "ODEN HAS WHAT?!" I admitted, "He just told me. It's better now." Phil stared at me. He asked, "Better now that your mate UNLOCKED her damn wolf?!" Oden said, "Yes, actually." I nodded. He said, "Rocket is going to berate Oden for us not knowing that." I said, "I'm not happy about it either." Gage chimed in, "Me three."

Phil powered on, "Moving on from that, what the actual fuck is Melanie McAlister doing in Black Path?! Why was she wolf less until she locked eyes with Alexander and BAM she gets her wolf? She

LOOKED into his eyes and her wolf came to her. That's weird. I'm not the only one who sees this as weird, right?"

Gage agreed, "No, that's easily one of the weirdest things I've heard, and I don't have a low bar for that." He wasn't wrong. Phil waved his arms shouting, "THEN my mate says I can't mark her. Can't, you guys. I assure you both, I could absolutely mark her." I went to say something, but he kept going.

"In fact, I can mark her two different ways. She can't explain why I can't mark her either but says after we go home, she'll pack up her stuff in her pack. THEN she can explain when she gets to Black Mountain." Oden growled, 'I don't like that." Neither did I.

Phil shouted, "I HAVE TO LEAVE HER IN BLACK PATH! You want to know what I can do about that? JACK SHIT because they HATE us! HATE! We can't go to Nashville without them pissing their pants and crying to the Supernatural Council about what the big meanie is doing in their territory."

Gage reasoned, "Just tell her you'll buy her new things, and she doesn't have to go back. She can call her parents. This is fixable." Phil snarked, "I already tried that! It didn't work. OHHHH! I am SO pissed right now!"

I had a feeling I would be too, but there was no reason for Melanie to keep up this facade of being in Black Path. I could conjure their things, but Sierra could have someone ship her all her things. Or Phil could have me conjure it, which they both knew. So, what was going on?

Phil whirled tome asking, "Can you just pop us to Nashville and do your 'explode all their heads' thing? My way solves a lot of problems for me and you. Like LEAVING OUR MATES WITH THOSE CRAZY ASS MOTHER FUCKING PEOPLE! I don't like it."

"Rocket likes it less than I do. My Hackura side is about to go all golden eyed about this. Do you how many of them I could kill going golden eyed? My hatred for that pack has grown SUBSTANTIALLY since we met our mates. What the hell did they do to our Luna and to my mate?! YOUR Beta Female?! The insults just keep adding up. The did something to ALEXANDER'S LUNA AND BETA FEMALE! Head should explode for that. I'm just saying."

Gage asked, "Did you ask your mates what the hell is going on?" I snorted, "Not exactly." Phil replied, "He didn't ask at all. He's an Alpha Blood. I asked subtle questions, but not many because, well she's hot. I'm a man and she smells so good."

I sighed, "I don't know what's going on either. Could Melanie have been recruited by the Supernatural Council to…?" I trailed off and ran my hand through my hair. I admitted, "I don't know. Go undercover? Maybe that's why she won't come home." Phil blinked several times while Gage whistled.

Eventually Phil asked, "And then they did something to her wolf?! Without her knowledge?" Gage scoffed, "Because they want Eric to kill them on all fronts. No, they want him to kill them for recruiting her. Then they want him to raise them from the dead to kill them again for doing anything to her wolf. That's insane, guys. They have to know the Werewolf Council would kill them for doing that."

I shrugged admitting, "I've got literally nothing on the deal with her wolf. We will have to talk to Corbin privately later. Maybe he can tell us whether or not that's even possible." Phil sighed, "I mean the Supernatural Council could've approached her about going undercover." Gage scoffed, "You seriously think they have a death wish?!"

Phil replied, "My dad said that they approached Drake about wanting to using Melanie several times when she was a pup." I growled, "What?" Phil sighed, "Yeah, plus you have a point. If they approached her, she would've been PISSED if they told her everything going on that her home pack did not."

Gage agreed, "They could've told her all the stuff we, and I say we loosely meaning Red Run, are hiding from her." Oden snarled. Phil jumped back in, "But how can the Female Lead Warrior of a pack in Nashville be in New York dancing all the time. When she's clearly also in Nashville a lot." Gage offered, "The answer is obviously magic. She's could have a Demon, Fairy…" He trailed of when I growled.

I argued, "It better not be a damn Fairy because I COULD'VE POPPED HER AROUND!" Phil hummed, "Don't say Hackura on this list, Gage." I pointed out, "You just did." He winked at me. Oden snarled, "We beat the shit out of a Fairy or Hackura if they helped without telling us." I agreed with that.

Gage picked up his list, "Or Witch/Warlock friend. She does like to be busy from everything we know about her." I admitted, "I've been thinking Ashley might be in The Resistance." Phil gasped, "Holy shit. I thought the same thing. It jives man. The Resistance wants to help YOU. Specifically, and it's ALWAYS coming back to you. Helping you, answering your questions, getting YOUR brother's mate home. You, you, you, and more you."

Gage chimed in, "That makes sense." Oden grumbled, "Except it doesn't." Phil clapped, "Right? Of course Melanie McAlister wants to help Alexander. Elise told him, and he told us, that she had a crush on him when she was a pup."

He smacked his own head, "I thought Ashley and Melanie were just friends or some shit. NOOOOO they are somehow the same person. Dude, your dad will literally call in both your uncles, Fairy and Hackura, if the Supernatural Council recruited a fourteen year old to do this stuff. What even is this stuff?"

Gage snorted, "You're speculating that they started The Resistance." Oden snarled. Phil groaned, "Oh god, we're going to kill people. Like a lot of people. Aren't we? Is this war? With...." He trailed off. Gage offered, "Everyone."

I answered, "It's looking that way. If the Supernatural Council kept Melanie from me, they are dead, but I think they lied to her about something else. She's afraid of something to do with us and that comes across in her emails." Phil groaned.

I continued, "Not to mention all our offers to have her do a workshop or come to Elise's birthday. If they told her we'd get hurt, or that we'd hurt her if we knew who she was, they die horrific deaths. Not to mention the pack LYING to us about being her hosting pack in New York. Let's not forget Black Path for having her in their pack and LYING about it using an alias."

Phil agreed, "Fair enough." Gage hummed his agreement. Phil continued, "Now that you brought it up. Let's talk about these Black Path assholes." Gage scoffed, "Nice transition." Phil retorted, "Thanks. Sierra is scared to tell me her real name and won't let me mark her. She HAS to go home first before I can mark her. What is that fucking shit?" I didn't know any more than he did.

Phil began to pace, "If she's not ready to be marked that's one thing, but that not what she said. Not even close. Not that she doesn't want me to mark her. She says I can't. I do not like those words. It does NOT give me the warm fuzzies. She looked VERY sad, and I feel like killing people would make me feel better."

"You want to know what else doesn't give me warm fuzzies? Either of our mates going back there. What if it's some plot and the Supernatural Council tries to keep them from us to continue doing whatever the HELL it is they are doing." Gage declared, "No way. That's not happening."

I growled, "I have been separated from Melanie long enough. I won't stand for it. EJ and I will declare war until Sierra and Melanie are back by our sides. Everyone would. The Supernatural Council cannot separate mates."

Gage supplied, "Plus, Dalton and Dakota could, and would, bury them for this. Melanie is their pack member, and they have no idea she's been so damn close to home this whole time." Oden grumbled, "Close yet so far."

I replied, "We don't know that they don't know." Phil snorted, "We do. Besides, the Supernatural Council can't just recruit teenagers to go undercover. Is this why Ashley holds Alpha Theo at arm's length? I have so many questions, and I have no answers. I HAVE to tell you both how much my Beta brain HATES this entire thing."

Gage chimed in, "My Gamma brain isn't thrilled either." Phil muttered, "I hate it from the depths of my being. I think my brain is actually itching from the lack of information I have. The questions just grow more complex. Because my buddy Beta T will FLIP SHIT if his baby sister is in The Resistance."

Gage agreed, "His head might actually explode from anger." Phils snorted, "Not to mention his poor head or heart if the Lead Female, formerly wolf less, Warrior from Nashville is his sister. Drake McAlister will actually lose his mind. I can see it now. Just..." He clicked his tongue made a mind blown gestured with his hand, "right out of his head."

I closed my eyes. Gage said, "Just ask them." Phil scoffed, "And have them run away from us? Have you met us? That would go poorly, and we'd hunt them down then mark them." I agreed with Phil, "We can't force them to tell us. All we can do is make them feel safe until they have to go back. We can get them to open up. If we push them, they could take off like Phil predicts." I growled that part. Oden snarled, "MINE!" I knew that.

Phil muttered, "Then we'd have to march on down to Nashville because that has to be where they'd run. I don't know what those guys are doing, but I KNOW it's bad. I also know that I don't want my mate, or my Luna anywhere near them. NOWHERE Alexander."

I growled, "Do you think I like this? Or that I want them near those people my dad has ALWAYS thought are shady pieces of shit?" Gage replied, "I do not." Our mates ran by us with clothes in their hands to the dressing rooms.

Phil snorted, "I actually think you want to go to nearest gym and beat someone to bloody pulp." I inclined my head indicating he was right. That's exactly what I wanted to do. I had to prioritize my wants here though.

I declared, "Melanie is my priority. She wants to spend this time before my mission just with us. She's reeling. I can't imagine being a Beta's pup and finding out I didn't have a wolf." Phil winced. I continued, "Only to find out at twenty years old you DO have a wolf."

Phil sighed, "Ok, I'll give you that, but it's not really fair when you think about it. You have Alpha blood. You're all about getting the answers, but you don't have the urgency I do. I NEED answers. I have to know all the things." Gage assured him, "I'll be finding out what I can, Phil."

We could hear our mates laughing. I looked at Phil practically pleading, "I need her, man. I need her not to disappear. She has a knack for being invisible and not around. I can't lose her now that I have her. No, that's not the right word. I WON'T lose her now that I have her. She's mine."

Phil teased, "And you're her Xander. It's adorable." I glared at him saying, "Only Melanie can call me that." Gage gasped, "She actually called him that to his face?" Phil answered, "Mmmhmmm." He grumbled, "And I missed it."

Phil rolled his eyes at me complaining, "I'm only your cousin and Beta but sure the Luna is the only one who gets special nickname privileges. I see how it is. Also, for the record, I said Ashley was meant to be my bestie. I'm obviously right, since she's my Luna."

I agreed, "Yes, ok fine. If it makes you feel better for us to acknowledge that you were right, that's easily done. She is going to be your friend because she's your Luna." Phil smiled, "It's so nice to hear you say that. I do so love being right. It's very fun for me." I rolled my eyes muttering, "Whatever."

Sierra came out with her arms crossed. Phil said, "Gotta go, Gage. My mate is annoyed." He snorted, "I'll look into some stuff." We hung up. I made the space heard before Sierra got to us. She looked a little suspicious but to my surprise she didn't address Phil.

She looked at me saying, "I told Ashley that you don't care what we buy. In fact, I made her try on a lot of stuff. She looks great in it." I glanced at Phil who shrugged. I admitted, "I don't see the problem." She threw her hands in the air shouting, "She just wants to get a coat!"

Oden growled, "We can afford more than a coat." I knew that. I told Sierra, "That won't work. She'll need a swimsuit and snowsuit. We have a hot tub and a pool inside the house, and I want to take her snowboarding." Sierra nodded, "I got her all that and then some. Yet she insists she only needs the coat." I winked at her.

Melanie ran out of the dressing room with eyes wide. She stammered, "Umm it all just… it's gone. I didn't do anything, and it all just disappeared! I was putting everything back on hangers then it was gone like magic… oh my gosh!" She glanced at me.

She whisper yelled, "SAMANTHA! You told Xander to conjure the stuff back to the house! I told you I didn't need all that." I kissed her stopping her rant. Oden said, "This is the most brilliant plan you've ever come up with. Kiss her to stop the ranting." It was because according to her family she did this a lot. Which means I'd be kissing her all the time. Darn the luck.

Oden grumbled, "Until she got that etiquette coach." Except she clearly didn't have that coach or stop talking the way they missed with each breath they took. Maybe the Supernatural Council had someone else writing their texts and emails and gave Melanie a script for their calls. They probably had her keep them brief because she couldn't lie well.

Sierra snorted, "So all we've needed this WHOLE time was him? We normally just let her rant." Oden purred, "We are exactly what mate needs." I ignored him enjoying the feel of her lips on mine. He said, "Freya said she also enjoys kissing us." Good.

Phil snorted, "How long could a rant actually last?" Sierra laughed "It depends but it could be a few minutes… or hours. If she gets on a tangent, or she's nervous, excited, angry, etcetera, it just goes on and on. There is no end in sight."

I pulled back and looked into Melanie's eyes. I told her, "I'll buy and give you whatever you want. I want to take you to do some things while we are here. I left the coats here because I want to show you around the town." She slowly nodded.

I grabbed her hand, and we walked out. Everyone we walked by was nodding to us. We'd been here enough our whole lives, they knew Phil and me. I caught a flash of someone familiar. I pointed at something for our group to look at, then I looked the other way.

I spotted my Uncle Bjourn in the crowd. I smiled broadly at him and winked. Melanie was excitedly chattering about everything around us. Uncle Bjourn raised an eyebrow then nodded to Melanie. I nodded back.

He linked me, "Is that who I think it is?" I answered, "Yes, it is and she's mine." He smiled and faded into the background. He sent me how happy he was for me in the bond. He knew the fact she was mine settled that piece of me that had been worried I was a possessive jerk.

I turned back around just as Melanie turned to look at me. She whispered, "This is so amazing, Xander." I said, "I'm glad you like it. It's just a walk though. I plan to dazzle you." She flushed, "I don't need to be dazzled. I just want to spend time with you."

I teased, "Aren't you sweet?" Melanie laughed, "Sometimes... I mean... well… some people would definitely not say that... some people really don't like me. I mean... they aren't… well they suck. I mean... I think they do. I'm nice to my friends…. Well, I used to be nice to more people… I'd never be mean to you… other people though… other people suck when you really think about it..."

I tilted her head up saying, "Anyone who says you aren't nice will not like the version of me they meet. No one will say an unkind word about you ever again if they know what's good for them." I kissed her again. I could admit I was addicted.

Hell, I was a lost cause. She'd owned me since I was fourteen years old, but now with her in arms reach, it was undeniable. Oden said, "Yes, well she could've been in reach longer if you'd listened to me about her being ours." I apologized, "I really am sorry, Oden." Especially since he'd felt pain since her sixteenth birthday.

I shook that off and showed my mate, and Sierra, around the town. I took them to a cookie shop in town. Melanie flushed scarlet red out of nowhere. Sierra laughed, "You ok, Ash?" She whispered, "They heard us! Oh my gosh… I talked about biting and licking a sugar cookie… and it was Xander!"

Sierra replied, "I mean you do plan to do that anyway. You've been fan…." She cut off her sentence and must have linked my mate. I linked Phil, "How the fuck can she link my mate? Melanie NEVER broke with Red Run." He replied, "You know what I do." I was going to murder someone was the other part of that.

Melanie playfully slapped her, "SAMANTHA!" Phil called, "No linking things like that, Sugar Lips. I definitely want to know the end of that sentence. Don't you, cousin?" I replied evenly, "I'm sure I can figure it out."

I whispered in Melanie's ear, "You're definitely free to bite or lick me anytime you want to." She made a choked noise, and the smell of her arousal filled my nose. I added, "You better get your cookie, Lovebug, before I throw you over my shoulder and take you home." She shivered and definitely not from fear.

Sierra grabbed her hand and walked to the counter. The whole while, Melanie was blushing. Phil linked me, "No one would believe me if I told them that YOU, Alexander Marcus Nathan Conners, threatened to carry a woman out of a shop in a sexual way. Not a fighting way."

He scoffed, "People will doubt me, in fact, NO ONE besides Gage will believe me. If you're going to say things like that, you have to warn your Beta cousin so I can get video evidence. Beta Dylan requires video evidence in situation likes this." Oden snorted.

I rolled my eyes retorting, "She's my mate. Of course I'll say things like that to her." Phil snorted, "You've spent twenty five years not talking to anyone like that. You've been waiting." I emphasized, "FOR HER. I was waiting for her, and you know it."

Phil chuckled, "Even before Oden was certain it was her, you didn't really show interest in anyone." I shrugged offering, "I'm like my mom that way. We are both more sensitive as Healers. I've wanted Melanie for over a decade though." Now she was finally here and officially mine. All the waiting. Every single moment before this one didn't matter to me.

All the loneliness I felt on holidays seeing my siblings in love and wishing for my own were gone. None of it mattered now. I had her, and I'd be damned if I let her go. Oden growled, "We will decimate anyone who tries. Ajax will be thrilled because she'll be home."

Yeah, they were going to be hurt too though. She'd missed a lot never coming home. She'd never even met her nephew. Our mates came back over with cookies. Melanie had sugar cookies, which didn't surprise me.

When we left the shop, I popped us to restaurant nearby for dinner. Melanie's eyes were wide with excitement. I pulled her chair as close to mine as I could then ordered for the table. The wine I'd selected was brought over.

I asked, "Have you had wine before?" Melanie shook her head, "Wine, no. I have not had wine before." I laughed, "Evasive. Have you had alcohol before?" Melanie nodded, "Yup… for sure. A lot… probably more than… that's not the point. Uhh the point is I'm a vodka cranberry juice kinda girl."

Oden growled, "What did that mean?" I replied, "If you were a Beta's pup and didn't get a wolf I'd imagine you'd attempt to drink that pain away." I didn't like that she had, but I could easily understand the notion.

I was shocked that she didn't come home though to try and figure out what happened. Maybe she was embarrassed? That tracked. Oden growled, "If the Supernatural Council did this then lied saying that we didn't want her because of her lack of her wolf, and neither did her family, we explode heads." I agreed, "Eventually, yes. Prior to that we torture them for six years." He conceded, "I do like that plan."

I playfully teased my mate, "You really like do like the color red." Melanie leaned over and kissed my cheek. She blushed admitting, "I do. It's my favorite color." I knew that. We ate our meal enjoying conversation as a group. We blended well together, but that wasn't surprising.

As soon as Melanie and I were done eating I was ready to go. I asked, "Do you want to get out of here?" Melanie laughed before telling me, "Samantha eats REALLY slow… for as fast as I talk... she eats the opposite way."

I smirked, "That sounds like a Phil problem." She touched my arm lightly. She giggled, "You're so bad." Her eyes told me she wanted to go though. Oden purred, "I do like that her emotions are all over her face but Freya said she did want to leave. They want to spend time with us." I did too.

Sierra urged, "We are fine by ourselves, Ash. In fact, it sounds like a lot more fun that way. Go on and get." Melanie blinked at her. Sierra waved at her, "You two get out of here." Melanie flushed, "Are you sure?" Sierra practically pushed her out of her chair.

They clearly linked again because Melanie blushed harder. Sierra smiled, "I demand you two go back to the house. There's no need to wait for me. Even though I maintain, I eat at a perfectly normal pace that allows my food to digest." Melanie laughed and I took her hand.

She smiled up at me a little nervously. I asked again, "Do you want to get out of here?" I was praying to every god and goddess I knew the name of that she'd say yes. She smiled shyly and nodded. With that answer, we ran out of the restaurant. More than a few knowing looks were thrown our way.

There was live music playing when we walked outside. I spun her around, pulled her into me, and started leading us in a swing style dance. She laughed delightedly asking, "You can dance?" I winked, "I can do a lot of things, my Lovebug."

I'd learned for her since I knew she loved to dance. My Uncle Aiden taught me all the different styles. I wasn't a bad dancer due to my Fairy blood. I wasn't surprised she picked up the moves and knew the style. Then she even started showing me moves. We were quite the duo.

People clapped when the song was over while we were both staring into each other's eyes. Someone yelled, "If you don't kiss her, I will!" Oden snarled, "ALEXANDER!" I growled and claimed her lips. MINE! She melted into me, and I couldn't help but note how our bodies fit together perfectly.

I pulled away from her with great effort. I grabbed her hand and took us to a secluded area before popping us back closer to the house. Oden grumbled, "Pop to a bed. Why are we here?" He knew why. I challenged my mate, "Race ya back." She giggled, "You're on Xander." Then took off.

I gaped for a half second. She really was FAST. Tristan and Jason talked about it all the time, but I thought they were exaggerating. Oden said, "Uhh we are going to lose if we don't move." I quickly took off after her. She actually beat me.

I looked over at her asking, "What are you? The Flash?" She answered, "Well, no… I've always been faster than most people. Plus, I follow your cardio training plans. Don't you?" I couldn't stop my smile or laugh. She gasped, "I mean… of course you do… that... wasn't... I didn't... I mean…."

I kissed her again. I really didn't mind if this is what I had to do to calm her down. I pulled back whispering, "You're funny and playful. You're perfect." Pain flashed into her eyes. She whispered, "I'm not." I tilted her chin back up declaring, "To me, you are perfect. Come on." We walked inside.

I sat down on the couch, and she followed. I asked, "So, how's having a wolf?" She smiled, "I... it's kind of weird having this extra voice in my head, but super cool at the same time. I keep almost answering out loud and sounding like a crazy person. I don't know how sixteen year old's do this and go to class."

I laughed, "Oh yeah? Were you the brainiac in your class?" Melanie looked away, "I used to be." Oden growled, "What does that mean?" I answered, "You know as I do that Ashley Griffen has a GED. I don't know if Melanie was ever dancing at that high school." He snarled in my head, and I felt exactly how he did about that.

I asked, "Why did you get a GED?" Ashley shrugged, "It was important to me. Black Path doesn't really put an emphasis on education. They especially didn't put one on mine. They were not thrilled that I got a GED, but they can eat lard."

I laughed, "I'd like to see that. I could also arrange it and make it happen." Melanie laughed, "Oh my gosh… that would be hilarious." Oden chimed in, "Let's do that then. Keep her happy." It really was easily done.

I somewhat warned her, "Just remember, your wish is my command. I'm a partial Fairy. I can absolutely make them eat lard." Melanie cackled. She managed to say, "You… have… no…. idea… how… funny… that is…."

I changed the subject, "When I come back from doing something for my uncle, will you be ready to move? I'd honestly offer to move to your pack, but I'm certain I would not be accepted there. Nor do I like most packs in the Nashville area."

She snorted, "Because they are mostly trash… there are good ones though… since ya know, Phil's friend… his pack is good." I nodded. I offered, "You could challenge and be the Female Lead Warrior of the pack that's mine if you wanted to." Melanie's eyes widened.

She replied, "You might not want me to move... I mean... I don't know if I can... I mean... Black Mountain is…. and I'm…." I interrupted, "I want you with me." She put her fingers in the corners of her eyes, wiping tears away before they fell. She whispered, "You might not say that once you know everything." Oden demanded, "Make her stop crying and tell her that's not true at all!" I was going to.

I pulled her into my lap and rubbed circles on her sides. Eventually I looked her in the eyes. I vowed, "There is nothing you could say that could make me not want you. We all have a past, and stories to tell. You can tell me yours when you're ready. I still want you to be ready to leave when I come back. I shouldn't be gone very long. It will be a few days at most." She put her forehead on mine.

She whispered, "I hope that's true. I want to be with you, Xander. Always. We have… a lot to talk about and work through though if you do too." I asked, "Like what?" She looked away before answering, "I have a lot of baggage."

I teased, "I'm good at moving things from one place to another. I'll conjure it all to Black Mountain. I can also carry quite a bit." She sniffled, "I mean emotional." I kissed her lightly whispering, "I know what you meant. I stand by what I said."

"Your baggage is mine too. I'm here for you. I'll help you carry the burden. I'm your mate and I'm here for you. I'll be here at every twist and turn. If you need time to explain things, that's fine. I'm still here. I'll leave you my burner number. You can contact me on it while I'm gone."

I stated, "I'm not leaving you. Not ever. Now that I have you, I'll never take a mission like this again if you can't be by my side. I know my uncle will agree. He might want to see your skill set, but your reputation speaks for itself."

I complimented her, "I'm so proud of you. I can tell you have some ghosts and some things that hurt you in your past. I don't think I can accurately express how much I hate that. I wish I had been there for you all along. I wouldn't have held you back, ever; however, I would've shared the burden. You don't have to take on the world and the injustices in them alone anymore. I'm here and I'll help you. Whenever you are ready."

Melanie didn't bother to try to stop her tears this time. She clung to me as if I was her lifeline. She pulled back, "I've… I'm… not exactly alone, but I am. I have my friends… and it's my fault they aren't as close to me as… well… I keep them further away than I should… it's just they don't understand…" Neither did I as things stood.

She continued, "They have become my family but… my wolf… not having a wolf was a huge missing piece inside me... and… you. I've missed you so much." I'd missed her more than I could express. I couldn't imagine thinking I didn't get a wolf. I'd had Oden with me my entire life.

I held her giving assurances, "I'm not going anywhere. You have me now. I'm sorry it took so long for us to meet. I've been fighting my instincts about popping down to Nashville to meet you in person. I was trying to respect your wishes. I was really worried about you last year. If those in Black Path know what's good for them, they will stay away from you."

She sighed, "Can… I…? You… well... I mean… about marking me…." I raised an eyebrow. Oden howled in delight. Melanie continued, "I want that…. like more than I can express… but... like… we need to wait… until we can talk… about everything… then you... umm can decide…. what you want to do."

Oden grumbled, "I do not need any details. She's ours." I replied, "I know that. Nothing, literally nothing, even her being a serial killer, could change that." He snorted, "She's not." I huffed, "It was an example. I know she's not."

I told her, "I'll mark you whenever you're ready. If we are waiting until we have some big talk, that's fine. I might have to bite a pillow at times though." I winked at her. She buried her hands in her face. I laughed, "We can take our time with all that because we have it."

She whispered, "I want to… I've just… I mean… I haven't…. and you're… like wow… and well… like you know what you're doing with stuff." Oden purred, "She's so cute. She said stuff instead of sex." I caught that.

I slid my hand on her neck and kissed her lips again. I pulled back, "I've never done this before either. I was waiting for you. I did get drunk at my birthday party one year and a girl kissed me…" She growled and I couldn't help but smile. It was an adorable growl.

I continued, "I pushed her off the second I could without hurting her and walked away. That's all I've done." Her eyes widened. She gasped, "That's it? I mean... you... but… like… LOOK at you! Plus… well… You said… but… they…."

I laughed, "Clearly you do not own a mirror. My Lovebug is gorgeous. You're so incredibly beautiful. I am a VERY lucky man." Oden growled, "She said they. It's like she was going to say something else." We could figure it out later. She knew I couldn't lie.

She asked, "Will you regret this if you find out later... I'm not who you think I am?" I replied, "There's nothing about you I will regret. You're exactly who I think you are." She whispered, "But what if I'm not?" I realized she didn't think I knew she was Melanie. Oden snorted. I smiled, "Then I'll enjoy learning more about you." I kissed her again.

We began making out and petting each other through our clothes. I groaned when I cupped her breast. I desperately wanted to play with her nipple. I reached to take her shirt off, but she pulled back. Her heart rate was near panic levels and her face showed it.

I asked, "Is everything ok? If this is too fast…." She cut me off, "No. I mean... I just… I don't want to take my shirt off." I was startled. I put up my hands saying, "Hey, it's really ok if this is too fast. We can go to bed."

I offered, "There are plenty of rooms here for you to sleep in if you don't want to stay in my room. You are absolutely welcome to join me though. I'll snuggle the fuck out of you." I'd also be sleeping on the floor outside whatever room she picked.

Melanie stammered, "I... No. I want to do this… I just want my shirt to stay on." I nodded, "Ok." That was confusing but fine. Before I could say anything else, her mouth crashed onto mine. I smelled Phil coming and popped us to my room.

I laughed, "Now I have more questions." She smiled, "You could ask them... or…." She took my shirt off. Her jaw dropped. She said, "OH MY GOSH! Seriously? I mean… good gosh… look at you! Are you kidding me? What the heck?! How do look better in person than your videos? That's insane…. Do you ever leave the gym? I mean… just wow… I mean…" I pulled her onto the bed and kissed her neck.

I kissed where her marking spot was, where my mark would be one day. She moaned. I gently nipped at the spot. She jumped, "Holy mother of pearl… what the…." I bit it again harder. She ground her hips into mine, whimpering. I couldn't stop my smile.

I muttered against her skin, "Maybe when I found out you were my top account viewer across several accounts I had that drilled down into the content you like. Then maybe I created more content just for you." She moaned, "Xander… oh… oh…" I kissed her body through her shirt.

When I got down to her jeans I slowly peeled them off. She was wearing boy short underwear. I gathered the hem of them in my teeth and slowly, with some shimmying on her part, slid them off her. I'd seen this plenty of times in the Hackura realm, so I had the basics.

Her eyes widened when I settled between her legs. I inhaled, "My Lovebug smells amazing." She flushed, "I mean… that can't be true. I should probably shower... I mean... OH MY GOSH! Why didn't I shower?!" I used my tongue to gently lick her clit. She jerked her hips.

I was just going to fake it until I made it since I'd seen this done a lot. She started panting and gripped the sheets. I slid my finger around her entrance. I groaned finding her dripping wet. I slowly slid my finger in.

She whimpered and came halfway off the bed. I slowly started moving my finger. Her moans steadily became more frequent and closer together. Suddenly I felt her walls clamp down on my finger and she screamed, "XANDER!"

I slid another finger inside her and kept going. I knew she needed to be prepared before I slid my dick insider her. I didn't want to hurt her. After her fourth orgasm she begged me, "Please… please Xander… Claim me… please…." I agreed, "With pleasure." Oden purred, "Finally."

I snapped my jeans off. Her eyes widened when she spotted my dick. Oden chuckled. She somewhat shrieked, "Ummm hold the phone... that fits in me? I don't think it does… mistakes have been made… that's like a massive weapon of destruction." She was good for my ego.

I laughed, "It fits. It will be ok." She raised an eyebrow, "Easy for you to say. It's not going inside you." I laughed again offering, "We can wait." She frowned, "No… I just… are you sure that's going to fit?" I nodded, "Yes." She pursed her lips, "I guess I'll have to trust you then." I laughed, "You can definitely trust me." Her eyes softened.

I kissed her slowly and lined us up. I pulled back admitting, "It might hurt for a second." She shrugged nonchalantly saying, "I'm sure I can take it." I did not like the sound of that at all. My Melanie, My Lovebug, should not be used to pain. Oden demanded, "Think about that later." I would.

I slowly slid inside her. When I felt her barrier, I used my healing light as I pushed past it. She purred while I slid the rest of the way in. She looked down asking, "That's it? You're like all in? You're not… there's no way that thing fit… you did say it would though… so… I'm confused."

I chuckled, "Yes, I fit." She admitted, "That didn't hurt at all… look at that… you do actually fit. Do I have a magical vagina?" I laughed, "I used my healing light so you wouldn't feel pain, and it's magical to me." I kissed her and slowly began to move.

Melanie closed her eyes. I growled, "I want to see your beautiful pale green eyes." Her eyes snapped back to mine. She whispered, "Gosh, that feels so good… like… better than imagined… which… well… gosh…"

I smirked and repeated the move, "That? That right there?" She moaned, "Yes!" I kept repeating it. I whispered, "I'm close." She whimpered, "Don't stop… just… I'm close…." When she came this time, I couldn't help but come right after her.

I groaned and nearly said her real name. I barely stopped myself. This was going to be harder than I thought. I was so focused on not saying her name, I didn't even realize my hand was glowing. I only noticed it when Melanie seemed to have a second orgasm out of nowhere.

I realized I'd shared my light with her. Oden growled, "That's not fair to your wolf side." I winced admitting, "I didn't mean to do it, and you know that. I mean I want to, but technically, she didn't actually say anything about my light. Just about not marking her."

Oden snored, "Fairies." I countered, "Loopholes. Plus, it settles a piece of you, I can tell." She was ours and marked in a way. He admitted, "It does settle me somewhat. It's a little less than nothing." It was more than nothing to my Fairy side, but I knew why it wasn't to him.

I slid out of Melanie slowly. I already felt like I was missing something not being connected with her. Aesir above! How did my mated siblings get anything done? I'd link Phil and ask if he knew but he might just challenge me to a sword fight if I did that. I could tell in the bond he was also having sex.

I went into the bathroom and washed myself off before grabbing a washrag for her. She was already asleep. I gently cleaned her up then conjured the wash rag back to the bathroom. I crawled into bed, pulled her into me, and fell asleep.

I woke up knowing I was missing something. I jolted up and realized it was a 'who' not a thing. Melanie wasn't with me. She was gone. Her side of the bed was cold too. I snapped on sweats and a hoodie and searched the room. Her bag was still here, and it caught my eye.

I stopped when I saw what was on top. Her toy wolf from all those pictures I'd seen was barely peeking out. Oden hummed with satisfaction. I couldn't help my own sense of pride about it. She still had it after all this time. Hell, she traveled with it. At least in some small way, I've been with her all along.

I quickly shook myself and inhaled. I settled knowing she was nearby. I tried to pop to her, but it didn't work. OH COME ON! I was beyond annoyed at myself for agreeing to that stupid promise all those years ago. She was mine and I NEVER should've agreed to that bullshit.

I charged down the stairs, jumped, and landing soundlessly on the ground. I followed her scent trail outside. She was playing music softly and dancing barefoot in the grass. I was immediately captivated. The videos I watched didn't do her justice. Seeing it in person was somehow more moving. She was the most graceful dancer.

Oden purred, "Mate is stunning. She can fight and dance. Plus, she's kind, and caring. Don't let her go back to those people, Alexander." I sighed, "Let her? Come on now. She's a person with free will. I'll make a strong case for her to just go home."

I paused adding, "Well, our home in Black Mountain since I'm not supposed to know who she really is. Or since she knows Cayden, I might be able to convince her to wait in the Hackura realm. I imagine she will actually have to go back to Black Path since she'll have to tell Alpha Edward she's leaving. She's the Female Lead Warrior. That could wait until I could go with her though."

Oden grumbled, "I don't like it." I asked him, "Has Freya give anything away?" Oden sighed, "No. They are just getting to know each other. She doesn't want to upset Melanie. Plus, she thinks that they both need to be ready to tell us."

I replied, “That doesn't sound good.” Oden growled, “It doesn’t.” I told him, “If the Supernatural Council did this to them and us; I promise you they will pay. She’s hurting and feels alone. She’s been missing Freya. I can’t even imagine, as a Beta’s daughter, how devastating this all was to her to think she didn’t have a wolf.” Oden growled, “I agree. Someone WILL pay.”

I watched her dance for another half hour. It was much less haunting than anything she’d choreographed for the last four years, but that now made sense to me in a way. Part of those dances were about missing her wolf.

A timer went off on her phone and she turned off her music. The wind blew my scent in her direction which had her whirling around. I complimented her, “You are a beautiful dancer. How is it that no one talks about what a great dancer Ashley Griffen is?”

Oden snorted, “Seriously. We’d have gone to see her because we’d have thought the coincidences were too much.” Which is why no one talked about it. She blushed, “I mean… I dance in fields. The pack’s not my biggest fan. They tend not to talk about me more than they have to.”

I growled, “Then they are idiots. I’d talk about you all the time. In fact, Black Mountain might just get sick of how much I brag about you. That’s a personal problem though, and they wouldn’t dare say it to my face.”

Also, it didn’t make sense that she wasn’t the hero to Black Path. She’d saved them more than once. Melanie laughed, “No, I doubt they would… say anything to your face I mean. You’re intimidating. I mean not to me, but I could see how people would find you intimidating… I mean... this is all sounding so wrong and I…”

I closed the distance between us and kissed her. I pulled back, “I find I am a fan of having to kiss you to stop your rambling. I’ll have to be on call twenty four seven. I can’t say I’m even remotely upset about it.” She blushed. I took her hand, “Let’s get back inside.”

I popped her back into our room. I noted that I could pop with her, but not to her. How obnoxious and annoying. Oden scoffed, “You never promised not to pop WITH her, just to her.” I retorted, “It wasn’t her specifically. It was the McAlister’s in general.” He growled “I remember.” He’d been just as pissed off about that entire ordeal as I had been. I got back into bed and fell asleep holding my mate.

When I woke up again, the same thing had happened. Oden and I both sighed. I’d have to tell her I wanted to wake up with her. Also, was she some type of ninja?! I was not a heavy sleeper. This time, I could hear her in the kitchen.

I snapped sweats on and walked downstairs. She was cooking up a storm. I couldn’t help but smile watching her. Oden purred, “She’s perfect. She does everything.” I replied, “I agree wholeheartedly.” Neither of us would care if she couldn’t cook. She was perfect to us no matter what.

She had bacon, biscuits, eggs, pancakes, waffles, and fruit all cut up and presented beautifully on a platter. Phil walked in sniffing the air. He linked me, “She made all this? Does she sleep?” I snorted, “No she gets up to dance first. I took her to back to bed, then she got up to fix this.” She was dancing around the kitchen, not paying attention to us.

I took in her appearance loving that she was wearing my hoodie from this morning. I instantly got hard. She casually said over her shoulder, “Help yourselves. I wasn’t sure what everyone liked... so I made a little bit of everything. The muffins will be done in a few minutes.” So, she did know we were here.

She added, “I wasn't sure what time everyone woke up… so I wanted to space everything out. I made chocolate and blueberry muffins. There are chocolate pancakes too. Those are for Samantha. They are her favorite.”

“Well… if you guys like them, I could make more… that’s a thing I could do. Sorry about the mess… I had to search for everything. Your kitchen is really well stocked though…” Phil linked me, “It’s too early for her to be using so many words.” I popped beside the refrigerator and kissed her.

When I pulled back Melanie bit her lip. She added, “There’s coffee too.” Phil brightened, “Coffee. I love coffee!” Oden snorted, “As if everyone didn’t know that.” Melanie laughed. I asked, “How much coffee have you had, mate of mine?” She blushed and her heartbeat caught when I referred to her as my mate. Her eyes shone with happiness.

She shrugged, “Some.” I laughed clarifying, “How much does some mean?” Sierra came in wearing Phil’s clothes. She snorted, “Some is either one or two pots.” Melanie stuck out her tongue at her. She declared, “Just the one pot… AND I made more. Plus, I made your favorite pancakes which I regret since you’re being mean to me.”

Sierra laughed, “But I love you, and your cooking so much. I also love you on coffee. Just not too much coffee. For example,” Melanie gasped, “DON’T YOU DARE!” Phil’s eyes brightened, “Dare Sugar Lips, please do dare.”

Sierra laughed, “The first time Alexander emailed her. You have no idea how much coffee she drank. You might have to pay Hendrick and Mason a chunk of change for all the coffee she went through. ALL NIGHT long!”

A wet dish towel flew at Sierra’s arm. Melanie was near tears. Oden demanded, “Fix it, Alexander.” I instantly took her in my arms. I told her, “Would it make you feel better to know that I drafted my email to you at least twenty times?” She blinked up at me.

Phil cleared his throat. I added, “I also made Phil read each and every one of them.” Phil snorted, “It’s true. He was VERY obnoxious about the first email he sent you. Then he just locked me out of the exchanges as if I didn’t have to read a billion drafts of the email that started it all before he sent it.”

He dramatically gestured between us saying, “Now, I get nothing. I just know you email each other. It’s maddening I tell you. Sometimes my Alpha and cousin is so very mean. Watch out for that.” I growled at him.

He smirked, “These eggs are amazing, Ashley. So fluffy. Where did you learn how to cook?” Melanie answered, “Hendrick and Mason King taught me how to cook. I work in the kitchen at the diner sometimes. They cook breakfast, lunch, and dinner. Mason’s burgers are the best, but Hendrick is the breakfast master.” She looked sad.

Phil linked, “Sierra, who you are calling Samantha because if I call her that she growls, told me that Mason and Hendrick are like family to Melanie.” I cleared my throat saying, “I’m sure we could find the perfect spot for them to open a diner in Black Mountain. I could conjure it for them even. I’ve heard they are impressive Warriors. They are more than welcome to come with you when you move.”

Melanie’s eyes shot to mine. Hope danced through them. She whispered, “Really?” I nodded, “Of course. If they want to come, they are welcome. We can even find a way to keep the diner they have now open and open a new one where we live. I have no problem with them joining you two in our pack.”

She wrapped her arms around me and kissed me. I deepened the kiss sliding my tongue into her mouth. Sierra laughed, which had Melanie pulling away. She whispered in my ear, “Thank you.” Her timer on the oven went off.

She ran over to the oven mitts and pulled out muffins. I got two plates and handed one to her. She looked startled and stared at it like it was a bomb, not a plate. I laughed, “You know that you have to eat with us.” She seemed stunned for several seconds but nodded.

She checked everything then came to sit by me. I snapped us mimosas and pitchers of more to drink later. Except for Melanie, I snapped her a cranmosa with a separate pitcher. Sierra laughed, “He’s got your number, Ash.” She smiled and we all ate.

Suddenly Melanie jumped up, “Oh gosh... I need to clean everything. I left your kitchen such a mess!” I replied, “I got it. You cooked.” She wasn't listening though because she was already running into the kitchen. She seemed panicked and her heart rate told me she was nearly having a panic attack.

I frowned asking, “What just happened?” Sierra sighed, “It’s complicated.” She raised her voice, “Ash, we are on vacation. It’s ok.” I walked into the kitchen and found my mate scrubbing a pan as if her life depended on it.

I snapped everything clean then conjured it all back to the original spots. Sierra raised her eyebrows muttering, “How handy.” Melanie turned around apologizing, “I’m sorry I shouldn’t have left everything out like that. Some of that needed to soak, and I just left it all out. I shouldn’t have done that… I can’t believe I didn't at least soak everything.”

I walked over and wrapped my arms around her. I told her, “It’s just dishes. It’s fine. As someone whose family owns the place, I promise it’s fine. I’m impressed that you can cook. Either Mrs. Blanch or

Zoe cooks my food or someone snaps it. There is an Omega who makes killer cookies, but that's it. I really appreciate you making us breakfast. Ok?" She slowly nodded.

Phil linked me, "Hey golden eyes, cut it the fuck out before she thinks you're mad she didn't wash the dishes." I closed my eyes and replied, "Why the FUCK would she be afraid over the fact that she didn't wash the dishes? I can promise you it's not anything the McAlister's did."

I paused adding, "Hell, I know it's not. Jase left dirty dishes in the sink for a week. Sam just let them pile up until he did them. Then she made him buy her a new cooking pan when he couldn't get all the stains off of it. Dirty dishes don't really bother them."

Phil sighed, "I'm sure Black Path has some weird thing about the kitchen being clean." I raised an eyebrow retorting, "Why would a Beta's daughter work in the kitchen? Or be yelled at for not cleaning a pan?"

Phil sighed, "That I do not know. She clearly likes to cook though, so I'm sure that's why she was in the kitchen." I snorted, "Black Path gives zero shits about people's passions." He admitted, "Ok, that's a valid point and true, but I was aiming for you being calmer."

Sierra said, "Let's just go sit out on the deck and have some more of these Fairy snapped alcoholic beverages and take in the scenery." I nodded saying, "We will be right there. You guys head out." They left quickly, holding hands.

I turned Melanie around. I studied her from head to toe. I asked, "Are you ok?" She shook herself, "Yes... I just…." I finished, "Panicked about dirty dishes. That you probably would've cleaned while we ate, but I insisted you come eat with us."

I tucked her hair behind her ear, "I can snap everything I want done or clean. I wasn't worried about the dishes. Even if we had to clean them by hand, neither Phil nor I would be upset about it. Hell, we'd have cleaned the kitchen. That's how things work with my family. You do the cooking then you definitely don't do the cleaning. If you do it's because you can snap it clean."

I chuckled, "My first memories of the holiday's that I can recall are of my mother making my dad pies for Thanksgiving and this Christmas cake he likes. You'll love said cake. It's called red cake, and it's aptly named. My mother can cook three things. Sugar cookies, cherry pie, and red cake."

"Every SINGLE time she cooks it looks like a bomb has gone off in the kitchen because she insists on making all these things for my dad from scratch. She's actually a good cook, but boy if she couldn't snap things clean, I think Mrs. Blanch would turn red from the state of the kitchen. She might even pass out, but she would never hurt anyone over it."

Melanie asked me, "What's your favorite food? I can learn how to make it for you if I don't already know." I replied, "I loved everything you made this morning. My favorite food is probably steak. Favorite meal would be steak, asparagus, and mashed potatoes or a baked potato. My favorite dessert is strawberry shortcake." It had been ever since I was fourteen years old and smelled her hoodie.

She seemed to make a mental note saying, "I'll remember that." I had zero doubt she would as a Beta wolf. Her heart rate was slowly coming down which made me happy. I asked, "What's your favorite food?" She was quiet before admitting, "I haven't thought about it in a long time."

I tapped her nose, "Think about it, and get back to me." She smiled, "I love sugar cookies. It's always been my favorite dessert. I'm not a fan of other cookies though… especially peanut butter cookies… they are… just a no for me." That was too bad. They were Karina's specialty.

She shook herself. Before I could ask why she didn't like peanut butter cookies she gathered herself. She said, "We should go outside." I disagreed, "Not yet." I kissed her gently then pulled back. I winked, "Now we can go outside, and talk about plans for the day."

Melanie asked, "What are we doing?" I answered, "I'm taking the group to Interlaken. We can hike and sightsee. It's very pretty. Then tomorrow I'm teaching you to snowboard." She grinned happily saying, "I always wanted to learn." I kissed her forehead, "Good."

Oden snorted, "You knew that. Ajax told me and Jase told you." He was right. I did know that, but I was going to use every bit of knowledge I had to impress my mate and make her dreams come true. I held out my hand which she quickly took.

We walked outside to join Phil and Sierra, who for some reason was still going by Samantha. Sierra reached over and squeezed Melanie's hand then handed her another drink from the pitchers I'd snapped. I had so many questions.

The most important ones were: What the HELL happened to my mate? And who the fuck hurt her? Because when I found out the answers to those questions, heads would roll. No one would get away with hurting Melanie. Ever again.

Have some Fun

Melanie is Twenty-Years Old

Melanie's friends were watching her closely. I found I was highly annoyed by that. No. I was annoyed by everything right now. Their looks of concern and the reasons for said looks of concern. The upcoming week and the Odette situation.

I couldn't find her. I'd lost someone…. me! She was being hidden by her horrible mother… and Odette needed me. It was insulting that I was being bested by that horrid woman. It had been over a month, and I was coming up empty on her whereabouts.

I was taking it horribly and I was grouchy. Hence all the looks from my friends. I winced thinking about how alone Odette must feel again. I couldn't help but remember when I met her.

Flashback

Melanie's computer went off. Everyone went on alert in my place. My off pack grounds secondary place was a popular hangout with our group for several reasons. I couldn't very well take down the Ring working out of Hendrick and Mason's house or diner.

Plus, we hated being in the pack because they sucked… well… mostly to me… they respected my friends… just not me. I quickly got to my desk and entered my passwords. I groaned, "Oh come on!"

Addison asked, "What is it?" I explained, "A girl who doesn't know about Supernatural's is about to be abducted. Apparently, she's very pretty and someone wants her."

I muttered, "A horrible reason to abduct someone… when you think about. Also, her mom is traveling and never around. They are moving quickly on her for some reason. They are being really light on the details."

Paige questioned, "The Ring wants a human?" I sighed, "That would be different. I can't imagine she's human… Plenty of people just don't know they are supernatural." I grabbed my gear. I announced, "If I'm not back in five hours, you know what to do." They nodded.

Dax offered, "I'll go with you." I pointed out, "You have a meeting you can't miss. I've got this." Avery asked, "Did they at least put in the girl's name?" I shrugged saying, "They did but they said it's not her real name. They put in Adair and a description of her." Avery nodded, "If anyone can get her real name, it's you."

Paige warned, "Be safe." I smiled saying, "Of course." Dax scoffed, "You know we say it to you because you are often not safe and do reckless things when you go alone." I argued, "You say I do reckless things when you're with me too … so, when you think about it… there is no winning on that front for me." He blew out his breath as I smiled at him.

I put my mask on and took one of our cars. The girl didn't live too far from here. Hopefully, I'd gotten the alert soon enough that I could beat them to her and she'd remain oblivious to the Supernatural world. Since I was me and this was my life… I did not get my wish of being on time.

I saw them throwing the girl, based on her description, in the back of the van when I got to the parking lot of her building, which absolutely should be condemned. They weren't even looking around and they were literally out in the open. Why the hell were they being so sloppy?

Something about the girl looked familiar, but I shoved that aside and followed them at a distance. The second they were on a service road I took out my gun and shot out their tires. They lost control. I actually yelled, "REALLY? Supernatural reflexes don't apply to the Ring people? Naturally…. Normally, they are better drivers… what the heck?!"

They hit a tree, and I could hear the girl in the back crying. I quickly went around to the front, putting my silencer on as I went. I shot both kidnappers on sight. They were Demons. I grumbled, "This is really on you… Because you should totally have better reflexes. Now I have to explain… to the girl in the back. You really made my life more complicated… you were just supposed to pull over because of a FLAT TIRE! Jerks."

I walked around to the back, hitting buttons on my watch that would text Valentina I needed a clean-up at my location. I timed it to send in five minutes, so I didn't have her shimmer in and have to explain that to the girl who didn't know about Supernatural's.

I opened the back of the van and looked at the girl who scrambled away from me, ready to fight. Interesting instincts. I tilted my head noting she was something for sure. I was certain she was a partial Werewolf mixed with something else. She felt exactly like Lux did to me. I'd never met anyone else the same mix as him.

I held my hands up saying, "I'll help you get home, I promise." She whispered, "You have on a mask." I reasoned, "Well, yes… that's true… but they didn't, and they kidnapped you. I'm rescuing you. I guess we are doing this back to front, in your mind…" Humans would easily expect the other way around and she had no idea there was Ring or opposition to it.

She studied me for several minutes then nodded. I cut her zip ties off and got her into my car. She was shaking really badly. She whispered, "Thanks for saving me from those weirdos. They were crazy." I took off my mask and she continued to study me.

I asked, "Why do you say that?" She snorted, "They said they were Demons. I think they actually believed that. Can you imagine? Demons. They need mental help." I replied, "We could all use some help. I'm Melanie but people call me Ashley. What's your name?"

She sighed, "People call me Adair around here." I asked, "What's your real name? Because… trust me, I'm kind of the expert on saying people call me Ashley… when my name is Melanie. So…" She admitted, "My mom said I can't tell people my real name."

I asked, "Where is your mom?" Adair sighed, "Off with her boyfriend of the month." I snorted, "Well, I won't tell your mom if you want to tell me your real name. I don't tell anyone that I've told some people my real name… I actually usually have someone with me to say my name. I've been told I'm a truly atrocious liar… which sounds harsh… I'm not great… which is annoying… but atrocious seems harsh." She snickered but didn't answer.

I put on the radio which Adair started to hum to. Wow… she had a great voice. I told her, "I play in a band. If you want, you could sing with us sometime." She smiled admitting, "I love to sing." I nodded, "I'd imagine so. You hum very well… so logically you are a good singer."

Adair said, "Maybe I could sing with you guys. I usually work to help keep the electricity on in my apartment. Do you guys pay?" I looked at her, "Your mom doesn't keep up with the bills? Yes, I pay people. We get paid for the gigs… so it wasn't like a for fun offer… though we do play together for fun sometimes…"

Adair sighed, "No, my mom doesn't pay for anything. The rent is usually paid by her boyfriend of the month. Sometimes her boyfriend's pay everything so I don't bother them. Or the landlord doesn't. My mom thinks I try to steal her boyfriends, but I don't. They're creepy." Fury filled me.

I told her, "Yeah my aunt's husband is a creep, so I get it. How old are you?" She smiled, "Thank you for saving me. I didn't say it back there, but thanks. I just turned sixteen recently."

I told her, "Saving people is my thing. Don't worry about it. I teach self-defense classes. You should stop by." Really, she should. She was Supernatural; she just didn't know it. Her Supernatural genes meant she'd be good at fighting; she just needed to train.

Adair's face lit up. She whispered, "Really? Where?" I parked at a hotel and wrote down the address. I told her, "Don't go back to your apartment. I'll get it shut down for some reason and set you up with a new place. Ok, Adair?" I was hoping if I said her name enough, she'd want to tell me her real one. I'd know better than anyone you just want to hear your actual name sometimes.

She whispered, "Odette. My real name is Odette." I smiled, thanking science for that win. I replied, "That's a beautiful name. What's your last name?" She sighed, "I don't have one. Well, not that I know of. My mom is super paranoid about someone taking me from her." Not paranoid enough considering someone had just successfully taken her.

I asked, "Why would she be?" Odette explained, "My older brother's dad took him from her. My brother didn't like her though, so I don't think his dad took him so much as he willingly left. I miss him." I offered, "I could help you find him." Odette smiled, "Thanks. I'm looking for him myself though. I'll find him."

I nodded, "If you change your mind, I'll help you." She nodded. I asked, "So is your mom scared your dad will take you too?" Odette frowned, "She says so. All I know about my dad is he gave me some blood disorder and doesn't want me. So, I don't know why she's worried he'll take me."

I frowned knowing that the chances that was a lie were highly likely. That was my guess since this girl had NO human blood and no Supernatural had a blood disorder unless they were being poisoned. I asked, "Do you move a lot?"

Odette nodded, "Oh yeah. Ever since my brother left, my mom shuffles us from one place to the next following some guy. They eventually break up with her. She has a few days of wallowing with ice cream and wine, then we move onto the next city and guy." I frowned.

I took out an extra phone I kept on hand and handed it to her. I said, "If you ever need me, call. If I don't see you Thursday for self-defense classes, I'll come looking for you. Your new apartment address and keys will be delivered to you tomorrow. The hotel is paid for."

Odette asked, "Why are you helping me?" I told her, "Helping people is what I do. My family abandoned me too, but I've made new friends. They've practically become my family. You can do the same." She nodded tentatively at me.

I explained, "The front desk clerk will just give you a key. Call if you need anything… seriously. I'll send someone… or come myself. It depends on what's going on." Odette smiled and got out of the car. I watched her get inside safely.

My inside man texted he'd given her the key. Now I needed to handle her new place. I'd make sure she had everything paid for so she could be a kid. She deserved that. Everyone did. I couldn't have it, but I could give it to Odette. I drove away planning how to keep her safe.

Flashback Ends

I shook off the past. I'd gotten Odette to open up with us. She'd learned self-defense and took to it easily like I thought. Now, she was just gone. I was supposed to be able to find people. My friends thought I was being obsessive about it… and I was… but people should NOT be able to hide from me like this. She needed us… needed me. She was only sixteen.

Because of this ordeal, my friends decided I needed a vacation after our gig in Louisiana. I did NOT need a vacation. LORD knows the trouble my brother could get into while I was missing for two weeks. Without me watching his dang back… he'd be dead. Multiple times over by now. My friends all PROMISED they would watch out for him.

This was all because of Morgana. That vapid, evil hiding Odette from me woman… If I could find the new name she was going by… I would be going to kick her butt to the east river! Morgana was Odette's missing in action mother. She'd returned, apparently.

I imagined she flew in on her broomstick. The Wicked Witch of Nashville was on the loose. I hadn't heard from Odette for a few days, then she'd missed a gig. She loved to sing in our band, and I paid her generously when she did.

She had an amazing voice everyone loved… she was popular with our band and fans. Odette was beautiful with blond hair and blue eyes. She was a sweet kid despite being abandoned by her mother. Even after being kidnapped... albeit briefly… she was still the kindest soul with a killer voice.

We were working up to telling her about the Supernatural world. Sierra came up with the plan because… I was not exactly subtle and usually blurted things out. Odette was skittish as it was… So we had a plan.

After she'd missed the gig, I'd gone to her apartment and found the phone I'd given her with a note. A note from Morgana to leave her daughter alone… she threatened me. ME! Like I would care. My life was in constant danger for a multitude of reasons.

I couldn't stop my snort. Leave her alone? Like she did? My mother would NEVER do what she did to Odette. It wasn't fair that my mom was murdered and mother's like Morgana were still out there. I didn't have much to go in my search for finding Odette's dad.

None of the men I could find linked to her wretched mother had a blood disorder, which confirmed my suspicions that Odette was taking some placebo thinking it was for a disorder, so she didn't look for her dad. I really didn't know what Werewolf could even have a condition. I'd never met the evil woman who happened to be her mother… so I couldn't tell. If she did have some weird disease she kept it on the down low.

I'd tried to get Odette to stop taking the tablets, but she'd shut down about it. I guessed that she'd tried that before, but she wouldn't talk about it. I couldn't get it out of her what happened. I just needed more time with her. Time I no longer had, because Morgana just up and disappeared with her.

Morgana always changed their names. I had to hope that Odette went to Black Mountain or one of their allies. I'd given her all the city names the good packs were in. I'd told her to try to convince Morgana to try them out.

I nearly screamed and smashed things. I ran The Resistance for goodness sake, and I couldn't find my friend! Odette looked up to me, and I was letting her down. I was trying to run down patterns of names Morgana chose for them.

I knew living in Nashville Odette was called Adair Vertend. Odette didn't tell me any of her other fake names though before moving here. Or who the hell they were hiding from. Gosh darn Morgana's timing! I just wanted to help Odette.

She needed someone to look out for her. She had a mother… in a way. She was alone in this world though. I knew what that felt like. I knew how much it hurt. My mom was dead, but I didn't get ferreted away in the middle of the freaking night because I made some friends.

At least the gun I'd given her was gone. Hopefully, she still had that to protect herself. Plus, I had the knowledge she could defend herself now. She was really good. I looked up at the sky, glaring. This was yet another failure on the part of Selene.

She was supposed be the Moon Goddess, but she was more like the moon's joke. At this point I was convinced Selene didn't know her head from her behind. She had to be the most worthless goddess of all time. The Resistance shouldn't exist because the RING shouldn't exist.

Selene turned her back on me when I was fourteen, but she'd turned her back on the people I helped long ago. When I'd arrived… I had NO clue how sheltered I was. I thought packs were like my home pack and the allies.

Now I knew…. when the Alpha is bad… it can all go south. People around here paid with Omegas lives for protection from Hunters. Instead of hunting them their DANG selves like ranked wolves were supposed to do, Black Path sent in wolf less and teenagers under the age of sixteen to help Hunters.

I still honestly couldn't believe they didn't know we hadn't been helping since I got here. I was a suspect several times, but I'd passed their tests. All because they wouldn't ever ask me directly. I was certain they thought there was no way I could outsmart them. My mind flashed back to the day I got the call about Jason. My heart had stopped.

Flashback

My phone rang. I frowned seeing who was calling. It was JC. JC was a wolf less pack member in Black Path like me. He'd never expected to get a wolf though… so he wasn't exactly like me in that aspect. He was with one of the other pack members who hadn't turned sixteen yet.

I answered, "JC, are you ok?" JC sighed, "I think you'll be mad if we don't tell you this." I questioned, "Tell me what?" JC sighed, "Your brother infiltrated a Hunting ring while you were being hunted by the pack then punished for winning." My breath caught in my throat.

I shouted, "HOW THE ACTUAL HELL DID WE NOT KNOW THAT?!" JC sighed, "You know how. You were being hunted by the pack and they kept it pretty close to the vest. He was doing great, but Dante showed up instead of Nate. He knew him."

I scoffed, “How could he be doing great?! They knew he was a freaking Werewolf the whole time. Where is my brother?” JC evaded, “He’s in bad shape. I don’t think he’s going to make it.” I couldn’t breathe.

Valentina came up beside me asking, “Mel, what’s wrong?” I demanded, “JC, you tell me where my brother is RIGHT NOW AND YOU MAKE SURE HE DOESN’T DIE BEFORE I GET THERE!” Valentina’s jaw dropped.

JC begrudgingly told me, “We are in that building on the outskirts of Nashville. I don’t know if you can save him this time, Mel. They worked him over good.” I warned, “You’d best get on YOUR KNEES and PRAY I can save him.”

A sob bubbled up, “He can’t die… so…. I can save him! You should’ve texted me the SECOND Dante made him!” Valentina said, “Sierra just got you out of the hole after you were being hunted by the pack. When was he going to tell you?” I replied, “He could’ve told someone!” She made a face that said I was right.

This was fixable… I could fix my brother. I had Xander’s number memorized. He’d come get Jason, and I’d deal with the fallout. He’d save my brother. They were best friends. This was fine. Everything was absolutely fine.

I hung up the phone then looked at Valentina. I told her, “I need to get to the Hunter building Dante prefers in Nashville. I’m honestly shocked this isn’t being done at his headquarters. Get me there and then get the hell out of there. Let everyone in the Resistance know what’s going on. I’ll do what I have to do to save Jason. That might mean I might not come back.”

Valentina’s eyes filled with tears, “Mel….” I shrugged, “If I have to... I’m calling Xander. If he rejects me… he’ll still save Jason. I just…” I cut off as a sob reached my throat at the thought of my Xander rejecting me. Valentina rubbed my back.

She told me, “You know I understand why you have to save Beta Jason, but you’re not old enough to be rejected officially. He could change his mind even if he says something hateful and stupid today.” I knew she understood why I had to save my brother.

Valentina and Virgil had an older brother. One who knew what had happened to them. He’d tried to help them, but in the end… it came down to his children or them. He’d told them he’d tried to get them taken to the nicest place he could. They still kept tabs on him and his family through me now.

That was the reason they understood more than any of my friends why I couldn’t just give up on my brother. These last few years... sucked, but there were fourteen years when Jason was the best big brother with Tristan. No matter what… he was my brother. That meant something to me, even if being his half-sister meant nothing to him.

Valentina grabbed my hand, then shimmered us outside the building. I could smell the blood from where I stood. I wouldn't have needed anyone to tell me it was Jason’s. I knew that scent like the back of my hand.

I promptly threw up my lunch. What had they done to him? Valentina rubbed my back, “It’s ok.” I told her, “Get out of here. Warn everyone. I don’t know what will happen to me after this.” Valentina had tears in her eyes.

She told me, “Let me know if you need me to take Beta Jason home. If they dare put you in a dungeon then we will get you out.” My gut clenched.

Ever since my sixteenth birthday… and what followed… I couldn't be in enclosed dark spaces. It wasn’t great before my birthday, but after… I’d have a panic attack. Maybe that would fade… one day…. It hadn’t happened that long ago… it felt like a lifetime since everything changed though, and I didn’t shift.

I could do a lot of other things… but dark enclosed spaces? I panicked. I shook myself and told her, “I’ll survive. It’s what I do.” Valentina rubbed my arm saying, “I know you believe your Xander is your mate. He can’t allow that to happen you if he is.”

“Even if, and I don’t think he would reject you especially when he officially can’t, you’re not eighteen. Causing you pain would hurt him.” She was hopefully right.

I nodded to her but she didn't shimmer away. She said, "I'm with you, always. If my brother was in there I'd need someone by my side to see him. This is a big moment for you to see him again." Ok… she was right. My hands were shaking a little bit. I was going to see my big brother for the first time since everything changed. We walked in the building together to see the shape my brother was in.

End of Flashback

Mason touched my arm pulling me back to reality. He asked, "Are you ok Ashley?" I shook myself because we had a gig to play. I nodded, my voice hoarse when I told him, "Yep, fine." Everyone looked at me like they didn't believe me.

To be fair, I was lying and it wasn't my forte. No matter how hard I practiced…my lying skills never improved. Evading? Yes. Lying? Nope. In truth, my heart ached. I missed Jason. I missed my home. My throat closed as I thought… I miss my Xander. I miss him. I miss my wolf… she had to be real… I was pretty sure she was.

Blair told us last year that her mate told her that Hunters can't fight so there was no way I had Hunter blood. Deep down, I knew that about Hunters because I'd been taught that. I just didn't tell them that. I did watch as they looked into it and discovered her mate was right.

They'd been furious and I admitted it hurt because Alpha Peter and Jason knew that. Every single member of Red Run did along with the allies. Every single person in my home pack knew that and I was still here rejected and banished by them.

Even though they REFUSED to acknowledge I was the one saving them, they'd always known I had exceptional fighting skills. They all knew, and they still abandoned me. Which meant Slade Carter killed my family…. and so far, he'd gotten away with. Alpha Peter had never questioned me about that night, so they didn't know I knew the identity of the man who'd shot them.

All that meant to me was either Slade was a different type of Supernatural working with Hunters and running their group. Or… hope filled me that my dad… that Drake McAlister really was my father. That thought brought up more questions.

Where was my wolf? Why did she abandon me? Did she really tell me to fight that night? If yes, that meant she didn't fail me. I'd failed her and I didn't like to fail. I was pretty bad at it actually. I took failure worse than most people I knew.

I shoved those thoughts aside as we walked out onstage and I let my mind go numb while playing the notes on the guitar and lost myself in the music. I remembered how Tristan had taught me how to play the electric guitar every time I played.

I missed his smile. I missed his voice. Not for the first time my thoughts went to the questions I had. Why did he have to come home that night? That same scenario had happened countless times. None of them had ever come home early. Why did it have to be that night? Where were the pack Warriors? Why didn't they save us?

Before I knew it the concert was over, and we packed up our stuff. Everyone was still eyeing me. Sierra touched my side gently saying, "It's a good time to get away. I know the past knocks on your mind harder with the upcoming days." She was right.

It was almost the anniversary of Tristan, mom, and Dad's deaths. I'd never seen where they were buried since it was in Red Run. I couldn't visit them or even say goodbye properly. I had my spot I went to be close to them though, with dedicated headstones for them though. I had them properly maintained so it remained nice.

Everyone else gave Sierra and I hugs. I looked at Hendrick before asking, "You've got Jason, right? I know Dax and Caine… just don't like him." Hendrick hugged me whispering, "Go be a normal kid and have fun on vacation. I've got this, I promise." I nodded, "I know." Hendrick squeezed me and let me go.

Addison pouted, "I wish I was going with you. My dad sucks." I snorted, "You are preaching to the choir. Literally all of us agree… but, you are in charge of the Warriors… which he totally didn't see coming and it made his face turn all red." She smiled agreeing, "That's true. Have fun guys!" She left.

I sat down struggling with leaving them with everything. Sierra sighed, "We need to get moving." She was right. We walked back out up to the box where a Ring member was. I quickly snapped his neck. We spilled alcohol on him staging the accident the way we'd planned.

Once we walked out the most delicious scent reached me. I turned in the opposite direction that we were supposed to go. It was hardly my fault… that scent was a sugar cookie…and I loved them. It was also a sugar cookie I desperately wanted.

My mouth was actually watering. I'd never smelled something so good. Sierra linked, "What are you doing?" I didn't answer because…. well. I didn't actually know the answer. I just needed to get to that cookie.

We could leave as soon as I had my cookie. It smelled even better than the ones my mom and grandma made at Christmas time. Sierra linked, "Seriously, you don't smell the chocolate pie?" No… I was pretty sure her wolf was crazy. Right along with her. That was NOT a chocolate scent.

I could tell I was getting closer to my delicious cookie. We turned the corner… and I was practically on top of it. Then the world shifted. My jaw dropped in actual shock because Sierra's mate was Phil… Xander's Beta. Phil Kruthers was here… but…that meant someone else was too…since he was always with Xander.

My knees shook when I heard my mate's voice. It was mixed with Oden declaring me his. His. He'd said I was his….That was everything I had ever wanted to be. Everything I thought I would never be.

I silently prayed, "Any god up there that's not a jerk… please…. Please let the picture he gave those models of me be from far away with dance make up on…. and when I was younger…. other women recognized the older version but he's a man… so… just do me this solid of not letting him recognize me… not yet. Just give me one night."

My gaze felt like it went to Xander in slow motion. Had time actually slowed down? I took him in and considered the fact that my jaw might need to be surgically repaired. Xander looked better in person than he did in videos.

His scent his me. Oh my gosh… HE was the sugar cookie! This is what I get for not letting Hendrick put his scent in the report. How dare no one EVER tell me from my old pack… Elise… She could've mentioned it.

I knew practically ever scent of everyone in his family, but I'd blocked myself out from knowing his. That was error on my part. A very big one….since I'd literally come drooling towards his…but there was nothing I could do about it now.

Our eyes met, just like the movies. Then an intense pain hit me hard. Did he reject me in a glance somehow? Did he know who I really was? I didn't even get to say hi. This was so not going like any of my plans, because I couldn't stop screaming in pain.

Logically, I knew I needed to stop screaming. We couldn't be seen here after everyone left… we'd killed someone. I couldn't stop though because this pain was killing me. Suddenly I felt warm and tingly all over.

Someone was holding me and based on the scent it was Xander. That made the pain somewhat tolerable. He was holding me. Did a god answer my prayer about the picture he had? Was it Aesir? Was he on my side?

The pain overwhelmed me, and I literally felt everything leaving my mind. It felt like someone was drilling into my head. Suddenly I felt tile beneath me and the warmth and tingles left. I needed to move…. Sierra needed me.

I tried to crawl, but the pain was unbearable again. The warmth and tingles came back. I heard someone urge, "FIGHT! COME ON! Mate is here this time! We can do this!" Fight? What in the French toast was going on? Who did I need to fight? Was Sierra safe? What had just happened? Everything was a blur.

Fight… well… If someone would stop drilling on my head... I was positive I could beat whoever it was. I leaned into the warmth I felt because somehow there was strength coming from it and… it was the most comforting thing I'd felt since the day I was sent away from my home pack.

I felt something prick my arm. I knew that feeling… it was a drug. Well… the joke was on whoever did that. I don't know if they wanted to sedate me, but it wouldn't work. I did feel lighter but that wouldn't last long.

I heard the most beautiful voice tell me I was ok. I'd believe that voice any day. Whoever it was… sounded like a god himself. Who could doubt him? Why was that voice familiar? Did I care at the moment? Nope. Not me.

I wasn't going to doubt him either… maybe if Selene sounded like that, I'd believe her too. I nearly laughed at my own joke. I'd never believe a word out of her mouth at this point, even if she dared to speak to me.

Someone sighed, "Finally." Who was that? Wasn't I with Sierra? That wasn't her. I felt so comfortable and safe. Those were odd feelings I'd not felt in six years. Why did I feel this way? I could've opened my eyes, but I didn't want to. I wanted to stay here forever.

Eventually someone said, "Open your eyes right now." Demanding and rude…. What an obnoxious annoying voice that I didn't recognize. I wanted to stay in the warmth with the god-like voice….that my brain was nagging me I knew…the nagging and the demanding voice needed to cut it out.

She growled, "Open your eyes." Ugh! I said no nagging. FINE! I opened my eyes and inhaled. Sugar cookie….that was right! I needed to find the sugar cookie! That's what I was looking for. I jumped up and looked around.

I found Sierra….but we were definitely not in the place I remember us being in. What the heck happened? She linked, "What the hell happened to you? You went down and screamed. I've seen you whipped without screaming that loud." Huh?

Well…to be fair it did hurt…a lot. Did I get shot in the head? That would've been….no…I touched my head but didn't feel a wound.

The nagging voice sighed, "Look AROUND the room. Remember the Sugar Cookie. I know you smell it. Come on you can do this. Spot the sugar cookie smell." Who was that and why were they nagging me?

Sierra linked, "Mel, get it together. No one besides me is talking." Rude…someone definitely was. The nagging voice sighed, "I know this is new and all but don't be a crazy person. LOOK for the sugar cookie." Again with the demands with no explanations.

Then Phil Kruthers spoke. I whirled and found him. It all came back to me….that was real….he was there and Sierra was his….but that meant….I turned and found Xander. His eyes looked worried but not angry…some god answered my prayer about that picture being far away and when I was younger.

The nagging voice purred, "MINE!" I screamed and covered my face. MY WOLF? MY WOLF HAD BEEN TALKING?! I looked at Xander wide eyed. I linked my wolf yelling at her, "WHERE THE HELL HAVE YOU BEEN?"

She answered, "Trapped in your mind. It was NOT fun. Let's not do that again." I questioned, "How were you trapped? Is that even possible? I mean…it clearly is…since…we are here. Seeing Xander unlocked you…that's….something…and weird….but you're here… Oh gosh…what's your name?"

She chuckled, "Yes, let's start this over. I'm your wolf, Freya. I don't know how it's possible the event is all fuzzy to me. I do feel there was magic involved but we will remember more now that I'm able to reach you as I should be." Magic.

Now that she said it was pretty obvious. I had suspects but they weren't powerful enough…even combined. Freya quietly said, "It will probably come slowly. I'm going through your memories right now. I'm so sorry. I know you needed me." Tears filled my eyes.

I replied, "You told me to fight and I failed you. This is my fault." She disagreed, "You did fight. You are the perfect choice and fit for me." At least she didn't blame me. I had her now thought and that meant everything…. could all be different. I had a wolf.

Jason could…..well he could take everything he'd said back…this was proof…I was his full blooded sister. Xander and I could be together. I could still stay out of Jason's way if that's what he wanted but…...I could be with Xander.

Xander spoke soothingly, easily figuring out why I was panicking. My wolf was talking to me. Yeah….that was a bit of a shock after four years of NOTHING! Freya snorted, "Hey! That wasn't my fault! It wasn't your fault either, but it wasn't my fault either."

I agreed, "I know it's not our fault. Am I going to shift tonight?" Freya sighed, "I'm too weak right now. I'm getting stronger though." Oh no. A horrible thought came to me. I blurted out, "Will we shift? Like ever? Or are you trapped in my head….like you were without being able to talk to me?" That would be horrible for her.

Freya replied, "We will shift. I just don't know when. I do know we need to stick by mate though." I replied, "You know that we can't do that long term…if you're going through my memories. He doesn't actually want us. I go by Ashley Griffen….and the odds are that's who he thinks I am. Sierra would've called me Ashley."

Freya growled, "That's not true. Oden and Xander want us. Your memories are strange, but the loophole of being with us is there if he even made that promise which I doubt." She was technically correct being Ashley Griffen was the loophole.

I was drowning in Xander's ocean blue eyes. I wanted to stay with him…forever. Freya said, "And we will." She was confident…that was good. Sierra appeared in the way of my staring contest. She linked, "Tori contacted Freya! You really have a wolf, Mel." She'd known how obliterating and hard it was for me not to have one all these years.

I didn't know what was going on and my emotions all came crashing down. It was all for nothing. All the horrible things Jason had said to me after my birthday….being banished…it was for no reason. The McAlister's had all abandoned me…but they were wrong.

Jason wasn't my half-brother. He was my full on brother. Drake McAlister was my father. It was as if several pieces of me clicked back into place. Freya whispered, "I'm so sorry you suffered so much Melanie."

I cried harder because she was in pain this whole time. She was with me but couldn't talk to me and that was horrible. How could someone do this to me? How could Selene let this happen? Freya whispered again, "I don't know." It seemed to genuinely bother Freya that Selene let us hurt this way.

Xander wrapped me back up in his arms. I was now hysterically sobbing because I never wanted to leave his embrace, and I'd probably have to. The odds were that he'd hate me when he found out the truth of who I was.

I asked my wolf, "Did it hurt you to be locked away?" Frey seemed to cringe answering, "You suffered, as did I." I cried for both of us. I told her, "If I knew you were locked away inside me…..I'd have found a way to bring you out." Freya replied, "I know."

I asked her, "It's because of Xander you're with me now, isn't it? You were freed because of him." Freya purred, "It does seems likely. Wouldn't you break any hold on you to get to him?" Yes, I would but she knew that because she had my memories and knew what I'd done for him.

Freya laughed, "Oden is actually pretty funny. You should say something to our Xander. He is very worried about you." I looked up into his eyes and the concern I saw reflected back melted me. It had been a long time since someone looked at me with that much love and concern in their eyes.

It made me feel like a fraud because he didn't know me. All the cute things I'd planned over the years of what I'd say to him….flew out of my head. I simply said hi. HI?! After YEARS of planning our first meeting….I went with hi? Open up the heavens and take me now.

Sierra linked, "That's so not on the list of the things you planned to say to him." I replied, "Please kill me here and now…Did I really just SQUEAK hi?!" She answered, "Yes, but he finds it adorable. Let's consider it a win you're not ranting nervously. This is such progress for you and I'm so proud of you right now." I wasn't!

When he called me Ashley Freya and I growled. I didn't like another girl's name coming out of his mouth. I linked Freya, "DANG, FREYA! Be cool! We are Ashley…too….so…he means us." Freya growled, "No. WE are Freya and MELANIE!" I reasoned, "He doesn't know that." Freya disagreed, "I wouldn't be so sure." I was sure.

He'd freak out if he knew I was Melanie McAlister. No one knew Ashley Griffen was Melanie McAlister outside of Black Path. He would leave and reject me. Freya snarled, "No, he wouldn't." I replied, "Just be glad he clearly has a picture from far away…obviously in full dance makeup mode to give to those model like girls he sleeps with."

She snarled, "I will rip all their lying heads off." I replied, "That's hardly …well…they….liars?" She scoffed, "He has no chosen mate. So, clearly they lied." I offered, "Or it fell through… not that I found any paperwork….about them staying in the Luna suites…and I looked." She growled, "Liars." Maybe.

I linked Sierra, "You heard him say Lovebug, right?" She answered, "Yes, and it's the most adorable thing I've ever heard." It really was. My eyes filled with tears. Because the endearment matched with what people called me for fourteen years. I used to be Ladybug.

My heart clenched at the loss of my family, but it wasn't as bad with Xander here. Phil was talking, but I couldn't hear him. My own thoughts and being lost in the fact that Xander really was here with me. We were together. I couldn't stop myself from touching his face…it was hardly my fault…. He was so beautiful. I was in his arms. This was real. I had a wolf….maybe…..maybe this could work out.

Xander conjured our things and mine to his room. Holy crap. Freya purred, "Good." Sierra linked me, "Hey, this is a good thing. You can finally live out those fantasies we've caught you masturbating to. Except this time Xander will be there."

I gasped, "SHUT UP! You guys were the ones who said I need an orgasm. Then you just waltz into my room...without knocking!" Sierra snickered, "You did need one." Yet they barged in…that was on them. Freya agreed, "It was. You have nothing to be ashamed of. Masturbating is perfectly normal."

Sierra linked, "Your Xander brings up a good question. Are you ok? This is a big deal." That was an incredibly complicated question. I had never been better….or more confused in my entire life. If I had a wolf….was everything for nothing? Every scar…..everything I'd let myself endure….No I still deserved that. My family was dead.

Freya whispered, "You didn't deserve any of that. That should never have happened." Xander took my hand, and I lost my train of thought. We walked outside. We were really out of the country. We were in a mansion in Switzerland.

I had this mansion and schematics plugged into ILYX in case anything happened here but I never thought I'd see it in person. I couldn't stop talking about it until Xander wrapped his arms around me and complimented me. No one called me beautiful anymore…Lux Bartlett did compliment me…but it was flirting…that probably still counted. Most men and boys just said they'd possess me.

Compliments outside my friends? Nope…those didn't happen. Well, Lux did…he was a flirt though and he was kind about it. I couldn't stop myself from melting into my mate which had Freya purring in my head.

I stuck my tongue out at Sierra when she commented on how Xander stopped my rant. Xander popped away with me when the alarm sounded. He would probably freak out if I put in his code…right? That would probably turn into a whole thing.

Freya snorted, "Yes, let's not admit we can turn of the alarm at all the Connor's homes." Fine…that was reasonable. That seemed like a later revelation to let them in on. He quickly put in a code. His muscles were distracting.

Freya linked, "He offered to give you a tour." I replied, "I know the schematics of this house. So, I know where all the rooms are." She snorted, "Just go on the tour." Ok…but I already knew where all the rooms were.

He called me his Lovebug and warmth filled me. Freya purred, "Let's go throw him down in the next room we get to. He's so sexy." He was very sexy. I replied, "I'm pretty sure if we threw him down he could roll... and pin us…throw is…the wrong word…we could tackle him." She hummed, "Fine. Tackling is also fine."

That didn't seem like the right move either. She groaned, "I don't mean as a fighting move." I replied, "How else does one tackle people? We aren't playing football…well.. American football…we are in Europe and they call soccer football…and you can't tackle people in…"

She cut me off, “You are funny.” It was good she thought that. I asked her, “How many humans have you had before me?” Freya answered, “None. You are my first. I’ve been around though for a long time because I have been waiting for the perfect human.” I apologized “I’m sorry you got me then.”

Freya snorted, “Nonsense! You’re perfect and none of this was your fault. I’m proud of you. You are so smart! You’ve invented things for Xander to be safer. You’ve started the Resistance and you’ve started taking the Ring down. Now with mate and his family we can dismantle them.”

I questioned, “You’re proud of me?” Freya answered, “Yes, and mate will be proud too. Your parents would be too. No one is going to be proud of letting yourself get beaten to a pulp but hey you can’t win them all. No one has a perfect record in life.”

For the first time, I felt embarrassed of my actions. Maybe Xander wouldn’t find out about that. Freya snorted, “Optimism. I like it. It feels like the first moment you’ve had it since I came to you.” I rolled my eyes at her while thinking she might be right. She should know my life doesn’t go anywhere near happy things happening in my life.

My approach to everything was the glass is half full and someone was about to drink it. It was a better way for me to view life. Xander said he had a mission he needed to leave for, but I already knew that. Freya snorted, “Yeah, maybe we wait on the whole knowing his every second and move.”

I replied, “He makes last minute decisions…that I have to catch up on….but this is a mission…of course I know about that. It was planned…that’s obvious.” She snorted.

I was happy that we had two weeks here though. Two whole weeks. Maybe it could just be us for two weeks before everything came crashing down. That’s more than I thought I’d ever get with him. I lived my life up until now on fantasy’s. I could literally go my entire life with two weeks’ worth of actual Xander.

Freya told me, “It will be a lifetime of memories.” She really was optimistic. That was probably good since I wasn’t anymore. Xander took me to the library and off handedly mentioned he’d read the *Thoroughbred* series. I physically jolted because I hadn’t read it since I left, but it was still my favorite.

It was a silly notion but I felt the book series let me down when no one in Red Run clicked onto my name as Ashley Griffen. Freya surmised, “Mate knows who we really are.” I reasoned, “Jason probably didn’t tell him I read that book series. He doesn’t know….he just might know that Ashley Griffen….isn’t my real name…or it’s just a general comment.” Which flustered me a little bit.

She replied, “Keep in mind, I know the answer to this question. What’s the probability he thinks the name and the name you gave for Sierra is a coincidence?” I admitted, “Less than one percent…but that doesn’t mean he knows I’m Melanie. He doesn’t. Because the probability he would react with anger is over ninety-nine percent.”

She hummed, “Those are based on things your brother, old Alpha, current pack, and family members said. Not our mate.” That was true…but it was still the probability. Xander walked over and caged me in his arms.

I’d imagine he’d gotten many people into this position who didn’t feel safe…except the model like blondes he liked…and had been with. Freya snarled, “Don’t think about them right now.” Easy for her to say…I wasn’t blonde…but he was attracted to me…so that was something.

I was trying to remember a time when I felt safer than I did caged in his arms, but I was drawing a blank. Freya was purring in my head. How did people do this? I’d almost answered her out loud a million times. All those thoughts flew out of my mind when my lips met Xander’s. It was better than I’d ever imagined…. and I’d fantasized about it a lot.

When he pulled back...I couldn’t help the small but loudly terrified part of me that was scared he would break me. He could. I needed him now that we’d met…this pull between us was different than I’d anticipated. Before all I had was longing for him now…it was all consuming.

What if he rejected me? Would I lose my wolf again? Freya whimpered in my head. She stated, “You will never lose me again.” She didn’t know that though. She was a new wolf. She huffed, “I’m an old wolf. I’m just new to having a human.” Interesting.

Xander was upset. Freya replied, "He thinks you are scared because he's an Alpha Enforcer." Well, I didn't know how to tell him....that wasn't the problem at all. I was scared he'd leave me. Because I was Melanie McAlister....the family killer.

Freya growled, "That wasn't your fault! Besides, there's someone off about that too." I questioned, "What do you mean?" Freya sighed, "I don't know yet. It just feels off. Besides, there you go. Mate just promised never to hurt you physically OR emotionally. Which means he won't reject you. He can't. He just promised."

I reminded her, "He also promised Jason he would reject me. What if this hurts him?" Freya sighed, "You don't know he really did that. Besides, we already discussed the loophole. You are still Ashley Griffen. Besides, Jason could've been hurting and he didn't want you to come home and see if Xander was really yours."

I bristled, "I've always known that he was mine." Freya chuckled, "I know." I startled a little because she didn't question that I knew. In fact, she knew that I knew. That was weird. Most people assumed I was a kid with a crush. Even the wolves.

My head was such a mess and my tears started all over again. This could work....really actually work now. It was unquestionable now that I was Drake McAlister's daughter. Maybe.....if I stayed out of Red Run's way....they wouldn't fight me being with Xander.

I didn't have to go to events or meetings there. It stopped being my home four years ago when Alpha Peter banished me. Xander made assurances to me. If only the problem was my lack of a wolf....it was far more complicated than my wolf being locked away.

I never really considered my lack a wolf the problem with Xander since I'd still been freakishly good at fighting without one. I was still a Lead Female Warrior. In fact, I was the youngest Lead Warrior ever ...male or Female.

Freya linked, "Because we are special." Sure. Special. That was me....the freak of a wolf. I asked Freya, "Will silver and wolfsbane affect me now?" Freya answered, "No." Then she clammed up. I didn't want to upset her since I'd just gotten her so....I physically forced myself to not keep talking.

Xander referred to our email where I'd said he was hot. Dang it....He had to read that part? Freya laughed but didn't say anything on insight from Oden about that. She told me, "I'm actually a little tired. I need to rest. It was exhausting working through that barrier. I'll be around though. I won't leave you again." I sighed in relief.

I focused on Xander. Gosh...he was like photoshopped or something. Definitely sculpted by the gods... for sure. He kissed me again. My thought trending towards touching him. Which was different. Freya snorted, "It's natural." I replied, "Not for me." I wanted to lick every inch of him She purred, "That's a great idea."

He called me beautiful again and stopped talking. Freya hummed, "He's normal." Yes, well comments about my body usually followed a guy saying they wanted to have sex with me. Lux was respectful and playful about it, but that was the closet I'd gotten to flirting.

To be fair, he flirted...I didn't...because I just only ever wanted Xander. I knew I wanted to just be here with him and forget the real world. I wanted to forget why as Melanie McAlister I couldn't be with my Xander. I wanted to be in this bubble....with him.

To my shock, he agreed. Freya said, "He is our mate. He will do anything to make us happy. Plus, he knows." I asked, "Did Oden say they knew?" She admitted, "No." I hummed, "So, he doesn't know." She argued, "I think he does." Thinking was not knowing.

I pondered his words again. He'd said the words what I wanted. I couldn't remember the last time an Alpha had said that to me. I couldn't stop myself from kissing him.... Gosh...he was perfect. Xander pulled back all too soon. I frowned then smelled other people in the room.

Sierra linked me, "One, I can't believe we actually got into a room without you noticing. You're already relaxed. More than ever. I like it. Second, kissing nice! I like it. You went from never being kissed to making out. I'm so here for this." I blushed.

We discussed some valid point regarding the weather. I sighed. I did actually have money, but what I had went to my experiments and the resistance. I could get myself a coat and Sierra could get whatever she wanted.

I just didn't get myself new things anymore. My money went to important things that didn't involve things I wanted that couldn't be used for the Resistance. Freya snorted, "Mate is paying." No. Freya reasoned, "He's insisting," I retorted, "Well, he doesn't understand. Once he finds out who I really am….he'd think I was taking advantage of him. I don't want his money."

Sierra linked, "Come on. Do this for yourself, for once." I felt like I did was repeat myself. I retorted, "He doesn't know who I am! He will be upset about this later. I won't take advantage of him." Sierra argued, "He wants to do it. You don't know he doesn't know who you are. I've seen pictures of you when you were younger. While you look different you also look the same."

I disagreed. He couldn't know who I was. ILYX's probability program told me that. Freya reasoned, "It's still not based on our mate's confirmed words. Just hearsay." I tried to compromise, but none of them were having any of it.

Sierra shouted, "AH HA! You're going to cave because he said it would make him happy." Fine. I'd let him buy a coat. Freya snorted, "You should probably let the probabilities you love tell you how you're not only getting a coat." Well, I didn't want to think about those right now. She chuckled.

Xander popped us out and kissed me again. I needed to get a handle on this because when he kissed me….the earth stopped moving. Everything stopped…even my brain…which was odd…my brain didn't even stop when I slept.

The fact were in, I was screwed. Eventually he stopped wanting me to go shop. I didn't want to leave him. My feet felt like lead. I don't know how long this could all last. We were in Switzerland so we'd probably make it the full two weeks without someone outing my real name. I just didn't want to spend a second apart from him.

Sierra linked me, "The faster we get done, the faster we are back in their arms." I turned and walked away. I let her fill my arms up with clothes. I told her, "We don't need all this." Sierra snorted, "Phil told me what your Xander would likely have us doing. So, for once you're wrong. We do need all this."

She touched my hand and linked, "Are you ok? You were right all along. He's yours." I shook myself, "I knew that." Sierra nodded. I added, "Things could be different….I do actually have a wolf." She hugged me, "I know, girl. That's a mind fuck but she's here now."

She whispered, "We are going to be together for centuries now. It's you and me forever with our mates." It was her and Phil unquestioningly for centuries. I was a question mark. Freya growled, "No we aren't."

I assured Sierra, "I'll challenge your dad when we get back….then you can go. You run to Phil and never look back. Promise me, Si." Sierra frowned arguing, "We can go together." I shook my head saying, "I'll meet up with Xander and explain after his mission. Then it will be his choice."

Sierra nodded, "Fine. You can have your moment but then we will be together for centuries. That's the rumors with pack that have Fairy's." I snorted, "It's not a rumor. It's true." I was destined to live a long and probably very lonely life.

At least that's what Paige had discerned from a coven she'd worked with a few times that I'd assured her didn't suck. She had told me that even though I was banished, I was born into a pack where a Fairy shared their light and joined the pack.

Apparently, the oldest lady in the coven dated a Fairy once upon a time. They traded in trade secrets with each other. Her for the Covens and him for the Fairies. Lucky me. One secret was about sharing light and what that would do to Supernatural groups.

Sierra ran us back to the dressing room. I tried on all the things she'd gotten for me. I liked it. Especially the red dress...Xander would...die….maybe….not like literally…but I did look good. I sighed looking at my reflection. She'd picked a dress with a back because I wasn't showing those hideous scars.

Freya snarled, "That boy will pay. Mate would rip him to pieces." I pointed out, "That would ruin our two weeks with him. He'd go confront Trevor and find out everything. I just want these two perfect weeks. We may never get more." She sighed, "We would but I understand your feelings and respect them." I sighed in relief.

Sierra squealed, "Let's get it all! You looked amazing in everything." I shook my head saying, "We can get the coats and some sweats...but we don't need the rest." Sierra snorted and left the dressing room. I was putting everything back when it vanished, like magically, except my red coat and Sierra's purple one.

I ran out then realized it wasn't like magic. It was magic. I looked at Sierra. She shrugged and linked, "He WANTED to get them for you. Stop thinking you don't deserve nice things. He's a good guy. Phil told me he's been waiting for his mate. Let him spoil you. You deserve it, Mel." I didn't though.

Freya disagreed, "You do. WE do." She did. She'd suffered all this time. Freya reasoned, "So did you." Yes, but I deserved it. She growled, "No, you don't." Xander kissed me again and every argument, every single one of them... just melted from my brain and off my tongue.

When he pulled back I'd forgotten what I was going on about. Sierra linked, "He's right. You DO need this stuff for our trip. Let's walk around the quaint adorable town and let our mates spoil us. Ok?" Only because it clearly made him happy.

Freya hummed, "Yes, you did do a whole study on how providing for their mate's increases and Alpha's happiness exponentially." Which is why Edward was SO unhappy. Not that he read the research I'd left out FOR HIM. It had been in an effort to stop getting him to be a jerk before I realized that would never happen.

Xander led us outside the shop. Sierra linked me, "The others will NEVER believe that this whole time we just needed your Xander. He holds the key to stopping the Melanie rant." I grumbled, "Oh just...shut it." Sierra snorted, "Uh huh. I'm right."

I looked back and noted she was wrapped up in Phil. I told her, "I'm so glad you've got a great guy. I knew you would." Sierra chuckled, "I knew you had one too." Of course she did. I told them who it was and he is a great man. So, that wasn't a novel thing to know.

I just hoped he wanted me when all was said and done. I shoved it all from my mind and looked around. I'd never been out of the country for fun. I'd been for work…and to kill people…and to meet with Anastasia…but never for fun. It was always Resistance related and I never went sightseeing.

I wanted to enjoy this. I wanted to enjoy everything about being with Xander….on a trip. A vacation. I hadn't been on a vacation since I was thirteen with my family. Pain threatened to overtake me, but I didn't let it for the first time in years.

Freya purred, "Mate wants to dazzle us." Yeah, well he didn't have to try. I was dazzled. He was dazzling. Freya warned, "I would stop talking about how much people don't like you if you want to hang onto that two perfect week goal. Oden is furiously asking what that means." Hopefully, she was a better liar than I was.

She chuckled, "I think almost anyone, if not literally everyone, is a better liar than you. I can easily put him off since I'm still going through ALL your memoires." Well, at least she had an excuse ready to go. I thought about Black Path and all the things they did.

A lot of men in Black Path despised me while simultaneously wanting to have sex with me. They hated my ideas. They hated that I changed things. Even though they were for the best. They did not like me.

I used to be sweet. Heck…I used to be nice. They'd beaten that out of me a long time ago….At least I thought they had. I could be nice to certain people. Freya replied, "No, they didn't." Xander had a serious warning about people who didn't like me.

Gosh….he was going to be busy if he didn't end up hating me. Sierra linked me, "The Ring and Black Path beware. Melanie's Xander is going on the hunt. Something tells me he excels at it." She knew he did because I'd told them.

He was an Alpha Enforcer and Squadron Leader who happened to be a Duke of Faerie and the Hackura. That would be serious trouble for the list of people I had that were bad. If he got it, they were dead much quicker than I planned on killing them. Xander was a see a problem, take it out kind of man.

To be fair…The Ring didn't actually know my identity as the Resistance leader….but they certainly didn't like me…since I did lead it…I was definitely on the top kill list for a lot of people. Xander's lips were on mine again.

Eventually he pulled back and led us all through the town. It was amazing. Freya hummed, "Yes, sightseeing has perks. You could enjoy other countries instead of just having meetings in buildings you own, killing someone, and leaving." I replied, "Well, I killed bad people so…." She snorted, "I am aware."

I loved everything about this town. When they took us into a cookie shop it hit me….They heard Sierra and I talking about their scents. Xander had heard me talking about licking and biting a sugar cookie…but it wasn't a cookie….it was him.

Embarrassment flooded me. Sierra tried to play it off. She linked me, "You've been fantasizing about you two together for YEARS. It's always him." I slapped her arm. Phil wanted her to say it out loud. I warned over link, "Don't you dare tell him that!" Sierra retorted, "One day, maybe even right now, he will find it interesting." I rolled my eyes.

Xander seductively whispered in my ear. Freya purred, "Yes, lick him everywhere." She was sounding weaker and I hated that. She snorted, "Focus on our sexy mate." His breath was tickling my ear and giving me ideas. This wasn't fair. That tone...that voice.

Sierra linked me, "Ok your scent of arousal is through the roof." I nearly shrieked, "Well…it's not my fault! He doesn't whisper like this to other people. ILYX doesn't whisper because XANDER doesn't on any audio I had access to."

I stammered, "He…it…I'm not prepared…and I'm not good in situation when ill-prepared." She scoffed, "You plan on the fly better than anyone I've ever met. Let's get our cookies." I practically flew up to the counter.

There was a she wolf behind the counter who winked at me. Oh good lord. Sierra linked me, "There is nothing to be embarrassed about. Our mates are hot." I'd always known Xander was hot. I didn't know he had a panty melting whisper he'd never used anywhere I could hear it. Or how his breathe on my neck would make me want to submit to him. I needed to do more research.

I ordered a sugar cookie. Sierra snorted, "Why bother? The best smelling one to you is over there." I stuck my tongue out at her and walked back over to Xander. He popped us to some restaurant he liked. I couldn't believe this was my life right now. This was happening. I bit my lip.

I glanced at my one of my best friends. It made sense when I thought about it…Sierra and Elise... I was always meant to be by their sides with our mates. I hoped….it could all work out. Sierra linked, "Aww you get to say you've never had wine." That was true, I hadn't.

I drank a lot though. Here shortly…..I'd see if I could dull the pain of the memories of my family dying with alcohol. Or maybe I wouldn't do that this year. Normally I put on music and drank. Not exactly the best way to cope….but it's what I had.

I was usually punished on that day too. Every year. This would be the first year I wasn't in Black Path….to be punished. Well, I'm sure it was waiting for me when I got back.

Sierra linked me, "How interesting he already knows your favorite color is red." I replied, "It's kind of obvious….and purple is a close second." She sighed, "You're being obtuse and I'm pretty sure it's not intentional." Umm rude. I didn't know what she meant but it felt like Freya did.

Once we finished eating Xander was ready to leave. Except he had no idea Sierra wouldn't be done eating for at least a half hour. Sierra urged out loud and over link, "Go. Be with your Xander." I asked, "Are you sure?"

Sierra snorted, "I'm beyond sure I want you to go be with him. For my own part, I'm getting some from my mate when we get home. Go get you some of that man. You've been crushing on him since you were three years old. I mean seriously the UNIVERSE threw you together. He wasn't supposed to be at the show." She was right.

He absolutely was not supposed to be there because I'd have known if he was…. and I would not have been there. Sierra added, "It's past time you had some fun. You haven't had any since I've met you. You train, you experiment, you create, you dance, but you don't have fun. You've had fun tonight. Go. Be with him. Trust yourself. Your heart is telling you he wants you. Don't listen to your head." I nodded to her….but my head was right. Freya said, "It's not." It was.

I could argue with Sierra that killing bad people could be considered fun…I also met a lot of interesting and new people…I was uniting the secret and unknown Supernaturals together. I had fun when Kinglsey introduced me to the Yule Cats. They were fun…so…I mean I did go kill more people while she had sex….but Grandma Yule Cat was fun.

I wondered if Benny was around. Maybe I could talk to him…or Alastair….JJ would be best. He was definitely fun… Xander would probably like to spend time with them too…since it was all on the down low anyway…Benny was being difficult about everything though.

Freya snorted, "But you understand his quest to do avenge his family himself." Yes, because I was on my own quest. I reasoned, "Yes, but we are with Xander and they are family. They know them." She hummed, "He can lie."

I asked, "Why would Benny lie about that? I've seen him with some of Xander's cousins anyway. He does leave really fast. This time he could hang out. If I need fun, he definitely does." She snorted but I was pretty sure I was right.

With that settled Xander and I ran outside. Several people chucked at us. Then he pulled me into him and began to dance. I couldn't help my smile. Fairies were good dancers, and Xander was no exception. I taught him some moves so we could do flips. He picked it up in a flash then kissed me again.

I swear this time I heard fireworks. Eventually we parted and took off again. He popped us closer to the house to race. Freya laughed sleepily, "He's in for it." He was. I was insanely fast and I always had been. With my wolf, I'd bet I was faster.

She hummed, "Good assumption and it's incredibly accurate." That made me laugh. I'd often wanted to ask Alpha Emmett to race me….just to see who was faster…probably him but I'd get closer to beating him than anyone else.

I took off knowing Xander wasn't going to catch me. He might be able to be right behind if he hadn't been so surprised. I teased him then wanted to slap myself. He just kissed me again though…Ok.. so he wasn't mad. Freya agreed, "He's definitely not mad."

It was ok by me if he'd kiss me every time I ranted. It was nicer than the things people usually said to try to get me to stop. Not that their way worked. My heart hurt when he said I was perfect. I wasn't. I was going to be a problem for him. Freya argued, "We are his best asset." Not really.

We walked inside and talked through some things. He seemed upset by several things I'd said. Freya hummed, "More like that this happened to you. Not that you said it." His eating lard comment set me off. I'd pay him….so much money to see that.

We discussed moving. Freya scoffed, "We are moving. I will not live with those horrid people. I'd kill that Alpha the second I was strong enough." I replied, "I could kill him." I just hadn't because while Caine was ready to take over now, the other packs weren't yet.

Caine also doubted he was ready but that was because of the years his dad had of putting him down…I needed Xander's mom psychology degree but… I didn't have one. I could get one though…food for thought.

Freya purred, "He offered to move for us and our position. He is a true Alpha." I agreed, "He is but they would never let him come." She scoffed, "If he wanted to come they could not stop him." I replied, "They would never let him see what truly happened in their pack. Besides, we don't know he will want us in Black Mountain after we explain it all."

I tried to explain that to him but it wasn't coming out right. I was trying to keep my tears from falling. I desperately wanted to hear all these words from him….but once he knew….that might not be the case. Freya whispered, "It will be. He already loves us." She didn't know that. She didn't understand.

Freya sighed, "I have all your memories Melanie. It may be slow going through them right now, but I know that no one should have blamed you. They were the ones who were wrong."

"Any family would've done the same to protect their pups. The Warriors should've helped. Hunters shouldn't have been in the heart of the pack. Someone had to help them." She was right. Someone had to let them in. Was Jason in danger? I'd have to figure it out.

I resolved to tell him the whole story the second his mission was over. If we went to Black Mountain together….Elise and EJ would recognize me in a second. I didn't know what either of them knew about my situation.

I was also certain Xander's dad, Alpha Eric Conners, would put it together too. He was on vacation and based on my projections Princess Luna Haley was likely in her concupiscence. So…he might be busy.

Freya snorted, "The amount you know about this family you never met deeply impresses me." That was good…since I knew practically everything about them. Xander made declarations about the emotional baggage I had and I knew at that moment my heart was gone.

It had been his for seventeen years when you really thought about it. When he said he was proud of me, I nearly jumped him. I'd been working so hard to make everyone from my past proud of me for almost seven years.

No one besides Mason and Hendrick ever said they were proud of me anymore. I felt all those lonely alone spaces in me begin to fill up. Freya was here now and Xander was too.

I didn't even know if Jason and I could have a relationship at this point. Maybe we could get over the hurt between us one day. We'd never be like we were though. Mom, Dad, and Tristan would want me to try though… I could try for them… we'd just need therapy. A LOT of therapy.

I broached the subject of marking. He couldn't do that until he knew everything. Freya grumbled, "I get it but…" I interrupted her, "It has to be his choice with all the facts… out there for him to decide… I can't take his choice away from him like that." Freya sighed in discontent.

I understood that feeling. I desperately wanted him to mark me, but he needed the full picture. Freya told me, "So tell him." I reiterated, "I want this time with him. Don't you?" Freya didn't say anything, but I knew she agreed.

She just wasn't as scared as I was that he would reject me. The words had haunted me for four years. I'd sat in my car outside the diner for five hours the day after my eighteenth birthday trying to decide if I should just go to Xander.

Ultimately, I knew the people of Black Path needed me. I didn't know what would happen once Xander rejected me. I knew that even strong wolves went down for at least a week. I didn't have a wolf at the time. His rejection could've literally killed me.

Freya groaned, "Mate thinks we aren't ready to be marked." I replied, "Yes, well… that's not the problem. The problem is whether or not he will want to be connected to me forever." He was teasing me about biting pillows.

I nearly groaned. Seriously? With that smirk and that voice? Was he TRYING to make me combust? I was so ready to jump him. Freya linked, "Thank god." I blew out a breath saying, "I just… he looks like a god and I'm… inexperienced."

I nearly fell over when he said he'd never done this before either. What in the Fairy loophole evasive statement was that? I linked Freya, "What does he mean by this?" Freya laughed, "You're cute." I replied, "You have my memories! They said…"

She growled, "And I told you that your projections were based on hearsay. Those people are obviously skilled liars. Your memoires reflect your hurt about it, but If I'd been with you…" She trailed off. She sighed, "One, they'd be dead. Two, I would've told you they were lying."

She could tell they were lying from a memory?! She answered, "Yes. Our counterpart told you they were lying." I snorted, "He was trying to make me feel better and…" She cut me off, "He wasn't. Those women were lying to you. I wasn't certain when we spoke about it earlier, but I am now that I've gone through every single memory involving those people."

She didn't know though. She snorted, "Our mate that can't lie just said he's never had sex. So, they did lie." She made a valid point. He could not lie nor was there a reason to… other than I wasn't his type… with my lack of blonde hair.

I was actually taken aback when he mentioned he was kissed against his will. HE WAS WHAT?! AND I MISSED IT?! That was a personal affront to everything I did for him. I didn't let people hurt or take advantage of my man. Freya purred, "Possessive. I like it."

Yeah, well I'd find out who it was and wring her neck! Freya was in complete agreement. I was easily still in shock that he'd never had sex. He'd just had one kiss. Freya snorted, "I told you those women were liars."

Well, I didn't have enough evidence to make that statement. It could be one of Xander's brothers they were with… and people couldn't tell the difference. I needed more data before I hunted them down TO KILL THEM ALL.

Freya said, "I told you mate knew who we were." I sighed, "I'm sure he thinks he knows all about Ashley Griffen. You've seen my memories. He doesn't know a lot about me… like my real name... He doesn't know I'm Red One, Bravo One, Swiffer…. so… he doesn't know what's happened to me."

Freya told me gently, "He will avenge it, and he won't judge you. It will hurt him, but we will get through it." It wouldn't hurt him... because he wasn't going to find out. Red One, Bravo One… he had to know about those if we were going to be together... eventually he'd figure it out so I had to tell him.

The rest of it? He never had to know. That was what I deserved. It was my cross to bear, not his. Freya disagreed, "You didn't deserve it. Not once. Not ever." Well, knowing I was Swiffer and how I'd fought would hurt him. So, that was not on the table to discuss. Freya snorted like she didn't believe that.

I lost myself in the feeling of kissing Xander. It was escalating and he went to take off my shirt. Oh no. We were in the light. Even if we were in the dark, he'd be able to see the scars. Supernatural's had excellent vision.

I'd never been this ashamed of them except those first few months after they happened. I didn't inflict them on myself. It had been done to me, but I didn't want Xander to see them. He was clearly confused but agreed to my boundaries.

Freya asked me, "How long can you keep that up?" I didn't know. I did know I could do it for at least two weeks. The swimsuit Sierra had picked was bikini bottoms with a swim shirt… like I was surfing. Not that I knew how to surf… I could learn though. She'd been thinking ahead on that one.

I had a bikini I wore in Black path, but everyone there knew I had the scars. Most just didn't acknowledge why anymore. They did acknowledge that their Alpha was a liar and coward after that. Especially once Trevor declared he was my mate.

Edward had been losing control on the pack since I was sixteen but the drastic downfall he'd gone through since I turned eighteen was historic for Black Path.

Xander popped us upstairs. I'd been popped before leaving Red Run by the entire Gamma Family. Jared had popped me first. My favorite time had been when Luna Emmaline Lyons popped me around my house.

That had been because I was so excited to meet her. It felt like a step in the right direction on meeting people. I'd been wrong, but at the time it felt like meeting her would mean meeting everyone else.

I took his shirt off and I was certain my eyes almost bugged out of my head. I thought I was prepared from memorizing his videos. Because… OH MY LANTA! You have GOT to be kidding me. Freya linked, "He's yummy. Go with your first plan of licking and biting him." She might have a point.

He teased me about knowing I watched his videos. FOILED BY PRINCE GUNNER! I knew it was him. My fake accounts to watch his videos weren't that deep but I didn't think he would look into it. I didn't have Prince Gunner level protection on those accounts because why would he check? I couldn't believe he catered his videos to me.

I nearly panicked because I watched the most on my actual account… that I never posted on anymore. But this conversation meant Xander knew Melanie McAlister watched his videos. Freya snorted, "And he clearly doesn't care. In fact, he likes it." He was talking about Ashley watching, not Melanie.

She replied, "Same person. I argued, "He doesn't know that!" His work in the gym showed. Thankfully, he didn't ask if he could mark me at that moment; because I'd have blurted out the whole dang story so that he'd keep nipping at that spot. He settled between my thighs and said I smelled amazing.

Well… that couldn't be true. I had sweat at the show and then there had been that whole writhing in pain then... OH MY GOSH! WHY DIDN'T I SHOWER?! How could I let him anywhere near me without showering?! Freya chuckled at me.

My train of thought abruptly left when I felt his tongue on my clit. It felt better than anything I'd done to myself. When his finger entered me, I was panting with need. It would be embarrassing if I cared about such things at this moment.

Honestly, he could ask me anything he wanted. I'd tell him everything. I was so beyond screwed. He made me come several times before he climbed up. Freya purred, "Good plan on getting claimed. It's odd to do so without marking but not unheard of."

Exactly. We could at least do the whole claiming sex thing. My brain might have broken when I saw his… .my books called it his manhood. My books were liars. Manhood… Pshhhh… that was a weapon. Of course it hurt when girls had sex for the first time. LOOK at that giant... hard…. Weapon. It was definitely a weapon.

Freya reasoned, "You did a study on Alpha wolves. You know all Supernatural's are well endowed and Alpha males more so." I replied, "There is reading and seeing… that's different!" She chuckled in my head. Xander looked so confident about this working without damage to my internal organs.

Freya chimed in, "I agree with mate. Trust him." The biggest problem right now was... I did. I did trust him. I was screwed. I wasn't even overly worried about the pain associated losing my virginity.

Which might sound insane. My friends talked about a pinch. Sierra and Addison, not to mention Paige, had broken it all down for me and Avery. The remaining virgins of our group. Heaven knows I could handle a pinch. I'd taken much worse than that. He slid inside me, and a peaceful euphoria took over me. I was pretty sure Freya was purring.

When I looked up Xander had stopped moving. I looked down. Son of a gun… he did fit. That must be magic. Was I magic? Or rather... my body parts? Freya told me, "I love you so much. This is comedic genius."

I hummed, "I'm pretty sure I am magic so… it's not actually comedy. Just facts." She laughed pretty loud in my head. I was touched on a level I didn't understand that he'd used his healing light on me to counter the pain. For a pinch?! He cared for me. I could see it in his eyes. Maybe everything would be ok.

He claimed me thoroughly and I enjoyed every second… so of course I embarrassingly came after he'd stopped moving. I berated my lady bits, "Seriously magic vagina? You don't come just because he's still inside us… you have great stretching powers that possibly extend to my belly button… and that's super cool and helpful…. Just, find some chill."

I waited to hear the response but my magical vagina didn't have the power to reply, I guess. When Xander slid out of me, I wanted him to come back. Maybe we could just stay here in Switzerland… or meet here every so often.

I just needed him to stay in my world. He was suddenly my air. I couldn't keep my eyes open any long… I was going to say that was because it had been a really long, strange... but wonderful day. I woke up and looked at the time.

I gaped at the clock realizing I'd been asleep for four hours. That... was a record since I'd left Red Run. I was usually up cleaning and making breakfast for everyone… but I'd had to clean up the pack hall and kitchen after dinner.

I didn't often get to bed until two in the morning… if I managed to get to bed. Even when I did… I had to get up at five. I grabbed some yoga pants and a t-shirt out of my bag. I needed to dance… for a happy reason for the first time in a very long time.

I went outside and put a timer on my phone. I played music and lost myself in the beat. I danced away all my feelings. When the timer went off, I quickly turned it off. I knew everyone here had super hearing. Hopefully, I didn't disturb anyone.

The wind blew and I smelled sugar cookies. I whirled around. How did Xander do that? I was normally very aware of people around me. Freya told me, "You trust and feel safe with him. You are alert about danger. He's different. He's mate." She was right about that and not at the same time.

I never felt unsafe with EJ... or my brothers… or my friends… but I knew when they were around. Xander was different though. We were different around him… it was definitely something to look into and research. I bet my cortisol levels were playing a big part with all the endorphins flooding my brain and system.

Xander commented on my dancing skills. He didn't mention Melanie though so that seemed like a win. Freya sighed, "I see you're going to cling to this idea he doesn't know quite hard." I replied, "Because he's not mad which means he doesn't know." She hummed, "I see."

Black Path would also never let positive rumors about my abilities go around. They tried to downplay what everyone knew about my fighting skills. They certainly were not going to mention me dancing in the fields around the pack.

Even though everyone knows where my spot is. Most of them left me alone out there. That was because most of those people didn't want to see me as a person. Even Trevor was nice to me for several hours after seeing me dance.

It freaked people out. Because then they didn't just see me as the person who shakes up the status quo of their pack. They might see a person instead of the devil. Xander cut off my next rant with a kiss. Freya purred, "Mate likes kissing us." Yes, well…. I was a fan of that too.

He took me back inside and we fell back asleep. I woke up two hours later. He was really going for a record with my sleep. I got bored sitting there though. I decided I should get up and make us all breakfast. I quickly got up and went to the kitchen.

Someone had stocked it pretty well. I put on the coffee first and drank several cups. I had to look around for everything I needed. I had the schematics of the house, but not what was inside. I clicked several buttons on my watch to scan it all and noted the placement of things.

I go to work once I had everything out, playing music on my phone as I worked. I could smell Xander and then Phil behind me. I had no idea how long they'd been there. Freya grumbled, "Then actually sleep."

I gasped, "I did! Six hours total even… and…" She complained, "That's not the record you think it is. It was also not consecutive." It was a record… for the last six years in fact. So, I was definitely going to count it and put it in the record books. She snorted.

Freya purred, "Mate looks ready to devour us. We should let him." I replied, "I need to clean up the kitchen, and wait for the muffins to be done." Xander kissed me though, which made my mind go to mush. I quickly told Phil about the coffee. Us Beta bloods needed our coffee.

Warmth filled me. I was officially a Beta blood again. Freya agreed, "You absolutely are and always have been." I shoved those emotions in a box to cry about later. Sierra joined us.

I linked her, "It was just the one pot today. I slept amazingly well." She asked, "Did you?" Freya grumbled, "No." I replied to my friend, "Yes. I got up to dance but Xander found me and made me go back to bed. It was so weird."

Sierra started to talk about when Xander emailed me the first time. Sierra linked, "He doesn't care Mel." I replied, "He could figure out who I am… and that…." Sierra cut me off, "Oh girly, I think they both know." I shook my head denying that.

Freya said, "I told Tori you're hanging onto your delusion with all your stubborn capabilities." I told her, "It's not a delusion." She said, "It very much is." She was wrong. Xander calmed me down. Phil even added humor to the situation.

He did make a comment I disagreed with. Xander wasn't mean… I don't think Xander could be mean. He was my big teddy bear. Freya snorted, "Yet you think he'd hurt you." I reasoned, "Extenuating circumstances exist here. He IS a big teddy bear, but Jason is his best friend." She groaned.

I nearly flashed to my first attempt at cooking when I'd been burned on the stove by Aunt Stephanie and thrown into the cupboard. Sierra linked, "Stay in the here and now. We are with our mates, and you made a killer breakfast." That was true.

I shook myself, thinking about Hendrick and Mason. My heart felt heavy. If things worked out between Xander and me... I'd be leaving them behind. I couldn't think about that. Sierra cooed, "Aww he really is perfect offering to bring Mason and Hendrick up. We were already bringing the girls. Caine and Dax will just have to take over." They were ready so that wasn't a big deal.

Tears filled my eyes. I knew the only thing that kept Mason and Hendrick in Black Path when they had offers to leave was me. Maybe… maybe this new life could really work out for us. I locked eyes with Sierra. For the first time in a long time, I felt hope.

I got the blueberry muffins out and nearly dropped them when Xander handed me a plate. I looked over wondering if he needed me to carry this to the table. Sierra linked, “I think he wants you to join us.” She was right because he clearly did. Well, that was a throwback to my old life.

I didn’t get to eat with ranked wolves... or even unranked. I usually ate after everything was cleaned up. I made sure nothing was still on then went to sit by Xander. Freya linked, “You are aware you were always a ranked wolf as a Beta blood, but you absolutely had a leadership rank being the Female Lead Warrior.” I replied, “They did not care about those facts.” She growled.

Sierra smiled at me, and I couldn’t help but smile in return. We all ate together. Other than at King’s diner… this never happened. Cayden and Micah would eat with me… .my friends would too… but this was an actual Alpha and a Beta eating with me again.

Not the future leadership. Not my friends. An Alpha and Beta who had their ceremony to have the title. I hadn’t done this since leaving Red Run. Our family used to eat with the Kyle’s all the time. This felt weird, yet normal.

Then it hit me, the kitchen was a mess. My mind flashed to being locked in the cupboard. The dark damp cupboard that locked from the outside had an additional deadbolt so I couldn’t get out. It was triple reinforced.

I’d even dislocated my shoulder trying to get out. I couldn’t be in a small space. My mind flashed to the hole. The hole that I’d been put in many times, including after not shifting. I ran into the kitchen. I couldn’t go back there. I should’ve soaked the pan. I began to scrub the first pan I found.

Sierra linked me, “Mel, they don’t care. We aren't at home. No one’s going to lock you away and I’m pretty sure they are freaking out right now.” She was probably right… but I couldn’t stop. I heard a snap, and my hands hit the sink.

One glance told me all the pans were clean now. Freya said, “You knew mate could do that.” Logically, yes… and now I felt bad because he looked sad. He was probably disappointed in me. I’d ruined this two perfect week goal already.

Freya disagreed, “He’s worried about you. He doesn’t care about the pans. Those rat bastards shouldn’t have done that to you. You were a teenager who had never cooked before. You didn’t know those things. It was unfair and they are unworthy of their titles for doing that to anyone.” Well, she and I agreed there.

Xander spoke in a soft and comforting tone. Maybe he wasn’t mad about the mess then. Sierra linked me, “It’s really ok. We aren’t at home.” I was being pathetic. I was a Female Lead Warrior for goodness sakes. I could beat up Alpha’s... Beta’s… Gamma’s… the list went on. Yet here I was losing it over dirty dishes.

Freya offered, “You’ve been physically and emotionally abused. Just because you are a badass doesn’t mean that doesn’t have an impact on you.” She was very wise for a wolf who had never had a human before.

Freya snickered, “I told you, I’ve been around for a while and I’m an old wolf. I was just waiting for you.” I still had no clue what that meant. She told me, “Now is really not the time for that conversation. Before you ask, I don’t know when will be. Your life was not to be this way. I need to figure out a new plan for us and our path.” Ok, fair enough.

Sierra suggested sitting outside. She knew being outside calmed me down. Xander hung back and comforted me again. I was really wishing he hadn’t noticed the near panic attack over the dishes. Freya chimed in, “For the love of god. You can’t lie and that panic attack over the dishes was obvious. You weren’t even lying.”

I replied, “I didn’t say that much… about it… mentally I thought it, but I didn’t say it.” She blew out her breath. “Melanie, I feel you think you pull off things you don’t. You were not calm. He is an Enforcer with amazing hearing. He could hear your heart betting erratically.” Ok, well that was true.

Xander’s story about his mom was super sweet. I had heard she baked things for Alpha Eric before though. I was from Red Run. They talked about it a lot. My mom even had some of those recipes. I changed the subject to his favorite foods.

Freya snorted, "You already knew his." I replied, "I had a logical guess based on his ordering history. I did not actually know." She laughed in my head. Mason had taught me how to cook steak. I was pretty good at it.

Xander's favorite dessert made my heart skip a beat. I smelled like strawberries. Could he know? He had to have smelled my stuff before... right? But then he would've known I was his before I left. Wouldn't he? The answer was he would so he didn't know I was Melanie.

Freya sighed, "You really are going to be very stubborn about this. You knew his favorite dessert too." I grumbled, "I had a logical guess based on the data of his orders." I practically felt her purse her lips at me.

My thoughts startled when he asked me in return. I honestly hadn't thought about my favorite food in years. Mason's burgers were good. I also loved sugar cookies though, not the evil cookies. Freya agreed, "Those peanut butter cookies do seem to be our enemy."

I was glad she was on my side about that. No one else used to be and it was VERY annoying. I sighed because if I could have my family back, I'd bake them their weird cookies every damn day. Which probably meant figuring out where the HECK they came from but I could do that now. I had skills I didn't then. Charles had really improved my dark web hacking skills.

We joined Sierra and Phil. Freya seemed excited about the hike and I found I was even smiling about it myself. Maybe Xander would shift for me. Freya purred, "Yes, I want to see Oden." I did too. Oh gosh…I needed to hide my Xander wolf at the bottom of my bag.

Freya asked, "Why?" I replied, "He would see it." She chuckled again offering, "He'd be flattered." I replied, "But he might recognize it… and that's problematic." She hummed.

Sierra linked, "Are you ok? You mentioned T was going to teach you snowboarding." We never got around to it, but he'd planned to teach me in Black Mountain's territory one day. I replied, "I'm fine." She reached over and grabbed my hand. I smiled at her. I reiterated, "I'm ok."

We sat there drinking for a bit in silence… which bothered me a lot. I was biting my lip, so I didn't fill it since I'd already embarrassed myself over dirty dishes. Freya disagreed, "You have nothing to be embarrassed about. The reprobates that are the reason you have trauma associated with dirty dishes do."

Sierra announced, "Ok, we are going to shower. You guys do the same. Alexander, please conjure a few outfits of Ashley's to my room. We will meet you downstairs in a half hour." Xander pulled me into his lap and kissed me. He agreed, "Alright."

Sierra led me to where Phil's room was. I told her, "I don't know how I can hide my scars…. I have some of my mark concealers… they don't make the words disappear though." Sierra knew that already. I'd tried to get the formula perfect, but those marks… the words Trevor carved into my skin… they wouldn't go away. Freaking Trevor.

Freya growled, "He will die." I agreed with that. I had several plans on how to arrange it. She snarled, "By my claws sounds good." Well, I could come up with more and new plans since I had her. Sierra rubbed my arms saying, "Your Xander won't care."

I snorted, "He will absolutely care." Freya agreed, "Yes, he will. He'll go full Hackura golden eyed Alpha Duke Squadron Leader about it." Yeah, he would. Sierra sighed, "Just get in the shower and we will figure it out." I quickly followed that directive.

Once I got Sierra wiggled her eyebrow suggestively. She commented, "You still smell like him. Did you get you some of that? I did, not your mate obviously. I meant mine. WHEW! That man…" She trailed off amending, "I mean my man knows what he's doing in bed."

I blushed, "Umm well... we... you know… did... things… and stuff." Sierra snorted, "You had sex." I nodded. Sierra jumped out of the shower and hugged me. She squealed. I quickly sorted through the stuff Xander had conjured in here.

I grabbed black skintight leggings and a green shirt with a black vest and gray beanie. I quickly did my makeup with my red lips. Sierra got dressed. She grabbed my hands saying, "It's going to work out, I just know it. It's you and me and once Caine and Dax take over, we'll get Avery and Ads to Black Mountain."

I asked, "Uhhh what about Paige? We will…" She snorted, "Paige will literally just follow you. She will curse Edward if he so much as tries to say a word to the contrary. Virgil and Valentina will shimmer wherever you are, and Crush will follow Virgil. So, that side of the group is handled." I smiled, "That would be perfect." Except I was certain some of my friends would be perfect with some people from my past in Red Run. I shoved all that from my mind.

Everyone could get to the allied territories and then I could find Odette and life would be rainbows and roses. Except my life was never rainbows or roses. Freya chimed in, "It will be now. Mate will make it so." That just wasn't my reality anymore. My life was dark, dreary, and cold.

We ran downstairs and Xander's eyes instantly found mine. He looked upset about whatever he was discussing with Phil. Phil quickly hung up his phone. Freya asked, "Who do you think they were talking to?"

I answered, "Gage. Xander's Gamma. Easily… it was definitely him." She chuckled, "I'll go with your guess." She could ask Oden. She hummed, "You are correct it was Gage and he's intrigued I knew that. Don't worry, I blamed you." I bit my lip so I didn't laugh. Our interaction practically struck me in the chest. I'd missed out on moments like this with her….but I had her now so…it was ok.

I asked my mate, "Are you ok?" Xander kissed me possessively until Phil cleared his throat. He broke apart from me. It looked like it took effort for him to say, "Let's get going." Sierra linked, "Look at you having sexy girl mojo! I knew you had it in you."

I asked, "Huh?" She snorted, "You kiss so well the man wants to claim you." I blushed. The truth was I'd read a lot about kissing. In book and how to's. I didn't want to be completely unprepared….just in case I did convince Xander to give me a chance. Or in case the mate bond just demanded he kiss me.

Xander popped us on a mountain that overlooked a beautiful town and lake. I gasped, "It's beautiful." Phil announced, "We will meet up for lunch. Are we doing that at the usual place, Cousin?" Alexander answered, "Yup." Phil opened a portal and he and Sierra stepped through.

I practically shrieked, "Did they just go to the Hackura realm? I just... seriously? They did… they totally did…" Xander laughed, "No, they didn't. They briefly stepped through it. Phil likes that mountain." He pointed to one that was three mountains away from us.

I asked, "Will you shift for me? I want to see your wolf." Freya purred, "Oden. You want to see Oden." I replied, "I know that….but he doesn't need to know I know his wolf's name… I've obviously known forever…but he doesn't need to know that." She reasoned, "A lot of people know his wolf's name." Fair.

I amended, "Oden. I'd like to see Oden." Xander's eyes went black. Oden asked, "Would you, little mate?" I nodded, "Yes… but I'm not really little… so…" He chuckled, "You are smaller than me." I asked, "So… what you're saying is everyone is little to you. Because you're a giant… got it."

He grabbed my hand, took me a little deeper into the forest, then started to strip. I blushed. Oden laughed, "You've seen all of me, little mate." I agreed, "Yes… but… it's like daylight… and… no you're just right." Oden smiled, "I know. I enjoy how you look at my body and so does Alexander."

I felt my face flame, "Umm well… you're like… sculpted… so…that's really your fault…when you think about it…and possibly all the gym sponsorships you have…definitely all the practices you do…for sure." He winked at me and I was certain that time stopped again.

In the next second... he shifted into a beautiful black wolf with white markings. He looked just like my Xander wolf. Oden tilted his head at me. I linked Freya, "Did I say that out loud? Say no… please say no." Freya said, "No, you didn't say it out loud. Isn't he handsome?" He was.

In fact, I'd never seen a wolf, other than my stuff wolf, that looked like his. I reached forward and started to stroke his fur. He shivered under my touch. I declared, "You're bigger than… other Alpha wolves I've seen… like, by a lot. I mean that was the rumor about your dad and your family's wolves… but like in person… wow… like… wow." He chuckled but this should be studied.

Freya linked, "Oden wants you to ride him." My hand faltered, "But… he's an Alpha wolf, Freya. They don't just let people ride them." Freya argued, "You aren't just people. Can you please do this for me? I can't shift and play with him yet." I felt guilty about that.

I was getting all our time with our mate, and she was still locked away inside me. Freya assured me, "I'm getting stronger. It helps being around Xander and Oden." I spoke out loud, "Freya says you want me to ride you." Oden nodded his head. I sighed, "Ok... if I'm too heavy... this is really on you." He snorted as I climbed onto his back. He leaped forward.

I couldn't help but laugh. I'd ridden my dad and brother's wolves before for fun, but this… I felt free riding on Oden's back. Just like when I was dancing. We stopped by a lake. I climbed off Oden, and he shifted back. I smiled, "This place is… quiet."

His voice sounded husky when he answered me, "It's off the beaten path. Only wolves could find this place. Or other animals." I looked up noting his eyes were full of lust. The look alone had my underwear dripping wet. Which he definitely smelled. Freya purred, "He does."

He gripped my waist then practically seared his lips to mine. We lost ourselves to that feeling. He pulled back barely even breathing hard while I was panting. He whispered, "Are you sore?" I shook my head, "No. Take me Xander." He growled and his lips were back on mine.

My back was against a tree as we ground into each other. I couldn't get my pants off at this angle. UGH! He snapped them off in the next second. I felt his finger at my entrance. That was so not what I was wanting at the moment.

I said, "I want to feel you… take me. I'm ready." Xander growled, "Fuck me, Lovebug." I admitted, "I'm trying." He chuckled, "You'll be the death of me." He slowly slid inside me. He groaned, "You're so damn wet."

I mean… I did tell him that…right? Maybe but my brain couldn't form that thought to say out loud. I could only moan. I didn't care that my vest was going to be ruined... I could only think about the pleasure I felt.

We didn't stop for hours. He'd even snapped us a mattress at one point. We fell apart in a heap. I snorted, "We are going to look like the hot mess express at lunch." Xander laughed and snapped us back to normal with our clothes back on.

I admitted, "Well… that's handy." Xander rolled on top of me, "Not really. Not when I already want you again." I blushed. Xander groaned, "My cousin has lost his touch. They are waiting for us already." He stood and pulled me up to him.

He popped us closer to where they must be. I nearly laughed when I spotted Sierra's sex hair. Xander snapped his fingers and fixed it. Phil nudged her saying, "I told you he'd fix it." She smiled at him, and he turned to face my mate.

Sierra mouthed, "Holy shit. That snapping thing is SO handy." It was. Phil announced, "Alexander, I ran into Elias. He'd like us to stop by the gym." I nearly squealed because I knew who Elias was because they hung out with him if they were here so I had a folder on him…I hadn't met him but he was a Werewolf.

Freya laughed in my head. I tried to calmly ask, "A wolf gym?" Phil nodded. I clapped asking, "Can we go? Please! They would be a challenge… their pack is good… I like challenges… I like to win… and I would… and…"

Sierra snorted, "I told you she'd be all about it, Phil. Just conjure our gym clothes here." Alexander agreed, "I can do that." We ate and talked for about an hour. I was really excited. I needed a good workout.

We went to the gym on the pack grounds. Xander handed me a bag with clothes. Sierra and I ran off to the girls locker room. I grabbed the yoga pants and the tight blue long sleeved pullover then pulled my hair back into a ponytail.

Sierra snorted, "They aren't ready for you." I admitted, "No one ever is. It's kind of… the running theme of my life. It's the literal one thing I can count on. So, let's go show them what's up." We walked out and I nearly tripped over my own dang feet.

Xander was already in the ring with his shirt off. I couldn't help but stop to watch him. He was so fluid on his feet. He was just warming up with his fight, but he still looked good. I glanced around the gym to see if everyone was as captivated by him as I was.

I growled at three women who were staring at him with bedroom, lusting eyes. They glanced sharply at me and found my glare waiting. I growled at them again but more menacingly. Sierra linked, "Whoa. Down girl." I replied, "MINE!" She agreed, "I know. It's officially and everything. Please calm down."

Freya linked, "That's right. You tell them what's up with your death glare. He's ours, and they can't have him." I looked back at Xander once they'd looked away. He shot me a wink and landed a punch. Phil was already fighting too. Sadly, I didn't see a camera set up. This would be GREAT content for him.

Elias joined me and Sierra. He smiled introducing himself, "I'm Elias." Sierra linked, "We could freak him out so bad right now saying we knew that."

I replied, "Not really. His pack is used to people knowing prominent members. It would be stranger if we didn't know him." She snorted, "Darn. It's always fun freaking them out with the knowledge." I made my friends study packs and their leadership along with prominent members just like my old pack did. They'd picked it up with ease.

I told Elias, "Nice to meet you." He chuckled, "Alright Phil and Alexander said you'd want to spar." I jumped in, "We do… like a lot." Sierra replied, "I personally have a reasonable amount of wanting to spar. She is far too excited." I shot her a look, but she just smiled at me.

Elias chuckled, "If you don't mind, we've got two guys over there, both mated, I feel that's vital information to give the area." I asked, "Why?" Sierra snorted, "Don't mind her, she's clueless." I gasped, "What? I am not… I…"

Elias added, "Ok, well those mated men would like to spar." I nodded. Sierra introduced us, "That's Ashley by the way. I'm Samantha." He nodded and pointed to our opponents. I hopped into the ring.

My guy told me, "I'm Ludvig. I heard your name is Ashley." I nodded, "Mmmm that's what my friend said…" It was true since it was one of my names anyway. We shook hands and he came at me.

I flipped him over my back and pinned him immediately. He took in a sharp breath. I smiled and offered a hand to help him up. He gaped at me for several seconds. He practically shouted, "Ummm what the hell?" I heard several whistles.

Ludvig grinned saying, "Again." He tried for a half hour, but he couldn't get one move past me. He always ended up on his back. One guy yelled, "Let me at her. You've got nothing, Ludvig!" Ludvig snorted, "Boy, I'm your Male Lead Warrior." Oops.

I didn't know he was that Ludvig… it was a common name here… and I didn't have his picture on my system yet. I knew my face turned red. Freya snorted, "Well, I am proud of you." I replied, "Male Lead Warriors don't like being embarrassed. He's going to kick us out."

She asked, "Would that happen in Red Run?" I snorted, "No, Zane would complement them but…" She cut me off, "We aren't in Black Path. We are back around good people." Ludvig looked back at me.

He quickly said, "Hey none of that. You're damn impressive. I'm aware that I'm a good fighter. We all know who Ashley Griffen is around here. I doubted your skills because of your pack, but you're amazing."

I admitted, "That's not exactly uncommon… knowing me… or doubting my skills." He winked and jumped out of the ring. He said, "Go ahead and line up to get your asses kicked by this amazing Warrior." Now, I was blushing for another reason. A wolf of rank complimented my skills openly.

I took several more guys down from their pack before Phil hopped in. He winked at me, "Bring it, Shley." I laughed, "Uhh... don't you mean Ashley?" Phil shook his head, "Nope. I'm calling you Shley." I laughed, "Ok then." He was good, but that didn't surprise me.

It took me a few moves to pin him. Phil snorted, "What the hell do they teach you in Nashville?" I laughed, "Nothing." He hummed, "Yes, well I think I recognize some of your moves. It's a combination of people I know." He gave me a look that said he knew Cayden and Micah had taught me.

I said, "Umm well… I… watch…" He snorted, "I know exactly what you watch." Oh gosh. Earth swallow me whole please. He wiggled his eyebrows, "In fact, you are the reason I didn't get beat within an inch of my life for some of those videos so thanks for the views." Freya cackled in my head.

Xander jumped into the ring. He declared, "Those are mostly all my moves, cousin. With some others." Phil chuckled, "This ought to be good sparring match." He jumped out. What was happening? Freya teased, "I think that's obvious."

I squeaked, "You… and me? Like… umm… now?" Xander replied, "I told you several times via email I wanted to spar with you." Yes, I knew that because I'd said he'd be too distracting. Sierra linked, "You've got this. You've always wanted to spar with him. Embrace the moment and enjoy it."

Before I could answer her, Xander came at me. He was fast, but I was faster. It felt as the fight went on, I could sense Freya getting stronger. I couldn't stop my smile while Xander and I were blocking each other's moves. I almost pinned him when he flipped it on me after an hour of fighting.

I was breathing hard but still smiling. He was really good. He closed the distance between us and kissed me. Cat calls echoed throughout the gym. Sierra said, "You always said you'd hold out for a guy who could beat you or give you a challenge, Ash." I flushed.

I linked her, "Some things can remain not said out loud. I meant him when I said it." She replied, "I know that." UGH! Xander pulled me to my feet. He told Phil, "See you later, cousin." He popped us back to the house.

I laughed, "You keep forgetting them." He pushed me back onto the bed. He kissed down my body through my shirt before he ripped my pants off. He jumped up and his lips were back on mine.

He growled, "Do you have any idea what you were doing to me? I watched you take them all down. My Lovebug, my mate, my little dancing Warrior, you are fierce. You even stuck with me. I have trained since I could walk to fight." I knew that.

He growled, "I need you. I need every inch of you. I'm so hard it's painful. I've never been like this. I've never kept an eye on another fight during my own." I locked my arms around his neck. I could feel how hard he was through his shorts. I flipped our positions.

Freya encouraged me, "You've got this." I shakily ordered, "Snap your shorts off." I'd heard girls in Black Path talk about giving head. Mostly Sierra, Paige, and Addison because I introduced them to good men and not the horrible people of Black Path. Angelique had lots of tips she offered about it when we talked or saw each other too.

I kissed his would be marking spot. His grip tightened on my waist as he groaned. I kissed and licked and nipped my way down his torso. Now Xander was breathing hard. I licked his weapon, as I'd decided to call it. Freya chimed in, "Dick. It's his dick." Or weapon… because it was one.

He groaned, "Fuck." I locked eyes with him as I swirled my tongue around the tip. His gaze seared into my very soul. I made an O with my mouth and took as much of him as I could. I looked up at him again.

He warned, "I'm not going to last long at all. Not with your hot mouth on me with your wide eyed, innocent look after you teased me in the gym." I had no idea what he was talking about. I didn't tease him at the gym.

Freya encouraged, "Just keep going with what you're doing. Think about that later." I could do that. I couldn't take him all in my mouth. Apparently, my mouth wasn't magical like my vagina. Freya snorted at me. I slid my mouth up and down what I could get.

Xander groaned, "Put your hand on what you can't get in your mouth, Lovebug." I did what he said and moved my hand with my mouth. He gripped my head. He whispered, "God, yes. Keep going like that. FUCK, ME…." His voice died off.

I frowned. I'm pretty sure I was doing that… well with my mouth… Did he want me to get on top? He came in my mouth, but he was still hard. Wasn't he supposed to be soft now?

He pulled me up off the ground and threw me onto the bed. He settled between my thighs again. Gosh I should shower, but he didn't let me up. He had me screaming in seconds.

Eventually he slid up my body with a smirk that could melt panties. He flipped me onto my stomach in one move. He entered me quicker than he had last night. I pushed my butt back into him. He moved faster than our first time.

I screamed, "XANDER!" He was so deep, and it felt so good. He bit my marking spot lightly. I gripped the sheets. He growled in my ear, "MINE! You're MINE!" I moaned, "Yours." He pounded into me. I'd come three times before he roared his release.

I noted feathers were suddenly floating around me. I looked up at him over my shoulder. He'd ripped a pillow apart to keep from marking me. Rejection slammed into me. Freya growled, "NO! He's doing what we asked." She was right, but it still felt awful. It felt like he didn't want me.

Which logically was insane… I'd asked him not to mark me. For some reason my feelings apparently didn't care about logic.

Xander snapped the room clean and gently laid on top of me not quite putting all his weight on me. He kissed my cheek, "Fuck, Lovebug." I laughed, "I don't know exactly what happened with the whole teasing you in the gym comment but... I work out like that a lot."

Xander growled, "I dislike seeing you on top of other men." I snorted, "It was in a completely non-sexual way." Xander slowly pulled out of me and laid beside me. He pulled me over, so I was snuggled into him.

He said, "I know it was. It didn't seem to help with my reaction though. I was so damn proud of you, but I wanted to tear them all to pieces. It's a new feeling for me." I laughed, "Ok." That meant he didn't want to tear people apart for Cheyenne.

Freya growled, "I don't like her from your memories." I hadn't actually met her, but I had been near her. Her perfume nearly gagged me.

Xander said, "I recognized the techniques I teach. You took them all to heart." I nodded because I'd memorized his training videos. I'd mimicked his moves until they were muscle memory. I told him, "Those videos teach so many people thing they wouldn't know… I'm so proud of you for putting them out there." My eyes were drifting shut.

Xander urged, "Get some sleep, Lovebug." I smiled, feeling completely safe and content. I was drifting off, but the feelings remained about not being marked. I'd asked for this. It wasn't even his fault, but it still hurt. Was this going to be my life? He could still want to meet me but never mark me. Yeah, that sounded like the Melanie McAlister lot in life.

To Be Continued in Volume 2

Made in the USA
Columbia, SC
20 June 2025

f9dc3a42-e62f-492e-a2b7-1fb3b3bbdd9bR01